Praise for *The Second Chances of Priam Wood*

2013 New York Book Festival - General Fiction - Honorable
2013 Readers' Favorite Book Award Con

"The best of this novel ech   it
imagination, storytelling, and l   1
ambitious, far-fetched premise tha   .t,
allowing readers to suspend disbelic   ...ıat John Gardener
referred to as fiction's 'continuous dream.' This is a moving story of
regret, salvation, of life as journey, and of souls as forever students."

- Writer's Digest

"The writing is flawless; the seven days that the character had to relive is told in details and isn't rushed...it is beautifully and genuinely
written. The lessons and inspiration that one can take from this
book are plenty: live life to the fullest, nothing lasts forever, and you
don't know what you have until it's gone. The depth of this story
was astonishing. This is a kind of book that you will want to read
while you are relaxing no matter where or when."

- Readers' Favorite

"Rigby is able to reach out to all audiences by capturing the
fundamental human experience: love and loss. As Priam Wood
retreats into several nightmarish days of his life, his ability to alter
the future allows us to understand the torture of regret."

- Calamus Works

"A fulfilling and interesting read, Rigby has produced an intelligent
and thought-provoking novel. At times poignant, at others
humorous, this novel contains an intense mix of heady emotions to
excellent effect."

- Alex Norris, Author

"The concept of Priam the artist and Ellie the ballet dancer has a
natural romance at its heart, and their glorious heady youthful love
through to the painful complexities of later years is beautifully
expressed."

- Wendy Janes, Reviewer

SASKATOON PUBLIC LIBRARY **MA**
36001402294770
The second chances of Priam Wood

The Second Chances of Priam Wood

Alexander Rigby

Copyright © 2013 by Alexander Rigby

All rights reserved. No part of this book may be used or reproduced without written permission from the publisher except in the case of brief quotations embodied in critical articles or reviews. For information address Maple Lane Books, 219 Elysian St, Pittsburgh, PA 15206

This book is a work of fiction. Names, characters, businesses, organizations, places and events are either the product of the author's imagination or are used fictitiously. Any resemblance to actual persons, living or dead, events, or locales is entirely coincidental.

Published by Maple Lane Books, Pittsburgh, PA, USA

LIBRARY OF CONGRESS CATALOGING-IN-PUBLICATION DATA
TXu 1-856-756

ISBN-13: 978-0615784984
ISBN-10: 0615784984

The text of this book is set in 11 point Goudy Old Style, designed by American printer and typographer Frederic W. Goudy (1865 – 1947)

First Edition 2013

Maple Lane Books
www.maplelanebooks.com

© 2013

To anyone who ever believed in me

January 24ᵗʰ 2012

As I lay here dying I realize there are many things I wish I could change. What is a life without regret after all? Never has a life been lived where things have fallen exactly according to plan. Not a single person has accomplished every instance of happiness that they wished to. I sure haven't. I'm filled with desires that seem to dig into my skin, my skin that is old and wrinkled now, covered with dark spots which seem to be laughing at me.

This isn't the way I thought my life would go. This isn't the way I thought everything would happen. If I had known when I was younger that I was still going to be alive at the age of seventy, I never would have believed it. When I was little I used to think I was going to die every day. I've always been afraid of death, but now, as I lay here alone, as I feel it slowly creeping upon me, almost as if death itself is some sort of smoke that is about to envelop me, I know one thing: I am ready to die.

As ready as I can be anyways. I realize now that I can't change those things that have already occurred. I can't go back and be a better man. I can't mend all of the hearts that I have broken. All I have now is myself, all I have is this seventy year old body that is slowly wasting away at a seemingly faster rate as each day goes by. We all start to die the moment we are born. The second we enter this world is the youngest we will ever be, after that instant we begin to lose our innocence, our life.

I have no one. I had a family once, but they are gone. I am alone in the world and for the most part, it is my own fault. Everyone who ever loved me has gone away and it's because I chased them, not on purpose, not because I wanted them to leave, but because I was afraid, I was weak, I was wrong.

I think of her face. I think of her sweet, soft lips, the twinkle in her eye and the way she laughed when I said something that pleased her. I think of the way her waist felt when I pulled her close as we danced, the sound of her voice singing in the shower and of the times we used to walk together in the park. I think of her delicate hands running down the small of my back while we laid in bed all day. I think of her, it's all I ever do.

She's gone now though. She isn't here. Like all of the people in my life, my wife, the only woman I ever loved is gone and

I know it's my fault. At least that's what I tell myself. I'm not sure why I was never able to realize all of the things I was doing wrong while I was doing them. It is as if I was drunk the entire time I lived, and now that I am dying, I'm finally beginning to sober up. The haze of my days is sliding away and I'm in a realm of understanding. It's too late though, time is running out.

I always told myself that I would never die in a nursing home, yet here I am lying in this bed at a center for the old and unfit. When cancer decides to take hold of the body, it sure is one hell of a bitch. The nurses are nice though, they take good care of me. I'm comfortable...well, as comfortable as one can be when he's dying of cancer in a nursing home all alone. Yes, I am alone, that word plays over again and again. Perhaps that's what scares me most of all, and not the actual fact that I'm dying. No, I think I've finally come to terms with that. I'm scared that I've failed. I'm afraid that my life was a waste, the days drifted by like a reverie I couldn't comprehend. I wasn't good enough, I wasn't good enough for them.

So I'm alone, and I suppose that is what I deserve. Besides, the people in my life I loved the most couldn't even be here if they wanted to be. They've parted this planet long before I have. I'm not dead yet. No, not yet.

It's coming though. I can feel death grabbing onto me more every day. The nurses talk to me and each time they feel farther and farther away. The rain outside doesn't seem like rain at all, but rather small droplets of dreams that I once had but can no longer recall. I know death is coming, and at last I wish it would. I'm tired of waiting to see what happens next, if anything does. I'm ready to go, to go to wherever we all end up going when we're gone.

I look across sometimes at the mirror on the other side of the room and when I do I wish the man who stares back at me could have been better. A better son, a better brother, a better husband, a better father, a better man. I wish I could tell the people who loved me how much I loved them, how much I do love them still, just one last time.

That's not how life works though. The secret surprise you thought would never happen hits you in the face and before you know it you're an old man dying alone in a nursing home bed. My life didn't amount to nothing, oh no, I did things, but not everything I wanted to.

As I sleep I dream listless dreams of faraway places I've always wanted to see but haven't. I dream of paint colored clouds drifting through the sky. I dream of the house I grew up in, in the town I feel I barely even remember at all and I dream of her, of course I dream of her.

My ballerina, my love, my life...Ellie was as sweet as the summertime even on the coldest January afternoon and somehow she was mine, she was all mine. Until the day she wasn't, until I made her change her mind.

My body aches. Seventy years of life is a whole lot of time while still being none at all. My body was born to betray me, it has always contained within it the workings of my destruction, it was only a matter of time before it decided to turn against me. Maybe today will be the day. As time goes on I begin to pray to sail away, from this life, from this place, from the fears I've always had, and from the mistakes I already made.

I still feel alive. It's not the same kind of feeling I felt while I was young and full of hope for the days of which I knew naught. It's the kind of feeling that I know though, the feeling of being within a space, residing in a place.

I think about my mother and what she would say to me now if she were here. I feel a cool moisture on my forehead and imagine it's her lying a washcloth on my face to help me feel better since I'm sick. When I open my eyes I realize it's not her though, it's just a nurse who has come to do what I had already previously asked. My dreams, my past and my present seem to all be colliding at once.

No, my mother is gone, just like Ellie she left me before I was ready; she left me before I knew what to do, what I could do, what I should do. I had to keep on living even though living wasn't always easy, and even though the way in which I lived wasn't always right, I still lived, I still loved, just with a heavier heart that buried itself deeper into my chest, further from the surface, hidden from those who tried to gain the key to open it.

My shoes feel thin. However, as I look down at where my feet are I realize I have no shoes on. Or rather if I do they are two very old looking shoes that seem to resemble the feet of an old man.

3

An old man, that's me, I recall, that's me.

This life I have lived was a life with myself. Sure, it was with others too, many people this is very true, but every day I've ever lived I was the only one who was always there. Even those I loved the most couldn't complete every step of the journey with me.

I've loved at great lengths and at various strengths, but I've never been able to truly love myself. For how can I after all of the awful things I've done? How could I love myself after all of the mistakes, all of the breaks that I myself have begun? I've cried tears of sorrow and those of pain. As those tears have fallen I've often looked within a mirror and told myself to feel it, to feel the misery, the madness, the sadness. For if I couldn't feel, how could I have become better? How could I have made those mistakes memories to learn by, in which to heal?

I reach out for her hand, to calm me down as I feel something within my chest burning now, burning bright red. Her hand isn't there though, no, it's not. Ellie's hand hasn't been beside mine for many years now and I know why. I have no hand to hold as death starts to take its final toll. No hand to hold but the hand that is my own. I lift up my right and grasp it with my left. I squeeze on both sides. The pressure seems to lessen the pain, but only for an instant.

I close my eyes and try to think of a day that isn't today, but nothing will come to my senses. I am here and this is now. This is the day I'm going to die, yes I do so believe, this day has arrived.

As I lay here dying I realize I actually am dying, currently... now. I want to yell out, to ask for help. I want to scream for my mother. Even though I am an old man I want her to console me as if I am a child. For I realize that death makes me feel young, it makes me feel unsure and unaware and naïve once again.

I wish Ellie were here to help me, or even my brother or my son. I wish I had someone. I wish the life I lived wasn't so contrived and contorted. I wish the happiness I once had lasted longer, I wish I had been a better man.

The pain is spreading now and I squeeze my eyes tighter as some sort of light seems to be trying to get in. I decide to open my eyes and see the sun is shining through the window. The past few days of rain have finally stopped, the light has come back. I can't help but laugh to myself, even though the laugh comes out more as some sort of choke. Light, as if I dying deserve any kind of light, yeah right.

I tried to be good, really I did, I always tried, but trying wasn't good enough. I let them down, I disappointed them, I left them, I angered them, I broke their hearts. I broke my own. I did the wrong thing simply for the sake of doing it, but instead of learning from my mistakes I just seemed to make more of them. I messed up, I gave up.

I stare out the window and when I do I see something in the distance running this way. It seems to be an animal of some kind; I think I've almost made out what it is when something else takes over my senses.

Death of course.

It's not a person who takes me, or some evil sorceress who finally breaks me. I die myself, with one last flash of pain, and with one last gasp of air I cry out. The light fades, my time is gone and death takes over. Everything fades out, completely to black.

I, Priam Wood, just a man, am gone. My time is up.

The blackness stays in place, but eventually it slowly starts to ebb. I am still aware in some sort of consciousness, but I don't know how it can be, for I know I'm dead. There isn't a single part of me that doubts this fact, it is a certainty.

The black begins to get lighter. I look down expecting to see a body, but I see nothing at first. I pull my hands up to my chest and I feel I am still there. The pain I was experiencing previously is gone, but I can tell my body is the same. I'm still seventy years old, I'm still a man.

The blackness fades even more and I can finally see my hands now, my feet, my fingernails, my body. Although I'm in the same body I've always been in, it feels different. Nothing hurts, I feel no aches, no stiffness, no nothing at all really. I am still residing within my body, but my being feels unlike anything else it ever has felt like before. Since I'm no longer alive, I suppose that makes sense. At least that is what I tell myself.

The black isn't really even black anymore. I don't know how long I have been standing here, I have no real sense of time. Perhaps it's been an eternity; perhaps it's been a second. No, it has to have been longer than a second, because the black has been getting brighter slowly, gradually changing over time like a symphony I can't hear or see.

Suddenly the black isn't black at all, it's white, it's bright, it's almost blinding. When this thought crosses my mind the whiteness fades a bit, the brightness falters, it pulls back. The changing of the light finally rests at a comfortable level so that my eyes no longer have to squint, a level where I can adequately see. My eyesight seems much sharper than before. Even though all that I'm surrounded by is a blank canvas with nothing upon it, I feel everything is at a clearer conceptual contrast. I wish for a paintbrush, I wish for tubes of paint, I wish to have the ability to cover this blankness and make it into something for me, something to look at, something more to see.

Then, I notice it, a faint pinprick of something in the distance. When I first realize it is there it is just a speck, a small dot of something in the middle of nothing. I wonder if I am just imagining it, perhaps I'm imagining all of this right now. Maybe I'm really not dead, just having a whitewashed dream. I know I'm not though, I know I'm gone. Whatever realm of reality I'm currently residing in is real, as real as these sorts of things can be anyways.

The dot is getting bigger, it's evolving. I can start to make out a color, a golden hue that is definitely growing. How far away is it? A mile, a millennium, a meter? I can't tell, but it is most certainly getting closer. It's on its way.

Finally, I realize what it is. It's a dog. I can make out the golden coat, the hairs brushing against the white as it runs towards me. I can see its tongue hanging out of its mouth, gasping for breath as it continues its journey on its way. It's a golden retriever, a dog that looks familiar. As it gets even closer, as it has almost made its way to me a chain seems to connect with another link in my brain. It's not just a dog, it's not just a golden retriever. It's my golden retriever, it's my dog, or, at least it was.

The last leg of the distance goes by at a much faster rate than the previous amount the dog has run. Before I know it she is upon me, jumping through the air and landing directly on my chest. I am knocked back and fall to the ground. She licks my face and I laugh as a cool wetness is rubbed all over with her tongue. When the sound escapes my voice I am surprised to hear it. I haven't laughed in quite a while. I wasn't even sure if I could make noise in this place, whatever this space even is.

I touch her coat and rub the soft fur back and forth. She stops licking my face and backs up off of me. I sit up and pat her on the head. She looks happy and content to see me, just as I am delighted to see her. She's out of breath, panting deliriously. I watch as a few drops of drool fall from her mouth. I wish I had water to offer her, but I have no idea how to access anything here. I understand why she is tired after that run, for it seemed to last forever and only for a moment all at the same time. I'm sure I would have probably doubled over after going so far, then again in this body that doesn't seem to feel any pain perhaps I could run a marathon. Who knows? I don't seem to know anything about where I currently am. If only there was someone who could explain it to me. At least I have my dog, she is with me. I'm no longer alone.

And then something completely unexpected happens. I hear a voice. It's hers. "Hello Priam, it's nice to see you again."

I look all around, trying to see if someone else has appeared from behind me, or from either side, but there is nothing, no one, nothing but whiteness, blankness, nothingness. It can't be the dog talking to me though. It can't be. Confused I look back to the dog; I look back to my golden retriever Chloe. I look into her eyes.

"Yes, Priam, it's me."

I'm sitting in a white abyss with my golden retriever who died before me. I'm sitting here and my dog just said hello to me. The afterlife is officially crazier than the most insane mental hospital that ever existed. I think I've officially lost it, even more than I've already lost before.

I try and find the words I want to say but all that comes out is a stuttered "Wh-wh-what?"

My breathing has quickened and Chloe seems to notice. She is still my dog, but something is different about her, she has become more human like, as human like as a dog can be that is. Since she just spoke, I suppose that would be logical.

She lifts her front right paw and sets it on my thigh. "I'm sure you have a great deal of questions Priam. That's normal, completely normal. I'm sorry if talking to you has startled you a bit, but that too is to be expected. You aren't on Earth anymore, this place is different. I have some things to explain to you."

It's weird because even though I know Chloe is speaking, it is not as if her mouth is moving. I'm not looking at some kind of cartoon caricature of a golden retriever. No, the sound is coming from the direction of her mouth, but when she speaks it just seems to emanate from inside of her and out into the stillness of the white surroundings before reaching my ears. Her mouth doesn't have to flap up and down in order to speak, instead, the noise just comes out and somehow finds its way to my conscious mind.

Thoughts of heaven and the afterlife and everything I ever thought might happen after I died start to swim through my brain. The fact that I had yet to even think about any of these notions surprises me, but now they feel vaster than an ocean, more complicated than I feel I can adequately comprehend.

"What is this place? Where are we? Why are you here? Why am I here? What does this all mean?" I ask, the questions falling out of my mouth one after the other as if they are train cars connected on railroad tracks.

"I suppose it is probably best to answer your questions one at a time, for all of them are very important and they all deserve answers. Luckily for you Priam, I am indeed able to answer them.

Let's just say, I'm your guide."

"My guide to what?" I ask incredulously, for this place we are residing in doesn't seem to need a guide. I may have needed her in my life to help guide me along, but here it is a completely blank slate, a nothingness that stretches on forever.

"This isn't heaven and it's isn't hell," Chloe begins as she pulls her paw off of my thigh. "Those notions aren't important here. Instead, this is a place designed just for you. A place to complete the unpainted parts of your life so that you can move on with the dignity you deserve."

"I don't think I deserve much dignity. I did so many awful things in my life, so many things I regret," I say to her. The thoughts start flooding in, so many memories of love and joy, yet so many moments of sadness and despair jumble all together within my head. I don't want to think about those moments, I don't want to think about how I was never able to be the kind of man I wanted to be, at least not completely.

"That's where you are wrong though Priam. You do deserve dignity, you deserve grace, you deserve a second chance, if that is what you wish."

"As I was dying all I could think about were the people I let down. The loves of my life I lost, and how I wish I could change things, to make them know how much I loved them, to show them how I truly did always want to be there. It was just-"I stop abruptly.

Chloe tilts her head to the side, the kind of movement a dog makes when it's curious, waiting, expecting something more.

I take a deep breath and begin again "It was just that life always got in the way. I let it get in the way. I messed up, I messed up so much."

"We all mess up Priam. We all make mistakes, that is how life is. We make the wrong choices and we learn from them, we move on and we fix things, we make them right."

"That's just it though, when I made mistakes in my life they just piled on top of each other, they all seemed connected. I felt trapped, I felt like I couldn't do anything right a lot of the time. I was blessed with so many wonderful things, but I also felt as if I was cursed. I couldn't escape the continuous reality of people being disappointed with me over and over again. I was never good enough."

As I state that last sentence which I believe to be a fact, I feel a tear well up inside my eye and fall to the ground. I am more aware of my body now than I have been previously in this place. Even though what I am feeling is sadness and regret, part of me feels alive again. Not that I feel completely dead, but I know what I am experiencing now isn't life itself, it's something else.

"I think you are wrong," she says to me as her amber eyes glisten. "That is what this is for, this is for you to make things right."

"To make what right? I can't change my life, I can't go back and relive my life and fix the things I messed up. It's over. No one is going to know how much I loved them, my life is over, it's done." As these words fill up my mouth and fall out into the air I realize how sad this truly is. I have no hope. Although Chloe has told me this place isn't hell, I'm starting to think maybe it is. All I can focus on are the things I did wrong, all of the things I was thinking about back on Earth when I was dying. Ellie, my mother, my son, my brother, my life twisting and turning into a sinking ship that is twenty thousand leagues under the sea, split apart into a million little pieces. I can't fix it. I can't pull it back up to the surface. I can't save it, I can't save them.

"That's where you are wrong," Chloe begins. "You are wrong Priam. Just as you were wrong many times in your life, you again are wrong. Your life can be changed. The decisions you made can be undone, you can become the man you were always meant to be. You can change your life. You can have second chances with the people who mattered to you most. You can show them your heart and you can give them the key. You can liberate your life and shed the strife you carry with you. You can change it."

As Chloe the golden retriever tells me these things I want to believe her. I have to believe her; the desire within me to change things, to make things right with my life is burning within me at a higher temperature with every moment that slides away. I have to change it, I have to save them. If that is what this place is for, to fix things, to make my life right, the way I always wanted it to be, I'll do it. I'll try my best, even if it means I'll fail again, I'll still try.

"I can really change my life? I can relive it? Is that what you are saying?" I ask.

"In so many words. This is the place where I am able to give you what you want more than anything else in the universe: a second chance. This is your wish, and let's just say I am your genie," Chloe says. She gets up on all fours and her tail begins to wag ferociously. "Get up Priam, come, follow me."

I push my hands off of the white abyss beneath me and stand up straight. As I look down at my body I wish didn't have the physicality of my seventy year old self, I wish I was young again, but that isn't what I wish for the most. Chloe is right, what I wish more than anything is for a second chance to make things right, to make the people in my life happy, fulfilled. I follow the dog, I follow my guide. This journey, whatever it is, looks like it is about to begin.

Chloe takes me a distance that seems to be about a hundred yards, but seeing as there is nothing to base off how far we have walked since the whiteness all looks the same I really have no idea how far we have gone before she stops. I wonder why we have stopped, because whatever Chloe needed to tell me seems like it could have been explained where we were before, this spot is just as white as the previous- but then, it's not. I notice something, just as I noticed the speck before that turned out to be Chloe, I notice a faint imprint in front of me. It's not a speck though and it's not just one. I seem to be noticing shapes of colors appearing. Faint at first and then brighter and brighter seven rectangular outlines appear.

They are all in a row, directly at the level of my eyesight, seven rectangular outlines of color. The bursts of color in this white space feel so refreshing to my eyes, that I can't help but smile. This place is becoming livelier all the time. The appearance of the seven shapes makes me long for a paintbrush, for although there is finally color here, the spaces within the seven colored rectangles are still blank, they are still bare.

"This is why we are here," Chloe says as she sits down underneath the seven rectangles and turns to face me, so her back is towards the newly added shapes. "We are here Priam, because you have the chance to relive seven days of your life."

I hear what she says but I still don't know how to comprehend it. I can relive seven days of my life? How is that possible? How is that logical? The more I start to think about it, the more it seems to tangle together into some sort of messy heap that is both nothing and everything that ever mattered all at once. I need to be able to understand this better.

"I'm going to explain it to you better."

"Can you- can you hear what I'm thinking?" I ask, as Chloe just answered the question I was rolling around in my mind.

"I don't need to be able to read your mind in order to know what you're thinking. As I told you earlier, I'm your guide. I will show you the way and explain the rules, for oh...there are rules."

"What kind of rules? And why is it seven days? Why can't I just relive my entire life?"

I'm not trying to be greedy, but as I'm thinking about it, there are more than seven days I'd like to change. More times I messed up with Ellie, more mistakes I made than just seven. Why can't I change it all? Why can't my second chance be to live my life all over again?

"It is seven days. The exact answer is a complicated one," Chloe begins. "You get seven days, seven choices and seven ways to change. Your life, as you lived it originally will be put upon a new course of trajectory. What you change on the first day will affect the next six days that follow. How those following days change is completely up to how you behave on the first one. You can make big changes, you can make little changes, but there are a few things you have to understand before you can choose the days you want to relive, the days you wish to change."

"What do I have to know?"

"First, you cannot directly save someone. In the manner of which you cannot stop someone from dying simply by deciding to."

At these words her face flashes before my eyes. Her smile fleetingly flickers through my brain and I am appalled that I know I can't save her, for of course that was the one thing I wanted to change more than anything, the one thing I thought of first. How can I be given the opportunity to change my life, but not the ability to save her? It seems unfair. Knowing this truth, I wonder if I really want to relive my life at all, even if it is just seven days, how long these seven days will feel. Will it even be worth it, if she doesn't make it?

"Why? Why can't I?" I'm angry and upset as the hope I had for this reliving is already beginning to falter. What other kinds of rules will there be to limit how I wish to change my days?

"Priam, life is a delicate thing. The fact that you are being allowed to change seven days alone is a stretch normally not undertaken, but as it is your heart's truest wish, your wish has been granted. Even so, the lives of others and how they end are not something you can change on your own. You cannot tell someone they are going to die. You cannot stop them from doing something you know will result in their death. You cannot be the keeper of the keys when it comes to the end of a life. That is something you cannot change on your own."

"That was the first thing I wanted to change though. I wanted to save her. To stop her from dying, to make it all right," I say as my heart swells with a longing depressed rage I cannot contain. I have to save her. I still have to try, even if there are rules, I will try to break them. I have to attempt it.

"Perhaps you can make it right in another way," Chloe says as she looks up at the rectangles above her head, acknowledging their presence for the very first time. "You get seven days."

I think of the days in my life I wish to change.. There are so many floating around I know it will be difficult to choose. I think about what Chloe has told me, that the days will affect one another, whatever I do in the first will affect what comes after.

"So all of these days are connected? Does the second affect the third, and the third affect the fourth and so on?" I ask, realizing I don't know what is true.

"Correct Priam, the days are a chain, they are linked. Whichever seven days you select will be relived in a chronological way. The time in between those days will be filled in by what can be best described as a sort of autopilot."

"What does that mean?"

"It means that the days, months, and years in between the days you are able to relive will not actually be lived by the conscious mind that currently resides within you. Instead, the changes you make on the seven days will adjust to your soul and the days in between them will follow according to how you yourself would have reacted. The days will sort themselves out as if you had actually lived them. Are you following me?"

"I think so," I answer, but in reality what Chloe has just said isn't something that I can easily comprehend. I only get seven days. I realize that much, but what about the days in between? I feel as if my mind is being incepted by aliens who are far too intelligent for me to keep up with. What happens in between my second chances will fall according to how I would have originally lived if I would have done things right the first time. I think I get it. I think it makes sense.

"You have seven days. The time in between will work itself out. You shouldn't focus too much on that. What you should think about though is those seven days. For once you select them, you can't change them. If you reach days towards the end and don't like how things have turned out you can't go back. Once the days are selected, you have those seven days to relive, seven days to change, and that's it."

The more Chloe explains to me the more this notion of getting second chances terrifies me. If I mess something up on one day it could potentially mess up the rest of my life. What if I make things worse than they already were before? What if the changes I make destroy the life I lived to a whole new level of infamy? I can't think like that. No, I can't. I know I have to relive these days, I know I at least have to try to make things right. For that is my wish, that is what I want, to make things right.

The seven rectangles in front of me are morphing into something else now; they aren't just colored rectangles anymore. Their lines of color are become corrugated and ridged in a wooden way. I take a step back and realize that they are seven wooden frames that are composed of different colors: yellow, green, blue, indigo, violet, red and orange. The colors of the spectrum, the only colors ever needed.

"There is one last thing you have to know about before choosing your seven days," Chloe says and I look down from the frames to her face, her golden face.

"Yes?" I ask, not even wanting to imagine what the final rule could possibly be.

"Well, you don't just get seven days of your choosing that you can change the way they happened. Before that, for each day you select, you first have to relive the original day, in the way it happened the first time, without the ability to change a single thing. You will be a sort of passenger within the body of your former self; you will have no control over anything on these original days. You will simply be watching, truly reliving in the way the days happened before."

My heart sinks farther down than it's even fallen before. The strings that were holding it up have been ripped to shreds. The thought of having to relive the seven days I wish to change in the way I originally lived them is a nightmare I don't want to dream of. How can I possibly make it through the days I wish to change when I have the burden of the original days pushing down upon my back? I don't know if I can live through missing her again, I don't know if

I can exist as some kind of witness to all of the horrible things I've done. Living through those days once was hard enough, but to have to relive them again without a chance to change them? I think of it as an impossible concept I won't be able to conquer, but then...I remember something. Once I relive these seven days, after I watch them happen in the way they originally did, I will be able to change them, I will be able to save her. Some way, somehow, I will save her, I will save them both, I will save them all. I will get my second chances.

"I know reliving those days the way they originally happened isn't going to be easy, but trust me," Chloe says as she lifts her paw and this time I lean down and grasp it and look into her eyes. "It will be worth it. With each day fresh in your mind, you will know what you want to change, what you need to fix. It will be as if the original day just happened yesterday when you wake up on the morning of the day you get to change, the same day as the one before, but the second time you're in charge."

"I suppose you're right," I say to her as I release her paw and she places it back down on the white abyss beneath us. "It's just going to be hard, that's all."

"Nothing about this is going to be easy Priam, I hope you realize that. As I told you before though, I think it will be worth it, I think you will find what you are looking for. I think you will find that peace, and the dignity you deserve."

"I hope so." I look at the seven frames and when I do, I know I have the days selected in my mind. After all of this talking I just want to get started, I want the seven days, each playing out in two different ways, to begin. I think I'm ready.

"Are you set? Do you know which days you want to pick?"

"I'm as ready as I'll ever be," I tell her, which is the truth. I don't think I could prepare myself anymore for what is about to happen, I just need it to start. I might not even comprehend all of this, but a part of me doesn't even care, I just want to begin. I need to ask something else before I pick my days though, one final question that has been drifting through my mind.

"Why are you the one who is explaining this all to me Chloe? Why are you here, and not someone else from my life?"

I decide to sit down after I ask this. I want to be on the same level as Chloe when I hear her answer, if she even has one.

"Do you think there is a certain reason why I am your guide?" She asks me. I wasn't expecting another question to my question, but I guess she has a point.

"I don't know," I say. "I just have a feeling there is one. Is it because you helped guide me in my life?"

"Well, there is a reason, but it's not that one. I don't know if the truth will make you feel any better about what you are about to do."

"Is it because no one else wanted to come? No one else wanted to see me? This has to be some sort of purgatory doesn't it? This can't just be my own version of the afterlife."

"Yes and no, Priam. I can't give you answers to those questions right now, not before your journey begins, but I can tell you why I'm here. I'm here because in your life, I was the last soul to love you, the last being who was present during the final years of your life. It's as simple as that. Since I was in your life at the end, I have the privilege of being the first one you see after your death. It's a sort of symmetry."

She's right. In a way it kind of makes me sad to be confronted with the fact that the last soul on earth to love me belonged to a dog, but at the same time, it kind of makes me smile. Chloe was my best friend towards the end of my life, the only one who didn't judge me for what I had done previously. I never felt bad when I was around her. It is probably for the best that she was the one to greet me in this place, if anyone else had even had the opportunity to come, I don't know if they would have.

"Well, I'm glad you are here Chloe. I'm glad you are here." I say twice, repeating the sentiment so she knows I mean it.

"And I'm glad I could be here for you Priam. Now, are you ready to pick your seven days? Do you need any more time?"

"I'm ready." After getting the answer to the last question from Chloe, my seven days are locked in my mind. I guess now I just have to make them official, as Chloe is standing up on all fours and looking towards the seven colored frames before us.

"These seven frames represent your seven days Priam. When you're ready all you have to do is place your hand into each separate frame and think of the day you wish to change, the day you wish to have a second chance with. Start from the first frame on the left, and then work your way down to the seventh at the end. Remember, the days will be lived in chronological order, so place them that way in the frames. When you're done, we'll lock the days in place and send you on your way."

I look at the seven frames and step up to them. I approach the first one which is the yellow frame and I place my hand into the white abyss that resides within the four lines. I think of the first day I wish to change and then something I didn't expect occurs, an image takes the place of the white space. Not just an image in fact, but a bunch of images flashing quickly as if it is a miniature motion picture. I step back in awe and realize the images that are flashing in the frame are images from the first day I picked, how it happened during my life.

I want to stop there, as I can already feel the tears flowing, but I know Chloe is behind me, watching me, rooting me on to finish the selection in her silence. So I go on, I place my hand into the next six frames and at each one I gasp as the blankness within the colored rectangle is filled anew with a mirage of images from a day in my life.

When I'm done, I take a step back; I take many steps back and sit on the ground once again. Chloe comes over and lays on my lap, I pet her on the top of the head, feeling her soft golden fur running through my fingertips. In front of me are the seven days I get a second chance to live. I'm looking at what is about to occur, I'm looking at my second chances. I see images of my mother, my brother, myself, Ellie, my son, the city, and a gun.

"Are you ready to go on your way Priam? Are you ready for these days?"

"I think so," I say with a voice that sounds thicker than usual, it's filled with an emotional resonance that seems to bounce around within my core.

"Alright, well then...it's time for me to send you on your way." Chloe gets up off of my lap and turns around. She lifts up her right paw and is about to place it on my head when I think of something I can't believe I haven't already asked her.

"What happens when the days are over? What happens when I've had all of my second chances?" I say as quickly as I can, screaming the questions out loud in a fervor that previews what happens next.

I don't get an answer. Chloe's paw touches my forehead and I can no longer feel my body, I can no longer feel anything. Everything once again...fades to black.

My Life
1941 – 1954

I was born on the fifth of July in 1941. My mother always said how she wished I would have arrived the day before, because that way the sound of the fireworks booming in the distance would have been able to cover up the sound of her screams.

Instead, I came out not on the day of our country's independence, but on the day of my own, for the fifth of July was mine and personally, I always felt glad I didn't have to share it with the nation. Of course, I often thought I would have been willing to, if it would have made my mother feel better about how much I hurt her as she delivered me into this world.

Entering this earth apparently wasn't easy for me and it wasn't easy on my mother, Moira, either. She had decided to give birth to me at home, just as she had done with my brother Daniel. Her best friend, who just so happened to be a midwife, helped with the delivery. She was in labor for sixteen hours, and when I finally decided to come out and greet the day, my mother had lost a great deal of blood. After I was born my mother got to hold me, even though she was in barely any condition to do so.

She used to say to me when I was little: "You were the most beautiful baby I had ever seen, right along with your brother of course. When I looked into your green eyes, I knew that every second of those sixteen hours was worth it. Even though I was in so much pain, so tired after trying to get you to come out and greet us, I thought I'd do it again if I had to, even if it only meant just to see those green eyes for a second."

Unfortunately she didn't have the opportunity to look into my green eyes for very long that day, because her best friend Susan had decided that she needed to be taken to the hospital after losing all of that blood. My father drove her there in his car since the hospital was only a few miles away. That's where she spent the rest of her day, without me. The doctors were able to stop the bleeding, which was caused by a postpartum hemorrhage. They told my father it was lucky he brought her to the hospital when he did, because otherwise she could have easily died. She didn't die on the day I was born though; she lived, thankfully.

Susan watched Danny and me the next three days, as my father, Patrick, stayed in the hospital with my mother. When she was feeling better, Susan brought me to the hospital so my mother could hold me longer, more adequately. She told me she always regretted not being able to spend that first night next to me, but it didn't matter to me. I was glad she made it through, I was happy she was safe.

I grew up in a small town called Alden in Northwest Pennsylvania, about thirty miles south of Lake Erie. It was the most wholesome American town that one could imagine. The older I got, the more I came to resent it, but later in my life I returned to it and I tried to think back on the good old days when everything seemed simpler, easier, and happier. It contained a sense of myself I was never able to completely recapture after I left it.

My parents met at an art gallery in New York City. My mother always used to tell me how she knew the moment she saw my father that she would fall in love with him. I remember one time in particular when I was twelve I came home from school and she was standing at the sink washing the dishes. She asked me how my day was, which I told her was fine. Eventually we got to discuss the topic of my father.

"He was the most handsome man I ever laid eyes on," she had said with a sparkle in her smile, as she dried off her hands with a blue dishtowel and pulled back her long blonde hair into a ponytail. "I knew that if I couldn't have him, I didn't want anyone at all."

"Well how did you get him to talk to you? You were strangers then weren't you?" I had asked her, not able to comprehend how two random people just come together like that when they don't know each other at all.

"We were strangers then, but not for long. I was only aware of your father's existence for about five minutes before we became something less than strangers. I couldn't help but stare at him," she had laughed as she set the last few dishes in the drying rack and came over to the wooden table to sit down next to me. "He was far more interesting to look at than all of that impressionist artwork that was hanging on the walls."

"What did Father say to you?" I asked her as I threw my book bag on the kitchen floor. It slammed to the ground with a thud.

"Priam! How many times do I have to tell you not to throw your things about like that? You need to learn how to take better care of your belongings, or I'm going to stop buying you anything at all."

She wasn't really scolding me, although the tone in her voice had most definitely changed. My mother wasn't capable of yelling at me. Instead, when she was annoyed with something that I had done her voice just went up an octave, as if she was underwater struggling for air.

"Sorry Mother," I sighed. I hated nothing more than to disappoint her. She was the sun in my sky, my golden light above that I only wished to please. I wanted nothing more than for her to always be proud of me.

"As I was saying you young whippersnapper," she said with a wink and pulled me close, as she could tell that her reprimanding had hurt me more than she intended it to. "I didn't have to wait too long to talk to your father, for he came up behind me while I was looking at a particularly fascinating yet equally peculiar painting and said 'I must say miss, I have absolutely no idea what this is supposed to be a painting of. Do you?'"

"What was the painting of?" I asked.

"A boat in the middle of the sea, or at least that's what I told him," she said with a smile.

The first words my parents ever exchanged were about a painting of a boat in the ocean. That was how the love affair started between Moira Kelton and Patrick Wood, the two people who I would not have existed without.

After dating for two years in the city, they decided to get married. My father was the son of a rich advertising executive, while my mother came from more humble beginnings. When they met, she was trying her luck in the theater, for she had a beautiful voice. She had some success and was in a number of different productions, some more lucrative than the others, but she decided to stop acting in musicals when my father asked her to marry him. I'm not sure if she regretted leaving the stage, but I think she loved my father so much that it didn't really matter.

They were married in Manhattan at what I've been told was a rather lavish ceremony, although it was kept quite small. I often looked at the pictures from that day, the look in their eyes was one of another world, a place where only the best kind of love existed. The two of them were meant to be, it was as clear as the clearest blue day could be. They decided to move away from New York together, as they had been city kids their entire lives and wanted a change. They ended up in Alden, the town that was the first place I ever came to know. Together they built a two story white house located on Elm Street, which was on the outskirts of town. The first thing my mother decided to do when the house was finished was to paint the door a bright shade of red. Every time I walked through that door I was reminded of her, and her fiery red spirit burning bright.

My older brother Daniel was born in 1939, so we were rather close in age. Growing up, he was both my best friend and my worst enemy. I suppose that is typical of brothers, but our dynamic seemed to be more dysfunctional than most. He was my brother though and I always loved him and looked up to him when I was young.

My mother constantly told me that the first few months of my life were the happiest she had ever lived. She had a beautiful home in a small town that she adored, two healthy sons, and the man of her dreams at her side. Sadly, her version of happily ever after started to crumble on that fateful day, December 7th 1941. Seeing as I was only five months old on the day the Japanese attacked Pearl Harbor, I obviously have no recollection of what it was like to live through it. My mother told me that she was in the beauty salon getting her hair done when the news came blasting through on the radio.

"When I heard the man's voice explaining across the air waves what had happened, somehow I just knew it was going to affect my life more than the average person's. Don't tell me how or why I thought this, I just did."

Unfortunately for her and for my family, she was right. Shortly after the attack my father decided to enlist in the Marines. He told my mother that it was the right thing to do.

"I've always had such a beautiful life Moira. I've been given everything a man could ever want, and I feel as if I have to do something selfless for once in order to really earn all that I have been given. I need an experience that makes me become a worthier man."

"Patrick, you already are a worthy man! You are the most wonderful, worthy man I know. If you enlist, God knows what will happen. You'll be sent overseas, in who knows what conditions, think about me, and think about the boys. Why go if you don't have to?"

I'm sure her voice was calm, but underneath her persevering strength I know her heart was breaking. Even at that time when the idea of him going to fight in the war was just that, an idea, it seemed to be splitting her core in two.

"I have to go Moira. It is for you, it is for the boys, it's for all of us as Americans. I feel it is my duty. I'm a twenty-six year old man in the prime of my life. I have to do this for all of us. Please don't hate me for it."

There wasn't a single bone in my mother's body that could hate my father, not even in the slightest. He was too good of a man, he was too good to her, and he was too good to us, even in the short time he had. My father enlisted in the spring of 1942, and he never came home. He died on the shores of Normandy on June 6th 1944, D-day.

The one thing I remembered my mother saying about my father's death more than anything else was this: "I just hope when he died he was looking out at the ocean, I hope his mind faded slowly, peacefully. I hope he saw a boat, a single boat on the sea, and as his vision blurred, as he saw that impressionist painting, that painting that we both first saw together, I hope he saw me." Every time she said it, I pinched myself. The pain I felt inside when I heard those words was too great to bear.

I don't remember my father, not even a bit. The days I had with him were limited, those days I don't even recall, not at all. How could I? I was only a few months old when he left for the war, and not even yet three years old by the time he died. He was a great man though, or so my mother always told me, as I had no basis to judge this fact for myself. Every time she told me a story about his life or a fleeting moment she had with him, I only yearned for his presence even more. My father Patrick Wood was a man that I always aspired to be like. Unfortunately, I don't think I ever achieved the amount of greatest he attained in less than half of the time I had to live.

I don't remember his funeral, I don't remember the way my mother sobbed when she found out he was gone. There was a picture of my father holding me just a few weeks before he went off to war, beside him was my mother sitting down, with my brother

Danny on her lap. The four of us together were a happy family, it just didn't last. That picture always had a prominent place in my home, just as it had an important spot in my heart. At our house back in Alden it rested on top of the fireplace, and later when I moved out, a copy of it was always on display wherever I lived.

My father dying was something I could not change. Something I wouldn't have even tried to change. For even though he died, he died with dignity, and I can almost assure you that he died while seeing a vision of that impressionist painting of a boat on the sea. I can tell you without a doubt he saw my mother's beautiful face flash across as a reverie in his mind, before he passed on to the other side. So no, the first day I chose to change had nothing to do with my father. Instead, it was a day I had selected for the beautiful effervescent glorious Moira, my wonderful mother, who I lived to please.

The days, months and years that followed after the death of my father were not as discouragingly depressing as one might think. My mother, although completely heartbroken and distraught by my father's disappearance from her sight, from this life, refused to be defeated. She knew that was the last thing he would have ever wanted. He never would have wanted her to give up, to back down, to live a life without happiness. For her happiness, her smile, and the twinkle in her eye was what he had always loved about her. He would have wanted her to maintain her tenacity and spirit for us, his sons, and for everyone else in Alden. Just because my father was gone, didn't mean that my mother was going to give up. That's just not the way she was.

After my father died, my grandfather insisted that she take some money from him in order to get by. At first, with her strong sense of pride she resisted, not wanting to take a hand out even if it was from family, but after a while, she realized she had no other choice. She had two young sons and it wasn't very likely that she would be able to work anytime soon while raising the two of us on her own. My father came from money. His father, my Grandpa Wood was a brilliant man who ran a very lucrative ad agency in New York City. He had money coming out of every crevice of his body. He probably even wiped his ass with it. Needless to say, the man had more than enough money to help support my mother, my brother and me while she got her life back in order. By the time I was six she was teaching acting and singing classes at the theater a few towns over. She didn't really do it for the money though, she did it because she loved it, and she did it to prove that she wasn't just that 'poor widowed Mrs. Wood from down the street.'

The beginning of my memories until that fateful day in October were as happy as they could be all things considered. My father was dead, but I was very much alive and so was she. My brother Danny rounded out our trio and we got by just fine. My mother's best friend Susan was a frequent visitor to our home and she always kept us laughing. The sound of my mother's laughter always gave me a case of the butterflies. I just wanted her to be happy. I didn't really know the man she knew, my father, her lover, my maker, but I knew that without him, she would never feel completely whole again.

She never dated another man, and didn't even try to, although many men attempted to court her. I told her once when I was ten that "It's okay if you want to find another man Mother. I won't mind."

She looked at me and smiled kindly and said "Well thank you for your permission dear Priam, but you know, I think I'm just fine. I think we're just fine, the three of us. Don't you?"

"Of course I do. I just wanted to say. You know?"

"Thank you baby, you're just the sweetest," she replied, as she grabbed me by the arm and twirled me around. I pulled her towards me, and we performed a sort of waltz across the dining room floor. Even though I only came up to her chest, the two of us together somehow seemed to act like we knew what we were doing. We didn't, but that wasn't the point. It was a moment of serenity, a moment where we just let everything go and danced.

That certain balance of tranquility and hopeful bliss our family had somehow maintained even despite my father's absence, but it didn't last as long as I wished it would have. For just three years after that peaceful day when I danced with my mother across the wooden floors, sliding my socks against the base boards, both of my parents would be dead. When I was thirteen years old, Moira Wood, the woman I felt I had everything to thank for, breathed her last breath and every thing in my life, completely and utterly crashed to the floor.

I feel fingers running through my hair and I try to brush them away, but they don't leave my head, they stay. The hand pats my head and then I feel a warm breath near my right ear whisper and say "Priam, baby, it's time to get up. Monday, Monday, it's time for a fun day."

I groan and kick my legs but since they are underneath the covers they don't move very far. "Priam! You almost knocked me off the bed!" The woman's voice yells, I open my eyes fearing that she is mad at me, but when I look at my mother I see that she is smiling. "Now get your lazy butt out of bed and start this day off right. I'll be downstairs fixing your breakfast. Chop chop!"

I sit up and lean against my headboard and watch her walk out of my room and down the hall, listening to her light footsteps flitter down the stairs until I can hear her no more. I stretch my arms up above my head and cover my mouth in a yawn. The fact that my mother considers Monday a fun day is an atrocity in my mind. As a thirteen year old boy I don't know why she would expect me to be excited for the start of another school week, especially when I have to get up so early in the morning to get to class on time.

I don't hate the seventh grade, but I don't really love it either. Being that it's my first year at Alden Jr. High it's a nice change of pace from that crappy elementary school I feel I outgrew long ago, but at the same time now I just feel like a kindergartner all over again. I'm at the bottom of the food chain. The fact that my mother still calls me baby doesn't help my feelings on this matter, but for some reason I've never asked her to stop calling me it. Even though it annoys me I guess I am her baby after all, so I suppose it's okay if I let her have her way and call me what she wants.

After brushing my teeth and putting on my outfit, I grab my book bag that holds a jumbled mess of papers and random things such as marbles, cards and a few wads of bubble gum. I see some of my other papers strewn across the floor, so I pick them up and shove them in my bag too. At least she won't be able to yell at me for having them scattered all over my bedroom now. When I reach the kitchen table my brother Danny is already sitting there eating some scrambled eggs and a bowl of cereal. "Hi fat face," he says with a smirk.

My mother turns around from the stove and glares at my brother. "How many times do I have to tell you to stop being so rude to Priam in the morning? I don't care if you think it's alright for you to pick on him just because you are the bigger one. Knock it off," she adds as she shakes the spatula in her hand at him in a disapproving manner. She turns back to the stove, flipping over a pancake that I know is for me.

"Sorry Mother," Danny says in her direction then looks back to me with a grimace and bellows out "Hi skinny face. You're looking awful skinny today. Better eat up or you're not going to be able to fit into that Halloween costume of yours." I glare back at him, just the way my mother had done. He's such a smart ass. I contemplate slapping him across the face, but then I know I would be the one in trouble then and I'm sure the punishment would be much worse than just a disapproving look and a wave of a spatula.

Halloween is only a few weeks away and I am planning to go dressed up as Superman. My mother had just recently started making my costume, sewing it together herself. I couldn't wait to run around town in my red and blue, the cape floating behind me in the brisk fall wind.

"I'm sure you will fit into your costume just fine Priam," my mother tells me as she walks across the kitchen and places the plate of pancakes in front of me. "I am the one making it after all, I think I know much better than your brother about whether it will fit or not and I'd vote yes. Those muscles of yours will make you the most regal, blonde version of Superman I'm sure the world has ever seen."

"Thanks Mother," I say. She always knows what to tell me in order to reassure me whenever my brother puts me down. Between the two of them, it was like an equalizer that I was in the middle of. She would fill me with hope, aspirations and dreams, and my brother would fill me with realities that would bring me back down to earth. Together, they've shaped me more than anyone else, although I like to think my mother has influenced me more, with her passion for life, with her grace.

"Superman isn't even blonde, why don't you just dye your hair?" Danny asks me as he shoves a huge mouthful of eggs into his face. "They have that spray on stuff down at the corner store, don't they Mother?"

"I'm sure they do, but just because the regular version of Superman has dark hair doesn't mean Priam can't go as a blonde. Look at me, I'm a blonde, maybe I'll go as Lois Lane." She says with a laugh and returns to the stove to take the pan off and put it in the sink.

"But Lois Lane has dark hair too! Gosh, don't you know anything?" He says to her with a lot of attitude.

"I know much more than you think Daniel. Much more."

Ever since I can remember I've always felt like my mother was much harder on me than my older brother. He could say disrespectful things and get away with it, while if I even so much as back sassed my mother in the slightest, I would receive a punishment far worse than anything he ever got. I tell myself it is just because she expects more of me, wants more for me, but that is just what I want to think, what I tell myself to feel better. As always, I live to please her.

I am impressed she even knows who Lois Lane is, I don't care that she doesn't know the color of her hair. Besides, I figure she just meant we could go as blonde haired versions of dark haired characters together. Perhaps Danny is just jealous because he isn't blonde like us. He had inherited brown hair from my father.

I eat my delicious pancakes as Danny continues to stuff his face with great fervor as my mother packs our lunches and places them in our book bags. She doesn't say anything about the jumbled state that mine is in, so I hope she hasn't noticed. Shortly after, I am tying my shoes and putting on my fall jacket and getting ready to go out the front door.

Alden Jr. High is only about a mile away so Danny and I always walk together every day. When we aren't around my mother, he is always so much nicer to me. Don't ask me why, I've always thought it made no sense, no sense at all. I just figure it is because he wants to show off in front of her, to appear tougher and stronger than me, so I let him do it. We are brothers, and we are friends. I love him, I hate him. I think the feeling is mutual.

I watch as Danny runs out the front door and sweeps his hand along the side of my mother's Ford Victoria that is parked in the driveway. Once he reaches the street he shouts back at me "Hurry the heck up Priam! I haven't got all day." He stops by our mailbox and starts kicking the gravel at his feet towards the direction of the car.

My mother comes out from the kitchen to where I am standing up by the front door. "What are we going to do with that brother of yours?" She says in a sweet tone, "sometimes I worry he is going to end up as some crazy vagrant on the street. Take care of him will you?"

"I'll try my best Mother, I'll try."

"I know you can do it. That's my baby," she says as she kisses me on the forehead and sends me on my way. A part of me cringes when I hear her call me baby again, but a part of my heart melts just the same. I meet Danny at the end of the driveway and look back at our house. My mother, still standing in the doorway is now leaning up against the side of the doorframe, waving us goodbye. I wave back, and start to walk down the street to school. I look back one more time before we are too far away, but her smiling face, her golden locks, her tall slender frame in her favorite blue dress covered in white polka dots, is gone.

The day at school is a rather boring one; then again I'm usually always bored at school anymore. I don't care about scientific experiments or algebraic equations. What is the use in learning something if there is no way for me to interpret it on my own? As I've been getting older I've come to hate math and science more and more. I despise the fact that they are just the way they are and that I cannot prove them wrong. I cannot interpret them, so in essence, science and math don't let me think for myself. They tell me what to think, and if I disagree, I'm simply wrong. Thus, I don't often pay attention in either of these classes, which is probably why I'm not doing too well. I'm not failing by any means, but if I actually paid attention I could probably get A's in both of them. I just don't care that much when it comes to disciplines that don't let me reflect in the way that I want to. I'd much rather be a philosopher, or an artist.

So today, in math class I once again am daydreaming instead of focusing on the blackboard in front of me. I don't care about the numbers or the addition signs in between them, all I care about is the story I'm creating in my head, about a magical man who has the ability to make numbers disappear, so much so that no numbers are left and nobody cares. I lay my head down on the desk, I'm feeling tired. Mother woke me up even earlier than usual it seems. This probably isn't true, but it sure feels like it. I start to nod off when I feel something wet hit me in the back of the head. I spin around slowly, making sure the teacher at the front of the room doesn't notice. What I see when I do is my friend Jimmy holding a straw pointed in my direction with a big smarmy smile on his face.

"Got ya!" He yells as quietly as he can.

"Knock it off you brat," I say back to him. "I'm not in the mood."

"Did someone wake up on the wrong side of the bed? Poor baby."

With that comment I am immediately contemplating why I am even friends with Jimmy, but I know he is just pulling my leg. I'll forgive him for the time being, he is my best bud after all. "Don't call me baby!" I say to him in the most serious tone I can muster. "Are you paying attention to this stuff?"

"Not really. Why should I? Anyways, do you want to hang out after school? I was thinking we could go check out the old Miller place. I hear some of the older kids were planning to turn it into a haunted house for Halloween."

"Really?" I ask, my interest peaked. "Yeah, that sounds fun. Do you think they actually have gone inside already?"

"Priam!" The teacher yells from the front of the classroom, so I spin around as quickly as possible, but it's too late. She's caught me. "Kindly pay attention to this lesson and stop talking to Jimmy. Neither of you have any excuse to be discussing anything right now. Nothing else in your life could possibly be more important than algebra."

"Sorry Mrs. Johnson," I say, even though I'm not really sorry. Algebra most certainly is not important to me. The idea of checking out the old abandoned Miller house a few streets over from where I live after school has me much more excited about this day, as excited as I can be while still trapped at school anyways. Suddenly something outside the window catches my eye so I turn my head to see what it is. It's a brown rabbit, running around in circles over and over again. I wonder what on earth it's doing, but before I can think about it for very much longer, the bell rings. Finally, math class is over.

I get up from my desk and head out the door, Jimmy and I make plans to meet up once the school day is over and I walk to my locker to get rid of my math book. My locker, just like my book bag is a distraught mess of papers and piles of random things. I don't need any books for my next period, because it's time for art class. The only class I actually care about.

My art teacher, Mr. Williams is the most marvelous man I have ever met. He actually used to live in New York City when he was younger and tried his luck in the art world. Unfortunately he wasn't successful, so he moved back home to Alden and got work as an art teacher. I don't know how he didn't succeed; he's the most talented person I've ever known. His paintings, his drawings, his sculptures, they are all so otherworldly. I aspire to be like him.

When I'm painting something, I just feel as if all of my problems melt away. I don't have to worry about what is going to happen next, or what has happened before, all I have to focus on is my craft, the colors I'm mixing and the molds I'm melting together in my mind in order to create a picture of the sky, or a fly, or something way up high. When I paint, when I generate something from my mind and put it on paper, when I use my paintbrushes and touch them to the canvas, I feel alive, and everything else fades away.

Perhaps I'll be an artist one day. Maybe I'll move to New York City just like Mr. Williams did. I could live in the city where my parents met. I could make it, or at least I'd try. As my mother always said "We never know what the world has waiting for us, but each and every one of us always finds out eventually. So why not find out in the most wonderful circumstances we can muster?" These words are a riddle to me, sure they make sense, but they puzzle me all the same. All I know is that I don't want to stay in Alden forever; I don't want to be in a suburb a million miles away from everything where everyone knows my name. I have to get out, I have to make something of myself, and I don't want to do it by sitting in an office and wearing a suit all day. I want to have a studio at the top of some skyscraper in the middle of the city where I can throw paint on the walls, roll around the floor and laugh hysterically to myself and not give a single care in the world to what anyone thinks of what I've done or what I've accomplished. Except for my mother of course, hopefully she will still be proud of me, even if I am a crazy artist who cackles away the day and throws paint towards the sky.

Once the school day is over, I meet up with Danny outside and we walk home together. He asks me what I'm going to do the rest of the afternoon and at first I am hesitant to answer. I'm not sure if I should tell him what Jimmy and I have planned. Eventually though I can't keep the secret to myself, I have to share it with him.

"I think Jimmy and I are going to ride our bikes on over to the old Miller place."

"What for?" He asks, looking at me quizzically.

"Just for fun Danny. You're welcome to come if you want to. Just don't tell Mother."

"Why don't you want me to tell her?"

"I don't think she'd approve," I say, which is most definitely the truth. The old Miller place has been abandoned for years. I'm not really sure why, but I've heard that it's because both of the Millers died in that house, only a few days apart, and that their kids couldn't come to terms with selling the house because it held so many memories for them. At the same time though, they couldn't come to terms with entering the place or taking care of it either, which if you ask me is complete baloney. Thus, the old Miller place stands in complete and utter disrepair.

"You're right, she wouldn't," he says, then turns to look at me. "I'll come though. You two goofs will probably need my help if you're going to see anything worthwhile anyways." That was Danny, always making it out as if I were completely incapable of doing anything on my own. He must have perceived me as an idiot, at least that's what I felt like most of the time.

When we get back to our house, we quickly walk inside and put our book bags in our rooms. Mother is in the kitchen, and from the smell wafting through the air I can tell she has already begun cooking dinner. It smells like pot roast, my favorite. I decide not to go in the kitchen to greet her because I don't want to have to explain where Danny and I are going, so I try to sneak out through the garage where my bicycle is waiting. I've never been very good at quietly sneaking about though, and this is proven correct because just as I am about to be free of her noticing me and exiting safely into the garage, I feel her hand on my shoulder.

"And where do you think you are going mister?" She asks me as I turn around to face her.

"Ummm...just to go hang out with Jimmy. Danny is coming too."

"Is he now? Did the two of you decide together that you weren't even going to say as much as hello to your mother before you went off on your way?" She asks me in a way that immediately makes me feel bad for trying to sneak in and out of the house without even greeting her.

"I'm sorry Mother, we're just in a rush that's all." I'm not really lying to her, I'm just not telling her the whole truth and as far as I'm concerned, I suppose that's good enough.

"Well alright Priam, although I don't know why you need to be in such a rush. The least you and your brother could have done was say hello to me before you left me once more."

"It won't happen again," I say, which is probably a lie, but at least at the current time I mean it. "Did Susan come over to visit when you got back from the theater like she normally does?" I ask, but before I get an answer we both turn to look in the direction of the stairs from where Danny has just stumbled down and is now standing beside us.

"Unfortunately not," she says looking back at me. "She had to take Margaret to the doctor. I guess she was up all night with a fever. Poor thing. Anyhow, you two better be back by six o'clock at the very latest, you hear? I've got a pot roast in the oven for dinner."

My nostrils were right, pot roast, my favorite.

"We'll definitely be back by then Mother," Danny says as he opens the door and basically pushes me through it. "We're just going to ride bikes with Jimmy for a bit. We'll see you soon!"

I almost fall face first onto the concrete of the garage floor, but luckily I catch my balance. I turn around and glare at Danny for shoving me as I pick my bicycle off of the floor and hop onto it. Danny does the same and my mother bids us adieu and adds at the last minute: "behave boys!" as we pedal away furiously, out of the garage and into the street. If only we had listened to her warning, if only we had actually behaved ourselves, perhaps the rest of the day wouldn't have ended up like it did. All I knew then was that we were going to the old Miller house and that some way or the other I was going to show my older brother Danny that I was better than him.

We race our bikes over to Jimmy's house and before I know it the three of us are on our way over to our final destination. The Miller place isn't too far from where we live, and its only about four or five blocks past Jimmy's so it doesn't take too long to get there. When we arrive, we park our bikes back behind the house by large evergreen bushes so that no one will see them by the driveway at the front of the street.

"Do you really think they're making it into a haunted house?" Jimmy asks us as he tries to peer into one of the back windows, which is covered in cobwebs and dust. "I can't see anything. This window is filthy," he exclaims as he wipes his dirty hand on the side of his pants, scuffing his previously clean khakis.

"It would be a great haunted house, don't you think? Even in the daylight it's pretty spooky," Danny says and he's completely right. I'm freaked out just being here and I begin to think that coming to the old Miller house wasn't such a good idea. A part of me wants to leave, to just ride our bikes through the neighborhood instead, but the other two are so fascinated with the house I don't think I could convince them to leave even if I begged.

"Let's go inside," Danny suggests, and at those words I want to run, to get away, to go back to my house and just sit in the kitchen and suck in the smells of Mother's pot roast until it is ready to enter my belly. I don't like this, not one bit.

"I don't think we should go inside Danny. What if someone sees us? We could get in big trouble. Mother would kill us."

"Oh stop being so dramatic," he says to me as he pulls his face back from the dirt-covered window to look me square in the eyes. "What's wrong? Are you chicken?"

"No, I'm not afraid," I lie. "I just don't think we should do it. Besides Jimmy, who even told you about this supposed haunted house? What kind of proof do you have those older kids are really working on one at all?" I ask, turning my attention to Jimmy. The more I think about it; wouldn't that kind of be a stupid idea? Even if they did build a haunted house in here, what would be the purpose of it? It's not like they could charge admission for everyone to go in without at least half of the neighbors noticing, and then they'd probably be arrested for trespassing. The Alden cops sure don't deal with any boohickey from young kids, that's for sure and if they caught us breaking in, I know we would be in deep shit.

"George Jones was telling my older brother about it. Apparently he asked him if he wanted to help. Maybe you're right though Priam, maybe I got my facts wrong." Jimmy says to me, as it appears he too is beginning to have his doubts.

"Well I don't care what you two babies think, we came all

the way over here, I'm going in. If you are too afraid to take a risk in your lives, then just stand here and watch me," Danny says to us in a scolding manner. He focuses his glare on me and gives me a look of utter disgust, and when he turns away all I can feel is my blood beginning to boil.

I don't often have a temper, but I too just like anyone else have a breaking point. Danny has been so arrogant and asinine towards me all day that I feel at this moment that I have to do something in order to prove to him that I am not a baby. I am sick and tired of the way he treats me. It is as if he can never be nice to me when anyone else is around. I am embarrassed, I am infuriated, I am going to show him he is wrong.

For a few moments I just stand there, not knowing what to do. Jimmy and I watch as Danny paces back and forth trying to figure out how to get into the house. He goes over to the porch door, whose paint is peeling chip by chip, but it's locked. He grabs the rusted handle and pulls on it with all of his might back and forth, but it doesn't budge. After a few more times struggling with it, he gives up on the idea of getting through the door and comes back to the window where Jimmy and I are standing, the two of us still doing nothing. Danny glares at me once again, as he moves up towards the window and grabs the bottom trying to push it up. I don't know what I ever did to him that made him act like he hates me so much. Sure, I understand he is my brother and I'm sure I can be annoying sometimes, but do I really deserve to be looked upon as if I am some heathen creature from the deep?

I continue to watch as he struggles with the window. I look over to Jimmy. "Do you want to get out of here?" He asks me.

I am about to tell him yes, let's just go, but I don't. The amount of unbottled rage inside of me won't let me leave. As I look past Jimmy's face something behind him comes into focus. A pile of bricks, probably five or six, are lying on the grass only about a few yards away. I walk past Jimmy and grab a brick. The faded crimson colored rectangle feels heavy in my hands. I turn back to see that Danny is still struggling with the window, clearly making no progress at all. When I pass Jimmy coming back towards the house with the brick in my hand I hear a slight whimper come from somewhere deep within his body. "Priam," he mutters, but I don't answer. "Priam, what are you doing with that brick?"

I approach the house. Danny is in front of me and has no

idea of what I am about to do, while Jimmy is behind me and certainly has some idea as to what I have planned. I hold the brick up high while facing the window. Before I move forward with my plan though, I finally decide to answer Jimmy's question. "Just watch me," I say in a voice that almost frightens me as it doesn't sound like my own, it comes out as a kind of uncontrolled snarl. My anger has taken over me. I feel like a passenger inside of a body that has lost control. At the same time though, I know exactly what I'm doing. I pull the brick back as far as I can, and push it forward through the air with all of my strength. It reaches impact at the top of the window and crashes through, with a loud sound of shattering glass emanating from the breaking point that seems to echo all around us. Danny falls back from the force and his utter surprise as to what has just happened in front of him. He has no idea what has occurred until he turns around from the ground, stands up and sees me standing there with a big grin on my face.

"What the hell Priam? Are you crazy?" He exclaims, clearly shocked at what I have done. Although he doesn't see the brick in my hand, since it is now lying within the old Miller place, I think he is able to figure out what just happened.

"Maybe a little bit," I say to him, still smiling. "Now you have a way to get in. You were obviously never going to make it in on your own. You needed my help."

"You could have killed me! What if you had missed the window and hit me instead?" He yells at me, not at all grateful for the help I have given him in his mission. To be honest, I hadn't even though about that. Maybe I should have warned Danny to move out of the way before I threw the brick. I hadn't wanted to warn him though, I wanted to scare the shit out of him, to show him who was boss; that I, for once in fact could be in charge, I could be the rebel without a cause.

I don't get to answer the question he has asked, I don't get to tell him that I was fed up beyond belief with how he had been treating me today. I don't get to tell him that this was my way of showing him that I wasn't a baby, that this was my way to show him that I was the brave one, I was the bad ass, I was the go getter. I don't get to tell him any of these things, my speech of valor and rage is never delivered, because suddenly we hear someone shouting in the distance, but the distance isn't far, and it seems to be getting closer and closer to us with each passing second.

"Hey! What was that? What the?" A man's voice exclaims and I can hear the sounds of his body running towards us, his footsteps crunching through the fallen leaves.

"Shit! We gotta go!" Jimmy yells as he runs to get his bike and hops on. I do the same and Danny follows suit once he is able to rebound from the shock of the brick explosion that just happened right in front of his face. We're on our bikes quickly, but it's not fast enough, the man arrives at the Miller house, right where we had just previously been standing and he sees the huge gaping hole in the back window. The shards of glass hanging out from the hole spread out around on the ground before it. While I'm pedaling away I can't help but turn and look to see the reaction on his face.

"You kids come back here! What in the hell did you do that for? Hey! Come back here!" He yells as I pedal faster and faster. I'm in front of both Jimmy and Danny on the escape trail, and we are almost out of sight when I decide to turn back one final time to see if I recognize the man, as before I was unable to focus due to my fear. When I do, I wish I wouldn't have looked back. Even though he is far away now, I am able to put two and two together. The voice, that tall physique, and especially that green pinstriped blazer, I recognize who the man is. I know him and not only do I know him, he knows me, and more importantly, rather, more unfortunately...he knows my mother.

Mr. Sanders, the owner of the Alden diner just interrupted our plans. As I pedal my feet as quickly as I can, propelling my bicycle faster than I think it's ever gone before I can only think of one thing: if I recognized him, did he recognize me? And if he did, will Mr. Sanders tattle on us, or more significantly, will he tell my mother about my brick throwing escapade? Will he tell her anything at all? I feel my rage melting away and transforming into something else entirely: a lump of guilt in the pit of my stomach, and a strong sense of fear, utter fear as to what my mother will do if she finds out. Disappointing her, embarrassing her is the last thing I want to do.

Jimmy rides his bike straight into the driveway of his house and I don't even bother stopping to tell him goodbye. I keep pedaling until I make it back to our house on Elm Street. I throw my bike in the front lawn right to the side of my mother's Ford Victoria, which is still parked in the driveway where it was before. I bend over and look at the grass below, the green color mixes around and starts to float away. Suddenly I feel very dizzy, I grab my stomach and I puke.

"What the hell is wrong with you today?" Danny asks as he sets his bike on the ground beside me.

"Everything Danny, just everything and I feel it's only going to get worse." I throw myself on the ground, not even caring that I'm lying next to a pile of my own sick. At least I'm home, at least I can pretend like things are alright, at least for a little while. That is, until Mr. Sanders tells my mother what I've done, if he ever does. If there is a God above, I need him now more than ever.

After lying outside in the grass for about ten minutes aiming to regain my senses, I finally decide to get up and go into the house. Danny had left me a while ago, so I had just been out there by myself. I wonder if he is as nervous as I am about Mother finding out about what we have done. Then again, it was really I who had done the worst thing; it was I who had thrown the brick. I don't know if Danny had recognized that it was Mr. Sanders who was yelling at us. I think about going up into his room and asking him but decide against it, I don't want to risk the chance of Mother overhearing our conversation. When I enter the house I see she is sitting in the living room, working on my Superman costume. It looks as if it is almost finished. I walk towards where she is sitting and plop down on the couch next to her.

"What are you two doing home so early? I asked your brother but he just completely ignored me and stormed up to his room. Is something wrong Priam?" She seems to notice the hint of distraught I'm holding and trying so hard to hide. A lot of things seem to be going wrong, but I don't want to tell her anything that has happened. I don't like lying to my mother, but I can't bare the notion of telling her what actually occurred over at the old Miller house so I make something up instead.

"Jimmy had to go home early, so Danny and I just decided to come back."

"Ah I see. Well, did you have fun riding bikes for the little amount of time you had anyways?"

"Yes. It was fun. I beat Danny in a race, I think maybe that's why he stormed up to his room without saying anything to you."

Even though my plan of being better than Danny in real life

was far more mischievous and poorly executed, this notion that I tell my mother about being faster than Danny on our bicycles isn't completely false after all, as I did beat him back to the house after Mr. Sanders scared us away.

"You two are so competitive with each other; I think you get that from your father. He always wanted to be the best at everything he ever did. I just hope that as you get older, you start to get along with each other better. You know, the three of us should really be able to depend on one another more and more as time goes on," she says a she lifts my costume and holds it up in front of her with a big smile that could light up the moon.

"It looks amazing Mother, I can't wait to wear it."

"I'm glad you like it Priam. All I have to do is attach the cape and it will be finished."

"I'll try better to get along with Danny. I swear we do get along sometimes, I just think he likes to rough me up to prove he's the one in charge. That's normal, isn't it?"

"I suppose it is to a certain extent, but you know, it's alright if you rough him up right back sometimes too. Don't let him walk all over you Priam, I don't want him to do that to you and I know your father wouldn't want that to happen either. You're a strong boy, I know I don't have to worry too much about you," she says as she stands up and sets my Superman costume on the chair. "I think the pot roast is almost finished. Why don't you go up to your room and get cleaned up. Since you boys are home sooner than expected, we can eat earlier. How does that sound baby?"

"That sounds wonderful Mother," I say as I get up and follow after her into the kitchen. I watch as she checks the oven and starts to pull out three pale yellow plates to set the dining room table. When she turns around and sees me standing there, she lets out a slight gasp.

"I thought you went upstairs," she says softly with a laugh. "Did you need something else?"

"I don't need anything Mother. I just wanted to tell you I love you," I say and then I wrap my arms around her waist.

"I love you too dear. You know that." She says and holds me close. We stand there for a moment and then I can feel her body start to sway side to side.

"What are you doing?" I ask, although I think I have an idea why her body is moving to and fro.

"Oh, I just figured we could go for a little waltz, you know, like we used to when you were younger. I feel as if we haven't put on our dancing shoes in a while."

"When did we ever have dancing shoes?" I ask her, confused.

"Oh Priam, I was just kidding. With moves like ours, we don't need any dancing shoes," she says and she grabs my right hand and pulls it up into hers. We sway and begin to twist to the silence that seems to be enveloping us. She pulls her hand away from mine suddenly, but only for a second. She turns on the radio next to the kitchen window and the room is quickly filled with the voice of Nat King Cole soulfully singing us the song *Smile*. She returns her hand back to mine, and twists me around. I can't remember the last time we danced together like this, but I feel it has to have been a while because I am almost as tall as she is now. Not quite though, but I'm sure I'll surpass her soon enough. The music picks up my spirits as the melody soothes us and generates our feet into a softly swaying beat. We continue dancing together, waltzing around the kitchen floor as if we are professionals, when in reality we are just two dancing fools.

"Isn't this nice?" She asks me, "It's really good advice you know, what that Nat King Cole has to say. Life isn't just a plum full of misery; there are lots of happy times too, like this, and even when things get hard, it's always important to smile."

"I agree, Mother. I most certainly agree," I say as the song slowly fades out and her hand parts from mine.

She kisses me on the forehead and then says "Now go on upstairs and get ready. By the time you come back down dinner will be ready."

"Yes, Ma'am" I say and go on my way. I don't get very far though before she calls my name. I look back in her direction, taking in her beauty, her long blonde hair swept to the side, her sky blue dress as elegant as ever, the white polka dots shimmering, and her face, her radiant face.

"Thank you for that dance, it was lovely," she says and offers me a charming wink.

"The pleasure was mine Miss," I tell her as I bow. I hear her chuckle as I swiftly run up the stairs, grinning all the way. Perhaps this day won't turn out so bad after all, and even if it does, I'll just tell myself to smile.

Dinner is delectably delicious, as always. I savor every morsel that meets my mouth with complete enjoyment. Mother asks us about our day, I tell her about art class and mention the rabbit I saw outside the window during math class too. I do not bring up our bike ride with Jimmy. Danny is quiet for the most part; I don't know what has gotten into him recently. He seems to shift from one mood to another so rapidly anymore. Perhaps, it's that puberty thing he's been going through. His voice has started to get deeper and he's much taller than he used to be. I don't think I've hit that stage yet, I still feel the same.

About halfway through dinner there is a knock on the door and I literally have to grab myself by the throat to stop myself from letting out a scream. Here it is, here is the moment where my day catapults straight into the ground. It's obviously Mr. Sanders at the door. Who else could it be?

"I wonder who that is?" Mother asks as she gets up and sets her napkin on the table next to her plate. I remove my hand from my throat and look over at Danny. He gives the impression of being terrified as well, but he doesn't seem nearly as freaked out as I am. We both watch as our mother glides over to the door and slowly opens it, so slowly I almost feel as if I am in agony from the suspense as to who our visitor is, even though I feel I already know. I'm wrong.

"Susan, dear, how are you?" I hear my mother exclaim as she opens the door as her best friend Susan walks in.

"Oh Moira, I'm so sorry to be bothering you and your boys, during dinnertime," she apologizes as she nods towards the dining room where Danny and I are still sitting glued to our seats. "It's just that Margaret still has a terrible fever and I've run out of aspirin. Do you have any I could have?"

"Of course I do. Don't worry about interrupting us, we don't mind, do we boys?" She asks as she goes into the kitchen and pulls out the aspirin bottle from the cabinet in the corner and brings it to Susan. "The least we can do is offer some assistance to help Margaret get better."

"Thank you so much, I really appreciate it. I shouldn't stay though, I need to be getting back to tend to her. Thanks again Moira," she says as she waves goodbye to us boys. My mother delivers a kiss on her cheek and then she is gone.

Mother closes the door behind Susan and comes back to the table. We finish our meal over the next couple of minutes. When my plate is clean I push it out away from me and put my hand on my stomach. I'm completely stuffed, I wonder if this is what being pregnant feels like. I think about asking my mother this question, but then decide otherwise. I'm so weird sometimes.

"Dinner was excellent Mother. I feel as if I don't need to eat for weeks."

"I'm glad you enjoyed it Priam. And what did you think, Danny?"

"It was great," he offers her with a smile that's slightly forced.

"Well whenever you boys want you can be excused, go work on your homework for a bit, and afterwards perhaps we can watch something on the television. I need to go buy some groceries at some point tonight. I realized that I'm out of pancake mix today, but I can probably do that later."

I don't really care if she gets pancake mix tonight or not, I could skip them for breakfast in the morning if I had to. I'm more excited by the idea of being able to watch something on the TV so I stand up and take my plate over to the sink. Breakfast foods are the last thing I want on my mind right now as I still feel full enough that it's possible I may explode. I run upstairs and start furiously working on my math assignment. Surprisingly I feel as if I am getting every problem right, even though I didn't pay attention at all to today's lesson. I'm not sure how much time goes by, but it must be at least a half an hour if not more. I hear Danny in the room next to me listening to his radio. Who knows if he is actually doing any of his schoolwork, but I don't really care. When I finish my algebra I decide to go downstairs to see if Mother has attached the cape to my costume yet. She had told me she was going to make the final touches after she finished cleaning up after dinner.

When I race down the stairs in a state of excitement filled with anticipation to see my costume and because of the television program that I will be able to watch with my mother, I am drenched in a certain sort of happiness that has apparently left me oblivious in thought to the day's prior events and former worries. For when I reach the bottom of the stairs and enter into the living room, I see that my mother is standing near the doorway with a man beside her. A man in a green pin stripped blazer. A man named Mr. Sanders, the last man on Earth I ever wanted to see in my home. I stand still, in a frozen state of shock. My mother is wishing Mr. Sanders goodbye, as he is putting on his hat. Her back is faced towards me so she doesn't see me in my stationary state standing as a statue in utter disbelief. He sees me though, and he tips his hat towards me.

"Evening Priam," he says. Those words are all he has to give to me. He wishes my mother goodbye, who still has yet to turn around to face me. When she does though, when she bids him adieu and sends him on his way, and turns around to see me, her face looks like one I am not used to seeing. It is a face of absolute disappointment, the worst face I can ever see her possess.

I knew I hated algebra for a reason. Those damn math problems completely distracted me; perhaps if I wouldn't have been upstairs doing them I could have intercepted Mr. Sanders before he talked to my mother. Maybe if Danny wouldn't have been playing his radio so loudly I would have heard him arrive and I could have explained myself to her before Mr. Sanders did all of the talking for me. I hadn't though, and from the look on her face, I was most certainly in trouble.

"I think we have some talking to do young man. You better call up to your brother and tell him to come down here," she tells me as she walks over to the chair where my Superman costume is lying. She picks it up and when she does I see the cape is attached, it looks absolutely glorious. I am in awe of how magnificent it looks, when suddenly she does something I never would have expected her to do: she throws it to the ground.

I gulp, swallowing what feels like a thousand daggers. I nod in her direction and turn around to go up the stairs to fetch my brother. Hopefully, I will be able to explain my way out of this one. It's unlikely, but it never hurts to try.

When I come back down the stairs with Danny behind me, I notice that my mother is sitting in her chair, with no expression of any kind on her face. She is staring down at her hands, which are placed one over the other on her lap. My Superman costume is still crumpled on the floor directly next to her. I can already feel my heart slowly beginning to melt. This isn't going to be good.

Outside the sun is setting, but light is still flooding through the large window in the living room. My mother is entrenched in a luminous glow that makes her look even more beautiful than usual.

The fact that she looks calm, almost serene, makes me afraid of what is about to happen even more so. I know she is not feeling at all at peace on the inside, even though that is what an outsider would believe if they were to see her still, sunlit face. Inside, her emotions are much more of a mess, I'm sure. She notices the two of us as we walk over and sit on the couch directly across from her. She moves her head ever so slightly but does not look up at first. It appears that she is still thinking over what she wants to say, forming her discussion points, deciding on how best to tell us that she is disappointed. For of course, she is.

"I'm sure you are both now aware at this point that Mr. Sanders came over to talk to me and told me of a little incident that happened earlier this evening," she begins as she looks from me to Danny with no sense of happiness in her stunningly glowing face. The sunlight that is streaming into the room is making this unbearable. I feel as if I am on fire. I wish the damn thing would just set already, or at least fall behind some trees so I don't have to deal with its presence anymore.

"He told me how he saw the two of you and Jimmy ride your bicycles out to the old Miller place. He didn't think much of it, but then as he was raking some leaves up in his yard he heard a giant crash that sounded like glass breaking. When he went to investigate what had happened, he noticed one of the windows was busted, and that the three of you were fleeing the scene. When he asked you to stop and explain yourselves you just kept on pedaling, as if you were criminals."

The fact that my mother just eluded that Danny, Jimmy and I had acted as if we were low life immoral thugs, running from the scene of the crime digs into me deep. In essence, that is what we did, but that's not exactly how it had felt at the time. I was running because I didn't want her to find out, I didn't want Mr. Sanders to tattle on us, but unfortunately that is exactly what he did. I don't care about feeling like a criminal, but I do care about the displeasure I can see swimming around in my mother's green eyes.

"Now, I'm sure there is more to the story than what Mr. Sanders bore witness to. So before I say anymore I want the both of you to explain to me what happened. And I want the truth," she says and then separates her hands and places them on the sides of the chair. She crosses her legs and sits farther back so that her face is no longer directly in the sunlight, now it is immersed in the shadows.

I turn to Danny, and try to swallow before I begin to speak, but he beats me to it. "It was all Priam," he says, throwing me under the bus.

"That's not true!" I shout interjecting to defend myself.

"Boys, we're not going to turn this into a fight. Let's try and discuss the situation in a civilized manner," my mother suggests. "How about you each get your turn to talk? Daniel, you can go first."

"Why does he get to go first?" I ask, not thinking it's fair.

"I'm older." He says, as if I need any reminder of that fact.

Mother nods in his direction, giving him the go ahead and so he begins. He tells her how going to the old Miller place was all my idea, that I told him Jimmy and I were planning on going to check it out after school. He tells her how I invited him, and how I had thrown the brick, almost knocking his head off in the process no less. He doesn't mention that he was the one who was so desperately trying to get into the house though. How convenient of him to leave out that little tidbit of information. In essence, my brother doesn't just throw me in front of the bus, he makes sure that the bus completely obliterates every part of my body. If this bus situation were to be real, I'd be dead.

When he is finished telling his part, which to be honest is pretty close to the truth minus the part he omitted about himself, I feel like there is no way in hell I am going to be able to talk my way out of this, but I'm still going to try.

"Alright Danny, we've heard what you have to say for yourself. Priam, you can go ahead and give me your viewpoint before I decide what I'm going to do about all of this," she says as she runs her fingers through her golden hair and pushes it to the side behind her other shoulder. I take a deep breath in, and then I exhale. After waiting for a few more seconds to think about what I want to say, I begin.

"What Danny said is true for the most part Mother. But he left out some things too, and I want to be able to explain what actually happened. I feel as if it looks much worse than it actually was. Jimmy and I did plan to go to the old Miller place together. We wanted to look inside because we had heard some of the older kids were making a haunted house there. When we got there we didn't see anything. I even suggested that we leave; I finally realized when we were standing outside the house that the whole thing was such a bad idea, and that it was wrong to be snooping and trespassing at the Miller place, regardless of whether or not there was a haunted house.

"That's when things took a turn for the worse. I tried to tell Danny we should leave, and Jimmy seemed to agree, but Danny didn't want to leave. He said that we were going to go inside, and that he was going to get us in. I disagreed with him, and that's when he called me a baby." At this point I start to tear up a little bit, I can't help it. The emotions come flowing out of me like a river that cannot be stopped. The dam has broken and the gates are flooding. The strength in my voice that was there at the beginning of my speech is now gone, my will is slowly faltering.

"When he said that, a kind of anger boiled up inside of me. I'm not a baby. I know you always call me your baby Mother, but it's starting to bother me. I'm thirteen years old, I'm growing up, I'm not a baby anymore." When I say this Mother looks as if she wants to interject in to say something. Just as the words are about to escape her lips she covers her mouth with her hands as if to stop them from coming out. She decides against saying anything, she didn't interrupt Danny, so she's not going to interrupt me. It wouldn't be fair.

"Maybe I should have told you earlier that I don't want you to call me your baby anymore, but I guess all that matters is that I'm telling you now. Anyways, when Danny called me a baby it just set something off inside of me." At this point I turn to look at him, "I feel as if you are always trying to make me feel bad, always trying to push me down and show that you are braver and stronger than me. Well today I decided to prove you wrong. When you were pulling on that door, and trying to lift that window with no success, I noticed a pile of bricks sitting nearby. I know I shouldn't have done it, I know it was wrong, but when I saw those bricks it was almost as if I couldn't help myself. I had to do it. I had to do the wrong thing, in order to show you that I could. In order to prove that I'm not just some perfect little well behaved baby, that I'm a boy, that I'm a young man."

Danny offers me a slight shrug, appearing somewhat sorry for his part in what happened. I notice it, but at the same time I ignore it. I look back to my mother and continue. "When Mr. Sanders started running over and yelling at us we all got scared and fled. I know that was cowardly, especially after I just explained to you how I was trying to be brave. I'm not claiming that what I did makes much sense, but it did at the time. I just wanted to show Danny that I could be a rebel too. I just wanted to surprise him for once, I wanted to feel alive."

At that, I end my argument and lean back farther into the couch, as all the while I was talking I was sitting on the edge of my seat using my hands in order tell my story as effectively and sympathetically as I could. I wipe the tears off of my cheeks and shove my hands into my pockets. I gave it everything I could; I hope she has some empathy. I hope Danny knows now how angry he makes me at times. If anything, hopefully this dilemma will somehow make my relationship with at least one of them better.

"I've heard what you've had to say and I appreciate you being so forthcoming," she says as she comes back into the sunlight and looks at Danny and then back to me. "Although, I'm sure you know that I can't let this act go unpunished, you both did things that I am disappointed in, things that I know your father would be ashamed of too." When she says this, it is as if my lungs close and no air can enter into my system. My mother rarely ever brings up my father when she is punishing us for something, but when she does, it is most certainly never a good thing.

"Daniel, for not telling me that you were the one who was trying to get into the house so desperately, and for all of the times you have been rude to your brother unnecessarily that have gone unpunished, I'm going to have to ground you for two weeks."

"What?" he screams. "Really? Two weeks! That's absurd! I didn't even do anything! It was Priam who threw the brick!"

"I understand that, but you were an accomplice, and what you did affected the turn of events, and for that I feel like you need to be held responsible. Besides, you are the older brother, you should have known better than even going to that house at all. When Priam told you about he and Jimmy's plans you should have told him not to go, instead you joined them. I think two weeks is a fair enough punishment for that."

"Fine," he sighs. He realizes that arguing his case any further will do him no good. I'm surprised his punishment is so harsh, but Mother has made good points for her reasoning. She looks at me, and as she does I notice that the sunlight is slowly fading from her face. I turn to look out the window where the light had been streaming in, and although it has not yet set, the sun is now hidden behind some maple trees. The light, might as well be gone altogether.

"I understand your frustrations Priam, and in part, I do almost feel as if I can comprehend why you threw that brick, but that does not in any way justify what you have done. I'm not going to ground you for two weeks though, I don't think that would be a fit punishment for your actions." I let out a sigh of relief as silently as I can, for I don't want her to notice. I think she does though. Perhaps my punishment won't be as bad as I originally thought. Perhaps I should have just been honest with her all along from the moment I got home this afternoon. "Instead, I'm not going to allow you to go out on Halloween. There will be no blonde Superman this year."

At these words I feel as if all of the happiness I have ever experienced in my life is being sucked out of me. How is this my punishment? How is this happening? This cannot be my punishment, it just cannot. I would rather be grounded for two weeks than to not be able to go out trick-or-treating. That's all I've been looking forward to this month, that's all I've wanted.

"What?" I scream, just as Danny had done only a few minutes earlier. "But, that's the one thing I want to do more than anything! How can that be my punishment?"

"Because, like you just said, that is the one thing you want to do more than anything else. You said you didn't want to be treated like a baby anymore, so that is what I am doing, I am punishing you as the young man you are, by taking away what you desire the most. I'm not happy to do it, but unfortunately I feel it is necessary in order to teach you a lesson."

"This is so unfair!" I yell, as the tears are burning my eyeballs once again and leaving streaks of fire down my cheeks. I can feel the snot starting to drop down into my nose, the sobs are getting heavier. I can feel myself losing control. Danny is silent behind me; I can't even bear to look at him. I feel as if this is all his fault. I know that's not true, but I wish it were. I wish I could go back in time and stop myself from throwing that brick, but I know that is impossible.

"I'm sorry you feel that way Priam, but I think this punishment will allow you to focus on how careless you acted. How would you feel if someone threw a brick through a window in our house?"

"But no one even lives in the Miller house! It's abandoned! It's a piece of shit!" The anger I felt earlier today, right before I performed the act that had gotten me into this mess in the first place is back and this time it's boiling hotter than ever. I've never had much of a temper before, but now it seems to be all I can feel, and as I stare into my mother's eyes, I feel it being directed towards her. For the first time I can remember, the sight of her makes me furious.

"Priam, don't say such things. I understand you are upset but try to control your anger."

I can't control my anger and for once in my life I don't even want to try. I feel as if I can't try. She stands up to console me. I know she feels bad that things had to happen this way, but at the same time she thinks this punishment is what I deserve, and for that I feel an emotion I have never felt for her before. As she begins to extend her arms towards me, I too stand up off of the couch and I push her away. I look her straight in the face; I make sure my eyes are locked directly with hers. The sunlight is gone, but her beauty still shines through, even though she does not look particularly happy, she still looks far more composed than I'm sure I appear to be. I am a mess, a thirteen year old boy who is sobbing uncontrollably with tears streaming down his face, with nothing in his heart at the moment except for the rage that has come upon him because of being denied the thing he wants more than anything, to wear that red cape on Halloween night, to fly.

"I hate you!" I scream at her, and as the words escape my mouth I can say no more. I look at her heartbroken face that is utterly stunned and I turn away. I run upstairs, down the hallway to my bedroom and slam the door as hard as I can. I throw myself onto my bed and curl into the fetal position and begin to sob even more uncontrollably, filled with anger towards my mother and my brother. As I lie there I have no idea that those are the last three words I will ever say to her. Those three words filled with fury, filled with rage will never be able to be taken back. My mother, my hero, my everything, Moira Wood would never hear another thing I had to say, for later that evening, she would be dead.

After a while I eventually am able to calm myself down and I wipe the tears off of my eyes with my bed sheet. I don't want to go downstairs; I don't want to talk about this anymore today. I just want to fall asleep and for everything to be okay. I watch the sun set in the distance, and as it falls behind the skyline completely my eyes slowly begin to drop down too. I'm just about to pass into unconsciousness when I hear a car starting right outside my bedroom window. I get up to see what is happening.

My mother is sitting in her black Ford Victoria, the car she got just this past May. It's a beautiful car, and it looks so crisp and concise right now in the little amount of daylight left that is still flittering about through the air. I wonder where she is going, but then I remember she told me she needed to buy some more pancake mix for my breakfast tomorrow morning. I really could go without pancakes for a day, but I suppose she figures since I'm so upset I'll need the comfort of normality when I arise in the morning to greet her. She probably figures it's the least she can do.

I watch as she pulls out of the driveway and continue following the Victoria with my eyes until it fades away into the night, the dusk enveloping the vehicle entirely. I leave the window and topple back onto my bed. This time, I decide to just get under the covers. It's still rather early but I don't want to be awake anymore, I'd much rather be greeted with the blank slate of sleep, or even a dream. Hopefully not a nightmare, as I feel as if I am already living one. Slowly, little by little, I drift off into a slumber.

While I am sleeping events happen that will change my life forever. I'm not aware of them right away as they occur while my mind is in another place. I find out about them later, I find out about them when I wake up, and in the days and weeks that follow. In a way, the events that happen as I sleep are sort of like a dream, but a dream they actually are not, for they are real, they exist in my reality, my life.

My mother had decided to drive to the grocery store just as I had thought, to get some pancake mix for my breakfast the following morning. She made it to the store fine, even though she was still distraught from what had transpired before she arrived there. She had figured it would be good to get out of the house to clear her mind and to reflect on things.

Danny would later tell me that she had told him where she was going and that she wouldn't be long. The last thing she had said to him before slipping out the door was: "Check on your brother will you? Make sure he's okay." He had done so, but apparently when he opened my bedroom door I was asleep on my bed and he had decided not to wake me, that sleep was what I probably needed most.

While at the grocery store my mother bought just two things according to Fred, the old man who owned the place. He was the one who waited on her. She had purchased a box of pancake mix and a carton of blueberries. Apparently she had decided regular pancakes weren't enough for me that following morning, I needed something special, something blue. I didn't deserve special pancakes after what I had done, or what I had said. In fact I didn't deserve pancakes at all that next morning. I wish she had thought the same. That wasn't my mother though. She was always thinking of us boys, always trying to see the good in us even when there didn't appear to be much good shining through.

"Hello, Mrs. Wood, how are you doing this evening?"

"Oh I'm doing alright Fred. Could be better though."

"What's wrong? I thought that pretty face of yours looked a little upset when you walked up to the counter. You always appear so happy whenever I see you around."

"Oh it's just my boys. They got themselves into some trouble and I had to punish them, and my youngest son Priam didn't take it too well."

"Well, don't let it get to you Mrs. Wood. Young boys can be awfully temperamental sometimes. I'm sure if he acted out it wasn't because he meant to."

"I suppose you're right. I just have never felt so much anger from him before. I guess I don't know how to process it, that's all. I'm sure by tomorrow morning it will be fine, I'm going to make him some blueberry pancakes. He is a good boy after all."

That's how the exchange had gone, that was the final conversation my mother ever had, about blueberry pancakes and a misbehaving son that she still believed was good. When Fred Thompson told me this a few days later at her funeral I felt so light headed I almost passed out. He had wished her a good evening, and instead of returning the sentiment, instead of saying anything in return, my mother had nodded her head and forced herself to smile, as she knew Fred would appreciate that more than anything she could say.

The last thing I ever said to my mother was "I hate you."

The last thing my mother ever said about me was "He is a good boy after all." The paradox of those two sentences haunted me forever. I've always wished to take back those three words. The seven words she offered me, the seven words she said to Fred that he delivered to my ears kept me sane and let me have some hope that when it happened, she didn't think so poorly of me, she still thought I was a good boy. I was her baby.

After she left the grocery store I have no idea what she thought, what she did, or even if the radio was playing in her 1954 Ford Victoria when it happened. I like to tell myself that the radio was on though; I like to tell myself that Nat King Cole's song *Smile* was playing and that the last thing she ever thought about before she died was me and her waltzing together around the kitchen floor, just two dancing fools. I hope that was her last thought and I hope the final thing she did before she left this world was exactly what the song told her to do: smile.

The truck hit her going sixty miles an hour and impacted her directly on the driver's side of her black Ford Victoria. Her car flipped from the impact, rolling a total of four times down a slight grassy slope before it finally came to a stop. I don't know why she didn't have her seat belt on. That part has never made sense to me as she always wore it and she was always making sure Danny and I wore ours to. I blame myself for that, I blame those three words, I think they must have distracted her. If only she had worn it, if only I hadn't said what I did, perhaps things would have been different. Those three words ruined a lot for me.

The truck that hit her was driven by George Jones, a senior at Alden High School. Apparently he wasn't paying attention and forgot there was a stop sign at that intersection. He was in a rush to go over to the old Miller place. There was some sort of Halloween project he and his friends had planned to start working on that evening and he was running late. Some sort of haunted house they had planned or something like that. The irony was too great to bear.

Back at home I am still asleep when it happens. When my mother doesn't return for over an hour Danny starts to worry. When more time passes he starts to worry even more. That's when the telephone rings, that's when I jolt awake.

I look at my clock and see that it's now 9:30. I look to the window and notice that outside it is black. I decide to get out of bed and walk downstairs. When I reach the kitchen I expect to see my mother talking to someone on the phone. Instead it is Danny, holding the telephone up to his face, which looks as if it has completely transformed into something I have never seen. I don't know how long I stand in front of Danny as he holds the phone up to his ear. It must be about two minutes. He doesn't say much, just a few okays and yes and alright. When he hangs up the phone he falls to the ground, his limbs crumple into a pile just like my Superman costume on the floor in the living room.

"Danny, what is it?" I ask, starting to come to terms that something must be wrong. Something has to be wrong. He begins to sob, just as I had previously done that day, gasping thickly for a breath that seems to be avoiding him. When he finally tells me, when I am informed of the reality of what has happened it is barely intelligible, but for some reason I am able to understand the three words he says: "Mother is dead."

I don't know why he delivers it as such. I don't know why there is no detail in what he has said, just a subject and a verb and a fact. Danny has found out about our mother's death on the phone and I feel horribly bad because of this. When technology interludes so directly with life it makes my insides squirm. Death and life shouldn't have to be processed in such a way. I'm sure there is more to what happened than the simplicity of what he has told me, as people just don't die unexpectedly without reason. I guess I don't deserve a reason right now though, that reason is too much for Danny to explain to me. It is all too much.

I scream. I scream so loudly I'm surprised that I don't break any more windows than I have already broken today. I continue screaming, unable to move, unable to do anything but let out a barbaric noise of fear, of complete and utter disbelief, a sound of unrelenting incredulity. This can't be, this can't be. Somehow though, I know it is.

From that point on the day is a blur. Eventually, Danny and I regain some sense of our humanity and run next door to Susan's to tell her what has happened. She begins to cry, but it is more controlled than how Danny and I reacted, perhaps that comes with growing up I think to myself, surprised I'm even able to think about anything else at all. Maybe she has experienced someone dying before. I never have, at least not like this. She drives us to the hospital, and finds out more details of what happened from the doctor. Over the next few hours I find out what has happened too. I find out that the Victoria is totaled, that George Jones only suffered a broken arm, that she was only two miles away from home, that she died upon impact, going straight from life into death's outreaching clutches.

She died while listening to the song *Smile*, she died with a smile on her radiant face, I keep telling myself over and over again. She died thinking of me, and our foolish waltz, thinking of a happy time, a time when she knew I loved her. That's all I can tell myself, for those three words I last said to her keep trying to come to the forefront of my mind. I try to push them back with my philosophy of her final moments, the two things battling for my attention.

We don't stay at the hospital long. Susan drives us back to our house and tells us she is going to stay over for the night. She tells us it's best if we just try to go to sleep. That things will be okay, that things will somehow get better. I look at her as if she is a crazy person. I feel like a crazy person. This can't be real.

As I lay in my bed I know I am not going to be able to fall asleep. I stare at my clock, watching the second hand circle around for what like seems like an eternity. I try to think of nothing, I try to not exist. I don't want to exist. I'm still awake when the clock is at 11:59. I watch the second hand go around and around as if it is trying to prove to me it is never going to give up. When the clock hits midnight, everything goes black. I don't fall asleep, as my eyes are still open, the day just stops.

Monday, October 11ᵗʰ 1954
Day One – *The Second Chance*

I feel fingers running through my hair and I try to brush them away, but they don't leave my head, they stay. The hand pats my head and then I feel a warm breath near my right ear whisper and say "Priam, baby, it's time to get up. Monday, Monday, it's time for a fun day."

Immediately at those words I jolt right up and wrap my arms around her, holding her as tightly as I can because I never want to let her go. It's really here, she's alive, she's here with me now.

"Priam, if you squeeze me any harder I think I'll explode," my mother laughs as she tries to loosen my grip a little bit.

"I love you, I love you, I love you," I say three times aloud. First and foremost that is what I want her to know more than anything.

"Were you having a bad dream or something baby? I've never seen you so excited to wake up this early in the morning."

"Something like that," I say as I finally release her from my grip and look up at her face. It's even more beautiful than I remember. It's like experiencing a sight so divine for the first time and I don't know how to handle it. I know I have seen this face before but it feels like it's been forever since I've seen her last, yet all the while it feels as if I saw her yesterday.

Yesterday. I'm not sure if my current essence, as in my mind that I'm in control of now was completely present during the original day that I relived, but I feel as if I was there experiencing it the way it originally happened. I feel as if I just woke up from falling asleep on that fateful night. I remember everything as freshly as I possibly can. I feel all of it, the happiness, the sadness, the confusion, and the heartbreak. Everything from that day is with me here now, as I am about to live it once more. This time though, as Chloe had explained to me in that white space, I'm in charge and I can change things.

Rolling over all of this through my mind I'm trying to compartmentalize things so it makes sense, but I know it never really will. What I'm going through currently is like nothing I have ever gone through before. It is an indescribable feeling.

"Well I'm glad whatever it was you were dreaming of is over

now if it frightened you so. I'm going to go downstairs and make your breakfast. Get ready for school, alright?"

"Yes, Mother. I'll be down soon," I say.

She gets up from my bed and I watch her walk down the hallway. When she reaches the top of the stairs; she looks back at me and smiles. Oh how wonderful it is to be with her again. I feel as if I cannot even begin to fathom what I can do with this day. I can do things my way, but...can I save her?

Her death is just as fresh in my mind as it could ever be. I touch my cheeks to see if there are dried streaks of tears on my face, but of course there are not. I remember the rule Chloe told me, as she said "You cannot directly save someone. In the manner of which, you cannot stop someone from dying simply by deciding to." What does that even mean? Thinking about the way she worded it now, or how I remember her saying it, is there a way to get around this rule? I cannot directly save her. I cannot tell her she is going to die tonight. I cannot lock her in her bedroom or anything of the sort, that much is clear, but can I somehow save her without letting her know that on this original day she died while driving her Ford Victoria? Can I change other things about this day which will lead to her living to see tomorrow? For tomorrow is a whole new day in this reality, this tomorrow will be different, it will be affected by what I do today.

This is only day one, only the first of my second chances and already my head is spinning. I decide to stop thinking for a moment about all of this and get out of bed to gather my things as my mother requested. I have no interest in going to school, I'd rather pretend to be sick and stay home with her, but I doubt she would believe me if I did so. She could always tell when I lied. Besides, the school day is where it all started, where I got hit in the back of the head with a spit wad that resulted in the plans to go to the old Miller house, where I threw the brick that eventually led to me saying those three words. One thing I know for sure, I will not say those words today. I will die before I do so. At that thought I begin to wonder if it is even possible for me to die in this reality of second chances. I decide not to dwell on it, as my seventy year old brain within the body of a thirteen year old can probably only handle so much.

Suddenly I recognize myself in the mirror that is in front of me. I know it's me, but it's a strange sensation that my eyes are evaluating. Seeing myself again in complete consciousness within my young, unwrinkled, untouched body is such an otherworldly experience. I begin to feel woozy. I look down and realize that everything is smaller than the last time I remember it being. Sure, I suppose I was in this body yesterday, or at least whatever yesterday can be classified as in my mind, but I wasn't in control then. I was simply a passenger within the body watching the day go by as if it were a motion picture. Now, I can actually stop and stare at myself, I can look into my own thirteen year old eyes. I drop my jaw as if in disbelief, simply to make a silly face. I laugh out loud. Oh, to be young again.

I get dressed and collect my mess of papers strewn about my room and shove them into my book bag. I throw the bag over my shoulder and then quickly brush my teeth before heading downstairs for breakfast. When I reach the kitchen table Danny is already sitting there eating some scrambled eggs and a bowl of cereal. "Hi fat face," he says with a smirk.

My mother turns around from the stove and glares at my brother. "How many times do I have to tell you to stop saying such things to Priam in the morning? I don't care if you think it's alright for you to pick on him just because you are the older one. Knock it off," she adds as she shakes the spatula in her hand at him in a disapproving manner. She turns back to the stove, flipping over a pancake that I know is for me.

"Sorry Mother," Danny says in her direction then looks back to me with a grimace and bellows out "Hi skinny face. You are looking awful skinny today. Better eat up or you're not going to be able to fit into that Halloween costume of yours."

I put my book bag on the floor next to my chair and am about to sit down, but instead I do something else. I walk over to Danny and slap him across the face as hard as I can.

As soon as it happens I can't believe it actually has. For some reason, I just felt I needed to do it. The look on his face is one of horror, one of total disbelief. "Like Mother said Danny, stop being rude," I tell him as I sit down at the table in a nonchalant manner.

He is silent, but the quiet only remains for a moment because after I take my seat I realize my mother is rushing right toward me, spatula in hand, and she's not planning on using it to serve me pancakes, instead she grabs me by the arm and pulls me off of the chair and smacks me with it, right on the ass.

"What in good heavens is wrong with you this morning Priam? Just because I told your brother to stop being ignorant doesn't mean I meant for you to start being the bad mannered one," she says in a flustered tone as she releases me and goes back to the stove. My ass is stinging, but I suppose I deserve that.

"Sorry Mother," I say. "I guess I just lost my temper." As I glance back at Danny I realize I'm not really sorry though. The look on his face is the most priceless thing I have ever seen. I think I just proved to my older brother that I am brave, that I can be spontaneous. I think I just showed my brother I'm no longer a little baby. One mission down, only a million more to go.

While eating our breakfast I decide to ask my mother about how the Superman costume is coming along even though I know she is almost finished with it. "I think I will be done with it later tonight actually," she says as she sits down at the table with us confirming the fact. "I'm sure you will look wonderful in it."

I wait for Danny to say something about how Superman isn't even blonde but he doesn't say anything. I'm beginning to wonder if me slapping Danny is going to change how he behaves the rest of this day. If it does, I suppose that is alright, as long as his behavior doesn't impede on me giving everything I've got to somehow save my mother's life.

"What are you dressing up as again Danny?" I ask, as I realize I don't recall what he was planning on being for trick-or-treating. Neither of us actually went out on that Halloween. I couldn't bear to put on the Superman costume after it happened. In fact, I could barely even look at it after she died.

"I was thinking of going as Dracula," he tells me. "I don't know though, I think I might be getting a bit old for the whole thing. Perhaps I'll just stay in this year and help Mother pass out the candy."

"Well whatever you decide to do is fine with me," she says. "But if you do decide to be Dracula you better let me know soon so I can start working on a costume for you."

"Alright, I will."

The idea of my mother making a costume for Danny, one that she would have to start another day excites me. I know Chloe told me I can't save her, but for some reason I no longer believe that is actually the case. I know there has to be a loophole. I have to stop her somehow from going to that grocery store, even if it is indirectly.

We finish eating our breakfast and she clears the dishes away for us as we gather our book bags and put on our jackets by the door. Danny runs outside first, without saying goodbye to our mother, but I decide to wait until she comes over and tells me goodbye. I want to take in every instance of her that I can. When she greets me at the door to say farewell she kisses me on the top of the head and wishes me a good day, and then says "I think I'll have to go to the grocery store later today. I just realized I'm all out of pancake mix."

My heart jumps up from my chest and hits my brain so that I feel as if all of my neurons are about to explode. I start to scream internally, I try to say something, anything, I try to tell her no, don't go, I don't need pancakes tomorrow, but the words won't come out. I am unable to say anything. This is fate telling me not to mess with its plan, this is what Chloe warned me about. I can't save someone from dying simply because I want to, if I even can save anyone at all. I am afraid this truth will affect me more than just today. All I can do is wish her a good day as well. "Have a splendid afternoon Mother. And I'm sorry for slapping Danny, really I am. I don't know what came over me."

"I appreciate the apology Priam, but I think perhaps your brother would appreciate it even more. Everyone loses control sometimes, but you know I expect better of you."

"I know. I'll talk to Danny on the way to school about it, I promise."

"Good boy, that's my baby," she says as she hugs me once more and leads me out the door.

I stare at the Ford Victoria that is parked in the driveway, and as I do I wonder if I can somehow slash its tires or hide the keys. As I approach it there seems to be some bubble of protection around it that won't let me get close to it since these thoughts of disarming it are floating through my mind, but then I think of doing something else to it instead and the invisible shield fades. As I'm walking down the driveway to meet Danny by the mailbox I stick out my hand and sweep it along the side of the car, petting it as if it is a dog. Somehow, I am going to become its master. I'm not going to let it become the tomb that causes my mother's death.

When I reach where Danny is waiting for me we begin to walk down the street. I turn around and wave to my mother one last time. She blows me a kiss and this time I decide to watch her as she goes inside. When I can no longer see her shining face or any trace of her blue and white polka dotted dress I turn to look at my brother. "I'm sorry for slapping you at breakfast Danny," I say in the most meaningful tone I can muster.

"It's alright Priam."

"Really?" I was not expecting to hear this kind of answer from him.

"Yeah, really. I think I probably deserved it."

"Well still, I shouldn't have done it."

"Maybe not, but at least you stood up to me for once. Usually I feel as if I can walk all over you, because you never do anything back to me. I don't know if this is weird for me to say, but I feel like Father kind of would have been proud of you for finally doing something to make me realize what an ass I've been to you recently."

"You really think so? You think he'd be proud?"

"I think. Besides, it's not like you got off scot free," he says and laughs. "It looked like Mother hit you pretty hard on the ass with that spatula."

"It definitely didn't feel good, that's for sure."

The rest of the walk to school with my brother is a pleasant one, we talk about going for a bike ride later, as long as it's not to the old Miller place, I think. If I would have known slapping my brother would have elicited such honesty and a new found respect in him for me I would have slapped him across the face many times before today. I guess that's what these second chances are for though, to find out new things about those I love, to make changes, to fix everything I possibly can and to be a better man.

The day at school is a weird one. I feel strange being surrounded by only thirteen year olds. I suppose I myself am only a thirteen year old, but on the inside I don't feel like one. Walking down the hallways of my high school is a strange experience. I hadn't been at Alden High for quite some time before I died. I suppose in some sense I was here yesterday, but was that really me? As in the me I currently am? Perhaps I'll never know. I'm here now, that's for sure and just as on this original day I'm having trouble concentrating on anything related to academics.

All I can think about is my mother and how I have to save her. I know a major part of my plan to do so resides within my math class. It resides in a wet gooey spit wad that is going to hit in me in the back of the head by none other than my best friend Jimmy. I wait for it to happen, and when it does, I spin around slowly making sure the teacher at the front of the room doesn't notice. Jimmy's face is just as big and smarmy as it was the first time. I want nothing more than to send a spit wad back in his direction.

"Got ya!" He yells as quietly as he can.

"What the hell do you want?" I ask, deciding to go with a more direct approach this time.

"Geez can't a guy just try to get his friend's attention without such an angry response?"

"That's the attitude you get for hitting me with that nasty spit wad of yours. Would you want me hitting you in the back of the head with one of those?"

"I guess not," he admits as he sets his straw down onto his desk.

"Anyways, what's up?" I ask, even though I already know what he wishes to discuss.

"Want to go to the old Miller place after school? I heard some of the older kids are planning to turn it into a haunted house."

"Nah, Jimmy that sounds like an awful idea. We'd be busted for sure."

"Wha-?" He begins to stammer but is cut off by the shrill voice that then emanates from our teacher at the front of the room.

"Priam Wood!" She shrieks, "Kindly pay attention and stop talking to Jimmy. Neither of you have any excuse to be discussing anything right now. Nothing in your life could be more important than algebra."

"Sorry, Mrs. Johnson," I say, even though she is even more wrong than the first time she said that sentence. Today I have to save my mother's life. I don't give two shits about algebra. In fact, I don't think it would be possible for me to care about it any less than I do currently.

I see something running around outside and turn my head to look at what I already know will be a brown rabbit hopping about. It is a brown rabbit, but this time, it's not alone. Instead of running around in circles like it did on this original day, the rabbit is running in a straight path along the side of the school, sprinting for its life in fact. Behind the rabbit is a dog that is chasing it, and it's not just any dog, it's a golden retriever. Without even realizing what I'm doing I get up from my seat and rush over to the window to get a better look. It looks just like...no, it can't be.

"Priam! Sit down! What on earth are you doing?" Mrs. Johnson shouts at me, even more irritated than before.

I try to get a better look at the dog chasing the rabbit but the two animals are already out of my sight when I reach the windowsill. I apologize to Mrs. Johnson and return to my seat. The dog I saw was the absolute spitting image of Chloe. She wouldn't be born for decades though. I suppose dogs do look alike, especially if they are the same breed, so I must be imagining it, that's the only logical explanation. Still, the fact that on this original day the rabbit was alone and is now being chased by a canine has me a little bit worried. What if I'm already changing too much? If a slap across my brother's face and a firm no to my friend's plans can elicit such a strange response in this new reality, what on earth will change in my life if I save my mother from dying? The thought scares me, in fact it terrifies me, but regardless I still know that I am going to do everything in my power to save her. It's what I came here to do.

When Algebra class is over, Jimmy meets me at my locker and tries to convince me to agree to join him to go to the old Miller place. I steadfastly tell him no over and over again. I reassure him that it is an insanely horrible idea.

"Besides, if we were to get caught snooping around over there, who knows what our parents would do to punish us. Mr. Sanders lives right by that house and he knows my mother well."

"Oh, I didn't even think about that. You're probably right, I guess we shouldn't go. I'm not going to go by myself anyways, that's for sure."

I grin and give him a high five. "Thatta boy! Finally using that noggin of yours for the first time in quite a while!"

"Hey! Are you calling me stupid?" He asks, but I've already begun to walk away. I've dissuaded him from going to the old Miller place. So in turn, I won't have to go. I'll never throw that brick, I'll never get in trouble, and I'll never say those three words to my mother. Even if Chloe was right and I can't save her, at least I will get to say something else to her before she goes. At least that's how I have it planned. I walk with my head held high on my way to art class, believing that I have actually made some progress on this day. Little do I know that October 11ᵗʰ 1954 has another thing coming. Time can't be changed as easily as one might think.

In art class I decide to start a new painting. I've already finished the assignment that Mr. Williams gave us, so while all of the other students are finishing theirs I pull out a blank new canvas and get to work. When I paint, I do so rather frantically, not taking time to plan out a process of any kind. Painting to me is like poetry, it flows from my fingertips which lead the brushstrokes onto the white abyss before me until it is white no more.

I paint a scene from a dream I once had in my life. In this life though, dreams can come true, because what happened in the past hasn't happened here. This is a place where I can start anew, if only time and fate decide to mate and let me pass through.

I paint a street with autumn colored trees and leaves falling to the ground. I paint Alden city hall in the distance too. I paint a car, a black Ford Victoria rolling down the avenue. I paint a boy in the sky dressed as Superman with green eyes and blonde hair, and in the car I paint a smiling woman with golden hair of the same shade, waving up and smiling at the boy. I paint her a blue dress, bluer than the sky in which the boy flies and I cover the dress with white polka dots that look like clouds. This scene is from a dream I once had long ago, but oh how I wish it to be real. I know that if my mother lives, if I somehow manage to save her, I probably won't actually have the ability to fly, but oh I'll try, at least I'll be able to try.

When I meet up with Danny after the school day is over to walk home I suggest that we ride our bikes downtown and get ice cream and then go to the park. He agrees on the plan and I sigh in relief thinking that I have made another step forward in saving this day when all of a sudden I hear someone running up behind us. It's Jimmy.

"Hey there boys, what are you all up to on this fine afternoon?" He asks as he pants heavily, out of breath from running to catch up with us.

"Beat it Jimmy," I say, trying to stop the chance of any of his suggestions seeing the light of day before they even form in his brain.

"Priam, he can come with us. Don't you think?"

"I guess," I say, even though I would rather he didn't. For some reason I feel that Jimmy is the direct connection to the old Miller place, and if he is around us, we will somehow end up there, and if we end up at that house, who knows where the day will follow afterwards. I tell him of our plan to go downtown and he seems to think it is a fine idea, but I know he is still going to have something else to offer.

"So we really can't go check out the old Miller place?"

"How many times do I have to tell you? No!" I scream. I'm almost tempted to slap him but I decide that slapping Danny this morning was already enough to fill my daily quota. I don't want people to think I've lost control of myself completely.

"What's this about the old Miller place?" Danny asks turning to face Jimmy who is a few steps behind us.

Jimmy explains his idea, tells him all about the haunted house he heard the older kids were making, and how he wanted to check it out after school, but that I wouldn't agree to go with him. "Why don't we go just for a little bit Priam? We can go downtown afterwards," Danny suggests.

"Absolutely not. We'll get caught snooping around, I'm sure of it. It's not worth it," I tell them both.

"Hmm. Well I'll go with you Jimmy, I'm curious to see if they really have done anything to the old place. Lord knows it basically is just an old haunted house anyways, might as well accentuate the spooky features for the entertainment value alone if anything."

This is all wrong. We aren't supposed to go to the old Miller house. If we go, what if we get caught, what if Mr. Sanders catches us? Even though I know there is no way in hell I am going to throw that brick this time, I feel that the more similar this day is to the original one the better chance there is that my mother will get into her car and go to the grocery store this evening. If she does that, the higher the possibility is that she won't live to see another day, she won't live to see her baby blonde Superman fly in the sky, or at least she won't be able to watch him try.

I continue to yell at them in an increasingly angry tone but it's no use, they're going with or without me. I decide it's better if I go with them, at least then I can supervise whatever it is that happens and have at least some sort of control over it. If I just sit at home with Mother I think I'll go crazy not knowing what is happening. We part with Jimmy and tell him we will meet back up with him soon. When we walk into the house I decide to greet my mother instead of trying to sneak out of the house, I know that won't work this time anyways. She's in the kitchen sitting at the table working on what appears to be a crossword puzzle. The smell of pot roast drifting through the air smells just as delicious as it always has.

"How many words have you found so far?" I ask her.

She looks up and smiles. "Seven." Of course it would be seven, I'm starting to wonder if any other number even matters.

"One for each day of the week," I say as I sit down beside her. "I think Danny and I are going to go for a bike ride with Jimmy. Is that alright?"

"Sure baby, just make sure you're back by six o'clock. I have a pot roast in the oven."

"Alright, I'll make sure we are back before then. I think we are going to go downtown, and maybe get some ice cream or something."

"Well don't eat too much before dinner, you'll need to have room left in that belly of yours. Isn't pot roast your favorite?" She asks with a smile.

"You already know the answer to that Mother," I say coyly as I lift her hand and kiss it. I get up from the table then to take my book bag upstairs. I throw it in my room and then come back to the ground floor where Danny is already waiting for me. When we exit through the garage he doesn't push me, instead he waits for me to walk out the door first. My mother wishes us a good time from the kitchen and reminds us not to eat too much.

"We won't Mother! I want to have room for the delicious meal you've made!" I say in a sing song tone as I hop on my bike and then we are on our way.

I don't need to prove anything to my brother. I don't need to show him I'm brave, or reckless or spontaneous. I don't need to throw a brick, I don't need to cause a scene. All I have to do is make sure that we are quiet, make sure that Mr. Sanders doesn't notice anything fishy and that we come home by six o'clock. It seems like a simple enough task, somehow though the feeling that is churning around in the pit of my stomach eating my insides tells me that it is not going to be an easy task at all. Chloe's rule, the only rule she gave me, wants that brick to be thrown, for fate is planning on this day being justified in such a way that it still gains what it came here for: my mother's life.

When we get to the house it looks just as foreboding as I remember. The white paneling is faded so that it appears to be an ominous gray. Some of the shutters are crooked and tilted off to the sides of the windows. We take our bikes to the back of the house so that no one will see them out front, just like we had yesterday, or what felt like yesterday to me anyways.

"This place gives me the creeps," Danny says. "If the older kids are making a haunted house here I definitely want to come back on Halloween to check it out. We should try to go inside to see what they've done so far."

"That's a horrible idea," I say, putting my foot down both physically and figuratively, stopping where I'm standing about ten feet away from the back window, the window where the brick crashed through, in that other place, in the reality I once lived.

"Stop being such a baby," Danny tells me. "No one is going to see us." The fact that he calls me a baby makes me angry just as it always has, but this time it's different, this time I don't have the naïve mind of a thirteen year old. I have the mind of an entire life worth of experience, an intellect full of memories that have the ability to strengthen my convictions, and so I'm able to tell myself to simply ignore his harsh words.

"You're the one who is acting like a baby if you're really going to try to go into that house. Mother would be ashamed if she knew what you were up to, she would expect better of you. I told you we shouldn't have come."

"Priam, it's really not that big of a deal," Jimmy says. "We're just checking out the place, it's not like we are going to set it on fire or anything."

I scowl at Jimmy. I feel this is his fault. If he would have kept his mouth shut my brother and I would be downtown already, eating ice cream and sitting in the park. Instead we are here, just as we were before. This is the last place I want to be.

I stand away from the house with Jimmy as we watch Danny try to get inside. He pulls on the window and yanks on the porch door with all of his might to no avail. He returns back to the window and tugs on it even more. I know he isn't going to get into the house, not this way anyhow. I decide to look over to see if the bricks are still there and of course they are, sitting in the same pile. I imagine each of them with a menacing look on their face, as if they are alive, as if all they wish to do is to be picked up and launched through the air.

This is the moment where I acted out, this is when I went over to the pile of bricks and picked one up. This is when my blood was boiling so much that I performed that reckless act, the act that put into motion the rest of that fateful day. The act caused my mother to punish me, which in turn lead to those three words, those words that I've always blamed myself for. I know it's probably not possible, but I feel as if those words alone took her life. Not tonight, not if I have anything to say about it. I'm going to save her.

The moment passes; I can feel my body being overcome by an irrational feeling of sensations in which all of my nerves are overloading with repetitions and axons of irritation. This is fate telling me that I am messing with its plan, that I am changing the day in a serious way. In a way it almost hurts, but at the same time I tell myself that it hurts so good. I am winning.

"Why are you two just standing there? Why don't you help me?" Danny asks us, clearly irritated at our lack of action.

"I'm not helping you Danny. I didn't even want to come here."

Jimmy looks at me, and then looks to his left where my gaze was resting only a few seconds previously. "There are some bricks over there; maybe you could use one of those to help get the window open."

"Jimmy!" I scream. I could kill him for even suggesting the method. This boy who is supposed to be my best friend is ruining my day more than anyone; he is suffocating my second chance at the life I wish to lead. He is advocating an idea that could lead to dire consequences of destruction.

"That might actually work," Danny says as he abandons the window and walks over to the pile of bricks. I imagine the faces of red changing their menacing looks to smiles; they just want to fly, to float through the air, to have a purpose. In that respect, I suppose the bricks are like people, aren't they? Don't we all just want to fly? I have to stop the flight. I leave the spot where I am standing and put myself in between Danny and the window. He has a brick in his hand, I'm sure it is probably the same brick that I threw, but it's not going to take flight this time, not if I can stop it.

I never imagined that the brick itself wanted to cause damage to my life so badly, for now it seems that is all it wishes to do. I think about the seven days I picked and realize that this first one has the ability to change my life more than any of the others. If I succeed, if my mother lives, if I save her, what follows will be different. Of course I hope some things stay the same, but I believe that this is why this day is so hard to change. On this day, what I wish to change the most is not only three words, it's about saving a life, it's about my wondrous mother, Moira Wood. I wish to see her grow old, even if it is only in this second reality that I am currently creating, at least I would still feel fulfilled, at least I would prove that I am worthy of her love, and she of mine.

"Get out of the way Priam," Danny says as he angrily stares at me. "We're going into that house whether you like it or not. The Millers probably won't even notice if a window is broken, they never even come here to take care of the place."

"No!" I scream as loudly as I can. The screech is so earsplitting I surprise even myself, but it doesn't seem to dissuade him from his plan. "Stop it Danny, you're going to get us all into a heap of trouble. Put the brick down," I beg of him earnestly.

He is standing right in front of me now; I stretch out my arms in order to block him, thinking that I will be successful. I'm wrong though. For even though I feel I know more than Danny, I'm not any bigger than he is. I forget that I currently reside in a thirteen year old body, a body that is prepubescent and weak. He extends his arm and shoves me down, I fall completely backwards in one swift motion, my ass hitting the ground first, before my entire body is touching the ground beneath me.

I don't know what else to do so I scream again, this time it's not a word that comes out of my mouth though, it's just a noise, one of complete desperation, a prehistoric punctuation of the predicament I am currently in. The noise is followed directly by a crash, the brick has taken flight, it has beaten the blonde superman to the skies, it has fallen. All of my efforts of this day up until this point seem to have amounted to nothing. Though I was not the one to do the deed, it didn't matter, the old Miller place has still been desecrated, at least in part.

"Danny! You stupid bastard!" I yell as I get off of the ground and rush towards him. I'm so mad I don't even think about what I'm doing. I tackle him to the ground and start beating him on the chest. "You ignoramus idiot! Why did you have to do that? Why?!"

"Get off of me Priam!" He shouts as he pushes me off. I feel the grass brush up against my face as I roll through the terrain once more. I push my hands off of the ground and stand up, I look to Jimmy who is still and motionless, simply taking in the sight before him. He clearly has no idea how to react to what has just happened. When the man's booming voice echoes off of the broken window and reverberates against our bodies though, everything changes.

"Hey! What was that? What are you kids doing?" Mr. Sanders says as he emerges from the foliage behind us, much closer to us than he was the first time.

"Shit!" Danny yells, and with that he is running, I look to Jimmy who is running too, they have no intention of staying to answer the questions Mr. Sanders has asked. All they are thinking is to get out, to get out as fast as they can. They have the brains of two teenage boys after all, what else can I expect from them?

I watch as they go. I stare at them as they hop onto their bikes and pedal away. I don't move though, since the moment Mr. Sanders has appeared I know I am going to stay. I have to try to explain what has happened, I can't run away. Something is keeping me rooted to the spot, and I hope it's not fate, I hope it's not the actuality of reality that I am battling. Rather, I hope I've decided to stay because I somehow believe that talking to Mr. Sanders will make things better. I hope that deciding to not run away will make me a better man, to face everything I've ever been afraid of and take credit for what has gone wrong, even if it was not I who did the wrongdoing.

Mr. Sanders stares at me, and I stare back at him in his green pinstriped blazer, at his tall frame and handsome face. I hope that he somehow respects my decision to stay; I hope that I can somehow convince him to say nothing, to speak not a single word to my mother. Moira Wood doesn't need to know about the old Miller place, about the haunted house that is to be made here, or about anything that has happened at this spot. I pray Mr. Sanders can be on my side, I hope that he chooses to team with me, instead of a predetermined destiny.

"Evening, Priam," he says as he stands in front of me. "Care to inform me on whatever it was that just happened?"

"Oh, I'll tell you everything Mr. Sanders. I'll tell you everything," I whisper to him in a voice that I try to keep as calm and collected as possible. I'll tell him a tale, but that doesn't necessarily mean it's going to be true. A man's got to do what a man's got to do, and in order to save the life of his mother, a boy has got to stretch the truth, he's got to do what is necessary in order to get by. How I'm going to make it past this first day to the next six which follow is something I'm beginning to doubt, but now, all I care about is day one. It truly has begun.

I take all the blame, I tell Mr. Sanders how we decided to come to the old Miller house in order to see if the older kids really were making a haunted house inside. I tell him that Danny was trying his best to get inside and couldn't find a way to do so, thus I took it upon myself to smash the window with the brick. Even though I didn't, even though I haven't even touched a brick today I know that I can't tell him it was Danny, I feel as if that would be wrong even though it's the truth. I suppose since I was the one who threw the brick the first time, it's kind of like I'm fessing up to that reality in this one. It's not like I never threw the brick after all, it's just that this time I am actually innocent. I hope that taking the blame will somehow work out for me in a karmic kind of way.

"Is that really how it happened Priam? You threw the brick?"

"Yes. It was me. I'm so sorry Mr. Sanders; I really don't know why I was being so careless."

"It was rather careless and destructive, but you know, I really respect the fact that you stayed behind to face me while the others ran away. That was very brave of you, very brave indeed."

It appears that I have gained some respect from Mr. Sanders, which I only hope can favor the outcome of this day. It at least can't make it any worse I imagine.

"I just didn't think it would be right if I ran away after what I did. I'm not some vagrant kid, I swear. Could I ask you a favor though?"

"What's that?" He asks as I put my hands behind my back and cross my fingers.

"Could you not tell my mother about this? Could we maybe work out some deal? I'll do anything I promise. I can do yard work for you, I can help you with chores of any kind. I just don't want her to know what happened. I know she'll be disappointed in me, and that's the worst feeling in the world."

"Well, you don't have to do anything for me. It's not my window that was broken. I suppose if I keep quiet about this no real harm will be done. Besides, I haven't seen any of the Millers for years as it is. I doubt they will even notice the window is busted, and if they do I'm sure it won't be anytime soon."

"Really Mr. Sanders? You won't tell her? Golly thanks so much!" I mumble out in a mess of words with as much ecstasy as I could ever contain. I reach out my arms and embrace him squeezing tight. He seems thoroughly surprised by the hug, but I don't care if it has caught him off guard, I'd hold onto this man for a million years if it means that my mother won't find out about what I had told him here.

On the bike ride home I feel as if everything seems brighter, lighter, faster, and more beautiful than it's ever been before. The wind that rushes through my shaggy blonde hair and brushes past my face feels brisk and cool. The red, yellow and ochre colored trees are filling the atmosphere with a warm hued pleasure that is spreading down the avenue and following me all the way back to my house on Elm Street.

I take my bike into the garage and put the kick stand down, so it's in the exact same position as it was when I got it earlier, not thrown in the lawn next to a pile of puke like it was on the first time I lived this day. Today is different, I'm making changes, I'm on my way. I don't see Danny's bike anywhere, so I assume he and Jimmy must have went downtown after all, they probably figured that I would have met up with them there. I'm sure when they find out that I stayed behind and talked to Mr. Sanders they'll shit their pants.

I'm alright with the fact that Danny isn't home yet, that just means that Mother and I have the house to ourselves. When I walk inside she is sitting in the living room, working on my Superman costume. I can tell that she is almost finished with it; it looks just as wonderful as I remember. I hope beyond all hopes that I actually get to wear it this time and that she gets to see me do so. I need someone to be my Lois Lane after all. I sit down in the living room with her and when she looks up at me I give her a smile.

"How was the ice cream?"

"I decided not to get any; I wanted to be able to enjoy your pot roast on an empty stomach."

"Oh really? Is my pot roast that good?" She says with a giggle.

"It's basically the best thing in the world."

"My, my, what wonderful compliments. I hope it lives up to its reputation."

"I'm sure it will."

"Did your brother and Jimmy decide to still get some then?"

"Oh yeah, they went downtown still. I'm sure Danny will be back soon though."

I pray he takes his time, I'm finally home with Mother and I don't really want my brother to interrupt us, especially after what he just did at the Miller place. I guess I can't be that mad at him for throwing the brick though, seeing as I did the exact same thing the first time I lived this day, but I'm still annoyed with his behavior nevertheless. I'm just happy that I decided to stay and face Mr. Sanders. If I would have run like the other two, I imagine that my mother would have found out what happened anyways. At least this time she won't.

She raises my costume off of her lap and I notice that it's finished. The cape is attached, it's complete. "What do you think?" She asks as she beckons for me to come over and hold it. I take it from her and place it up against my body, it looks perfect, it might as well be the real Superman costume, because as far as I'm concerned...it is. I realize that since I stayed longer at the old Miller place and pedaled back to the house slowly on my bicycle taking in the fresh air and falling autumn leaves that my mother had more time to work on my costume, she finished it earlier than she originally had.

"It's amazing."

"Why don't you try it on?" She suggests.

When she says this I just look at her. I look at her face, her long golden hair and her emerald eyes. I look at her and I just wish, oh I just wish that I knew now how this day was going to end. I wish I could tell her not to leave the house tonight, not to go anywhere at all, but even when I start to have those thoughts my mouth starts to feel constricted. It's fate telling me no, no, no. If she wants to go, then she will go.

I look at the costume that is in my hands. I'd never tried it on before, it didn't seem right after she died. She hadn't felt I deserved the costume after what I had done, she had punished me, she had said that taking flight as Superman was what I wanted most, and thus she took it from me after what I did on that day. Even though she was gone and there was no one to enforce her punishment, I knew I couldn't put the costume on, I just couldn't. I always kept it though, throughout the years of my life I would often pull it out of storage and just hold it, I would look at it longingly and realize that it wasn't the thing I wanted more than anything else anymore, what I wanted more than anything else was her, for her life, for her love, for her to be here with me again. And she was, at least for now, and she was telling me to put it on. That was what she wanted, and I wanted it too.

"Alright, I'll go upstairs and put it on and then come back down to show you."

"Sounds great, I'll go check the pot roast while you are trying it on, I think it's almost done."

We exit the living room together. She goes to the kitchen and I race up the stairs. I enter my bedroom and stand before the mirror gazing at my thirteen year old face. When I was young I used to always stare at myself and imagine what I would look like when I was older. Now, it is almost a kind of reverse effect as I know what I look like as an older man, now I am trying to comprehend my young face, the thirteen year old face that currently contains my brain that is bursting with thoughts and desires of dreams and reveries. I undress, taking off my light green button up shirt and my khaki pants, so that I am only standing in my underwear, in my boxer shorts that are a simple gray. I take the costume and put it on. When it touches my bare skin, my legs, my chest and my arms tingle as a certain sensation encompasses me. I zip up the back and push the cape down so that it is flowing behind me. It feels right, it feels super. Once everything is in place, I turn back to the mirror and flex my muscles, what little muscles I have anyway. I laugh to myself and then run out of my room and down the stairs, entering the kitchen to where my mother is standing at the sink, her back towards me.

"Well hello Miss Lane, how are you doing on this fine day in Metropolis?" I say in the deepest voice my vocal chords will deliver. She turns around to see me and as she does the largest grin covers her face, so much so that she begins to laugh with delight and covers her mouth as if she is a shy school girl embarrassed by the amount of glee that is running through her veins.

"I'm doing wonderful now that you're here. Always saving the day."

"And how do you think I look?" I ask as I flex my muscles again.

"As epicly super as a superhero could be."

I walk towards her. I see the radio sitting on the counter and turn it on. A song is just ending, I'm not sure what it is, but when the music fades away the announcer's voice says: "And now the new hit from Nat King Cole, this...is *Smile*." I don't know how it's possible, because this isn't the same time of the day that we danced before. Perhaps Mother had changed the station earlier, perhaps something I did differently today caused the song to be delayed, at the moment though I don't think about it too much. All I think about is what I'm currently doing, walking towards my mother with my arms outstretched.

"Care for a dance?" I ask and then laugh, unable to hold in my happiness.

"Oh, I think that would be lovely," she says as she takes my hand. I twirl her around and then we come together, swaying side by side as the song fills the air around us. So it is, I waltz with my mother once again to a similar song, with me in my Superman costume and her in that same blue dress which is still covered in white polka dots. I lose myself in the moment, not wanting to say anything to disrupt the essence of clarity the dance contains. As we glide back and forth around the kitchen floor, I begin to cry. I can't help it, the amount of emotions that I've felt today are too much to hold in. I try not to make any noise so that she doesn't notice, but I should have known better than trying to evade her senses.

"What's wrong Priam?" She asks as she looks down upon my face which is streaming with tears.

"Nothing's wrong Mother. Nothing, I'm just so happy that you're here. I'm so happy that I'm here with you."

"Awe, baby, I'm happy too. I'm glad we're both here, and we will be for quite some time. I can promise you that."

As the song fades, as I wipe the tears on the shoulder of my Superman costume, as my mother and I slow down the pace of our waltz until we are standing still it's all I can hope for that what she said will be true. I need her to be here longer, I need her to live. For if this first day doesn't turn out the way I want it to, will the six days that follow even be worth living at all? Only time will tell, my battle

73

with fate is still a journey uphill.

After our dance, I go back upstairs to take the costume off and when I return to the kitchen Danny has returned and the meal is ready to be served. Dinner is just as tasty as the first time I tasted it, having my mother's pot roast two nights in a row, or at least what feels like two nights in a row is a treat I've never experienced before. I'm able to enjoy this one more, without the worry of whether or not Mr. Sanders will come beckoning, for I know he won't. There is still an interruption though, as Susan comes by asking for aspirin just like she did the first time. Margaret's fever still burns. Danny is talkative and enthusiastic at dinner. He mentions how when he and Jimmy were downtown they saw the mayor and that he actually bought their ice cream for them. Pretty good luck if you ask me, especially since I didn't think Danny was really worthy of any sort of reward after what he did at the old Miller place, but that was a different matter.

I don't think he has any idea that I stayed behind and talked to Mr. Sanders. He hasn't asked why I didn't come downtown and I haven't told him. When dinner is over, Mother tells us to go upstairs and work on our school work so that we can watch a television program with her later. "I think I'm going to go to the grocery store too, I need to get you some pancake mix Priam," she says with a smile.

I stare at her, wanting to scream, wanting to rip out my heart and throw it on the floor, wishing to do anything that could convince her not to go. I can do nothing though, all I do is stare at her silently trying to look as crazy as I possibly can so it at least gains her attention.

"Are you alright Priam?" Danny asks me, as he has noticed the look of terror plastered on my face at Mother's suggestion. "You look like you've just seen a ghost." Really, I sort of have. Mother has been a ghost to me all day. The last time I was with her, the last time I talked to her was this day, October 11th 1954. It had been almost six decades since I saw her last, before I woke up today, before I relived yesterday.

"Oh, I'm alright Danny. Don't worry about me." I am worrying enough for everyone in this family; I want the two of them to be as calm and collected as they can possibly be. I just have to figure out how to dissuade her from going to that damn grocery store, if I even can. If I can't I guess I'll just have to send her on her way with as much love as I can muster. I'll say goodbye by sending her away with a speech that is poetic and poignant, words to live and die by.

The two of us tell our mother how delicious dinner was and then get up to help her clear the table. Afterwards, I go upstairs to start on my homework, but I know I'm not actually going to do any of it. I just have to pretend like I am, until I can come back downstairs, until enough time has passed so that she doesn't suspect that I'm actually slacking. I am not going to be here tomorrow, regardless of what happens tonight it's not actually going to be me who deals with the dilemma or lack thereof that comes afterwards. I won't be in control again until day two, version two. I start to think about the second day I chose to change but I stop myself. I can't start worrying about that when this day isn't over yet. Day one, day one, it's still only the first one.

I hear the telephone ring downstairs and it cuts into my thoughts like a blade ripping through my head. Who could be calling now? No one called before that I remember, the only call that happened this day, the first way was when...no, she's downstairs still, I know she is. She's not dead. I get up off of my bed and look out to the driveway where the Ford Victoria is still parked. She's still home, I knew she was, but now I have the clarification I need. I run down the hallway and sit at the top of the stairs trying to listen to what she's saying but I can't make out most of it. When I hear her say what I think is a goodbye I get up and rush down to the ground floor as quickly as I can.

"Who was that?" I ask as I come around the corner and enter the kitchen to where she has just hung up the telephone onto the receiver.

"That...was Mr. Sanders."

"Are you shitting me?"

"Priam! Watch your mouth. No, I'm not kidding you. It was Mr. Sanders, he had some very interesting things to share with me. Go fetch your brother, I need to have a talk with the both of you."

I thought that bastard had promised that he wasn't going to tell my mother what had happened. Apparently crossing my fingers and hoping for the best had done nothing to help my case. The man in the green pinstriped blazer still told on me. And now the talk that lead to those three words was about to begin. This time though, I hope, no...I know, it has to be different.

I go into Danny's room to tell him that Mother wants to talk to us. I simply tell him to come downstairs, but he won't let me get away that easily. "Why didn't you come downtown with me and Jimmy? Where did you go?"

"I didn't go anywhere."

"I mean, why didn't you run? Why didn't you follow us?"

"I stayed behind and talked to Mr. Sanders."

"You...what? You talked to him? What in the hell did you do that for?"

"I felt like it was the right thing to do. And in fact, I took the blame for you. I told him it was me who threw that brick. So if you ask me, you're the lucky one. Mother wants to talk to us because he just called her on the telephone. I thought I had convinced him to stay quiet about the whole thing but I guess I was wrong. I'm about to be punished for something I didn't even do." At least not this time, I think.

"Why did you do that? Why did you stay?"

"That's all you care about, why I stayed? Shouldn't you be thanking me for covering for you?" I ask him, upset that he hasn't even acknowledged what I did for him.

"Oh, right. Thanks, I guess. You didn't have to do that."

But, do it I did. I took the blame for the brick that in this reality was thrown by none other than one, Daniel Wood. And now, because of that I am about to be punished by my mother. I suppose I'll have to sit there and take it, apologize, tell her that I love her, and that I am sorry. Those three angry words will not escape my mouth, that much I know. Fate can't control me completely.

When the two of us come downstairs to face her, I notice that she is sitting in her chair, just as she had before. The sun has already set, so there is no warm sunlight to light her face this time, instead she has turned on the lamp next to her chair, so that the light that is present to portray the scene is one of a much dimmer tune. We sit at the couch across from her, just as we had before. Her face isn't as expressionless as it was the original time though; instead it seems to hold a look of confusion, an utterly beautiful bewilderment. Moira Wood doesn't know what to do, or what to say, at least that is what it appears to be, to me.

"Do either of you have any idea why I want to talk to you?"

"I think...I might," I say as sympathetically as I can.

"Danny?"

"Not really," he mumbles, even though I know he is aware of what this is about as I had just told him.

"I just got off the phone with Mr. Sanders. He told me that he saw the two of you near his house earlier today, over at the old Miller place, but that's not all, he told me that he saw one of you throw a brick and smash a window."

"I'm sorry Mother; I don't know why I did it. We were just trying to get in so badly and I had a moment of weakness. Punish me in whichever way you see fit. I deserve it," I spit out as quickly as I can, just wanting to get this conversation over with.

"Stop it Priam. I know it wasn't you," she tells me in a tone that is inflicted with seriousness.

What on earth does she mean? She knows it wasn't me? But how is that possible? I had told Mr. Sanders that it was I who threw the brick, I confessed, I had taken the blame, there was no logical way that he would have thought otherwise.

"Mr. Sanders told me how he talked to you, how you took the blame for throwing the brick into the window, how you asked him to not say anything to me about it and initially he had agreed to stay quiet. The more he thought about it though, he decided he had to say something to me, because Mr. Sanders saw what really happened. He knew that you didn't throw the brick Priam. He saw your brother do it."

At this I look to Danny whose face is a blank white slate of surprise. He hadn't seen this coming, this is the last thing he expected to happen. "But...how?" I ask, confused as I can be.

"He told me that he saw you boys park your bikes by the old Miller place and thought nothing of it, but then after a while he heard you screaming, Priam. When he heard you, he came over to investigate, and that's when he saw what was happening. He watched as the three of you were standing there, he saw you begging your brother to leave, to let go of the idea of getting inside. He saw you Danny," she says as she looks my brother dead in the eye with a look of earnest disappointment. "He saw you throw the brick and then run away after he asked you to stop. Do you have anything to say for yourself?"

"I...I'm sorry. I didn't mean to cause any trouble, honestly," he says. I look at him, full of despair for how he must be feeling, but at the same time I feel nothing. He doesn't have much to say for himself, no reason of explanation of why he did what he did. He had nothing to prove with that brick, no causation or possible reconciliation for what happened. He did it simply because he wanted to, and for that I am not sorry.

"I'm going to have to ground you for a month. No bike rides after school, no trips downtown, no Halloween. Nothing except for school and this house. I'm disappointed in you, and I know your father would be too." He starts crying then, but he doesn't sob like I did when I was in his position. He apologizes to my mother, and I believe he means it. I think my brother is truly sorry for what he's done, but that doesn't take back what happened. He goes upstairs so that it is just me and her sitting across from one another.

"Why did you take the blame for your brother Priam? Why didn't you just tell Mr. Sanders the truth?"

I don't know how to answer her. I did what I did because I thought it was what was best. I did it because in a way, I was taking responsibility for when it was me who threw that brick. I can't tell her that though, I can't tell her I'm a seventy year old version of her son reliving this day, and I know that even if I wanted to do so I wouldn't be able, because I'm sure that would classify into one of Chloe's rules of disrupting the equilibrium of fate and the existence of the universe.

"I...I just didn't want Danny to get in trouble I guess." This is true, but I also did it because I needed to come to terms with myself. I had to take the blame for something I didn't do in order to feel that I was getting somewhere, in order to feel that I was accomplishing something, so I could start down the path of becoming a better man.

"Well, to be honest I'm surprised you did so," she says as she gets up from her chair and comes to sit next to me on the couch. She places her arm around me and I snuggle into her so that my head is lying on her shoulder. "I don't think I would have been brave enough to do what you did. When I was a little girl I tried my best not to be noticed, to not stand out. It wasn't until I got older, when I started to become more comfortable with myself, when I started to sing in front of people, and when I met your father, that I became who I was always meant to be. Your father inspired me; he was always the brave one. I know he would be proud of you for what you did, for taking the blame even though you didn't deserve it, for sacrificing yourself in order to save your brother."

I think she is giving me far too much credit, more than I deserve, more than I am capable of accepting. I just sit there with her, taking in the moment, taking in the fact that she is proud of what I have done, and that she believes that my father would have been too. I realize in this moment that this is what I wanted, for her to have proof of the good boy she always thought I was, to have an instance, a recent example that proved to her that I was on the right track, that she had taught me well. We sit there for a while, not saying anything at all. The only source of bright that emanates over us is from the lamp across the way. I don't want her to get up, I don't want her to leave, but I know it is coming. I know it has to, she has no control over it, fate is calling her to go.

"I think I'm going to go run to the grocery store to get that pancake mix. When I get back how about we watch some television?"

She stands up and she looks at me with a smile. It's then that I decide that I have given up. If my mother has to die today, if she has to go, I don't want to think about trying to save her anymore, instead I want to relish these last moments with her, I want to take in her beauty, her warmth, the perfection of her complexion and enjoy it for what it is, the love that she has given me, I want to give back. If these are my last moments with her, I want them to be good.

"That sounds like a grand idea," I say, stretching my arms back behind my head on the couch as I watch her go to the closet to put on her coat.

"Good, I won't be gone long. Do you think your brother's okay? Should I go check on him?" She asks as she slips on a pair of white high heels.

"I'm sure he is alright, I'll check on him while you're gone," I say, as I get up off of the couch and go stand next to her at the door. When it appears she is ready to go I embrace her for what I'm sure is going to be the last time, second chances or no second chances, I believe this is goodbye. I cannot save someone's life simply by deciding to do so.

"I love you Mother, I love you with all of my heart. Thank

you for always believing in me, thank you for showing me how to be a good man."

"Oh Priam, you may be intelligent for your age, but I think you still have some time before you can classify yourself as a man," she says as she pulls away from the hug and bends down so that she is level with me. "Besides, you've probably taught yourself much more than I could ever teach you. Regardless, I love you too baby, I love you too."

That is when she starts to walk away from me, when my mother slides away into the night, the evening of fright that could only be classified as a chilly October eve. When she reaches the doorway she turns around and offers me a wink. I laugh and return the gesture. The door closes behind her, and I start to accept the fact that she is gone.

After I hear the Ford Victoria start up and pull out of the driveway I decide to go upstairs and put on my Superman costume again. I feel that when the telephone rings notifying me of her death it will help me to feel stronger than I felt the first time that it happened. I'm going to answer it this time; Danny shouldn't have to deal with it again, even though I guess it would be the first time for this version of him. When I leave my room and walk past his door with my costume on I hear his voice. "Why are you wearing that?"

I'm not even sure how he saw what I am wearing as his door is only open a crack, but I've stopped questioning things at this point, this day doesn't make sense and I have accepted that. Life and love and destiny are all forming some sort of interplay that has its own mind and can create whatever it wants to. I step into his room and say "because I want to." He's lying on his bed, his head hanging off the edge, upside down.

"You're such a freak sometimes," he tells me, which hurts. Up until this point of this day Danny has been much more supportive of me. I feel the emotions I felt on this original day rushing back towards me now. He goes on, saying "Get out of here; this is all your fault. I hate you."

So there they are, the three words had to be delivered after all, they had to escape someone's lips and reach another's ears. Now more than ever I know that time is not easily changed. I may have stopped myself from saying those three words myself, but they had to be distributed somehow, they had to be felt, they had to be real. Danny hates me, and I know it's my fault. I changed what I changed and this is the result. It is not ideal to have my brother have such hostile feelings towards me, but I tell myself it is better than having said those three words myself to my mother only a short time before she died. It was worth it, this day was worth it even though my mother is currently on her way to death, at least I know now for a fact that she will die without a doubt in her mind about my love for her. She will die knowing that I am a good boy.

I leave Danny's room without saying anything. I shut his door slowly and walk down the stairs. I decide to sprawl out on the floor right in front of the entrance to our home, pushing my cape up so that it is stretched out above me like a red cloud of confusion floating high. I can't think, I can't do anything at all, so I just lay, and as I do, I imagine myself dying all over again. I think of my mother, and for the first time today I think of Ellie. Maybe a part of my thirteen year old brain had taken over to prevent me from doing so before. I don't know if it's because I shouldn't know of her yet, but I do. I think of her face, and I think of the days yet to come that I still have to save. Even though Chloe's rule was right, even though I couldn't save my mother, I still know that in actuality, in this life of second chances I can save her, I can save Ellie, my wife, at least in some way. Time floats by and the spots on the walls that I either see in reality or in my mind fade as the front door opens and hits me on the top of the head.

"Ouch!" I shout as I begin to sit up slowly, rubbing my skull, for it hurts.

"Oh, I'm sorry Priam. What on earth are you doing on the floor?"

I sit up, my vision a little bit foggy, expecting to see Susan requesting some more aspirin or something, but when I calculate the face in front of me I can't handle it. I fall back to the ground, I faint.

What lies beneath me is squishy, soft, and what is on top of me is wet and cool. "What the-?" I begin to mutter but I feel a finger push up against my lips, silencing me.

"No need to talk baby, just keep your eyes closed." Of course as soon as I hear that I open them as wide as I can. It's her, she's before me and she's alive and I don't know how it can be. My mother, with her golden locks, her emerald eyes and her charming smile, my mother is still alive.

"How?"

"Shhhh...be quiet now. All of the excitement of this day must have left you with a bit too much to handle. Everything is okay, I'm here."

I lift my hand up to my forehead and realize that there is a wet washcloth lying on the top of my face. I feel her hand running down my arm, her fingers circling in patterns that soothe me.

"Did you get the pancake mix?" I ask, it's all I can think to say, after all.

"Oh I got it. I almost died on the way home, but I suppose the risk was worth it. My baby needs a good breakfast in the morning," she says in an airy tone of lightheartedness.

I don't need to ask what she means, for I already know the answer. Somehow, everything I changed today was enough. Sure, my mother still went to go get pancake mix at about the same time that she did on this original day, but what I did was sufficient. George Jones never hit her with his car, the Ford Victoria wasn't totaled, it never flipped. Fate had decided to deal me a win, it decided in the end that my first day could be changed in a dramatic way. As Chloe had said, I couldn't stop anyone from dying directly, and I hadn't. My tongue was tied, my feet were buried in concrete, but yet I still prevailed. I proved that I learned something, I earned my mother's life. As I lie in bed thinking about all of these things I start a celebration within my mind. Day one is almost done, and day one, I've won. Moira Wood, my mother, my wondrous mother will live to see another day, she will surprise the morning with a smile and search for whatever she can save.

My mother didn't need saving though, she saved herself. She saved me. I realize now that her patience, her grace, and the goodness she always held inside finally rooted itself deep within me on the second version of this day. It finally won out, and because of that, we won. She lives.

"Goodnight Priam, I'll see you in the morning," she whispers into my ear as she removes the washcloth from my forehead and kisses me right where it had been. She gets up and walks to the door. Before she shuts it though, I hear her gasp silently and turn back towards me.

"I almost forget, guess what song was playing on the radio

on my way home? It was that song we danced to earlier, that Nat King Cole song. *Smile*."

"How absolutely wonderful," I whisper back to her, and with that she closes the door. My body quivers with an overjoyed absolution. My mother has lived on in this place, and now I have learned one thing about how that first day played out, I now know something I had wished to be true, but now have confirmation of. Even when she didn't make it through, my mother wasn't sad, she still believed in me. Nat King Cole was crooning in her ear and as she died on this original day, she had a smile on her face, and an image of us waltzing across the floor wandering through her mind. She was happy then and thus, as the colors of dark blues and purples coalesce around me, the day fades, I fall asleep and I am gone.

My Life
1954 – 1959

October 12th, 1954 was the day that I realized I was an orphan. No mother, no father left on this Earth to guide me. Sure, I had my brother Danny, thankfully, luckily...but the two people who made me, the two souls that I never would have been alive without, were no longer living themselves. Neither of them would be there in the days of my life that followed, they wouldn't see me grow, they wouldn't know the man that I would become.

Her funeral was a few days later. The one thing I remember about it most was talking to Fred, the old man who owned the grocery store. I remember him telling me how my mother still believed I was good, even though I had told her I hated her, even after how horrible I had acted that day, she still had faith in me, her baby boy. Other than that conversation with Fred, what I remembered most was being hugged by a lot of people I had never seen before. I remember pretty women, handsome men, fat women, sad men, ugly women, tall men, old women, stupid men, and I remember what they said to me, for it all seemed the same. "So sorry for your loss Priam, so sorry indeed."

I don't know how they knew my name, I sure as hell didn't know most of theirs and I didn't care if they were sorry for what I had lost. I didn't give a damn if they were sad about my mother's passing, they only needed to multiply whatever it was they felt to the utmost power in order to understand how I was still reeling. The pain I felt at her funeral was too great to bear, I didn't feel alive, I didn't want to be alive. I wish it had been me. She didn't deserve this, but I believed I did, or so I thought then.

Danny and I stood next to her coffin, I tried not to look over at her often, but when I did I just tried to pretend that she was asleep, for even as a corpse my mother still beat out everyone else in terms of beauty. Her skin still looked soft and supple, her hair as golden and glowing as it ever had been. It wasn't fair how gorgeous she looked, even though I knew she wasn't there, that the vessel that had once held her spirit was just that, a container for where she once resided. What was lying in that coffin wasn't my mother, just the case she had left behind when her time ran out.

I blamed myself for her death, I may not have been the one who hit her, but I knew that what I had done that day had caused the event nevertheless, or at least that's what I told myself. The shame and anger I felt for how I behaved that day and for what I said to her wrestled inside of me like a monster that couldn't be tamed. It would haunt me for the rest of my life. After that day I was never able to feel as happy as I know I could have been if she would have lived. Ever since that day a part of me was missing, for up until that point my mother had been the most important force in my life, she had been the sun to my stars, and I had let her down, I had let her set before the dawn.

Beside Danny and me next to the coffin that day were my mother's parents, Grandma and Grandpa Kelton. My father's parents were also there, Mr. and Mrs. Wood, and of course Susan too. The seven of us were the closest people that my mother had known, both she and my father were the only children in their families. I remember her always telling me that they had wanted to have a big family because of the feeling of growing up alone. They had planned on having at least two or three more kids after I was born, but of course a little thing called World War II got in the way of those plans, just as death had. Still, she always told me how happy she was that my brother and I would always have each other.

When she died, I had no idea what was going to happen to me and Danny. We obviously weren't old enough to take care of ourselves, so as I stood there next to those five adults that day, I knew that there were three different ways it could play out. I would either live with my mother's parents, my father's parents, or with Susan and her family. What ended up happening in reality was more of a mixture of all three. My mother left a will. This surprised me seeing as she was only thirty nine years old when she died, I imagined she didn't often think of her own mortality while she was still alive, but I was wrong. I suppose my father's death had influenced her in that way, so as a precaution she wrote a will, so that if anything ever happened to her things would be taken care of, and we, her two sons, would be taken care of in the way she wished.

In her will, she expressed that she wanted us to stay in Alden. She wanted us to grow up in our small town and she wanted us to stay enrolled in Alden High too. That was why she and my father had moved away from the city after all, to expose us to a life of simplicity in the suburbs. Apparently she had discussed this issue with Susan before, and Susan had agreed to become our guardian if anything were to happen to her. Unfortunately, something had.

Thus, Susan, her daughter Margaret, and her husband Steve moved into our house with us. Our house was a great deal larger than the one they lived in, so it made sense that they would move in with us rather than the other way around. Besides, I think everyone figured it was better if us boys were able to at least stay in the house our parents had built for us, since we were unable to be with them, at least we would have a connection to them through the home which they had made.

So a new sort of family was formed, in a way it was kind of like Susan and Steve became our adoptive parents, but I never considered them as such. To me, they were just older friends of mine who happened to be able to tell me what to do. Margaret never became my sister, she was just the young girl who lived in my home. They all were just visitors in my house to me; I never really saw it any differently than that. Of course I became close with them, but I never let myself forget who I was, that I was Priam Wood, and that my parents, my real family never had much of a chance. At least I still had Danny.

I wasn't shocked that my mother had wanted us to grow up in Alden. Part of me wanted to escape the small town as soon as I possibly could, but at the same time I wanted to hold onto it. It was the only place I had ever called home, it was where my parents, young and in love had come to make their life. It was the best connection I had to them, well that, and New York City of course. For the city contained the two other components of the arrangement she had put together for us. Danny and I were to stay in Alden during the school year, and then to spend our summers in New York, split between our grandparents equally. For all of June and half of July we would live with my mother's parents in Brooklyn in their modest apartment, while for the second half of July and all of August we would live with my father's parents in their glorious penthouse in Manhattan. I didn't know it then, but those summers would help to both challenge and inspire me more than anything else had up to that point...until I met Ellie, of course.

"Don't you think he looks like George Washington?" Danny had asked me when we were back at our house, sitting upstairs in my bedroom after hearing the decision from all five of them a day after the funeral.

"What on Earth are you talking about?"

"Grandpa Wood, doesn't he look like Washington? I've always thought that."

Although Danny had apparently compared the face of our father's father to that of the first President of the United States I barely had even looked at any of their faces at all when they told us how we would be shuffled around between Alden and New York City. Now that I was thinking about it though, I could see the resemblance. It's not like this was the first time I met my grandfather after all.

"I suppose he does a bit. And what do you think about Grandpa Kelton looking like Abraham Lincoln?"

"Are you nuts?" He said with a laugh. "Grandpa Kelton doesn't look anything like Lincoln, I'd say he looks more like Harriet Tubman."

"That is the dumbest thing I have ever heard."

"That's a lie," he continued, as he flicked me playfully on my shoulder. "You've heard much more idiotic things than that, in fact, those things have come out of your own mouth."

"Never!" I yelled as I pushed him to the floor and we began to wrestle. Although I started out on top of him I didn't remain there for long. My brother was much stronger than I was and before I knew it, I was pinned. I pushed him off of me, but we didn't get up, we laid there laughing for a while. It was the first time I had laughed since it happened, the first time I had temporarily forgotten that she was gone. That was the beginning of Danny the good, Danny the wise, Danny my protector. I don't know exactly why he decided he wasn't going to pick on me anymore, but after she was gone he rarely ever did. He was the perfect older brother, he helped me, he supported me, he stood up for me and because of that he became my favorite person in the world. I looked up to him more than anyone else. In a way, I wanted to be him.

Of course I didn't gain that respect for him on that day we wrestled around on my bedroom floor laughing about Washington, Lincoln and Tubman. No, it occurred over the next few years, as I grew up and as he grew up too. It happened between the slowly changing seasons in Alden and the hot summers immersed in the fast paced concrete jungles of New York. Slowly but surely, Danny became the one person I relied on more than anything; he became the one person I completely trusted with everything...until I met her.

It was a few weeks before my eighteenth birthday, I was staying with my Grandma and Grandpa Kelton in Brooklyn just as I had the previous five summers during June and the first half of July. Danny had graduated from Alden High the previous year and was now going to college in the city, majoring in advertising. Grandpa Wood had inspired him to do so and had offered him an internship to work at his firm during this time as well. Danny was incredibly smart and everyone who met him always seemed impressed. I had a lot to live up to.

I was sick of school; thankfully I only had one more year left before I could finally do what I really wanted: move to the city for good and completely devote my energy to my art. I was tired of listening to lectures of older adults telling me that this was this and that was that. I didn't believe in science or math or any other discipline that wasn't navigable or changeable. I needed leeway; I needed freeway in order to accept anything as being true. In essence, I only believed in what there was no evidence for.

After my mother died, I poured my soul into painting just as I poured paint on the canvas bit by bit. Art became an escape for me, one that I could create a serene symphony with the colors on the page. When I painted I was able to forget about the things that made me sad, I was able to enter a new plane of reality that was all my own. That's what it was for me, something that I had complete control over, no one else to influence how I brushed the stroke or how I envisioned things to appear. There had been so many instances in my life that I felt hopeless and lost, my art brought back a dream for me, it made me believe.

It was late one Tuesday afternoon and I had decided to go to Central Park in order to paint a landscape portrait. It wasn't very often that I painted things from life but for some reason I had a desire to go outside into the bright sunlight that day. I often had wondered what my life would have become if I had just decided to stay inside instead. If I had simply situated myself in the corner of the bedroom I used while at Grandma and Grandpa Kelton's house and created an abstract illusion on the white canvas in front of me, would anything have been the same?

I didn't stay in though, something pushed me out to greet the day, to smile at the strangers who rushed pass, to look up at the sky and the clouds floating by, to imagine that I knew the people that I saw, pretending as if they were visiting from the future and that I would know them then, someday that had yet to come. I arrived at the park and took a seat on a large rock and set up my easel and canvas before me. I dumped my tubes of paint and palette onto the ground and quickly got to work painting a scene of the green stretched before me with the random citizens of the city floating past, as the harsh grey lines of the skyscrapers poked up from behind the foliage in the distance. I painted for a while, filling up the canvas at a steady rate. When I was almost complete with the scene I set my brush down for a second to get up and stretch. And that's when I saw her.

She was across the way leaning with her back up against a massive tree and pulling her fingers through her chestnut brown hair, stroking it softly before she put it up into a bun on the top of her head. She was wearing a white strapless dress, one that was fitted at the top accentuating her breasts while leaving her shoulders bare. The bottom of the dress was wide and freely flowing, giving her room to move about without restraint. After taking in her appearance I noticed that she was beginning to stretch, just as I had gotten up to do so, before I became rooted to the spot due to the sight of her.

I set my paintbrush down and watched her, there was nothing else I could do at the moment, every part of my body was focused on her presence, it was as if a spell had been cast on me. She was the most beautiful girl I had ever seen. Her skin looked silky and smooth; her tall slender frame was perfectly proportioned. I suddenly became very happy that I had decided to come to the park that day.

She stopped stretching, threw both of her arms into the air directly above her head and began to move her hands about so that they swiveled at her wrists. She jumped up and down a few times and then she seemed to lose control of her body, and thus, she began to dance. I'll never forget the way she moved when I watched her dance for the first time; it was as if every combination of serenity, sensuality, poise and grace was exiting her body through the movements she made. I was transfixed, for the way in which she moved was so peaceful, yet so strong and glorious that it almost made no sense to me. I couldn't comprehend how she was able to do the things she did. She looked so happy, so free. She was twirling around near the edge of the sidewalk in front of the tree that she had been stretching and I noticed that she had not only gained my attention, but also that of other passersbys who were taking in the girl in the white dress.

I looked back to my painting which was almost finished and decided to add a figure in the bottom left corner. I sat down on the rock and studied the girl with fleeting glances until I had completed what I wanted: a girl dancing in a white dress, one leg lifted elegantly in the air. My portrait of Central Park was now finished. I looked at it before me, trying to decide if I wanted to make any more additions before I started to pack up for the day. No, I decided it was done; the girl was the last touch. I returned my gaze to where she had been dancing and was heartbroken to not find her there. When I was studying my painting for the final time deliberating whether or not it was complete she must have pranced away, to dance another day.

"It's beautiful," a sweet voice said softly into my ear and as I heard it my limbs flailed and my legs propelled me upwards as I quickly spun around.

"What in the hell?"

"Oh, I'm sorry. I didn't mean to frighten you. I thought you saw me walk over." It was her. She was releasing her hair from the bun and I watched as it fell down, finally resting upon her shoulders. I felt as if I couldn't breathe for the girl who I had watched dance so intently was now right before me. From a distance her beauty seemed exuberant, but from up close I almost felt as if I couldn't handle it, wasn't worthy of it. Why was she talking to me? Suddenly I became very aware of my unkempt shaggy blonde hair, the acne on my face and my paint covered hands. I'm sure she was thinking about what a mess I appeared to be.

"I-I- sorry, I uh, didn't mean to react in such a way, you just surprised me that's all. I was putting the final touches on my painting so I must not have noticed when you were coming this way," I spurted out as quickly as I could, hoping she didn't think me a fool.

She tilted her head to the side trying to look around me to where my painting was sitting on the easel. When she moved in the direction of where it rested I stepped in that direction too. The last thing on earth I wanted was for her to see what I had painted. What if she hated it? I realized I cared an awful lot about what this girl thought of me, when really I had no idea who she was at all.

"When I was finishing up dancing I saw you over here and realized that you were working on a painting. Immediately I became curious what it was that you were creating, I tried not to stare at you but it was almost as if I couldn't help it. Then, I saw you look over at me too."

I'm not sure how I didn't notice her looking back at me, perhaps it was when I had started to add the figure in the corner of my piece, when I had begun to look back and forth between the canvas that was no longer white and the girl in white herself. She had spotted me.

"Ah - well it's really nothing. I'm not that good of an artist; it's just something I like to do to pass the time." I told her, trying not to let her get any closer to my painting. I was embarrassed, I felt as if she saw my landscape and the figure in the corner she would think of me as a creep. This girl, who had awoken a feeling in me I hadn't ever felt before simply with her presence, could probably crush the sensation currently flowing through my veins with only a simple disapproval of what I had created. That was the last thing I wanted to happen.

"Oh come on," she laughed, flashing a smile that made her alluring beauty even more charming. "I'm not an art critic, I promise not to be harsh."

I melted into a pile of goo. The smile had rendered me helpless and as I lost control of my body I slid to one side so that the girl in white could see the painting of the park that I had just finished making. She glided up to it effortlessly, as her dress billowed in the cool breeze that passed us by. My heart was beating so quickly I could hear it louder than any of the other sounds that were taking up the city around us. I stared at the painting from behind her, hoping that she didn't hate it, hoping that she didn't think I was a weirdo for adding a character in the corner that was clearly her. After taking in my creation for what felt like an eternity, but was only a few seconds in actuality, she turned around to face me and said "I think it's absolutely marvelous Priam. You're really talented; you shouldn't be so hard on yourself."

I didn't know why she was being so kind to me, I mean I supposed the painting wasn't exactly horrid, but I didn't think I would call myself really talented or claim that anything I had ever made was marvelous. Sure I thought I was good at painting, but that's not why I did it. I painted because it made me feel like myself more than anything else ever did. The fact that she thought what I had made was of any quality made me feel wonderful. I wanted to ask if she had noticed herself depicted, but then I realized something else. "Well thank you for the wonderful compliments miss, but I'm sorry, how did you know my name? Did I tell you? I don't remember doing so."

She laughed again, flashing her perfect teeth as she pointed to the corner of my canvas. Not the corner where her replica resided, but the other one. The corner where I had signed my name, as I did on all of my paintings, for there it read: Priam Wood.

"Oh right, how silly of me."

"Don't worry, I can be scatterbrained too, but now that I know your name, I suppose you should know mine. I'm Ellie Donahue. It's a pleasure to meet you." She grabbed her dress with both hands, curtsied and then extended her hand before me.

I looked at it, then back to her face and as I did so she winked at me. I felt my face getting red so I looked away as quickly as I could and then grasped her hand to shake it. When I touched her hand, her sweet skin residing up against mine, I felt as if I was on fire, not in a way that I would be burning alive, but a kind of fire that made me feel alive, a warmth of pleasure that gave me a sense of truly being me, similar to the experience of what painting did.

"It's nice to meet you too Ellie. So very nice to meet you," I said in a voice filled with strength and composure, something I felt I so often lacked. I smiled broadly and met her gaze. I didn't know what came over me at that moment, but I decided to wink back at her. She laughed once again and then sat down on the rock on which I had been perched upon earlier and said, "So tell me your tale Priam Wood. Tell me everything there ever is to know about you. For some reason I feel as if I should be aware."

I sat down on the rock next to her, and placed my paint covered hands on top of my olive colored khaki shorts. I was about to begin but then I swiftly lifted my hands from my thighs and pulled on the front of my grey buttoned up shirt, for it felt as if it was unexpectedly choking me all of a sudden, even though I knew it wasn't. Instead, the idea that this girl, this beautiful girl named Ellie cared to know anything about me had left me stunned and was making me imagine things that couldn't possibly be happening, such as my shirt struggling to strangle me.

Once I got going with my story not a single part of me

resisted or held anything back, the words started to come out faster than I could say them. I told her of my life in Alden, I told her of my father, my mother, and Danny too. I explained to her how I loved the city and couldn't wait to make it my permanent home. I'm not sure how long we talked for, because it wasn't just me who told my tale, it was her too. After I had begun to talk about my life, hers unfolded before me as well. We went back and forth creating a tale of two seventeen year old kids who dreamt of the stars and didn't very often limit their visions of the future. Before we knew it, an hour or so had passed and the sun was beginning to fall behind the trees. We got up together and I collected my things, stuffing my paint tubes and brushes into my bag. I took the painting off my easel and asked Ellie to hold it. I folded the easel and then told her she could hand me the painting back.

"I think you already know that you aren't getting this back."

"What? You mean-"

"I mean, if you'll let me of course. I'd love to keep it."

I couldn't tell her no; besides, it felt right to let her keep it. She was kind of the inspiration for it after all. Thus, our relationship began, as she danced in her long white dress next to the tree, I painted the city, the sky and the people that passed by. As Ellie Donahue moved gracefully, my hand guided the brush resting within it, making a motion similar to an ocean, to see. For that was the day that I first felt truly alive again, the day that the part of me that had gone away when my mother died, returned.

Ellie was the girl who saved me, and all I ever wanted to be from that point on was the boy who saved her in return. I was nowhere near what she actually deserved, but for some reason there would come a day when she realized I was what she needed. There came a moment when we were both underneath a painting created years before by a kid who was talented with a brush, inspired by a girl who could fluidly move, when that boy was a man, and that girl was a woman, and they realized their love was strong enough to get them through. Love really was all I ever needed, until there was only one, for when there was only one, then it was just me without any form of love.

I haven't had pancakes for breakfast in a really long time. I've tried to eat them, but the taste in my mouth has never been the same. In fact, the smell of them alone turns my stomach. I used to love them, but after my mother was gone, I never wanted to have pancakes again.

When I wake up in the morning, I stretch slowly and convince myself to get out of bed in order to prepare for the day ahead. After using the restroom, I put on a white button down, a black tie and a pair of dress pants. Tonight is the big basketball game against the Sommerville Saints and whenever we have a game coach insists that we dress up for the school day. I never thought I'd play sports in high school, but seeing as I now stand at six foot three it almost would be a waste if I played nothing at all. Thus, I decided to go out for the basketball team freshman year. It turns out I'm actually pretty good and I'm one of the five starters for Alden's team. If we win tonight, we will be in first place in our region. I'm nervous because I really want to win, but I've been trying not to think about it much the past couple of days. That plan hasn't worked too well so far.

As I walk downstairs and enter the kitchen I see Susan and Steve sitting at the table with Margaret who is eating a bowl of cereal. I pour myself one too and join them. "Big game tonight. Are you ready?" Susan asks.

"As ready as I'll ever be."

"I'm sure you will do great Priam. You honestly are the best one on the team," Margaret tells me, offering her support.

"I'd predict a win for the Alden Panthers, with senior center Priam Wood the leading scorer with seventeen points," Steve adds as he sets his newspaper down to look at me.

"You're far too kind," I say in a quiet voice as I shovel a big spoonful of cereal into my mouth and begin to chew the crunchy oats. "I'll be happy with a win alone, even if I don't score any points."

"Come on Priam, you know you're going to score points! All of the girls talk about how good you are! I think half of them are in love with you," Margaret says as she quickly averts my eyes.

Sometimes I think Margaret is in love with me from the way

she acts. I don't know about any of those other girls though, I've never had a girlfriend before. Even though I am talented at basketball and with my art, I still don't feel confident about myself as a man, or with how I look. Sure, I am tall with a muscular frame and my blonde hair and green eyes don't hurt my case either, but my skin often breaks out in zits that I can't seem to control no matter how diligently I wash my face. My acne isn't that bad, sometimes I barely even notice it at all, but when I do, I pray that no one will look at me, or notice the ugliness I see. I don't know how to talk to girls, I always feel as if they are staring at me, or giggling behind my back. The only girl I can really talk to is Ellie. Since that day in the park when we met she has become my best friend. We spent practically the entire summer together, running through the streets, exploring art exhibits, visiting the beach and going to the ballet. We danced and painted our summer away. Having to leave New York at the end of August was horribly wretched.

"I'm going to be back before you know it," I had told her. And I meant it. As soon as I graduate from Alden, I am moving to the city for good. I am going to find a big apartment and turn it into my studio; I am going to devote my life to my art and to her, in whatever way I can.

"You'll write me, won't you?" She had asked.

"Of course I will. I will write you everyday if that's what I have to do so you won't forget me."

"I could never forget a boy like you."

So we wrote. I wrote what had seemed like a hundred letters since that day when we said goodbye. We had talked on the phone a few times too, but Ellie's family didn't have much money so we couldn't do it very often since long distance calls weren't cheap. I would see her again over the upcoming holidays when I visited my grandparents in the city, but that was still three weeks away. I wanted to see her now. I didn't want to wait anymore.

"I doubt that all of the girls are in love with him," Susan laughs bringing me back to the conversation before me, as thoughts of Ellie fade from my mind. "Although I'm sure quite a few of them are."

"Stop it Susan. You're making the poor boy blush," Steve adds as he nods his head in my direction. He could tell that I was starting to get uncomfortable with all of this talk about girls who are supposedly in love with me. I only want one girl to love me and as of yet, I don't believe she does. Ellie is too good for me, she is too beautiful, too sweet, too everything. Sure, we get along famously and always have a great time together, but as the time has passed since this summer I feel her slipping away. I haven't been able to see her smile, to see her laugh, to see her dance. Letters and the fleeting phone calls can only do so much. I want her here. Why did Alden have to be so far away from the city?

I finish eating my breakfast in silence, as the three of them chat the morning away. When I am done eating I take my bowl to the sink and go back upstairs to collect my book bag and jacket. Margaret does the same, as we always walk to school together, just as Danny and I used to. I haven't seen my brother since the summer either, we talk on the phone more regularly though. Besides, missing Danny is a completely different kind of missing than the way that I miss Ellie.

Margaret and I are just about to leave when Susan calls out my name from the kitchen. "Yes? What is it?" I ask.

She comes towards the front door where the two of us are standing. "I can't believe I forgot to tell you. Your brother called a few minutes before you woke up and said he was going to come to your game tonight."

"What?" How could Danny be coming to my game? He lived in the city; it was over a seven hour long car ride from there to Alden. The idea both excites and terrifies me at the same time. It would be great to see Danny, but it also makes me feel even more nervous about tonight than I already did. He is the last person I want to screw up in front of. Ever since Mother left, Danny has been so good to me and he has done so much for himself as well. He is successful, he's good looking, he's smart, he is a citizen of the city and a full time citizen at that. He is everything I want to be. If he came to my game tonight, what would he think if we lost? What would he think if I failed? Susan tells me that my brother has decided to skip his classes today and tomorrow so he can come watch me play tonight. Apparently he had said it was more important to support me than to attend a few lectures that he could easily catch up on. Grandpa Wood had let him borrow his car. He was already on his way.

"But why?"

"What do you mean but why?" Susan asks me with a

wondering look on her face that says she can't understand why I am acting so weird about this. It is good news, I am happy, but I am terrified too. "Your brother is coming to watch you play because he cares about you and wants to see you succeed. He wants to be there when you win."

I nod my head and smile at her, and then walk out the door into the cool December air as Margaret follows behind. That was just it though, what if I didn't win? What if Danny drove all the way to Alden from the city to see me fail? I couldn't think of how horrible that would make me feel. I guess I just have to try even harder than I was already going to do in order to succeed. Danny is the only member of my four person family left besides me. All of the glory I hold within me that would have been used in order to please my mother and my father has manifested all towards him. He is my older brother, he is my hero, I look up to him in every shape and form. I live to please.

Danny wouldn't be the only one I had to perform my best for that evening. Alden, my small town that never held any sort of surprises that I cared for was going to deal me an even bigger one than that of my brother coming to watch me play. When I returned back to my house, when the school day was finished, the nerves that were jumping around inside me were going to reach an all new high, they were going to take my body over as I realized what lay before me.

Everything is discolored, the day and the way it fades. While at school I walk through the halls with nothing on my mind except for the game tonight and the fact that Danny will be there. I try not to concentrate on my nervousness and how it has been fully exacerbated since I feel I have to prove myself more than I already did. The sensations inside me are multiplying and I realize that tonight is when everything will divide.

All of my classes are unbearable to get through, especially physics and calculus, but I keep telling myself to power through, that each time the bell rings I am one step closer to tonight, to seeing my brother and winning the game. The only class I really care about, the only one that makes me feel sane is my art class, which unfortunately isn't until my last period of the day. By the time I make it to the art room I feel completely worn out from all of the thoughts and expectations that have been running through my head. I'm sick of having conversations with people about tonight. I don't want to talk about it anymore; I just want it to happen. Until then, I will paint.

Art class is where I belong; if it were up to me I would just stay in this room all day and listen to Mr. Williams talk about when he had a small studio in New York City. When I was younger I always used to want to be like him, now I know in a way that I can be. Hopefully though, unlike he, I won't have to return to Alden and settle for teaching art to students. I want to make art for others, but most of all, I want to make it for myself, on my own terms. Since I am in a senior art class, we are able to come up with our own project ideas; we don't have to follow any specific guidelines, which is nice. I like being able to let my creativity flow uninhibitedly, I like being free from boundaries, free of constraint.

Currently, I'm working on a surrealist painting, one that is similar in style to what Salvador Dalí has painted. It's of a dream I had in which a lion was chasing me. So far what I have depicted on the canvas is a man running naked overtop of a brown and red shaded cliff that is melting towards the center of the space and mixing with the sky. The lion is jumping through a hole in the air behind him, escaping from a black and green vortex. In the top right corner I'm planning on painting a woman in a red dress sitting in front of a vanity on a golden hued cloud. Recently, there's always a female figure present in whatever I paint.

I get to work, devoting all of my attention towards my brush and the picture before me that is unfolding, trying to forget about the stresses of today. I want to dissolve into a realm where all I have to concentrate on is my painting in front of me. I don't want notions of basketball or impressing my brother getting in the way. Instead, something else entirely comes to my attention.

"That looks spectacular Priam."

I pull my brush away from the canvas and turn to my right from where the voice came. It's Mr. Williams, who I assume had been watching me work for a while now without saying anything. He knows that I don't like to be disrupted while I am at work. As a fellow artist, we speak the same kind of dialogue, both internally and externally.

"Thank you Mr. Williams, I don't know if it will make much sense to anyone else, but it makes sense to me."

"Art doesn't have to make sense and besides, it's visually

very intriguing, so I think that's all you need. You know, a great deal of people came up and told me how much they enjoyed your work after the showcase last week."

Alden puts on a yearly art showcase at the beginning of December, and this year's had been just a few days ago. I had three paintings on display: one was an ocean scene, another was inspired by suburbia, and the last was a tangle of the buildings and streets of New York that I love so much. I knew that people had complimented my work, as Mr. Williams had already told me, but I still didn't know whether or not to believe how good I really was. I don't want to have a big ego; I paint simply because it is what I love to do. I don't need for people to love or even accept my work, but it is true that it makes me feel better about it. I think Mr. Williams knows that, hence why he keeps telling me over and over again how well my paintings were received by the adults and students from the community alike. The inners hiding in the dark part within me need to be told I am worthy of praise repeatedly in order to accept it.

"I'm glad that people enjoyed my paintings. Although I'm sure they liked some of the other students' more."

"Eh, I don't think so," he says as he rests his arm on my shoulder. "You know Priam, you are extremely talented. Probably the best art student I've ever had while teaching at this school to be honest, why won't you believe that?"

I want to believe it; I just am unable to do so. Sure I think I am good at painting, but not a single part of me believes that I am great. I long to become an artist in the city, someone who will one day be able to make a living solely off of my work. Do I think I will actually be able to do that? Not really, but that isn't going to stop me from trying. I still give everything my all, even though as time goes on and life becomes more real, my dreams seem less so, but regardless I still never want to give up on them. I know my mother would have wanted me to follow my heart.

"Perhaps I'll believe it one day, when I feel I've really earned such praise."

"Well, speaking of praise, I wanted to talk to you about something. I know you have said you are planning to move to the city after graduation to start a studio, but are you sure you don't want to go to art school at all?"

"I'm just so sick of school. I'm fed up with being told how

to think, how to feel and what to believe. I want to believe in my own philosophy."

"I get that and I respect that," Mr. Williams says as he sits down in the chair across from me so that my canvas is halfway in between us. "But, I talked to a contact of mine at the Parsons School of Design on your behalf and they wanted me to urge you to apply."

Parsons is one of the most prestigious art schools in New York City, in the country in fact, if not the world. Why on Earth would anyone from there want me to apply, especially if I had not taken the initiative to do so myself?

"I don't understand."

"An old friend of mine happens to work in the admissions department at Parsons. When you told me you didn't want to go to art school, I couldn't believe it. Perhaps I shouldn't have, but I took a few pictures of some of your most recent paintings and sent them in. Needless to say, they thought they were wonderful, and they want to see more."

"You sent in pictures of my paintings? And they thought they were good? Just from black and white photographs? Are you serious?" I can't believe it, part of me is angry at Mr. Williams for going behind my back and sending in my stuff without my permission, but I suppose I can't really be mad at him, as the result is residing highly in my favor.

"Yes, Priam, I'm serious. I think you should apply, you have a good chance of getting in. You have my support, that's for sure."

"Thank you Mr. Williams, I'll have to think about it. I'm going to get back to working on my painting though, if that's all right," I tell him as I pick up my brush again. I can't talk about this anymore, I feel as if my mouth is no longer able to formulate words. I watch as he nods and walks away to go and talk to some of the other students who are sitting on the opposite end of the classroom. Here I am perched over in the corner, as if I am already better than the rest of them. I hope they don't think that, I don't ever want people to think I am selfish, or think too highly of myself. That's why I don't want to believe in the idea of Parsons, that's why I can't accept that my paintings are as good as everyone tells me they are, I'm afraid of standing out too much in any way.

When I was younger, when she was still alive, my mother was there to reassure me, to tell me that things were true even when

I knew they already were. I needed her to make me believe, to make me see what was right in front of me, to accept the truth and deliver it. Ever since she had died I had a hard time digesting reality, I had difficulties with people thinking highly of me. Compared to Danny I always felt like the afterthought. He was so good at everything he did and although I was good at art and at shooting hoops, I never thought that would amount to enough, but maybe, just maybe, it would.

With thoughts of attending Parsons in the city and winning the big game tonight floating through my mind, I am beginning to believe that perhaps I can get everything I want after all. As long as that means Ellie too, for I realize as I start to paint the girl in the red dress on the cloud at the top of my canvas, I am really painting her. I am always painting her, and in doing so I feel as if she is mine. The one thing I want more than being an artist, or a basketball star, or a good brother, is for her to love me back, in the way that I love her.

When the school day is done I meet up with Margaret by her locker and we begin our journey home. It is rather cold, as when I step outside the air seems to hit me in the face with a fist of fury. If I had to guess, I would say it is certainly below freezing temperatures. We haven't had any snowfall yet which is surprising since we normally get a ton of lake effect snow in the winter. Maybe we'll get some tonight; it sure feels as if we could anyways.

"Do you think Danny will be at the house when we get back?"

"It's quite possible, seeing as your mother said he was already on the way before school started. I guess enough time has passed. Are you excited to see him?"

"Of course I'm excited, but aren't you excited even more?"

"I am. I just hope that we win tonight. I don't want him to have come all the way here to watch us lose."

"I'm sure you're going to win Priam. And even if you don't, I don't think that matters much to Daniel. He wants to come and support you, no matter the outcome."

I know she is right; I guess I should probably try and lighten up. The game is going to unfold tonight in one way or another, hopefully in my favor, but even if it doesn't it's not the end of the world. It's just a basketball game.

We walk home the rest of the way in relative silence. When we approach the house I can see that Grandpa Wood's silver Cadillac is parked in the driveway. Danny has made it home. He's inside the house right now. Margaret enters the front door first and I follow directly behind. I see Susan and Steve sitting in the living room, but Danny isn't with them. They see me and say hello and that's when he steps out from the kitchen, into my field of vision.

"Hey there little brother, you ready for tonight?"

I don't answer right away; instead I just walk over to where he is standing and give him a hug. I hold onto him for a few moments and then pull away and say: "You know you didn't have to come all the way from the city just to watch a stupid old basketball game."

"I know I didn't have to, but I wanted to. Besides, I could use the break from school. I brought some of my assignments with me anyways, I can work on them after you win tonight," he says with a smile. "And everything will be happy dandy then, I'm sure."

"As long as we do win, that is. You all know that's not a guarantee," I say to everyone sitting in the room. Susan, Steve and Margaret all offer me a warm glance in return, as if to say they still believe wholeheartedly that there is no way we are going to lose, but I find something puzzling about their expressions. It is almost as if they are focusing their attention on something behind me. At first I just think it's Danny, but then I realize it can't be, as he is moving from where he was standing to come around and join them on the sofa in front of me. I hear a flutter of footsteps in the kitchen, ever so slightly, but still present as they seem to be heading this way. I begin to turn around, but before I am able to face whoever it is that is coming towards me, they make their presence known even more.

"Oh you're going to win, there's no way I bummed a ride all the way from New York City to watch you lose!" The last word escapes her mouth just as I have fully turned around to face her. Somehow, she is standing right in front of me now. I wouldn't have to wait until the holidays to see her stunning face, to witness her laugh, to see her sway from side to side as she moves towards me in her red dress. All at once she leaps into my arms. "Surprise!" She giggles as she puts her hands around me and pulls me close.

Ellie Donahue is in Alden. She has come to watch me play basketball tonight. As I hold her I feel as if a thousand fireworks are shooting through the sky, but all the while I simultaneously feel as if

I am starting to drown in the middle of the sea. I am ecstatic that Ellie is here, but the pressure seems all too much to bear. I have to win tonight; I have to make sure of it. Losing in front of my brother would be disappointing, but losing in front of Ellie would be impossible. I have to show her that I am good enough, I have to prove myself worthy of her affection, if I even can at all, tonight is the start.

I release her and look at her in front of me, still trying to take in this reality. I forget about the others sitting behind us, all I can see, all I can think about is her. "How did you get here?" I ask, even though I'm pretty sure I already know the answer.

"Your brother of course, he told me he was coming and asked if I wanted to join him. There wasn't a second thought about it after he asked; I knew I had to come see you, to watch you win."

"Golly, if I lose tonight I'm going to feel like the biggest failure in the world." Which is the truth, I think to myself. I just want the game to be over already and it hasn't even started yet. With the three Henderson's in the stands along with Danny and now Ellie too I know I am going to feel as if all eyes are on me, watching my every move. The people I care about most in the world are expecting me to succeed.

"You won't lose," she says as we walk into the living room and I realize the rest of them are getting up to leave.

"Where are you all going?" I ask, confused.

"Oh I'm sure you two want some alone time," Susan says. "I'd imagine you have things to catch up on."

I don't know how much there is to catch up on, with the regular letters we write to each other and the phone calls, however fleeting. I know everything that has been going on in Ellie's life recently, but I won't argue with the idea of some alone time with her. If the others want to leave, I'll let them. Besides, it won't be too long before I have to go back to the high school to prepare for the game.

We sit down in the living room, which everyone has just vacated and talk for an hour or so, not once does anyone interrupt us. I feel bad that I haven't had a chance to speak with Danny for very long, but I imagine he is working on his assignments upstairs anyways. I owe him one for coming all the way here, but especially for thinking to invite Ellie to come along too, there would have been no way she could have made it here on her own otherwise. She tells me of her dance classes and about the ballet she is performing in, which just so happens to be a rendition of the Nutcracker. It opens in a few weeks and I was planning on going to see it over Christmas break while I am in the city, but that task alone seems insufficient now since she has come to surprise me and watch me play. Maybe there will be some way I can go to watch her dance on opening night, before she expects my presence in the stands.

"I'm surprised your mother let you come the whole way to Alden. What did you have to do in order for her to allow you?"

"She doesn't know."

"What?" I ask, thoroughly shocked.

Ellie's mother was very protective and often overbearing towards her only daughter. Sometimes it was a struggle to even get her to let Ellie hang out with me in the city, let alone receiving her permission to drive across the entire state of Pennsylvania to see me play a basketball game.

"I knew she wouldn't let me come if I told her the truth, I left her a note saying I was going to be out late because of rehearsal and that I might just stay over at Juliana's if it got too late so I didn't have to venture across the city late at night. I'm sure she won't even notice."

"I don't know about that. I hope you don't get in trouble."

"Even if I do it will be worth it Priam. I wanted to see you play. There's nothing she can do to take back tonight now that I'm here."

I suppose that is the truth. She's going to be in the gym watching me play; I look up to the ceiling and say a short silent prayer for a win. I don't know if the spirits above watch high school basketball games, especially ones in small towns like this, but if they do I beg of them to please help my team win. In return for the assistance, I'll do my best to be a better man.

I sit in the room with Ellie and listen to her talk about the beautiful costumes and the wonderful choreography of her show. I take in every sensation of the conversation I can. I don't want to talk anymore, I only care to listen. I wish I could skip the game and just stay here with her, to go out for a walk in the cold winter air, or to sit by the fireplace and paint her a picture. I know that can't be though, I have to play, I have to win. The time ticks by, and before I know it I have to go upstairs to get my stuff ready for the game. I don't want to leave. Ellie helps me pack my gym bag and admires the new paintings I have hanging in my room. It's the first time she's ever been here. I tell her of the one I'm working on at school and she says that she'd love to see it. It's not finished though, it's not finished I say. After we leave my room she heads downstairs to help Susan and Margaret with dinner. I decide to stop in Danny's room briefly and as I do I see that he is sitting on his bed working on one of his assignments he had mentioned. There is a great deal of papers strewn across his comforter and I see that his briefcase on the floor is stuffed with folders and other materials too.

"College sure looks tough, how many assignments did you bring home with you? A thousand?"

He looks up at me quickly in a start, and his face looks scrunched from the way he reacts to my presence. I approach him and when I get closer I see that there is a picture of a car in his hands. "You startled me Priam, I hadn't realized you had come into my room."

"Oh well you know me, ever the super sleuth."

"I don't know if I would go that far." He says as he sets the photograph down, placing it underneath some of his papers. "Anyways, I'm working on my final advertising project for the semester. It's a campaign for a new model Ford."

I sit down on the bed beside him and look down at the papers he's studying. I realize now that they aren't all papers, for there are more pictures piled within his belongings than just the one he had been holding. I pick one up which looks similar to the one he just had and quickly realize that it's not just any Ford that Danny is doing his project on, it's the new model of the Ford Victoria. It's the newest version of the car that my mother died in. I rapidly become dreadfully angry. Why on earth would Danny do an advertising campaign for this? Perhaps it wouldn't be a big deal to many, but it is to me. Ever since that day I always feel a shiver go down my spine whenever I see a Victoria drive past me, it's as if a ghost walks over her grave every time my eyes are faced with the tomb of her destruction. I hate that car, the car that killed her and every other car that is built to look anything like it.

"Are you shitting me?" I ask in the calmest voice I can, for although I am terribly disturbed by his project, I don't want to yell at him, as he did just drive all the way to Alden to see me play. He came all the way here, he brought Ellie, but he brought this project too. I already hate it and I don't think there is any way he can explain it to me so that I won't stop despising every single picture of the new Ford Victoria that he has lying across his bed and floor.

"Priam! Watch the way you talk to me. I'm sorry I guess I should have said something to you before you started looking at what I've got so far. I wasn't able to pick the product I had to make a campaign for. It was assigned to me. There was nothing I could do."

"I don't believe you."

Danny looks at me and rolls his eyes. "Oh come on, Priam. Do you honestly think I would choose to have a final project that reminds me of my mother dying every time I sit down to work on it?"

"Who knows, with you sometimes I wonder. I don't want to start an argument though. I came in here to tell you that I'm happy you're here and I wanted to thank you for bringing Ellie. Nevertheless, the least you could have done was talk to your professor about it. Did you even do that?"

"I didn't see the point. I doubt he would have changed the subject of the project."

"You didn't even try. Mother would be ashamed of you. Just as I'm ashamed of you for promoting the vehicle that killed her. Maybe it wasn't the car's fault or even Ford's, but still, it makes my blood boil. Everyone is always saying how great of a guy you are, if you're such a great guy you should have done something to get out of this. You should have stood up for her memory. I would have if I were you. I bet if you told your professor your mother died in this exact car he would have changed it for you. I'm sure a Buick would do."

I throw the picture of the new 1960 Victoria on the ground. I feel bad that I've spoken to Danny in such a way, but at the same time I don't. When I'm angry, all filters dissipate. I've never been one to silence my emotions, to mask my feelings with pretend triviality. I don't want to be in his room anymore, I don't want to be surrounded by pictures of that car; I don't want to feel as if I'm reliving her death all over again, I've done that enough times before. I storm out of his room, I hear him calling my name but I don't go back. I just want to get out of this house. I can talk to Danny later, once I've won, once it's over and everyone is happy with me, proud of me. I'll talk to my brother once I feel better about my life, once Ellie has congratulated me, and the feelings running through my veins, those feelings of which he has done our late mother a disservice have evaporated.

I grab my gym bag in the hallway and rush downstairs. I ask Susan to pack dinner in a box for me. I tell her that I forgot that coach wants us to come to the school earlier than usual because of how important tonight's game is. She seems upset that I won't be able to eat with them and in a way I am too, as the look on Ellie's face is one of disappointment when she hears me tell my lie. I can't be in this house any longer though, I don't want to have to talk to my brother, I need to cool down, I need to go to the school and prepare for the game. I have to focus. Susan reluctantly prepares a box of food for me and wishes me luck. Ellie does the same; she gives me a hug and walks me to the door.

"I'll be there right in the stands the whole time. If you're scared, look to me."

"I'm not scared, Ellie." I say to her, lying again. "But I'll look to you, I always do." I peck her on the cheek, which up unto this point is something that I've never done before. I don't even realize it until I pull away and notice that she is blushing. I throw on my letterman's jacket and open the door. I hear Danny coming down the stairs, so I exit quickly, not wanting him to see me go.

"Goodbye dear," she says with a wave as she stands in the doorway, leaning up against the frame in her red dress, just as my mother had done all those years ago in her white spotted blue. "And good luck!" she adds, yelling loudly so I hear her as I begin to run down the street, the cold air filling my lungs and my feet propelling me faster and faster. I don't know why I've started to run; my body just decided to, my mind never thought of it, not until this moment now anyways. I'm getting away from everyone at the house, the people who I have to make proud, the people I love more than all others alive.

I wish she were here, I wish my mother could let me know that everything was going to be okay. I wonder if she knows, wherever she is, what is going to happen tonight. If I will win, if Ellie will ever love me, if Danny hates me, for I feel as if he does at times, even though I should have no reason to believe such an idea. Something feels off. I need my mother's reassurance and I know there is no way to receive it, at least not in any natural or scientific way. I run to Alden High. My mind and my body have no idea what the score of the basketball game will be, how many points I will score, how many buckets I will miss, the anger that will follow the outcome, or what I will do both because of that anger and as a result thereof that will subtlety, yet every so strongly, change my life forever.

When I get to my school I sit in the locker room and stuff my face with the dinner Susan has prepared for me. I take one bite after another, not taking much time in between to digest what I've already eaten. After I finish, I put on my uniform and then my warm up outfit over top of that. No one else is here yet so I go into the gym, find a basketball and begin to shoot around. I try not to think about anything at all. At first, thoughts of Ellie, Danny and that damn car are bouncing back and forth in my brain, just as the ball that I am pushing against the ground is, but eventually they fade. I focus on what I am doing: shooting, running, dribbling. The motions of the game overtake me and I remember why I play basketball in the first place. An amount of time passes, I'm not sure how long, but I begin to hear my teammates going into the locker room, the door slamming shut when they let go of it every time. I decide it's time I stop warming up, as spectators will soon begin to fill up the stands.

In the locker room, my teammates quietly get ready. No one says too much, I imagine they are all just as nervous and anxious as I am. Not much later, our coach comes in and talks to us. He gives us words of encouragement and tells us to do our best, to play as we have been playing and that we will succeed. I am only able to half listen to what he has to say. I just want the game to begin. And then, after what I feel has been almost an entire lifetime, it finally does.

I don't look out into the bleachers until the game is just about to begin, as the starting five from both teams step onto the court, myself and my best friend Jimmy included. When I finally do, I don't have to search too long to find Ellie. Her red dress stands out in the crowd, as does the fact that she is waving frantically at me with a smile on her face that seems hopeful, supportive and endearing. I gulp, swallowing the small amount of spit left in my mouth which now feels very dry. I nod my head in her direction and force a smile her way. I notice that she is sitting next to Danny, who appears to be sitting very close to her. He's not looking at me though, he seems distracted, gazing off into the distance, maybe thinking of that final project of his, that stupid car.

I enter the circle in the middle of the court where the referee is standing with the ball, along with the tallest player on Sommerville's team, who I clearly am going to have to jump against in order to determine who will have possession. I shake his hand and say "Good luck." He shakes my hand in return as hard as he possibly can, almost to the point of crushing it. He stares at me intently; he utters not a single word. This bothers me as I wonder what the hell is wrong with him. At the same time however, he lights my fire to reach the ball first.

The referee asks us if we are ready, to which we both nod. I crouch down low, with my hands ready at my sides. The referee blows the whistle and at that instant I push myself off of the ground with all of the force I can so I am floating towards the ceiling, my right arm outstretched. I feel the ball in my fingertips and push it back with my hand as vigorously as possible in the direction of our team's point guard. When I come back down to the wooden floor beneath me I glance to the direction of where I moved the ball, as I know that I reached it before the boy I was jumping with. The ball is in the Alden Panther's possession. At least I did that much right; the nerves rolling around in my stomach may not have gotten the best of me after all, at least not yet.

The start of the game is a fast paced back and forth brawl for control of the ball and the scoreboard. Both teams score a similar amount of points and I have two lay-ups and go two for two at the line for a total of six points. When the buzzer rings at the end of the first quarter. My team has a total of 18 points with Sommerville right behind us at 16.

We huddle around our coach who tells us to keep up the good work, and suggests a few pointers to help our offense progress further. I try to listen intently, but I can't help the urge to look back up in the stands to get a glimpse of Ellie. This time, she's not looking in my direction, instead she and Danny seem to be deep in conversation as they are both looking intently at one another, after a few moments she bursts into laughter and sticks out her hand and playfully pushes it up against his chest so that he backs up a little bit in his seat.

Coach calls for all of us to put our hands in the middle of

the huddle and as the rest of the team shouts "Go Alden!" I say nothing at all. I walk out to the court, my eyes still on the two of them, who have yet to look back in my direction. Does Ellie even care that I'm here? Does Danny have feelings for her? Is that why he brought her all the way here to Alden? I had introduced the two of them during the summer in the city and they interacted other times before this, but I had always been there with them. I never dreamed that the two of them had any relationship of their own that didn't involve me.

Ellie never mentioned spending time with my brother in the city in her letters, but now all I can think about is that I have been so naïve to think that I actually had a chance with her, that we would ever be anything more than friends. Danny and Ellie are in love, I had just seen them flirting in the stands and they had not even noticed my watchful glare or my breaking heart. The pieces are crumbling. How could she know of my feelings? I had never told Ellie how I truly felt about her. No wonder she blushed when I pecked her on the cheek when I left the house. She is in love with my brother, the older, smarter, better looking one. How could she ever love me? We are friends, just friends, that's all we will ever be.

The second quarter starts and I realize that everyone else is beginning to run to one side of the court while I stand still here in the middle, motionless. I shake my head from side to side trying to empty out the thoughts of my heartbreak and I run down the court, but I don't get there before Sommerville scores. It's now a tied game.

The rest of the quarter goes in a similar fashion as the first, although I mess up a great deal more. I only score one bucket, and I miss all four of my foul shouts. I drop a few passes and the referees call me for walking twice. I can't focus on the game, in a way I don't even care about it anymore. I want to run out of Alden High, out into the streets and cry. I want to go back to the house and go through my mother's old records; I want to listen to the one of her voice that she had recorded when she was still singing in the theater in the city. I want her to be here, she would know what to tell me, how to deal with Ellie and Danny.

The minutes pass faster and faster and before I know it the buzzer is ringing once again, this time though, we are no longer winning, the score is 32 Sommerville, with my team trailing behind at 29. This loss is occurring in all of the ways around everything that

I want. We go into the locker room and sit down as my coach begins to speak. He says that we are still doing well, but we need to pick up the intensity, we need to focus on our offensive abilities and not miss any more foul shots.

"Priam, are you alright?" He asks me suddenly. I've been staring off into the corner of the locker room towards where the showers are in the back, not looking at him or any of my teammates, not even Jimmy.

"Fine," I lie, right through my gritted teeth.

"Well you don't look fine, and you haven't been playing fine this past quarter either. It's as if all of the force you had in the first quarter just randomly decided to disappear. Bring it back the rest of the game okay? We need you."

"I'll try Coach, I'll try." And try I will, for even though I don't want to, I have to. I'm the boy who will never stop trying. The amount which I am able to do so though is not always under my control, as the third quarter begins, I once again look to the stands. This time Susan is waving at me and I nod, acknowledging her, but I can't make myself smile. My eyes pan to the two of them beside her and I see that Ellie is looking right at me; she looks happy, but also concerned. It's as if the look on her face tells me that she knows I am upset, she can tell something is wrong.

I think of running over to where she is sitting, so I can actually hear her voice, so I can say something to her, but just as I think to do so, someone else acts first. I see his hand reaching out behind her shoulders and then slowly resting upon them before he pulls her close, the way that only couples do. I don't see her face, I don't see how she reacts, I don't see anything at all because I immediately turn away. I can't look at them anymore, I can't bear to witness the happy couple that is the girl I love and my brother. I used to look up to him, but now all I can think about is how he is such a smug bastard for stealing her right from under me. I had no clue about it whatsoever.

The third quarter is different, I'm angry, in fact, I'm furious. I become a crazy animal on the court, a freight train that can't be stopped. Although Sommerville has brought out a similar amount of passion onto the wooden floors, I charge through the boys as if they are simply dominos in my way, knocking one down after the other. I score eight points, and have three assists, not messing up once. By the time the quarter ends the score is 48

Alden, 46 Sommerville. We've reclaimed the lead, the third quarter's the key.

During the huddle before the final quarter Coach is very enthusiastic telling me "I like what you're doing out there Priam. I guess you were listening to me in that locker room after all." Really, I wasn't, but he doesn't need to know that. I have improved my game for another reason entirely, to show my brother, to show them both that I am good enough. Maybe Ellie has decided on the elder Wood boy, a decision I didn't even realize was plausible or possible before tonight, but I'm going to make her regret it. I'm not only going to win this basketball game, singlehandedly if I have to, but I'm going to become the better brother in every aspect in the long run. I'm going to be more successful, smarter, and hopefully as I grow older, more attractive too. I will make them regret this day, this day when they shoved their relationship in my face, regardless of if they did so willingly or not.

The fourth quarter unfurls at an even faster pace than the third. Before I know it the last minute of the game is upon us and the score is 57 Alden, and 56 Sommerville. There is no room to breathe, no room to think, even though the thoughts in my head won't stop buzzing, can't stop buzzing. Although I feel as if I am on fire with passion and force, inside my emotions are melting into a miserable mess of despair.

We have possession of the ball on our side of the court so we pass it around for a while, trying to kill some time since we are ahead. After about twenty seconds the point guard passes the ball to Jimmy, who then passes the ball towards me. It never reaches my hands though, a scrappy player from Sommerville intercedes and grabs the ball and then dribbles it down the court towards his goal. Everyone on my team chases after him, but none of us are fast enough. He scores and their fans cheer wildly. We are now the ones who are losing by one. I look to the scoreboard, there are only twenty three seconds left. I never wanted it to happen like this. I didn't want to have to feel as insane as I currently do, with the basketball game and with my emotions too.

The point guard for our team gets the ball from under the hoop where it has just fallen through for Sommerville and we quickly get it back to our side. I run under the hoop knowing that our best chance to score is if I get the ball and make a lay-up.

Apparently that is what the rest of the team believes too,

because shortly the ball is in my hands, I stretch towards the hoop, but before I can push it through the net the center from Sommerville, the same player who crushed my hand so mercilessly before crashes into me, smacking at my hands so that I miss the shot completely. The whistle blows and the referee calls a foul. I have two shots, two shots at the line. This game is going to be either won or lost, entirely by me. As if I should have expected any less, it's almost like I knew it would turn out this way all along.

As I approach the line, I look to my fellow teammates and when I look to Jimmy in particular, I am reminded of that day five years ago when I threw the brick, when I told my mother I hated her, when she died. I feel a rage inside me, an anger I wish I could suffice, but all I can think about as I stand at the line waiting for the ball to be in my hands is how I wish I could change that day, and how I wish I could change this one too.

I think of Ellie, sitting in the stands with Danny. I can't help but to look at her and when I do, I am surprised to see that Danny is no longer sitting so close. He looks as if he is almost ignoring her in fact. He sees me looking at him for the first time the entire game, he nods his head and gives me a thumbs up, apparently that is his method of encouragement. I look to Ellie, she mouths words to me, which I recognize: "You can do it." I've stared at her lips for far too long not to be able to know what they are saying even without hearing anything.

I turn back; the referee passes me the ball. I dribble the ball a few times, everything is frozen yet spinning faster. I bend my knees, I lift my arms above my head, I shoot...I miss.

The crowds on both sides of the gym seem to fall silent; in fact the entire world becomes mute at this moment as the ball hits the ground, up and down, up and down. I'm not surprised I missed the first shot; in fact I almost knew I was going to. It was too much pressure to bear. I tried, but I failed.

This last shot, this final shot is still before me though. We are only down by one point, all I have to do is make this shot and the game will be tied. We will go into overtime and then someone else can make the final shot. I don't want it to have to be me. I look to the scoreboard, only two seconds are left. If I miss this, the game is over; I doubt anyone would be able to shoot again in time. I take a deep breath and the referee passes the ball to me again. I take my time, dribbling the ball up and down, up and down. I bend my knees, I lift the ball above my head, I snap my wrist and release it. The ball floats through the air in slow motion, I watch as it flies towards the hoop in what appears to be a perfect arc, it is right on track, I couldn't have made a better shot.

Except I don't. The ball falls in between the rim, but as it does, just as I think it has gone in, it bounces, it slams across both the back and the front of the orange circular hoop and decides to fall, not in, but out. I miss the shot. It falls out of the rim, Jimmy tries to grab it, he tries to put it back up, but he never even gets to touch it. It falls within the hands of the massive Sommerville boy, the one who smashed my hand. The buzzer rings. We've lost.

The Sommerville fans go wild, their student body runs onto the floor surrounding their team, screaming, cheering, liberating their spirits that had been held captive by the four quarters of this basketball game. They have won, we have not. I've lost.

I glance back to the stands, where Ellie is now standing up, where everyone is standing. Her hand is covering her mouth, tears are slowly streaming down her face. I look away as quickly as I can. I can't look at her, I can't. I've disappointed her, I've disappointed everyone. I wanted to prove I was good enough, I wanted to prove I was better than him. I wanted to prove something...anything. I wanted them to believe in me. I can't handle the feelings that are inside of me, I can't deal with the chaos I feel inside of my soul. I have to get out of this gym, I have to get out of this school. So I do. I begin to run, out of the gym, out of the hallway, out of Alden High, out into the freezing cold air in nothing but my basketball shorts and my tank top which bears the number thirteen. I run.

By the time I make it back to my house I feel as if every bone in my body is frozen. Running out of the gym with nothing else on except for my uniform was probably not the best idea I've ever had, but at the time it seemed like the only real option available. I couldn't stay in that gym any longer, I couldn't face her, I couldn't face any of them. I enter through the front door of the house, which is never locked. As the warm air inside surrounds me, my ears slowly start to burn from the abrupt change in temperature. I go into the kitchen and pour myself a glass of water. I start chugging it as quickly as I can; I lean against the wall and slowly slide down to the floor.

After all of the day's anxiety, after all of the worries I had about how things would go this evening, I never in a million years thought they would turn out so horribly. When I woke up this morning all I was worried about was losing and even though the loss did come true, a loss I feel is completely my fault, so many other elements I didn't anticipate went wrong too. I never thought Danny would be here, let alone Ellie, but they both were, they were both in that gym and as the control of winning the game fell from my hands, so did my heart. I am still in a state of shock and disbelief from the fact that there is something going on between the two of them. Sure, I can understand it in a way, it makes sense to me that Ellie has chosen my older brother over me, but that doesn't mean I want to accept it.

As I sit on the ground in the kitchen, the glass of water perspires in my hand as the cool sweat runs down my back. I lift my hand to wipe away the wetness on my forehead. I think about how angry I was when I saw him put his arm around her, how upset I was when the two of them were laughing together, flirting, having fun, enjoying themselves...without me. I think about how their interaction made me feel weak, how I started to play like shit in the second quarter and then how it angered me into a rage that fueled me into an unstoppable frenzy that scored all of those points during the third. In the end though, I didn't score enough, as I took those two final shots all I could think about was the two of them, their happiness, the pleasure they were experiencing while I was left alone out on the court.

Maybe this isn't entirely my fault. It can't be, I didn't lose the game singlehandedly. The more I think about it, my teammates didn't matter much in my destruction, only one person affected that, and that one person was my older brother Danny. Sure I'm upset with Ellie too, but I can't really be mad at her even if I try; besides I don't blame her for seeing all of the wonderful qualities my brother has to offer. I do blame Danny though. I blame him for going behind my back and scooping Ellie up without even thinking about how it would make me feel. He had to know how I felt about her. Even though I hadn't told him outright that I cared about her as much as I do, he knew. I spent every waking moment with her this past summer, and every instance since thinking about her, writing to her, talking to her, dreaming of her and wishing for the day that we would be together. He knew what he was doing, I am sure of it. As I stand up from the floor an idea crosses my mind, an idea that I realize is the only way I can rightfully get back at him, the only way I can think to make myself feel better; to exact some sort of vengeance that in a way almost seems perfect. What I have to do, what I have to destroy, is sitting upstairs in his bedroom.

I imagine everyone will be arriving back shortly. I know they saw me run out of the gym and even though I sprinted the entire way home I'm sure that the car will bring them back to the house quicker than I probably even realize. If I am going to act on this, I have to do it now. I climb up the stairs and enter his room. I stare at the images of the car, that evil car, the one that took her away from me. Sure, these images are newer than the one that stole her life, that made her leave this Earth, but if anything, the cars that are pictured in these photos in front of me are just the descendants of the devil himself. They are still to blame; they still infuriate me simply by the sight of them being present in my field of vision. I have to get rid of them, all of them. My anger on this day began when Danny told me about his final assignment, and the only way to get rid of the feeling inside of me is to make things equal. I have to get rid of his project, I have to make the images of the 1960 Ford Victoria go away.

I collect all of his papers and pictures, the ones on his bed, the ones on the floor and the remaining few that are still in his briefcase. I throw them into a pile at my feet. A picture of the Ford Victoria is lying on top. I pick it up, and stare at it for a few moments and tears well up in my eyes. I think of that day, I think of her death and when I do all my anger and sadness explodes inside of me, down from my heart and into my hands which begin to rip the image apart, into a thousand pieces so that the car is no longer a car, rather just slices of what used to be a motor vehicle, littered on the floor in front of my basketball shoes.

I look around his room until I see his steel wastebasket in the corner. I take out the plastic trash bag and drop it on the floor. I kick the can over with my foot until it is centered in the middle of the room. I dump the papers in, every image of the Ford Victoria, every paper he has for his final assignment. I grab a pack of matches off of his desk and strike one against the back of the pack so that a flame emerges in my hands. I drop the match in the bin, and the images and papers quickly begin to melt. I set it on fire not just because of what it is, but for what he's done. All of his hard work, all of the hatred I have for that car, for that project, for him and for stealing my girl are beginning to slip away. I snatch the ripped up pieces of the image I destroyed earlier and let them fall on top of the flame, as if I am sprinkling pinches of salt and pepper onto my cooking dinner.

I stare at the flame, taking in the sight; the warmth begins to raise the temperature of my body, which still feels raw and numb with cold. Dancing within the orange and yellow glow is everything I have experienced today, all of the people and places and faces and mistakes that I've made seem to be going away. I know what I've done is rash, but I believe it is the only way to make me feel okay with the way things turned out tonight; it is the only way to make me feel alive again. The flames have me transfixed, so much so that as I take in the dancing fire before me I don't hear any of them come inside, I don't hear their footsteps flitter and fall on the stairs. I don't hear when they call for me, I only become aware of the fact that they are home when they enter the room.

"What the hell?!" He yells from behind me. My shoulders jerk up at the sound, surprised from the sudden noise that I was not expecting. My destruction of Danny's project had taken me over completely; I had forgotten that anyone else would be coming home. I had lost myself in the flames. I don't turn around; I don't need to, for before I know it my brother is in front of me, his eyes filled with anger. It's not the same kind as mine though, whereas my emotions have always been dominated by heartbreak, the current situation that resides with him is one of complete and utter disappointment and confusion. His heart isn't breaking, he is a man filled only with the shock for the scene in front of him.

"What are you doing? What are you burning? What is going on?" He asks, one question after another. I don't answer. I can't answer. I stare at the fire that has a grip on my soul. He looks around the room, and then a glint of light flicks through the irises of his eyes. He realizes, he notices that his project is gone, all of his work, all of his papers, all of his images. He looks back to me.

"What did you do? Why? Why?!" He screams now, begging me to answer the question which I feel he at least partially knows the answer too.

I feel another presence in the room, I feel her spirit behind me and then it floats to my side, her red dress illuminated by the light of the flames. She stands right beside me and I can tell she is looking at my face, but she says nothing and I do not look at her, at least not directly. She resides simply in my periphery, as the girl in the red dress, the girl who, as it looks from the light reflecting off of her, as if she could be on fire herself. She's not though, the only thing burning are the papers below and they are beginning to run out of steam, they are amounting to nothing but ashes.

"You know why I did it," I finally say. "I had to do it. I can't believe you Danny. When you came here today I thought it was for me, but it wasn't. It was for her, it was so you could shove your relationship in my face. You've always had to be the best; you've always had to show me that you were better. I'm sick of trying to compare to you, I'm always going to lose, just like I did tonight."

"What on earth are you talking about Priam?"

"You know what I'm talking about Danny. You brought Ellie here because you two are together, you didn't invite her for me, so stop pretending like you did."

"Priam," Ellie interjects. "It's not like that Priam. It's not, I swear."

I look at her face that's lit up by the flames and I'm reminded of the last day of my mother's life, the day she was encased in the setting of the sun, her glory and her beauty drenched in the sunlight. The parallels seem to persevere through the precipice of this moment even though I try to shake it away. I can't look at her anymore; the hurt is too great to bear. I loved her, I love her.

"I can't trust you Danny. I thought you were supposed to be the one person that was always going to be there for me, to support me, to show me the way. I looked up to you, but I won't anymore after today. I don't even want to have to look at you at all. The game, I lost it and I feel like a big part of that was because of you. I wish you wouldn't have come at all."

"Just let me explain, you have it all wrong." He says as he looks down to the flame which is beginning to die down. "Why did you destroy my project? I've been working on that for months. Do you realize what you've done?" He's yelling again now, his voice quivering with an unruly discontent.

"I destroyed it just as it destroyed our mother. I hate that car and every example of it. I don't understand how you don't too. After I got home from the game it felt like the only thing I could do, the only logical step in order to release the anger inside of me that came about from losing, from seeing the two of you..." My voice trails off, and as it does, Ellie comes back into my view, standing across from me and next to Danny. The sight of them together in such a way turns my stomach, though they are not even acknowledging each other, the image of them beside one another in the frame of my mind is enough.

My frozen bones begin to feel weak as they are now filled with warmth and are beginning to expand. An ecstatic energy is whizzing through my body. I look down at the basket and realize that only a small flame is left, it flits to and fro for an instant and then becomes a much more miniscule spark before it fades entirely. Blood is pulsing through my veins, I look at him and then I look at her. The anger and confusion in his eyes has a similar residence within hers, but where he has anger she holds sadness, and a simple sense of longing. He looks as if he wants to strangle me; she appears to want to console me. As they both begin to move forward towards me, arms outstretched, I back away. I can't, I can't, I can't. Not now. I have to leave. So I run, again I run. Away from them, down the stairs, past the Henderson's who are standing in the living room with perplexed looks on their faces, out the front door, out into the cold air once again. I run.

I don't make it very far, for the truth is I have done an awful lot of running today, between the game itself and the two flights I've taken trying to escape my fears, trying to get away. It's even colder now than it was before. It's somewhat of a struggle to propel by body through the brisk air as it seems to bite at all of my appendages with every movement I make. I end up at a nearby park, one that is not too far away from the old Miller place. I think about going over to the house, to see if the window is still broken. The last time I checked it was, but I decide against it. I've thought about that day enough already. I just want to empty out all of my emotions; I wish I could pour them out onto the street.

I sit down on a swing and begin to kick the dirt beneath my feet. I push my legs off the ground so that I slowly sway back and forth. I don't have enough energy to propel myself high up into the air right now; I don't deserve to be on an elevated level in any regard anyways. I think about what I've done and if it was right. Was destroying Danny's project really the answer to the day's events? I wonder, and as I do I start to swing a little bit faster, so that my feet are no longer dragging beneath me, I start to take flight.

My airborne experience doesn't last long though, at least not on its own, neither do my fleeting feelings about the outcomes of my actions and how it has affected the people who matter the most. She appears in the distance, small at first, but even when she is far away I can still see her clearly, her red dress shimmering in the night, like a star illuminated with a maroon moon. As she approaches she says nothing, she just keeps looking at me, our eyes connecting in an unwavering dance. She slinks into the swing beside me and slowly begins to propel herself so that she is swaying in a similar fashion, and when the two of us are moving in a symmetrical way, she speaks.

"Are you okay?"

The question seems so simple, but at the same time it is the most appropriate one she could have possibly asked. It lets me knows she cares, it shows me that she wants to know how I am most of all.

"I've been better Ellie, I've been better."

"I'm so sorry about the game Priam. I hope you don't think the loss was your fault though. You played great; you were the high scorer you know. You shouldn't be so hard on yourself or take all of the blame. You did everything you could."

"But it wasn't enough."

"You tried your best, I know you did. I watched you the entire game. You were fighting out there, you were strong, brave, you played beautifully. The way you moved around the other team's players almost reminded me of a ballet. I became entrenched in the elements of your physicality, even though you lost, you impressed me. You amazed me."

Those last three words echo in my head. Hearing them from her makes me feel better. Maybe today wasn't a total failure after all, but still, she doesn't want me. She made her choice, she, like everyone else sees Danny as the better one, the stronger one.

"Well that's kind of you to say Ellie, but I'm sure even if I moved in an impressive way, it was still nothing compared to how you do," I say, and then pause before going on. "Can I ask you a question?"

"Of course, Priam."

"Why did you come to Alden today? What was the main reason? Please be honest."

"Priam, the number one reason I came was to see you, and

to see you play. I wanted to be here to support you, just as I knew you would come to support me if you had the opportunity to do so."

"Really? So you watching me play was more important than getting to spend time with Danny? I saw you two up in the stands, that's why I was so angry during and after the game. I saw both of you...it's okay if you're together you know," I say, even though it's not. The thought of it still makes me want to die, but if it is what Ellie has chosen, I have to support her, I can't not support her. "I just wish you would have told me, before I had to find out...like that."

"Priam, I don't know what you saw in the stands, but there is absolutely nothing going on between Danny and I, nothing but friendship. He asked me if I wanted to come with him to watch you play. There was never any other underlying reason for my visit."

Our swings slow down now so that we are both hovering on the seats in the middle of the ground where the dirt below us is compressed in a divot. I look to her for the first time since she's sat down next to me, and when I do my heart begins to beat faster, the blood races through my veins as if it is on a race across the world.

"You mean, the two of you aren't dating? You aren't together?"

"No! Priam, of course not! I can't believe you would even think that. I barely even know your brother. Today was the first time I was around him without you."

With these words I'm beginning to regret ruining Danny's project, for setting it on fire. Sure, even with this information I still hate what the assignment was, but I don't think that fact alone was enough of a reason to destroy it. I had started the flames for what I thought he had created with Ellie, a relationship that I assumed he was attempting to shove in my face. I was wrong.

"It's just that I saw you two laughing and flirting together in the stands. I saw him put his arm around you too."

"Well you must have looked away as soon as he did that, because if you would have continued watching us you would have seen me pull away. I can't lie to you and say that your brother didn't try to flirt with me tonight, because he did. He asked me if I would like to go on a date with him back in the city, but I said no. I said no, Priam."

"I guess I made judgments too soon. I should have talked to

you before I reacted like I did. I just feel like Danny is the perfect one, I never feel good enough next to him. When I saw the two of you together, it just made sense to me. I wasn't surprised that you had chosen him, or so I had thought. Ever since that day, ever since she died you know...I guess I'm just hard on myself. I always feel like the messed up one, the one who ruined everything. I never feel good enough, not for him, not for anyone."

"You're good enough for me Priam. In fact, you're more than good enough; you're simply just so hard on yourself that you don't see."

"What don't I see Ellie?"

"A lot of things, but I guess the one thing more than anything else is that you don't see me. At least not in the way I actually am." She begins to push her feet off of the ground beneath so that her swing leans to the side closer to mine; I decide to do the same so that we are now right next to each other. She reaches out and grabs my hand and holds it in her lap.

"What do you mean? Of course I see you. I see you even when you're not here. I think about you all the time, I think about this summer, and the times ahead and how I always wish you were here in front of me. I see you, Ellie, I do."

Her hands are warm, and as she holds mine I no longer feel as if I am developing frostbite. It is the middle of winter after all and I am still wearing nothing but my basketball uniform which is not the most appropriate kind of attire. The number thirteen that is emblazoned onto my back barrels into me through the cold. I look at her face, and as I stare into her blue eyes, I feel as if I can see her soul. Ellie Donahue, the girl I love more than anyone else on this earth is before me and she believes in me. Not only that, she's amazed by me. I think about all of the times I've wanted to tell her how much she means to me, that she's not just a friend, that she is everything I want, everything I feel I need.

I exhale slowly, and as I do my breath becomes illuminated by the park lights and the cold air, which makes it show up as fog between us. We laugh together, I see her smile and then without any further deliberation I go for it. When our lips touch, a new sensation enters into my experience of existence, one that seems to transcend reality for it makes me feel more alive than I ever have before. The kiss seems so good that I wonder if it could stop death, stop wars, stop heartache and all pain completely. The kiss only lasts for a few seconds, but within the time it occurs I feel as if I lose myself in a realm that goes on and on for ages. When I pull away, I slowly open my eyes, and I see her. I see her.

The snow begins to fall slowly at first, then faster and faster with each white teardrop of the heavens frozen in what feels like a fictitious faction of surprise. I never thought this day would end with a kiss from the girl I missed, the girl who is here now with me, the girl who chose me, me...Priam Wood.

*Tuesday, December 8*th *1959*
Day Two – *The Second Chance*

I'm conscious, and I think I know where I am, but I don't want to open my eyes. This bed feels just as it did yesterday when I woke up in the morning before the big game. It's time to do this all over again; it's time for day two, my way.

The last thing I remember is her kiss, the first kiss we had, the first one I had ever had and I just got to relive it again. The second day felt just as the first one did, I was there, but at the same time I wasn't. I felt her lips, I lived it again, but I couldn't hold her closer, I couldn't hold her any longer, and I sure as hell couldn't apologize for all of the things that were yet to come.

After we kissed in the park we went to Mr. Sander's diner. We got two large milkshakes and talked until midnight, when the day ended, when it faded away from me and brought me to this bed, where I am now. It feels as if I am traveling not only through time, but space as well, as I have apparated from the diner directly to this spot beneath my covers.

I don't want to open my eyes because even though the last sensations I have of this original day are good memories with Ellie at the swings, sipping on milkshakes still in my uniform which made me even colder than I was before, and of taking in that she was my girl, the bad ones come back too. My brother Danny clouds my senses as I see his face in the darkness of my closed eyelids, staring me down. I never went back to the house to see him, to talk to him, or to apologize. Instead I was even more selfish than I had already been before and spent the rest of the evening with Ellie, I never went back. I never fixed things and by the time the next morning came Danny was far too mad to even talk to me. The flames of his burnt project and the ashes they had become were still too hot and the fact that Ellie and I didn't come back to the house until late into the night must have made him even angrier still. In a way, I not only ruined his project that night, I was the brother who won Ellie too. Danny wasn't used to losing to me.

I have to change this day because of him, this is the day where our relationship started to end. After I destroyed his project he refused to talk to me for weeks and when he finally did everything was different. Sure, I apologized eventually for what I had done, but it wasn't enough as far as he was concerned. He became even more distant as time went on. He was hurt, and he never trusted me completely again after what I had done that day, this day.

The months and years went on and things were never the same. There were other instances, other occurrences along the way, but this is what started it all. When I set that project on fire, I burnt our relationship as well and it never fully recovered. It slowly charred into a crisp that couldn't be saved. That's why I knew I had to change this day, that's why I selected today as day number two. I have to win Danny back; I never wanted us to grow apart. I have to stop myself from lighting that match, from creating the spark that set our brotherly love ablaze.

The past is passing by like images swirling on the inside of my eyelids, as if the moments I am thinking about are painted upon them. The back and forth between the original seven days and the one day I have already changed has confused me slightly in a sense and as I think about those changes, I realize that some have already been made. Immediately my eyes fly open, in fact I can't believe they have been shut for so long. Perhaps it was necessary to collect my thoughts, to prepare myself before I came to face this second day, this second way. I remember that this day is already different at this instant without me having even to get out of bed. The exhaustion I felt only a few seconds ago has left me. My mother is still alive, and if I have to guess, I would assume that she is only just down the stairs.

I throw off the covers and lift my torso up from where it was resting. When I place my two feet firmly on the ground beneath I take in the room around me. It looks the same for the most part, although the paintings on the walls are not the same as the ones that were here originally. I'm glad to see that the auto pilot version of myself has stayed true to who I am, just as if I myself had lived each of the days in between.

To be honest, I was terrified when Chloe explained to me the rules of this seven day journey. She told me I would relive the days as they initially occurred and then have to deal with the things I would change being filled in by an entity that wasn't entirely myself. Hell, I'm still terrified by this idea, but I trusted my dog when she told me so, and I still trust her now. I can't think about it too much more though, because whenever I focus on anything else besides the day at hand and what I have to do it starts to hurt, not only in my head but in my heart, my entire reality of being is pained. I wonder if this is an unwritten rule Chloe never described to me: to focus on what is here, focus on what is now. So that is what I'll do. From now on I can't think too much ahead, or too much behind, all I have is the potential of this day, and as I leave my room and walk down the hall with my arms outstretched running my fingers along the walls, I think about how much potential it has, for this day is another way to make myself a better man.

I clamber down the staircase hurriedly and as I do I notice that there are photographs along it that were never there before. I see one of my mother and Danny at what appears to be his high school graduation; I see one of she and I where I am wearing my basketball uniform, and finally one of all three of us standing in the driveway with the Ford Victoria behind us. Seeing my mother represented as an older being in these photographs than what I've ever experienced her to look like is an otherworldly experience. I stare at them, taking it all in, but after a few minutes I pull myself away, I want to see the real thing, I want to see her.

When I walk into the kitchen a familiar smell fills my nostrils, one that I have never been able to appreciate since that day. The scent is that of my former favorite breakfast food: pancakes. She's at the stove with her back turned towards me, the green dress she has on shows that she is still in as good of shape as she was when she died five years ago, her frame is just as slender and tall. Her blonde hair is shorter though, whereas it used to fall well beneath her shoulders I see that it is cut right above them now. She is whistling a tune, I'm not quite sure what it is, but it makes me smile. I've never been able to whistle. She always used to try to teach me how to, but I only spit out soundless air.

"Good morning Mother."

She turns around and grins at me and it lights up the room just as it always used to. I feel my heart turn into a pile of goo, the fact that she is before me now, five years older than the last time I saw her is almost too much to comprehend, too much to take in. "Good morning Priam. Big day today isn't it? Are you ready?"

I sit down at the kitchen table, she turns back to the stove and flips the pancakes onto a plate and then brings them over to me. The syrup is already in front of me, she has perfect timing still, she always did. My mother was the queen of punctuality. Unfortunately I never inherited these skills from her.

She sits down in the chair across from me and I can't help but to stare at her. I notice there are a few more lines on her face than the last time I saw her. She's five years older than she ever was and it appears that a lot has happened in those five years. I hope they were all good things, I hope they were filled with smiles, laughter, grand decisions and only a few tears. I don't actually know what has happened to her since that day, the first day I changed. I know I have to ask her things, but I can't make it come across as if I don't know the answers. I recognize the possibility that could skew the day and create problems for the ones that follow. I can't tell her that I am reliving seven days of my life. No, I have to act as normal as I possibly can, I have to be a better man.

I grab the syrup and pour it over the pancakes she has delivered to me. They look as good as I remember them being. I begin to cut into them. I take a bite and chew, still silently staring at her as unobnoxiously as I can. It's her, my mother. I saved her.

"Did you become mute overnight? Or are you really just that excited to eat those pancakes and look at my face?" She says in a playfully sarcastic tone.

"Both," I mumble as I continue eating the pancake that is sending a sensation of warm delectability down my spine.

"Well that's a lie. Boys who are mute can't say the word both."

I swallow and acknowledge my mistake. "Good point."

"So do you think you boys will be able to clinch a win tonight? Sommerville is pretty good, aren't they?"

The game. I can't believe it's actually still scheduled tonight even after the major changes made on that first day. I mean, I did save a life after all. I suppose my mother never had much to do with arranging basketball schedules though, and apparently I was always destined to play, with or without her, as the picture on the stairs so adequately displays.

"I'm sure the game will be a close one. They're very good, their center in particular is a pretty aggressive player, believe me, I know," I tell her as I imagine that monster squeezing my hand as hard as he can. It feels like it just happened yesterday and in a way it did. At least I know I can jump higher than him.

"Well, I bet you and the rest of the Alden boys can take him and the rest of their team. I believe in you. Plus, you're a rather aggressive player too you know, it's not like I haven't been at every game watching you play."

This delights me. I always used to feel strange not having either of my parents watch me play, or to watch anything I did from the age of thirteen on, really. I wore the number thirteen in her honor, it was my way of keeping her with me, for that was the only version of myself that she knew, that thirteen year old boy, the blonde superman that never came to be.

This life is different though, for my mother who is sitting in front of me now has always been here, she never died, she never missed a game, I never said those words to her, she saw me in that Halloween costume, and many more I'm sure. She saw me play basketball, she saw me grow up. So far only one day has been changed and it already feels so much better than the life I led the first time around. I feel so blessed for these second chances, so happy that I get to spend any more time with her at all, even under the current circumstances of not knowing how real this can be.

"I suppose you're right I say," as I take another bite and look away from her for the first time since I've sat down. I don't want to freak her out after all. At the rate I was going it was as if I was trying to get her to have a staring contest with me. "Is Danny planning on driving down from the city?" I ask, trying to get a feel for how I am going to fix this day, to change the reason I selected to relive it in the first place. I imagine that since the game is still on, he is still going to come to watch me play, he'll still bring Ellie, he'll still bring his project. Maybe all of those major things will be the same.

"The city? What are you talking about Priam?" My mother looks at me as her eyebrows furrow into a state of complete confusion.

Here it is, this is the start. The beginning of when I begin to wonder how easy it will be to make these second chances the way I want them to be. How can I create the life I want when I am not in complete control? How can I plan the perfect life when all I have is seven days?

"Danny. I mean, isn't he going to come and watch me play tonight? I figured he would, especially since it's such an important game."

"Oh...Priam. I'm sorry baby, you know how hard I tried to convince him to come. I always try to make him come to your things, but ever since he moved out I can't really force him to anymore. I wish you two were able to get along, really I do."

As she calls me baby, as she tells me in so many words that my brother is not coming, I realize that I didn't only save her life that day, I made changes that affected me and Danny's relationship. Whereas our relationship began to fall apart on this original day, on this second version I am beginning to understand that it already has fallen, fractured, and broken apart completely. The damage I came here to undo has already been done.

"But I thought...maybe since this game meant so much to me, he would change his mind. You really don't think he will come?"

"I talked to him yesterday and he said he wasn't going to be able to make it. You know how busy he is working at the shop and going to his evening classes at CCAC."

When she says this, I become the one who is confused. What shop does he work at? Danny isn't supposed to have a job; he is supposed to be in New York City going to school so he can work for Grandpa Wood when he graduates. He shouldn't have to be working now, he doesn't need to be...does he? CCAC is the community college of Alden county; it is where people go if they can't afford to go to a more traditional school, or if they aren't smart enough to get in. Danny was brilliant and surely we had the money to pay for his tuition. Grandpa Wood had helped us out with everything, the Henderson's never had to use much of their money to pay for anything Danny and I ever needed. They gave us their time, that was enough.

I realize the answer is sitting right in front of me in one, Moira Wood. She gets up and takes my plate away; it has been scraped clean by me in fervor I was mostly unaware of. She rinses off the remaining syrup in the sink and puts it in the dishwasher. I take my gaze away from her and direct it out the window to where I know the cold air is swirling about, abrasively chastising all who come into contact with it.

Grandpa Wood never became our source of financial dependence like he had been originally; he didn't need to be because my mother never died. I'm sure he still helped out, but my mother's pride would never have allowed him to pay for Danny's school, at least not completely. That day, the day that he was the one who threw the brick, when he was the one who said those three words, to me nevertheless, his life changed more than I ever thought possible. I didn't only save my mother's life that day, I ruined Danny's and because of that he took a different path, one in which he despises me, one where his dreams became limited, for in this reality it appears that Danny is the brother who never thought he was good enough. In this reality, I am the good son.

"Do you know what time he has to work today?" I need to find out where he works, but I don't want to have to ask directly, I should obviously know this information; I don't want to alert her to anything suspicious.

"The same time he works everyday Priam. Nine to five. And I think his night class is at seven, right around when your game starts. Apparently they have a test tonight, he told me he was studying all of yesterday evening."

She returns to the table and sits down across from me; she reaches across and grabs my hand. "Are you sure you're okay baby? You're acting awfully strange. I've never seen you so excited to see me or to eat my pancakes, let alone mention your brother so much. I guess it's good though, maybe it's time that you try even harder than you already have before to reach out to him. It never hurts to try."

"I'm just happy to see you that's all. I had this strange dream the other day that you were gone, and ever since then I just want to appreciate all that I have, I don't want to take anyone important in my life for granted, not you, not Danny, not Ellie."

"Who's Ellie?" She says as she releases my hand, returning hers into her lap as she smoothes out the green fabric of her dress against her legs that she has crossed.

As soon as she lets go of my hand I feel the Earth fall from underneath me. I feel the apocalypse approach and take me over just as quickly as it has arrived. Who's Ellie? These two words burn oh so much brighter within my consciousness than her question about the city did. I can deal with Danny going to school locally, I can deal with our relationship being strained, for it always was strained, thus why I came to this day to fix it. Yes, I hadn't planned on it going sour earlier than I had destroyed it originally, but me and Danny's relationship is something I can fix, but Ellie? How does my mother not know who Ellie is? Perhaps I never told her about her, but I can't imagine that being true. Anyone who knew me since the time I met Ellie knew of her. She was all I talked about half the time, ever since I met her in the city that summer.

Summer. It's all beginning to fall in place in my mind, when I saved my mother I changed not only the length of her life, but the course of mine, and the lives of those who were most directly impacted by that fateful day, the day the Victoria was totaled, the day she died. Mother and Father moved to Alden to get away from the city. Sure, they loved it there, but they wanted their children to grow up in the suburbs, to have the all American life, a simple life. Since my mother is still alive, there was no need for us to live in New York for the summers. I realize now that since she never left this place, neither did we, at least not for extended periods of time. I'm sure we visited the city occasionally to see our grandparents, but when we did our mother was there too. I never went to the park to paint, I never saw her dance, I never met her, I never loved her. Not in this life, not this second one. I've only changed one day so far, and already I've changed so much.

"Ellie Donahue. The love of my life."

I know I shouldn't have said it in such a way, but I couldn't help myself. After processing the reality of how things are here I can now comprehend that I have never met Ellie, at least not this version of me. But at the same time that's not true, for all I can think about currently is her face, her frame, her smile, her body dancing through the trees, twirling about and saving me, saving my life, just as I saved the woman's in front of me.

As every minute passes I realize how complicated this is already, I'm only on my second day. How can I make it through five more? Am I a strong enough man to do so? I came here to make things better. I'm ecstatic that my Mother is alive, but if her being alive means I will never meet Ellie, how can I live myself? Can I even live at all? No, no, no. Just as I will fix things with Danny, I will figure out a way to find Ellie, I will have it all. I have to know everyone I've always loved and let them know so in the way I should have the first time around. I will have my second chances, I will strive, I will try until I die, again, if I even do. I will go on, regardless of the difficulties and challenges along the way.

"Well that's a very pretty name. Ellie Donahue," she says as she glances at the clock above the stove. "I'm sure she's a lovely girl. Does she go to Alden?"

"Oh, no. I met her in the city once. You know, the last time we went to visit."

"I see. Why haven't you told me about her before?

Especially if she is the love of your life."

"I guess I forgot."

"You forgot to tell your dear old mother about the love of your life? That doesn't seem like my baby. You tell me everything."

"I guess this time it's different. She means so much to me."

"Well I'd love to meet her," she says as she looks to the clock again. "You know, you should probably get ready to head to school. If you don't hurry up you're going to be late. And lord knows that wouldn't go," she says as she runs her fingers through her hair, pushing back the piece that had fallen in front of her face.

"Can I borrow the car?" I ask abruptly. Through the discussion of Danny and Ellie with my mother, I've realized that there is only one way to save this day, to get everything back on track the way I want it to be. In order to take full advantage of this second day I have to combine the two into one and the only way to do that is to use something I've always hated more than anything else in the world: that car.

"What on Earth do you need the Victoria for? You've never driven it to school before."

"I wasn't exactly planning on driving it to school, to be honest."

"Have you lost your mind? If you would have just said you wanted to take it so you wouldn't be late I would have considered it, but why would I give you my permission now when you are telling me that you're planning to skip school? And for what Priam? For what? If you don't go to school you can't play in tonight's game. Wouldn't that be selfish of you? I'm sure your teammates would be let down." Her face isn't one that glows anymore, it has changed into a look of uncertainty. It's clear that since I saved her that day the autopilot version of myself was the perfect son, doing everything to please her, doing everything to honor and obey her. This rash and inconclusive behavior I am presenting before her now is something of an entire kind completely, she doesn't know how to process it. I don't blame her, for in the end, everything is still my fault. These are my second chances and even though every aspect isn't in my control, I am still the keeper of the keys, the one holding the reins.

I reach out across the table, laying the tops of my hands against the grain of the wood so that my palms are facing up, beckoning her hands to join mine. My mother has always been fond of using her touch, to soothe me, to comfort me and to let me know she loves me. I decide the best way to convince her of my plan, the best way for her to understand it and accept it, is if I act in a way that she knows, to come from a way of love, of compassion, of grace. I nod my head looking at her face and offer her a smile. I look from her eyes down to my hands and watch as she places hers in mine. I wrap my fingers overtop of hers and try to somehow project the unrelenting force I have inside of me upon her. I have to make her understand.

"If I could perfectly explain to you the reasons why school isn't important today, why even the so called crucial basketball game doesn't matter to me now, believe me I would. Life isn't like that though, for sometimes the days we think are going to be the most important don't end up mattering at all. It's the moments and memories that surprise us, the ones that at times come out of nowhere that can matter the most. Tiny miracles can come from beyond to save us, to liberate our spirits and set us free. If today is going to matter in the long run, if this day is going to make any difference, it's going to be because of the people I love. It's going to be because of you, because of Danny, and because of Ellie too."

The confused look that was on her face previously is starting to fade away, the apprehension she held before is gone and a sort of contemplating appreciation of what I am saying is starting to matter in her mind. After all, most of what I'm saying has been influenced by what she taught me. Even though I only had thirteen years with her, the majority of which happened ages ago, the lessons she taught me still ring true, I still hold them in the most sacred chamber of my heart.

"I have to make things right with Danny and fix our relationship. I know I've tried before, but believe me, this time it's different. I have to talk to him, I have to make him see things from my point of view."

"That's very brave of you Priam and I can empathize with your reasoning. Believe me, I feel I know more than the average person how your life can change on a dime. I feel it was only yesterday I was meeting your father for the first time and falling in love. Sometimes days pass you by like a wonder you never even knew. But why today? Can't you just wait until this weekend? I'd have no problem with you borrowing the car then."

"There's no day but today. I have to go today Mother. It's

for a rather complex reason, but it isn't worth trying to explain it. Can you trust me? I promise you that it will benefit everyone in the long run, yourself included."

"Well baby, I've always trusted you, you know that. I don't quite understand why you are giving up the chance to play in tonight's game though, I know how much it means to you. However, at the same time, if you are skipping school, if you believe that going to see your brother is more important than this basketball game, then I believe it too. I believe you."

She grasps my hands tighter than before and moves up and away from the table and pulls me toward her. It's a rather weird sensation as we hug, for all of my life I was always shorter than her, looking up to her beauty above. Now I tower over her in my eighteen year old body, my six foot three frame. She holds me close and her head brushes up against my shoulder. Her soft blonde hair touches the bottom of my chin and I laugh, for it tickles. It's a nice moment, having my mother hold me close; it's nice to know that she cares utterly and completely. We separate and as she pulls away we stand there in the kitchen, looking at one another, as if we are seeing each other for the first time in quite a while. In a way it's true, even if she's not aware of it, this reality we are living is a certain sort of new.

"There's one more thing though," I continue. "I don't want to tell you only half of the truth."

"Yes? What is it? I don't know how much more my heart can handle Priam. You know, I am getting old."

"Oh stop it, you're just as beautiful and youthful as you've always been."

"You're far too kind to me," she says as she heads over to the counter and puts on her apron, then turns around to give me a playful wink. Her spirit is still as lively as the day I left it. I stand where she parted from me, unmoving, still. "Well go on then. If this day is as important as you say it's going to be, I imagine time is of the essence."

I laugh and then say "Well, it's just that after I make up with Danny, as long as it all goes according to my plan, I'd like to take the car for another ride, with him as my passenger."

"And where would you be taking the car to?"

"The city," I say as I hiccup in both fear and anticipation. I feel I need her approval for all parts of this day; I need things to fall into place as smoothly as they can. I remember how hard it was to save her on that first day, how everything and everyone seemed to be fighting against my success. I feel that if I get the important players on board, if they know what I'm doing, perhaps the day will agree with my plan, maybe then I can be successful.

"Why do you need to go to the city?"

"For Ellie."

"Ah yes, I should have known," she says as she comes back towards me. "This girl has quite the hold on you, doesn't she?"

"Most definitely."

"And what makes her worth an entire trip across the state and then some, especially on a school day? This girl must be very special if you are willing to give up playing in your game tonight."

"She's more than special Mother. She's everything. She's my life. I want you to meet her, I know you'd love her."

"I'm sure if you do, I would too."

As she stands in front of me, I am reminded of a memory that once took place here, my mind goes back and I can hear Nat King Cole singing a sweet symphony. I remember our dance and how we waltzed across the floor to and fro. I remember in that moment feeling a sense of clarity, I could feel the sounds, smell her touch, see the emotion. It was salubrious splendor, that dance of ours.

"When I met her, she was dancing in the park. In a way, it reminded me of you, how we used to dance together when I was younger. Do you remember that?"

"Of course I do. How could I forget?"

"The way she can move, it sets your spirit free just by watching, it reminds me of a dove flying through the air in a revelry of serenity. She truly is a remarkable girl. I have to see her today, and I feel that Danny should accompany me on my way."

"I'd ask you for a dance right now, but somehow I feel as if the sooner you go, the better," she says in a heartfelt and fully finished way as her eyes light up and she starts walking out of the kitchen towards the front door. I follow her until both of us are standing in the hallway of our house, the grayness of the winter outside somehow sparkling inside with a white light that blurs.

"You mean...you'll let me go? You'll support my decision, even if it sounds crazy?"

"You've never been normal Priam, I realized that a long

time ago. What you have said doesn't make sense to me completely, but it does click in certain means and that's all I need. You have to go, for your brother, for Ellie, and even for me it seems. Like I said, I believe in you, I always have, you're my baby and you will be forever. I might not agree with your rationality, or your simplifications, but I do agree with one thing, the thing I trust completely...your heart," she says, as she places her finger on my chest, right on top of the organ we humans associate with love.

"Oh thank you Mother! Thank you so much," I say as I embrace her once more. A part of me doesn't want to leave her, but I know that this day wasn't chosen for her, it's for Danny. I have to fix things with him and in doing so I have to find Ellie as well. This day was the day of our first kiss and somehow, some way, I know I need to make that happen again during this second chance too. I peck her on the cheek and throw on my coat, which is hanging beside us on the rack. She hands me the keys to the Victoria which are hanging up on the wall.

"Just promise me one thing," she says, asking for one final request as she opens the door.

"Anything."

"Be careful...and succeed."

"Oh, you betcha Mother, you betcha. I'll do everything in my power to make this day everything it was ever meant to be. That's a promise."

I jog out into the driveway to where the car is waiting. The cold air greets me briskly with a smack to the face. I feel as if the car is glaring at me, but I try not to take any notice. It appears worse for wear than the last time I saw it, but nowhere near what it would have looked like if things hadn't changed that day. As I sit down in the driver's seat I feel a shiver slide down my spine. I hate this car and yet, it's the only way I can make today be the day it needs to be.

I look up and see my mother standing in the frame of the doorway, just as she had done on that day. She's older now though, with shorter hair, a few more wrinkles and a bit more life behind her. She lifts her hand and waves, and I wave back. I give her my final farewell and it's then that I realize I have no idea where I am going. Danny works at a shop. What shop? It could be anywhere, what my mother told me literally gave me no clue. I start to feel frantic and as I do my eyes start to dart back and forth around the interior of the car. Luckily for me, because of this I notice something, a receipt of a bill that has the name Moira Wood written at the top of it. As I lift up the piece of paper I realize it's an inspection of the car from Monty's Auto Shop. I glance to the bottom of the page where I see something familiar: a signature, but more importantly, a signature that belongs to my brother...Daniel Wood.

I begin to pull out of the driveway now that I am aware of where I have to go first. As the car gears into motion I can't believe my luck, that my mother has let me take her car and that I've figured out where Danny works without even having to ask her. This second day seems to be cooperating with me so much more than the first one ever did. Then again, I'm not trying to save a life, just hoping to resolve strife with my brother, and to find the woman I love, to find my future wife. I pull away from my house on Elm Street, where my mother waves goodbye one final time and then disappears inside. I honk the horn of the car as I pass our house. I'm on my way, today...today, I'm on my way.

As I drive through Alden in the Victoria I can't help but to think about how strange it is. Never in my life did I ever consider an experience such as this; one where I, as an eighteen year old, would be driving my mother's car throughout the town I grew up in, on a mission to save my relationship with my brother, in order to meet the girl I already met so long ago. By now I've come to realize that these second chances are never going to completely compute in my head in a way a normal day would. These aren't normal days though, so I suppose that is okay. This is my time to make things right and even if the changes I make on the days that come before the others lead to unexpected outcomes, I know that in the end everything will end up okay...it has to. At the very least, I know it will end up better than it did the first time, I can't screw up any worse than I did during my life, before I died. No, that's just not possible.

Monty's Auto Shop is on the other side of town. I'm actually rather surprised I still remember where it is after all of these years. When I come to a stop at Alden's only traffic light I take in the sights around me. I see men in suits going into work, women holding the hands of young children who are all bundled up in their scarves and mittens to stay away from the clutches of the cold. I see older kids walking on their way to school, their faces red due to the nippy atmosphere. I'm glad I'm inside of the car with the heat blasting. The memory of running all about town in nothing but my basketball uniform still feels fresh on my flesh, so I am delighted that nothing about this day has anything to do with me embracing the winter air.

It takes only about ten minutes from when I pulled out of the driveway to when I can see the auto shop approaching in the distance. As it comes into view my heart starts racing. What am I going to say? How is Danny going to react? Can I change things...or is it already too late? I can't think like that, I have to strive on even if it's going to be hard to convince Danny to forgive me, to let go of his grievances, whatever they are. In reality, besides that day that I already changed, I have no idea why the two of us grew apart so much sooner than we had originally. In this chain of events I had never set his project on fire, his project didn't even exist any more. Perhaps it all stemmed from those three words, it must have begun when he threw the brick and I got off scot-free. That's when all of this had to have started. Regardless of whether it was due to a brick or a burning, we're still brothers. We always will be.

I pull up to the shop and see some guys working on a car in the garage. I don't see my brother though so I park the Victoria and step out, slowly walking towards the entrance of the shop as the freezing air bites at my collarbones. When I walk inside it seems that no one is in the office, maybe I should have just walked into the garage straightaway. I'm about to go back out the front door and around to the garage when I hear my name.

"Priam? What in the hell are you doing here?" It's him, and as he walks towards me I am taken aback by his presence. It's Danny alright, but the Danny I knew never looked anything like this. His hair is shaggy and unkempt, his hands are dirty and it appears as if there is grease on his face. The uniform he has on is oversized and soiled. He doesn't look very happy to see me. As the scowl on his face persists he lifts a cigarette to his mouth and takes a long drag. The Danny I knew never smoked a single time in his life. This can't be him.

Danny was always so well put together, with short-cropped hair, dressing in well-tailored suits that were always crisp and clean. Not this Danny though, this Danny is anything but well put together, he doesn't only appear distraught from his outward appearance, but also from the look emanating from his face. He walks across the way and stops in front of me only about two feet away from where I am frozen to the ground, unable to move, unable to say anything at all. What I had done had not only changed our relationship, it had changed him as well.

"I...I wanted to come to talk to you. I wanted to try to work things out between us. I want to fix things Danny, I want to make it so that we are okay, I want us to be alright."

"What the fuck is that supposed to mean? We haven't been alright for years. What is the point of trying to fix it now? We don't get along. So what? Not all brothers do you know. I love Mother and I know you love her too. That connection is the only thing we share, the only thing we have in common at all."

"That's not true," I say desperately. "We share so much more than that. We were close once, we were best friends in a time you probably never even knew. We are more than just similar DNA. We were close, we shared times together, we grew together. I want that back, I need that back, and perhaps you do too, without even realizing it."

"Why aren't you in school? How did you even get here?" He asks as he walks past me basically ignoring everything I have said and sits down on a bench near the main office where no one seems to be. The shop is strangely empty, everyone who works here is in the garage. Maybe Danny is in charge of the office today, I really don't know.

"I skipped school, talking to you was more important to me. I drove the Victoria."

"You skipped? Why on earth did you do that? Don't you have some important basketball game today or something? Mother was begging me to come. I don't have time. You know how busy I am."

"Do I?"

He glares at me, and then takes a final puff of his cigarette before crushing it on the ground beneath the power of his steel toed boot. "You should. Anyways, I thought you hated that car. Have you ever even driven it before? How did you convince Mother to let you come? I can't believe she let you skip school, and for me of all things. Lord knows you're her favorite. I'm surprised she cares that we have a relationship at all."

"That's just it though Danny. Do we even have a relationship? Screw the car; screw that damn Victoria and everything that it caused. I don't want to think about that stupid brick or days where you told me you hated me. I want to move forward, I want to fix this, to fix us. I want us get back the state of brotherly love that we used to have."

"Have you gone insane? I think we are beyond ever achieving that again. That brick throwing incident was so long ago, what does it have to do with anything? So much more has happened since that."

"Well it's just that it feels as if it occurred two days ago to me. I think that's where we started to grow apart, where things started to change, where you changed," I say as I walk over from where I am standing and sit down on the bench next to him. I don't know how I am going to be able to convince him to come to New York City with me, but I know that if I don't succeed on this day, there is no way that I can achieve anything with the next five days I have left. Everything is dependent on what comes before, what happens now, and how I get those I love to believe in me.

"How have I changed?" He asks as he turns his upper torso to the side so that he's facing me. "Tell me Priam. It seems you have all the answers, so why don't you fill me in." His sarcastic tone digs deep into me and it burns. Just as the fire I created on that night which got us into a similar situation in another life, the flames are spreading and spiraling out of control. The longer this conversation goes without an uptick in hopefulness the harder it will be for me to fix it, or so I have decided now. I take a moment and try to figure out my approach, to calculate a rational way that I can convince Danny that once he was different, that his life wasn't always this way and that he was the good son, the one everyone loved and compared me to. Suddenly it all clicks in my head, the only rational way to get Danny to change, to get him to think of anything I say as important or inflecting is to deliver the most irrational speech I can muster: to tell him the truth.

I begin by trying to explain the unexplainable and say "Try to imagine a life we already lived, one where things turned out differently, major events happened to change us, to shape us, to build the relationships that mattered most. In this life no one was there but the two of us, we were the only two members of our family left and thus we had to depend on each other. As the older brother you took care of me, and in doing so I looked up to you. You showed me how to be a good man, how to be strong, how to be the best I could be. You excelled at everything you ever did, you won, you conquered, you strived for the stars and you reached them. I couldn't help but stand back and watch and be in awe of your honor, your strength.

"You were there for me, and I was there for you. At least I tried to be. I wasn't the good one, you were. You moved to New York City, you went to college and even ended up taking over Grandpa Wood's ad agency. You did everything you wanted to do. I was nothing compared to you, but that's not the point. The point is that we were close once, we were the kind of brothers we were always meant to be. I messed it up then too though, but it wasn't until today. It wasn't until this day when I did something out of anger, out of jealousy and rage that tore us apart. I know this might not make much sense to you, but it's the only way I can think to tell you. To dream of something that doesn't make sense and align it into a parallel paradise that you can see, one where you can live, to make that place be here, be now.

"I need you to know that I love you Danny. That I have always loved you as my brother, you have shaped so much of who I am, and you taught me how to live when she..." I stop myself, realizing that I shouldn't say anything about Mother dying specifically, somehow I know that would make this story be too farfetched, too unfathomable for anyone to believe, especially this Danny. For this Danny is different, and somehow I have to get him to be the man he is meant to be, and to do so I cannot tell him that our mother died in another life, I just can't. "When she couldn't," I continue. "Whenever she was away it was you that pointed out the way. In this life, you were not only a brother to me, you were a father figure too, the guide I needed to show me how it was done. Unfortunately I wasn't able to live up to your example, but that's why I am trying to fix all of that now. I want to fix our relationship before it's too late, to show you how much I love you, and to let you know how badly I want us to be okay, for it to all be okay."

As I finish what I want to say I realize that since I started my explanation I hadn't taken many breaths to stop. I've watched his face watch mine, his eyebrows furrowing at certain parts just as Mother's had earlier this morning. He didn't interrupt me throughout my speech, from what I can tell he was listening intently, trying to digest the alternate reality where things were better, when things between the two of us were alright, until I ruined them on the original form of this day. The silence begins to envelop us so he looks from the ground at which he has been staring at for the last minute or so while I was speaking and turns his attention back to me. He stares at me now, saying nothing and then slowly his blank face evolves into a grinning one and he begins to laugh. I smile nervously back at him, not knowing how to react as he has yet to respond. He pulls out another cigarette from his shirt pocket and lights it and takes a deep hit. He exhales the smoke and blows it away.

"You always were quite the character Priam, that's for sure." He says as he looks back at me and takes another puff of his cigarette. "Did Mother put some drugs in your pancakes this morning?"

"Something like that," I say as I nudge him in the shoulder. He nudges me back.

"What you have said is all well and good. But it's not like that, and you know it. This alternate plane of existence you speak of isn't us, this is who we are, this is how the two of us are, here...and now."

"I know that, but I just wanted to tell you in some way that it is possible for us to be close again, like we once were when we were little. Just because we grew apart and got upset with one another back in the day doesn't mean our paths have to continue to grow farther and farther apart. We can bring them back together."

"And how do we do that Priam?"

"By going on an adventure," I say as I stand up quickly from the bench and turn around to face him. He flicks his head to the side in order to get his long greasy hair out of his eyes. He takes another puff of his cigarette and then he gives me a look that seems to say he believes I legitimately am a crazy person.

"An adventure? What kind of adventure? You realize I'm at work right? I can't just get up and leave. I have night class tonight too. Just because you decided to lose your mind and dream up a life we never lived doesn't mean I'm going to do the same."

We did live that life though, I think to myself. What is here and now isn't what always was. Things were different once, and even though I messed them up then, I am fully committed to fixing them now, no matter how hard the task may be to achieve. But what if I can't? I've already told Danny my story, the tale of the life we once lived, and although he seems to have lightened up a little bit since I first arrived at the shop, the look in his eyes is telling me that he isn't convinced we can fix this, our relationship...our brotherhood. I have to try something else to get him to come with me. I have to tell him about her.

"I need you to come with me to New York City. There is a girl waiting there for me, a girl that I love and without your help, I don't think I can make it, I don't think I can secure the life I want unless I have your support, unless I have her affection."

He throws his cigarette to the ground and stomps it out, even though there is still more than half of it left. I seem to have gotten his attention, his interest is piqued. Although he was listening to the story I told before, he is now doing so more intently.

"Her name is Ellie Donahue and I know that she is the one for me." I continue, trying to make my words sound as earnest and meaningful as I can make them. "Imagine a girl who makes you feel as if your entire body is tingling with happiness every time she looks at you, and every time she says your name or tells you a tale. That's what she is for me; she's everything I have ever wanted all wrapped up into one person. She's beautiful, kind, caring, endearing and wonderful. I want you to meet her Danny. Besides Mother, you're the most important person in my life and I think you're the one who can help me find her, the one who has to help me make things right."

"You say this girl is waiting for you, but you also have to find her too? That doesn't make much sense Priam. How can it be both?"

"It just is. It's a complicated situation I can't thoroughly describe. It's like love you see, for how does one describe what it's like to be in love? It's as if every cell in your body explodes whenever you are with that person creating this unimaginable sensation. When you're in love all of the colors blur into one, time stops and fast forwards simultaneously, for when you're in love nothing else matters but how you feel and how that person feels for you in return. Love conquers space and brings you to a whole new place; it's a feeling of unrelinquishing contentment, a symphony of sweet melodies that never ends. Love is a lion that can never be defeated; it's the pearl at the bottom of the sea. It's forever and so full to thee."

"I've never been in love," Danny admits as he stands up and walks towards where I am standing. "But, I suppose if I had been, it would feel something like that."

"You'll be in love Danny. One day, I know you will. You're a great man, a man I look up to wholeheartedly." After I say this he stands right in front of me and looks me in the eye. His face seems to be confused, going back and forth from a look of enlightenment and anger all at the same time. Slowly though, the anger fades and he embraces me. He holds me tight and pats me on the back two times.

"I may not understand much of what you said to me, especially since most of it seemed a bit over my head and too much to comprehend, but I can understand one thing," he says as he lets me go and jogs over to the front door of the shop where he pauses. "You believe every word you've said. If you believe in yourself, if you really think we can fix our relationship, that we can find this girl and that you need me to help you, boy...I'll do it. I suppose it's the least I can do for treating you like crap for so many years. I've never missed work a day in my life and I should go to this night class, but screw it, you're my brother. This is more important."

I can hardly believe it. Danny is actually going to accompany me on my drive to New York, on my mission to find Ellie, the girl who doesn't even know me yet, the girl I spent my life with, who in this realm of second chances is still not within my plane of existence. She will be though, by tonight, with the help of Danny, Ellie Donahue will know a boy named Priam Wood, she'll know me.

Danny runs into the garage and tells his manager he has to leave for the day. He says something along the lines of a family emergency and before I know it I'm in the driver's seat of the Victoria with him at my side. "You really are crazy, you know that right?" He asks as I put the car in reverse and back out of the shop's front lot.

"Aren't we all a little bit crazy though? As humans, what would be the fun in a life full of straightforward nothingness? If you never learn to let go of yourself, you'll never be able to hold onto anyone else."

"Good point little brother, good point," he says as he slaps me on the thigh. "I suppose we are all a tad crazy."

With that, the two of us are driving down Main Street, taking in the sights of the bundled up people bracing themselves from the cold on this Tuesday morning. We're on our way out of the small town and towards the big old city. Somewhere in the concrete jungle that awaits is the girl of my dreams, Ellie, my sweet Ellie. I just hope that nothing I have changed in this world has made her any different from what I remember. I hope and pray that I can find her, I have to find her. As we drive on, I try not to think too much about it. I know this journey is not only about her, but about my brother as well. The adventure has started with him and I know as we drive across the state and on I have to earn back his trust, I have to build back up the relationship I ruined, not only in my life, but through my actions on that first relived day too. We're on our way.

   The wheels on the car are moving faster than I ever thought they could and we are steadily making progress on the way to the city. The Victoria hasn't crashed yet, even though every time another car is near I grip the wheel as tightly as I can, bracing for impact as if a collision is going to occur, just as it had before, with her. An impact doesn't come though; we glide along through the plains and valleys of Pennsylvania on our way to the city ahead. Danny and I talk a lot along the way, of everything from dreams that haven't happened to mistakes in the past we wish we could change. The tension I felt between the two of us at the shop slowly fades until we have entered into a realm of comfortability with one another. I'm starting to feel like I have a brother again, even though it's not the same version of the brother I once knew.

   "Do you ever wonder if anything really matters at all?" He asks me suddenly after a few minutes of silence while we are passing through somewhere near the center of the state. We still have a little over three and a half hours to go if my calculations are correct, but it's only a bit past one in the afternoon, so I'm sure we will get there in time. There's still time to find Ellie, time to make things right not only with him, but with her as well before this day is done.

   "What do you mean Danny?"

   "Sometimes I wonder what life is really about. What is the point of it all? Bad things happen to good people all of the time, and sometimes horrible people get by simply by having good luck. I get depressed thinking about it."

   "I get where you're coming from, but I still think life matters. I've never been able to take anything I've done lightly. Believe me; I have a lot of regrets."

"You're still so young though, you have so much life to live ahead of you. I'm sure you can't have that many regrets."

"It's funny you say that Danny," I say as I smile and look at him where he is slouched down in the passenger seat of the car with his legs up on the dashboard. "Because sometimes I feel as if I've already lived an entire life, as if I already have a life full of mistakes that I need to make up for."

"You mean like a past life?" He asks me as he straightens up his posture a bit and takes his feet down from in front of him. "I don't know if I believe in all of that garbage. I think we only get once chance, we either succeed or we're completely screwed."

"I've always believed in second chances."

And just as quickly as those words escape from my mouth I see it in front of me, the golden blur that flashes onto the road so unexpectedly that I gasp and grab the wheel and quickly turn it to the side trying to avoid the collision. I miss the thing, but since I was driving so fast the car begins to veer sharply to the side. We slide on a patch of ice and I try my best to slam onto the brakes. I hear a loud bumping noise and then a screeching sound erupt to my left. I get the car under control and it starts to slow down. I look back and see that the rear tire has gone flat and fallen off. The bottom of the Victoria is touching the ground and we grind slowly to a stop, the vehicle drags it's ass as if it is trying to wipe its own butt on the cement. This damn car, I should have known better than to try and drive this thing to the city.

"What in the hell was that?" Danny yells, but he doesn't wait for me to give him an answer. He hops out of the car and goes to inspect the damage. I get out of the car too, but I don't care about looking at the car right at this instant, instead I'm more worried about whatever it was that caused the accident. Whatever ran in front of us seemed like it was purposely trying to get me to stop, trying to intercede my mission. It's nowhere in sight though, whatever it was...it's gone. I imagine it was just a deer, running through traffic like they always do. I didn't get a good look at it though, Danny and I had been talking and I was more focused on the conversation than the road in front of me. Sometimes when you're driving you melt into a zone of tranquility and you're able to escape into some place inside of your mind, somewhere where you don't even remember you're driving at all. It had to have been a deer, I'm sure of it. Somehow though the only image that keeps flashing behind my eyes is one of a dog, a golden retriever I once knew, a dog named Chloe, the old girl who would always look out for you.

Could it be? I think back to that first day and how the rabbit had been chased by a dog that looked just like her and how it had made me feel then. If Chloe really is making cameos on the days I get to change it doesn't seem like she is trying very hard to help me out. In fact, it's as if she is trying to sabotage everything I am trying to accomplish. The Chloe I knew wouldn't do that. I can't understand it at all. I continue staring off into the distance as the cold air slams up against me and brings me back to the situation at hand. I hear Danny call my name so I turn my attention back to the car to see how bad the damage really is. The tire is completely gone, as I look towards the ditch to the side of the car I see it sitting at the bottom, lying on its side as if it has given up on everything. It's no longer interested in serving its purpose, no longer concerned about getting us to New York, or getting me to Ellie. The tire is detached from the situation, in all kinds of the way.

"How bad is it?" I ask Danny as he stands up from where the tire was previously attached.

"Well it sure as hell ain't good. I've never seen a tire fly off like that. This is some freaky shit," he exclaims as he lights a cigarette, takes a hit and pops open the trunk.

"You know, you really should try to stop smoking, it isn't good for you."

"Give me a break kiddo. After all I'm doing for you today; I might as well blow the smoke in your face."

I guess he has a point. I don't really have the right to tell him how to live his life anymore than I already have today. I got him to come along; I guess that's all that matters. It's okay if Danny continues to smoke, I just hope the next time I see him he's given up the habit. Seeing as how the Danny I knew never smoked a cigarette in his life, I have faith that if I figure things out and fix them today the small details will somehow start to align themselves in the way I want them to be.

"Where is the spare?" He asks me with a blank look as I stand completely still by the place where the tire once was.

"You mean it's not back there?"

"If it is, I sure as hell don't see it," he says as he puts the cigarette to his mouth and takes another puff. I go to the back of the car and inspect the trunk. He's right; the spot where the spare should be is completely empty, barren, desolate.

If we are going to get this car fixed, it'll be the old fashioned way. We'll have to walk to the nearest shop, or flag someone down to help us. Cell phones don't exist yet, there is no either way. The cold wind starts up again and beats me in the face with its frozen hands over and over again so that I feel as if the icy ground beneath me is starting to seep up through my feet and reach for my heart. I can't breathe, I lose control and start to become something less of what I was only moments earlier. Danny notices something is wrong with me and rushes over from behind the back of the car and grabs onto both of my shoulders and shakes me.

"Get a grip of yourself Priam, it's not the end of the world you know. We'll figure this out, we'll still get to New York before the night is over. I've failed you enough times before. I won't fail you now. Grab the keys, lock the doors, bundle up boy, we've got some walking to do." He says as he throws his cigarette to the ground and starts jogging down the road in the direction of where the next exit sign is about a mile ahead.

He's right. I have to get a hold of myself, this isn't the end of this mission, there is still so much time left in the day. We can still make it. Just as when I had to save my mother, this day too seems to be fighting back against me, but I won't let it win. I'll have my day the way I need it, the way it has to be so that my second chances are back on track. I quickly follow after Danny, looking up at the clear sky that seems to be enveloping me with its frosty air. Somehow, some way, the two of us are going to make it through, if it's the last thing we do.

About an hour and a half passes before we are able to find an auto shop. Although the town's exit off of the highway is only about two miles from where we leave the car, the town itself is even further. No one stops to help us along the way and by the time we go indoors my teeth are chattering from the cold. The coat I have on isn't as useful against the winter weather as I thought it would be, but at least it's better than a basketball uniform. I let Danny explain to the man at the shop what happened to the car, I figure since he works with cars everyday he will be able to explain much better than I would be able to. I sit on a bench outside of the main office waiting for Danny to come back to tell me the verdict. When he returns and walks up towards me, my heartbeat begins to thump faster, drumming up a noise that emanates from inside causing me more anxiety. It strangely begins to warm me up, thankfully the coldness from the journey here is finally leaving my body.

"So what did he say? Does he think they can fix it?"

"Yeah. He said they can fix it."

"That's it? That's all he said?"

"No," Danny responds as he sits down beside me. Suddenly the scene from this morning in the auto shop in Alden is replaying in my mind. I didn't think we would be anywhere but in that car and in the city after we left. Life has a way of delivering a repetition of a former reality whenever you least expect it. What is the same and what is different is never really all that undecipherable, especially for me, not on this passage, not on these days I'm living through.

"Well what else?" I ask.

"They said they can fix it, but that they probably wouldn't have it finished until tomorrow."

The heart palpitations I felt drumming inside earlier are no longer just beating rhythms of unease at these words he delivers. Instead they are starting to bang faster and harder as if my heart wishes to escape my body. My spirit wishes to escape too, from this predicament, my bad luck, and from that dog on the road or whatever the hell it was.

"Are you kidding me?!" I scream as I stand up and start pacing, extending my hands and pushing myself off of the walls every time I come into contact with one, as if I am a rabid animal trapped inside a cage. I have to get out of here.

Danny stands up and grabs me. "Calm down Priam. I told them we have to have the car back today; I told them how important it was for us to get to New York tonight. It wasn't easy, but I was able to convince them to fix our car before some of the others they're supposed to do today. So they told me they could have it done by tonight."

"Oh thank god," I say, sighing with relief.

"He said it should be done around eight o'clock. They are going to pick it up and tow it here now. I told them where we left it. We've got some time to kill, might as well go into town to try and distract ourselves until its ready."

Danny and I leave the shop and already I'm trying to

calculate the time in my head. If we leave here around eight this evening, we should still get to New York around 11:30. That only gives us about a half an hour to find Ellie and for me to get everything back on track. As we step back out into the cold air I shake my head back and forth out of frustration. Is this even going to work? Are we going to get there in time? What if all of this is for nothing? What if I never meet Ellie in this life? Or even worse, what if she never even knows I exist?

I feel an arm fall behind my shoulders and then lift up and rub me hard on the top of my head, but it doesn't hurt. I can tell the touch is one of an affectionate, playful manner. "Don't look so down on your luck kiddo. It's going to be alright. I'll make sure we get there in time. I'll even volunteer to drive the rest of the way, I have a way of getting places rather quickly you see," Danny tells me as he offers me a wink.

I think of all of the times my mother used to do the same, how she would use the rhythm of living to make me see, to let me know that everything was going to be okay, even if it didn't happen in the way I wanted it to. I've always been the kind of man who has tried to plan every accordance of his life, but really, the only time you will ever be able to reach your goals is when you let go completely and team up with the truth and accept that life has its own plans, you just have to go along with them and never give up.

Maybe this day isn't going as smoothly as it's supposed to be, but as I laugh and start jogging along the main street of some random town in the middle of the state with my brother at my side, I realize that this day doesn't have to go exactly according to my plan. For I realize that the most important thing about it all, about this day, is so far going right. Danny is at my side, and I feel the brick walls that were built up between the two of us are falling down, in a subtle yet strong way. I'm getting my brother back, the brother I loved, the one I looked up to, the person I relied on so much while growing up. That's what this day was all about anyways, fixing this bond of brotherly love and somehow through all of the insanity that seems to be enveloping me it is working. I'm getting him back and for now...that is enough.

While the car is being fixed Danny and I waste our time in the small town we have found ourselves in. There isn't much to see, or do for that matter, so we spend most of the afternoon in a small diner near the center of town. We sit in a booth by the window and watch as the townsfolk rush by bundled up in their heavy overcoats, scarves and hats. The cold sure isn't letting up, and if I had to guess I'd say there will be snow falling by tonight. Then again, I've never really been a betting man.

There isn't much to do but talk, so that's what we do. We cover a wide variety of subjects, ranging from Mother and Father, to Alden itself and how much we both have hated high school. I even end up telling Danny about how I met Ellie in the city. Or at least, I tell him how I originally met her. I suppose in this life I am only meeting her for the first time tonight, but he doesn't need to know that, at least not for now. He asks me about my plans after graduation and I tell him how all I want to do is to go to New York and become an artist, to live by expressing myself, to never have to live a boring life of conventionality, sitting inside an office typing away with nothing around to fill the time except for the monotonous movement of a boring life. No, that's not what I want at all, I need the right amount of freedom where I can come and go as I please, where I live only to make art, to make it for myself, and to make it for others based off of my own conclusions.

"What do you want to do Danny?" I ask him when I finish telling him of my plans. "I always thought you wanted to move to the city too."

"I used to," he answers sheepishly, as if he is embarrassed to admit it.

"Well what happened? What changed?"

He takes a deep breath and turns his head from side to side, looking out the window behind me, his focus distracted. It appears he doesn't really want to answer the question, but I feel that I have to find out why the Danny in front of me never moved to the city, never followed the dreams he once had, the dreams I once knew.

"Well?" I ask again, not letting the silence settle.

"I guess I just didn't think I was good enough."

"Why did you ever think that? You're more than good enough. You're great. If you wanted to go to the city, to get out of Alden, I know you could have done it. Hell, you can still do it."

"That's nice of you to say Priam, but I don't know. What would I even do in the city? I'm barely scraping by at the community college as it is. You were always destined for bigger and better things; you've always been the one to succeed. I'm happy we're patching things up and fixing our relationship, but it's okay if you leave once the school year is over. I always thought you would," he says as he finally makes eye contact with me for the first time since the topic of him moving to New York has been brought up.

"You can do whatever you want to do. As long as you try, as long as you give it an effort that's all that really matters. Isn't that what Mother has always told us? Just to give it a go and see what happens, for if you don't, think of all the things you might miss."

"I know...it's just too hard. I don't think I'd fit in there. Whenever we visit our grandparents it feels like another world, an alien encounter. I don't think I could handle it alone."

"Then don't," I say with conviction.

He looks at me with a confused expression on his face for the umpteenth time today. I've lost track of how many times people have looked at me so, with a puzzle piece staring back.

"What do you mean?"

"I mean...don't go to the city alone. In June, once I graduate I plan on moving to the city. Come with me. We can do it together Danny. If you don't think you can do it alone, then I can be there to help you. I'm sure we could make it together, two small town brothers from Alden. Let's make 'em proud."

"You'd really let me come with you? You'd do that for me? You'd let me impede on all of your dreams of moving to the city and having a fresh start? You'd let me interrupt that?"

"You wouldn't be interrupting anything Danny. You'd be making it all the better."

The light in his eyes flicker, as if everything before him has changed. And in a way, I know it has. Just as I am altering things in this life of mine today, I'm shifting the lives of others as well. As this conversation point comes to a close and Danny thanks me thoroughly, I know that the days that follow this one will consist of my brother and me building back up our relationship to where it used to be and making it even stronger than before. He will come to the city with me, we will live there together and make it even better than the first time when I went to the Big Apple to follow his lead. In my life, I always needed him; I always chased after his ambitions and tried to make mine even better. This time though, neither of us needs to do it alone, what both of us really need is to be there for one another, to be the brothers we were always supposed to be.

Hours pass and as we sit in the diner and eat a great deal of food, the daylight begins to fade away. We anxiously discuss ideas about what it will be like to live in New York and we also talk about how the city isn't too far away from us currently, as the asphalt forest will be within our grasp this very evening. Finally we step out into the frigid night to return to the auto shop to where the Victoria is waiting. When we arrive it is almost finished. I can barely even breathe; I'm over the moon about the success of this day, about fixing things with Danny and somehow making them better than I ever thought they could be. The day is not yet done; somewhere in the city we have yet to reach where she waits, unaware and unaccustomed to the notion that I even exist. I have to change this today too, for if I don't, many more years will pass before Ellie Donahue knows my name. It has to be today.

We get the word that the car is finally fixed and after what has seemed like an eternity we are once again on our way. Danny offers to drive and I let him. I don't think I can do anything besides sit in silence and stare out the window, hoping and praying for the moment when the lights of the city finally come into view. The few hours left of the journey seem to pass ever so slowly, even though I know Danny is speeding like a bullet cutting through the mesosphere. I glance through the glass directly to my right and try to think of nothing; instead a thousand thoughts of thinking tell me tales of travesty. I can't let them win though, I will see her tonight, and in doing so, she will know me. In one life, and in all.

By the time we arrive on the outskirts of Manhattan I see that the clock reads 11:33. So little time left, yet so much to do. I contemplate telling Danny just to pull over so I can call her on a payphone, but I know that won't be enough. How could that ever work? No, I have to see her, I have to try to make her understand. It's not like this is going to be easy. For how do you tell someone who has never met you that you love them? She is all I've ever wanted, all I've ever needed, now...and forever.

I tell him how to get to her apartment, I whisper the rights and lefts back and forth over and over again in a sequential order and then, finally, we are there. I quickly glance at the clock one last time before I exit the vehicle. It reads 11:57. I run out of the car and across the street to where I see her door in front of me. I stumble up the steps as quickly as I can and then ring the buzzer over and over. Please, don't let me be too late. No one answers right away, but I won't give up, I can't give up. I ring the buzzer again and again. Finally I hear someone behind the door heading my way. As the door opens I feel Danny walk up the stairs behind me and put his hand on my shoulder. When the door opens fully there is a beautiful woman standing before me, but it's not her. It's not her. I know this face though, it's as if the Ellie I expected to see has aged twenty years, and then I realize who this woman is. It's her mother.

"Mrs. Donahue, I'm so sorry to bother you this late at night, but is Ellie here? I desperately need to speak with her."

"What was so urgent that it couldn't wait until the morning young man? I think you should just come back tomorrow," she tells me, clearly perturbed.

"No!" I yell. "You don't understand!"

She's about to close the door when I hear a flutter of feet fall down the stairs behind her. I see long slender legs slinking towards where I stand as if they are gliding across the clouds. She's wrapped in a silvery white nightgown that somehow glows and is even more personified in my eyes by the cold air that is floating from the frigid realm I'm living in, into the one that she is coming forth. It's Ellie, my sweet Ellie is before me once again, in this life, and in every one I've ever lived.

"Wait Mother. Don't close the door." She says as she intercedes the closing of the wooden block that would have ruined it all. "Let me..." and then she looks at me for the first time since I have been standing here. She takes in the sight of me before her, and she breathes me in. "Oh!" She gasps. "It's you!"

I feel Danny's hand fall from off of my shoulder and then the temperature starts rising to one of a sweltering heat. I feel the beat of my heart quicken and then slow. I try to speak out to answer her, to say anything at all, but I am unable to do so. The sounds around me fade and I feel my eyes shift and then darken. The clock has reached midnight at last. My day here is done.

My Life
1959 – 1966

I got out of Alden as quickly as I could. For as much as I loved the place, I hated it too. Somehow, everywhere I looked reminded me of her, even though many years had passed since she had last seen the street light change or walked the halls of any buildings, she was still there for me. In a way, my mother and Alden would always represent one and the same. The town was a personification of everything she had ever been to me: stable, caring, supportive, small, yet strong. Nevertheless, I had to get away.

I couldn't stay. There were too many bad memories lingering on the lips of those around me. I didn't want to be the boy with no parents, I didn't want to be known as that Wood boy with his fanciful art dreams, I didn't want to be anyone that anybody knew. The city was calling my name, as was the girl I loved who lived there. Graduation came and went and shortly after it concluded Steve, Susan and Margaret drove me to the city with all of my belongings in tow. After Mr. Williams consistent urging, I did indeed finally apply to the Parsons School of Design, and to my surprise, I was accepted.

Ellie and I waited to make it official until I was actually in the city with her. Sure, since that day we kissed on the swings we were basically a couple, but something told us both that there was no reason to rush it. We wanted the first day of being together, as boyfriend and girlfriend to be the first day of many that we would spend in the city together from there onwards and evermore. I suppose there is so much to say and yet so little I feel I actually can tell about how those years made me feel. When I came to New York City as an eighteen year old boy I had my entire life in front of me, all of my dreams seemed obtainable and reachable, as if they were floating directly in the sky above me.

As the years passed I realized that some goals would succeed and others would fail. I never stopped trying though, just as I had up to that point I always gave it my all. Sometimes though, my all wasn't enough. There were some things I was not meant to achieve, or so the world seemed to be telling me. My experience at art school built me up and also tore me down in an equally adequate fashion. When I arrived to Parson's I didn't think I was the best artist by any means, but I did believe in my talent. Once I began my classes and saw the artwork of my fellow classmates I realized how much more I still had to learn. The professors there didn't change my view; instead they guided it in the direction that made the most sense. They showed me where to take my work, how to make it brighter and darker all at the same time. After four years of studying art, tearing apart every piece I had ever made and dreaming of all of the ones I had yet to create, I finally felt like I was the artist I was supposed to be. I had many exhibitions over the years and Ellie was at every single one of them. She always complimented my work even if it wasn't as good as it could have been, she believed in me and she let me know it. My grandparents would often come to my shows as well and every once in a while the Henderson's would drive all the way from Alden to make an appearance, just to let me know they supported me, that they loved me. Danny never came though. Not to a single one.

I guess it was my fault, after all I was the one who had set everything ablaze. After that day it was never the same. I tried to call him a few weeks after he and Ellie had left Alden to return to the city, but he never returned my calls, so I eventually stopped trying. I figured that with time it would all sort itself out. I believed that blood was thicker than water...and fire too. I thought that when I moved to the city we would hang out like old times, that we would become loving brothers again. That, or any inkling of that notion alone, never occurred.

Sure, I saw Danny from time to time, but it was never really on purpose, at least not on his part. We would have dinner with our grandparents often and he was almost always in attendance. He would be joyful and completely content at the dinner table, he would tell them jokes and silly stories of events that had occurred at the ad agency, but he rarely looked at me. Every time dinner ended I would always want to take him aside so we could talk, so that we could actually have a moment for our own relationship, outside of the realm of everyone else. I didn't though, at least not for a while until enough time had passed that I finally mustered up the courage to confront him.

About a year after I had started school at Parson's, we were having dinner at Grandma and Grandpa Kelton's place in Brooklyn. We usually got together there about once a month since I had moved to the city. Most of the times I would bring Ellie along, but this one specific time I had decided not to, and I did so for a reason. I'm not sure if Danny was really ever in love with her, but I did believe he had fallen for her, at least partially in some respect. There is no other reason for his behavior, or for the fact that day when she chose me over him was the day that ended any relationship we would ever have. Was it more that I got the girl and he hadn't, or was it that I got the best girl of all? I was never able to figure it out. At the dinners that had come before this one he wouldn't ever address me, but I would catch him glancing from me to her with contempt when he didn't think I was paying attention. I'm not sure if he was jealous, or still just upset with me for turning my back on him and destroying that damn project. One thing I did know for sure though was that I had to talk to him; I had to tackle our issues once and for all. No more putting it off, no more.

After dinner that night he said his goodbyes to our grandparents as he always did, with some excuse that he had to get home to work on a campaign that was going into production soon. I stayed sitting at the table as I always did as he kissed my grandmother on the forehead and shook hands with my grandfather before wishing them goodbye. He then turned to me at last and nodded his head, but no words escaped his mouth, none ever did. This was how he always handled my presence at these dinners, the only acknowledgement that I existed to him at all.

This time though instead of just sitting there blankly as I had previously done before, as he turned around I shouted out "Wait!" He stopped in his tracks, but he did not turn around. My grandparents looked at me, as if they were shocked that the normal turn of events had suddenly shifted. I hopped out of my seat and followed after him, as he had started to continue to walk down the hallway again. When I caught up to him we were walking down the length of the hall which was rather long in fact, our strides seemingly in key with one another as both of our legs pushed us forward in sync. Finally when we reached the end he turned away from the front foyer and put his face right in front of mine.

"What do you want Priam?"

"Hey now, no reason for such contempt," I said with a small grin, trying to lighten the mood.

"As you just heard me say, I have a project I need to complete this evening. I don't have time for any nonsense."

"Who said that what I have to offer is nonsense?"

"Oh I don't know, it just seems that's all you ever have to

157

offer these days. I do listen to you talk at the dinner table you know. About all your artsy fartsy friends and the ballet shows in which Ellie moves so beautifully," he bellowed with a slight sneer.

"She really does you know, have you ever seen her dance? You really should come sometime." I said as he rolled his eyes. That really bothered me. "She never did anything to you, you know." I added, trying to get him to feel something other than his annoyance for me. He glared at me then and I'm pretty sure his face turned a ruby shade of red at the idea that he had anything against Ellie. He would never admit it, but he never treated her the way he should have, it was because of me and what I had done.

Sure, ruining a project might not have seemed like such a monumental thing in the long run of a relationship between brothers that should have lasted a lifetime, but to Danny it was enough, and in part I understood it. When our mother died, he became everything I needed; he got me through the hardest of days and never asked for anything in return. After she was gone, he never did anything to me that I could even partially classify as cruel. When I set that project ablaze, when I destroyed those pictures and those papers of that damn car I really did mess up. I shocked him into oblivion, for up until that point I don't know if he thought I was capable of such malice, such blind rage and jealous discontent. So yes, what I had done couldn't be classified as the most horrible thing, but to Danny it was enough. I betrayed his trust and in a way, I understand why he never forgave me. Little did I know at the time that was only half of why my brother hated me so, as the conversation continued to unfold I wasn't aware I was on the brink of finding out the entire reasoning he had previously kept from me.

"If all I had to do was paint pretty pictures of the city and the trees perhaps I would have more time to watch your lovely girlfriend flit around like a little princess on stage," he growled as he grabbed his hat and staunchly shoved it on top of his head. "Some of us have real jobs you know."

"That's not fair Danny. Don't act like what I do isn't good enough. I would never judge you for the choices you've made. Art is all I know, it's the one thing that gets me through."

"If you say so. I just don't have time. It's nothing against Ellie, I guess I shouldn't have said that. I honestly mean no disrespect to her. She has you though, I'm sure that's enough."

"That's not the point," I said to him as he grabbed his coat out of the closet and threw it on. "It would still mean just as much to me if you acted like you cared about us, if you acted like you cared about me at all."

"I do care about you Priam. I just don't like you very much."

When those words came to fruition and reached my ears I felt as if my eardrums had untangled the words incorrectly. Was this really going to be the way it played out? Was there nothing I could do to save what had already begun?

"I'm sorry." It was all I could think to say.

"For what Priam?"

"For everything."

"You know, I may have appreciated hearing those words before, but they could have come a little earlier."

"Like when?"

"Hmm...I don't know. When you ruined my project, when you took everything I had done for you and you set it on fire. When you purposely and hatefully distanced yourself from me just because of some silly little girl."

"She's not some silly little girl! You know that. I love her. She means everything to me."

"Well then apparently you have all you need. What do you want with a brother like me?"

"I still want to be a part of your life Danny! And I want you to be a part of mine!" I was raising my voice then and in the distance down the hall I could hear my grandparents talking and getting up from the table to see what was going on between the two of us.

"I am in your life. I always will be, but we can't have the relationship we used to. It's just too hard for me, not after what you did. I'm sorry I can't forgive you."

"What am I supposed to do? What can I do to make you change your mind?"

"Nothing. It's just better this way. Even though you want it to work, maybe it's just better if it doesn't. We've already had to deal with enough pain in this family Priam. Let's just be civil to one another and not worry about much else. You live your life and I'll live mine."

"This is ridiculous! Why can't you just let it go?"

"I just can't."

"Why?!" I screamed, begging for him to give me a resolution.

He stared at me then, with his dark black top hat and his olive green pea coat. My handsome, smart, successful brother stood before me with a look on his face that projected every emotion I've ever seen him have, and yet a certain sense of nothingness at the same time. He looked full of so many things, but empty all the while. What he said next was anything except for that though, for in his heart, it was true. "I often wonder what would have happened that day if you wouldn't have done what you did. I wonder if things would have turned out differently."

"It was just a stupid project Danny! For Christ's sake!"

"I'm not talking about that. I'm talking about that old house, I'm talking about what you did, when you threw that brick, and what you said to her afterwards, before she left us forever."

I put my hand out in front of me, for all of a sudden I felt as if I had lost my balance. My body shifted from one side to another, and for a moment I thought I was going to faint. Slowly, I regained my footing and focused my glance to him, right before me.

"I think she might have lived you know. I think what you did that day probably caused it, somehow or the other. I've even had dreams about it. When you don't throw that brick, when you don't tell her you hate her, she lives. I guess we'll never know. Goodnight Priam."

With that he opened the front door and stepped out into the Brooklyn rain that had begun falling down, splashing the concrete below. He left the door ajar, and as the smell of the wet asphalt filled my nostrils, my legs collapsed beneath me and I crumpled into a heap on the ground.

He thought it was my fault, he blamed me. As my head hit the hard wooden floor it all made sense. Danny couldn't forgive me for destroying his project, because he already held an animosity for me before that day even occurred, he had been holding this in all along. What I had done had set him over the edge. He had put his anger aside and pretended like he was fine, he had convinced himself that he would ignore his feelings so that he could be there for me since she no longer could be. When I chose to throw that away, this time deliberately, this time so forcefully in a flash of fire, he gave up on me...completely. That's when I knew, there was nothing I was ever going to be able to do to change his mind. That was the day I finally gave up on Daniel Wood, just as he had given up on me.

Living in New York City was mostly everything I thought it would be, but that's not to say that there weren't some surprises along the way. I always felt like I fit in there though, every day as I walked through the mess of mangled misters and misses I adored the notion that no one I passed had any idea who I was, where I was going, or what I was doing. The sense of anonymity made me thrive. Yet, it killed me too. For in a way, I wanted strangers to know who I was, I never thought I would classify my life as a success unless I had somehow made a difference in the world. Sure, I suppose I made a small impact in the lives of those I knew and loved every day, but that wasn't enough for me. I wanted to create a legacy that would last, at least I did then.

While I was studying and creating work as a student at Parsons, my professors always seemed interested and encouraged by what I made and the things I said. Every showcase I ever displayed my work at was a success and I even sold a great deal of my paintings to enthusiastic critics and lovers of art. After graduation the compliments seemed to come fewer and farther in between. Sure, I still made paintings, more even than I ever had before in my life and I sold some too, but I was beginning to realize how hard it was to become a successful artist in what many considered to be the creative capital of the world. In essence, I started to struggle.

Shortly after my twenty-fourth birthday, in the summer of 1965 I met an eccentric artist by the name of Andy Warhol who grew up in Pittsburgh, which wasn't too far away from Alden actually. A friend of mine from school had invited Ellie and I to a party that Andy was hosting at a place people called 'The Factory.' We decided to go, as I figured it would be a good way to meet other artists and to network. Mostly though, I just wanted to meet Andy and see what all of the fuss was, as there was a rather noticeable one. In the long run, the party didn't really end up mattering that much, nor did the fact that I got to meet Andy Warhol, who would become one of the most famous modern artists of the twentieth century. No, what mattered to me was that at that party Ellie and I had a conversation that started to elicit a change that shaped the rest of our lives.

Ellie was a dancer at the American Ballet Theatre in

Manhattan. I often went to go watch her dance and each and every time was just as magical as the first time I saw her move so beautifully in Central Park when I was just a seventeen year old boy. As far as I was concerned, there wasn't a more perfect ballerina anywhere, none as flawless as her. While living in the city, and after finally accepting that Danny and I were never going to be close again, Ellie became the one person that I depended on more than anyone. I loved her with every ounce of my being, and for some reason, she loved me. I often felt that she could do better, that she deserved a rich, successful husband who could buy her a house in the suburbs and give her everything she wanted, but she always told me she didn't want that, she wanted me.

Life is an extraordinary thing. What shapes the person you become more than anything else is not the places you go, or the ideas you know, instead what constructs your soul and makes you believe are the people who help the blood flow, throughout your body steadily, to fill up your heart completely. As a young boy until the age of thirteen, that was my mother for me. When she was gone, my brother Danny took that role and when he left me once and for all, Ellie became the one and only I decided I'd ever need from that point forward and on.

On that night in the summer of 1965, I walked to her apartment and waited outside for her to come down. Although we had been together for around five years, we still did not live together and we had yet to get married. I liked to consider myself a traditional man, so I didn't want to live together until we were husband and wife. In turn, I couldn't propose to her until I felt I was more financially stable and able to take care of her in the way I wanted to. I needed to know that I could give her all of the things she deserved. Thus, until I knew that my art career was going to be able to support the two of us and eventually children as well, we would wait.

After standing outside for only a few moments she emerged from her building and flitted down the granite front steps to greet me. The air billowed along the ripples of her majestic peach colored dress, which only made her soft skin look even more smooth and beautiful. When she reached me, she clicked her white high-heeled shoes together and planted a kiss on my cheek.

"Hello my darling," I said as she pulled away.

"Oh no! I've gotten lipstick all over your face."

I looked at her and laughed, realizing the bright red lipstick she had on most certainly would have left a mark. I didn't care though, even if it made me look a fool. "It doesn't really matter dear."

"Oh of course it does. You want to impress people tonight don't you? Here let me fix it," she said as she pulled a handkerchief out of her purse and wiped the red lipstick stain off of my face. "There we go, all better. Now that handsome face of yours looks as grand and strong as can be. I wonder...are there any other artists in New York City as good looking as you?"

"I guess we'll find out tonight," I said with a chuckle as she laced her arm within mine and we walked down the street to greet the evening with a sense of how we still felt so free.

The Factory was located in midtown Manhattan at 231 East 47th street. The building didn't look like much from the outside, but when Ellie and I entered inside we were surprised to see a hustle and bustle of people filling out a large studio space that was covered in silver. There were even silver colored balloons drifting about the ceiling. Music was loudly playing and everyone who was in attendance seemed to be screaming at the tops of their lungs, as if whatever they had to say was far more important than everyone else's opinions. Therefore, the noise only continued to escalate with every moment that passed. Ellie and I just stood there in the doorway at first, arm in arm staring at the scene before us, both of our feet frozen to the ground unaware of what we should do or who we should talk to. We had been to some crazy art parties during my years at Parsons and I often joined Ellie after her shows to celebrate with her troupe, but it was never anything like this. This was something quite completely different than what we had ever experienced before.

As I watched a crazed looking girl with purple hair and dark green eye shadow run past us after a cat, I finally spotted my friend Thomas who had invited us to the party in the first place. He came over to greet us and immediately pulled us into the crowd of people and started introducing us to everyone all at once. Ellie never let go of my arm while we talked to individuals from all different walks of life. I chatted to a brawny, muscular sculptor from Denver, a poet with pigtails named Louise who lived in Chelsea, and a small, timid middle aged gentleman who said he only painted still lifes. Ellie stayed by my side, she stayed right there with me.

I tried my best to make the people like me, but I imagine the only reason they were interested in anything I had to say was because of the beautiful girl beside me. She didn't say much, but when she did offer something, whoever it was that I was talking to listened with earnest intent. They all seemed so much more enamored with the beautiful ballerina than with me. Perhaps I would always only be a small town boy from Alden, PA with his wild art dreams, or so I had thought then.

Thomas floated away eventually so we helped ourselves to a few drinks. I was beginning to give up on the idea of meeting anyone who would be able to help me with my artistic ambitions, so I decided to ask Ellie if she wanted to dance. About fifteen people or so were in the corner of the large room under the balloons, grooving to the tunes that were reverberating every which way.

"Of course, I'd love to dance with you. Would I, could I ever say no to such a request?" She asked with a smile as she took me by the hand and started to lead me over to the dance floor. Before we got too far though I felt someone come up behind me and tap me on the shoulder, I grasped Ellie's hand tighter than before so she would know I needed to stop. Just from that simple application of pressure she slowed down immediately, waiting for me to regain whatever sense of composure the person behind us had taken away from me. I released her hand and turned around. It was Thomas who had sought my attention, as he was standing right behind me now with a man with shaggy blonde hair. The man had an inquisitive look on his face, but I couldn't read his expression very well as he was wearing a pair of circular sunglasses. His black and white stripped t-shirt only confused me further as the horizontal lines seemed to be blurring together in my brain. The man of course, was Andy Warhol. I looked at him in disbelief, hardly believing he was before me, as I had almost forgotten he was the host of the party. I felt Ellie return to my side, once again linking her arm in mine.

"Well aren't the two of you just the most perfectly handsome couple I've ever seen."

"How kind of you to say Andy," Ellie said with a hint of pleasure.

"This is Priam Wood, the artist I was telling you about Andy," Thomas told him. "And his lovely girlfriend Miss Ellie

Donahue."

"Pleased to meet you both. I'd love to hear about your work Priam. Although, I must ask first, did I hear you correctly Thomas? You mean to tell me that these two lovely people aren't even married?"

I felt my stomach turn at his words, as Ellie clung onto my arm stronger than before. "No, we're not married Mr. Warhol," I stammered out.

"At least not yet," Ellie added with a smile.

"I see, I see. Well I'm not the biggest fan of marriage, but it seems to me that a couple as beautiful and happy as the two of you appear to be probably would be fine with going ahead and taking that next step. After all, it is okay to be traditional in some respects."

"I guess you're right. We're just waiting for the appropriate time," I tell him.

"Time? Time is never right. What are you really waiting for?"

At that, nothing else Andy had to say to me mattered much. Ellie tried to explain to him that I was hoping to become more established in my art career before we tied the knot, but as the words she delivered reached his ears it was almost as if he didn't care anymore. I imagine part of that was because what Ellie was saying to him she didn't really even believe herself. I was the one who was holding out; if it were up to Ellie we would have already been married by then. She didn't want to wait another day. It was I who was caught up in my ideas of needing everything to be in order before we took that next step. Ellie, Thomas and I talked to Andy for about another ten minutes after he had asked me that question. He asked us to attend the next party he was hosting at The Factory the following week, but we were never to return. Not after what happened after some random partygoer with dreadlocks whisked Mr. Warhol away. When he was gone and no longer in our field of vision, Ellie led me over to the dance floor, where we originally were heading before the conversation with the pop artist had begun.

The music was somewhere in between the tempo of fast and slow, as the pulsing beats were serenaded with a certain amount of rhythmicality that Ellie quickly started to glide across the floor to. We danced, with my hand around her waist, yet separate too. Dancing with Ellie was always like a small symphony. I didn't want to take my hands off of her, but at times I knew I had to, to let her dance to the rhythm on her own accord, to free herself from the reality of life and to escape through the movements of her body. Holding onto her while dancing, and dancing on my own as I watched her move were both equally enjoyable to me in different ways.

I don't know how long we danced for, and I couldn't tell by the songs that played as they all seemed to blend into one another. After a while though, I began to notice that everyone was slowly beginning to leave the dance floor and enter into the fray of fellow partiers until it was only the two of us left. The beautiful girl in the peach dress, her red lips so luscious with her chestnut hair pulled up elegantly on top of her head, and the boy in the pale blue suit with his black skinny tie admiring the way she moved to the music. Ellie and Priam, how it'd always be, or so I believed.

Suddenly, Ellie stopped dancing, and thus I did too. "Do you want to go get another drink?" She asked as she started moving away from me.

"Sure, why not?" We walked over to a table on the edge of the dance floor where the bottles of alcohol were uncountable. I imagined that at this point everyone who was drinking was well beyond wasted. I had a comfortable buzz going, but it was nothing that I couldn't handle. I made two gin and tonics for us and handed one to Ellie.

"Thanks. Let's go sit down." I followed her across the room, as she weaved in between all of the people, creating a type of maze made out of humans. When she reached the opposite side of where we were previously, she found a large red couch that wasn't near anywhere else and took a seat, and so I sat down beside her.

"Are you having a good time?" I asked.

"Oh, it's perfectly fine." As soon as she spoke I knew something was wrong. Ellie never described anything as being fine, unless there was an underlying reason that was bothering her. If something truly was fine to Ellie she would describe it in much more grandiose terms. She could have called the party amazing, ridiculous, splendid, charming, interesting, or even swell. But, when she told me she thought it was perfectly fine I knew immediately that she no longer wished to be there.

"What's wrong?"

She turned to look at me and took a sip of her drink.

"Nothing's wrong Priam. Why do you ask?"

"Ellie, you just said the party was fine. Come on, I know better than to fall for that."

"It really is fine dear, there is no reason to be dramatic."

"Well why aren't you having a great time? Why does it only classify as fine?"

"I don't know Priam. I just...we shouldn't talk about it here."

I reached out and put my hand on her thigh then, and the texture of her peach dress tickled my palm so I uncontrollably made a strange face of surprise. She noticed, as she was looking right at me, but she didn't acknowledge it.

"Talk about what? You know you can always talk to me. If I had any idea you were having a bad time I would have asked you about it earlier. We can leave if you want to."

"I don't want us to leave just because of how I feel. I came to this party for you, so I'll stay here for you too."

"Well will you please just tell me what it is? I can take it."

She put her hand on top of mine then and I saw tears forming in her eyes. They glistened as if they were moon rocks slipping through serenity unseen, except they weren't unknown to me, for they were all I could see before me. "It's what Andy said. The entire time we were dancing it just kept running through my head over and over again. The more I thought about it, the more upset I got, until where we are now, sitting here as I'm emotionally tearing myself up on the inside. I'm sorry dear, but I just can't take this anymore."

I lifted my arm from her thigh and tried to put it around her shoulder but she brushed it away. I felt a chill rush down my spine. Ellie had never turned my affection away in such an abrupt way before. "You can't take what anymore? I don't understand," I said as I turned my body towards her more, so that both of my hands rested on my knees.

She then turned her figure towards me too and said "That's just it Priam. I've told you a million times and you still don't get it. You still don't understand. What are we waiting for?"

It all clicked. She was tired of waiting, tired of making her life linger in the balance between the past and the future as I tried to figure out what I was doing with myself. Andy had struck a chord with her that had already been placed on the harp ages ago. He plucked the chord and pulled, and in doing so he made Ellie realize that she wasn't happy with waiting for me to decide what I was going to do, or when I was going to become the artist I felt I needed to be in order to marry the woman I loved.

"I hadn't realized how much this was bothering you," I said in a sincere tone, trying to calm her down. "I've told you before, you deserve the best. We can't get married while I'm still so financially unstable. I want to be able to provide for you, to give you the life you deserve."

"You already do. You're everything I want and more. I don't care if you feel like you aren't where you want to be yet. Every day we wait seems to cut into me deeper. We've been together for five years; almost all of our friends are married. I don't know how many times my mother has asked me why I don't have a ring on my finger yet. I don't even care about what other people think about us, but I do care about how I feel, and I feel as if it's like I'm the one who isn't good enough for you."

The idea that she thought that made me feel a retched sense of horridness I never expected. For Ellie to think that she wasn't good enough for me was not even the littlest bit logical. I had always thought that she was too good for me, not the opposite or reverse.

"That's not it and you know it. I love you with every ounce of my being. You are perfect in every way. You are all I've ever wanted, all I've ever needed."

"Then prove it."

I thought about proposing to her then and there, but it didn't seem right, and even though I knew this was breaking her heart, I couldn't think of anything in particular to say that would put her mind at ease. I thought about taking her by the arm and leading her out of the party. I wanted to apologize some more and then make love to her, but I knew that wouldn't work either. For all of the outwardly physicality of her beauty, Ellie's inner beauty was even greater and thus stronger than the grandeur of grace her frame presented to the world. This issue wasn't going to be one that could be solved so simply.

"I don't want to be the desire that holds you back. I want you to succeed, to soar, to be happy, to have everything you ever want. I've never thought you weren't good enough for me, because in fact, I've often thought you were too good for me," I told her.

The tears she had been trying to hold back in her seeing vessels fell then and I watched as the droplets were pulled through the air by gravity, they seemed as if they were falling in slow motion before they finally splashed onto the peach colored fabric covering her legs below.

"The only thing holding me back Priam is your unwillingness to let go. Life is never going to follow the plans you have for it. Life is unruly and wild, it will slap you in the face one moment and kiss you the next. It's a sandcastle collapsing in the surf, it's a thunderstorm a million miles away you don't even know is coming. If you aren't ready to let go, if my love isn't good enough for you to move on to the next step of our lives, I don't know if I can do this anymore. I need you to be willing to take a chance. I need you to be able to take a chance, for me."

What she said raced through my ears and spun around in a circle so that what I wished to say next needed to be of an appropriate reasoning, something that would actually help put her mind at ease. I waited too long to formulate anything though. The one thing Ellie didn't need from me was any form of hesitation, and when she recognized it was present in my eyes, she threw her drink on the ground. I watched as the glass shattered, as her legs uncrossed and the peach fabric billowed past me as she started to run away, her white heels clicking against the silver ground.

I watched her go, for only a moment, but it was a moment too long. I got up as quickly as I physically could, as her words had almost seemed to stick me to the spot. I was too late though, I finally caught up with her outside and the heat hit me like a truck, but so did the rain, which was falling steadily now, creating a mixture of both the hot and the cold. I saw her slowly running down the street, her arm up in the air as she hailed a taxi which quickly pulled over for her.

"Wait! Ellie! Wait!" I yelled, choking on the words, but she didn't hear me. Or maybe she did, but if she had, she didn't care. She got in the taxi, and I watched her go as the rain soaked my suit so that it begun to cling to my skin. I watched as the yellow car drove away, with Ellie inside, getting further and further away from me with every passing second. Ellie didn't want to wait anymore. It was no wonder she neither heard nor heeded those words I had just called to her. She was tired of waiting, upset that I couldn't let go.

I hear my alarm buzzing and awake with a start as my hand reaches out and slams the button that I know will turn it off. I roll out of bed and it's then when I realize that I am completely naked. I guess I was more drunk than I realized last night, it's the only explanation for why I would sleep completely in the nude. I pull on a pair of underwear and head to the kitchen where I brew a cup of coffee.

My studio in Brooklyn is just that, a studio. While my bedroom, kitchen and bathroom are all very small, the space where I work on my art is quite massive, at least for New York City standards. It contains high ceilings that stretch about twelve feet up into the air that are supported by four wide wooden beams scattered across the space. I have canvasses everywhere, on the floor, on the walls, set up on easels, some finished, some not. On the main wall I have an enormous canvas that measures about twenty feet wide and eight feet tall. As of now it's still empty, I've been sketching out a bunch of ideas that I've thought of painting on it, but nothing has been right.

Ellie and I had gone out with her ballet troupe last night after one of her shows. It was a rather enjoyable evening, but from the headache I'm sporting now and the recollections I have of the evening I am most certainly sure that I had far too much to drink. I guess the frustrations of the past week really were getting to me after all. Ever since last summer when the two of us went to The Factory things have been slightly different. Sure, we had made up a few days after the tiff, but our relationship never went back to how it was before. It was as if we were walking on a combination of ice, broken glass and nails. We had never experienced something like that before, we had never disagreed so vehemently, never been so at odds with our ideas on how to move forward. I had promised her I would get my life together and we would start moving on with everything, that my art would somehow turn into more of a viable living than it was, and that our engagement would be right around the corner.

However, I still have yet to buy a ring and to be honest, I don't know when I'm going to. I'm still struggling; I still haven't found that niche that I've been so desperately searching for. I'm still just some artist that nobody really knows, nobody that matters anyways. So that's why I have decided to take this meeting today, even though it's the last thing I want to do. I have to do it for her; I have to do it for us. It's not fair that I have made her wait this long. Sometimes in order to make the ones you love the most happy, you have to give up what makes you happy the most.

Grandpa Wood has been trying to get me to work for him ever since I graduated from Parsons. He claims that I could use my artistic abilities within the advertising field and although I know that most of what he says is true, I have been hesitant to contemplate the offer. Sure, I imagine that I could still use my creativity if I took a job at his advertising firm, but there are two things that have prevented me from doing so up until this point. One: I wouldn't be my own boss, I wouldn't have complete control over myself, my ideas, or what I make. I would become just another salary man, another drone in the monotonous undertone of Manhattan that has to follow some sort of protocol in order to make clients content. In short, even though I would be able to create art, it would be limited, it would be controlled, it would be stifled. Two: I don't want to be anywhere near Danny. He works for Grandpa Wood's agency and has a rather high position within the company. I don't want my brother to feel uncomfortable because I'm encroaching on his territory and to tell the truth, I don't think I would enjoy having to see him every day, not the way things are, not with how much he hates me. Yet, all things considered, at this point I don't seem to have too much of a choice. If I don't make a change fast, I don't know how much longer Ellie can take it, regardless of how much she loves me. I have to at least show her that I am trying, because I haven't made much progress recently, working on my art alone isn't cutting it anymore.

Thus, I've agreed to meet with my grandfather downtown. We talked a few days ago and he promised me that he could get me a job at a different agency through some of his connections, that way I wouldn't have to work with Danny. He called me last night before Ellie and I went out and said he had scheduled a meeting for me today with the executive of a company he thinks I would enjoy working at, one that would be more accommodating of my creative expressionism, or so that's what he told me. I just don't want to feel like I'm abandoning my art, whatever the costs.

I drink my cup of coffee slowly in my small kitchen and I contemplate the day before me. Will this day make much of a change in the life I have ahead of me? Will it really matter at all? I guess I won't know until I live it. Some days can have the biggest plans and amount to nothing, while the most average of days can have the most altering occurrences. I finish the rest of the dark hot liquid while staring out the small window above the sink. A few robins float by, but there is not much else to see, besides the blue sky and the reflections of the sun bouncing off of the particles of the atmosphere and spreading out through everything.

I go back to my bedroom and put on my best suit. It's a dark grey color and it fits me tightly in all the right places, or so Ellie has always told me. It's still conservative enough for this meeting though. I look into the mirror at the face before me as I tie on my crimson skinny tie. The shaggy blonde hair I once had when I was young is long gone, as my golden locks are now cut more into a kind of crew cut. The sides are shaved short, but the top still has some length to it. I push my bangs up and slick them back, so that on top of my forehead there is a nice golden crescent that adds another inch or so onto my six foot three frame. I adjust my tie and pull on the sides of my jacket to button it. I take one last look at myself after I put on my dress shoes and then wink at the young gentlemen before me, taking in his green eyes. As I do so I can't help put to pretend that it's my mother who is sending me on my way, with a wink and a smile, and that it's not just my own reflection bidding me adieu. I see her in myself sometimes, I see her everywhere.

I clamber down the seven flights of stairs and enter out into the brisk air of the day. I walk to the nearest subway station and get on a train that will take me downtown. Random strangers smile at me on my way, as if they know me, as if I was the one who mattered the most to them in a previous life. Some don't even look my way, but the ones who do really seem to see me, as if they know a part of me that I am not yet familiar, as if they have the keys to a locked secret I still have yet to find. My mother once told me to smile at as many people as I could, to greet the day in a pleasant way that would build up an air of optimism so that each and every person I encountered would love me. She didn't believe in holding pride of unjust confidence, rather she acknowledged that if we would all try to love everyone all of the time, and if we tried our best to be happy the world would be a much less melancholic place. I had always aimed to follow her philosophy, but recently it had been difficult to do so. Nevertheless, on this day, for all of those who greet me with a sign of content, I will return the sentiment with a grin and continue on my way.

As I sit on the subway I feel a bubbling boil up inside of me, not nervousness per se, but rather a kind of curious click pushing forth, trying to reach its way out to figure how this is all going to end up. When it's my time to get off, I exit the subway car and walk up to the ground above where the constant pulse of people rushing past in a hurry flows by me on all sides. Although there is a slight breeze present, the day is a sunny one; it's warm enough, but still has a sense of cool. Even though the area around the agency is crowded with citizens of the city I feel at ease suddenly when I arrive, the wind has stopped and it feels as if the calm air has taken control over my previous uneasiness. The hangover I had earlier is gone; the pounding in my head that I felt formerly when I awoke is no more. I enter the building and take the elevator to the twenty second floor where Grandpa Wood's agency is. As I slowly transcend further and further up and away from where gravity wishes it could pull me back down I anticipate what will come next.

It comes, and then it passes. I have the meeting, and then it is over. It lasts only about an hour, and I feel it goes as well as it can. Grandpa Wood really seems to have tried to find a position that I would feel comfortable and although the job sounds a lot better than I imagined it would, it still doesn't feel right. Mr. Haversmith, the CEO of the company I would be working for shakes my hand one final time as I stand outside the office where we held the meeting. He says goodbye to my grandfather with a shake of the hand as well and we walk with him towards the elevators which are waiting to take him down back to the ground. He pushes the button to beckon it, and then turns back towards where the two of us are standing behind him.

"You won't regret working for me Priam. I can assure you, I think you would fit in very well at Haversmith Inc. We could really use your talents, your all seeing eye. I bet we could make some fantastically beautiful advertisements together. Your grandfather will probably be kicking himself that he didn't hire you first."

"Believe me, I would if I could," Grandpa Wood chuckles as a dinging bell sounds and the elevator door opens. "I think Priam is meant for something more than what we could offer him here though."

"Well, I hope Haversmith can give you what you're looking for." He says as he steps in the elevator.

"Thank you. I will let you know my decision soon." I tell him, and then the door closes.

"So...what do you think?" Grandpa Wood asks me, expecting complete honesty now that it is just the two of us.

"I can't think. I can't think at all."

"Well, take your time. Haversmith's a good friend of mine. You can decide when you're ready. The job will be waiting for you."

"Thanks Grandpa. I really appreciate you doing all of this for me. I don't deserve it."

"Yes you do Priam. And besides, I understand where you are coming from. Just because times are tough doesn't mean you have to abandon your art. Regardless of what you decide to do, I know your work will live on, maybe just in a different form."

"I hope so."

I look at him then, I mean I really look at him, and for a second I see the face of my father. The man I owe so much to, yet a man I never knew. The generations between us collide and divide and suddenly I feel as if I don't even know who I am anymore. What, oh what am I going to do? Art is all I have ever understood, it's all I've ever had, the one constant in my life that hasn't left me, hasn't puzzled me, hasn't made me yearn for something more. Can I really give it up, even partially? I don't know. I glance at my watch and realize I'm late.

"I have to get going Grandpa. I told Ellie I would meet her for lunch, and if I don't show up on time she'll wring my neck."

"Alright Priam. Well, it was good seeing you. If you want to get together any time soon to talk more about the position just let me know."

"I will. Thanks again," I say as I shake his hand and push the button for the elevator to return. My grandfather walks away, the elevator comes and I enter inside of the small moving room that has the ability to lift you up or pull you below. Before he gets too far away though, he turns back to me and says one final thing: "Whatever you decide, whatever you do, at least don't let that girl get away. She really loves you." The doors close then, and I am unable to answer him. All that rings through my head is 'she really loves you,' over and over again. And I love her. I love her so much. I hope I don't mess this up, I hope I make it through.

I rush to the spot where Ellie and I had agreed previously to meet for lunch and when I get there I see her silhouette appear out from the crowd as she approaches the food stand, tip toeing along until she gets to the end of the line. I look both ways before crossing the street and run across, reaching her just in time before anyone else has the chance to get in line behind her. I tap her on the shoulder and she turns around.

"Oh! When did you get here?"

"Just now my dear. Right on time."

"I'm surprised, I figured you would be late, as per usual."

"What! I'm never late," I shout as I wrap my arms around her waist and pull her in for a kiss. Her lips feel so smooth and warm as they reach mine.

"I guess you are punctual...sometimes," she giggles as she reaches down and grabs my hand and begins to walk forward, leading me with her, as the line is moving to the front counter of the food stand. She's wearing a white silk halter dress, the top reaches around her neck like two swans' heads meeting behind her to steal a peck, or perhaps to share a secret. Her hair is wrapped up in a yellow headscarf, so that only a few ringlets of her beautiful chestnut hair are peeking through. Whenever I see her wearing something new I always try to take in every detail, every part of what it is that she has put together. As an artist, I like to experience the canvas of colors and prints that my Ellie uses to paint the elegant blank slate of her body. When we are at the front of the line we give our order and I pay for the both of us even though Ellie offers to pay for her own. The least I can do for my girl is to cover the cost of lunch. The food comes out quickly, and when it's ready we carry it over to the small park right behind the kiosk and find a bench that rests beneath a big old willow tree. The leaves on it are just beginning to bloom, as I notice small green buds on the end of each and every branch. We open the containers of food and begin eating, I hadn't realized how hungry I was until the first bite of the sandwich reaches my mouth.

"So...how did it go?"

For a moment I had forgotten all about the meeting. I cover my mouth with my hand so as not to talk with my mouth full, or at least so that I don't show her the food I have already chewed up and answer: "Oh. It went well. It went well."

"What did the guy have to say? Do you think you would want to work there?"

I swallow and say: "Possibly. I have some time to think about it, Grandpa Wood said the position would be there whenever I decided."

"Well that's good," she tells me as she takes a bite of her sandwich and looks away. We both watch silently as a young mother pushes her infant past in a strawberry colored bassinet. "Would you still be able to paint though? Did he say you could use your art in the advertisements?" She asks after a few moments when both of our mouths are empty again except for the words which we are loudly whispering to one another.

"Yes. I would. That's why I'm seriously considering it. I would still be able to make art. It's just the fact that it wouldn't really be on my own terms. I wouldn't be painting for myself, what I want to create. I'd be making things for ads, for clients, for customers. I'd be limiting myself to the ideas of others, I'd be letting go of the control I've always had. I'd be succumbing to what I've never wanted to: the outside world."

She doesn't reply right away, she turns to look at me and then she looks away. She takes another bite of her sandwich and I do the same. We sit there in silence for a few minutes, letting the still of the day surround us with its tranquility. A breeze comes along after a while though, returning from whatever place it went to this morning, and as it brushes by I feel it tingle down my spine. I turn to look at her, and when I do I see the yellow headscarf shake ever so slightly and rustle her hair beneath. Our food is finished, our lunch is done, but I know this conversation has just begun. She takes my hand, and finally decides to challenge what I have said head on.

"What do you want more than anything Priam? When you close your eyes and think of a perfect life, what are you doing in it? Are you painting in your studio in Brooklyn? Or are you sitting in an office in Manhattan talking to executives about the kind of picture they want you to create? Are you a man who follows his heart and goes for what he wants, or do you compromise in order to make things easier, to make things manageable?"

She's asked me so many questions, but somehow that doesn't faze me as I realize that I know the answer to each and every one. "I want to be an artist of my own accord. I want to paint, in my studio, or wherever my current inspiration takes me. I don't want to be some office drone, even if it includes an aspect of art which I can control. You know that I've always tried my best to follow my heart Ellie," I say as I squeeze her hand gently. "But how can I do that anymore? How can I keep blindly following my dreams when it's holding me back, when it's holding us back from moving on?"

"I'm not going anywhere Mr. Wood. I know I've gotten frustrated before, and yes, I am tired of waiting for the day when I finally become Mrs. Wood, but I've accepted that I know that day will come sooner or later. I just might have to be patient for it. I want you to follow your heart; I want you to do what makes you happy."

"You make me happy," I tell her as I lift my hand she was holding and put it around her shoulder to pull her close. She tilts her head sideways and lays it on my shoulder, so that it rests right against the lapel of my suit jacket, her breath glides out and skates across my tie as it drifts away and enters the atmosphere further from us.

"I know that love, but you'd be lying to yourself if you were to say that I am all you need. I love you with all of my heart, but I know that even so, loving you alone wouldn't be enough to make me happy. If I couldn't dance a part of my soul would feel incomplete. And believe me; this is coming from the girl who has been in love with the idea of love ever since I was old enough to comprehend it."

"I would never want you to sacrifice your dreams for me, I always want you to be able to dance," I tell her.

"Exactly. That's my point you see. I never want you to sacrifice your dreams for me either. I know a big reason why you would decide to take this job is for me, so that you'd have a more stable career, a more reliable source of income, what you think we need in order to get married."

"But-"

"But nothing. Only take this job if it is what you want. Don't take it for me. If I have to wait a little bit longer, if we just have to hold out on the marriage plans until you are ready, when people finally start recognizing your talent on a wider scale, I can wait. I've realized that your happiness is more important than my impatience."

"That's just it though Ellie," I begin. "I don't want you to have to wait anymore. You shouldn't have to, but you're right about the rest of it too. Art is what I do, and I can't imagine my view being directed or limited by anyone else. It won't be an easy decision, that's for sure."

"Well, whatever you decide. I'll still be here. I'll always be here Priam."

"Why though? What makes you stay by my side? Sometimes I wonder why you even love me. How am I good enough for a girl like you?" I ask as the selfishness of what I have done to her over the past few years seeps through. Often, I feel like I am only holding her back.

"Are you asking me why I love you?"

"I suppose in so many words."

She lifts her hand up to her brow, and pushes it along the side of her face before lifting it back up again to her forehead where she grabs her yellow headscarf and yanks it off, so that her long brown hair tumbles down, as if it has just been released from an unwanted containment. She tilts her head quickly to the opposite side of me and when she straightens her neck, her hair bounces back into place, perfectly framing her face. She takes my hand, the one that had previously been around her shoulder before and begins.

"I love you because of your dreams Priam. I love you because of your kindness, your simplicity and your honesty. You are the only man I've ever known who never gives up, even if the path ahead seems a most difficult one. You're true, you stick to the person that you are and never fade from it. You don't believe in a lot of things, but at the same time I know you have always believed in me. You mess up at times, but when you apologize to me, I can always tell you mean it. Not only that, you've been in my life for such a long time, I can't imagine anyone else loving me more. When I think about how we met that day in the park it all just seems like serendipity, like we were meant to be together. I love you because you not only complete me, but because your generosity and charm surprises and delights me every day. I love you because I know you will never give up, not on me, not on us, and not on your dreams."

I look at her then, when the words stop and she has finished what she had to say, I feel tears welling up in my eyes. It's as if what she has said has set me free, as if the most beautiful score from a film I have never even seen is playing in the background. I have no idea how to reply, how to top anything she has said, for the amount of love I have for her is nothing that is manageable or predictable, it is just there because it has to be, it's all I seem to know, all I want to feel. I lean forward and kiss her, slowly at first and then more passionately as the seconds wane on. She puts her hand behind my head and pushes my mouth into hers further, I wrap my arm around her and hold her close, inhaling and exhaling and feeling every part of her that I can. The bench we are sitting on seems to fall away and all I am aware of is this girl, this woman, and how much I love her so. I forget the worries I have and enjoy the experience I'm undergoing with Ellie. It's a moment of clarity. For even if everything goes wrong, at least I know I'll always have her making it right.

We stop kissing, and as I pull away I look into her blue sapphire eyes and say "I love you. I always have, and I always will. No matter what happens, I know that more than anything I have to follow my dreams, and my number one dream is and always shall be, to be with you."

She smiles then, flashing her perfect teeth and while I savor the sight I step up from the bench and throw away the food containers from our lunch into the rubbish bin beside us. I beckon her to come with me and she does so. We start walking out of the park back towards the street, she leaves my side and runs up in front of me a bit, lifting her arms in the air as she begins to spin, pirouetting repeatedly ever so gracefully down the sidewalk. I take in the view of her white dress moving around her body, highlighting everything I've ever known about this girl, the only woman for me.

I don't know what to do. A part of me has already decided not to take the job at the ad agency, as it's telling me that I have to follow my dreams, no matter how hard or difficult they may be to achieve. The other part of me tells me that I need to take the job, that I can't keep yearning for something more when I already have so much, that I shouldn't be so selfish, that I should take this job and compromise so that I can give Ellie the life she deserves. Either way I don't really win. If I take the job, I could propose to Ellie right away, we could get married and I know we would be happy, but I wouldn't be the artist I feel I am meant to be. If I refuse to take the job, if I decide I'm not going to give up on my aspirations, who knows how much more time will pass. After all there is a chance I will never be recognized for my work.

For now though, I simply try to forget about it. I watch as Ellie dances in front of me, twirling around one more time and then landing back on the dirt path on her own two feet. The trees on either side of where we are walking surround us with empathy and an underlying energy of desire as she links her arm around my bicep. Together, we glide out of the park, where the tranquility of the natural fades away as we step out into the street, as the cars honk and the passerbys shout, all I can hear is the beating of my heart.

Ellie and I part as she goes into the theater for a rehearsal for an upcoming show. After I kiss her goodbye I turn around to leave, but then turn back and watch her go. Right before she enters into the building she glances back at me, for I'm sure she somehow knew that I was watching her walk away. She blows me a kiss from the doorway and disappears inside. I walk to the street corner and stand there for a few moments, listening to the traffic rush past, taking it all in. I decide I should go home to my apartment. I need a paintbrush between my hands. I feel a primal urge egging on my entire being, I must create something. It's the only way I can sort through all of my thoughts completely.

I take the subway back to my apartment and when I reach my studio on the seventh floor I walk up to my turntable and put a Beatles record on. As the song In My Life begins to play I sit down on the floor in front of the massive blank canvas and stare at it. The stillness is gone as the lyrics fill the room. This song has reminded me of my days ever since the first time I heard it. It pains me yet lifts me up at the same time. I've always been that weird guy who loves depressing music the most. Somehow the sadness sets me free. The melancholy and the misery sung out helps me feel better. So many songs make me think of her. How could they not? Every melody tries it's best to compare, but nothing is as good as she will ever be. I often wonder what the soundtrack of my life would be. What songs would play during the most important moments I have had?

As the abyss of nothingness in front of me envelops my eyes and the song fades out I feel a chill push through every single skin cell of my body and then retreat back into me. I get up and pull the record off. I walk over in front of the canvas to where my brushes and cans of paint are sitting. I pick up a brush and run the tip over the tops of my hands, the bristles running back and forth, smoothing out the skin that holds all of the pieces I own together.

I lift the brush up and think of what to do. I close my eyes as my arm waves back and forth in front of me, trying to understand the undergoing I am about to choose. This blank canvas mocks me as a metaphor of my own life. It's empty, oh so empty and I have no idea how to fill it. I open my eyes, drop the brush to the ground and go to my bedroom where I take off my tie, my jacket, and my shirt. I look in the mirror, tilt my head to the side and then decide to take my shoes, socks and pants off too. The only thing retaining any form of my modesty are the boxer briefs clinging to my nether regions. As I exit my room I decide I need a finishing touch to my near nakedness, so I grab my gray fedora off of my bookcase and jam it on my head.

I go back into my studio and grab the brush. I clench it tightly, hoping for something to come to mind, a reverie or anything that will help me decide what to do. Nothing comes though, for I realize that what I need the most is to simply let go. I drop the brush again, and this time I know I will not be picking it back up. Something swallows me, taking control and I'm sure I know what it's related to: frustration, the feeling of being helpless, of being trapped in front of a speeding steaming engine that will soon run me over completely if I am unable to find the power to leave, to move, to go on.

I grab a can of green paint; I hold it in my hands and slowly walk backwards, shuffling my feet across the wooden baseboards. I look at it and think of all of the trees I've ever seen, their leaves that fall every autumn which could fill up all of the rooms I've ever been in and more. I stick my hand into the bucket, and as the cool thick liquid fills all of the lines on my palm and surrounds each one of my fingers entirely I gasp, and then try to breathe as the air in my lungs doesn't seem to be staying there or entering in at all actually. I swirl my hand around the inside of the jar and then lift it out and propel my entire body forward, with my arm moving first so that drops of paint leave me and splatter all over the whiteness. The green dots land and then start to slide down as gravity wishes to meet them more than the white fibers of the canvas desire to keep them. I watch as they fall and after a few moments I avert my eyes from the canvas and focus them on my hand which I place in the bucket again, repeating the same motion as before, over and over as

I run back and forth along the entire width of the canvas, spurting green drops of paint over as much of it as I can.

I set the bucket of green down and grab the next color. Soon, I have done the same with every color of the rainbow, my arm entering into buckets of blue, purple, red, orange and yellow too. By the time I am done dipping into the last color my arm feels heavy as the layers of paint have crusted over upon me. I think about going to the kitchen to wash it off, but I decide against it. Although there are many specks of color on the canvas now, the whiteness still seems to be searing through.

I look back to the pile of brushes and pick up the one I had been holding before. I decide to use a similar technique with it as I did with my arm, but this time instead of the paint flying off my arm in smaller specks, the brush projects the paints onto the canvas at a much higher velocity, thus the colors begin to blend together to cover up the white more and more. The specks from my arm and the long lines and gashes of colors from my brush slip together like a symphony. When I have done this with all of the colors I once again step back to look at the massive canvas before me. My frustrations of what to do with my life are being carried out in a rhythm of painting which I am trying to make help me decide. Do I continue to paint as I currently do, how I want, under my own terms, under the guise of my own moods and dreams? Or do I sacrifice that freedom, do I learn how to compromise? She deserves it after all, she more than deserves it and I know that. Even if she has recently been pretending like the fact that we aren't already married no longer bothers her, I know it still does.

I can't think, and there is still too much white left. I feel as if it's mocking me. I look to the left of my studio and then to the right, searching for something more, anything more. Then, I notice a can of paint I hadn't seen before sitting off to the side, not in front of the canvas but in a space all its own. I walk over to it and pick it up. I pull off the lid, and when I see the blackness residing within I have to laugh to myself. Of course it's black, as I peer at the midnight blue of all colors combined while still having none at the same time, I become acquainted with the black and I make it my friend. In doing so I move back in front of the canvas, positioning my body so that I am located directly in the middle of it.

I put both hands on the bucket and pull my arms back, as I feel the muscles in my arms bulge and then slacken, I reach a point of no return and then I swing the bucket forward with all my might. The black paint inside flies out from its vessel in slow motion, slamming into the canvas like a dark demon from the deep. I watch as the blackness covers the colors, the specks and lines of lightness and brightness. I watch as the black continues to flow from where I am standing, killing the white and making it night. I watch as the darkness of the day covers it all away. The black slides down, dripping to the floor. I run to the left side of the painting and whip more of the shadowed color along the canvas; I walk down the length of it and cover as much as I can. When I'm done I drop the bucket to the floor at the right side of the canvas. I return to the middle of my studio, with my back facing the canvas and then once I am located where I want to be within this room I turn around to face it and then sit down on the wooden floor, in nothing but my underwear and fedora.

What I see before me is a mystery that holds every answer to my life. I see highlights and shadows, I see color, I see white, and I see blackness. I can't help but to think of Jackson Pollock and his fractal paintings. Although what I have just created is nowhere as sophisticated as his pieces, somehow it seems to ring more true, at least to me. It's chaos, uncertainty and everything colliding and coalescing. It's life and death, it's misery and pain yet happiness and laughter too. I can see the death of my father on the battlefield and my mother in the Victoria driving by on the streets of Alden. I can see Ellie dancing up on stage, and I can see Danny behind the colors of a flame. And I can see me; I can see myself in every speck of color, in every flash of white, and hidden within every drop of darkness. This painting is my life, contrite yet concealed, delighted yet destroyed, hated yet hopeful.

I still have no idea what I'm going to do, but somehow creating this mess has made me feel better. I sit for a few more minutes and then realize I can't look at it anymore, at least not now. I did my work, I made my piece, now I need to go outside, into the air so that I can make myself breathe properly again, as I realize now that I feel as if I have been holding in all of the air I've taken in over the entire time since I've been home. I rip off my underwear and throw them in the corner of the room; I toss my hat to the floor and then walk into the bathroom where I start a shower, and then get in. I watch as the water washes the colors of the paint off me, as they all swirl together in the drain I say goodbye to them silently, never to see these molecules again. As the hot water cleanses me I feel new. I dry off, go into my bedroom and put on a pair of khaki slacks and a white t-shirt. I pull on my brown loafers, grab my keys and then leave, down the stairs of my building, and out into the streets of the city as clean and blank as I can possibly be, as the canvas I just transformed previously was.

I don't know why, but for some reason I feel like walking back towards downtown, even though I was just there earlier in the day. When I think about where I want to go it's all I can really come up with, so I decide that I should follow where my mind is leading me. After I make it through my neighborhood and the outskirts of a few other ones, I eventually reach the Brooklyn Bridge, which seems to loom before me with a grandeur of grey wistfulness. It's about the end of the afternoon and the sun up in the sky that was higher before is now starting to come back down, its golden light creating shadows and highlights over all of the various parts of the city before me. I step onto the bridge and begin walking across it, passing all sorts of people as I go. There's a woman covered in pearls who has a poodle on a silver colored leash, a young couple pushing twins in a stroller for two, an attractive man going for a jog with a green bandana stretched across his forehead, and a girl with auburn hair of about thirteen years old riding her bike quickly along. These people pass me and others do too, but for some reason I notice these ones the most. Its funny how some individuals you encounter strike you, they come into focus and leave an imprint, even if it's only for a second. When I think about all the people I have previously walked past in my life, our stories intertwining for only a moment and then separating again, I often think about what they are doing now. Are they happy? Do they have what they want? Are they sad? Do they feel as if they still need something more?

All of these questions collide in my mind as I reach the middle of the bridge, halfway across the East River, between the two towers that suspend the bridge across the way. And that is when I see him, right before me, coming directly towards me, my brother, Daniel Wood. He has on a nice navy blue suit that he has paired with aviator sunglasses to block out the light. Since his eyes are covered I can't tell if he sees me when I first notice him. I don't know how he couldn't though; we are walking as if we are two magnets that are being pulled together, unable to escape the force

184

that is asking us, requesting us to collide. We're two marbles on glass, sliding together and there's nothing we can do. As my legs keep me going, I slowly stop as he is finally only two feet before me, neither of us changed our direction, we just kept walking on, almost as if we wanted to see if the other would stop, or give up.

"Hello Priam."

"What are you doing here Danny?" I ask, confused as to why my brother would be on his way to Brooklyn, let alone why in the hell he would be walking there.

"Nice to see you too."

"Don't give me that bullshit. You are the one who stopped trying to be a good brother to me, there is no reason for formalities and I'm not going to pretend, so you don't have to either."

"I guess you're right," he says as he takes off his shades so I can see him completely. "I was coming to see you actually. I was on my way to your place, kind of funny I didn't even have to make it all the way there before I saw you."

"Why? Why were you coming to see me? And why didn't you just take the subway?"

"How many damn questions are you going to ask me? Jesus. I just felt like taking the long way there, inhaling a little fresh air before I told you what I wanted to say."

"What do you want to say?" I ask.

"I guess the questions won't stop coming. Not that I should be surprised after all. That's how you've always been. One question after another, always wanting to know all of the details, all of the answers, even to those questions that no one has them for."

For some reason, Danny is in an interesting mood today. I don't remember him having such a playful demeanor angled towards me in this way in quite a while. All it is anymore is a cold shoulder and a grin of disappointment. The fact that he is acting as if he actually has something to say and that he is seeking me out on his own has caught me off guard. I don't know what to do; I don't know what to say. All I can think about are all of the questions I want to ask, all of the answers I wish of him to give me, even though I know I won't get many, if any at all. The sun falls lower and lower into the sky and people pass us on either side of the pedestrian walkway, cars rush past beneath us, going from Manhattan to Brooklyn and the other way as well. The stones hold us high above the water, and as we stand still, in that moment I know that everything is about to change. I feel as if my life is teetering on a precipice of perpetual perfection that I may never be able to reach. It's just too far away, too high up on that shelf tucked away in the clouds.

"I was coming to talk to you about this job offer. I wanted to give you some advice."

"How do you even know about the job?"

"Grandpa Wood told me, of course."

For a moment I am furious with my grandfather, but then again I never explicitly told him that I didn't want Danny to know that I was considering quitting my artistic career to become an everyday man in the advertising world. I figured he wouldn't tell him though, as he knows how we don't get along, he knows the reason that I didn't want to work for him was because that meant I would have had to work with Danny. I can't really be mad at Grandpa Wood though, for in reality, I suppose I knew he would tell my brother all along.

"And what did he say to you? What did he tell you I had decided?"

"He said you hadn't. He said you were still contemplating what you wanted to do."

"Yes...that's true," I say in a whisper, so softly I'm not even sure he hears me because of the sounds of everything surrounding us.

"Well you're an idiot if you don't take it. You've tried this whole art thing and clearly it's not working. You deserve better. Ellie deserves better. Sure, you're talented, we all know that, but it's time to come back to reality. You're lucky you're even being offered a job like this. Haversmith is a great ad agency, shit even I would work for them. You don't have to act like you're above a normal life Priam, because you're not." He pauses and when he does I am tempted to reach out and strangle him, right then and there, while we are suspended in the air above the East River. As the Brooklyn Bridge holds us up, all I feel like is that I wish to fall down, to crumple to the wooden boards below, but I know I can't. I feel a rage and a sadness simultaneously. I wish my brother would love me, I wish my brother didn't just think that art was just some silly fantasy to me.

"Since when do you give a damn what I do with my life?" I shout, and as I do the passerbys look at me as if I have lost my mind, and perhaps I have. I fog them out of my periphery, so I can focus only on the man before me. "Or rather, since when should I have to listen to any of your advice? You lost that privilege when you kicked me to the curb. As far as I'm concerned, we aren't even brothers, you're just some guy I used to know."

"Always so dramatic, aren't you Priam? Maybe we're not close like we used to be, but I'm past thinking about all of that stuff. I thought you were too. I just thought that perhaps you could use some advice, regardless of whether you wanted to hear it or not. Mr. Haversmith is giving you a chance to make a life for yourself, and he's even been gracious enough to let you have leeway, to use part of your art within the position. I'd say you're pretty lucky."

"The only luck I've ever come across is the luck I've made for myself. And to be honest, I haven't had too much of it. I work my ass off as an artist, and yes I've been struggling, but I wouldn't give up that struggle for anything. I'd rather be a poor happy fool than a rich miserable soul any day of the week. I don't want to end up anything like you Danny. I want to veer as far away from you as I can."

"I guess it was a mistake to try to convince you of actually making something of yourself. I shouldn't have come the whole way out here. What a waste of a day," he says as he turns to walk away, but before he can separate himself from me completely I grab him harshly on the back of his shoulder and pull, so that he turns around.

"I'm sorry that all I am is a waste to you, but let me tell you one thing. Regardless of what I do, I'm never going to stop trying, and I'm going to end up happier than you. Mark my words Daniel Wood. I'm going to make it through."

"Well I hope so Priam. Good luck with that. Apparently you're going to need it. You know, if Mother was here I think she would tell you the same thing I've just told you now. She would tell you what a fool you're being, what a fool indeed." He reaches his hand out to me then, offering it to me so that I grasp it and shake it. I just stare at it, the words he has just spoken searing into my consciousness. I won't take it, I won't accept it, I won't touch him. After the seconds pass and I don't look up, or grab his hand either, I think he realizes that this interaction is done. He begins to walk away and this time I don't grab him, I don't make him stop.

I do add one final thing though, for I would never have

been able to live with myself if I just let him walk away as I stood there in silence. As he is about ten feet away, as I watch him go, with the city of New York before him, I yell out at the top of my lungs: "Mother would never have told me such a thing! She would have told me to follow my dreams, 'til the very last day I lived! She would have told me to never stop trying! To never give up! To never surrender!" I wonder if he hears me, as he doesn't stop, doesn't turn around, doesn't add anything more. How could he not have heard me? I think the entire Brooklyn Bridge shook as I screamed. After a few more seconds pass in painful silence, after he is a few more feet away, he lifts his right arm up in the air, pumping his fist once. For some reason, he decides to acknowledge my words and that, makes all the difference.

I watch him go for a few more moments and as I do so I realize that my entire life I have felt as if I have been standing still. I feel as if I have always been watching people go, watching people leave, watching people give up on me. I feel as if I always try my best to accomplish all of the things I've ever wanted and more, but no matter what I do I never truly succeed. I'm never good enough. I'm close to what I want, only inches away, yet there are many miles in between.

I turn back to the way I came, towards Brooklyn, and I begin to run, off of the bridge and back to my side of the city. When my lungs begin to heave after about ten minutes of jogging at a rather quick pace I finally see what I am looking for: a payphone. I pull out change from my pocket and jam the coins into the metal slot. I dial the operator and ask to be directed to the number I need.

"Thank you for calling Haversmith Inc. This is Betty speaking, how may I help you?"

"Hello, this is Priam Wood. I had a meeting with Mr. Haversmith earlier this morning. I was wondering if I could speak with him?"

"Of course. Hang on one moment please Mr. Wood." As I wait for a voice to once again pulsate sound in my ear through the telephone I notice how heavily I'm breathing. I try to take a deep breath to calm down my lungs, but it doesn't seem to do much good. I did just run a decent distance after all.

"Priam?"

"Yes. Hello, Mr. Haversmith."

"How are you doing young man? I didn't expect to hear

from you so soon."

"And I didn't expect to be calling you so soon, but I've made up my mind. I would love to take the position at Haversmith Inc. I think it is in my best interest to do so."

"That's great Priam! I knew you'd come around. You'll fit right in, I promise. I'm about to head out of the office for the day, but I'll get in touch with you again tomorrow to meet together again and go through more of the logistics of the position. Have a good evening!"

"Thanks sir, you too."

I hear the dial tone and then I hang up the phone. I pull the door of the telephone booth open, but I don't leave the metal chamber. I lift my hand to my forehead and wipe away the sweat on my brow. I've done it, I've really done it. All day I have been torn up about what to do. I've had my own thoughts and then those of my grandfather, Ellie, and now my brother too. And while those all factored in heavily to what I've just done, another notion influenced me more: my mother, or rather, the lack of her presence being here. Although I know what I yelled at my brother was true as he left, that she would never have called me an idiotic fool for following my dreams, that she would have wanted me to do whatever it was that made me happy, even if it wasn't easy, that isn't what caused me to change my mind. No, I know that Moira Wood would have supported anything I chose to do. She would have loved me no matter how I decided to live my life, but since the moment Danny brought up the idea that she could possibly be disappointed in me, that if I failed, if I continued to strive for something that wasn't realistic and was out of my reach that could cause her to look down upon me in any way, I knew that I had to stop trying. She would tell me to go on, but the reality of it all is, is that she can't. My mother isn't here anymore and she's never coming back. I have to please those people that are still on this Earth. I have to try to do what's best for me, and for the future too. Ellie doesn't deserve to be strung along like how it's been any longer. And even though I don't want to admit it, I still wish to impress my brother. Although a part of me hates him, a bigger part wants him to admire me, at least in some shape or form.

Thus, the dream I've had since I was a little boy, the notions of living to create an artistic expression of my own, to paint pictures of unknown entities only I can envision, to follow no rules and live each and every day being inspired by beauty both in this world and in the figments of my own imagination can no longer be. The dream I've always had has ended today. My dream has died. Although I continue to breathe, as my lungs take in air and my heart pumps blood through my veins, a part of my being, a slice of my soul is no longer here.

The rest of the afternoon and the beginning of the evening pass in a blur. After I leave the telephone booth I sit outside at a park near my apartment and watch as the daylight fades away, the sunshine saying goodbye to all that it knows and embracing the other side of the earth, saying farewell to the city of New York until the next day comes. I watch the pigeons as they waddle past my feet. I think of how ugly they are, what filthy and dirty creatures they can be, yet while thinking so, as the dark gray of their feathers burn into my eyes I notice the colors on their necks. I see the green hues and purple blues that fade into one another in such a way that they become beautiful. I realize then that even the most common kind of bird in this world has highlights of loveliness.

It's hard not to feel depressed. I'm unable to leave this bench seat and as the darkness surrounds me and the coldness of this spring eve becomes more and more frigid I fade away into a realm where time doesn't matter and the future is a thing that will never come. I don't know how long I remain here, but I know that it is a while; when I finally leave and walk back to my apartment I see barely anyone out and about on the sidewalks, rarely a car in the street.

I reach the seventh floor and unlock my door where the silence and the stillness of my studio apartment surrounds me, enveloping me like a small fish in the sea. My stomach growls, begging to be fed, but I ignore it, nutrition hardly seems necessary on a night like this. I pretend like I don't see the huge canvas splattered with paint in my studio mocking me, for at this moment it is the last thing I want to see. I go into my bedroom and look at my clock to check the time. It is half past eleven. I have no idea where the day went, but that's just it, it's already gone. I suppose there is no point in thinking about how it left me so quickly. I hear a knock on the door and go to answer it. I say a silent prayer hoping that the person behind it is the only one I want, the only one I need, and of course, it is her. As the door swings open she embraces me immediately, as if she knows that all I need right now is her love, her warm embrace.

"Hello my love," she whispers in my ear as she gives me a kiss, a sweet soft kiss.

"Hi," I croak, my voice sounding hoarse. We walk into the studio, hand in hand. She drops her bag on the ground and takes off her coat. I notice that she is still wearing her leotard and tights from her rehearsal. The velvety maroon fabric clings to her body, accentuating her perfect breasts and small waist. The tights cover her thin, muscular legs, holding everything in place.

"Make love to me," she coos as she places her hand on my chest, running her fingers down my abdomen.

"Oh Ellie, I don't know if I can."

"What ever do you mean?" She asks, and as she does so, I take her hand and lift it up above her head, so that she turns around and leans into me, her back up against my stomach. I wrap my arms around her, we stand there, up against one another, looking at the painted canvas before us, taking it in. I hear her exhale loudly, realizing that the white canvas she had left the last time she was here is no more and that in its place resides the crazy, frantic mess of colors, blacks, blues and more, all ringing true throughout the space where we currently are, in this place.

"It's intoxicating Priam. It's deliciously furious and revolutionary. I can feel so many emotions instantaneously just from the sight of it. You really are brilliant."

"Stop it," I plead, not wanting to hear how great she thinks I am, for I am not, I cannot be.

"Come on now, let me compliment you. You deserve it you know." I hold her tighter then, lifting my arms up to her bosom and then turning her around to face me again. I kiss her on the lips, tasting the sweet desire emanating from her soul. I slowly pull away, and when I open my eyes, I see her blue ones gazing back at me.

"I took the job," I say as calmly as I can.

"You...what? You took the job? Already? Why didn't you-"

"It's just what I had to do."

"Priam...that's great dear!" She exclaims, trying to cover her surprise with a sense of excitement. I know that she is happy for me, for at this moment she believes it is what I want, but really it is just what I need. Or so I have told myself.

"I suppose it is."

"Are you alright?"

"I'm as fine as I can be."

"It's okay if you are sad. I expected you to be if you ended up taking it. I understand my love. It's hard to let go of things we care about so much."

"I just feel like a part of me has died."

"Then why are you taking the position? I hope it isn't for me," she says taking a small step back. "I told you, I don't want you to sacrifice your dreams for me, regardless of what I may or may not have said in the past. I can wait."

"You shouldn't have to wait. You have waited long enough."

"Then why?"

"Just because," I lie, as the faces of my mother and my brother flash through my subconscious.

"Make love to me, let's go into the bedroom and forget about this all for now. I know it will make you feel better, to just escape into the moment with one another, to let go of reality for a time."

"I don't think I can Ellie. I wouldn't be any good tonight. I'm in a kind of funk. I'm glad you're here though. You being here is all I need."

"Are you sure? Is there anything else I can do to make you feel better?"

I look at my beautiful Ellie and an idea comes to mind. I let go of her hand and take a step back, so that there are a few feet between us, similar to the distance that Danny and I had stood earlier today. I look at her chestnut colored locks, waving down to the sides of her face and the leotard that fits her snugly. I look to the ground where her feet are bare. I hadn't realized she had kicked off her shoes when she came in.

"I can only think of one thing that would help," I say.

"What is it?"

"I'd love to watch you dance."

She smiles, and slowly begins to walk backwards towards her bag that lies on the floor next to her coat. "Of course," she tells me as she pulls out her ballet slippers, sits on the floor and ties them on.

I back up against the wall, so that the massive canvas is before me, with Ellie in the left corner of the room. I watch her as she laces up her dancing shoes. When she finishes, she walks over to the record player and puts something on. As the slow rhythmic piano begins to play, the chords strike me deep, etching into the lines of my heart. She bends backwards, her arms reaching high above her and as the music guides her she glides across the floor, turning around one time after the next. She lifts her foot to her thigh and touches it there, then points it out; stretching her leg as far as it will go. She twirls in place then releases herself and leaps across the room, landing on one foot and lifting the other up behind her. The melody of her movements puts me in a trance, as I continue to watch her, with my hectic painting as the backdrop behind her, the music plays on and on. Minutes pass and finally I can take it no more. I lean back further up against the wall and slide down to the ground; the tears begin to flow and then fall. I cry, I cry tears of heartbreak and hope, from the beauty and the sadness of it all.

Tuesday, March 30th 1966
Day Three – *The Second Chance*

I can feel something running down my back, but since it is doing so in such a light, lovely manner I don't open my eyes right away. I'm awake, but for the time being I just wish to absorb this feeling and enjoy the sensation. As it continues up and down, I realize that it is being caused by someone running their fingers along my spine, swirling circles and creating paths of perception with the softness of their ending digits.

"Mmm," I groan in a soothing moan. "That feels wonderful."

"You've always loved being touched," the voice says as the fingertips pull away. I open my eyes, and as the light floods into my pupils they focus and I take in the view before me: a beautiful woman with long chestnut colored hair, blue eyes and sensual skin. She has a seductive smile on her face, she doesn't grin and show her teeth, but rather her mouth is slanted up in one direction, which causes a stirring feeling inside of me.

"Good morning Ellie," I say.

"Good morning Priam," she counters back.

There are a million questions I want to ask already, first and foremost how are we here? The last thing I remember is the day before, this same day and how I watched her dance in my studio, how I lost control of my emotions and cried, how I gave up on my dreams and succumbed to the pressures of that reality. I think of this day and the way I lived it first, but my third day isn't the only chronicle running through my mind. No, I think of that second day too and how it ended. Ellie didn't even know me then, I had rushed to the city with my brother to make things right, to meet her, to get my life back on track in this second course of events. There were those words she had said, as I recall them and they echo in my ears now. 'Oh! It's you!' That's what she had exclaimed before it all had faded to black. Had she known me after all?

Its feels rather strange to have to think about two different lives I've lived and how they are different and yet how they are the same. This is the third time I have woken up in a reality like this one that has yet to be lived. Even at this moment when I am lying in bed with her I cannot grasp all of what has happened, and what still has yet to occur. It's hard to keep this all in order in my mind.

Waking up on these second chances with the original day ingrained within my consciousness as if was just the day before is a sensation I will probably never be able to handle fully. Chloe explained what would happen to me in that white abyss as best as she could, but I realize now there was only so much explaining she could really do. Thus, even though I know I will continue to think in such ways when I awake on my second days, I realize I have to stop thinking now, I have to start doing things instead. I begin by leaning forward and kissing the woman I love. When I pull away and look around the room I realize we are nowhere that I recognize. This isn't where we were before. In a way, these days give me the ability to apparate and time travel too. Somehow, my consciousness and my body went from watching her dance before me in my studio apartment in Brooklyn, to lying in bed with her in an apartment I've never seen.

"How are you feeling this morning? You look rather scared," she says, recognizing all of the confusion and uncertainty contained within my eyes.

"I feel fine, I'm happy that you are lying here next to me more than anything. I suppose I just have a lot on my mind."

"Oh. Like what?"

"I was just thinking about the time we first met," I begin. I need to know how that happened, since apparently it wasn't when I rushed to the city with Danny on that second night. When I had seen her then, even though it was only for a moment, I saw recognition in her eyes. We had to have met before, in this string of second chances. I must have met her in the days in between, while the so called autopilot was in control. Thus, I have no recollection of the encounter. I need to know how I met her and what happened when everything faded to black while I stood there on her stoop that night in New York with her before me and my brother behind.

"What do you remember about it the most?" I ask. I don't want to act like I don't recall things from my end of the spectrum; I just want to bring up the topic so we can discuss it and so that I can understand how it all happened. I need to know this not only for my own sanity, but so that this day can go forward.

"You mean besides the fact that you literally slammed into me and knocked me to the ground?"

"Wha-?" I start to ask but then stop myself. I suppose in some way I was there, but I have no recollection of this meeting whatsoever.

"Are you suffering from some kind of dementia?" She laughs as she gently pokes my ribcage. "Did you really drink that much last night? I mean, I know we were at the party for an awful long time, but I didn't realize you had reached this level. I suppose I can refresh your hung over mind about the time we first met."

Apparently I was always destined to drink heavily on the night of March 29th. Even though I don't feel hung over now, it doesn't hurt that Ellie thinks so. I suppose I can use this as my excuse, even though it's not a very good one. "I guess I just want to hear it from you, we've never really talked about it in such a way before."

"Well I don't know if that's necessarily true," she says. "But nevertheless, I suppose I can humor you."

"How kind of you," I say with a smile.

"I remember I was in a rush to get to my dance rehearsal, and I wasn't paying too much attention to where I was going. Apparently you weren't either because we slammed into each other on the corner of Park and 59th. We both fell to the ground from the force of the impact and then looked up to see what we had hit, only to find each other looking back."

"It was my fault I'm sure. I've always thought so," I say. I deem it necessary to feed off of what she says as if I remember it. Even though I don't, acting completely oblivious about the encounter will seem strange. Chloe never gave me any rules about how to find out about the things that occur between these second chances. I believe if I act like I remember nothing at all or tell anyone this isn't the way this day originally happened for me, it will result in some kind of black hole that will swallow us.

"Well, maybe it was kind of your fault; you were carrying an awful lot of things in your hands. That easel alone was rather cumbersome, but you know that I was to blame as well, I wasn't paying attention to where I was going, I was running late. In the end though I suppose I'm glad, otherwise none of this would have ever happened. I like to think it was fate," she says as she places her arm around my neck and pulls me closer.

"Do you think we were always meant to be?" I ask as I rub my hand across the back of her neck and down to her shoulder blades. "If we hadn't run into each other that day do you think we would have ever ended up together?"

"I'm not sure, how can anyone be? I like to think so. I like to think that you had decided to go paint in the park that day for a reason. I like to think that fate conspired with time and caused me to be late to my rehearsal. I believe everything happens for a reason really, the good, the bad, and everything in between. And for us, I suppose that reason was each other."

"I had some great luck that day, that's for damn sure."

"We both did."

"What made you decide not to go to your rehearsal?" I ask, putting myself out on a limb, for I really don't know that she skipped it, but I have a feeling that our encounter lasted longer than just a few moments.

"Well, when you got up off of the sidewalk and walked over to me and extended your hand, I just felt something when we touched, a feeling I had never experienced before. It was otherworldly. I don't know if it was love at first sight, but from the moment I met you on that day you were all I ever thought about."

"I'll never understand why I gained your affection."

"Oh Priam, stop it. I don't know why you always act like you aren't worthy of me. You're the best man I know."

"If you say so."

"From the moment you apologized wholeheartedly for running into me I couldn't look away from your face, I couldn't unlock my gaze. The way you spoke was as if there wasn't a single ounce of your being that believed the collision had been my fault, when in reality I like to believe it was equally our mistake and equally our good fortune."

"I'd say so. I was only ever in New York for a weekend at a time back then, before I moved here for good that is."

"And so you had told me then. You were leaving the following day, so we took advantage of our time and went to the park, the place where you had been heading all along. I decided to perform my dance for you, as I had skipped my rehearsal and you painted me doing so. We finished our original plans for the day, but in another way, and we did it together. We killed two birds with one stone, but in reality...we let them both live and then we let them fly away."

"I didn't want to say goodbye to you," I say to her then. I never wanted to say goodbye to you Ellie, I think. Never, ever did I desire to do so.

"But say goodbye we did at the end of the day and what a

197

beautiful day it was. As the sun began to set behind the trees in the park, after we had shared stories of our lives thus far and tales of our dreams, the day decided it was time to go. I had met you and you had met me. Priam Wood, the boy from Alden, Pennsylvania and Ellie Donahue, the girl from New York, New York. And honestly then, that's all I thought it would ever be."

"Why didn't we exchange phone numbers, addresses, anything? You never even told me your name. We never made plans to meet up when I moved back to the city. What were we thinking?" I ask, taking a note from the fact that my mother and brother had never heard of Ellie and from the surprise in her voice on that second day, I know now that when we had met this way, nothing else had been planned for the future, or so I tell myself, creating a confidence I know naught.

"I imagine we weren't really thinking, to be honest," she tells me. "I think we were too in awe of each other and too afraid to ask anything else. I would have given you all of that information and more if only you had asked. I guess I sort of thought you wouldn't ever really come back to the city anyways. I could tell you wanted to desperately, but people talk of moving to the city all of the time, less than half of them actually do it. I didn't want to give you my heart when I had no real way of knowing you would give me yours in return. Thus, we said our goodbyes that day. I thought I would never see you again."

"Of course, you did though."

"The next time I saw you is something I will never truly understand, but it may be the one thing I am most thankful for," she says as she stretches her legs out underneath the covers and entangles them in mine. I feel her silky smooth legs rub up against my coarse hairy ones. The touching of different textures tickles me and I laugh out loud.

When my lungs return to normal after I release the feeling of glee I ask: "You mean how I found you that night, or why I even came at all?"

"Both really. I suppose I understand why you came, I thought of you almost every day since when we met that summer, but I had no way of finding you, no way of ever knowing if I would see you again. Then, somehow late one night you were standing on my doorstep."

"Maybe it was a certain sort of fate, like when we met," I

suggest. "Then again, perhaps it was more than that. Maybe the fact that we both had done nothing but think of one another since we parted was what brought us back together. I've heard this theory that says that if two people are both thinking of one another enough, it isn't a chance encounter that reunites them, rather it's an unexplainable force that works through the cosmos that pulls them together like magnets in the sky."

"Possibly, or maybe we were always just destined to be together. Sometimes I think that we must have been in love in another life." At those words I can't help but to slightly convulse, my body jolts for a moment at the inscrutable illustration she has just created for us. If only she knew what she had just said really was true, for I do, I do.

"Do my words really affect you so?" She asks as her hand returns to the small of my back, tracing circles with her fingertips again, succumbing me to shivers. "I always believed since I was a little girl, that no matter what I did I would end up with the man I was supposed to, and that was you Priam, that was you."

"I'm the luckiest man in the world, that I ran into you that day in the summer and that I found you again that winter. Somehow, the universe dealt us the most perfect hand. We won."

"I'm just so happy that you did come that day and that you convinced your brother to help you find your way. I think you got scared when you finally saw me again. You were quiet for a while; Danny had to help explain why you had come. Of course, I already knew."

"And your mother wasn't all too pleased."

"Oh no she wasn't, but I made her keep the door open long enough so that we could make plans to meet up the following day."

"Danny and I slept in the car that night. It was pretty cold." I say, spurting out facts I'm not completely sure of, yet somehow I feel as if I have unknown intuitions of what occurred now that we are discussing the actual details.

"I appreciated you waiting for me. That next day came, we had lunch, exchanged our addresses and telephone numbers. We made plans to stay in touch until you and Danny both moved back to the city the following summer."

"And move back to the city we did. Everything worked itself out, I feel as if I had to barely do anything at all, somehow it all just clicked after I found you again. Danny started working with

Grandpa Wood at the agency and I still went to Parsons." I say, again spurting out sentiments that I feel are facts even though I am not sure of them, they flow off my tongue and drop down the air. "Maybe you and I really were predestined to end up together after all, perhaps it was only a matter of time before we came together, it very easily could have been planned from the beginning."

"Yes, and no," she says. "I think the universe may have guided us to one another, but I believe the connection of our souls is one of such that has the ability to take its own reins. Even if we had no help, we would have found one another eventually, I just know it."

I kiss her then, as passionately as I can, for now that I have the details that I sought, I no longer wish to think of how we met in this life or any other for that matter. I don't want to think about how we came together or how we fell apart. All I desire to do is encase this moment in my mind forever, to keep it as a memory that will never leave me. As our lips collide and I feel her hand grasp my back firmly I reach for her thigh and pull it towards me. We lose ourselves together, in that bed, in those minutes and seconds in between the reality which we have, and which we have yet to let go. The passion lingers above us and then takes hold. We make love in a sweet serene way, releasing all of the thoughts we have so that the only thing that exists any longer is each other. The moment of clarity extends and then takes control of all of our senses, creating a culture of undeniable fulfillment. As I hold her close everything fades and the world around us ceases to exist. For the time being, all that is real in this world is us and our love that seems so unbreakable. Unfortunately on the ends of my consciousness I know that isn't true, I know our love has been broken before, but I won't let that happen again, not this time. As the love we make continues on and on, those thoughts eventually grow faint and we slip into a tranquility of intelligibility. I have my Ellie once again, and she has me.

After it is over, we lay in bed for a while longer. The sun begins to make its presence known more and more as light starts to flood through the cracks in the blinds. Ellie gets out of bed and takes the sheet with her, wrapping it around her body so that she is covered in a long stretch of white fabric. This action leaves me on the bed alone, completely naked, but I don't really mind. I hear her rustling about in the kitchen and as the smell of bacon, eggs, and pancakes fill my nostrils, eventually I rise and walk over to the dresser, where I pull out a pair of green boxer briefs and slip them on.

When I move to close the drawer I notice a picture frame on top of the dresser. I pick it up and pull it towards me to have a better look. It is an image of Ellie and myself along with my mother, Danny and a woman I have never seen before. The unknown woman is in what appears to be a wedding dress, and the rest of us are in our finest as well, with both Danny and I in black tuxedos. Danny's hair is cut short again, like it always used to be, the shaggy locks and scruffy appearance he had sported on that second day are gone. From the greenery that is behind the five of us in the image it appears to be a beautiful summer day. I can't help but to be puzzled by the picture. Is Danny married in this life? Did my actions on those first two days change his life that much? As I stare into our five faces all I can see is happiness emanating forth from the image, yet I can't stop thinking about how the things I change on these days affect not only my life, but also the lives of everyone else I know.

"Priam! What are you doing in there?" Ellie calls out from the kitchen. "Come eat breakfast. You're going to need energy for all that you have to accomplish today!"

"I'll be right there," I yell back. I set the picture back in its place and walk out of the bedroom. When I exit the room I enter into a long hallway, I can see Ellie at the end of it in the kitchen finishing up our breakfast. Before I get to her though the hallway opens up on my right side to a huge room that looks not that unlike my old studio in Brooklyn. Instead of the massive canvas that I covered in colors, what I see are approximately fifteen easels holding different paintings.

I approach and see that among them is a cityscape of futuristic buildings floating on an island in the sky, and one that depicts two women swimming in an underwater bog, their faces screaming. Another shows a little boy sitting in a chair on the edge of a red rocked cliff, teetering on the precipice between the ground and the emptiness below. Finally, towards the back of the room I notice a painting showing a tree in the middle of a field, covered with a flock of ravens, which lies underneath an enormous orange moon and contains a woman resting below, leaning up against the trunk wearing a blue dress covered in white colored polka dots. As I'm surrounded by these paintings, pieces I know I have created, yet of which I previously knew nothing, I start to feel like this is all just a dream, that there is no way this is real and that I can't actually have been given a second chance at anything. Do these days I have really even matter? Are the people I have loved in my life really still here with me now? Are they actually conscious of these second days, these second ways in which I make things right? Is anything worth it at all? Somehow I know that I won't find out the answer to these questions on this day, or probably for some time to come. I have to just keep going, no matter how much doubt tries to seep into my soul. I have to move on.

I hear quiet footsteps behind me getting closer and then she is standing at my side, still draped in the white sheet she took from the bed. "They're all wonderful you know. Tonight's show is going to be perfect. You're on your way to greatness. In my eyes, you have already achieved it."

"They all are like dreams to me, as if when I painted them I wasn't even aware of what I was creating," I say to her and as I do, I know the words I speak are true.

"Maybe that's why they are so mesmerizing. It's okay if you're afraid for tonight. I know you have a lot to decide today. Regardless what you choose, I know every little thing is gonna be okay."

"What I choose?" I ask, puzzled. She walks back out of the room of paintings so I decide to follow her into the kitchen where the breakfast she has made is waiting. We sit down at the table and I begin to eat, suddenly aware of my ravenous hunger.

"Whether or not you are going to take the job at your grandfather's agency of course," she says and then takes a bite of bacon; the crunch of the strip seems amplified in my ears as she chews it through.

"Oh yes, yes of course," I counter back. Even though my mother still lives, and Danny and I are the kind of brothers we used to be, one thing about this day still remains the same: I have to choose between a career for stability, a choice of security, or the art form which allows me to live my own way on my own terms. Although the revolutions and reservations that are caused and collected may change, the axis of every earth still remains the same. I realize that my original days and these second ways will always have a way to counter and balance themselves out, for if they don't, how would there be any symmetry?

"Are you going to tell him today after all? I know you said you were going to, but you know honey...its okay if you wait a little bit longer. He understands how busy you are with how hard you've been preparing for your show tonight. I'm sure he wouldn't mind you taking your time."

I drink a sip of coffee and as the hot liquid fills my mouth and then falls down my throat it warms up the core of me. I know that the reason I came to change this day has presented this challenge before me on purpose and thus I am not going to dilly or dally. I will accept it head on and put it in the ground once and for all.

"I've decided Ellie. I'm not going to take the job. Sure, maybe I could be happy there working with Grandpa and Danny, but I could never truly feel fulfilled if I had to limit my vision. As we just stood in that room with all of my paintings around me I felt a feeling of nostalgia and hopeful yearning. Painting makes me feel alive and when I think of the life I wish to lead, a life of me and you, the only other thing I see besides us two is a paintbrush and a canvas with the world before our eyes, begging to be explored."

She reaches across the table and takes my hand, the sheet falls lower so that more of her flesh is exposed. "I agree with your decision wholeheartedly. I knew this is what you would choose all along and I think it's right. You've never been the kind of man to give up on your dreams and for that, more than anything, I not only love you, but I admire you too."

Her words mean so much, but as the joy I gain from them reaches me, another part of how this happened before plays out in my mind. Once I didn't follow my dreams, once I gave up, once I let go, once I did what I thought was right, even though it was wrong. And in so many ways, it was the beginning of my undoing. In my life, letting go of my art and taking the job at the agency changed who I was. The freedom I had always held inside started to disappear, over the months and memories that formed next and the ones that didn't.

"I hope it's for the best," I say and as I look down at her hand which still does not have an engagement ring on it, I decide to add one more thing. "We'll get married soon too; I promise you that Ellie, we will."

"I've waited this long, don't worry, I'm not going anywhere," she says as her hand leaves mine, slowly and wistfully pulling away.

We finish our breakfast and talk of the show tonight. Apparently over a hundred people are expected to attend. It's in downtown Manhattan in a courtyard pavilion. Some of my work will be displayed in the gallery while other pieces will be located outside in the patio area that opens out into a small park with the city stretching beyond. I work delicately and quickly to get the facts out of her without ever making it seem like I don't already know the details. It isn't easy to do so, but somehow I manage the feat. When I have the information I need, I get up to wash the dishes. Ellie returns to the bedroom to change, as she has to leave to go into the theater for her daily workout and rehearsal. When she comes back out into the foyer by the front door I kiss her goodbye.

"I'll see you tonight love. Enjoy lunch with your mother," she coos into my ear. She fleets away from me quickly and exits the apartment, slamming the door shut behind her. I return to the kitchen and call the number for the Wood Advertising Agency. When the receptionist answers I am relieved that the number is still the same. As I'm learning, some things never change. I tell my grandfather that I am very sorry but that I cannot take the job, that I have to keep striving on with my art, for it is the one true passion of my life. He sounds disappointed, but he also claims to understand my reasoning. He wishes me all the best and tells me he will see me tonight at the show before he bids me adieu. When I set the phone down on the hook, I notice a pad of paper beside it. Scrolled on the front page is a note that says *Mother's Hotel: Hilton East, Number:* 986-8800. I thank my good luck, realizing now that I have no idea of when I am supposed to meet up with my mother or where. I dial the number, ask for Mrs. Moira Wood and then after a minute or so I am delighted by the sound of her voice.

"Hello?"

"Hi Mother, it's Priam. How are you?"

"Oh splendid dear. Are you still going to have time for lunch this afternoon?"

"Absolutely. I just wanted to call to change our plans if that's alright," I say, realizing that the best way to meet up with her is to not ask about the plans we've already made which I know nothing of, but instead to make plans of my own for the two of us, on this day. "How about we go to Botecilli's at half past noon? You remember where that is right? On 52nd and Lexington? It's not too far from your hotel."

"That sounds wonderful. I remember going there with your grandparents when you and your brother were little."

"Precisely. I thought it'd be nice to return to a memory we've already made before."

"Perfection," she says with a hint of glee in her voice. "I'll see you soon then dear. Goodbye."

"Goodbye Mother." I say and then hang up the phone.

I know that seeing my mother again will be an interesting experience, one which will probably unground me just as it did before. Seeing her at an age she never lived previously, in a time of my life where she was never able to be is both thrilling and unnerving, thus, the reasoning for having it located in a place we both have been before.

The days go on and on and even though they often collide they never really get to meet one another, except for that ephemeral instant. Instead, they move one from the next, as separate compartments of antiquities. They start the same and end that way too, but none of them can ever be identical. Every day we live is a poem all its own, it cannot be replicated or reduced; each day is a mystery which can never be deceived, never completely delivered.

When I am standing across the street from where we agreed to meet, I see my mother sitting at a table outside. It's technically been a little over six years since I've last seen her, but to me it feels as if it has only been two days. When I cross the avenue and walk towards her she sees me heading her way and gets up to greet me. It's then that her features come into focus. Her hair is even shorter than it was when I saw her last. She looks older too, but the years have been kind to her beauty, keeping it restored in a simple and elegant manner. I quickly try to calculate in my mind how old she is today, but the numbers don't click before she embraces me.

"So good to see you Priam! I've missed you dear."

"You have no idea how good it is to see you too. I'm always missing you when you're gone," I say to her. I've missed her for a lifetime, these new memories I am able to make with her are the kind of fantasies I had only ever previously dreamed of. I used to always think about what I would say to her if I ever saw her again, but now I don't think of that, all I can ponder is just how glad it makes me to be with her for a time anew. We separate and sit down at the table. It's not exceptionally warm, but for a spring day it could be classified as fair. The sun is shining and I am glad to be sitting outside, taking in the sights of the people passing on the sidewalk and the hustle and bustle of the city. However, in a way all of that fades to the background, as all I am able to concentrate on is my mother before me.

"So how are you? How is everything back home in Alden?" I ask.

"It's as peaceful and as nice as can be. I keep busy at the theater working on various productions. It's great to interact with the young students, some of them remind me of myself you know. And of course the girls and I often get together. Just two days ago I was playing bridge at Susan's. They were so impressed with the fact that you are having your own show this evening in the city. Everyone is proud of you and your brother. I'm lucky to have such wonderful sons."

"We're lucky to have you."

"That's sweet of you to say. I only wish your father was here to see your success. I know he would be so proud of you. People always say that the pain of missing someone gets better with time, but I've never really believed that. When you love someone so utterly and completely the aching you feel inside when they're gone never goes away. Maybe it lessens in some extent, but for me it's never faltered, the only way I was able to move on was because I still feel his presence, in both of you."

"Awe, Mother..."

"Oh don't feel pity for me. I'm content with my life I swear. I know I'll see him again, after I leave this world, I know I will and when that moment comes, our love will still be as strong as the first day we met in front of that painting."

"If you could have told yourself then, at that gallery, that the man you had just met would be your husband, the father of your children, and that the two of you would have a son who himself would become an artist, would you? Do you think you would have been able to believe it at that moment, both the magnificence and the irony of it all?"

"Hmm. Yes, I think I would. I knew from the moment that I met your father that he was going to mean something to me; I suppose I just didn't know how much. Maybe the fact that we met in front of a painting somehow passed through our bones and into you. I sometimes think the universe has its own special method of working things out in whimsical ways like that."

"It's an interesting idea to consider," I tell her, and as I do I think of how the universe has dealt with me and these seven days I'm currently meandering through. There has to be some order to it, even if at most times everything seems so haphazardly placed.

"Everything happens for a reason. I like to think that even the bad things somehow end up leading to good."

"It'd be nice if that were true."

The waiter comes over and takes our order and shortly thereafter he brings us our food. We enjoy our meal and discuss more about Alden and my life in the city. I tell her that I had decided not to take the job at Grandpa's agency and she supports my decision, just as Ellie had. We talk about my gallery opening some more and I can tell that she is very excited to see it. Although I'd love to discuss the things I already know about, I have to start asking questions about the things I still don't understand. When our meal is finished and all of the plates are cleared away so that the only thing left on the table is the slight reflection of the sunlight bouncing off of our water glasses, I decide to start with the hardest questions first.

"Do you remember the first time I ever told you about Ellie?"

"You mean the day you asked me to drive the Victoria to see your brother and then all the way here? How could I forget?"

"I suppose that did seem rather odd," I say to her. "I guess all of my emotions had been boiling up for a while and on that day they spilled over. I often wonder why I never told you about her before then. We've never had secrets and if I loved her then as much as I do now, I still don't know why I kept it to myself."

"Well, the two of you had only shared one day together, and no matter how wonderful that day was neither of you had any idea that you would see each other again. Then again, the deepest of love doesn't have to be the longest you know. So I don't think that was it."

"I don't get it. In any other situation I still feel that I would have told you. Even if Ellie and I had only seen each other for a day, why do you think I didn't tell you?"

"You were a seventeen year old boy, in love for the first time with a girl from the city who came into your life in a flash and then disappeared just as quickly. If you and your brother had been closer then I imagine you would have told him. I never really thought much about you keeping it from me. Perhaps you were unsure of how I would respond to the strong urging desire you felt for this girl you barely knew. Maybe you thought I wouldn't understand and for that I don't blame you."

When I met Ellie in my life, we not only had one day together, but an entire summer. Danny and I were still close then and the Henderson's heard all about her too, but I never had the kind of relationship with any of them that I did with my mother. I realize now that she is right. The reason I didn't tell her was because I would have been too afraid that what I thought was love, or lust, or some kind of fanciful fascination wouldn't have seemed as important in her eyes. Sure, it is unlikely she would have dismissed my feelings as unworthy, but the autopilot version of myself that lived those days in between didn't know that. So in a way, I guess I do understand, because if it were me, I suppose I would have done the same.

"You did understand though, when I finally told you about her I must have sounded crazy. Yet you still let me go, you let me go see Danny and drag him along with me. Why?"

"Because I believed what you said. You explained to me how much this girl meant to you. What kind of Mother would I be if I stood between you and your happiness? And besides, it clearly all worked out for the best. If I hadn't let you leave the house that day, who knows if you and your brother would have made up, who knows if you and Ellie would have ever found one another again. Everything happens for a reason Priam, even if it seems simply mad at the time."

"You've lived longer than I to know." She smiles at me then, and when I think about what I have just said I wonder if it is really true. She's sitting before me now in her early fifties even though during my life she never even made it to forty. Yet here and now on this day all of those facts have changed. It makes no sense and it most certainly appears to contain a million notions of madness. Then again, perhaps it's supposed to seem simply mad, maybe the universe has a way of balancing itself out without us ever truly understanding it.

"That I have," she tells me. "And that reminds me, I brought something that I want you to have." She reaches down to her purse, which is sitting on the ground next to her chair. She pulls out a small jewelry box and slides it across the table to where my hand grasps it. I slowly open the dark blue felt box and am astounded to see what is inside.

"But this- you can't-" I begin to stutter.

"I can, and I want to. I want you to have it. I want her to have it."

Inside the box is the engagement ring that my father had given to my mother decades ago. I'd recognize it anywhere. I remember being amazed by the size of the diamond when I was a little boy, often asking my mother if I could touch it. She always allowed me to and as my finger glazed over the surface I'd dream of a day when I was rich enough to purchase such an extravagant thing. From what I know about the ring, my father had spent nearly all of his money on it, and then borrowed some from his father too, which he was still paying back in increments until the day he died, or so I had been told.

"It's your ring though. Don't you want to keep it? It's one of the most special things that Father ever gave you. Really Mother, this is far too generous," I say to her, trying to make her reconsider and take it back.

"It will be even more special to me if you finally propose to that girl with it. That is what will make me happy. She deserves the best, just as your father thought I did."

"Of course you deserved it. You deserve everything and more. Thank you. Ellie will be amazed." I get up from my seat and give her a hug and a kiss on the cheek. I return to my seat and am about to suggest that we leave and then I remember the other question I had been meaning to ask her. I realize I can find out the answer without having to ask it directly, the perfect opportunity to cover up the fact that I don't know about it.

"Why didn't you give this to Danny? Don't you think he would have wanted to give it to his wife?"

"Oh, I thought about it. But you know how quickly Daniel and Rebecca got married. There was barely even any time for me to get to know the girl before she became my daughter in law. Not to say that she isn't a lovely girl, because as you know of course she is, but it just didn't feel right. Besides, in a way, you and Ellie remind me of your father and I. It just felt right to give it to you."

Danny's wife is named Rebecca, and they got married quickly. I think it over and over again so I don't forget, seeing as I will probably be seeing the two of them tonight. Although her name and the knowledge that they got married fast isn't much to work with, at least it's something. I've made progress on patching this puzzle of days and second ways together as best as I can, at least for the time being.

"Well that has to be the greatest compliment you could give the two of us," I say. "If the two of us amount even near to the wonderful relationship you two had, I know I will be a happy man."

"You will, and my guess is, you'll surpass us."

"No one could ever pass the two of you."

"I guess we'll have to wait and see," she says with a wink.

I take a deep breath and take it all in, the day thus far, my afternoon with her, and all that has yet to come. Although it was only lunch, I feel this meal with my mother has changed things for the better. With what I've learned from her, and what she has given me, I've decided to do something tonight that I hadn't originally thought of, or planned. When I do so, I know it will change the continuation of these second chances even further and hopefully as I believe, make them even better.

"I should probably start preparing for tonight. I still have a lot to do. How about we get out of here?" I ask her as I stand up from my seat and extend my hand to help her up.

"Sounds good to me dear, I'm sure you have a lot to prepare. Thanks for making the time to see me before your show. I know how busy you are."

"Never too busy for you," I tell her. I missed a lifetime of moments and memories with my mother, every second I get to spend with her now is a blessing I never thought I'd experience. Even when you're a dead man, like me, you can never give up; you can never stop trying, because who knows, maybe everything is happening for a reason. Even though the situation you are currently undergoing can seem like utter madness, perhaps it's going in such a way because it's all going to lead to a second chance.

After I leave my mother I realize I actually don't have that much to do to prepare for this evening. Most of the artwork is already at the gallery, so I only have to take a few canvases in. I know this only because when I return to my apartment I find a map drawn out of a floor plan of what the gallery is going to entail. I see the titles of the paintings listed that are going to be shown, complete with descriptions, and from what I can surmise, I see that only three more have to be taken in. I wonder how I am going to get them there. I suppose I could take them on the subway but that would be a pain in the ass, and I don't feel like paying for a taxi from Brooklyn to downtown. I'm about out of options and ideas when I hear my buzzer begin to ring. I push the intercom and ask "Who is it?"

"It's me," I hear Danny's voice say. "Are the rest of those paintings for this gallery of yours ready? The damn thing starts tonight doesn't it?" He laughs, his last question clearly a rhetorical one. I buzz him in.

This must have been the plan all along. Lucky for me that the details of this day seem to be filling themselves out as I string myself by the side of everything blindly. This day is far more complicated than the first two, as there are more singular elements that I am not aware of. When Danny enters my apartment he looks very much like he had yesterday, or should I say this same day, the first way. I am glad to see that his hair is cut short again, and not the shaggy mess it was on that second day. He looks happier than I ever remember him being.

"How ya doing today kiddo? Ready for the big show?"

"I'm as ready as I'll ever be I suppose. I'm just happy all of the people I love the most in this world are going to be there. I'm happy you guys believe in me."

"Of course we believe in you. You're one talented guy."

We take the paintings down to his car which is parked on the street right in front of my apartment building. Shortly we are on our way downtown, driving across the Brooklyn Bridge. As we do so images of the conversation we once had on the pedestrian overpass above fill my head. I think of how Danny didn't believe in me then, I think of how he convinced me to give up on my dream, to stop painting for myself, to succumb to the pressures of everything around me, to let go.

I look across to the man who is sitting beside me now, grinning from ear to ear for seemingly no reason at all. I think about how good this all is, how wonderful it makes me feel to be able to wake up next to the woman I love, to have lunch with my gracious mother and to be riding in an automobile across one of the greatest bridges in the world with my brother, my best friend. I don't know what I did to deserve a second chance at anything, but one thing I do know is that I've never felt so complete. Happiness can exist in all terms of reality, but it's so much better when I am able to share it with the people I love.

The view of the city stretches from my peripheries and slams together in the middle, forming the front of what I can see to create a marvelous picture of poetry made of steel and glass. I wonder about the little parts that came together to make all that New York City is constructed from and I decide that every one of them is just as important, each functioning to complete an assembly of the adventure.

"How did you know that Rebecca was the one for you?" I ask my brother, wishing to know more about how his marriage came about and why he felt the timing to ask her was right.

"Because one morning I woke up next to her, and I couldn't imagine not ever doing so. When you love someone that much, you just know. I'm not sure if I can really explain it."

"But why did you ask her to marry you so quickly? Weren't you afraid you might have been going too fast? You never thought you were rushing it?"

"No. I felt her heart connect with mine in a way that I had never experienced before. And on the day that I asked her to marry me, I felt as if it was the way it was always supposed to happen. I felt as if there were so many signs around me telling me what I had chosen was right."

"Like what?" I ask.

"Little things. I called her favorite restaurant to try to make reservations, and even though I was certain they'd probably be booked, they had a cancellation that day so they could fit us in. A street performer was singing our favorite song on our way there. While we were in the restaurant, it poured down rain, but when we were finished eating it stopped and was beautiful again. When we stepped outside, Rebecca mentioned how venturing out after a storm made her feel happy, like everything was clean again. And I realized then, that was one of the first things I ever remembered her telling me before. The night unfolded before us in such a way that I knew I never wanted her to leave my side."

"That sounds so lovely," I tell him.

"It was Priam. I'm a lucky man."

"Do you think I can make Ellie happy?"

He looks at me then as if I'm crazy, as if I've just asked the stupidest question I could possibly ask. "Are you kidding me? That girl adores you. I've seen the way she looks at you. I think you are the only man that could make her happy. I don't know what you're waiting for."

I glance out the window as the city that was previously ahead of us is now beginning to swallow us, surrounding us on all sides. I reach into my pocket where the box my mother gave me is resting. I roll it around back and forth between my fingers and feel the velvety softness on my palm, knowing what is inside, trying to decide whether or not I should do this. For the first time on this journey I am trying to plan ahead, I am not thinking of how to fix this day as I suppose I already have done what I came to here to do. I'm not going to be working for Haversmith Inc. or any ad agency for that matter. I am not going to take the job that will ruin my life, my marriage, my love. No, that much has already come and gone. On my first and second day I was fighting for what I had come to fix until the very last second and then some. This third day is different, this day has let me fix what I came to quickly, it's given me extra time, to plan for the future of this experience, to change even more down the line.

"Neither do I Danny, neither do I," I say to him as we become immersed within the sights and sounds of Manhattan. "Today might be a day I decide to do something different, to follow my heart and only my heart, to let the music and the melody sway me, to let go and let love in, completely in. I think today I can do that. I think she deserves that. She deserves all of the happiness in this life that I could never give her before; she deserves all of it and more."

"That she does, Priam. And you know what; I think she'll get it. Your paintings alone are enough to make any girl proud. It's going to be a beautiful evening."

The wheels of his car roll us into the throws of downtown and then lead us to the gallery. When we get there, I take a look at the space and admire all of the pieces that are already there, both those inside and the ones in the courtyard near the park. I put everything else in its place, so that every last painting is hung. When I'm finished, I know that my choice is made. Every sight has to be seen, all chances have to be taken, no song can be left unsung, let this evening come.

Far more people attend my showing at the gallery than I imagined. Professors I had during my time at Parson's, fellow artists and friends I had met over the years, even Mr. Williams, my high school art teacher made the journey all the way from Alden. Of course my grandparents are in attendance, as well as the Hendersons, my mother and Danny too, with Rebecca at his side. Then there is Ellie, she might as well be called the gallery VIP from the way that she fleets from one group of people to another, chatting them up, making them laugh and smile in the most endearing way that she can before she moves on to the next. I mostly just watch the night unfold before me, sure I talk to people and accept a great deal of compliments about my work with gratitude, but I try my best to be a fly on the wall, or rather to hang up against the white as if I am a painted canvas myself. I walk back and forth around the inside part of the gallery, and when it all seems too overwhelming I venture outside to the courtyard where more of my paintings are located. I feel the show is successful, by the amount of people who come and from how much everyone seems to like my work. Perhaps I really could live my life as an artist, existing solely to create, or at least during these days that is how I could be I tell myself.

Andy Warhol shows up as the evening is winding down, exclaims to everyone that my work is brilliant, gives me a pat on the back and leaves just as quickly as he has come. I suppose that is the cherry on the top of the cake, but to me it feels more like the filling.

The night begins to head towards that moment where I am in control no more, when the clock strikes midnight and my Cinderella curse takes hold. I know I don't have much time left in this day to accomplish more. I have to act swiftly in order to enjoy these last few hours with those that are here, those that I love. I see Ellie standing over by a group of her dancer friends and walk over to them and wrap my arms around her waist. "Would you ladies and gentlemen mind if I steal this lovely lady from you for a few moments?" I ask. They tell me of course, go ahead, to take her. So that is what I do. Our hands interlace and we walk over and stand in front of a large painting of a woman in a red dress who is dancing in the savannah, with two enormous male lions running towards her on either side.

"So...what do you think?"

"It's great! Don't you think so? I can't imagine your show going any better Priam."

"Yes, I think it went pretty well. I suppose I could have tried to be friendlier and talk to more of those who came, but you kind of did that for me," I say with a smile.

"Oh you know me," she begins. "Always moving about any room you put me in to make the people happy. My mother always used to tell me to be kind to the people around me and to smile as much as I could so many people would love me. I suppose to this day I follow her advice so I don't end up alone on my dying bed, whenever that day may come."

"My mother told me something similar once," I say. "But that'll never happen Ellie, you'll never be alone, not if I have anything to do about it. Besides, although I think our mothers' advice may have helped us, I know people would have fallen in love with you regardless, just as I have."

"Awe, that's sweet of you to say dear," she tells me as she slightly blushes.

"It's true though. I don't know if I say it enough, but I love you with every ounce of my being," I tell her as I grab her hand and lift it towards my chest and place it over my heart. "You are everything I have ever wanted; you are everything I will ever need. I've loved you from the moment I first saw you, and I will love you until I exist no more. I've loved you in this life and I will love you in every life I can ever possibly exist in. Things have been a mess at times, believe me I often have felt lost, but the one thing that always brought me home has been my love for you. Ellie Donahue, you are the one constant in my life, the love, the woman, that I can always depend on. In my eyes you are perfect, you are so elegant and beautiful and kind. That's why," I say as I pull the box out of my pocket and bend down on one knee, "I want to spend the rest of my life with you. I want you to be my wife. I want us to be together, in this life and all of the lives that follow. Ellie, my love, my everything, will you marry me?" I ask as I open the box, so that she has a view of the ring inside.

I see a tear swell up in the corner of her eye and slowly slide down her cheek, her face looks like porcelain, so still and serene. Suddenly though that tranquility disappears and she breaks into the biggest smile she could possibly muster. "Yes!" she shouts, "Yes! Yes! Of course I will marry you Priam! I love you, I love you, I love you," she says over and over again as I lift the ring out of the box and push it on her finger. I get up from my bended knee and embrace her. She jumps on me and as we hug I twirl us around in a circle, making everything in the background behind and around us swirl together. For that moment in time, it is just her and I. When I set her feet back down on the ground and we kiss, I hear people clapping in a round of applause. When our lips part and we look out at the people who still remain in the gallery we notice that all of their eyes are on us. I see my brother and his wife, and my mother too, as well as countless of other recognizable faces. A few shout out "Congratulations!" and even "Finally!" I take it all in, the only person I'm really thinking about is the one that is right beside me. I look to her and say "We just changed the rest of our lives! I hope you're ready for what comes next."

"I've been ready for quite a while Priam. I'm more than prepared to be your wife. I'm just so happy that you finally thought so too."

"It was time," I say as I look at her, imprinting this moment deep within my mind so that it becomes a memory forever. It all seems far too good to be true, I wish I could freeze today and keep it with me always, but I know that can never be, even in the current situation of how things are. I know that when this day ends, the fourth day I chose will come, a day I will have to relive again, before I am able to return to a second chance where I hold the reins. "It was time," I repeat.

We leave the spot in which we are standing and go out to mingle with the crowd where we are showered with more congratulations and well wishes. Many people ask to see Ellie's ring and are astounded by the size and grandeur of it. I go over to my mother and give her a hug and thank her again for everything.

"I'm so happy for the two of you," she says. "I wish you a life full of everything you've ever wanted and more."

"Thanks Mother. I couldn't have done it without you," and as my words reach her ears, I can tell she knows they're true.

Slowly as the minutes pass the crowd begins to grow thinner as more and more people leave the gallery and head home. I thank everyone for coming and walk outside to the courtyard, which I imagined would be completely dark, but it isn't because it is encased in artificial light from the spotlights hanging up overhead, flooding the spot with brightness. Before long, the only people left are my mother, brother, Rebecca, Ellie and myself. The five of us stand in a semi circle as the evening breeze blows past us.

"So do you know when you're going to have the wedding?" Danny asks.

"I think sometime next summer would be nice," Ellie says.

"Next summer it is then," I say, allowing Ellie's suggestion to be the answer to his question.

"We'll all be looking forward to it. I'm sure it will be a beautiful day," Rebecca says.

"Indeed it will," Mother adds, then pauses before continuing. "We should get going Priam. It was a fantastic evening, you should be very proud of yourself for all that you've accomplished," she says as she hugs me. "And of course I couldn't be happier for the two of you," she goes on as she hugs Ellie too. "You're going to make such a beautiful bride."

"Thank you Moira. I hope I can be as beautiful as you looked on your wedding day."

"You'll look better," she tells her.

We say our goodbyes to my family and watch them walk out of the courtyard to the street where Danny's car is parked. Ellie and I stand there arm in arm and wave to them as they drive away. As the air outside swirls around and envelops us in its control, I can't help but to feel as if every little thing is going to be okay; including the days that will follow this one. I began this journey as a man with a broken spirit and even though it hasn't been easy reliving those days which broke me in the first place, the reward of these second chances has given me reason to feel alive again. Life seems so much lovelier, so much more clear than it used to. I feel as if every color I see now is brighter, bolder, more richly tinted with stains of silver and gold that I never thought I'd know. In essence, I never thought I'd feel so happy again, in my life, or in any plane of existence at all.

After the moment of clarity passes and I refocus on where I am and what to do next, Ellie suggests that we take down the paintings that are on display in the courtyard and bring them inside the gallery so that nothing happens to them overnight. A few of the paintings are hung up rather high, so I go and ask one of the attendants if there is a ladder we can borrow. A young man brings a ladder out for us and we start to take the paintings down one by one. It doesn't take much time and after I have taken down all of the paintings but one, Ellie asks me if she can go up on the ladder this last time instead.

"Why on Earth do you want to climb up on a ladder in your dress and high heels?"

"Sometimes it's nice to be elevated above the Earth, to gain a different perspective on it all." She tells me. "And besides, I just remembered you have to go get a copy of the keys so we can come back tomorrow to pick up everything. Go get them, then meet me out here and we can head home for the night mister."

"Alrighty. I'll be right back." I say as I move the ladder beneath the last painting that is hung up higher than any of the other ones were. She starts to ascend and I tell her to be careful as I begin to walk back into the gallery to fetch the keys.

When I'm back inside I look around to find someone, anyone, but it seems as if everyone has disappeared. All I see are my paintings staring back at me. I look back out towards the way from which I came where I see Ellie going up to the very top of the ladder so she can grasp the painting and bring it down. I'm about to shout out to her, to tell her to be careful again, when suddenly I feel as if an invisible hand has grabbed me by the throat, closing my vocal chords so that I cannot say anything at all. I am reminded suddenly of that first day in October, when I was trapped in my thirteen year old body while trying to save my mother's life. This feels like when I wanted to tell her not to go, but I was unable to say anything at all. I wish to scream not only because Ellie is heedlessly teetering on the top of the ladder, but because of what is currently rushing right towards her from out of the park and towards the courtyard at full speed. It's her again, it has to be. This time though, she isn't alone. A black labrador is galloping through the greenery and heading straight for the ladder on which Ellie is carelessly perched, while the golden retriever that is present is chasing the black lab, forcing it to barrel full speed ahead.

Ellie is up so high on the ladder that I can't even see her now, her body is blocked by the building from which I remain within. All I can see are the dogs heading straight for the ladder where I know she remains on top. Finally the golden retriever abandons the chase, but the black lab keeps on going. I watch as the golden one changes its tracks and turns and goes in the other direction. I try to run to Ellie, but my legs are melting beneath me and I feel as if I am still unable to form any words as I try to yell out again. The only thing I am able to do is lift up my right hand and reach out aimlessly to try and save her as I become close enough that I am able to see her once more and in that moment she finally grasps the painting and pulls it off of its hook. I look back out into the distance where I see the black creature still galloping forward, but the golden one is gone completely, out of sight. As Ellie holds the canvas in her hands she lifts her right foot off of the ladder step and starts to move it down towards the one beneath, but it never lands there.

She looks to me and sees my arm outstretched, and just as our eyes meet, mine are filled with an utmost sense of urgency and fear as she notices nothing wrong at all. The only emotion I see resounding in her eyes is one of complete contentment. That's when the black lab slams into the bottom of the ladder. The force at which the dog was running doesn't make the ladder teeter; no, instead it knocks it down completely. I watch helplessly as Ellie falls, from fifteen feet up in the air. I try to extend my reach even further, to stretch my arms out to catch her, but it is no use. I am nowhere close enough to save her; I am not able to catch her when she falls.

She is pulled down through the air by the gravity that I wish didn't exist, her face turns away from me so that I can't see her gasp out in pain when her body slams into the hard concrete beneath. I can't see her face as her back breaks. I don't know what expression she makes as her leg fractures. I don't know, I can't see, I won't let this be. How can this be?

The sound of surprise she makes as she meets the ground lasts only for a moment and then fades. As the world unfreezes around me and I regain my legs I watch as the black lab quickly gets up and then runs away, back in the direction from which it came. I contemplate running after it and killing it, as well as the golden retriever who chased it, but then I remember that it might have been Chloe, or some incarnation of her anyways. Why does she keep showing up? I realize now that she's made an appearance on all three of my second chances. Just when I think things are going right and everything is going to be okay the being that sent me on this journey in the first place comes to throw a wrench in my plans. Why, oh why, oh why? It makes no sense at all.

I can't run after the dogs. Even though I wish to bludgeon

them both, to make them feel the pain they've created, I know I can't chase them. Somehow I know that even if I tried to find out if the dog really was Chloe, I would be unable to do so. By the time I reach where Ellie is lying, the black lab is merely a speck in the distance, searching for it's golden companion I'm sure. She is unconscious. I put my hands underneath her and pick her up. I scream. I yell for someone, anyone to come, to call an ambulance, to get help. The same young man who brought us the ladder runs out and sees the scene where Ellie is in my arms and puts two and two together. He sprints back towards the office and calls for an ambulance.

"Oh Ellie, oh Ellie," I say with melancholic breath. "Why did you have to go up so damn high?" I ask, even though I am pretty sure she can't hear me. I look down at her hand, the one with the engagement ring on it and as I look at it and then back to her face that looks so still, I can't help but think this is all my fault. It always is.

An ambulance comes shortly, and when we get to the hospital they have to take her away from me. I sit in the waiting room, tapping my feet on the tiles in a rhythm, trying to create any sort of order that will make me feel better, but no order out of the madness comes. Before long I stand up and start pacing back and forth, wondering what I could have done differently so that this wouldn't have happened. I never should have let her climb up that ladder; I never should have left her side. After what feels like a thousand years, the doctor finally comes back out to tell me how she is doing.

"How bad is it?" I ask.

"The good thing is that she's awake now. When she fell she hit her head and has a slight concussion. That will get better rather quickly though."

"That's great to hear," I say, relishing any good news that I can.

"Indeed. However, when she fell she dislocated her spinal cord and broke both thoracic and lumbar vertebrae. She also has a fracture in the fibula bone on her right leg."

"What does that mean? She's going to be okay right, doctor? She's going to be able to walk and dance again." I say, purposely not asking it as a question. She has to be able to walk; she has to be able to dance. For whom would Ellie be if she couldn't dance?

"With time and physical therapy I am confident the damage will heal itself and she will be able to walk again."

"Thank God," I say as I exhale heavily.

"Yes, she'll be able to walk with time. Unfortunately though Priam, I don't think she will ever be able to dance again." I hear the words, but they cannot be real, must not be real. I tell myself that this doctor doesn't know what he is talking about. He can't be right. I make a promise to myself then, there in that moment that I will do everything in my power to make sure that Ellie recovers from this accident and not just partially, but completely.

"Can I go see her now?" I ask, wanting to escape his presence and be with the woman I love, the woman I am going to marry, the one person in the world I need more than anything. It is clear she needs me now more than I need her.

"Yes, of course," he says and then leads me to her room. When I open the door and see her lying in that hospital bed all I can think about is how badly I don't want to be here, how I don't want either of us to be here. Just a short time ago everything was so perfect, my second chances were all falling into place and I thought it was all going to end up okay. How very wrong I was. I force a smile so that she knows I am trying my best to be strong for her. She tries to smile back, but it only lasts for about half of a second. I can't help but notice the clock that is on the wall behind her bed, it reads 11:55PM. I don't have much time. I sit down beside her and reach out to hold her hand.

"How are you feeling beautiful?"

"As good as I can I suppose."

"You're going to be okay the doctor said," I lie to her. I'm not sure what she knows, but I can't bear to tell her the full diagnosis, at least not now. Not in the final five minutes of this day.

"Did I just lose my balance? It felt as if something knocked the ladder out from underneath me, but I don't really remember what happened."

"It wasn't your fault Ellie. Dogs were running around the park, one was chasing another and it ended up slamming right into the ladder, tipping it over. You did nothing wrong. It was simply bad luck...horrible luck. You're going to be okay, that much I know," I say as I squeeze her hand lightly. "Listen though; I need to talk to you about something. You know that wedding of ours?"

"How could I forget?"

"Let's have it on May 4th of next year? Okay? How does that sound to you?"

"Why that day?" She asks with a quizzical look.

"Because I had a dream once that we got married and that was the day it happened on. In the dream I kept seeing the date all over the place and it was that one. May 4th 1967. It was everywhere I looked."

"Was it a beautiful day?"

"The best." I tell her.

In reality, I never had a dream like that. Sure I had dreamed of Ellie and I getting married before, but it hadn't occurred any time recently. No, the real reason I have proposed this date is because it is the next day I get to live, the next day I get to change. May 4th 1967 is the fourth day of this journey, which I had chosen back in that white abyss with the dog that seemingly caused her to end up here. For the first time I am planning ahead, so that after I relive the fourth day the original way, I will know what to expect when I wake up the following morning, my second way. I need to marry Ellie that day, I want to be there when it happens, really be there. I want to see her walk down that aisle, and I want to feel her embrace as we dance together as husband and wife for the first time, all over again.

"May 4th 1967," she says aloud. "It sounds like a good day."

"Promise me Ellie. Promise me we will get married that day," I say as I look back to the clock, the second hand five ticks away from reaching the twelve.

"I promise," she tells me. When I hear those words I lean down to kiss her. The last thing I feel is the wet coolness of her lips, and then once again, I turn into a pumpkin, the clock has struck midnight, I've lost control, this day is done, and I'm gone.

When I took the job at Haversmith Inc. I thought that it would mean a new beginning, a new way to live my life that would eventually lead to bigger and better things. In reality though, once I started working at the advertising agency I didn't have much of a life to live. While the position sounded good on paper and brought about many monetary benefits, it quickly began to overtake all of my time, so much so that I felt as if my days were actually being shortened by hours and hours.

Sure, I still got to be creative in my position as the advertising art director, but it was a different kind of creativity, one that I wasn't used to. Instead of making art that formed in my mind on its own, I had to create a certain kind that was necessary to please clients. Paintings of evergreen clouds and movable mountains flanked by the feasts of famine and desire, dancing through the streets of the sun no longer had a chance to grace down through my arms towards a paintbrush stroking along that white, white canvas. Instead, I was told what to make and because of this, a part of my spirit started to break. What I thought was right, what I told myself had to be right, felt so very wrong.

Out of all of the unexpected came one thing that wasn't though, a few weeks after starting my new job, I began searching all across the city of New York for the most perfect ring I could find. About three months after I started my position, I finally proposed to Ellie. When I thought about how I should ask her the one question she wanted to hear more than anything else in the world, I could only think of one place it could occur: in Central Park, at the spot where we had first laid eyes on one another, where our story, our journey began.

I waited for a beautiful day when the flowers were in bloom and the approach of summer was wafting through the air. The citizens of the city seemed happier, livelier and friendlier than they had during the previous cold and dreary months that had come before. I hadn't hinted to her that I was going to pop the question, but I think she somehow knew that day while we were on a stroll through the park that when she left it she would leave as my fiancé. I can't remember exactly what I said and I know it wasn't eloquent, but what I do know is that I loved her endlessly when I asked her to be my wife. The love I had for Ellie made every day I spent with her feel like a glorious lifetime. She said yes, of course she said yes, in the most ecstatic joyful way she could possibly say so. After I got up from my bended knee and slipped the ring on her finger we embraced and kissed passionately. We swayed back and forth in each other's arms, taking the moment in. During that time, the worries of my new career and the hopelessness I felt from letting go of my artistic dreams seemed to wane. The longing I had for the outdoors and for my freedom remained in that moment as the monotonous days in the office faded away.

If only the day that I asked Ellie to be my wife would have been the beginning of the upswing, the catalyst I needed to make everything right and to go forth and become the man I always wanted to be. I thought that's how it would be anyways, I imagined that as soon as she became my wife we would live happily ever after and I would somehow figure everything out and no longer have to worry about money or further means of fulfillment. We didn't know then as the sun shined down on us in a cacophony of randomness, fleeting back and forth between the clouds and the blue sky that held it, that we wouldn't be swaying back and forth joyfully for very long. In fact, less than a year after the day we became engaged, we would be engaged no more. Not only that...we wouldn't even be together. Ellie Donahue, the girl, the woman I had always loved would have had enough of me at that point; she would have suffered enough disappointment, and enough heartbreak to decide that she had to let me go. The idea of that notion alone always made me feel as if I was drowning in the coldest of melted snow.

We had a lovely summer in the city during that year of 1966. Well, as lovely as a summer could be when you yourself are locked up in an office and feel not so very free. When I left my job each day though, I always had her to look forward to; she could always brighten up my spirits even when they were made up only of the darkest of hues. We spent most of our nights together, but as time went on and I learned the ropes of the advertising agency I started to have to stay in the office later and later. Some nights I would come home and throw myself on my bed and pass out immediately, too exhausted to even see Ellie at all. Although we were engaged, we still lived in our separate apartments. We had agreed not to move in together until we were married. I guess it was slightly strange that we didn't live together just for the sake of being traditional, especially since we had made love so many times I had lost count ages ago, but our living quarters remained separate regardless. It was impossible for us to resist the lust and passion we had for one another, but it was indeed possible to live in separate dwellings made of stone and brick.

After our engagement I thought about calling Danny and telling him the news, but I never did. I hadn't seen him or spoken to him since that day on the Brooklyn Bridge. I thought he would have been happy to hear from me, to know that Ellie and I were finally going to get married, but I couldn't bring myself to talk to him. I loved him, I hated him, I felt so many feelings of every little thing that I could possibly feel for him. In the end, I decided that he didn't deserve to know, at least not then.

One particular day that autumn all of the pieces that were culminating to a head finally reached their tipping point and boiled over and flowed into a bog of branches, wetness, unfinished mazes and disaster. I had been working at Haversmith Inc. long enough that it felt like an undesirable normalcy and my engagement to Ellie had sunk in and become an unrequited reality. Thus, I lost control of myself, and of my mind.

I sat at my desk that day, staring out the window, peering at the skyline beyond that stretched on for what appeared to be forever. I imagined myself bursting through the glass, falling down immediately and then somehow gaining a certain sense of buoyancy that would allow me to float high above the streets and glide alongside the silvery buildings and their gray sisters. The ides of everything and nothing coalesced at once and I began to fade out, I tried to forget about it all for a moment and let it go. I didn't want to think about my parents who were long gone, the brother I couldn't talk to, or the woman I loved but whom I only disappointed anymore, even though I had finally given her the one thing she wanted most. I had missed two of her opening nights the past few months because of staying late at work to finish projects that I was behind on, and even though she had said she forgave me for it, I could see the heartache flamingly glint in her eyes for a moment and then extinguish itself in a bout of dissatisfaction. "I promise I won't miss another one of your opening nights Ellie. I promise that to you with all of my heart," I had said.

"You know how much it means to me to see you in the audience. If you aren't there, I feel as if the dance I am performing can't be complete. It can't be the best it can be, just like I can't be without you."

"Ellie, even if I'm nowhere near you when you're dancing, we all know how beautiful you can move, with or without my eyesight focused on you."

"Maybe so," she had said in a slight whisper as she ran her fingers down the middle of my arm making motions of back and forth s's that connected to each other and created a path to the end where my palm lay softly waiting. "But I don't ever feel at my best unless I'm with you, in whatever I do. You make me a better woman."

As I thought back to that conversation, I pulled my gaze from the window and what laid beyond it and brought my attention back to where I currently was, in a drab tan colored office, sitting at a wooden desk with nothing before me but two blank storyboards. I put my head down and rubbed my hands through my hair, trying to not focus on anything. I never stopped thinking though, I couldn't stop thinking of my life, all that had come before, all that was happening, and all that had yet to come. It was all spinning undone, coming apart at the seams and separating itself into a slovenly hysteria of hectic decay. My life was not what I wanted it to be. Whenever I tried to fix it, to take a chance, to make a change and strive for something better, it never seemed to work...at least not fully.

"Priam, are you okay in here?" A man's voice asked from a short distance away, so I lifted my head up immediately and turned to the hallway from which it came.

It was Mr. Haversmith, who was leisurely entering my office albeit at a rather hesitant pace, as if he was trying his best not to startle or disrupt me, even though I wasn't really doing anything.

"Oh I'm sorry sir. I was just thinking about a lot of things, and it got to me. I'm fine though. I'll be fine."

"I hope so. You're doing great work here you know."

"I'm trying my best."

"I know this job might not have been everything you wanted, but at least it's something. It's hard to achieve all of your dreams in a city like New York you know. It's difficult to be successful, especially when it seems like so many people around you are failing."

"I guess you're right." I said, trying not to sound as depressed as I currently was. Mr. Haversmith had a point though; I needed to stop feeling so sorry for myself. That wasn't the man I wanted to be. I needed to pull myself together.

"How's that fiancé of yours?"

"She's great. She's the one part of my life that never lets me down. Even when I mess up she's still always there for me. For some reason she sees the best in me, even when I don't see it myself."

"Well that's what love is, isn't it? Seeing your partner at their worst and still admiring them for their best. You two are gonna make it. You two will be okay. I believe in you Mr. Wood. Make sure you believe in yourself too," he said as he gave me a salute and left my office.

I was always the guy who was trying, striving, and aiming for everything in the sky and beyond. The blue bells hidden in the heavens above that no one ever knew were the things I desired the most. I wanted nothing more than to make a difference, to achieve something nobody else ever had before and to make each day count. That's what I had always told myself. Really though, I just needed something to believe in. As I looked back out my window and saw the sight of the city before me once again, I realized that the only thing I needed was love. Her blue eyes, soft chestnut hair and sweet smile floated through my mind. Ellie was the only prayer I needed in this place, or even on this planet in order to make it through, in order to be delivered from the beginning to the end and on. I realized at that moment, even though the day seemed slightly hopeless, that life was far too beautiful not to believe.

Following my conversation with Mr. Haversmith I felt much better at the state of current affairs my life was in. I became productive and accomplished a great deal of work that day, starting an entire new ad campaign from scratch and finishing it as well. As I labored along in a frenzy, I lost track of time and when the instant arrived when I realized how late it had become, everyone else in the office had already left for the day.

When I looked at my watch and saw where the two hands were resting my heart dropped down into the lowest chamber in my stomach. It was seven o'clock in the evening, far past the time I was originally planning on leaving. I hurriedly dropped what I was doing, grabbed the jumbled mess of papers strewn all over my desk and shoved them into my briefcase. I got up to leave, slamming my office door behind me and then I ran down the hallway to where the elevators were. I had told Ellie I would be home no later than six. She had wanted to make dinner for me at her place and then discuss some of the plans for our wedding. We had to go over the guest list one final time, decide on the florist and the photographer, as well as pick the location of where the actual wedding was going to be. Needless to say we had a lot to discuss.

I rushed to her place from my office in Manhattan across the river to Brooklyn. All I could think about was the fact that I had just added something else to our plate on what we needed to talk about: how I kept messing up, how I kept breaking my promises and disappointing her over and over again. I didn't know why it kept happening, it just did. It was as if I had lost control of being prepared for anything anymore. Once the moment where I walked through her front door occurred and then passed I knew that I was in trouble. The dining room table before me contained no one, nothing but the meal she had prepared that hadn't been touched, it had lost its warmth quite a while ago. I looked to the living room but she wasn't there either.

"Ellie?" I called out. "I'm here. I'm sorry I'm late. I got-"

"Caught up at the office again?" I heard her voice say as she slinked out from the kitchen and into my view. She looked stunning in a bright coral colored dress, her brown hair pulled back with a silvery diamond pin, her lips were painted a crimson red. In her hand she held a glass of white wine that she was swirling around within the tumbler.

"I- I-" I started to stutter. I didn't know what to say to her. I hated letting her down. I had to stop letting her down. In a way I was never quite sure who was more upset at those times, her or I. For even though it was my fault, I never did it on purpose. It just happened; I just couldn't pull myself together.

"It's okay Priam. You're busy. I know that. I suppose I just have to stop expecting so much. Maybe we shouldn't make plans in advance anymore," she said as she walked back into the kitchen, behind the green painted wall so that I couldn't see her any longer.

I set my briefcase down on the floor and followed after her. When I entered the kitchen her back was facing me, she was staring out the window that only had a view of another window of another apartment behind it. What a view, from out of one seeing station and back into another. I placed my hand on the small of her back and then wrapped my other arm around her waist. "Don't be ridiculous Ellie. We can still make plans. I just need to learn how to keep them. I have no excuse. I screwed up again, and for that I apologize. I'm not going to say it won't happen again, but I will try my best so that it doesn't."

She turned around and pulled my arm off of her. "Priam Wood, always the man who is trying. Try he might, but will he ever really succeed? I always thought you would, at everything, but recently I'm beginning to wonder."

Her words cut at me deep, and I felt a slash of pain run down the inside of my body as if someone was tearing me in two. This was a version of Ellie I used to rarely see, the side of her that wasn't happy with her own life or me. I hated seeing it and I always wished to never see it again whenever it came out. I wanted her to be delighted and pleasant all the time, but I knew that even the most beautifully ideal women in the world like my fiancé had their days of darkness, moments in time where they felt ugly and upset, corrugated by the disappointment the world had caused them.

"Don't say things like that Ellie. I know I'm not great, not by any means, but you know I would never do anything to hurt you. I'll make it up to you. I swear," I had said as I moved closer to her again and kissed her on the cheek.

"Alright dear. I hope so."

"Can we reheat the dinner you made? Or is it ruined?"

"I suppose we can try."

So that is what we did, the dinner was salvaged and it tasted almost just as good as it would have if I had arrived when I was supposed to. I ate the meal and thanked her for cooking it. I looked into her blue eyes, and for the first time in my life it was as if someone different was looking back at me. Of course, it was still Ellie, but instead of the naïve, joyful and enchanted eyes being there, what was in their place instead were two seeing pools of an unruly discontent, ones that were neither mad nor sad, just displeased. I knew then that she was beginning to feel as if things were starting to slide downwards and not in the upward direction which she had so longingly been searching for.

That day my dreams died, that day where I took the job at Haversmith and watched as she danced before me in front of my chaotic canvas of colors was supposed to be painful for a purpose. It was hypothetically in place so that things would become better, easier and more blissful. Instead, it was complicating our lives all the more. I didn't know if it was just that life got more and more intricate as it went on naturally regardless of what I did, or if I myself was the cause of the start of our destruction. I looked at her and I thought of how much I loved her, but as she looked back at me I realized I no longer had the guarantee of seeing Ellie as something to look forward to. Not because I didn't love her, and not because she didn't love me, but because things were starting to change. The honeymoon was already over even though our wedding day was still ahead of us. Life had grabbed a hold of our souls and shaken them for a stir. All I appeared to be doing anymore was disappointing her left and right and in between. I told myself at that dinner table as we talked about everything but ourselves, that it had to change. I had to make our love turn out all right.

When dinner ended we went into the bedroom and looked over the notes she had taken about the wedding decisions we needed to make. I couldn't focus much on the details. I didn't care what color the flowers were in what church that day, or who captured the pictures of us either. All I could think about then and from every moment of my life before and after that, really, was that I just wanted us to be happy. I didn't care if Ellie and I got married in a room full of daffodils or pansies. I didn't care if the ceremony took place in a church or on a pebble stoned beach on the coast. I didn't care if everyone I knew was there or if it was just the two of us. What I did care about though, more than anything in the world, was pleasing the woman I loved. As she went on and on in excitement about the preparations and the decisions that needed to be made, all I could think about as I took the silvery clip out of her hair and then ran my fingers through the softness of it was that I needed to do better. For not only did she deserve it, but I wanted it. Life had to improve.

"Priam, are you even paying attention to what I'm saying?"

I looked at her then, our faces were seven inches apart and I realized I couldn't lie to her. "How could I pay attention to the details of a day that is so far away when I have the most stunning woman, the one person I love more than anything else in the universe lying here right beside me?"

She tilted her head slightly to one side, and as she did so I saw that look of disorderly restlessness ease and then disappear completely from the blue seas of sapphire in her eyes. As it faded I watched the youthful, carefree fascination that had been there before return. She pushed the book of wedding options away and lifted her arms up and draped them around my neck. As we looked at one another, our eyes connecting in the way they were meant to, she said aloud "Somehow, that was the most perfect thing you could have said to me right now."

I smiled, and as my mouth closed I moved it towards hers and kissed her pleasantly. As our lips collided and our tongues began to intertwine our bodies did the same. All I could think about was that we were going to live again. Not that we weren't living then, but I wanted us to feel alive in a whole 'nother way. I desired a perfect place in the sky where time didn't matter and decisions about the future wouldn't care what we thought of them. All I ever wanted was for the love story of Priam Wood and Ellie Donahue to begin and end with a jolt of manic and magnificent movement, with all of the most vibrant velocity of a color cannon shooting vivid explosions of stars through the atmosphere above, beyond, and forever.

Thursday, May 4th 1967
Day Four – The Original Way

I wake up twisted among my white sheets that stretch around my legs and envelop me in their affection. I try to slowly break free and reach out across the bed to the woman beside me, but when I do so I realize there is no one there.

In the dream I was having Ellie and I were floating through a green field full of yellow flowers that sang sweet songs to us as we passed them. We touched each one with our fingertips and felt a sensation of sugary confection pass from the end of our digits up into our limbs and run through our bodies lifting us up above the meadow onto white feathery clouds of cotton in the lavender colored sky. We had been laughing and sharing the joy of the mystery of it all together. There was no questioning of how these impossible things could be happening, we did not seek to know the answers. Instead we simply were enjoying the moment for what it was: unexplainable absolute satisfaction. The recollection of the dream fades and I pull myself free from the colorless linens that have been surrounding me and I sit up, swinging to the side of the bed and putting my feet firmly on the hardwood floor. I remember that I am alone; Ellie hasn't fallen into unconsciousness in this bed beside me for over a week now. We used to sleep together almost every night, but recently those occurrences have been spreading themselves out fewer and further between. I haven't even seen her in four days. I've been so busy with work and she has had an eventful week preparing for her new ballet, which opens this evening.

I will see her tonight, I promised her that I would go to the opening of her show and there is nothing that is going to stop me from doing so. After I see her dance, after a night of celebration and revelry around the city of New York and the parties that will surely commence in the streets, Ellie and I will sleep together in this bed again. I tell myself that tonight we will both become entangled within these white sheets. I touch the softness of the fabric and it is as if I can feel each and every thread contained within. I lift my body up, putting all of my weight onto my feet, ready to face the day ahead of me.

I have to attend the show tonight and see her perform because I've missed her past few opening nights. Although I offered her my deepest regret for doing so, I don't believe she deemed it sufficient. On top of it all I have a major ad campaign presentation that I have to give to the CEO and the top board executives from a multimillion-dollar bubblegum company.

Double Bubble Smacks Gum is one of Haversmith Inc.'s most important clients and I have been working on the artwork for this ad presentation for months now. I think I have a great advertising campaign to show to the executives and to Mr. Haversmith himself, but one can never be too sure. Jason Brock worked with me on the design and structure of the ad as well, but in reality he kind of just threw his opinions out into the open air. I mean, I guess he did do some work, but every day when the clock struck five he would be out the door. I was the one who stayed late many nights; I was the one who poured my heart and soul into this process, trying my best so that I could impress Mr. Haversmith with the responsibility he had given me. I wanted to knock the socks off the people who ran Double Bubble Smacks Gum. I wanted their damn bubbles to burst and explode in the best way possible. If I am going to sacrifice so much time with the woman I love to slave away in my office at the top of a building in Manhattan that so often consumes me, I want it to be for a good reason. I want to succeed.

The thoughts of what I want to achieve and what I feel I can swim around my head as I step into the shower and soak my body with the warm waters that fall from the nozzle above. I stroke the soap across my skin until everything feels lathered and clean. I let the bubbles slide down my face as I scratch my head with both soothing shampoo and calming conditioner. I sing a song aloud to myself, not really knowing the words, only practicing the melody. When the residue of the suds fall away and I can't remember the tipping point of the tune any longer, I slowly slink down to the bottom of the shower and sit on the ground of it, letting the water overtake me, succumbing to the tranquility of its nothingness. I sit there for a while, trying not to discover anything new or let anything old make me its servant. I don't want the day to start, but in reality the day has already begun. With or without me time will go on, I could sit in this shower forever and let the water drown me in its constant stream. Nothing really ever waits, everything must go on, nothing is eternal, or so I have been told, but I like to think that some things last.

After a while I push my hands off of the tiled bottom of the shower and lift myself up. I move my head back and forth as the water cleanses my face and makes me even cleaner than I was before. I reach the cold steel handle and turn the water off gradually. It fades away and then all that is surrounding me is the air that feels the lightest part of all. I step out, dry myself off, throw the red towel on the floor and walk to my bedroom completely naked. I stop in front of the mirror and admire myself. Somehow, I am still in excellent shape even though I never work out. At six foot three, I'm normally the tallest one in the room; but of course there are always exceptions. My blonde hair is short now, gone are the days when it was long and shaggy, but its golden color still shows through. I walk over to my dresser, pull on a pair of underwear and then apply the pieces of my suit onto my body, as if each part is a portion of a painting that I am constructing onto the canvas of myself. The last touch is my burnt orange skinny tie that I wrap around my neck and fasten into a knot, straightening it out against my shirt so that it lays flat. I look into the mirror one last time and point both of my index fingers towards my reflection with my thumbs pointed up, as if I have two smoking guns in my hands. "Here we go Priam. You can do this," I say out loud to the person beyond the looking glass. I slide on a pair of my loafers at the door and then without a hitch I'm on my way, taking the city in as it surrounds itself around me.

All that is occurring now is the madness of Brooklyn and the rest of the city that lies further beyond which I'm sure is preparing to cloak me with its daggers, throwing danger, desire and fanciful delusions my way. For that's all New York City is and ever has been, a place where people come to fulfill their utmost longings, a place where dreams are born...and where they die.

When I enter my office Jason is there waiting for me, I'm quite surprised that he has actually beat me in today, as it is an occurrence that rarely ever happens. He's staring out my window to the city skyline beyond, I call out his name to alert him that I have arrived and as I do so, he turns around to greet me. Once the pleasantries are over with, we get right to business.

"How did the pamphlets turn out?" I ask, as these packets are the pieces of information that the clients and Mr. Haversmith will have directly at their disposal while we give the presentation later this afternoon. Jason motions towards my desk where I see a small stack of them sitting.

"See for yourself," he tells me. I go over to inspect them and am relieved to find that they turned out exactly as I hoped they would. The front cover and the pages included within are full of color and pizzazz, every image and slogan is bursting off of the page and will surely snatch the attention of whoever looks at them. I only hope that the CEO and the other board members of Double Bubble Smacks Gum are impressed. My heart is already beating faster just from the thought of it.

"They look great," I tell Jason. "Is there anything else we need to do to prepare for the meeting?" I ask him.

"Nope, everything is in place. All of our boards are already in the conference room. The only thing we have to do is pass out the pamphlets to everyone when we walk in, and of course then we have to nail the pitch. With all of the hard work you've put into this, I'm sure you'll do great Priam."

I find it comical that Jason acknowledges how much I have done by addressing all of the work I have put into this campaign, without really giving himself any credit. I appreciate the sentiment and although I do feel that I worked my ass off a lot harder than he did, he was still a good partner overall. I suppose I just find it hard to relate with people who don't give it their all, for I have always been the kind of person who has tried his best no matter the cost or the sacrifice.

"Thanks Jason, as will you," I say as I pat him firmly on the back.

"I'll see you at one o'clock then," he mutters as he slips out of the room.

"See you then," I respond. I glance at the clock on my desk and see that it is only a few minutes past nine in the morning. There's still a decent amount of time remaining before the meeting. I wish it would just get here and be over with. The anticipation that has been building up inside me over the past few weeks will finally be released and hopefully relinquished today.

I sit down at my desk and look at the picture of Ellie and me that is there. It is held in a golden frame that is etched with a design of tree limbs on either side, each holding a sparrow in the uppermost branches. The photograph is one from two summers ago; it was taken after one of her ballets. Her lips looked so red and full, her brown hair was pulled back and shining in the light of the flash. The emerald green leotard she wore was clinging to her body accentuating her perfect frame. Next to her I stood with my arm outstretched around her shoulders, I was wearing a dark velvet suit jacket and an unbuttoned white shirt. The image had caught me in the middle of a laugh from a joke the photographer had told and although I can't recall what exactly it was that he had said, I still can't help but to smile in a similar way every time I see this photograph. Although Ellie's teeth were not showing through, the sweet smile she held was one of an utmost serenity. We looked as if we belonged together, we appeared as happy as could be. I pull my eyes away from the image, even though it had been pulling me in. I try not to think of the times when things seemed both easier and harder. It was as if my life acted like it would never truly balance itself out. Although when that photo was taken Ellie and I were somewhat more stable and secure in our relationship and devotion for one another, I myself had been struggling because of my failing aspirations of an art career. I had the kind of love I wanted but not the means in which to secure the life I wanted for the two of us.

Then there is now, I have a great job where I am making a great deal of money, although it isn't the kind of thing I want to be doing specifically. I miss the freedom that my own schedule of paintings used to create for me, when I was still able to express myself in my own way. Sure, I hate the humdrum day to day repetition of office life and I long to explore the outdoor parks and streets of the city more like I used to do every day, but the view of the Manhattan skyline from my office with its shimmering glass and silver façades makes everything a little bit better. However, it seems as if this job is starting to kill the relationship Ellie and I once had. The instances we normally spend together have been cut in half in recent months and as time goes on and I gain more responsibilities at the agency it seems to be getting only worse. It has caused me to miss her shows, and I can't even begin to count how many nights I wasn't able to see her, unable to sleep next to her. We are engaged and for that I know she is happy, as am I, but it isn't enough, like we had both thought it would be. This job has brought about the security of a salary that I will be able to use to start our married life together, but I am beginning to wonder if it is worth the sacrifice of time with the woman I love. I know she is frustrated, and even though she has brought it up a few times, she never tries to press about the situation, even though I can see it seething inside of her.

She has to use all of her composure and self control from letting herself show how upset she truly is. Ellie knows I am giving up a lot for the two of us and that I am doing what I think is best, and because of that, she believes that eventually everything will work out the way we want it to.

With the job at Haversmith Inc, I will be able to secure the kind of life we both seek, but will I still have her love when it is all said and done? Only time will tell...and if it doesn't I will shake each and every clock I come across until the bells chime and the ticks and tocks team together to tell me a tale of how it is all going to end up. I will refuse any news except that of the best, that Ellie and I will have our happily ever after that I believe we both so thoroughly deserve. We have been through enough of the dull difficulties and complications that life has thrown our way. I just want us to be.

I flip through the pamphlets once more, turning the pages back over and over, reciting the points I wish to say aloud at the meeting again and again in my head. This pitch has to go over wonderfully, because if it doesn't, I don't know what I will do. I need this first part of the day to fall into place so the rest of it follows suit. I have to show Ellie tonight how much she means to me and that this job isn't ruining everything we had hoped to gain and achieve. As the sunlight shows itself in through my large office windows and encases the tan colored walls of my office in a warm glow, I close my eyes and feel the light on my face. I pray that it is a sign that all will turn out okay, that one link in my life will settle itself and then lead a path of preciseness on and forward. Tonight, I will see her dance and afterwards I will assure her that everything is going to be okay. Everything has to be okay, because if it isn't, I don't know what I will do.

I should have known better than to think that it would all work out the way I hoped it would. Nothing was ever easy for me, Priam Wood. As I sat there that day in the office, searching for something in the moments that passed me by, pleading with the universe to grant me a break, I tried my best to keep the notions of failure far from my mind. They were the last things I had wanted to think of. But oh, failure was coming right for me as I sat there motionless; I was a stationary pinprick in the middle of one of the biggest cities in the world. I was a stranger to the disaster that was about to occur and even though there were far larger travesties than what would occur to me on this day it seemed greater than all of the seas combined. I didn't know it then, but that Thursday, May 4th 1967, was about to become one of the worst days of my life. A day I would always think of with dread, a day I always wished to change, even though all along I was only doing what I thought was right.

When the meeting at one o'clock finally comes I feel like I am as prepared as I can possibly be. The ad campaign Jason and I have devised is a good one and thus, even though I am nervous for our presentation, I am confident that Mr. Haversmith and the executives of Double Bubble Smacks Gum will approve of all of the hard work we put into it.

I'm standing in the front of the conference room with Jason next to our poster boards; he's holding the pamphlets that we created. Mr. Haversmith and five other men all dressed in staunch gray suits file in one by one and as they do so my heart jumps. All of the time and energy I put into this campaign comes down to this. If they like what I have come up with, I will feel such relief and in some way I know it will make all of those nights I missed with Ellie worth it. I smile and nod to each of the men as they take their seats as Jason hands out the pamphlets to them. Only Mr. Haversmith actually looks at the material, the others are all just staring up at me, waiting for me to begin. I swallow and as the lump in my throat seems to metastasize and explode, I know it is time to start. Jason returns to his spot beside me and then we're off.

"When you hear the words 'Double Bubble Smacks Gum' what comes to mind for me is a product that is fun. I can still remember the days when I was a young kid, riding my bicycle in the sun and chewing on a piece of your gum. It's a mouthful of flavor and fruitiness and as all of the kids used to claim, it's the best kind of gum to have if you want to blow the biggest bubbles," I tell the men as I flip the first board over, exposing the first ad which depicts a close up of a young boy riding his bicycle down the street with his hands outstretched at his sides, blowing the biggest pink bubble you could ever possibly achieve. The colors of the advertisement are exaggerated, when I painted this piece I thought of vivid dreams of saturation that elicited a feeling of excitement. In the bottom corner of the ad the words of the company are written in a wavy, bold font, the letters strong and secure, yet still amusing and interesting to the eye. The second line of font reads 'Bring back the fun to gum!'

"What we tried to achieve with this ad campaign is to take

Double Bubble Smacks Gum back to its roots. The target audience for chewing gum these days is children and young adults. Priam and I created these ads to appeal not only to young people, but to the kid in everyone." Jason says to the audience as he turns over the remaining four boards. "The bright colors and the images we created are the kind that will remind you of some of your favorite childhood memories, when everything seemed so much easier, so much more fun."

The other four ads have a similar feeling to the first one. When painting the original pieces that we designed for this project I decided that I wanted each one to have one color featured the most prominently in each ad, but regardless of which color was chosen, the pink bubble was always going to be the highlight of the image. The boy on the bicycle is encased in the rich green of the trees, a girl on roller blades blurs past a blue sky, three teenagers sit in the park as the orange sunset encases their happy faces, a family of five swim in a purple lagoon and in the last piece a boy and girl lay in a field of yellow daisies. In each ad someone is blowing a ginormous pink bubble, with the name of the company placed in the bottom corner, as well as the slogan we had come up with.

"I want people to associate this product with the happiest times of their life, I want Double Bubble Smacks Gum to fall harmoniously alongside the idea of good times with the people you love the most. I want this ad campaign to make people go outdoors and enjoy all of the beauty around us, to take in the day and make it an adventure. I want them to chew your gum and to enjoy doing so," I tell the executive board. I try to read the expressions on their faces, but it as if they are the most expert poker players. I have no clue what any of them are thinking. Mr. Haversmith looks pleased, which helps slow my beating heart a little bit, but his approval alone won't be good enough. If the CEO and the other board members don't like what we have come up with, none of it will matter.

"If you look inside the pamphlets you were given, you will see these five ads as well as descriptions about the campaign and how it can go from here. We wanted to make Double Bubble Smacks Gum fun again, to bring it back to its roots when it was just a small company that made a delicious fruity candy for children," Jason explains.

"But kid's aren't the only ones who chew gum," a voice from the conference table calls out. The silence that follows his conclusion couldn't be cut even with the sharpest of knives. This is the first comment from the men who hold the outcome and fate of this project in the nooks and crannies of the cracks and corners of their hands. If they don't like it, if any of them feel like the advertisements we came up with aren't good enough, I will feel as if we failed.

"This is true," I tell him, trying to spin off of his negative comment. "But the way that we designed this campaign is so that everyone will be able to associate your product with a time when they were young, a time they felt more free."

"I just think the colors are all a bit too much, I like the idea, but not the execution. The images are good ones, but it's just as if they are too overworked. I'd prefer if they were more simplified, less chaos and more simplicity. I don't think Double Bubble Smacks Gum should be portrayed in such a carefree and fleeting manner as the one you have chosen," another man says. This is the CEO, Donald Grexa. I know so because I have seen him come out of meetings with Mr. Haversmith before. He appears to be over a hundred years old even though I know he isn't. The skin on his face sags on both sides in opposite directions in an unusual manner. He isn't ugly per se, but the characteristics of his appearance make it hard for me to look at him, and the words that he has just delivered make it even more difficult.

"The ads are supposed to be carefree though," Jason counters back. "We wanted the gum to be portrayed in a way that could be associated with no worries whatsoever."

"And I get that," Grexa continues, "but this isn't what I would have chosen personally. I think you two are off to a good start, but I think you still have a lot of work to do. I'd like a little less color, a little more diversity and a tad bit more serious atmosphere for the product to be placed in. With advertisements like these, no one over the age of ten is going to pay any attention and as we all know ten year olds don't have much money," he says and then chuckles, his rotten teeth shaking around within his mouth, the old skin on his face bouncing. After a few laughs are released and leap abound the otherwise silent room he coughs and then seems to choke on his own saliva. I want to strangle this man, this thousand year old crypt keeper. He might think he is right, but I find him to be so very wrong.

I don't know what to say. I don't know if I am capable of

saying anything. I want to slap his old face and bury him six feet under the ground. I feel as if the power he holds over my head has the airs of unrequired simplification and rightfully so. I hate being told what to do, what to think, how to be, how to see. I detest the notion that I am not fully in control of my life when it can be so easily affected by other people like this, people that really don't matter to me. I wish it were different, but when I took this job I gave up on the liberty of a career of nonchalant nothingness that was my everything. I let it go.

"Do you think you can reimagine what you've come up with to Mr. Grexa's terms?" Mr. Haversmith asks me.

"I suppose we can try our best. After all, the most important thing is to please the client," I say as I force a smile, a grin that is the fakest thing I have ever contorted my face to hold. I don't care about what he thinks of the campaign, for I believe with every ounce of my being that he is wrong. I've done the research and I know that the ads that I have placed before him would be a success and would bring him more money than he could ever know what to do with. Apparently Mr. Grexa believes otherwise though and I suppose I can change what I have devised so that he's happy even though it makes me furious to do so. I'll make the ads more boring, less spontaneous and colorful. I'll give him the grays he wants, the grays that he wears and carries with him every day of his life. Some people are unable to handle the freedom and happiness of a listless life; some people take the beauty of what is delivered and desecrate it with the weaknesses of their own humanity.

"Great, how about we all meet again tomorrow? Same time, same place, with the improvements made and then go from there?" Grexa, the thousand year old CEO asks.

Tomorrow? He wants us to reenvisage this entire campaign in twenty four hours. He must be insane. Jason and I poured more than two months into devising this presentation. To think that we would have to redevelop it entirely to this man's liking in such a short time is a treacherous tragedy. Obviously it's not possible. Before I have a chance to say anything, Mr. Haversmith answers for me. "That will be fine," he says to Mr. Grexa and then turns his attention to Jason and me, "You boys better get to work." I can't accept the fact he actually expects us to achieve anything in such a brief amount of time. I stare in blatant disbelief in the direction of all of the begrudgingly dressed men before me, wanting to slam all of their heads together so that they fall into the deepest of comas. They stand up, slowly at first and then the overlapping moments speed up, as if to show that the amount of time I have to finish what they want is going to be even more unfeasible than I first thought. The room empties out until only Jason and I are standing alone at the front, still in shock from what took place.

"I guess we better get going," he says finally.

"What the actual fuck," I say in a wheezing exacerbated way. It's the only thing I can communicate, the only thought running back and forth across my mind like a speeding dragon that wishes to burn down every castle with the hottest fires of its breath. I feel there is no way we can finish what they wish of us, but I know we have to try. I'll have to quietly kill my pride and give them what they want, and though it hurts me to do so, I know that sometimes you have to swallow your honor in order to succeed. If only the world worked in such a way that you could always follow your heart, wouldn't we all feel freer?

Although the meeting ends far before the clock has hit two, I know I am never going to have enough time to achieve all that has to be accomplished. Mr. Grexa asked us to change the entire ad campaign that Jason and I came up with and he asked us to do so in less than twenty four hours. Once I regain my sanity and try to control the thoughts of strangling the old man that flash through my mind over and over again, I return to my office and get to work. I sketch out new advertisements in my book while Jason goes to the supply closet to retrieve five new canvases for me that I will have to paint the new redesigned ads upon. All I can think about is the fact that this man requested us to tone down the livelihood of what we came up with. It makes absolutely no sense to me. Why would anyone wish to stifle the livelihood of color and youth? Why would anyone ever want to dilute and dissuade the happiness we had portrayed in these ads?

I imagine that old age has gotten to Mr. Grexa, I don't want to understand how he sees the world, because I don't ever want to be in his position. No matter how many things change and how many days pass, I will never let the bright colors and the beauty of this world fade. I will see everything in the most vivid of hues if it's the last thing I do. So while I sketch out images of people sitting around indoors, chewing gum in gray colored kitchens and charcoal skewed cars, I tell myself that I will never succumb to the blandness that living life can drag down from you. I will pull away and continue on even when everything in my being tries to tell me otherwise. I won't let weakness win.

The hours pass on and on. I don't believe in what I am creating for the revised advertisement campaign, but Jason reassures me that what I am coming up with seems to be exactly what Mr. Grexa and the rest of his board desire. It just doesn't sit well with me. I can't fathom why any man would prefer simplicity and dullness that sits behind a shade of the screen and doesn't say any name aloud. It makes no sense from an advertisement standpoint. No one is going to notice these ads, at least not in the way they would have noticed the original ones we developed. If one has to choose between the darkness and the light, most people would always select the latter. For who wants to disappear into a realm of nothingness when one of everything and endless possible walkways of glee can be seen?

The way that I aim to get the work done can be classified as robotic. I use the skills I've honed in the best way I can, but what I am using my artistic ability for is nothing that I am proud of. I create images that look aesthetically pleasing, but the content of them is anything but what I am able to understand. I finish my sketches and then begin on the boards that Jason has retrieved for me. While I work on the images, he is in his office trying to come up with a new slogan to use for the campaign. There really isn't much else he can do at this point. I think of the men from Double Bubble Smacks Gum and how badly I want to Double Bubble Smack them all across the face. I wish I could knock some sense into their dull brains and explain to them how incredibly thick they are being.

Painting has always been something I've loved, but it is an art that takes time. In normal circumstances, I would never rush through something in such a fashion as I am doing now, but there isn't any other way to accomplish it all without doing it as quickly as possible. I slam the gray colors and nude tones onto the canvases with a frantic precision while still maintaining some sort of control, even though I feel I have lost it all already. One thing fades into the next just as all of the strokes I've been creating blur into one another. I'm no longer wearing my suit jacket; instead it lies on the floor next to my tie crumpled into a ball. All that contains and surrounds my upper torso is my buttoned down shirt, with the sleeves rolled up squeezing the ends of my biceps. I've gotten a few flecks of paint on it, surely ruining it for good but that is the least of my worries at the moment. The only worry I have is getting this done, so that this job doesn't take over me completely, in terms of time and the sanity of my mind.

After a great while has passed, I am interrupted when Jason returns to my office. When I see him enter, I set my paintbrush down on the small wooden shelf at the bottom of the easel and look his way, waiting for him to tell me what he has come up with. "So, 'bring back the fun to gum' is no more. Clearly these men don't want their product to convey any sort of silliness or amusement. What I've come up with is not really something I would pick myself, nor do I think it will be as successful as our original plan, but I think it is along the lines of what they want."

"Look at my paintings," I say to him. "We appear to be pretty much on the same page."

He steps up to the two and a half canvases that I have completed so far and for a few moments says nothing at all. He takes the images in, examines them and forms an opinion in his mind fully, before delivering it to me.

"Priam...they're...so dark, but at the same time, they're great. You really are talented. I think they will like them."

"Even though I hate them."

"I guess this isn't about us."

"No...clearly it's not. Our research, our ideas, our decisions don't matter. I think we learned that today," I say. "Anyways, what's the new slogan?"

"What should you do? It's easy really: chew."

I can't help but to laugh immediately when I hear it. It's so beneath anything either of us could have ever devised, but at the same time, maybe that's what Double Bubble Smacks Gum wants, something that they can claim was all their own, an idea and an uncomplicated message that even the dullest of individuals can identify with.

"You think it's horrible...don't you?" Jason asks me with the most sullen look on his face.

"I think it is as perfect as it could possibly be for what they want. If they say anything negative about your slogan, I'll personally kill each and every one of them with my bare hands."

"Well thanks Priam. If they don't like your paintings, then they can make their own for all I care."

"Yes, I agree," I say and smile, the first time I have felt any real sense of lightheartedness emerge since the presentation fell so horribly off key. I realize that what I want more than my own success is a life full of instances like these, when I decide not to fret over what others think of me and what I create, but what I do with myself in the mean time. I wish for a life of the most complicated simplicity. I desire an oxymoron that is the smartest thing that can ever be created. I want to make my bed and lie in it too.

"Do you think you're still going to be able to make it to Ellie's ballet tonight?" He asks.

The devil rips out my heart and cuts it in two, then slices it further making a mess of what used to be the one thing that kept me alive more than anything else. He stomps on the pieces and desecrates the organ that meant everything to me, or that's how it feels as Jason's words reach me.

"Shit, shit, shit!" I repeat three times. I turn to look to the clock and see that I have only an hour and a half before her opening night is set to begin. I'm relieved to know that I haven't missed it yet, but the foreboding of it all ahead of me is an obstacle I don't want to deal with.

"When does it start?"

"In less than two hours. There's no way I am missing it. Even if this isn't finished, I can try to complete it in the morning."

"Just try your best Priam. I'll understand if you leave before you get it done. I wish there was more I could do."

"You've done enough," I tell him.

He sets the slogan down on my mess of a desk and walks out of the room. I work furiously to complete the piece I'm on and as I do so I know there is no possible way I can get this all done before I need to leave. I've never been the kind of man who only completes something halfway, but when it comes to finishing a job or disappointing the person I love most in the world, I'd rather have a sluggish struggle of an atrocious atmosphere surround my work than an air of a similar manner crush the hopes of my dear sweet Ellie.

I work a little bit longer, getting as much done as I can before I know it's the latest time I can go without being late for the beginning of her show. I run to the bathroom and scrape away the paint chips that cover my skin with a thick bar of soap. As they flake off and fall down the drain, twirling around with the hot water that falls from above I wonder for a moment where I would be right now if I had never taken this job. I think of a reality where I still was free to do what I wanted, with no commitments but the ones I made for myself, but just as I think of them I make them disappear. It's no good to regret the regrets you've already let slip away. When I'm cleaned up I return to my office, I roll down my sleeves over my slick skin and fasten my tie back on. I throw on my jacket which covers up the flecks of paint I had gotten on my shirt and look to the window to see the slight reflection of myself showing itself back to me. I run my fingers through my hair and then turn to the paintings that are a completed jumbled mess of grayness. I suppose I don't hate them, as I have never ever truly allowed myself to feel that kind of emotion towards anyone or anything, but I am not particularly fond of them either. I guess if anything, they're just there, being all that they were ever capable of being. Thus, in a way, they're just like me.

I leave my office in Midtown and take the subway to the American Ballet Theatre, which is at Lincoln Center located on the Upper West Side. With the time I have allotted myself I can get to the theater and sit in my seat before Ellie has any idea that I was rushing furiously to make it. I know she will notice if I'm late though, she has a seat reserved for me right towards the front, just close enough so that she can spot me in the audience with ease, but far enough away that I can see all of the stage and witness the entire complexity and perplexities of the show.

The trains go just as fast as they always go, not speeding up because I wish them to do so or slowing down to hinder me further. Everyone else goes at the pace they always go, not getting out of my way or helping me along because they have no idea who I am or where I am going or what in the world I am doing. That's how New York City is and how it will always be, a massive collection of mostly strangers who don't care about you or what you do, yet we all share some kind of strange bond. After all, we're New Yorkers, every single one of us breathes in the same city air and exhales it too. No matter how we think of the foreign people we pass on the street and no matter if we never see one another again, we will always be collected together in between the rivers and steel and coalesce together randomly as one. We live in a fake empire. When I come up from below the ground and start to pace down 66th street towards Lincoln Center where Ellie's show will be, I am relieved to know that I still have a few minutes to spare before the dancers come on the stage, before she realizes that I am still not there, before anything else today falls amiss. I'm three blocks away when fate decides to deal me a different hand, a stack of cards that I don't want, but have no other choice to accept.

I notice her from the first moment my eyes see her and even though I try to look away I can't. The young girl with chestnut colored hair is on her own, walking across the thin sleek black railing as gracefully as she can, stopping only to lower her body and gain her balance before lifting up her right leg and pushing it up and out to her side. All of the people who pass her seem to pay no attention. They don't have time for her, they don't know who she is and they don't care.

The girl can't be any older than seven, and from the looks of it she just finished with ballet practice and is continuing to work on her technique, even though her lesson is done, she's trying to perfect her rhythm and her movements so that they are the best they can possibly be. She is still wearing her pink tutu and her ballet slippers. I stand there looking at this girl, frozen to the ground even though I know I can't stay and watch. She reminds me of Ellie, of course she does, not only because of her appearance and her apparel, but because of the look in her eye that I notice from afar, even at this distance I can tell she is never going to give up on her dreams. I watch for a few moments more and then push on; telling myself I have to get moving or I won't make it to the show in time. Just as the girl is a centimeter short from being out of my eyesight she lifts her leg too high; she loses her balance and slips off of the railing. She plummets to the ground. I see it happening and I attempt to stop her from impacting the concrete, but there is no way I can save her. She hits the sidewalk and lets out a scream of pain. I rush over and hunker down to her side and aim to console her in the best way I can.

"There, there," I say as I stroke my hand alongside her soft brown hair. "Are you alright?"

"Ahh!" She yells out, clearly in pain. I look down to where she is holding her leg and I see that her tights have ripped and that her leg has been scratched so that a small amount of blood is pooling through the hole in the fabric. I open my briefcase and pull out a handkerchief and put pressure on the scrape to stop the bleeding. After a minute or two, when the girl has regained her breath and the crying has faltered back I pull the cloth off of her cut and examine it. The bleeding has slowed and I realize that she is going to be okay. It's obvious that her tumble didn't feel very good, but she will be feeling fine soon enough.

"Thank you mister," she says through her stuffed up tears and thick sobs that cover the vocal chords in her throat. "Thank you for helping me."

"You're welcome miss. It was the least I could do."

"I'm Marjorie. What's your name?"

"My name is Priam, Priam Wood. Glad to meet you."

"And you as well."

"If I can ask, what on earth were you doing up on that railing?"

"Perfecting my technique. My teacher says I have a lot to learn."

"Well I'm sure you could learn a lot more in safer circumstances. You're lucky you're alright. Did you just come from a lesson? Where are your parents?"

"I don't know. You sure ask a lot of questions Mr. Wood."

I can't help but to laugh. "That's how I've always been Marjorie. Always wanting to know everything. You can learn a lot just by talking to people, everyone has a story to share."

"I suppose you're right. Well...I don't know how good my story is. I've been waiting for my mother for over an hour. She was supposed to pick me up right after my lesson but she never came. I don't know how to get home from here."

"Has she ever been late before?" I ask.

"Well...a few times before..." she says trailing off. "But she always comes."

"I'm sure she will be here soon. I can wait with you, if you'd like." I offer, wondering what kind of mother would forget about her young daughter time and time again.

"That would be nice. Thank you Mr. Wood."

"You can call me Priam."

"Thank you Priam. If it weren't for you, I probably would have just laid here on the ground after I fell and cried as people stomped over me."

"I'm sure someone else would have helped you if I hadn't."

"I don't know. You'd be surprised as to how few people have the decency to help one another out in this city. Everyone is in it for themselves."

"I'm sure I can be selfish just like the rest of them at times," I tell her. "But I was raised to help out others whenever I possibly could," I say as an image of my mother and the lessons she taught me overtake my mind.

"As was I. And I was always told not to be late," she says and then looks to me with a slight smirk. "I guess my mother doesn't hold that idea as close to her heart as she expects me to."

"I'm sure she didn't forget about you. I bet something came up."

"That's how it always is, isn't it?" Marjorie asks me.

"I wish I could answer that."

I extend my hand and help Marjorie up off of the sidewalk. We relocate to a bench on the side of the street only a few yards away from where I had been crouching next to the place where she had impacted the earth. She asks me what I do in the city and instead of telling her that I work as the art director at an ad agency I simply tell her I'm an artist. I reason that she will be able to understand that better, and after the day I have had at Haversmith Inc, it's the last thing I want talk about. I'm reminded of what I'm doing here in the first place and my heart thumps within my chest as I realize Ellie's show has to have started by now. I can't help but feel as if I am suddenly drowning in an unfamiliar air to know that she has most likely noticed my empty seat at the front of the theater at this point. It pains me to think of this, but I know that I can't leave Marjorie, it would be wrong to do so. I can't win, not in this situation, or in any matter that occurs today. Instead of focusing on this unfortunate truth any longer, I ask Marjorie why she enjoys dancing. I expect some epic answer of wise knowledge beyond her years like the things she has said before, instead though, what I get is a simple response that makes the most sense.

"Because it makes me feel like I am good at something. Even though I know I'm not the best dancer, I know that one day I can be if I work hard enough. It's worth striving for something if you love it enough."

"That it is," I tell her.

The seconds and minutes fade on and as Marjorie and I

talk about our respective lives, her seven year old adventures and my twenty five year old failures, I know that Ellie's opening night is slipping away from me. I know that I have already missed the beginning. I know I will have disappointed my fiancé once again and that she will be upset about it. I hope that Marjorie's mother will arrive soon, but in the meantime I just keep talking to the girl, trying to keep her mind off of the ache that is sure to still be emanating from her leg where the scrape that she just recently received resides. I try to tell her stories of my life that are of happy times, when I lived in Alden as a young boy and everything seemed so much simpler, of the journeys Ellie and I had gone on in the city and all of the people we had met. I try to keep her smiling; I try to talk to her in a way that I wish adults had talked to me when I was young. I aim to achieve a certain sense of splendor, so that when I part from her she will remember me forever, even though our time together has been brief.

Marjorie is in the middle of a tale about she and her younger sister building a giant sandcastle on the beach when we are interrupted by a frantic woman with long blonde hair of about thirty five years running up to us. "Marjorie! Oh Marjorie! I'm so sorry, I'm so sorry! I lost track of time and then Josephine got sick all over the kitchen floor and I had to tuck her into bed and then your grandmother called and I just got caught up in everything and I can't believe I'm so late and I really-" She stops suddenly and runs her hands down the front of her crumpled lavender dress smoothing out the fabric that had become wrinkled from the way she had been running in such a scuttle to find her young daughter who she had accidentally forgotten about, unintentionally of course. "And who are you sir?"

I stand up and bow towards the woman, although she isn't really that much older than me I can't help but to feel like a child myself in her presence. I suppose it's because she herself has a daughter, a young girl named Marjorie who I had the pleasure of meeting and in a way, saving today.

"My name is Priam Wood ma'am. I was just sitting here with your daughter until you arrived. I happened to watch her take a tumble earlier and-"

"He saved me Mama," Marjorie interjects. "I was being foolish and practicing my ballet high up on a railing and I fell. I would have bled all over the street if it weren't for Mr. Wood coming to my aid. We need to do something to thank him."

"Is that so?" her mother asks, looking from her daughter and then back to me. "How very kind of you sir. I thank you from the bottom of my heart for coming to Marjorie's assistance. Is there anything I can do to reward you for your generosity of spirit?"

"There is no need. Talking to your daughter was enough of a prize on its own. You have a good one here."

"Indeed I do," she says.

I walk closer up to her and whisper in her ear. "Try not to forget about her again." I don't know if it is my place to say it, but for some reason I feel like Marjorie's mother is often late to retrieve her, not only from dance lessons but from other things as well. This little girl doesn't deserve to have to wait, not for her mother, not for anything.

"I'll try my best," she whispers back.

I walk a few steps further, finally again on my way to Ellie, whose ballet has to be far more than halfway over by now. I realize this with a heavy heart, regretting how the evening has turned out, yet still wondering if it all was supposed to transpire this way from the beginning of every inception that ever occurred. Before I leave, I turn around to say goodbye to Marjorie.

"It was a pleasure to meet you little miss. Keep practicing those dance moves of yours, just in safer places please. I'm sure that one day I will be going to see you perform at Lincoln Center, as the star in the American Ballet Theatre Company."

Marjorie's face blushes and she sheepishly responds to my sentiments with "I will Mr. Wood. I promise I will. Thank you again."

"Oh, you are more than welcome," I tell her and then give her a wink, before I am on my way once more. I walk slowly at first, before picking up my speed to a steady gait, which quickly transforms into a jog and then a hectic sprint, hoping beyond hope that I haven't missed every movement that Ellie has to offer the stage this night.

When I walk into the main hall of Lincoln Center and the chandeliers stare and blink at me with crystal covered eyes I know immediately that intermission has already come and gone, all of the attendants are cleaning up, closing the refreshment booths and re-organizing the ticket stands. I hear the music emanating forth from the theater but I am too afraid to go in. I want to watch the rest of the show, what little may be left anyways, yet I can't help feeling like there is no point.

She knows. Ellie is aware that I haven't made it in time, she is conscious of the fact that I didn't arrive when I was supposed to. It pushes on me from the outside in to know that all the while she has been up there dancing she has had to deal with the idea that her fiancé, the man who is always and forever supposed to be here, there and everywhere for her, hasn't show up when he promised to. I've failed her, with good reason or not, I was unable to keep my word and even if it was for helping out a little girl who needed it, I know that Ellie needed to see me sitting in that seat from the very moment that this show started and I wasn't there, I wasn't there.

The music coming from the theater swells and then begins to fade. I make myself find the courage and slowly push forward towards the two large oak doors that glare at me with their bulk, daring me to move them with any bone of my being, trying their best to become as heavy as they can possibly be so that I won't be able to get from this side of the space towards the other where the ballet is taking place, the ballet that is getting closer and closer to the end. I do make it through the doors though and I'm relieved to see that the show is still ongoing. About fourteen or fifteen dancers are on the stage, an equal amount of men and women prance gaily from one side to another, moving their bodies in unique ways, all which transgress and repress what is known and what is not. I can't recall what the title of the ballet is, but all of the dancers are dressed in costumes made up of either black or white. They sway from side to side and the men lift up the women so that they float above the flat level center of the stage and glide across to and fro and further past. The men set the women back down and they pirouette again and again, it is unbearable to believe that they can turn around so many times without becoming dizzy or losing all sense of reality and where they are.

I look for Ellie frantically from my position at the back of the theater, where I am encased in shadow where no one can see me. I search the faces of the girls up on stage in their alternating black and white but she is nowhere, not on the stage, not present before me or anyone else in the audience who are experiencing this ballet coming to an end. The dancers continue their routine and I can tell that it is all building to some dramatic climax and

252

conclusion. The movements they make are becoming larger; they dance in frantic ways as if to foreshadow something greater that is about to occur. The women spin faster and the men jump higher. The fabrics, black and white, stretch across their muscular figures tightly, keeping them in place all the while setting them free.

The glow of the stage is suddenly blocked out immediately and totally as the dancers who were visible can now be seen no more. The music pulsates through the theater and I can feel it surround my heart and take it over. In the darkness the orchestra transcends through the reverie and warns of what is about to come. The light flashes back on and when it does I see her. There, in the middle of the stage, covered in feathers of every shade and every color that there ever was. Orangutan orange, red velvet, purple blues, golden glued hues that shake and shimmer in the spotlight that encases her exquisiteness. She is the most effervescent tropical bird and as she bends and begins to move the throng of the violin beats steadily to the texture of what she is wearing, which is unable to overcome her frame. Green leaves are twisted through her chestnut colored hair that is sleekly slicked back on the sides and pulled into a tight bun. Her arms float to both of her sides and perfectly hit invisible barriers that accompany the tune of the chords to a key. Her legs are like rotten cotton candy that is both sturdy and soft. She points out her feet and lifts her entire body into the air all the while slowing when need be and bending back so that her body creates an upside down L that is indescribably irreversible. It would be impossible to say what it is like to see Ellie dance, for watching her move is such an experience on its own. I can try to tell a tale of how she moves, but my words will never be enough.

She is the star of the show; I can hear awes emanating from the spectators in the audience as the men and women in black and white from before return to the stage and surround her, circling around Ellie as she continues to move, they flow together in a magnetic progress that evolves from what it is to something else while maintaining its signature and original ensemble. They run around her, leaping and bounding and floating through the air, spinning and singing silently with no sound as the music speeds up and grows stronger. She begins to spin, pirouetting in the middle of it all as the vivacious colors of her feathered dress seem to fly, creating an illusion that she is a bird taking flight. The one and only to be noticed, admired and revered. Ellie Donahue, my life, my love, the belle of the ball.

And just as it all begins even though I wasn't present for the actual start, it ends, quicker than I could have ever noticed without actually noticing so. She bends back one final time and then the fellow dancers stop, pose and hold their bodies still so that everything appears to take on the image of a photograph, frozen still. The crowd erupts into applause and the sounds of the orchestra fade as the instruments are put down, the players taking rest as the dancers on the stage aim to catch their breath. The ballet is over, and even though I only caught the last few minutes, I feel as if I was watching for hours, transfixed by the tragedy of it all, wishing for an answer that could make the colors and the lack thereof find a path that they could both take. I wish she would have been able to see me here standing at the back for the finale, but it is most likely too little too late anyways. The dancers bow and the audience applauds some more, when Ellie bows on her own, the cacophony of clapping is of the highest uproar. The dancers soon disappear and the lights on the stage go off again. I have to go backstage and see her to offer all of the regards that I retain.

I've visited Ellie backstage after shows a few times before, so I know where to go. One of the guards recognizes me as her fiancé and lets me pass without trouble. The atmosphere is that of excitement, buzzing sounds move from one person to the next as there are many people about. I have to push my way through many elated strangers to find Ellie's dressing room. When I get there she is not alone, she is surrounded by more than ten people, dancers and others, most of whom I do not recognize, except for her friend Juliana who glares at me harshly. Ellie sits in front of a mirror that is framed by large circular light bulbs that shine upon her face in all its delicate splendor. She is still wearing the colored feathered tutu that she had on during the finale. She doesn't turn when I walk in; even though I am sure I see a hint of recognition in her eyes flash when I enter, off of the looking glass and towards my direction. I don't want to interrupt her moment, I want her to enjoy it, I know how hard she has been working to prepare for tonight's opening and she deserves every compliment that comes her way,

"Ellie you were marvelous, I couldn't take my eyes off of you," says a man in a blue suit.

"Even better than in rehearsal."

"If only Dame Strousburg could see you now," Juliana

swoons as she rubs Ellie's back.

"You might as well be featured on every billboard for the American Ballet Company."

"No wonder we were all fitted in black and white."

"Even without your colors though, we all knew you would still burn the brightest."

The compliments go on and on from all different directions, from these people who encircle her. After the many thanks she offers them over and over again they slowly file out of the dressing room. They look at me as they leave, some acknowledge me and nod their heads while others just give me a look of contorted confusion, wondering why I am even here at all. Juliana is the last to leave us and although she offers me no words, I can feel the anger she is directing my way as she pushes past me. Finally, it is just the two of us.

The makeup table beneath her mirror is covered in flowers and as she runs her fingertips over them and pulls them towards her nostrils so that she can breathe in the sweet scents I realize I failed yet again by not even bringing her a bouquet. I move from where I am standing up against the wall and come up behind her. I put both of my hands on her shoulders and look at her face, though not directly, for what is seen in actuality is just her face being reflected back at me. She feels warm, yet cold and clammy simultaneously. She doesn't turn to look at me; instead she lifts her hands to her head, removes the greenery from her hair and pulls the clips out so that it falls down in a tumble.

"Ellie- you were perfect," I start to say.

"How would you know?" she asks, with a cold glimmering present in her seeing beings.

"I saw you, I saw you dance."

"What part of it, the last second? The closing frame of the ending scene?" Her voice echoes off of the reflective glass in front of her as she makes eye contact with me for the first time since I entered the room, even though it is not completely true as she still has yet to turn around to greet me wholly. It's the only the mirror she sees me through.

"I'm sorry, I know I wasn't here when I was supposed to be. There's no excuse, but I saw this little girl-" I begin but she interrupts me.

"I don't care Priam. I can't deal with your excuses

anymore."

"They aren't excuses Ellie. I swear I tried to be here on time. Life got in the way."

"It's always something with you anymore," she says.

"Won't you turn around and look at me?" I ask.

"I can see you fine," she tells me, still looking at me through the mirror, which seems to separate us further apart as the moments pass even though I am standing right behind her. I take my hands off of her shoulders and take a small step back.

"How can I make this up to you?"

"You can't."

"Ellie, I love you."

"And I love you Priam, with every ounce of my being. But is love alone good enough?"

"What do you mean?"

"We seem to be falling apart quicker than I can keep track. You know, when you took that job at Haversmith and we finally got engaged I thought everything would be better. Instead it's worse. I always get my hopes up and all you ever do anymore is let me down. I know you don't try to, but as you just said, life keeps getting in the way. You keep breaking my heart. I try to ignore it, but the pieces don't seem to fit together anymore. I don't know what to do."

"I don't want you to be upset."

"But I am. You are the one person I depend on more than anybody, and recently I feel like I can't depend on you at all. I can't keep living like this. I want to be your wife; I want to have children with you and dance around in the park and inspire you to make paintings like I used to, but you don't make paintings anymore Priam and I can't even remember the last time we danced together. I feel like your spirit is dying, and I can't save it. I can't save you."

"Ellie, you save me every day, just by being there for me."

"That's just it though Priam," she says as she finally turns around, breaking her gaze from the mirror and facing me, only the oxygen hanging between us to separate the situation. "You aren't there for me anymore and you haven't been for a while. I've been struggling with this for some time now and tonight broke me in two. I felt as if I was dying there onstage without you. Maybe you were there at the end, but you weren't there at the beginning, and for me...that made all the difference."

She lifts her hand up to her face then and pushes it into her cheek, rubbing off the rouge with her palms and then wiping it off into a cloth located on the table next to her. The light in the room catches her engagement ring and it sparkles in my eye, momentarily making me blind. I regain my eyesight and lean down to try to kiss her. She moves away, out of my reach so that I am unable to do so.

"I always felt that without you I would die so fast in this city, but now...all I can think about is the fact that I won't be able to live with you in the way which things are now."

"I'll change Ellie, I swear I can make this up to you," I plead. "This won't happen again."

"I know this isn't completely your fault Priam, but I love you too much to go on this way. It might not make much sense, but I know that if I don't put my foot down now, the love we had will never have even mattered in the first place."

I catch it, the past tense version of the word. For if we don't have love now, if the love we had is all that is here, then how do we even love at all?

"What do you want to do?"

"I want to give you this," she says as she slips her engagement ring off of her finger and places it in my hand.

"What are you doing?" I ask as the cold diamond feels so icy against my skin. "Why are you giving this to me?"

"I'm giving it to you because I can't wear it anymore. I can't be engaged to you Priam. Not now anyways, not until you realize what the word marriage means. I need to know that we can be together in a way that we are meant to be, forever and for always. I want to see the Priam that I fell in love with return. I know I expect highly of you, but that's only because I know you are capable of such greatness. I know you can love me in the way I love you."

"Ellie please- I promise I can fix this."

"Don't promise me anything Priam, show me. All I want for you to do is to show me, like the paintings you used to make in the park, create something and help me to believe in us again. I'm sorry to say for the time being I've lost the understanding I used to have."

She stands up then, and pulls her costume off. I watch in utter disbelief as she undresses and puts on a silver silk taffeta dress. I am unable to focus on her beauty because all I can think about is how badly this hurts. As I do so, I wonder if this is what she has felt like all along these recent months. I think of how I have upset her and that if how she has hurt me now equals out the score, but I know this isn't a game. She goes to grab her things as I remain where I am, still transfixed by the realness of it.

"Please don't go Ellie," I beg.

"I have to go Priam. I have to."

"But why?"

"Why not? Who knows, maybe we've always needed this. If we don't die now and regain ourselves from the ashes like two fiery phoenixes, was our love really worth it at all?"

"I don't know. I don't know," I murmur in repeated words.

"Only time will tell," she says as she exits the room. Her gown shimmering in the light, her chestnut colored hair flowing like the richest fire colored cocoa.

It happened as said even though it was neither what I desired nor saw coming. I don't follow after her. I wait a few minutes in the silence of her empty dressing room. I take a piece of purple cloth off of her table and put the engagement ring in it. I tuck the swaddled diamond into my pocket and leave the room, just as quietly as I had come. I don't know what to do so I let my feet guide me, out of Lincoln Center and into the streets. I wander for a while as I often do when nothing seems right and I end up in Central Park. I walk until I come upon water and watch as the swans swim around in circles, dancing on the pond as if there is no day but today. As they turn around in spherical motions that I know will never end, I wonder how I got here, this place, or whatever space it is. I think of Ellie and how I have done her wrong. She expects the best and I know I haven't given it to her. I've failed her so many times and I can't blame her for giving up on me, for wanting me to prove what I am worth, what the two of us are worth together. For if we can't even make it now, how are we going to succeed in a life that we aim to build together?

Ellie Donahue may have lost faith in me tonight, but as I stare at the reflection of the moon on the water, as the birds circle it and surround it, I tell myself that I will win Ellie back. I will show her that we are something that is worth it all, every star in the sky that has fallen and bounded back up, the candle that melted and burnt out, only to be relit again. I will show her that we are the city that rises from the ashes, the shadow that cannot escape the light. I vow never to give up on her, to never give up on us.

Another morning I awake and as I open my eyes I wonder where I will be or what will have changed in the automatic days that filled themselves in between the moment when I floated away from Ellie's bedside to wherever I may be now. The light floods in and I sit up slowly, taking in the view of the room around me. I must admit I am surprised to see that I am in my childhood bedroom in my old house in Alden. I had prayed today would be my wedding day. I turn my head to take in the full view of the room and I realize that it has changed quite a bit. There are no longer any instances of my youth, instead it simply contains many small prints of paintings I have made, some which I recall creating, others that I don't think I've really ever seen before. I get out of bed and walk over to my closet to put on some clothes to greet this day and whatever it may hold. I slide the large wooden doors open and see that there is only one thing hanging up inside...a black tuxedo, lonely on the hanger.

I am elated at the site; for I believe my plan has worked. Telling Ellie to have our wedding on this day has come to fruition, or so my hopes are begging me to believe. The juxtaposition of losing Ellie yesterday on this original day in her dressing room in front of the lighted mirror and the memory of her in that hospital bed on that third day has created a current urgency within me. I try not to focus on what has already come to pass in both what happened in my life and this current journey I am on now. I can't focus on them. The days have to be relived the way they originally occurred for a reason, or so Chloe had said. Although it pains me to relive the days that I messed up so thoroughly, I know there is a greater purpose for why I have to be imprisoned within them like some aimless passenger without a voice or a choice in any of the matters that matter.

I move away from the closet and greet my old dresser, I pull out a plain white t shirt and pull it over my head, lifting it down to conceal my previously uncovered torso. I find a pair of khaki shorts and put those on too. My outfit isn't a tuxedo by any means, but it is enough to allow me to leave my room. Besides, I am hopeful that the tuxedo will grace my skin with its slippery silk touch later today.

As I walk down the stairs I hear voices. The reverberations of the different sounds that are coming from at least three various people are noises that I recognize. Suddenly as the wooden stairs creak beneath my feet I am aware of my seventy year old mind that is still the keeper of all keys. I may currently reside within the body of my twenty five year old self, but I still have all of the memories of my entire life. I know what has come before and what will come after. Yet again, this journey that I am in control of actually has no boundaries or limitations. I don't know what will occur or come next when I wake up on each morning of my second chances. Is anything really ever written in stone? If we wish to strongly enough, can we even undo what we previously thought was unable to be undone? The mind can hold so many memories after all, countless times, trials and tribulations that all add up to create the person that you are. Memories are all that we will ever really have; the moments that we have already lived are the only things that can never be undone. Or can they? For what am I doing now? Am I undoing all of the wrongs I've already done?

Time tricks me to think so, but I know the mistakes I made still happened, they occurred in the ways in which I originally made them. No, I'm not able to undo anything, I'm just able to redo them in a different way, in this plane of reality where things are different, in this life where I am given seven second chances to be the man I always wanted to be, to make the life I always wanted to create, to paint the picture in the sky I always felt was so nigh, yet so high above me.

I reach the bottom of the stairs and enter the kitchen where the three voices I hear surround me, as do the faces that they are emitted from. At the kitchen table sits my mother, one year older from when I last saw her. That one year hasn't done much, she still looks as good as when we had lunch in the city, as graceful as she appeared when she came to see my art gallery that last evening that I was the pilot of. Directly to her right is Danny, my brother is home and it gives me the chills since I haven't experienced the three of us together in this room in any reality since the night that she died, and the night that she lived. Both those days whichever way, I was only thirteen years old in one way or the other. To his side sits Rebecca, looking as beautiful as ever. Of course, I have never been able to compare any woman to the majesty that my Ellie contains, but if any one could come in a close second, I would have to admit that Rebecca, with her fair skin, soft dark hair, and twinkling smile would be the one.

"There's the man of the hour!" Danny shouts.

"Glad to see you have awoken to welcome the day," Rebecca adds.

"Good morning Priam. How are you feeling my love?" My mother asks.

I sit down at the table, joining them, and as I do I realize the table has a great spread overtaking it, with blueberry pancakes, bacon, sausage, scrambled eggs and toast covering every inch except for the spaces where their hands and elbows rest. The seat I occupy has a bare plate before it and I ravenously begin to fill it up and as I do so I wonder if switching between the life I lived and the one I'm enduring now somehow has the capability of starving me in my unrequired unrelenting sleep that occurred in between. I take a bite full and answer her, "As good as I can possibly be Mother. I feel like yesterday was a terrible day, but I hope that today will be a good one."

"How on earth could you feel as yesterday was a terrible day?" Rebecca asks me. "It was one of the most beautiful days I have ever experienced. You and Ellie look so in love. Her speech at the rehearsal dinner made me cry and shiver from all of the sentiment."

"Really?" I ask, wanting to believe her words, but I am unable to shake the feeling I have resonating within my bones from when my Ellie, the one I knew from that day in her dressing room left me with all of the pain that I was unable to hold in or bare.

"Of course. She spoke so eloquently about why you two love one another, you make each other stronger. Neither of you are able to be as strong alone as you are capable of being together. I think that's what marriage is all about after all," Danny says. "That's how I've felt with Rebecca anyways," he adds as he looks to his wife.

"Marriage is an institution that was established to strengthen the bond of two people who can't live without each other," my mother adds. "It's an idea that in reality means nothing yet everything all at the same time. For really, two people can be hopelessly and effortlessly in love without being married, but marriage itself has the ability to strengthen that bond, to solidify the essentiality of it."

"And today is my wedding day," I say, both as a statement and as half of a question because even though I am even more certain of it now than I was when I saw that tuxedo first thing this morning, it has yet to be confirmed by anyone I know or love.

"Today is your wedding day Priam Wood. And it's going to be your best day, or at least one of the best days that you will ever live," my mother says to me as she wraps her arm around me and kisses me on the cheek. "Ellie is going to look so beautiful when she walks down that aisle."

When she walks, she is going to walk I think to myself. Her broken back is healed and she is going to be able to make her way to me as I wait for her. I would wait for a thousand years if I had to, to the end of the sea and underneath reverse mountains that stretch to the center of the earth. I only wonder if she will be able to dance. For how could Ellie be Ellie if she was unable to move in the motions of the oceans that I had always known her to do so? I believe it will all be okay, and that this life cannot stray too far from the one I've already lived, even though it already has in some confused ways. I tell myself that even the most messed up things happen for a reason.

"She's all better, after her fall, after all of the time that it took her to heal. She's alright...right?" I ask, again half as a question and half as a statement. Of course I should know, but in reality all I know is from what they have told me. In essence, I've been in a coma for a little over a year.

"She's resilient. She's a strong woman. I don't know if most women would be capable of striving through all of the pain like she has, but she's done it," Rebecca says. "I admire her, really. Ever since that day in the hospital when the two of you agreed on this date, she hasn't given up. She was determined to be okay."

"And so she is," Danny says. "And you are too Priam. You're both going to have a wonderful life together. Today is just the beginning."

"The feelings that surrounded us all last night at the church during the rehearsal and the dinner afterwards are only at the forefront of what the two of you are going to share. You will live a beautiful life regardless of the challenges that life throws your way, that I know," my mother tells me.

I take the last few bites of my breakfast, as I had been eating it all the while the three of them had been reassuring me that everything was going to be okay, that everything already was okay.

"I wish I could hear the speech she gave again. So that I could focus on every word she said, to take it all in and hold it within my heart forever," I tell them as I set my fork down and push my chair slightly away from the table so that I have more room to breathe, as I am starting to feel overwhelmed. For in reality, Ellie and I were already married once, although it wasn't like this. None of the three people before me were there, they were unable to be there, unable to know that it was occurring. This wedding day is the way I wish our original one had happened, but I guess this just goes to show that sometimes things are better the second time around, even if you have to wait for those dreams to be delivered.

"Maybe you will one day. I often imagine that in heaven we can rewatch the most memorable moments of our lives, like picture shows that we used to know," my mother offers up. "If you want something bad enough, anything is possible, even if it's not in this life."

Her words ring poignantly through me and as they do all I can think about is what Ellie will look like in her white dress walking down the aisle toward me, the greatest sight that can ever be seen. I know I can't see her until that moment, but oh how I wish I could see her now. I can't though, and for the time being I must settle with these three wonderful people who surround me. Although I must admit it really isn't settling under the current circumstances. For I have my mother near me, who still lives and breathes and graces this day and those that are yet to come with her persistent beauty. My brother, Daniel Wood, who I know without even having to ask will be my best man and his wife Rebecca Wood, who will fill the role as Ellie's maid of honor, finishing out the trio and then overcoming any expectations me and my wife ever could have thought of.

I think of her then, Ellie Donahue, who in a few hours will become Ellie Wood once again. My mother, brother, and sister in law sit before me, with no notion of what I have already lived and what I have already lost. They are instead only thinking about the beauty of this day and all it will hold, so I begin to wonder if I can think that way too. I beg myself not to think of the pain I still have to relive and to only focus on today, to take each day as it comes and to live not for a memory or a moment, but simply for the sake of living, to live and to be, as effortlessly as I can.

The sun shines through the kitchen window and the warmth encases my back as I am unable to face it, afraid to disappoint Ellie again, even though I feel as if I can't. I think of her in a white dress walking towards me with the most colorful stained glass windows shining through on either side, but as their brightness fades she is the only thing that matters, the one thing that I have always loved the most, the mate of my soul, the being that completes me more than anything ever could. I think of my ballerina, my love, my life, and I think of how I am going to marry her again, that tonight...she will be my wife. The bliss engrosses me and I get up from the table, ready to move forward with this day which I tell myself can only be what I've always desired.

Rebecca stands up and says "Well I better get going. I have to help Ellie get ready after all, as the maid of honor, it's my duty." I can't help but to smile at the fact that my assumption about Rebecca standing up there beside Ellie today is correct. Ellie was an only child and I certainly didn't have any sisters. There were various girls she was close with in New York, especially Juliana, but it makes sense that in this reality Rebecca is the one she is the closest with.

"Do you want me to drive you?" Danny asks her as he begins to stand.

"No dear, don't worry about it," she tells him as she rests her hands on his shoulders and slightly pushes him back down into his seat. "You all know as well as I do that the Red Rose Inn is less than a mile away. It's such a beautiful day; I can walk there in no time. Besides, the three of you should spend some time together before all of the festivities begin. It'll probably be the last time you have in quite a while I'd imagine." She kisses Danny on the cheek and waves goodbye to my mother and I. "I'll see you all at the church then," and with that, we watch as she leaves the kitchen and walks out of the front door, only letting the sunshine stream in for a second before the door closes behind her and she is gone.

I can't help but to think of Ellie once again, getting ready in one of the elegantly furnished rooms at the Red Rose Inn Bed and Breakfast. The two of us will probably end up there at the end of the night as well, as it's the only place to stay in Alden. I'm sure Ellie will do her own hair and her own makeup, as she always has, but her mother and father will be there, along with Rebecca to help her if she requires anything. I'm sure the white dress she has picked out for today will not be an easy thing to put on.

As the illusions I am creating about what she will look like today dissipate, I can't help but to think that everything is happening faster, time itself seems to slow and then quicken simultaneously. I ask myself if that makes any sense and I know it doesn't, but I still can't help to believe in it. The philosophy that has been filling my mind is at its peak; not only on this day but so it felt on that third day as well. I suppose that is because I am at my intellectual highest, or so it could be argued. Even though I was still in control those first and second relived days, I was in the body of a thirteen and eighteen year old boy, respectively. Perhaps the body and the mind are more connected than we think. Regardless, my thoughts suddenly escape me, getting lost in the flow of a river that's beating too fast, as I realize what Rebecca had said was right, at this moment, it us just the three of us at the table, I have to stop thinking and start living once again. I'm reminded that the last time the three of us sat here was during that last meal, when the pot roast was made in both instances of that day, from where things changed in one way or another in each case. I know all of the details from where that day went during my life and it digs at me to know there were days that competed for the title of a worse one. From where I am now though, I don't know what is going to happen. Of course, I hope it is good, I think of how time can never really be touched when it is still before you. I wonder if fate is real and if it is, how I will ever make it surprise me in a simple yet fulfilling way.

"What do you think Father would have to say if he was sitting here with us now?" Danny asks my mother, cutting through my ridiculous thoughts at last.

"I don't know if he would have much to say to tell you the truth."

"What do you mean?" I ponder.

"Your father often enjoyed taking the moment in for what it was. I know he would be proud of you and he would tell you so. He would wish you good luck and all of the happiness in the world for your marriage with Ellie. But mostly, I think he would just enjoy the fact of sitting here with us, to know that he had done a good job in raising you, as I'm sure he would have if given the chance."

"Isn't it horrible, how he never was?" Danny wonders.

"It sure wasn't the way I would have chosen it to be," she begins. "However, since it's happened it's hard for me to imagine it any other way. I miss your father, but the reality is that he passed away years ago, and even though I can still feel his presence in my heart everyday, I haven't felt his touch in decades." Her eyes glisten then, not due to any serenity of the sunlight coming through the window, but because of the water that she is trying so hard to hold in. Tears of sadness are nothing that she wants to release today; instead I know that she wants this day to be one full of happiness.

"I'm sorry Mother, maybe I shouldn't have brought it up."

"Don't apologize Daniel. Just because it can be hard to talk about your father at times like these doesn't mean we shouldn't acknowledge that he lived and influenced us all so much, even in what little time he was given. I think that just goes to show what a good man he was. I know he would be proud of you both."

To hear her say that at this moment feels like the one thing I need more than anything, to make the over thinking of the universe and my life from flowing so freely. I never would have thought my father would have been proud of me for the life I lived the first time around, but maybe she's right in saying he would be in this one. Either way, I have to let it go for the time being. Today is my wedding day, I have to stop thinking, I have to simply let it be.

"And he'd be proud of you for being the best Mother," I tell her. "If it weren't for you, neither of us would be the men we are."

"That's sweet of you to say Priam," she says as she stands up and begins to clean off the table. Her light yellow pants and teal blouse billow from the movement as she goes back and forth to the sink until the kitchen table is sparkling and bare. Danny and I just sit there, he stares out the window behind me, where the sun is shining and begging for us to get out of the house and surround ourselves in its light.

When she returns from the sink for the last time she doesn't sit down again. Instead she holds out both of her hands, one in each of our direction, her palms facing up towards the ceiling, beckoning us to grab ahold and get up, to get ready for the wedding, to leave our house on Elm Street and embrace this day where more changes will occur, the kind of day that is the turning point, a central element that makes up a crucial compound of life. I reach out and grasp my mother's hand and Danny does the same. I can't help but to laugh as thoughts of the kind of science that I wish I didn't have to believe in filters through. I imagine the three of us being the most important compound there is, that of water, the only thing that life cannot live without. My mother Moira, the oxygen forcing us to breath at the middle, her two arms the bonds that connect Danny and I to her on either side, functioning as the two hydrogens who complete the cure. Together, we are enough.

The tux fits me as perfectly as it can. I get ready in front of the mirror in my bedroom upstairs and am satisfied by my appearance. I'd like to believe that this is the best I've ever looked, which I am happy to accept, as it is what Ellie deserves to see. Even if I haven't always been the best I could be, the least I can do is make my appearance as diligently dutiful and handsome as is possible. Compared to a beautiful woman like her, I don't know if I will ever truly measure up, but I tell myself that no matter the comparison, we make a good looking couple, if not for the sheer features of our faces, then for the smiles that emanate from them when we are together.

I take one final look at my reflection and I acknowledge that the black of the tuxedo and the white of my shirt, vest and tie are the perfect contrast. For a man who has always embraced colors, it's actually nice to reject them on such an important day, at least for the time being. I'll let the color come from the moments and memories that are made today, which will imprint themselves within the consciousness of all of those who are in attendance. I smirk and then burst into a smile at the absurd idea, flashing my teeth and then winking at myself before I lift up my hands at my sides and shift my weight back and forth between my feet, doing a little dance of pure delight to know that everything has arrived on this day in a way that I feel glad. Now that I know Ellie can walk and that today is indeed our wedding day, I realize that I have nothing else to fix or change on this day. I can simply enjoy it for the milestone that it is. I've made it halfway.

Then again, that's what I believed on that third day after I refused the job at the agency and although the gallery showing was grand, it ended with Ellie lying in a hospital bed. I hope something like that won't happen again, I tell myself to be on the look out for any dogs, especially ones of golden hues that may appear and change the course of what could easily be close to perfection. The fact that a golden retriever has appeared each day in some capacity has not been a fact that I've forgotten. I won't let today be messed up, for this day more than any I feel like I need utter bliss and no mishaps to misshape or make any more mistakes than the ones that have already been made.

I look up to the ceiling. It is corrugated and contains so

many undesirable images of dragons and devils, yet it also contains the faces of happy people that I once knew. I remember lying on my bed at night as a young boy and dreaming up all of the things I thought I could see in the random patterns of the white and the shadows which they fought with. I stare at the ceiling for a few moments more and then I close my eyes. I bring my two hands together and let my fingers overlap before pulling them up to my mouth. I say a prayer, to anyone or anything that is listening. All I ask for is a day of effortless elation and beauty. Is that so much to ask?

Unknown to me then, life, or something like it, was going to decide to give me a break, to let me live in a state of pure joy with no interruptions or unexpected expectations. That beautiful sunny day was always destined to be my one reprieve amongst the seven repainted frames that I was able to make. Fitting that it would be the day that I married Ellie, the love of my life, for whom without, life never really seemed worth living.

When I walk downstairs with my tuxedo on, my mother is sitting in her chair in the living room. She sees me, stands up and walks towards me, and as she does so she places her hand over her mouth before pulling it away as if in surprise. "You look so handsome Priam."

"Thanks Mother. You look stunning."

She is wearing a pale yellow dress that perfectly accentuates her golden hued hair that is pulled up into a neat updo. The white pearl necklace she has around her neck completes the look in a most elegant manner. Even in her mid fifties, she still looks beautiful. "I have a little something for you."

"Oh? What's that?" I ask.

She lifts up her right hand that is closed into a fist and brings it level to my eyesight; her wrist rotates so that her hand turns around so that I can see her fingers. They separate slowly and open up to reveal what appears to be a golden pin of some kind. The sunlight that shines in from the window bounces off of the surface of whatever it is and reflects in my mother's eyes. Before I can get a better look she smiles at me and then removes the object from her palm with her other hand and beckons me closer towards her so she can pin it onto my lapel.

"This was your father's. He was wearing it the day I met him in the art gallery. I've held onto it especially for this day. I thought it would be appropriate to give to you as you and Ellie start your life together. You being the artist in the family after all, it only makes sense that you should have it, just as she has my engagement ring."

"That's so sweet of you," I say as I glance at the pin. Looking at it upside down I can't really study it adequately, but from what I can tell the golden metal is formed into the shape of an eagle with it's wings spread.

"I'm not sure where he got it, in fact, he wasn't even sure where he got it. He said he had it for as long as he could remember. I'm sure it was just something he found at a shop in the city one day when he was young. Regardless, it'll be like he's with you today in a sense with that close to your chest. He'd be happy to have you be wearing it the moment that Ellie becomes your wife. I wanted to give it to you earlier when we were all talking about him, but I thought now would be a more appropriate time."

"This moment where we are in the house the two of you built together, all the while on the edge of leaving it for the day," I offer.

"Exactly."

"With this, it's like everyone I love will be surrounding me in one way or another during the moment Ellie and I become man and wife. I couldn't think of anything better," I say with the utmost resolve. Although I wish my father truly could have been here too, I knew from the very beginning of this journey he was never going to be able to be saved. No, day one started with my mother, when I was thirteen years old. Some, no matter what, you have to let go.

Danny then bounds down the stairs and arrives to the spot where we are standing. He's wearing a tux that looks identical to mine, except instead of a white tie and vest he has on a black vest with a dark forest green tie in place. He too looks as good as any time I can recall. If it's any indication of how the rest of the day is going to be, I'd say everyone is going to look swell.

"Are you both ready?" He asks us.

"Ready," I say steadfastly. I'm ready to leave 157 Elm Street to embrace the sun and welcome the fresh air flow across my face. The Catholic Church in Alden is only a little over two miles from our house. Everything is close together in Alden after all, the sprawling sights and heights of New York City were never anything that I had to deal with here. The two places are as different as they could ever possibly be.

Danny slides past us and opens the front door for both my mother and I to exit before him. I can feel the warmth of this fine spring day as soon as we step onto the front patio. That's when I see it sitting in the driveway, as black as it's ever been: the Ford Victoria. It looks much older than the last time I've seen it, but it is still in a fine condition nevertheless. My mother must have taken very good care of it in the days that filled themselves in between the last time I rode in it. I look up to the sky and hope to myself that nothing of a similar nature that happened to Danny and I on our way to find Ellie on that second day will occur today.

"I've got the keys!" Danny says from behind us as I open the car door for my mother. She slides into the middle of the front seat so she can be in between Danny and I. My brother and I close our doors at the exact same time with a double resounding thud that pounds through our ears. Danny turns the key and the engine roars on.

"Here we go," he says as he puts the car into reverse and we pull out of the driveway and leave our house behind us. My mother puts her hand on my thigh for a moment and when she does so I turn to look at her. My brother looks in our direction for a second too, only taking his eyes off the road for an instant, of which I am glad, the last thing we need today is an automobile accident of any kind. I am elated and I am thankful for that fact because it is exactly how I should feel on a day like today...my wedding day.

The elm trees on either side of the street stretch their branches out over top of us and protect us from the glare of the sun. When we leave their territory and turn onto Main Street the sun returns and shines on us all. The little stores and city buildings of Alden appear drenched in the light, the windows functioning as eyes and the main doors opening as mouths with people pouring out into the day as if to wish us on our way. The women in their colored dresses walk alongside men in their buttoned down shirts. The only stoplight in Alden that is located in the middle of town is green, which I take to be a good sign as we continue on through. The children play in the small park in the middle diamond as we pass further downtown. The main stretch fades behind us as we reach the edges of town and come upon to where St. Agatha's church sits by the creek. Danny pulls into the church's parking lot and stops the car. I open the door and extend my hand to help my mother out. The two of them walk towards the church; it's tall white steeple stretching towards the sky before us. I watch them go as I stand by the Victoria for a moment and then I begin to move in a slightly different direction, out of the parking lot and towards the creek to where a small field with tall grass lies.

"I'll be inside in a minute," I yell to them as my mother turns around after a few moments when she realizes I am no longer at her side. "Go and say hello to Ellie for me!" Lord knows I can't see her for a bit longer anyways, I think. I'm sure that she and her parents along with Rebecca arrived from the Red Rose Inn a while ago.

"Alright dear, that we will do."

I turn back around and walk into the field, skimming the long grass with my fingertips as I enter into it. There isn't a path per se, but it looks as if someone had walked through here recently as some of the strands are pushed down. I feel a sense of déjà vu, even though I've never lived anything like this before. Then again, perhaps I have, it's starting to get a little hard to keep track of all of the moments and memories in order within my head. I push on further through the field, following the path which was trodden before me and then I arrive to where I wish to be, on the edge where the grass meets the creek in the most direct manner. I turn back slightly to my left to look at where the church shines white in the bright May sunlight. We couldn't have asked for a more perfect day.

The water current pushes the molecules of H_2O past me and I wonder if anyone or anything is really going anywhere at all. If so, then where do we end up? Is there an end in sight or do things just get reused and recycled, like drops of water that flow through circles for eternity? My thoughts of how things are and how they should be are suddenly interrupted when I hear a noise behind me. As I turn, I can feel the presence of someone close to me. When I am face to face with whom it is I cannot believe it. Even though I know I should be able to believe it from all of what has occurred up to this point in some seemingly ordered yet random way, I still cannot.

It's Chloe. There is no doubt about it; she is sitting two feet before me, her golden coat hinted and hued with the sunlight that shines down upon her. The green grass that was walked upon before had to have been from her, she knew I would come to this spot all along. I gasp, not in an exacerbated way but in such a tone that my breath becomes slightly irregular. She tilts her head to one side as if to ask a question, but she never does. I half expect her to speak, but no words emanate out from within her. I stare at her for a minute or two longer, not wanting to move, as I am afraid to shake up some balance that was put in place for a reason. My guide is before me, and as I take note of this fact, I realize now that had to have been her those three times before too. She never told me she was going to make an appearance on each of my days, but so she has.

"Chloe?" I finally ask. She doesn't answer. Of course she doesn't answer. Dogs can't talk, at least not here. Instead, she lifts up a paw and I reach out my hand to shake it. Before I am able to touch her though, she jumps back suddenly and begins to run away at a speed so fast I only half realize that she is going away before I am able to start sprinting after her. "Chloe! Chloe!" I yell as I stumble through the grass as quickly as I can, trying to catch up with her as her four legs propel her faster and away at a greater speed than that of which my two can take me.

"What are you doing here?!" I yell through stifled breaths as she gets even farther out of my sight. We reach the edge of the field to where a forest of trees stretches out across the edge of the water and then back into where there is only darkness from the leaves that cover every inch of the woods that go on from there. I see her turn back to me at the brink, her eyes burn into me and as I stop to look at her directly, it is almost as if she nods, but I may have just imagined it from this distance and the distortion my vision has taken on from running after her and returning back to a still position. She enters the woods then and when I can see her no longer, I know she is gone.

I'm not sure if she has been showing up to help me, or to hinder me, as it could really be either position at this point as I think of how she has shown up before. Her actions caused Ellie to fall and crash to the ground. It was because of Chloe that Ellie had to learn how to walk again, it was her fault. I wish I could find her so that she could somehow help me make sense of this, but I know I can't. Deep down inside I know now that I will see Chloe again on the remaining three days I have left to change, but I believe that I won't get any answers to the questions I want to ask until this journey is done and I end up wherever it is that I will.

I readjust my tuxedo jacket and turn around, away from the dark woods so that I face the green grass again, where the blue waters of the creek and the tall white steeple of St. Agatha's fill out the painting of my life. I know my bride and everyone else I love is waiting inside. I push on, as the grass remains downtrodden I walk above it and forget about what for now shall remain as insignificant as it can. Although, even the smallest of things can be important I remind myself, no matter how strange or trivial they may appear, the most miniscule of details always have the possibility to make all the difference. I won't think about that any more now. All I want to think about is that shortly I will see Ellie in her white dress and somehow I know it will look even brighter and more beautiful than the white of the church shining in the light shed down from the heavens. I will push on, for now and forever, as today...today, is my wedding day.

I enter the church and the sweet scent of the fragrance from the yellow flowers hits me with my first few steps. The light shines through the colorful stained glass windows on either side and I walk from the entrance and make my way back through the sacristy to where Danny and the priest are waiting.

"You okay buddy?" my brother asks me when I arrive to a spot beside him.

"I'm fine," I reassure him. "I just wanted to get one last breath of fresh air on my own before I came inside. That's all."

"Understandable."

The two of us exchange pleasantries and small talk with the priest and as the conversation goes on I slightly fade away. The minutes pass and as they do I know I'm getting closer and closer to seeing her, in just the way I've always wanted to. After a while Danny exits the room and goes out into the main part of the church to help usher guests to their seats. I have to wait a bit longer with the priest before it is time for us to go stand up at the front.

"Your Ellie is a great girl," he tells me.

"Thank you sir," I say to the priest, realizing I don't even know his name. He's around sixty years old, short and squat but with a kind face that contains the rosiest of cheeks. His demeanor is a pleasant one and I am glad of this fact. I wouldn't want a holy father of faltering means officiating our service. This man seems sure of what he's doing.

"I can really tell how much she loves you, even from last night at the rehearsal alone. I'm sure you will have a beautiful life together."

"That's what everyone keeps telling me," I say to him somewhat hesitantly. "I sure hope it comes true."

For it hadn't before, even when everyone still thought the same thing. In any reality that has existed for me, people always thought Ellie and I were perfect for each other, even when sometimes we weren't. They always told us that we would have a beautiful life, and that when things went wrong they would somehow end up right. At times they didn't though, at times, things fell apart beyond repair, but it's different here, or so I keep telling myself. This is a new trajectory of seven days that are connected together to give me a second chance at the life I've always wanted to lead. Even if things go wrong, at least I still have a chance to try to fix them, to make them right.

"Anything can be true, all you have to do is believe," he says to me. I look at him and nod, trying to accept the sentiment he has offered. At that moment before I can say anything else Danny returns to the sacristy to where the two of us are standing and tells us it's time. The guests are all seated and the procession will begin shortly. I follow him out to the front of the church as the priest trails along behind me.

The sunlight is filtered through colored glass and the shining quality of it dazzles me when I first take my spot. Before looking out to the people who I know are sitting there I look straight up into the rafters, to where dark red oak beams of wood hold up the white brick steeple and the church as a whole. Every piece of the building functions for some purpose, for some reason, and as I think about this I wonder about God for the first time in quite a while. Although I said a prayer this morning, I don't know if it was specifically addressed to God, for I've never fully decided if I believe in one. I've died, but then again have I really? I still feel very much alive even though I know this isn't any normal kind of life. Was it God who decided that I should get seven days to relive, seven ways to have a second chance? Perhaps I will find out eventually, when they are over. And then again, perhaps I will not.

My eyes drift down from the rafters and when they do I take in the people who are sitting in the pews lined up in front of me. On my side of the church I see my mother first, sitting in the front row in her yellow dress. I'm so glad she is here. Beside her are her parents, as well as Grandma and Grandpa Wood filling up the rest of the lane. Behind them I see all kinds of people from my life in the city and from Alden too. I see Susan, Steven and Margaret Henderson, Mr. Williams, as well as Jimmy who looks much older than the last time I've seen him. Friends from Parsons are in attendance and so are some people I don't recognize. I suppose for all of the overlap that has happened, there had to be empty spaces from all of the changes that have occurred. For the entirety of the individuals I've known in both versions couldn't be complete, it wouldn't be logical if the Venn diagram of this experience was even on both sides. I look at Ellie's side then too, and the first thing I notice is that both her mother and father are sitting in the front row. I find this strange, seeing as I assumed Ellie's father would be at the back of the church, walking her down the aisle like the tradition goes.

The music starts then and the doors at the back of the church open to reveal Rebecca, who looks stunning in a forest green colored dress. I turn to look at Danny to my left and as I watch him watch his wife I can see how much the two of them are in love. It makes me happy to see this kind of experience occur for my brother. I wonder why he and Rebecca never got married in my life, or even yet if the two of them even met then. The Danny I knew never had a woman like this, or at least if he did, I never took notice of it. Maybe the 'real life' Rebecca was the one who got away. Even though Danny and I didn't remain close in life, and as years went on we fell even further and further apart, he was still a decent man. I had always imagined he had to have had a woman, at least for some time. Perhaps things had just gone wrong, perhaps he had been like me, just another man who had messed up with the woman who mattered the most. When Rebecca takes her place on the other side of the church with the priest in between us, the music changes and the congregation stands up. I turn to Danny, for I have to see if he knows the answer to my question. I have a feeling he does.

"Why isn't her father walking her down the aisle?"

"She wanted to do it on her own Priam, to prove that she could."

It all makes sense then. Ellie, after struggling for the past year to walk again, wanted to show the world and all of the people closest to her that she was a woman who would never give up. Even when things went wrong she would challenge them head on and prove that nothing bad could get her down. As the door starts to open I am covered in a feeling of ecstasy that can only be described as the kind of chills that freeze you to your core and then melt you in warmth ever so quickly. The moment before I see my bride to be I feel like a puddle of pure outer body extension, as I know that Ellie is far stronger than I have ever been, or I will ever be.

When the doors open completely the white light from outside shines through so that all I can see is an ethereal glow. In time though, she emerges from it, her white dress just as flawless as I expected it to be. She walks towards me, down the aisle on her own and I don't see a single hint of pain in her eyes. Instead, she walks with strength, an epic smile on her face that I know will play on repeat in my mind for the rest of my life or whatever eternity I have the ability to reside in. Her dress is covered with delicate white lace embracing the curves over her shoulders, arms and breasts. Tiny white buttons go down the center of her chest, leading to her waist where thick white cloth is wrapped around her middle, accentuating her tiny frame. From there, the gown expands, as the bottom part of the dress fills out, creating a full hoop of white taffeta and silk that bounces in an ephemeral way with every step she takes. The thin veil that covers her face is unable to hide the beauty that emanates through it. The dress itself is just as I thought it would be, it's what I wanted it to look like and I know it is the kind of dress that Ellie had always wanted to wear on her wedding day. Even in her marriage to me, her true spirit shows, not only that of stunning elegance, but the slight traces of a dancer, as her white dress takes on the silhouette of many of the costumes she had worn on stage in the New York City Ballet. From the perspective of a man who has lived in this time period and many more decades yet to come, I realize that Ellie's loveliness is timeless. She could look as she does now in any occurrence and would be accepted and praised for the goodness she holds. I smile at her the entire way, we don't take our eyes away from each other and for the time that she is walking towards me down the aisle it's as if no one else in the room matters. Everything fades away and all that it is is just the two of us, finally achieving what we sought for so long to attain.

When she reaches me, I extend my hand and take hers in mine. I feel the coolness of the engagement ring upon her finger which juxtaposes against the warmth of her small hands. Our bodies touching, I already feel as one, as I've always felt with her. Even though I feel as if she knows what I'm thinking, I say aloud: "You look as beautiful as I ever thought you could be, and then ten thousand times better on top of it."

She smiles and says "Thank you Priam. You look so handsome. We've made it. We're here." And so we are. The priest begins to talk and the moment we exchanged still remains, as I look at her further, not able to let go or leave the safeness of her gaze.

The ceremony happens, readings are read and gospels proclaimed. I vow to Ellie to love her forever and she vows to do the same. I slip a wedding band on her finger, and she slips one on mine. The traditional rituals of the wedding itself are not what I will remember the most. What I find supreme is that we made it, that even though Ellie was trapped in a hospital bed only a little over a year ago with not much hope to hold onto, she never gave up and I like to think that I never gave up on her. Even after all of the times I messed up in life, I've never stopped loving her. I am unable to do so. This wedding is what I always wanted us to have, and now, the actuality of the fact will forever be ingrained within my mind. It is a reality. The ceremony comes to a close and as the stillness surrounds us it is broken by an exclamation from the priest.

"I now pronounce you man and wife. May I please introduce to you all Mr. and Mrs. Priam Wood!" The congregation claps and I'm smiling ear to ear as Ellie beams back at me, her splendor setting fires of unforgettable freedom inside of me.

"Priam, you may now kiss your bride!" he yells, his rosy cheeks even redder. I put my hand around her waist and pull her towards me. Our lips meet and it's the best kiss that there has ever been. No other kiss can compare to the creativity that concludes between the two of us in this moment. The sound of the applause disappears and I lose myself with her, as I often used to do. She is all I need, the only one I ever wanted. I've got her, and she's got me. If only this was the way it would have always been.

The reception is held outside, underneath an enormous white canvas tent that is set up by the edge of Woodboro Lake, which is only about five miles away from the center of Alden. The grass that would normally be present underneath our feet is overlaid with timber tiles that piece together to create a hardwood floor to dance upon.

A white limo delivers Ellie and I from the church to where everyone is waiting for us by the lake. It seems that the theme of the day is always going to be encompassed in white, and as I think of this thought, my mind wanders back to the white abyss where this journey started. I don't stay there long though, where I am in the here and now is too good to drift away from. The driver opens the door for us and we step out and are greeted by hooting and hollering as our guests are once again applauding our union. I look to Ellie and grab her by the hand and together we walk into the tent to the middle of the floor, which opens up as the one hundred fifty guests spread out and then surround us so that the two of us are centered in the circle, with just enough room to dance.

Dance, that single word bounces around the room and I can tell that everyone is expecting us to do so now. But can Ellie dance? I pull her from my side so that she will be right in front of me and I see the terror in her face as she realizes too what everyone wishes to happen next. The silence encompasses us and I don't know what to do.

"Priam, what's going on? I thought we agreed that we weren't going to do this."

I don't know what to say. I have no idea what we agreed upon and even more than that I have no clue as to what I was thinking yesterday, or the days in the year before, as I wasn't really there to witness them. I hear a needle hit a record somewhere in the distance, like a pinprick in the middle of a place no one thought existed. The speakers drown in the volume that plays as the orchestra bounds forth and pulsates as the music invades us all. I recognize the beginning of the song, it's *At Last* performed by Etta James. It's then that I know that I, myself, had planned this all along, at least the version of me that was here in the interim between when I actually was around to tell Ellie on her hospital bed that today would be the day we would get married. The doctor had said she would be able to walk in time, but he never believed she would be able to dance. I however, didn't believe him. I believed in her, then, now, and forever.

"You can do this Ellie," I tell her. "You were born to dance."

Her eyes imprint upon me a look of utmost suffering and fright. At the same time, I see a glint that I know she wants to try, but she is afraid. She doesn't think she can do it. "I can't Priam. I just can't."

The crooning voice of Etta James is just seconds away from

blasting through and the two of us are still only standing here, facing each other and wondering how this is going to play out. Although the Ellie I know has never been one to give up, as she proved earlier today when she walked with strength, all by herself down that aisle towards me, dancing was something else altogether. Walking was one thing, but to Ellie, dancing was so personal, even if it was only a slow dance with her husband to a song she had always loved, dancing was a part of her and if she couldn't do it at her best, she didn't want to do it at all.

"You can. All you have to do is believe that you can." I put my hands on her waist and I motion that she lift up her arms to wrap them around my neck. She does so, ever so slowly and that's when Etta's voice fires up, starting the lyrics that will be stuck in my head for the rest of the evening. I begin to move my feet side to side and back and forth. Ellie is still rooted to the spot, but after a few more moments she finally decides to let go and move along with me. I turn us around, so that the circle of people can have another view. That's when the foreboding from her face disappears, and she smiles for the first time since we reached the middle of the floor.

"I should have known better than to think you wouldn't force me to dance on my own wedding day," she whispers into my ear, the warmth of her lips feeling so close.

"I knew you could do it."

"Well, I guess moving side to side with you as my guide isn't really that much of a challenging dance," she says, not letting herself feel pride for being able to accomplish this much.

"You stop that right now Ellie Wood," I say, calling her by her new name for the first time today. "You've done so much already, you've overcome what so many women would have given up on. This is the first dance of many more to come. Even if you can't get back to the ballets you used to take part in, the two of us will have other dances like this one. I can promise you that."

"I guess I just needed you, to help me overcome my fear of trying."

"You've never really needed me. You just happen to think so. I'm not upset about that fact though, because as you know, the one thing I've always been good at is trying. Sure, I don't always succeed, but that doesn't mean I won't give it a go. And together, think about all of the things we can achieve."

"I can't wait to see what our life holds in store. I'm sure that sometimes we'll fail, but in the end of it all. I know we'll succeed."

I kiss her then, for all of the faith she holds in me, and the ability to believe even when it isn't easy to do so. Ellie had her insecurities and vulnerabilities but at the end of the day she never gave up, at least not completely. Ever since I had met her when we were seventeen, she was the kind of person who would even hold onto the things that she let go of. That was what made her special, that was one of the millions of reasons why I loved her. The music plays on and it tells a tale of a love that feels similar to the one we have. Our dance continues, for a few more minutes until the sound fades away. I push out my arm and propel Ellie from me so that I can then twist my hand around and twirl her in a circle. It takes her by surprise, but by the look on her face when she returns to me I can tell that she is glad I did it.

"I've never felt happier than I do right now," she says.

"Neither have I," I tell her.

When it's over we separate, but only for an instant before our fingers link again and we walk into the crowd of people who are around us, as they compound upon us, shouting in excitement and offering congratulations. I look to Ellie in that moment and she looks at me too with a smile. We revel in the utmost glory of it all.

The night goes on, and even though Ellie doesn't dance again, I know that she will again one day. Both Danny and Rebecca give toasts and I feel myself tearing up at their kind sentiments. Dinner is served and it's even more delicious than my mother's cooking, which is saying a lot. I'm so happy with the way that everything has turned out, and I'm so relieved that nothing has gone wrong. My confusion of coming face to face with Chloe outside of the church is still present in my thoughts, but I don't let it come to the forefront. I try not to think about this day as a second chance or a version of a relived life, instead I simply try to go through it as if it is just any other day, even though I know it's not.

At the end of the night, before Ellie and I head back to the Red Rose Inn we all leave the cover of the tent and it's hardened floors and gallop out into the night to where the moon shines down and covers us in it's gilded glow. The light reflects off of the strands of waxen looking grass which are sprinkled with tiny amounts of dusken dew. When we come to the edge of the lake there are twenty white paper balloons sitting about that have been set up a few minutes previously by the reception attendants. The crowd breaks apart and separates, gathering in groups around each one, ready to light the bottoms so that they may fill with hot air and drift up into the sky to greet the silvery splendid night. With the white paper balloon at our feet, myself, Ellie, my mother, Danny and Rebecca circle around it. We are the first group to be given the flame, and Ellie and I light the bottom of it together. The others help us guide it up and we all watch in awe as it begins to float away. Shortly it is joined by all of the others. The small groups that were in place mix together then, as every person is intertwined, staring up at the stars, the moon, and the new additions to the night, the bright white paper air balloons that are leaving and going away. With each of the balloons that fly I wish for something great, even though I don't really know what I'm wishing for.

There isn't much time left in the day when the two of us make it back to the Red Rose Inn B&B, but there is enough to make a few more memories of the night with my wife. I carry her across the threshold of our suite and we stumble in together as one, laughing all the way until we collapse onto the bed, covered in pillows and fluff filled blankets, every single one of them the sprightliest of whites.

We make love, for what feels like the thousandth time as well as the first. Her body feels new again and I feel an entirety of continuation within myself that I've never felt before. I ignore the large scar on her back and pretend it's not there. My limbs are in an accordance of harmonious rhythms that I can't understand but don't have to plan. Her body is an extension of my own and I feel at one with her and the movements that we make. It feels great. If I could express how sweet it is to touch her next to me once again I would, but some things are far too unimaginable for words. When it's over I turn and lay on my stomach and she begins to trace her fingers down the small of my back, creating a soothing sensation that cools the temperature of my body immediately. I enjoy the impression she makes, but realize what I would enjoy more is seeing her face for a few moments more before another one of my day slips away from me again. I turn around and when I am in a comfortable position she adjusts so that her head rests upon my chest, her long brown hair swirling around in a chestnut colored pool. I run my fingers through it, the softness introducing itself to the tips of my hands, the ends of my being.

"How many children do you think we will end up having?" She asks suddenly, disturbing the silence that was in place and starting a conversation anew. "I've always wanted a house full of children."

"As have I, but even just having one child with you would feel to me like a miracle unto itself," I reply. I don't think before I say it, it just comes out. When it hangs there in the balance between us though, before she is able to answer what I have said, it all comes rushing back to me, a million different feelings and unreturned requests that were asked to give me an absolution that would ease what was done.

Charlie. My consciousness concentrates on him now. I realize as I lay here that Ellie has unintentionally reminded me of what day will come next. The day I feel I regret more than any, or at least, the day that I caused the worst thing to occur. It was my fault. Sure, it wasn't I who directly caused the action, but I put the wheels in motion. I wasn't the kind of father to him on that day that I should have been.

Charlie Wood, my son, the only one Ellie and I had, was the sweetest boy that could have ever lived, until the day he didn't. There was so much life to be had and so much hope to hold onto, but while there was life, there was the opposite too. I lived a life where there seemed to be endless death. At least in the terms that the ones I loved the most were the ones who always left too soon.

I could have done things to change it, to stop it, or at least try to make it better. Although this day, my wedding day with Ellie has been nothing but sheer bliss, it begins to end now on a sour note, one that seems to dig down inside of me to plant a flower that will burst through my heart and tear me asunder. I saved my mother on that first day, even though I was unable to do it simply by deciding to, I changed enough to help her make it through. I tell myself right now that I can do the same for Charlie. I have to. Especially since I considered what happened to him to be more of my fault than anything else. Oh, regrets can take you over, shrivel you up and sound you out until nothing else seems real except for what you wish to change. And so I can try, day five is nigh.

With the changes that have been made already I start to wonder if Charlie will be different, or born in another month or year. I can accept that happening, but could it be that perhaps there will not even be a Charlie at all? I can't believe that. A fifth day where he doesn't exist would serve no purpose; there would be no justice in it. I know that one way or another, Charlie will be there when I wake up and am conscious of everything again. I know that Ellie will be there too, the woman who is beside me now. Many years will pass, more years than have passed on autopilot than any other gap that has taken place up unto this point, but I believe that there is a certain order to the universe and that the seven days and their original ways have to balance out in some manner with those that are to be changed. Just as I told Ellie to believe on that dance floor that everything would be okay, I listen to my own advice for the moment and let all of these worries coalesce and then rest in the side compartment of my mind.

"I consider everyday a miracle, as long as it's spent with you," she says then. Although I have had so many thoughts in between what I had said and what she tells me then, really only a mere moment has passed. Time can speed up and slow down simultaneously without any right or reasoning.

I kiss her on the forehead, my lips feel a cool layer of sweat encasing her. I lick my lips and then open them to say: "I love you, this, and everyday." I hold onto her even more tightly than before, my heart beats faster, each pump increasing upon the last, summiting to the top until the moment when our wedding day is over, no more. I close my eyes knowing that the day that I have to live through next will be the one that I've tried to forget more than the rest. I'll make a change for Charlie. That is something I can promise. I never meant to hurt him in the way I did, I never meant to send him to the end. This time the only conclusion that will be read is the kind that leads to a new beginning of something better. As the feeling of being taken away returns to me I know it is time to go. I die there, in a way, as I leave Ellie for another day, not to see her again until more than two decades have past, hoping beyond all hope that no matter what happens, some things will always last.

It was months before I saw Ellie again. After the day when she turned me away I called her as frequently as I could. I never heard her voice though, most of the time it just kept on ringing. Once someone picked up, I'm not certain whether or not it was her, but I heard the sound of someone breathing into the receiver. "Ellie? Is that you? It's Priam. Please...we need to talk. We have to-" Before I could say another word there was a loud click and then the drone of the dial tone was ringing in my ear. Whoever it was, Ellie or not, they didn't want to talk to me.

By the end of that first week, I realized I needed to stop calling her and just man up and go to her apartment to talk with her face to face. It was easy to hang up on me, but I figured if I was able to put myself in front of her, if she had to look me in the eye she might let me stay, at least long enough to get a word in edge wise anyways.

I left my apartment and drudged out into the pouring rain on just another manic Monday. Everyone was rushing as the commute to the city was in full swing. I too was hurriedly dashing to where I wanted to be, but it wasn't because I needed to be there at a certain time, rather, it was because the feeling inside of my body wouldn't stop ticking. When I made it to her apartment, I put my fingers to the doorbell and felt the smooth grooves on it prick me in an unexpectedly unexplainable way. I had rung this bell a million times before and never felt such a reaction from it. I rang it and waited for someone to answer. All I wanted was to see her again. After a minute, I heard someone coming down the stairs and I felt relieved that I would finally be able to sort this all out, I would be able to tell her what a mistake she had made and that everything would be better this time around. Even though I had told her similar tales before, this time I absolutely meant it. I never got the chance, at least not that day. Ellie didn't answer the door, somebody else did.

When the door opened, a large and hairy man stood before me. He was wearing a white tank top that stretched thin over his protruding belly. He looked down at me and scratched his head with one hand as he pulled a cigarette out of his pocket with the other, lifting it to his face and lighting it. I didn't know what to say, so I didn't say anything at all. He stared at me for a moment longer and then seemed fed up with the silence, breaking it. "Whattya want?" He asked in a gruff, harsh manner.

"I'm looking for Ellie Donahue. She lives here. Who are you?"

"It don't matter who I am," he responded in an unapologetic way. "And she don't live here anymore. I do. She moved out a few days ago."

My heart sank. Things really were changing, just like Ellie said they were going to. If she had moved away, I had no idea where she had gone. The city was an enormous one after all, she could be anywhere, I had no idea where to find her. The only lead I had was the unpleasant man in front of me. "Where did she go? Did she leave a forwarding address? Can you help me? I desperately need to speak with her."

"Sorry. No can do." And then he slammed the door in my face. The only lead I had, that horrid man who was my one hope at figuring out where Ellie had gone didn't give two shits about me or my problems. He had no desire to help me find the woman I loved. She was gone and it would be even longer still until I would find out where she had went.

I didn't know it at the time, but Ellie had moved in with Juliana, her best friend and fellow dancer from the New York City Ballet. We had met a few times and unfortunately she despised me for reasons I would never truly understand. If it had been up to her, Ellie never would have seen me again. Luckily, Ellie had a mind of her own and although Juliana influenced her decisions a great deal during that time, she didn't have the final say in what Ellie chose to do when it came to me.

After I had been turned away at Ellie's old Brooklyn apartment, I went to her parent's place and although they answered and wished me well, they were unable to tell me where Ellie was. Not because they didn't know, but because she had asked them not to. She had covered her bases, in a thick chalky dust as if someone just kept sliding into home, just as her new home was unknown to me.

The only other strategy I could think of was to sit outside Lincoln Center whenever I got the chance, hoping to catch her on her way out after practices and shows. While I sat there, I could hear the symphony play and I imagined her dancing on the stage again. I longed to go into the theater and watch it firsthand, but it didn't feel right to do so. I told myself I couldn't watch Ellie dance again until I knew she wanted me there. I wouldn't take advantage of the fact that I could buy a ticket and sit in the audience and watch her, especially when in the past that was all she had wanted and I had missed her ballets so many times. I never saw Ellie walk out of the theater and I figured it was because she knew better than to come out in such a way so that I could see her. She knew I would be waiting. That fact alone should have made me realize then she was thinking about me just as much as I was thinking about her, but it didn't feel like that at the time. The only thing I was aware of was how badly I ached for her to come back to me.

One evening, Juliana walked out of the theater while I was waiting. It was about a month after I had stopped by Ellie's apartment, a month since I had found out that I had no way to find her, no other option besides to sit and wait as the days continued to add up and multiply, passing me by. I recognized her from afar and quickly got up from the smooth granite wall on which I was sitting and approached her. We made eye contact and as soon as our gaze connected she looked away and turned, trying to get away from me before I could reach her.

"Juliana!" I yelled, chasing after her. "Wait! Please wait!" She stopped in her tracks, but she didn't turn around. I put myself in front of her, so she would have to look at me. "Do you know where Ellie is living? I really need to talk to her. Nobody will tell me anything. Please..."

"I imagine that is because Ellie doesn't want to be found," she began in a crisp, cool and collected way. "If Ellie wants to talk to you again I am sure she will make herself known, in the mean time I would suggest moving on Priam."

"I can't move on. I won't move on," I told her steadfastly.

"Don't be ridiculous. You and Ellie were never going to work; I could see that from the moment I met you. You both have different priorities, you want different things, you come from opposite ends of the world."

"You're wrong. We're the same, in every way that two people who love each other need to be the same. Sure, we have our differences, but they aren't anything that should keep us apart. I know I messed up, I just need to see her again, to apologize."

"She's heard enough of your apologies, she tells me so before bed almost every night." At that she gasped and put her gloved hand to her mouth, as if to shut herself up from saying anything more. I don't know if I would have thought more about what she had said if it weren't for her reaction to her own words, but because of it, I knew that what she had said contained a clue of Ellie's whereabouts.

"Every night? She tells you that every night?"

Realizing that it didn't matter much anymore, Juliana went on, removing her hand from in front of her face and speaking in an unrestricted way. "She tells me that and many other things. I give her my opinions too."

"And what are those?" I asked her.

"That she can do better than you. Have a good night Priam," and with that she walked away. I stood and watched her go, her dark plum colored dress shifting in an unnatural way as she moved further and further away, into the night and out of my sight. It wasn't a pleasant exchange, but at least I had somehow bartered out of it the thing I wanted to know most: where Ellie was. It was obvious to me then, she had escaped to a place where she knew she'd be told everyday to stay away from me, by the one person who disapproved of our relationship: Juliana.

It made sense, I knew Ellie was mad at me when she ended things, but I had thought she would have doubts and come back to me. She hadn't though, it had been almost five weeks and she had not so much as let me know she was still alive. If she had tried to get back in touch with me, or even thought to do so, Juliana would have told her not to. Juliana would tell her over and over again that it was time to move on, to find a man worth living with, a man worth living for, and in her opinion, that wasn't me. Ellie put herself in a place where she knew she would be told to stay away from me and she had done so on purpose. As I would learn five weeks later, Ellie wasn't sure she had done what was right for us, but she had been told she had done what was right for herself, and for the time being, that was what mattered to her. It was only when she realized down the road that she couldn't love anybody else but me that the light would shine through the iron covered drapes and break down the glass that destroyed us in the first place.

Once I knew that Ellie was staying with Juliana, I began to

make regular calls to their place. I figured that if I was persistent enough, Ellie would eventually crumble on her regards of not seeing me and give me at least a few moments of her time. Time was something that stretched on for longer than I imagined though. It was roughly three months after that night backstage, when all she would give me was the reflection of her beauty through the looking glass rather than looking at me herself, until I saw her again.

I was sitting on the steps of the stairs to the entrance of the building where she resided, staring at the willow tree planted deep down within the ground before me, as I so often did anymore with no real rhyme or reason as to what I thought would unfold. Juliana would pass me by occasionally, glaring at me every time, yet still nodding her head ever so slightly to acknowledge my presence. She never said a word though. Ellie was never with her and I was beginning to give up on the idea that she was actually living with Juliana after all. I would had to have caught her coming or going from the place at least once with all of the times that I stayed around hoping to catch even a glimpse of her. Then one day I did. It was the beginning of August on an unusually temperate day for what was normally one of the hottest months in the city. I watched the willow tree before me sway in the breeze, it was the only friend I had at that place. It entertained me with a dance to make the minutes meet one another, over and over and repeated. Then, suddenly coming across the street and emerging from behind the branches there was a woman wearing a yellow pea coat and pale lavender pants. Her brown hair was cut short, so that it angled in along her jawbone in a harsh yet refreshingly clean manner. Her lips were bare, and I realized, as she got closer to me that she had absolutely no makeup on whatsoever. She looked so fresh and there was a certain iridescence about her, yet she didn't look like the girl that I used to know, at least not completely. I stood to get up, but when she was standing in front of me, holding a brown paper bag of groceries at her side she motioned with her one free hand that I should stay sitting where I was, on those uncharacteristically cold stone steps that had become my second home, just as the apartment behind me had become her new one.

"You don't give up, do you?"

"Never," I told her.

"Well I guess you were right in saying you never stop trying to get what you want."

"I want you Ellie. I want you back, that's all I want."

"Oh Priam," she said as she set the bag down at her feet and took a seat next to me. She was so close I could feel her, yet at the same time I couldn't because there was a space in between us that kept us separate. Even though it was only inches, it felt like the widest expanse of the ocean. "I don't know what to tell you."

"Tell me that you will give me another chance. Please," I begged.

"You've already been given more chances than any rational woman would give you. It's all my friends have said to me when I tell them how you aren't giving up. They wish you would, and in a way, I wish you would too."

A sensation flowed over my body then, and it was not a refreshing one, instead it was as if a million tiny pins slid into my skin and then ripped themselves out. Tears welled up in my eyes, but I tried to hold them back. It didn't work though, for how could one hold back a waterfall simply by trying to impede gravity's wishes?

"I can't give up on you. It's impossible for me to do so," I tell her in a voice that sounds softer and quieter than my own. "Not when I still think there is a chance at fixing all of this for the two of us." I try to reach out for her hand then but she pulls it away. The ocean in between us remains.

"But that's what you have to ask yourself Priam...do you really think that chance is real? It's been three months; I've started to move on with my life. I wanted us to work out, believe me I did, but every time I thought we were going in the right direction, we wound up taking two steps back. I felt as if I was the only one trying to make it right."

"I tell myself that it's real everyday. I tell myself that there is no one else on this Earth I want to love except for you."

She looks at me then and when I see her, I see someone else. Not a different person per se, but a woman who has come to her senses. She wasn't going to deal with the bullshit I had given her before, that much was clear. She had always been strong, but I had never felt resilience emanating from her pores. She wasn't going to do anything she didn't want to do. But that was the question of the moment that passed us by as we sat there on those stairs...what did she really want anyways?

"I used to think that too Priam, but you can't force love to be real if all it wants to do is be a figment of a reality that isn't achievable."

"Our love is reachable Ellie. It's right here," I said as I stretched out to touch her again and this time she let me. When my hand touched hers, and hers mine I felt a spark light up in the heavens and burst into the brightest of white even though it was the middle of the day and there would be no way to ever see such a light amongst the contrast of the clouds. I felt it and she did too, her body quivered in an unconventional way. I expected her to pull away again, for even though she had let me touch her things felt different, but part of them still felt the same. The Ellie who left me was not the same one who sat there with me. Separation and thoughts multiplied by time, anxiety, and loss had the ability to change a person even in relatively short spans, but even through the wide open spaces of life, it was possible to find your way back. Sometimes though, other ships you never thought would set off to sail get in the way.

"Priam, I'm going to be honest with you. There will always be a part of me that loves you; it would be foolish for me to say otherwise. And even though I still feel something special for you as we sit here now, I just don't think I can do this anymore. Things are different, things have changed."

"What's changed Ellie?" I interrupted.

"I've changed. Our timing has changed. Things have happened in the in between."

"What can I do to get you to come back to me?"

"Nothing. I have to decide that for myself. I've had plenty of second thoughts and in the weeks that directly followed the last time I saw you, I almost came running back to you multiple times."

"But you didn't."

"You're right. I didn't. And there was a reason for that. We have to let go."

"I'll never let go. No matter what happens Ellie, you're the only one I want." What I said was true. I couldn't imagine loving another woman. I didn't want to love anyone else besides the person who sat beside me then, my hand still holding hers, our bodies touching in an elementary way when compared with the ways in which they had collided before. And just as I thought that, they were touching no longer, as she pulled herself away. She stood up, and as she did so I tried to too, but she motioned again for me to stay where I was.

"It was nice seeing you Priam, but I have to go inside. I have plans tonight that I have to get ready for. Maybe we can get together again sometime, I would like it if we tried to remain friends."

Even though her response came from a place of kindness it was the worst thing I could possibly hear at the time. No one ever wanted to hear those words come from a former lover. The idea of going through life with her just as another person I knew was an idea that I couldn't wrap my head around. I would never feel okay with her living her life unless it was with me. I didn't know what to say to her then, I didn't know what to do. She began to walk up the rest of the stairs and when she got to the doorway and pulled out her key I finally got up from where I was rooted and followed up the incline after her. I put my hand on her arm and spun her around. I was determined to kiss her and make her realize what a mistake she was making. I thought that if my mouth impressed upon hers she would be unable to deny what she felt: an unending, all enduring love for me. Before I could do so though, she forcefully turned away and pushed me off of her. She did not want to feel my kiss upon her lips. She wanted to let go.

"No Priam. No. I love you, but I can't kiss you. Not now. I didn't want to have to tell you this, but I've started to see someone else. He's a good man, and I can't keep playing these games with you. I've moved on."

The situation just kept getting darker and darker; the spark that existed in the sky before when we first touched again went out completely as I slowly walked backwards down the stairs away from her. "How?" It was the only word I could say. The only question I could ask.

"It just happened. He's a fine and respectable man. I've known him for years; he's a production manager at Lincoln Center. His name is Theodore Granderson. I think you met him at one of the after parties once. Apparently he always had eyes for me but kept his distance because he knew the two of us were together. He's been a gentleman about it all; he waited until just last month before he made his advances. I didn't want to go out with him at first, if I'm being honest, but I convinced myself that I have to see what else is out there. I've never been with another man."

"That's because you belong with me," I told her, my voice harsh, coming out choked.

"How can I know that if I have nothing to compare it to? I'm sorry Priam, but this is just the way it all turned out. I didn't want to leave you, but you gave me no other choice. I can't settle for love no matter how great it is if it always finds itself in a certain sense of mediocrity. If we are meant to be together, it will work itself out. If not, we have to let go Priam. We have to move on and respect one another. You have to respect my decisions."

"I just can't."

"And I can't talk about this anymore. Goodbye Priam," she said as she finally unlocked the door, with a new key to her heart that I no longer possessed. Ellie wanted a love that was pure and true, but not only that, she wanted one that would be present with her all of the days of her life. Up unto that point I faded too frequently from her reveries. I wasn't there when she needed me, and now I wouldn't have her in such a way when the roles were reversed. She walked through the archway, into the darkness and away from me. The door shut slowly, and I turned and left, going out into the city and on my way. Trying my best to think of nothing, but unable to shake the feeling of the heartbreak I felt. What I had tried to tell myself would all get better in due time had just gotten worse. I didn't know what to do. Behind the doorway in a place I didn't know, Ellie ripped her yellow pea coat off and threw it on the ground. She dropped the bag of groceries onto the floor and they spilled out, heaping into an unintelligible mess. She slid down along the wall in the entrance by the door and covered her face with her hands and wept. All she had ever wanted was to love a man named Priam Wood, but he had made it so hard to do so. She had to let go, even though it was tearing her asunder inside of the organs that made living and breathing through every dance possible.

Theodore Granderson was a man of many talents. Not only was he handsome and smart, he came from a well to do family on the Upper East Side that had millions of dollars. He didn't know what it was like to struggle, he had no idea what it felt like to fail. He held all of the possibilities and opportunities for the kind of life Ellie always dreamed of having. He had wealth, security, and access to the high society circles that I never would have been able to achieve. He was everything Ellie could have ever wanted in a man, but he wasn't me. For some reason Ellie and I were like two elements that were unable to form bonds with anyone else.

After that day when I talked to her on her doorstep I started to give up, for the first time in a really long time. It was the primary instance that my giving up on thinking I could make it work occurred. As I started to let go, Ellie started to think more prudently about her life and the decisions that were dwindling through her days. As she got closer to Theodore Granderson, she got farther away from me. And although her life had a new sense of grandeur, it was beginning to lose its vibrancy.

A month of further separation passed after I saw her last escape behind that closed door before she sought me out. After that, we began to see one another regularly. Not at night or in any personal proximity, but for lunch dates at small cherry colored cafes and for walks in Central Park. She saw him, but all the while she saw me more and more. The hold he had on her began to loosen and the regularity of my presence in her life began to increase. She didn't allude to it at the time, but she would later tell me that at night, during those dark times I wasn't allowed to see her, she would feel as if her heart was begging her to choose me finally and completely, while her mind urged her to surrender to Theodore's advances. Yet at the same time, how could her heart tell her anything without going through her mind? When she pondered this notion towards the end of 1967 things begin to click into a new kind of machine that had never been produced before.

Christmas Eve 1967 was the day that changed everything. Ellie awoke with the dawn as the sunlight that was present in the sky showed up in her eyes as it reflected off of the white snow on the streets and up through the glass and into her bedroom. As she rolled out of bed and tiptoed into the bathroom, the cold water that splashed across her face felt chillier than usual, its icy surfaces covered her completely, or so it seemed.

The two of us had lunch that day, it was just as all of our other visits had been, regular yet extraordinary. I still loved her with every ounce that I had. I didn't want to be her friend, but I had begun to let go of the idea that I either had to have her all to myself, or not at all. The middle ground was better than nothing. I was settling for her presence before me, as every time it occurred it was like a present I found beneath an evergreen tree. She was distracted, I didn't know why and I didn't ask. Although I figured it had something to do with the evening that was still before her. She didn't often mention Theodore or the things they did, but when she did the words bore holes into every crevice that I contained and stayed there for what felt like forever. She had told me of some fancy rooftop dinner that he had planned for the evening to celebrate the holiday in the grandest way possible. She had told me as we walked to the café that she would have preferred a quiet evening at home in front of the fireplace, but that was not how Theodore Granderson operated. He did everything big, as even the tiniest of details somehow became grandiose. I left her that afternoon with a kiss on the cheek, which was the closest we had yet come to any certain sort of centrality of our previous love affair. It was just a friendly goodbye and happened without either of us realizing anything amiss, but as we both began to walk in different ways we simultaneously felt separately as if something had changed. Was anything really changing though? Neither of us were making decisions except for the ones that we kept on living with one another in our lives.

As she walked away from me she moved closer to him. And that night, on top of that building that was higher up in the sky than I had ever even been in my life, he asked her one question that changed it altogether.

They sat at a white linen covered table that was sprinkled with rose pedals and had a small green wreath wrapped around a red cinnamon scented candle at the center. Towards the end of the meal his hands reached across to hold hers. She let him do so, but when his skin touched hers it felt differently than it ever had before and she wasn't sure why. He was talking about something, but it was nothing that she could hear or comprehend because at that instant she realized his touch felt differently because it was the first time he had placed his hands on her since she had felt my lips impress upon her skin again. Touching another man in such a romantic way no longer felt right as my lips had, in a way, reclaimed her love for me.

Suddenly she came back to the words he was writing in the air and listened to the last sentence he had to deliver which in this case was the most important one. It elicited the response that turned the spinning table back down to a level one, rooted firmly to the ground.

"Ellie Donahue, I love you and want to spend the rest of my life with you by my side. Will you marry me?" He asked as he pulled a small royal blue colored box out of his pocket and popped it open in front of her. The diamond that resided within in it was the biggest she had ever seen in her life, the largest that she would ever see entirely. Even with all of its magnificence, as she stared into the sparkles that circled around each other for what seemed like forever she knew that she couldn't accept it. She couldn't let this man go on any longer this way when she knew deep down inside that it could never be. She had tried, but she was unable to love someone else when she still loved me.

"No," she answered him with that simple word, yet how complicated it was with its single syllable. She didn't know how else to say what she needed to, so she just let the words escape out of her mouth further without any restraint. In hindsight, perhaps she could have let the poor gentleman down a little easier.

"I'm so sorry Theodore," she said as she unlocked her hands from his and pushed away from the table and the strong smell of Christmas time. She was standing then, above him, looking down as she realized that he was already heartbroken. Even though he hadn't known her, he had loved her, or at least he loved who he thought she was: a trophy wife, a beautiful woman who he could show off at his side. Ellie was more than that; she was a sphinx that could spiral her own papyrus and write down a secret that had the ability to save us all, even if she was never truly able to save herself.

"I don't understand..." he mumbled.

"I can't marry you. I'm so sorry I've strung you along like this, but as we've continued to see each other I've just felt more and more of a disconnect that I would never be able to mend. I love you in a way, for your kindness and for all of the things that you've shown me, but I can't promise myself to you when I'm still in love with someone else."

"Priam Wood."

She had never mentioned my name to him when the two of them were together, but she hadn't needed to. He knew well enough that she was never going to be able to let me go. He thought she had, although not completely, but at least in some way. He had just judged inadequately the amount to which she still and always would hold onto me.

"Oh Theodore," she said as she walked behind his chair and put her hands on his shoulders. "You deserve someone better than me anyways. I'm a mess and I probably always will be."

He closed the blue box then and the diamond's shine slipped away from the night, to never be seen again. "I guess it's better for you to tell me the truth rather than to continue on like this when you know deep down inside that this can never be. You should go and tell Priam how you feel. He deserves to know. He's a lucky man after all, he's acquired what I wanted more than anything else...you."

She leaned down and kissed the top of his head and let her hands slide away from his shoulders as she disappeared into the darkness of the night. Theodore Granderson didn't turn to watch her go; instead he stared at the table in front of him and wondered what would happen next.

When I opened the door that night and saw Ellie standing there in a lavender colored dress, with white pearls around her neck and a glint in her eye that told me that something had fallen apart all the while resulting in something else coming together, I didn't exactly know what to do. She was holding a large rectangular parcel covered with brown paper in her hands. I hadn't been expecting her and I had no idea how to properly react. I didn't have to do anything though, for even though no words were spoken, the point made itself known as she set the package down and leaped off of her feet and threw herself in my arms, kissing me passionately.

"I want to wake up next to you everyday for the rest of my life. I don't care if it's not easy or if there is strife. I've decided that I can't live without you and I can't stop loving you no matter what happens or what goes wrong. I'd rather live a mess of a life with you and still know that at the end of whatever it is that occurs between us our love will still remain, than have an easy life with a man that I only feel a slight adoration for. While what I had with him was one grain of sand, you and I are the entire stretch of the sea."

"Ellie." I just said her name and nothing else; it somehow had the power to convey the message I wished to share, which was just that I was so happy she was there.

We made love that night and all throughout the next day, over and over again in front of the fireplace, as we laid covered in thick red blankets on the floor. The parcel Ellie brought rested on the mantle place above us, as she had unwrapped it as we entered and showed me what it was. The rectangular shape just so happened to be the painting I had created when I met her, the artwork that I had painted that day in the park when I first met her. She had kept it in her possession all of those years.

We didn't leave my apartment at all that Christmas day. The only reason we would have was to get married and since it was a holiday we had to wait until the sun set and rose again the next day. So thus that is what we did. Ellie became Mrs. Wood on December 26th 1967. We eloped at city hall with no one to witness it except for the people employed at the building where we wed. I had all but given up, as had she, on the idea that we would ever be married in the way that we wanted to be, and even though the ceremony was nothing much to remember, it was the fact that it occurred at all that mattered the most to us.

Life itself, for some reason had forbade us to let go or give up completely as we had held on to the fragments and figments that we had built together. Ellie was finally my wife, the day had finally come and as we left city hall together hand in hand, the snow fell down and we kissed on the front steps of the building, surrounded by falling white flakes just like that day on the swings when our mystic mouths touched for the first time. Life repeats itself and goes backwards and forwards all at the same time, delivering out the present instances that depend on who we are and how we feel. At that moment, all we felt was love, and on that day, it was enough.

Ellie moved out of Juliana's place and into mine. For the first time since we had known each other, everything was different, yet strikingly similar considering how much had changed. It all felt right. As my wife, she shared everything with me, every moment of the days that we lived together in my studio in Brooklyn. Even though the two of us were busy with work and rehearsals, we rung in the New Year of 1968 just us two, singing and dancing and painting together underneath the high vaulted ceilings and the bright white walls that surrounded us until they were colored entirely.

On New Year's day of that fresh and free year I thought of calling Danny to tell him that Ellie and I had finally tied the knot. I didn't call him though, instead...he called me.

"Hello?" I had answered that afternoon with no clue as to who it was or what they were calling for.

"Hi Priam."

"Danny?" I asked in some sort of shock.

"Yes it's me. Happy New Year!" He shouted as unenthusiastically as a shout could possibly be.

"To you as well. How are you? What can I do for you?" I asked, as I figured he had to be calling for something.

"I just wanted to call and wish you well. How are things?"

"They're swell," I started, wondering if I should tell him about Ellie and I. I was just about to spit out the words when instead he interrupted me to tell his own tale.

"I'm glad to hear it. I'm just a little bummed right now, that's all. The girl I was seeing slipped away last night. I don't know how and I don't know why, but she's gone. Gone, baby gone." I pondered then if Danny was intoxicated. The slur of his words seemed to mend together and leave no space for any breaths in between. I meant to ask who this girl was, or what she meant to him and how she got away, but I didn't, I couldn't, as the rectory of our rhetoric changed and ripped through the rails of a wintertime wail.

Ellie clambered out of the bedroom then and came to sit on my lap. She wrapped her arms around me and asked me who was on the telephone but I didn't tell her. I wished no longer to speak to my brother or think of the memories that he was attached to, for now that I had my wife there with me I stopped caring about my brother on the other end of the line who needed me more than I then realized. He had lost the love of his life, just as I had previously. Unlike me though, he would never get her back. I would never meet Rebecca during my life, but Danny still always loved her just the same, it's just that in life, unfortunately for all, she got away.

"I'm sorry Danny," I said to him then, "maybe it'll all work out. Perhaps we can get together sometime to talk. That'd be nice."

"Yeah, I think I'd like that. Well Happy New Year again!" He said with a whimper that I didn't notice, too entrenched in my own happiness to notice the neglect of necessity in his voice. I let him go with one more pleasantry, unaware that he would sulk the rest of the day and never feel as happy again as he had the year before, when Rebecca Whitmore was the one and only woman by his side, the one that spirited away.

Years went by and while the happiness that Ellie and I found was substantial at first, eventually it didn't feel like enough. I didn't hate my job the way I would later grow to despise it as it eventually took all of my time away from me, but I never loved it either. I wished for the days when I could waste away painting all of the things I ever wanted and for all of the dreams I could never remember or muster together in my memory. I saw Ellie dance as much as I could, I didn't miss her shows, I went to all of her opening nights and sat right there in the front row. I had told her I would be there and so I was. I wanted to prove to her that marrying me and leaving what could have been a life of luxury was purposeful and more perfect than what people said it would be.

We were happy, but as time went on we were getting older and as the days faded by us the damage that was done to us required more and more of what we had to give. We wanted a family, not just an apartment that contained our love, but a place to share it further and make it grow. We wanted children desperately, and even though we had been trying since the minute we got married, no seed had yet been sung.

It wasn't until the summer of 1971 that we finally got the news that we had been hoping for. After a long day of work in which I had to give three presentations and paint three other advertisement campaigns for the next day, I came home expecting to greet an empty apartment that contained only the paintings I had been working on. Instead, when I arrived back to where we lived I tumbled on in past the ballet slippers that were thrown halfheartedly in front of the door discardidly. As soon as I tripped over them I knew that she was home. I followed the bright white light that poured out from the corner bathroom that was smushed in between the studio and our bedroom. The door was open just a crack, and as I moved forward I saw her sitting there, on the toilet with a small little plastic fortune teller in her hands.

I stared at her for a moment before she realized that I was there. I watched as she lifted up one hand and pushed her hair behind her ear, so that it held it in place and exposed more of her face. What I saw painted upon her was a look of terror and a prescription for rejoicing. She was scared, yet as I looked at her closer I realized that the other sentiment was showing through further. She was elated at the news that she had been told not by a person, but a linear equation as simple as the horizon in the high tide. She saw me then, as she looked away from the news before her, she turned to me standing in the doorway and leaped up and embraced me, wanting to share what she had just only moments ago discovered.

"We're having a baby!" She said through tears of joy, "What we have been wanting for all of this time is finally here! You're going to be a father!"

I held her tighter then than I felt like I ever had before, not wanting to let go, as she contained every essence of my life that I had always longed for. I was elated at the fact that our family would grow. At that moment all I felt was the joy that emanated through my body as my touch bounced off of hers. I couldn't have been happier.

People always say that pregnant women glow, but Ellie didn't. I hate to sound conceited but she was my wife after all, and within her grew my child, a person that I was yet to know. She didn't glimmer in a ho hum sort of way, instead she shone, as bright as the light and whiter than the utmost snow of any blank canvas that I had ever bought or sought to show. Her pregnancy was a beautiful one, and those nine months although not easy, were days and weeks that I would never forget. The time that built up to the production of a soul that I had such investment in creating was an experience that I had never felt before.

Charlie Kelton Wood was born on June 23rd 1972. From the moment that I laid eyes on my son, the world never spun in the same direction. Although everything still moved forward, I felt as if it all went so much quicker than it had originally done.

I don't really know how to describe all of those years in between, when Charlie morphed from just some little soul that I could hold in my hands into a fine young grown man. It was as if every day that passed us by had something new to offer. I remember his first smile, when he was able to walk on his own for the first time, and when he called out to his mother not by saying Mommy as most children do, but by simply saying "ELL-EEE!" He must have heard it from me, as I often let those two syllables roll off my tongue in adoration whenever she was around.

To me, Charlie was a perfect little boy and I know his mother thought so too. Yet at the same time he was different than all of the others. I think deep down inside both Ellie and I always knew that things with Charlie weren't going to be easy, he was too smart and aware of life to accept it simply in the way that it already was. Even as a child we could see in him a fire for life that begged to rebel against the regularities that the rest of us realized.

Although he was born in New York City, he never came to

know it as Ellie and I had. We decided that we didn't want to raise our son in the hustle and bustle of everything that the streets contained, so shortly after Charlie's first birthday we picked up our lives and moved to Alden. It wasn't something that I would have predicted for us, but as we moved back into the house that I grew up in, as the Henderson's insisted that I take it back from their possession, it felt right. I often saw visions of myself and my mother dancing on the kitchen floor and Danny and I wrestling in the bedroom, but just as those visions appeared they went away too. Instead I saw realities of Ellie twirling around as she cooked and Charlie racing small toy cars along the way.

I was able to take a similar yet better paying position at a branch office of Haversmith that was located in Erie Pennsylvania, which was only about a half hour commute north of our small town. Ellie had reached her peak dancing and thus surpassed it, so although she was sad to leave the theater and the city behind, she found joy in opening a small dance studio in the center of town where she taught young girls the art of ballet. Our lives adjusted as we watched Charlie grow. We both wanted what was the best for him and we told ourselves over and over again that bringing him back to Alden to grow up was the best thing we could have done. Later in time though, we would wonder if it was the mistake that made our future memories muster into a stain that would never go away.

One day when he was seven years old I went to pick him up from his Elementary School. I could see that unlike the previous times when I came to get him he wasn't standing alone on the cobblestone sidewalk against the black iron fence. No, instead a woman with fire red hair was standing beside him, holding his hand in hers. I was puzzled at first, but then I realized the woman was his teacher.

"Hello Mrs. Cavendish," I announced as I stood in front of her and my little boy, luckily remembering her name even though I was sure only two seconds previously I had no idea of it. It just happened to come out of my mouth even though my mind was unaware. "Is everything all right?"

"Oh for the most part Mr. Wood," she said. "I just wanted to let you know that Charlie had a little accident today." She didn't look down at him, and when I left her gaze to give him my own he didn't accept it. He stared down at his shoelaces, one of which was untied and green, while the other was brown and jumbled in a knot.

"What happened Charlie?" I spoke directly to my son, trying not to have to go around the subject and hear it from his teacher; I wanted to hear it from him. He didn't look up though; he kept on with his faraway silence without saying a single thing.

"Charlie, why don't you go over and play in the grass behind the fence for a few minutes while I talk to your father? I think I saw a bunny hopping about over there." With her words he immediately released her hand and ran away behind the black fence as she had suggested. I watched him go, and sure enough as he bounced along his way, a small brown rabbit hopped into sight. He stopped in his tracks and stared at it intently, trying to figure out what it was thinking, and where it was going.

Now that it was only Mrs. Cavendish and I, she got right down to it. "When I say that Charlie had an accident, I don't mean a serious one. In fact, it happens to quite a few first graders, but the circumstances of this one seemed different."

"What do you mean?" I asked her as I set my briefcase down on the sidewalk.

"Well, today Charlie wet his pants, and normally I don't think it would be too much of an issue to worry about, but it's what happened before and after the accident that I thought you should know about."

"Yes?"

"Well, it so happened that I was reading a story to the children and Charlie and a young girl by the name of Betty had volunteered to act it out for the class. It was a tale of a husband and wife who had gotten lost in the wilderness while trying to drive to Alaska. Anyways, that part is not important. Everything was going fine and the kids seemed to be enjoying themselves until Betty got a little too immersed in character."

"What do you mean?"

"She grabbed Charlie around his waist and kissed him right on the lips."

"Are you kidding me?" I asked, slightly flabbergasted. "Are you sure this Betty is actually in the first grade?"

"She is. I know...I was caught by surprise too, but things like this happen more than you think. Kids watch what adults do and try to follow suit. After her kiss parted his lips, his accident happened."

"Well no wonder!" I exclaimed. "This little first grader molested my son!" I couldn't help but yell.

"I think she's just a curious girl."

"Well I don't know what all of the fuss is about. She obviously frightened and embarrassed him."

"I think he was more embarrassed after the fact."

"What do you mean?" I asked as I turned away from her for the first time since she started to tell me what had happened, only to see Charlie perched exactly where I saw him last, still glaring at that rabbit he didn't want to look away from.

"He started screaming. And not just like a temper tantrum that I would usually expect in the situation. He kept screaming the same line over and over again. I think he scared some of the other children."

"Well I don't really care what the other children thought to be quite honest," I told her.

"I understand Mr. Wood, but what the other children think of your son will influence him a lot more over the next ten years than what you'd like to believe."

"Whatever," I said to her, a bit annoyed with all of this nonsense. I just wanted to get to the bottom of whatever it was that had went wrong with Charlie. "What was he screaming?"

"Girls are the worst ones."

"That's it?"

"Yes. But he seemed so angry when he said it. Charlie is such a sweet boy, in fact he is one of my favorite students, but the young man who said those words did so in a way that I couldn't recognize. It was as if something had taken him over entirely."

"I don't know what to tell you Mrs. Cavendish. I suppose his mother and I will have to talk to him about it. I think he was just scared. Little Miss Betty obviously rubbed him the wrong way."

"So it seems..."

"Well thank you for your time," I said as I bid her adieu. I called out to Charlie and this time he turned to acknowledge me. The bunny bounced away and although he looked sad as he turned back to watch it go, when he returned back to my side he had a smile on his face. It was as if the trauma of the day had never even occurred.

I didn't know that he had already hidden it in the back of his mind. Unfortunately for him, it was only the beginning of the times in which he would feel embarrassed and confused as his peers were around him. Charlie Wood was the best kind of son and even though I always thought of him to be the most special one, as the years went on kids began to wonder more and more what was wrong with him, as he didn't fit into the cookie cutter mold of what they expected him to be. He forged his own way.

I never mentioned to Ellie what Mrs. Cavendish told me that day. Through the beginning of our marriage as we raised Charlie together we communicated everything, but for some reason I felt that this one should be left unsaid. So that is what it did, I let it bounce away into the thick green grass and slide between the black iron fence. It was just that I should have caught the bunny then, or at least stared at it more intently. If only I had done so, perhaps I could have saved it. Instead, that little brown rabbit ran across the sidewalk and into the street, where death did it meet.

We wanted to have more children and believe me from the amount of love making Ellie and I did in our thirties you would have thought we would have given birth to half of the babies in Pennsylvania. Negligence never missed us; instead it consumed us in the fact that Charlie was our only one. We tried to give him a sibling and once when he was ten those lines showed up on that little plastic device again and we found out that Ellie was pregnant.

The child grew within Ellie for seven months, we knew that we were going to be having a little girl and that Charlie would become a big brother to the daughter we were going to name Alma. And name her that we did, but she was never conscious long enough to realize it. Instead of making it all the way through to nine months as most babies do, she wished to greet the world sooner and was born two months early as well as arriving with various other complications. Ellie was fine, but our sweet little Alma wasn't.

She only lived on this Earth for seven hours and seven minutes. This was a number I never knew exactly, but I could have bet on it if I had rolled the dice. Getting over the appearance and disappearance of Alma was hard for all three of us. Charlie wanted a sibling so desperately, and Ellie and I wanted to give him someone who would be able to be there for him when we were gone. Unfortunately things didn't work out that way and Charlie Kelton Wood remained our only child, our son. After the heartache of losing little Alma, who we never really knew, we came to the conclusion that we would stop trying, that he was all we needed to make it past all of the time that could never last.

The eighties flashed past us in a certain sort of neon green and blue that was mixed with purple hues. As one year lead into the next things began to change more rapidly. It was a happy time for my family for the most part. We had accepted the fact that it would always just be us three and we became okay with it. Charlie grew from a little boy into a young man. His mother and I tried to expose him to as much as we could, while still protecting him too. Even though we lived in Alden we still took trips back to the city. We didn't want to be disconnected from it completely.

Ellie and I were in love and those years were strong ones for us. The decade in between the strangeness of the seventies and the notoriety of the nineties was a good one, especially because most of its days passed me by without much notice, primarily because we didn't encounter any significant problems. Obviously this time was one of serenity, as not a single one of my seven days would happen during this period of my life. Sure, things went wrong, Ellie and I got into fights occasionally and we had to discipline Charlie for acting out in various ways, but as a whole everything was okay, as okay as it could be for the three of us anyways.

The stories you tell about your life even if placed in a transient paradise are always the ones encountered with strife. It's funny how no one ever really wants to hear the perfect pattern that you found one day. Sure, they want the happy ending, as we all do, but it can't have been too easy to achieve. All of the struggles from day one until you're done have to be filled with frantic and furious instances of absurdity, otherwise, frankly, no one really gives a damn.

So thus the eighties slipped away, and we were met with a new decade when the clock changed from 11:59 to 12:00 and January 1st of 1990 was upon us. A new feeling of feeling nothing was in the air. Unfortunately the simplicity and well workings of what had settled down was about to be shaken up before I would be ready to handle it. Hell, I never would have been able to prepare myself for what would happen to us that year.

I was still working with Haversmith Inc., and while I couldn't believe it, it was the reality I knew. Working in the branch office in Erie was not as stressful as it had been in Manhattan, but it still had the same monotonous tone. The old actuality that I used to live in, where I dreamed up a life where I could create anything I wanted simply for the sake of wanting to was long gone. Sure, I still painted on my own from time to time, but the instances where I bought new canvases were less frequent. Our house in Alden didn't have a studio and even though I made my childhood bedroom into a room where I could paint, as the years passed by I went into it less and less. The oak door that lead into it was often shut and the blank canvases that rested inside were not regularly introduced to color.

I don't know if moving back to Alden stifled my soul in any way, but it did almost feel as if it forced me to let go of my creativity. People in northwestern Pennsylvania weren't as vibrant as the insane slovenly souls that you could find in New York. I missed the city quite a lot, as when I was young all I desired was to escape Alden for the vivacious views that I had never really known. Yet the three of us had all we could really want, and we all seemed as content as we could be. However, looking back I wonder if we were just all pretending to be happier than we actually were.

I tried to be a good husband and a good father too, and while I don't think I failed, I think I could have been better. Even though I never missed any of the concerts or sporting events that Charlie participated in, or the recitals that Ellie put on for her young girls at the local theater, I was often late for no real reason. I blamed it on work, but to tell you the truth I never really had to stay late at my office in Erie. Instead, the times where I didn't show up on time were because I used to walk up to the great lake and stare out at all of the water that stretched before me. I wondered how the body of water in front of me could look like an ocean even though it was only a lake, no matter how great.

The idea of something appearing as one thing and giving no evidence of being anything else, yet still being aware of the fact that it is not what it seems due to indications that you know, has never been something that I had an easy time accepting. I created things that made no sense during many phases of when I lived, but that never meant that I was ever able to fully understand the lessons that I should have learned. As I got older I didn't have the answers to everything, and eventually I realized that some things were better not known. All the while however, I still yearned to grasp the fathoms of the past and the future that fell before me.

Ellie and Charlie never really got mad at me for the times

that I showed up delayed, instead they just focused their energy elsewhere, as they merely stopped expecting everything of me. They realized that while they knew I loved them both with all of my heart, I was a tad bit lost in life and there was no real way for me to be found. So thus, they let a little bit of me go, all the while holding on to the part they had always known.

During the first week of June in 1990, the three of us left Alden for a few days and drove across Pennsylvania to return to the land where every instance of our trio had met and loved each other during one time or another. Recently Charlie had seemed far more distant to the both of us than he ever had before. He was about to begin his senior year of high school and although he excelled both academically and with his extracurricular activities he seemed ashamed of something that made no sense to either of us. It was a problem we couldn't understand, as the end of his junior year had concluded wonderfully in the most concrete of terms, but it was the foundation and the façade beneath it all that was beginning to crumble. Charlie Wood had a secret that was eating away at him each and every day, and even though he had tried to tell his mother and I many times before, it never came out, at least not until that summer.

Before we found out what was going on with our son and why he felt so sad, we had those few days in our city, as I always felt as if New York belonged to the three of us just as much as it belonged to anyone else. We visited museums and even walked past our old apartment in Brooklyn where our family was formed, before eventually descending upon Central Park, where we always ended up.

"Do you think you would have liked growing up in the city?" Ellie asked Charlie as we started to get further and further away from the skyline and became more immersed within the green realm of the world around us.

It was a strange question to ask and when I heard her ask it I wasn't quite happy that she had done so. For a boy who seemed to be teetering on the edge of a certain kind of sanity I didn't know if a question like that would be beneficial for his well being. Nevertheless, he began to answer her with gusto. Perhaps his mother understood him better than I did.

"I would have loved it," he told us both as he walked along

our side. As he began to give his reasons I interlocked my fingers with Ellie's and we strolled continuously. "New York City has everything I feel Alden lacks. It has spirit and spontaneity, it contains people who think outside of the box and doesn't rip up the ideas and differences of those who rebel against what is perceived to be normal, instead it accepts those who are thought to be freaks."

"That's a good point to make," I told him. "But as you know some people here could be less accepting than certain individuals in Alden. It just depends what kind of apple you pick from the orchard."

He laughed at my words then. "Oh Dad, always so philosophical with the most simple of imagery. I often wonder why you don't paint anymore."

"I still paint..." I halfheartedly said without really having much evidence to show for it.

"Not as you used to," Ellie mentioned, partnering up with my son.

"Well it doesn't matter if those days are done," I told them. "This isn't about me or what I say or how I create. Weren't we discussing life in ways that it could have been different if only certain things had been changed?"

"Indeed we were, I suppose any little thing could be different if any circumstances were altered. Relativity will never relate to my senses however," Charlie said and then randomly burst into a sprint, running away from his mother and I.

"Charlie! Wait!" Ellie yelled out, but he just kept on running. In that instant a memory of myself running down the streets of Alden in nothing but my basketball uniform in the dead of winter came to my senses. Wood boys were always running it seemed, even if they had no idea where they were going.

We began to walk faster, trying to catch up with our son, who was experiencing quite the opposite temperature of what I had run through. Whereas I encountered winter winds, he was pushing forward through the hot sun. We watched his pace fade as he came to a certain spot and threw himself on the ground underneath the shade of a massive tree located at the corner of a path.

When Ellie and I finally caught up with him all I wanted to do was scold him for running away from us while we were in the middle of a conversation. I didn't know what was wrong with him, but I found it highly disrespectful the way he was acting. I didn't get the chance to do so though because when we reached where he was Ellie let out a small gasp of realization. Our son was lying spread out on the ground beneath us and we stood above him, as if we ourselves were two trees rooted to the surface offering him more shade than I thought he rightfully deserved.

"Priam...do you recognize this spot?"

I hadn't, and at her words I tried to think to make it compute. And then it did, the three of us faded away, and my viewpoint was pushed back to atop of some rocks that were further in the distance. The massive tree that was hovering over us then was the same one that Ellie had danced underneath when I first laid eyes upon her. We were at the spot where everything had once begun. We were only seventeen years old that day we met in the place where we were then, just as the son we had together was the same exact age, in the same exact spot where in a way, the story of his life, his history, had originated.

"It's where I saw you." That's all I said.

She smiled at me then, before returning her attention to the boy who laid at our feet. "Charlie! Open your eyes, guess what?"

He only opened one, not deeming what we had to say as completely commanding of his attention. "What?"

"You stumbled across the spot where your father and I laid eyes on one another for the first time. Remember the story of how we met? This tree is the exact one that I was dancing under as your father watched me from right up over there," she said as she pointed to the spot where I had painted that painting all of those years ago.

Instead of thinking that the notion was a worthy one, he questioned it. "How do you know this is the spot? There are a million trees in Central Park that look just like this one."

"I just do," she said to him. "Isn't it the one, Priam?"

"It is."

"Well that's wonderful. I'm glad that your love has been so easy."

"What do you mean by that?" I asked of him, as I was slightly angered by the idea that anything his mother and I had ever done or achieved was to be considered easy. Our love might have been strong no matter what happened between us, but one word I would never classify it as was easy.

"You found each other without even looking, you fell into each other's lives and even when things went wrong they still went right. I just can't feel happy for the two of you when you were lucky enough to find your soul mate at the age of seventeen."

"Charlie...stop it," Ellie said to him then, tears welling up in her eyes. She knew he didn't necessarily mean any harm by his words, but she too, just as I knew what we had was never simple or grand. Our love story wasn't handed to us in a bound completed book. Instead the fairy tale created was written by us, complete with struggles that at times seemed impossible to overcome.

He stood up then and looked at us. I don't know why, but he felt as if it was two against one. Instead of thinking of us as three, all he felt was that he was an outsider to our love. Instead of believing of his existence as a miracle of the affection that Ellie and I had planted from a seed that sprung into a tree as massive as the one we were under, our son couldn't let go of the despair he felt for thinking that he would never have what we did. And thus, the culmination of everything he had felt for so long exploded in that moment.

"I can't stop it Mother! I'm not like you or Dad or anyone else I know! People think I have everything I could want, but how can I when I know for a fact that I'll never be in love? People kill themselves everyday over this thing that isn't even a tangible entity of anything. I don't understand it and I'm afraid I never will."

"What on earth are you talking about?" I asked him then, confused as I could possibly be as to what he meant.

"I'm bitter about the way that my body tells me I should believe. There is a disconnect between what I feel, what I know, and what I feel I should know. Nothing makes sense to me anymore. And I'm sorry but hearing about your love just makes me want to puke."

I reached out to grab him by the neck then, to wring his ears and smack some sense into him for his insecurities. I didn't have the chance though, for before my hand even rose above my waist my ears were already becoming acquainted with the noise that was created by Ellie's hand slapping across his face. As soon as it happened I know she regretted it, but she had lost herself in the moment. The fact that the product of our love had spoken so negatively about what we went through to be where we stood appalled her and thus the primal urge she felt to quench the clamor that was throwing dirt on our tale had won out, and brought about the start of what would soon be done.

Charlie stared at her then, as tears welled up in his eyes, he couldn't comprehend what his mother had done. All his life Ellie protected and portrayed everything for him, she had never been the one to paint the exit in a place where one didn't exist. Usually I was the one who had to deal out the discipline, but this time, Ellie took matters into her own hands and with the impact of it to the forefront of Charlie's senses, his hope in knowing what Ellie and I knew faltered even more rapidly than before.

"Goodbye Mother," was all he said before he ran away again. He offered me no words, and sprinted past us and on into the park. I started to run after him, but as I heard Ellie yell from behind me to stop, that is what I did.

She returned to my side and said, "We have to let him go. He needs some time on his own. If we follow after him it will only stifle him more. I shouldn't have done that, it's just made matters worse."

"I didn't know they could get any more so with him."

"Things can always go downhill Priam, even at the bottom of the mountain, things can go lower still."

"I just hope they don't," I said. "Why did he say goodbye to you in such a way, without even saying anything to me?"

"I don't know." And she probably never did. As the world continued to spin on and our son continued to run through the park, we stood back by where our love story had begun and wondered what was the matter with the boy we loved. For something was most definitely wrong with him. We never figured out what it was until it was too late, when the worst and last day of Charlie Wood's life ended and commenced in reverse orders that made no prescription of the penalty love could create, and take.

Friday, July 6th 1990
Day Five – The Original Way

I wake up to the sounds of Ellie screaming. My body quivers and shakes itself conscious as her voice loudly reverberates across the room and into my eardrums. When I bring my body forward from its lying position and begin to turn to where she should be next to me my heart skips a beat, as I'm afraid she won't be there. In that moment I worry that something has happened, that something has gone horribly wrong, but next to me is where she remains, as she sits at my side clutching her chest, her eyes open, filled with a terrorized look that I haven't seen her hold before.

"What's wrong?" I ask immediately.

"I have no idea," she says as she lets the trepidation slowly slide away from her sight, accepting the summer light that flows through our bedroom window. She leans into me and wraps her arms around my waist. "I guess I had a nightmare. It's weird though; I can't remember what it was. I just woke up in this state, the disconnect between my dreaming mind and my risen body seem to be at larger odds than usual."

"Well whatever it was, I hope you never have that dream again."

"Ditto," she offers, and then we let the silence succumb for a second.

Ellie and I are no longer as young as we once were. Although the years of our marriage have been good ones for the most part, I often wonder how time has passed us by so quickly. I used to wish for the days when everything would be simpler, when I would have the family and the life that I always longed for. I haven't been able to achieve all I have wanted however, and by this point I realize that I probably never will. I don't like to focus too much on my regrets, but the truth is...I have many.

Yesterday was my forty-ninth birthday and as a whole, it was a lovely day. We spent the afternoon with the Henderson's; as Margaret is once again our next door neighbor in the house she grew up in. The picnic that Susan, Margaret, and my wife put together was splendid, but there were so many people who weren't there that should have been. For starters, the July sun didn't have the opportunity to introduce itself to my parents, who have been gone for so long now that I sometimes have to remind myself that they were ever here at all. When I feel like this, memories of my mother eventually flood back to me and as the tide of her presence returns, I look at a picture of her that I carry in my wallet, never letting her stray far from me. The shores of her love may rise at different tides, but the water is always present with me, no matter how far I sail away.

I haven't seen Danny in years, so he wasn't at the picnic either. I sometimes wonder if he would come back to Alden, to visit the house he knows better than all others if only I would just invite him to do so. But that's just it, I don't, and a part of me won't. I occasionally think of him and I wonder how he is doing back in the city, but I never call. It's gone on too long like this. I feel I've lost the brother I once knew, pretty much completely.

Charlie wasn't able to attend either, as he has been at a varsity basketball camp in Pittsburgh all week. I suppose that's okay though. My son is still here, unlike the other members of the Wood family, I still have him. Things have been difficult recently, as his mother and I have been worried about his well being. We have been unable to crack the code of what secret he holds within the inner most chamber of his heart. I love him, and I know Ellie does too, but sometimes I wonder if he loves us enough, if he can't even tell us what is the matter.

I feel the warmth around my midsection dissipate, as my wife releases her hold upon me and gets up from our bed. I watch her walk out of our room and into the bathroom. She removes the pink satin nightgown that she is wearing and as I become acquainted with the sight of her naked body from afar, I am put in a sudden sense of disbelief by the reality of how good she still looks. All of those years of dancing did her well, as she remains just as fit as she was during her twenties. We still make love like we did when we were young, it just doesn't happen as frequently as it once did. When it does though, I still lose myself in similar ways.

She turns the shower on and steps inside, I lay back down temporarily, listening to the sound of the water hitting the stones of the shower and drip dropping off of her body. I can't hear the sounds well, but it's as if I can feel them. The sunlight gets brighter now and I have to place my hand over my eyes as closing them alone doesn't do enough. The darkness that is the inner part of my eyelids isn't what I wish to see either though, so I open them up again and let the sunlight of this July day collide with my senses and accept

313

me. Summer days will never cease to drift away and amaze me, even when they really do nothing at all.

I took off work yesterday, and I have off today too. I don't often do so, but I felt the need to this year for my birthday, or rather, Ellie begged me to. Furthermore, this afternoon we are going to pick up Charlie from the basketball camp where he has spent all week and Ellie didn't want to drive to get him on her own. I suppose I understand since it is about two hours away at the University of Pittsburgh. She wanted some company and even more than that, she wanted me to be there when she was reunited with Charlie for the first time in a week, as the rate at which he could have another issue has been becoming harder and harder to surmise. Some days he is fine and the happy go lucky loving boy that we cherish, and other days he paints himself into dark circled clouds that he can't free himself of. It all turns from sunshine to sadness with the flip of a coin.

When I walk downstairs I see Ellie in a similar position that my mother once was in, cooking at the stove in the kitchen, although I know better than to think for a second that she is making pancakes. I haven't had pancakes for decades. Instead, when I sit down at the table and she turns to me, the smell of bacon and eggs wafts in my direction. No cakes created in pans will be served in any shape or form this morning.

"It's seemed rather quiet this week, don't you think?" She asks me as she piles together a heaping plate for me to eat. Apparently she doesn't think we ate enough yesterday. I'm not as thin as I used to be, but by no means am I large and in charge, as the serving that Ellie is dishing out appears to make me.

"Jesus! Why don't you split that in half? I think you gave me enough for the two of us!"

She looks down at the plate, almost as if she is seeing it for the first time. "Oh dear, I think you're right. You know how I am anymore, always making too much food. If we would just get a dog like I've been begging for years, all of the leftovers would have a place to go."

"We're not getting a dog Ellie. They're pointless."

I had never had a dog and to be honest I didn't really understand them. Maybe if I had one growing up then I would be more acquainted with their purpose, but I didn't relate to the idea of having another being in my house that was furry and liked to slobber and make messes all over the place. Cleaning up after Charlie for the past eighteen years was enough. Even though Ellie promised she would take care of a dog if we got one, I knew that I would end up doing most of the work. I wouldn't put my stamp of approval on our acquisition of a new creature that could clamber through our house and be destructive.

"Hmph," she sighs as she sits down beside me, giving up on the discussion before it has really even begun because she knows I won't budge when it comes to this topic. "Anyways, you never answered me," she continues. "Hasn't it seemed quiet around the house this week?"

I think about it, and I suppose she is right. I'm not at the house as much as she is. Her dance studio is in Alden, so when she doesn't have ballet classes to teach, she can come and go as she pleases. When I'm at work I'm trapped. I can't leave unless the workday is done, and even when it is I often feel I can't come home until I stare out at something for a while to clear my mind. Whether it be the lake that I journey to frequently, or a parking lot full of people running around like maniacs, consuming all of America as they buy more products than capitalism could ever contain or calculate for them.

"I guess so. Do you mean because Charlie hasn't been here?" I ask.

"Yes. I mean, that would be the main reason, but then again, it almost seems as if the house is getting progressively quieter as time goes on. Maybe we should have a party, a giant romp that's so out of control that the police are called," she giggles as she playfully lifts her feet off of the floor and rests them on my legs as she forks a bite of eggs into her happy mouth.

I want to scold her for being stupid, but then I catch myself and in that moment I realize it's times like these that make me love her. She's the silliest song that could have ever been written and somehow it's been sung just for me. Her request of a party makes no sense, first and foremost seeing as we just had a party for my birthday yesterday, but it's the spontaneity of the idea that I almost wish I could accept, and even though I can't, I love her for it.

"Ellie, even if we did have a party, like something we used to go to back in New York during your dancing days, I doubt anyone would call the police. Margaret sure as hell wouldn't, you know she would be here doing keg stands until she capsized and her dress fell overtop of her head."

She laughs even more at this idea I have painted for her. Although Margaret is a few years younger than the both of us, the notion of her behaving in such a way at her age and the accompanying inkling that we would be the hosts of such a soiree that would get her to behave so is anything but what seems possible. The dreams that we are able to picture ourselves in, no matter how real or unreal have that stain of uncertainty attached to them, thus somehow forcing us to deal with the actuality of our lives again.

"Oh Priam," she says through stifled hilarity. "You'll always be the one who makes me the happiest." She pulls her legs off of my lap and leans in to kiss me. In that moment it is a beautiful day, at least for the time being. "If only you were to buy me a golden retriever, I would feel my happiness becoming less measurable and more into what is infinite," she continues as her lips touch mine and then she pulls them away.

"The only dog you're going to have is this old one right here," I say pointing a finger at my own chest as she resituates herself in her seat. "And that should be enough."

If only it was.

After that day in the park Charlie apologized to both his mother and I for what he had said about our love. Ellie also said how sorry she was for slapping him. It wasn't an easy thing to talk about after it happened, because I knew that all three of us had felt betrayed in some way or another, but we were able to work through it together, as only our trio could.

Charlie seemed better, but he still remained distant. There were days when the three of us would go on walks from our house to downtown Alden and visit the ice cream parlor, telling stories all the way about times that had passed and ideas we had of how we could spend the future together in the most absurd ways we could muster. Together, the three of us worked as a team, we loved one another and we supported each other in our happiness. Yet even on those sorts of simple days when I watched my son and the woman I loved eat frozen milk condensed and mixed with sugar in apathetic ways, I wondered if I should have been doing more to give them a better life.

I pondered quite frequently if maybe it would have been

better for all of us if we had stayed in New York to live out the rest of our lives. I missed it. Just as I had longed for it during my adolescence in Alden, there were occasions when all I wanted was to never have to leave the boundaries of that metropolis again, but we had. Ellie and I had decided it was the best thing for us, and for our son. I wonder if things would have turned out differently if he had been in a city like New York, where more people would have simply accepted him for the way that he was. Perhaps I too would have understood him better then. That wasn't the way it happened though, that wasn't the way it was. For whatever reason the balance of everything dealt itself out in kings and queens and spared the joker until the last moment, when we were expecting nothing of it's kind to come above the surface to show it's face. It surprised us; it died within and without us.

Later in the afternoon, after a few carefree hours spent around the house and walking through the neighborhood with my wife at my side to pass the time, we get in the car and head down the road to Pittsburgh. I drive, as I always do when I'm ever in a car anymore. I don't like riding in an automobile without being in control, as I know all too well how every turn you make could lead to terror showing up out of nowhere. I've never bought a Ford. Even though they don't make Victorias anymore, I still would never consider purchasing one of theirs. I suppose the way my mother died wasn't necessarily the manufacturer's fault, but I still don't approve of them.

So on we go, in our white Chevrolet to Pittsburgh. It's a beautiful day, and Ellie and I roll the windows down so that a fresh breeze can come in. We listen to the radio, as songs of previous decades greet our ears. The basketball camp that Charlie attended was held at the University of Pittsburgh. I hadn't been to this city much, as the city I had always known was New York, but the few times I had visited it I did enjoy it quite so. After all, it was much closer to Alden than New York City was, but even still, it felt farther away from me.

When Ellie and I get close to the campus, the looming and gothic Cathedral of Learning rises before us. It appears as a tall pinnacle out of the blue, looking down upon us as if we are tiny babies that have to be taken care of. It seems very tall for a university building. Upon looking at it, I wonder if Charlie has any plans to apply to school here, even though I would prefer him to go somewhere in my city, perhaps it would be nice if he went to college a little closer to home. Pittsburgh has always been so unique and welcoming after all.

When we pull up outside of the gym I see Charlie standing outside on the curb waiting for us. He has a large bag slugged over his shoulder and a few more at his feet. He's wearing only a tank top jersey and basketball shorts, the number thirteen emblazoned on his chest. I shake my head quickly, thinking I have seen the number wrong, but no, I saw it right. I am reminded of the day I ran through the freezing cold streets in an outfit almost identical to his: the day I set my brother's project on fire, the day I lost, and the day I gained Ellie with the kiss of her lips for the first time.

His mother waves to him feverishly and yells at him out the window. "We'll be right there honey! We'll go park the car and come and help you with your stuff." He says nothing back. He simply lifts up his hand and shows us the five fingers attached to his palm to let us know that he heard her. He looks lost, as if he is on a sailboat in the middle of the sea, with no compass and no direction.

After we park the car and walk back to where we originally found him, I notice something along the way. While all of the other boys who are clad in basketball tanks and shorts are clustered together in a giant group waiting for their families to arrive, it appears that Charlie is the only one out on the periphery, standing alone, as if he wants nothing to do with any of them. When he sees us getting closer he looks up from the ground and grins in our direction, the idea of us taking him home seems to be one he is happy to accept. When we reach him, Ellie gives him a great big hug and asks him how the week went.

"It was good. I was the leading scorer for my team in every league game we played," he says softly.

"Sounds just like your father back in the day," Ellie laughs as she pinches my side. I bat her hand away and grimace at her playfully. "Here, go ahead and give us your bags, I'm sure you've done enough work these past few days."

"Thanks Mom," he says as he hands off his book bag to her, and his two large oversized gym bags to me. We turn to go, but before we have the chance to do so, I see one of the boys emerge from the huddle and run over towards us.

"Hey Charlie! Wait up!" Charlie doesn't turn; in fact he

acts as if he hasn't heard the boy call out at all. He keeps walking, even though his mother and I have slowed. "Charlie!" The boy calls out again. "I said wait up!" He ignores the call still, not accepting it as anything that is real.

"Hey buddy, I think one of your friends wants to say goodbye to you," I tell him, wondering why he hasn't stopped.

"He's not my friend," my son says as the boy finally reaches us. Ellie and I look at the short and scrawny young man who has approached us and we ask him what his name is. Charlie doesn't turn around to look at him, at least not completely; he is staring off into the sky, as his blonde hair is ruffled by the wind that suddenly blows by.

"My name is Zach. You must be Mr. and Mrs. Wood?"

"That's correct," Ellie says. "It's nice to meet you Zach. Were you and Charlie on the same team?"

"Something like that," he says. "I just wanted to ask both of you a question."

Charlie turns around now, and when he does I can see a look of terror in his eyes, one that I have never seen before.

"And what's that Zach?" I ask him.

"Are you aware that your son is a homosexual?"

"Excuse me?" Ellie asks as her vocal chords crack. "What on earth are you talking about?"

Zach says nothing; he just looks from myself to Ellie and then back to Charlie. In the distance I notice the other boys are beginning to point in our direction, most of them are laughing. It takes a while for me to register what he has said, to realize that Charlie is turning around again, away from this boy and the other ones too, he covers his face with his hands, he backs away from it all.

"I ought to wring your neck for saying such a thing you little twerp," I shout out in anger as I take one step towards where Zach stands and look down upon him with a lot of resentment. "To insinuate something is complete bullshit. I'm sorry if you suck at basketball and are jealous of Charlie's skills, but how dare you say something about him like that, especially to his mother and me. Get the hell out of here!" I scream in his face, so enraged by this boy that I watch as tiny drops of spit fly out of my mouth and land on his face. I do so unintentionally, but my words were lined with a physicality of myself, and I don't feel sorry for it. He wipes the wetness off and runs away, back to the group of boys who envelop him, surrounding him in a circle so that he disappears.

"What in the hell was all of that about?" I ask as I look to Charlie, who is already walking away, away from where we had just been. It is clear that all he wants is to no longer be in this place.

"Can we just go home? All I want is to go home," he says to us as we follow behind him, his bags in our hands.

"We're going home right now sweetie," says Ellie as she shuffles faster to catch up with him. She tries to put her arm around his shoulder, but he brushes it away.

"Not now Mom. I'm sorry, I know you're trying to help, but I just don't want to be touched right now."

"Okay honey." So we walk on, we put his bags in the trunk as he climbs into the backseat. He slams the door shut, so that it is just Ellie and I who remain outside. I look to her for a resolution, or at least some sense of understanding of what just occurred.

"Do you have any idea why that just happened?"

"I don't have the faintest clue," she says to me.

"We have to talk to him."

"We will."

We separate and move to the front of the car and get in on either side. As soon as we sit down in our seats, we both turn back simultaneously to look at our son. He is sobbing hysterically. It sounds as if he can't even breathe as he gasps for air that is eluding him. Something happened at this basketball camp, I don't know what it was, but it has deeply affected my son. Charlie Wood is a strong boy, but as his mother and I have known for a while now, something is digging deeper and deeper within the route of his consciousness and planting a seed of distress in his core. Incomprehensively, unconstitutionally, he is falling apart.

I'd be lying if I say I know how to react right away, because I most certainly do not. I want to ask what's wrong, but I figure that he won't tell us anyways, so instead of addressing the situation, I start to drive away. I want to get us away from this damn basketball camp, away from the punk ass boy who asked that delirious question, and away from the city of Pittsburgh altogether. So, I start to drive. Ellie climbs over the middle consul as we begin to move and sits beside Charlie in the backseat, putting her arm around him. This time he accepts her touch. "There, there honey. It's going to be okay."

"It's never going to be okay," he says. "Not for me."

"Don't talk like that. It will get better. Whatever it is, it will all get better."

I look back at the two of them in my rearview mirror and watch as Ellie hands Charlie a tissue out of her pocket. He lifts the white cottony material up to his face and wipes away some of the tears, then he blows his nose as a great deal of snot is released. Ellie rubs his shoulders, trying her best to calm him down.

"You have to tell us what's wrong Charlie. Tell us what happened."

"I don't want to."

"You might not want to," I say, "but you have to. And besides, if I had to guess, I'm sure it will make you feel better. Your mother and I are your biggest fans. You can tell us anything."

He takes a deep breath and then sighs. He turns to look out the window, as we have now gotten back onto the interstate. The city fades behind us as we are beginning to be enveloped by hundreds and hundreds of green trees again, the kind of scenery that Charlie is more used to than anything. Soon enough, we will be back in Alden. Perhaps that's all he needs to comfort him.

"What happened there, as the both of you saw, is pretty much how the entire week went," he starts as he maintains his gaze outside the window, looking longingly for something that doesn't appear to be there. "Zach wasn't the only guy who talked to me like that and said those kinds of things. Guys were saying that kind of shit to me all week."

"But I don't understand why they would do that," Ellie says, half as a question, half as a statement.

"People have called me gay, faggot and a priss for as long as I can remember."

"Why haven't you ever told us any of this before?" I ask him, looking back into the rearview mirror once again, trying to catch his eye, but I am unable to do so. It's clear he doesn't want to look at either of us right now.

"Because it's embarrassing. It's something I don't really understand. Why they call me those names I mean, but it's something that I have gotten used to. I figured maybe it was just some sort of monotonous undercurrent of similarity that I was going to be forced to deal with. The guys at Alden are simpletons, the ones who say this shit to me. They're C students who don't play any sports and couldn't get girlfriends if they tried. I ignore them for the most part, but sometimes it doesn't work."

"It sounds like they're jealous of you Charlie," Ellie suggests.

"I've thought that before, but then I came to a camp like this one and the same thing happens? The same kinds of insults fall out of the mouths of city boys who barely even know me? Maybe there really is something wrong with me."

"There is nothing wrong with you," I tell him.

He looks away from the window then, and I catch his eye for the first time since the wheels of the car started moving, since this discussion had begun. I see him through the reflection of the mirror. "I just want everything to be okay. I'm ready to go to college, I want to go to a place like New York City where people won't judge me for the little things. Instead they'll accept me for who I am, as a whole, not pulling out the tiny pieces and tearing them apart."

"I think you would love going to school in the city," Ellie tells him then as she removes her arm from around his shoulder, letting a little bit of him go. "You would thrive there, I'm sure."

"Maybe. I guess we'll see. I just don't want people to judge me for the way I am. I have a lot of girl friends, and maybe I'm a bit too in tune with my emotions. It doesn't help that my voice is a bit higher pitched than most guys too. Maybe it's my fault...I'm artistic, and I love the ballet, but that's what you taught me. I love every part of you both, you know. I look up to you so much and if that makes me be perceived as being gay, then fuck it."

Usually Ellie would have become angry with him for saying the f word in such a way, but she lets it go this time. How could she not after the sentiments he has said? It pains me to think that the way that Ellie and I have raised him has caused this kind of backlash from his peers, but if it means that Charlie will end up succeeding in life more than any of them combined, I'd rather him undergo this kind of pain and learn from it rather than stay in a certain kind of simplicity and never know his true self.

"You know how much we love you Charlie," Ellie says then. "And when you get out of Alden so many more people are going to love you too. I know you'll change the world. You change mine everyday."

"Thanks Mom," he tells her as he wipes away the remaining

tears and then he turns to look at her as she kisses him on the cheek. "I'm starting to feel a bit better now."

"That's what we're here for son," I say. "How about we go to the diner when we get back to Alden? You can order whatever you want."

"That sounds perfect," he answers back. "I just want to relax and not have to worry about anything for a while. I want to escape into what I already know, as the future scares me too much right now to think about it anymore."

All you need to worry about is the here and now Charlie, I think to myself, but for some reason, I don't say it out loud to him. How I wish I would have.

The rest of the ride back to Alden is a positive one. We try to forget the event that happened, even though I know deep down it's all we are thinking of. Before long however, we make it back and stop at Mr. Sander's Diner as promised. It still looks nearly identical as to how it did when Ellie and I came here all of those years ago when we were both eighteen, after our first kiss, after the snow fell from the heavens and we hadn't much to miss. Charlie loved the diner since the first time we brought him to it, and the truth was, we had been bringing him to it for as long as I could remember. It was a memory that we all shared, it's silver white walls, straight lines and simple design were all we required. Sure, the atmosphere of its insides were a bit old fashioned and out of date, but the food still tasted just as great no matter which decade we ate it in.

When we were there, it was as if nothing else mattered, as if all time and meaning and hope for the future slipped away and the only thing that we noticed was each other. That night was no different, as we ate burgers and fries we laughed about stories that only we would understand. I would relive it if I could, but in a sense I wouldn't either, I couldn't, as that dinner remains one of the most personal moments of my life. It was the last happy time I ever had with my family, just us three. I remember him smiling and I recall him telling stories of all of the slam-dunks he had. I imagine that he flew above all of the other boys, floating through the air overhead of the rest, as only a blonde superman could do, as his father once dreamed to.

If I could have recorded that night, or watched it as a different patron at another table I wish I had been able to, yet at the same time I don't. That dinner, the last supper, was all I ever wanted our lives to be, simple and serene, yet filled with a sense of security that our presence brought to one another. During our meal as I looked across at the two people sitting before me, I realized that I had a good life. I had a wife who adored me, whom I cherished more than anything else, and I had a son who regardless of the strife that he was undertaking, still was able to end the night with a smile. At least until the dusk approached the dawn, when the yawn of the wolves began to howl and the terror of what lay before us all approached. If only I would have known what would befall us that night, maybe I could have changed it.

I couldn't though, as I silently embraced the love before me without action, I wasn't able to realize what could be lost. I didn't accept the situation for what it was, instead I tried to compartmentalize everything in ways I expected them to be. Instead of loving the love I had for the sake of which it was, I was too afraid to understand it as being different. I backed away, and for that, even as I was living it, I know I would have told myself that I was sorry. Mistakes are made every moment of every day, but only under certain realizations of what life truly is, do we understand how to fix them.

When we get home after our splendid meal at the diner, Charlie goes upstairs to unpack his things. I plop down on the sofa and take a deep breath, pondering over all of the things that occurred today. I'm still worried about our son, even though we just had a nice time together over dinner. I still think there is something he isn't telling us, there has to be. Why would those boys act in such a way towards him? He is such an endearing young man. Maybe that's it though; perhaps he is too endearing, too lighthearted and gentle for the rough ways of society. It seems he is not what people expect him to be.

After storing some of our leftovers in the fridge, Ellie returns from the kitchen and sits down next to me. She places her hand on my thigh and croons in my ear before giving me a soft kiss.

"Do you think he is going to be all right?" I ask.

"I wish I had the answer to that Priam. I'm glad that the three of us were able to have a nice time at the diner and let the unpleasantries of earlier go on the back burner for a while. Still, maybe we should talk to him about it some more."

"That's what I was thinking. But what should we say?"

When I look at her then I can tell that she is just as dumbfounded about what to do in this situation as I am. I never dreamed that being a father would deal me scenarios like this. Then again, I never really imagined half of the things that have come to pass in my life. Every year holds hidden desires and heartbreak that emerge from trysts of tyranny. One can certainly not know what secrets and promises fate will fetch for us, at any time or anywhere.

"We could ask him to tell us the truth, the whole truth. What he really thinks has elicited this bullying, not only at the camp but in Alden too. I'm not saying he is to blame," Ellie goes on as she moves her hand from my leg and interlaces her fingers with mine. "But maybe there is something rooted down deeper that we are unaware of. There has to be something, don't you think? He's been unhappy for a while now. Maybe this isn't the only thing that's bothering him. Maybe there was a girl, maybe she broke his heart."

"I don't remember him ever talking about any girls though," I tell her. "Do you?"

I think back to the days after I met Ellie and how I talked about her to anyone who would listen. In fact, that is pretty much all I ever did. No, I don't think Charlie had fallen in love with a girl, or fallen out of love with her for that matter. I would have known, I would had to have known.

"No. I don't," she says. "We just need to make sure he knows that we support him no matter what the cause of this unhappiness is. He needs to know that we love him unconditionally."

"Of course. I think he knows that already though. Haven't we already told him that?" I wonder.

"Maybe we haven't told him enough."

"You have," his voice sounds from behind us.

Ellie's hand pulls away from mine then as we both turn to see Charlie standing behind us, having come down the stairs, apparently so quietly that neither of us heard him arrive in the living room. He could have been standing there the entire time our conversation was going on for all I know, but somehow I have a feeling that he just arrived now at the end of it.

"I know that you both love me. You've shown me how much you love me since the day I was born. Even at the times we got into fights and I rebelled against your authority, deep down, I still knew that you loved me, even then when I didn't feel like I deserved it," he says as he sits down at the chair across from us, so that he is facing us both.

The sun is shining through the window now, and it begins to lower down further amongst the blue sky, the hanging clouds encircle it, as they feel it is near, and in doing so the light starts to envelop the boy before us. The sun sheds its pure properties onto Charlie and he gleams from the bright. I am reminded almost instantaneously of the last day of my mother's life, when she sat before me in this very room and was illuminated in a similar way. I miss her presence, and I miss her grace, but then as I think these things, I realize that a part of her is still here, not only within me, but within the boy who sits before me too. She lives on, through the blood that flows through the hills and valleys of my vessel, and that which I passed on to Charlie as well. Her spirit, and his spirit have always reminded me of one another. I know that if they had the chance to meet they would have gotten along like two peas in a pod. They would have escaped into the rabbit hole with Alice and drank all of the tea and journeyed on without ever looking back. Except for whenever it was that I came calling, they would have returned for me, if I needed them.

He goes on. "I've always known that you have loved me with every ounce of your being and every one of your bones. That's not what I need to be reassured of," he states with conviction, as the sunlight heightens the gold in his hair, the youthful flesh on his face and the liberation which he seeks, but still has yet to find. "What I need to know more than anything else in this world...is that you will accept me."

"Of course we accept you Charlie. We accept you just the way you are. We've watched you grow from a baby into a young man. Why would you think that we wouldn't accept you for the person that you are?" asks Ellie, trying to reassure our son that everything is going to be okay.

"Because I have something to tell you now that may change your mind."

"I doubt that is possible," she says.

I sit where I am, still, silent. I look at him as the light glows further and begins to fade ever so slightly, I wonder what it is that he is going to say. I can't imagine anything making me see Charlie differently, but lights can change ever so quickly and sometimes, they can go out entirely.

"I don't really know how to begin with this. So please bear with me," he says, appearing rather nervous. I know my son well enough to tell that he is uncomfortable with this conversation, but he is pushing forward, as whatever it is that he needs to say is something that he has been holding in for quite a while now. I realize currently, that Ellie and I are finally going to find out what has been bothering him for all this time.

"We're here," I tell him. It's all I can say.

He takes a deep breath, his lungs heave and then ho and he is still again. The sun is sliding away from his presence, but traces of it still remain as he continues and begins anew again.

"Like we talked about in the car, it's obvious that I've never been the boy who fits in. No matter how hard I try, there have always been people who don't like me. I haven't always been sure why, but recently I believe I have started to figure it out. People are sometimes unable to accept me for the way that I am because I'm different. I go my own way and strike my own chord and some individuals have a hard time accepting that. It's not only guys that have given me a hard time and called me insulting names. Girls have done it too. You would be surprised at some of the things that teenage girls say. They can be even crueler than the boys sometimes. What Zach said to you both today, even though it was bad, it wasn't the worst I've heard. At times I've thought it was going to end, that people were going to stop calling me gay and stop harassing me and accusing me of being something that I'm not. But then what are we and who are we? That is a question I have been asking myself more and more recently. I think about my future all of the time, and sometimes I have a hard time seeing it. I have a difficult time imagining that there is a place for me."

"Of course there is a place for you Charlie! Don't talk like that," Ellie interrupts, her voice quivering.

"Please let me finish," he says and then his face becomes flushed. "I'm sorry Mom. I don't mean to sound rude, but all of this is hard for me to say. And I would rather just say it all at once and then have you both react when I'm finished."

"Okay baby, okay."

"Anyways," he continues. "I know now that life is never going to be as easy for me as it is for some people. I am never going to have a simple life. I will never live in a place where people are able to understand me completely; at least I don't think so. That's how I've been feeling you see, and thus the dark clouds have surrounded me, tightening their grasp with every passing day that doesn't get any better. I always try to tell myself to be positive. I always try to be optimistic as you both taught me, but sometimes it's hard when things never change. I'm tired of being the faggot who lives on Elm Street. I'm tired of being the pussy boy who likes ballet and I'm tired of being the homo also known as Big Wood. I don't want to be any of those things. I just want to be me.

"And that's where the problem lies. As you see, how can I be me if I rebel against the very idea of what everyone is proclaiming me to be? The last thing I ever want to be is gay. For how can I be? It's all everyone has ever made fun of me for. It's why all of those people who say those things to me despise me so much, because they aim to understand something that I don't even quite understand myself. They seek to label me and categorize my life into a compartment that is compact, even when all I have ever wanted is to be free from everything, the worries and wonders and whimsome memories. All I've ever wanted was to simply just be. But I've learned that you can't exist in such a way when you've been lying to yourself all along. Even though I don't want to admit it, and it pains me in a way to do so, I know that I have to accept myself before anyone else can and thus, that is why I am here before you now. To tell you, once and for all, and finally, that what everyone has been accusing me of being all the while is actually true. I am gay."

The sun sets behind the trees, and the light that was filtering through the window and placing itself over Charlie, almost as if it was a blanket of elegant energy to protect him, disappears then, entirely. I'm not sure if the silence that follows in the seconds that come next are actually in place or if I dream them up, but in this moment I feel as if my eardrums go numb. I can't hear anymore and I don't know if I want to. Charlie's charade is done, and I realize this boy I thought I knew I have never really known at all. Or so, that is how I feel. How could this be? Is this reality? I look at my son who sits across from me and I wonder how he could possibly be so different from me, yet so similar all of the while. I do not understand. I cannot understand.

"Oh Charlie," Ellie says, pushing away the silence and tranquility that had arrived at the end of his speech. "It's going to be okay." She moves from off of the couch beside me and goes over to sit on the chair with him, her arms draping over him. "You know that we still love you. We will love you no matter what."

It's the cliché kind of answer that a son hopes to hear from his mother, the being who brought him into this life and will never leave him, even when unexpected occurrences such as this one arise and refuse to hide from the tide. Is this news really that much of a surprise after all? I would be lying if I said I expected Charlie to tell me he was a homosexual, but now that I am mulling it over in my head, it makes sense. In fact, I can't believe I never thought of it before. I'm surprised that this truth is something that neither Ellie nor I was able to figure out, on our own, or together. It was staring us right in the face, or so it seems. As I contemplate the curiosity of all of this, images of beautiful girls dance in my head, like the woman who sits before me, her arm resting on our son, trying to help him realize that it will all be okay. Are these all of the women that Charlie could have loved, but never will? I can't understand it. I see the beauty of Ellie and I imagine her feminine figure in every way that it has ever been and I can't comprehend Charlie not being able to accept that or a similar elegance for what it is. I can't imagine him turning away from the lovely female form and accepting the male one instead. I cannot understand what I do not know, what I could never know.

"How long have you felt this way?" She asks.

"For as long as I can remember," he says. "I haven't been able to accept it until recently and even still I haven't wanted to. But I realize now that there is no other way I can be. You're the first two people I have told."

"Thank you for telling us," Ellie tells him. "I wish you would have told us sooner. You know we will always be here for you."

"Thanks Mom."

I try to form words, but I can't. I don't know what to say. What can I say? I am too afraid to speak, uncertain of the noises I would create and how they would affect him. The last thing I want to do is hurt him any further than he has already been, but I still know that deep down inside I don't want to accept this either. They both look at me then, I know they are waiting for my input, as it is important to the two of them equally. My silence stretches on and slices the night that has arrived into something that shouldn't have to be shaded into any kind of gray, but as the darkness consumes us all, so does the lack of interpretation of this current station.

"Dad?" He finally asks, not being able to wait any longer.

"Charlie." I say his name.

"Are you okay?"

"I'm fine son. I'm fine. I'm glad you were able to tell us this." I know he wants me to say more, but what can I say?

"Do you still love me?" It sounds like an absurd question, but apparently he is doubting almost everything now and he needs to know the answer for clarification.

"Of course I still love you Charlie."

"Good."

"We will always love you Charlie," Ellie tells him. "You are the best thing that has ever happened to us. You are half me and half your father. We made you out of a place of love and will love you all the same."

"That's one way of putting it," I whisper, but they both hear me even though I didn't intend them to. Their ears perk up and they look away from one another and back to me. I switch the lamp on that rests on the small side table next to me, as the darkness due to the setting of the sun was beginning to become too much. I need to see what is before me, every line and every detail of each of their faces.

"What's that Dad?" He asks.

"Oh nothing son. I guess I'm just a little bit out of it," I say, even though really I feel insane. I feel high, it's almost as if I am in the middle of some orange candle, melting down around the wick in a molten pool of wax. I'm stuck, and I have nowhere to go, no chance of escape or understanding to free me from the confusion that has commenced. I don't understand my son.

"What do you mean Priam?" Ellie asks, saying my name, which triggers the truth. I don't know why, but it does, and off I go.

"I guess I just can't understand the fact that you're gay. How can you be gay? Is it something we did to make you so? Did we do something wrong?" I ask as I look from his face, which looks different now, to that of his mother's, which stays in place. "Have you ever even given girls a chance? I don't remember you even trying to be straight. So if that's the case, how can you know you're gay?"

"Dad...it's not like that," he says, his voice trailing off.

"Then what is it like? How do you know? There has to be certain reasons or some kind of undertaking to come to this conclusion. I just can't figure it out. I look at your mother as she sits right next to you and I'm filled with a sense of sadness in the fact that you will never know a love like ours. As it is, my relationship with her has been the one thing that has gotten me through. I want you to have that Charlie. And now as you tell us this, I know you never will."

"Priam, don't talk like that..." Ellie says, upset by the words that I deliver even though they are notes about my love for her. Even though what I say could be positive in a way, she knows better than to accept it, she is aware how it digs into our son. In part I am too, but I keep going, not able to stop, pretending that what I am saying is what he needs to hear, even though deep down inside I should know it isn't. We ignore parts of ourselves at times in order to move forward even if later it only ends up pulling us back. We don't know what lies before us, just as we don't always contemplate the words we create.

"The fact that you will never know a woman is depressing, and I don't know how to pretend like I am not disappointed by the way this has all turned out. You are a wonderful boy, you are brilliant and artistic and kind. And although you will always be loved, a part of me will still always wish that you weren't gay."

The glint in his eye flashes then and that is the moment he removes his gaze from me. Ellie glares at me with an upset tone and tries to stop Charlie as he gets up to leave, but she can't. He walks quickly towards the stairs and is about to run up them, but before he does, he stops and turns to me.

"All I ever wanted to do was to make you both happy, to make you proud. I guess I am never going to achieve that."

Ellie gets up and follows after him, reaching him before he leaves, embracing him in her arms as she hugs him close. Even though he towers above her now, with his tall lanky frame at a similar ratio as to what mine would have been to my mother's, I see the smallness inside of him, and he shrinks in her arms, letting go, if only for a moment, to accept her embrace and cherish it.

"You make us happy every day Charlie. Even if your father can't realize that now, he still knows it. As your mother, I have the capability to speak for us both."

"I just wish you didn't have to," he says. He turns to look at me, and although I see the kindness in his eyes, I don't get up. I don't go to him. I stay glued to where I sit, unable to move, unable to do anything at all. For how can I go on and accept something that I don't understand? If only I had learned more from the books which were never written in a reality where I could write them myself, maybe, just maybe I would have had the perseverance and strength to get up and tell him how special he was to me, but I didn't. I didn't.

I'm dumb struck, but not enough to enact any sort of action, at least not right away. Charlie has gone upstairs and I remain where I have been since this news hit me. I don't wish to cause my son any more strife than he has already endured, but as my wife returns from where she let him go, I wonder if I should have reacted differently. I don't know what time it is, but I would say at least an hour has passed since the sun set on the dialogue that was delivered and another forty five minutes after that before Ellie has returned. I'm sure she talked to Charlie some more, but I notice when she walks by the opening at the top of the stairs she goes back into our bedroom first before she decides to come back down to face me. It's somewhere near eleven o'clock in the evening and even though the night is almost done, it's almost as if it has just begun.

The chair where I sit encompasses me in a way that I can't control; yet I don't want it to swallow me, as it feels it may. The suede fabric of its outer being is soft to the touch, but coarse when it rubs against me in a wrong way. It as if the life I have led is pushing back into me and acknowledging all I have done wrong. My senses collide and introduce themselves to each other, even though they come from opposite ends of the symphony, they still all collaborate to create a similar tune.

And then she is before me, back fully and I know immediately when I see her face that she is disappointed in me. She handled the news Charlie gave us in a completely different manner than I did, and to her, how she dealt with it was the correct way and how I reacted was wrong. To her, I could have done better, I should have done better.

"Why did you talk to him in such a way? I just had to console him for almost an hour as he cried on my shoulder. You know how much your opinion means to him. I can't believe you tried to justify your viewpoint of it by using our love as an example."

"What else could I have used? Our story is the one I know best."

"I don't care Priam. For once you should have put something else before the high pedestal that you hold our love upon. You know, regardless of how much we love one another, some things are more important. Like our son for instance, like the soul that only exists because we held onto each other so desperately for all of these years."

"What do you mean desperately? Are you saying we are clinging onto something simply for the sake of what it once was?" I ask, offended.

"That's not what I mean. I just don't think you should have tried to compare his life to ours. It's completely different and unrelated. If he is gay and wants to be with a man you shouldn't try to lessen him for that. You shouldn't have brought our story into it."

"But isn't all love similar in some way or another?" I wonder.

"Every love is different. The young boy who loves his teddy bear may believe that the plush toy that sleeps in bed with him every night is all he needs, but as he grows, he will realize that love evolves, love changes, it shifts and it shapes our lives in many ways. But it would be blasphemous to try and categorize love into different compartments. No love is the same, not even ours," she says with conviction and in listening to the strength of her words, I know she means it.

"Maybe you're right..."

"It's not about being right, it's about the times like these when you are wrong and you are smart enough to realize it. I think you owe our son an apology. I think he is waiting for one, rather, hoping for one. I know you'll do the right thing." She tells me, and as she approaches where I sit in my chair and kisses me on the forehead, I know I have to go upstairs and talk to Charlie, man to man, and let him know that I am sorry for the way I tried to simplify his life. She goes, away from me and back upstairs, and as I watch her silhouette fade and disappear up and away and then turn down the hallway to where our bedroom is I know that she will not talk to Charlie again this evening. I know that the final word will be left up to me.

I wait. A little bit longer, thinking, trying to come together with a story that will make him realize what my life has been and what I want it to be. It's only as the grandfather clock in the hallway chimes at 11:45 that I decide I need to get up and talk to him before he falls asleep, before he can escape from the tears that may drown him. I wish to lift him up, to row past in a boat in which I can carry him to a place where everything is okay; somewhere that includes his father's admiration and respect for him. I push myself out of my chair and the fabric, which is a maroon color similar to that of a red merlot, runs against my grain and plants a new harvest that I will be surprised if I ever see again. My senses collide and as I slip away from where I sat, I let them go away. The stairs creak as I clamber up them, the wooden panels that piece together to make them have aged since the days when I was a child and ran up and down them multiple times a day. I realize as I go to see Charlie, that as this life goes on, everything changes.

When I reach his door I push it slowly, and the old oaken rectangle groans as it slides open. I see his empty bed and am elated to know that he has yet to fall asleep. It is only when I look to my left, to where his closet is that I realize something else entirely. He has fallen asleep forever.

There he is, my boy, floating through the air, yet grounded by a strap of leather that rings around his neck and connects him to the metal bar that holds him up and brings him down, as gravity suffocated him at the will of his own hand.

I can't breathe, and rightfully so, as this room is now the chamber where my son has died. I can't believe, won't believe it, and as I wake myself up from the slumber that I thought he might have taken, I realize he is already gone. Even as I run to where he hangs and lift his limp body up, untying the long leather belt that suffocated his neck, wringing out the life and the lust and everything he ever had to offer to this Earth, I know that he is gone.

I want to scream, I have to scream aloud, but the agony is too great for my senses to understand. I can't understand this, won't understand this, don't want to understand this, just as the lack of comprehension helped to create this in the first place. I hold my son in my arms, his body just as big as mine, but so much younger, all the while getting older with each passing second as the life is gone from him and he is beginning to decay ever so slowly. As everything is temporary and nothing lasts forever, I realize that the words I offered led him to this decision. I wasn't the kind of father I should have been. Regardless of whether he was gay or not, it didn't have to end like this. Charlie Wood is dead.

I cry, I let tears of tyranny slide from my eyes, as I am unable to accept this fortune before me. I slightly slap his face, hoping to wake him up from the sleep that he has chosen, but I know it is for nothing. He is gone and he is never coming back. The pang in my stomach burns harsher as I realize that Ellie is sitting in the other room. She has no idea that her son is no longer living. She doesn't know what has befallen these wooden boards that hold us up, these broken bones that pull us down. She doesn't know that he is gone, and that it's my fault he has chosen to be. My tears leap off of my cheeks and fall down, some splashing onto his face, and as I wish for a miracle, as I hope that somehow my crying can revive and rejuvenate him, I realize it will never happen in such a way as more minutes pass.

I pull myself away from him, not wanting to, but having to, as a cold breeze blows through his open window and knocks a few sheets of paper off of his desk, which land on the floor near where I sit with his body on top of me. The wind feels too cold for July and I know that these papers are meant to be read by me, as they reach out to make themselves known. They are the last things my son ever had to say. The three pages rustle together as I collect them and look down upon them and try to concentrate on what they have recorded. I read them to myself slowly, as they are slightly crumpled yet still clean. The words enter into my brain as I still hold the hand of my dead son next to me.

To Ellie and Priam,
The names of the two people I feel I only sort of knew.

I wish to start by saying I'm sorry. I know how selfish this is of me and I want to apologize for it before my reasons for why it occurred can even suffice, because I know they never will. You are both beautiful and wonderful souls, and I owe you so much. Though neither of you are perfect, even with your wrongdoings you always felt mostly right to me.

But that isn't what this is about, what it is, and what it was, is that I have never felt like I have belonged here, or anywhere. Not in Alden, not in Pennsylvania, or even in New York. Even at the times I felt happy I still always have felt as if something was missing. I've always been gay, and I've always known it, even though I have never ever wanted to accept it for the fear of rejection, the kind of misunderstandings that happened here tonight.

I don't blame you Dad, I can't blame you for not being able to comprehend how I feel or what I have always known, but I would be lying if I said it didn't push me even closer to the edge, closer than I've ever been before.

I don't blame you; I don't blame either of you. I just can't do this anymore. I never feel like it is going to get better. I can't see a future where I am happy; I can't imagine an America where I as a gay man am treated equally. I know that is sad, but people are too afraid, too constricted by Gods that may not even exist to accept what is different from what is considered normal. I wish to be free, and I have never felt that here, and I fear I never will.

As I sit here now, and look out of my window, I can see a dog in the distance. I don't know whose it is, as I have never seen it before, but its golden coat seems to be shining, even though the sun has set hours ago. How this is possible I don't know, but the point is, that it is running free. It has no constraints or restrictions holding it back. I want that.

I don't want to hold you back. I don't want to be a connection that stifles your love or makes it harder for either of you to love one another. Because as long as I have been living the one thing that I have admired the most is your love for each other. I've been jealous of it all the while, yet still; I have been in awe of it just the same. I had hoped one day I would meet a man and have a love in a similar way, but I have decided my fate and there is no going back. The only love I will ever know is the love of Ellie and Priam. And at this moment, as I watch a golden dog run away, ever so free, I realize that is okay.

I wish to do more than just exist. I wish to be more than just a memory. I wish to be free. Forever.

Love to you both, now and always,
Your one and only son,

Charlie Kelton Wood.

I heave ho, and I faint, unable to exist for now anymore. I collapse in a temporary state, in a comparable one to the boy who lies next to me. Only even as I fall, unaware of what is happening, I still know that I will awake, and that he...he never will.

Friday July 6th, 1990
Day Five - **The Second Chance**

This time, it is the sound of my own screams, which awake me with a jolt. I arise from my slumber and clutch at my chest in a similar fashion as Ellie had done originally. I hear her stir next to me, at least I imagine it is she. I haven't seen her face yet, but there is no one else it could be. "Priam, what's wrong?" The sound of her voice asks. It's her, of course it is. I feel her hands rub gently up and down my bare naked back and I relish the feeling of her skin up against my skin. It feels as wonderful as it always did.

"I was having a bad dream I suppose," even though I know it wasn't a dream, but rather the reality where I found my son who had just ended his own life. I lift my hand up to my face and I feel the residue of streaks of wetness underneath both of my eyes. The tears which I had cried that day had somehow manifested in this actuality as well, showing themselves as an example of how wretched that experience had made me feel, crossing borders of where rules should have been by breaking them. The fifth day in it's original way rings in my ears and burns in my heart. The lessons I should have overcome are too true to me still. I can't comprehend them fully the way they happened. I will always remember my son in a certain way, as I only had eighteen years with him. Five more than what I had with my mother, but all too few just the same.

As her soothing touch continues to calm me, the memory of him lingers and slowly fades, as the distance to which I was with him in the night before, or what felt like it anyways drifts away. I wonder if Charlie Kelton Wood even exists here. How does one ask his wife if the son he had and lost is still a perpetual being who continues on? This life that I have reworked for myself has already changed so much. How can Charlie exist here when Ellie and I got married on a different day, in a different way? Our times of love making varied and we changed how we laid. If every human is distinct and if our souls are created in the moments of love and lust by the two people who construct us, are we truly singular? Or are the lives which are meant to be lived always going to be made in some certain way even if all of the other factors change? I wish to find out at this instant, but I know that I will find out soon enough.

This bed and the room where we reside now is not the same one it was yesterday, on that day that occurred on this exact date when I lived it the first time in the summer of 1990. Although the décor has a similar kind of style, this room is larger than the bedroom Ellie and I shared in my mother's old house, and then when that idea hits me I realize the explanation lies there within it's reasoning. We can't live in the house I grew up in on Elm Street because my mother must still be living there, just as she was the last time we left her on our wedding day in Alden, where I was completely present last, where the memories I created anew with the woman in the bed next to me were as perfect as they could have ever been. Even though she had been knocked down on that third day, she rose again on the fourth and greets me on this fifth. Through perseverance and tolerance we've been delivering on and I can only hope that even if more difficulties are met with the angst of these second days we are still able to continue on this journey. As Chloe told me, these last few days will continue to be even more different than the original ones. The paths are splitting and getting wider apart.

I'm surprised that we still decided to move to Alden, as I was almost sure that I would have woken up back in New York, never having left to come back to the town I grew up in as we had chosen to do in my life. I figured that my art career would have made me stay in the city, that Ellie wouldn't have wanted to be far from the theater, even if she couldn't dance. Yet, I suppose it made sense that the small town had called us home. Whereas the painful memories that I experienced here had pushed me away, the good ones always brought me back.

"You've been having an awful lot of nightmares recently," Ellie says as her hands finally leave my back and she slinks out of bed. I watch her go, just as I had on the first version of this day as she leaves me. Although her body is still just as beautiful as I remember it, I notice the large dark scar run down the middle of her spine as she escapes from the bedroom and goes into the bathroom which is on the opposite side of where it was the last time. Her back had been broken, and the doctors had to piece her together again so that she could walk. The crash of the fall had left its mark, imprinting itself upon her. They said she would never dance and although the kind of movements she had once been able to make were no longer possible, she still was able to sway to the music in a simpler way. The tune of the chord would always be struck by her body, just at a more modest mixture moved by the melody.

The room I am in now is far more eclectic than the country clutter collection of decorations I remember being in the bedroom that we had shared together in my mother's house. The pieces on the wall are brighter and livelier too. It appears my artistic influence has made its presence better known here, and I imagine the rest of the house will have a similar feeling. The house on Elm Street was ours, yet it contained so many other elements of my life and the one I wish I had but didn't, that I'm not sure if we were ever truly able to make it our own. In comparison, this house clearly was designed by Ellie and Priam Wood, uninhibitedly.

She doesn't get in the shower this time, instead she comes back to me after a couple of minutes pass and returns to the bed where she wraps her arms around me, cuddling in close and kissing me sweetly on the lips. The aroma of her entrances me and I get lost in the scent. The moments collide together and dissipate just as quickly as they came. I'm brought back to the qualm of the currency that lingers before me, as I continue to wonder about the possibility of our son and what happened to him, a presence enters the room that we are entangled within.

It's not him, and somehow a part of me knew it wouldn't be. Instead, a young girl who looks to be around the age of ten enters. She comes in slowly, her chestnut brown hair is tangled and ruffled as it appears she just awoke like the two of us recently did. She says nothing when I look at her. She smiles though, and then lifts up her leg, bringing it to her side in a point, before twirling around on the wooden floors of our bedroom. She is a tiny ballerina, one of the smallest I have ever seen.

"That was perfect form Alma. I'm impressed, especially first thing in the morning," Ellie tells her, and the girl giggles loudly before jumping up into the bed with us. I try to catch my breath, but I can't. I look at the child beside me, as I watch her cuddle up against her mother. My body breaks apart from the both of them, even though I only move a few inches away, the disconnect feels greater, as I have to separate myself in this moment to understand the reality that is present.

Alma Moira Wood is a little girl who can see, smell, breathe and dance. She decided to incubate longer, to stay within the womb her mother had made for her and so she was born on the right day. She didn't greet the world too soon, instead she waited with patience until her body was ready to carry her soul all of the way through. Alma didn't die on the same day she was born in which she only claimed a few breaths of her own. Instead in this life she claimed them all, as our daughter lives to tell tales and inspire memories within us and all of the people she knows. Alma.

I'm astounded and I try to process the acceptance of a life I had once created but never really known. It truly is a lot to do. I don't know what this all means as far as this day goes, but I am ecstatic to learn that Ellie was granted the daughter she always wanted. She may not have been able to dance in this life for as long as she had before, but at least she was able to pass on the art of her fluidity to a piece of herself that lives in Alma. I touch my daughter's head and slide my hand down her face lovingly, smiling at her as she giggles once again. She leans away from her mother and pushes into me, snuggling up against my chest and breathing a heavy sigh, one of utter contentment, as she seems to be in her element when she is sandwiched in between us, loving us the way we have always loved her.

Alma is an unexpected presence here and even though I am beyond any measure of joy and elation, I still can't help but to long for Charlie, the son I always knew, the boy I failed. I hope he is here, so that I can make things right with him, so that I can save him and our bond, as I was able to do so with the three other people who mattered the most to me in the days that had come earlier. From what I had changed during the second chances I have been granted, I was able to make it so that my mother lived to see a much larger magnitude of days, I saved the relationship I always wanted with my brother, and the woman who was part of my soul and the answer to everything for men never left me and still remained with me. I knew fixing things with Charlie and making it so that he never gave up was one of the most important things I had yet to accomplish, or this journey would only be partially fulfilled. He has to be here, he has to...and then he walks into the room, as my eyes leave Alma and my wife and focus onto the doorway where he has just entered through. He looks exactly the same as when I left him. When my gaze reaches his eyes he smiles at the sight in front of him, delighted by the vision of the early morning gathering of his blissful family.

"You three have way too much energy. I could hear Alma giggling from my room at the end of the hall," he says.

"It's better to have too much than not enough," Ellie tells him. "Why don't you join the party Charlie? There's enough room for the four of us."

He looks down sheepishly, moving his right foot around on the ground in a circle as if he is embarrassed, but then suddenly he looks up, right at me and the two ladies next to me and he gallops quickly straight towards us. He jumps and lands on top of us all, combining into the pile that we have made as we all laugh furthermore and relish in the dignity of this day and the ones that have yet to come.

Charlie is here, and in this moment as I look at the three faces that are near me, I realize that some things can be saved, including the lives you lost and the loves that only briefly lingered. For it appears to be a decree that the lives that endured once always have to exist here and anywhere, and that canceling an existence cannot occur, but rather only a shortening or lengthening of a soul's presence can. Fate doesn't pick and choose who comes or who goes completely, rather the choices we make and the combinations that collide in a certain tide are able to affect not who we love, but for how long.

After staying in bed for a while longer, we leave the comfort of its grasp and filter down the stairs one by one. Ellie pours us bowls of Frosted Flakes and I laugh as Alma slurps her milk and Charlie crunches on the sugary oats. The noises they make are normal ones, but they are comical to me just the same. Ellie puts the box of cereal back in the cupboard and joins us at the table. This kitchen is much bigger than the one in the house on Elm Street and all of the appliances seem newer too. I wonder where all of the money has come from for this house, which seems much nicer than the one I remember, but I don't have a chance to ask before my wife begins to speak.

"You know, I'm so happy I have all summer off. It's so nice to spend every day with you three. Not that I don't love teaching, but those fifth graders can sure be pretty darn rambunctious at times."

"We're not that crazy Mom!" Alma says sweetly as she giggles before putting another huge spoonful of cereal into her mouth. "At least I'm not. I'm a good girl."

"Well for the most part you are, but you still have a little bit of a wild side. I blame your father for that," Ellie says as she looks at me.

"If I recall correctly during your dancing days you had a pretty bright and burning flame going," I say to her. "I remember a lot of the after parties that followed the opening of your ballets to be quite the ordeal. And you were always the shining star, both on the stage and off of it. The combination of us both equally probably resulted in the way our kids are, if I had to guess."

"I think you're right Dad," Charlie says. "We're all just a bunch of free spirits, and we probably always will be. We'll always have each other though, no matter how free and far we fade away, our heart lines will always bring us back together."

"What a nice thing to say," Ellie tells him.

"I try," he says. "Maybe I'll write about it."

"You should, and let me read it!" Alma says. "I love your poetry."

I don't remember Charlie writing poetry before, so I am surprised to hear this, but then as I ponder on it further, I remember that letter he wrote to us, the last thing he ever wrote, the last thing he ever communicated to anyone, to anything. And it was beautiful, it was tragic, but it was elegant nevertheless. I read it a million times over the rest of my life and every time it affected me just as deeply as it had the first. If only he had more time. Now he does, he's here today, this won't be his dying day, it can't be.

I know I have to save him, just as I saved my mother. I feel it won't be as difficult, as so many things have already changed. Whereas the trajectory of her day was nearly exactly the same as when I had the chance to make her go on, this day is already so much different than the last day I saw my son. Maybe it will be alright. Then again, something completely different could happen, something like what happened to Ellie on that third day, when her bones were broken, when she lost the ability to dance like she used to. Things can go right in some ways, yet fall apart in others.

"Do you miss dancing?" I ask my wife. Even though I already know the answer, I have to hear it, whatever it is. I need to know that the things I have changed have been worth it, and that her losing what she loved didn't damage the temperament of her soul. I need to know that she has gone on in other ways and flourished within and without certain elements that used to mean so much to her.

"Of course I miss it. I miss it everyday, but I was never delirious enough to think I would still be dancing ballet now like I used to when I was young. I did imagine that I would be able to teach it though, to young girls like little miss Alma here," she says as she reaches her hands out to our daughter who holds onto them. "But as we all know even that isn't possible, not with my back the way it is. I'm just glad I can walk, and that every once in a while I can sway to the music with you," she says as she looks at me, where I sit across the table from her. "I take joy out of teaching in another way, learning ballet is similar to learning mathematics and history you see. Your body is still becoming aware of what it previously did not know, the only real difference is that I enlighten the mind instead of the limbs."

"What an eloquent way to put it," Charlie offers. "No wonder I write in the way I do with words like those falling from the lips of your mouth."

"Oh I don't know how much I'm to thank for your talent Charlie."

"More than you probably realize," he says.

"You should thank your father. He's the true genius in the family. I'm sure the hundreds of patrons who have bought his works over the years would agree. His ability alone helped to build this house and give us this life after all."

"The artist and the ballerina," Alma says. "I think we should thank you both."

"Here, here!" Charlie says as he lifts up his bowl of cereal as if to give a toast. "To a wonderful life with the most magnificent people. I couldn't ask for a better family to be surrounded by."

"Oh..." I say as I start to feel my nose twitch from the sentiments that have been spoken. "I'm going to get all choked up from the nice things you're all saying. I just feel so fulfilled in this moment."

"You should Daddy. You've done everything right," Alma tells me, as she releases her mother's hands and gets up from the table and spins around on the kitchen floor, like the little dancer she is. Somehow, I know that even though Ellie can no longer move in the way she used to, she still taught Alma everything she knows about ballet. When her turn is complete and she's come back down to the ground beneath her feet, Alma moves over to me and gives me a hug. My arms wrap around her tiny body and I pull her close. I never had the chance to embrace my daughter like this before. I have so much more than I ever thought I would. This little girl is mistaken though, even though she may think I've done everything the right way, she's wrong. The things I regret still haunt me now, even as most of the days are behind me, they sting just as harshly as they did before.

She lets me go after a few moments and when she does I look back to her brother, my son, Charlie. "Want to go outside and shoot a few hoops?" I ask.

"Oh Dad, you know how much I hate basketball. There isn't any point in pretending I like it anymore. You always beat my ass in P-I-G anyways. I'm through with embarrassing myself," he says and then laughs.

"I appreciate your honesty."

"Besides, we have to go to Grammy's!" Alma screams.

"Geez Alma," Charlie glares at her playfully. "Don't break our eardrums. I think we are all aware that Dad's birthday party is today."

"A birthday party? Today? Correct me if I'm wrong, but didn't I turn forty-nine yesterday?"

"Indeed you did," Ellie says as she gets up and collects the empty cereal bowls and takes them to the sink. "But as you know, your mother was in Florida until just this morning. Apparently she decided you turning forty-nine wasn't as important as another day in the sun."

"Oh how she loves the sun," Charlie says. "I'm sure she'll be tanner than a Cherokee Indian when we see her."

"I can only imagine," Alma says somewhat silently, her tone turned down after her brother warned her of her loudness. I notice this and am enticed by her sweetness and the affection of her personality.

"We will find out soon enough," Ellie tells us as she comes back over to the table, and finds a seat on my lap instead of the chair that she was previously perched on. "Here's to a beautiful day celebrating the man who made all of this possible."

I look around at the three faces surrounding me and I melt, into a puddle of pure bliss, as the addition of everything together in the way it is is just too good to be true. And it is, it's just that I don't know it yet. Life giveth, and life taketh away, and it will only be later during this day that I will be confronted with the certain kind of fears I thought I had escaped. For even though time is current and I am living now and don't know what is going to happen next, the future has the capability of coming back to take hold of you, as does the past. For anything can happen, and happen it will.

After breakfast is over and before we have to leave for the picnic at my mother's, I wander around our house and try to lose myself within it, which isn't too hard to do seeing that it is quite large. The pictures on the walls and in the nooks and crannies on corner tables of my family are all too much to see, as they are memories I don't necessarily recall, but I know that they happened, at least in some way. The one thing about these seven days that has bothered me the most is not being present in the interim. For even though I trust an essence of me has lived then, have I really? For what is living if you are not actually there? Can that really be considered living after all? I wonder if these days even exist. Regardless, I suppose the most important thing is that I am here on each of these seven days and that I have been given the chance to fix them at all. As Chloe said to me in the white abyss, this isn't a wish that is granted very often, but as it was my deepest desire, somehow, I was deemed worthy.

I end up walking out of the house and embracing the sunlight. I pass the lonesome basketball hoop in the driveway to come across a large two story garage which is separate from the house. I walk inside and see three cars parked within. A black Mercedes Benz, a vintage looking pale green Volkswagen Bug and a dark blue Land Rover. Someone has expensive taste, I wonder if it's me. At least the Victoria isn't parked here, I hope that car has shit the bed by now.

I leave the cars behind and walk up the stairs and when I reach the top I realize that I have come across my studio. In a way, it reminds me of the one I had in my apartment back in Brooklyn, especially due to the large wooden beams that hold up the vaulted ceiling. Yet, it's different too. There aren't any big blank walls, instead there are paintings upon paintings that are either half way done or already finished. I walk around and look at them and see that the majority of them have tags hanging from the bottom of their easels, each with names and prices attached. Every price is over a thousand dollars and every one contains the word 'sold.' I admire the paintings: the mermaids swimming in an upside down blue lagoon hanging off a mountainside, a small boy running amongst the clouds as a horde of trolls chase him, abstract images of blocks of colors that have no subjects but collide all the same, and a girl in a white dress dancing on a stage located in the middle of a busy intersection where buildings made all of glass contain hundreds of little people who look out to her.

I don't know how I became so successful, but I don't question it. I accept it as a sequential surprise and I'm happy because of it. I never thought I would have everything I wanted, especially here in Alden, but it seems I do. Perhaps not abandoning my art was the most beneficial thing I could have done for my life. Taking the job with Haversmith affected more than just my happiness after all, as it ended up ruining the contentment of others. I am glad that I was able to realize how giving up on my dream corrupted my soul. I always felt that my art was a part of me and the elation I feel from experiencing this outrageous success warms my spirit greatly.

When the paintings fade from the forefront of my mind I realize that there is a large mirror located on the far left wall, on the opposite side of the stairs. I go over to it and look at the man before me. I recognize him, but at the same time he has a face I have never seen before. I'm somewhere in between what I last remember seeing and what I last know I was. The seventy year old man that I concluded living as has been gone since the beginning of this journey, even though I know he still resides within me now. The thirteen, eighteen, twenty four and twenty five year old versions have left me now too, as the forty nine years that I have aged approached me yesterday, or whatever the day was that came before this one.

My blonde hair is gray, and even though it is still light in tone, it's not as golden as it used to be. I examine my face and see the firm impression of wrinkles that are not yet deep, but will become so soon enough. The green eyes look back at me as I push my face closer towards the mirror. They look tired, but they aren't dead, they still have much left to see. I'm stuck in between the recollection of recently feeling young, all the while recalling how old I felt as I laid in that bed in that damn nursing home, dying all alone. I don't want to go back there, I don't want that to be my reality, at least not this time. Will I die again? This is something that I do not know.

I am alive now, at least in some sense of the word. I run my hands down my chest and smooth them out over the button down shirt that I am wearing. My stomach doesn't feel as firm and flat as it was on that fourth day, our wedding day when we made love in the hotel room and I left her, not to return until today. All the while I am still in shape for a man who is almost fifty. Things could be worse.

"Admiring yourself, eh Dad?"

I turn away from my reflection to see a different one looking back at me. For it's not me, but instead just a part, as Charlie has clambered up the stairs and now stands in the middle of my studio looking at where I am.

"I suppose you could say so son. I was just thinking about time and how it changes, and how you yourself will always be evolving too. Not only what you can see on the outside from the reflection of a mirror, but on the inside too."

"I guess that's a good way of putting it," he says as he sits down in the middle of the floor. I find this strange, but instead of questioning it, I move over to where he is and do the same, so that we are on the same level, both of our legs crossed beneath us. The anxiety I feel inside of myself about what I want to talk to him about has been hiding inside of me ever since I woke up this morning. I've tried to ignore it, and a part of me has been able to do so, but it's still there, and I can feel it rising up now, wanting to make itself known.

"What does it feel like to be forty nine years old?" He asks suddenly. "I know it's really not that old, but to me, at only eighteen it feels like such an enormity. I can't comprehend it. Sometimes I feel like I'm never even going to make it past twenty."

"Don't say that," I say harshly. "Don't even think that. You're going to live a long and happy life. That's what I want for you more than anything."

"Isn't that what we all want?"

"Good point," I mention as I ponder further how to go about what I wish to discuss. How do you ask your son if he's gay in such a random way? Then again, is it possible that this Charlie isn't even gay at all? I wonder. People always argue about homosexuals being born the way they are and that there is no way to change their orientation. Then others say it has to do with how they are raised, and the environment they grow up in. I've always speculated, but I never really made any conclusions about the subject. After Charlie died it was painful to think about homosexuality, especially because of the fact that I hadn't accepted him for who he was, who he would always be. I had pushed him closer to the edge than he had ever been before, so much so that I might as well have shoved him off of it. At least that's how I felt after what he did, what I did.

"Dad, I just wanted to thank you again for yesterday. I know I probably didn't pick the best time to share this news with you, but I just couldn't wait anymore. I had to tell you, we've always been so close, it felt like an injustice to keep it from you any longer."

I know immediately what he is talking about. Somehow, the fact that Charlie Kelton Wood always hid from me had delivered itself in a different way, one day earlier, and I know now that my initial reaction has already occurred. He's already told me. I am relieved, yet I feel a pang in my heart as to not have been there to experience it firsthand. There were so many things I wanted to say to him this time around when he told me. I had so many dreams after he was gone where he told me he was gay and all I did was hug him and tell him I loved him over and over again until it was ringing in his head. I wish that is what I would have done the first time, but I didn't and I never had the chance to fix it. At least not then.

"You're welcome Charlie. You know that I love you for the person you are and I don't ever want you to have to feel like you have to hide any part of yourself from me. I'm your father, and I always will be, but just as importantly, I'm your friend."

"You're one of my best," he says.

I hug him then, as we sit there on the floor of my studio where the paintings surround us and the colors collide as I hold him close and imagine this is the dream that I dreamt up all of those times before. Except now it isn't a dream, it's real and things are alright.

"Mom told me it would be fine you know, she said you would be okay with me telling you, but I was scared. She's known for about six months and I made her promise that she wouldn't say a word to you. I know that was hard for her, I know you guys don't keep anything from each other, but she kept it a secret, for me, and that just meant so much."

"You're mother is very special person."

"She sure is."

"I'm glad you told me when you were ready. And you know really, I can't think of a better birthday present than what you gave me yesterday. You gave me a part of yourself that you were scared to share, you gave me something more important than cake or balloons, you gave me yourself, in the way you are, and I cannot thank you enough for being willing to share that truth with me. I know it was hard."

"You're going to make me cry Dad," he says as I can see his eyes are beginning to well up. "That's such a nice thing for you to say. I didn't know how you would react for sure, but I'm so happy to know that you're okay with the fact that I'm gay."

"You're still the same son I've always known Charlie. I'm here for you no matter what. I want you to have a good life and I want you to be in love. I want you to feel the kind of love I've felt with your mother all of these years. You deserve that and I've come to realize it doesn't matter who you love, what matters is how you love them. You can love another man, someone of another race, or even a person of another religion, those things don't matter to me anymore. What does matter though is that you can feel the kind of love that I have been blessed to know, I want you to experience that more than anything."

"I'm sure I will one day."

"I know you will," I say even though I am uncertain of it. I believe that Charlie Wood will not give up today, or let go of his future when tonight gets dark. He will go on and I know I will be there too, at least in some way, to watch him age and reach places I had never let him know.

I put my hand in my pocket, not for any reason in particular, but when I do, I feel something small and solid touch my fingertips. I pull it out, and look at it, analyzing the details of what lies in my hand. It's the golden eagle pin, the one my mother gave to me on my wedding day, the one my father owned. I had never known it in my life, but it had introduced itself to me in this one. I look at the heavenly bird coated in the element that we desire most and I know then as I look at it that it was placed in my pocket for a reason. I'm not aware of the exact details of what yesterday was, but I know now that as I sit here with my son, that I meant to give this pin to him today. It will function as a sign of moving forward, of attempting to not focus on the past in the terms of regrets, but instead to think about the memories which brought us to where we are.

"What's that?" He asks, as he notices that I have been staring at the object in my hand.

"This, was given to me by your grandmother on my wedding day and it was your grandfather's before that. It's something that represents this family, in ways that have been known and are unbreakable like the gold that coats it, and in a way to show that everything goes on, just as the eagle does through the sky. I want you to have it," I tell him as I pull him closer to me and grasp his shirt so that I can attach it to him, making it a continuation, an extension of his being.

He looks down at it as it is connected to the cotton that encases his upper torso and admires it from where his eyes fall above. "It's amazing. Thank you Dad."

"You deserve it more than I ever did. And who knows, perhaps one day you can pass it on to your own son, on a special kind of day, just like today."

"It seems so weird to think about a day like that will ever come," he says and when he does it's almost as if I can feel his mind wander into the future that is not yet known to any of us, not even I, who have already lived one.

"The days will come before you know what to do with them, so take each one as a surprise and cherish every moment you are given, especially the ones with those you love, because you'll never know when they'll be gone," I tell him.

"I'll hold on to every single one," he replies. "Especially today."

When I look at him then, I see a part of myself residing in his bones, just as I used to recognize a trace of my mother living in me, even after she was gone. The transgression of the transition that can be present through the blood of those that both create and break us can never truly be lost. I realize now that no matter when they greeted me, or left me, my family, the ones I always loved more than any others, will always be with me, no matter the cost, no matter the consequences. My family, the Woods, always has been and will forever be one.

When we arrive at my mother's house on Elm Street it looks very similar to how I left it. The only real difference that I notice is that the front door is no longer painted a bright shade of red. It is now black, and the contrast of that darkness up against the white siding is something that stands out to me. It leaves a potent imprint upon my consciousness.

Seeing my mother at the age she is currently is something that is even harder to accept than being introduced to ten year old Alma this morning. While I was always aware of the soul of Alma existing, I didn't have anything to compare her to when she jumped into our bed this morning. In truth, she was very similar to what I imagined her to be. My mother, as she is now, is nothing that I ever expected I would see. I study her appearance as she embraces every member of my family, until she finally comes to me. Her hair is cut in a short pixie, her blonde so light that it's almost white. She is in her seventies and even though I can still see traces of her beauty shining through, the years have affected her nevertheless. She's older than I ever thought she was capable of being. The turquoise colored dress she has on is free flowing, but I can still tell that she is in good shape for her age. I imagine she is very active, rarely sitting down or taking it easy. Her skin is tanned, just as Charlie guessed it would be as she had just returned from the Sunshine State. When I see her face up close to mine as she squeezes me, I realize one thing hasn't changed, the look in her eyes when she looks into mine.

"Happy Birthday Son! I'm so happy you all could come!"

"Thanks Mother, we're glad to be here. It's wonderful to see you. You look great."

"Oh, I'm sure I look like an old sack of potatoes, what with how dark my skin is. I swear, I don't even try to soak up the sun, it just comes right on over and crisps me up."

"Well, you look great to me Grammy," Alma tells her sweetly.

"How kind of you little one," she says in response as she pats her on the head. "Are you all hungry?"

"We're always hungry for your cooking Moira," Ellie says.

"Ain't that the truth!" Charlie adds.

So we go from the living room into the kitchen. It looks the same as I remember it, even the table that I grew up with remains in place. The appliances are new and so are most of the decorations, but it is close to what I remember. I am surprised to see a man cooking at the stove, but no one else seems to think it's anything out of the ordinary.

"Hello Jeffrey," Ellie calls out to him and it's then that he turns around to greet us all, with a big toothy grin on his face.

It's Mr. Sanders, Jeffrey Sanders, the man who watched me throw that brick all of those years ago, or rather in this chain of events, the one who watched Danny do it, the man who explained to my mother how I took the blame for my brother's actions. This is the man who owns the diner that played a part in my life in a few different ways, on some of my best and worst days. He is here in my house now, cooking at my mother's stove and it doesn't appear to be anything unusual. However, I can't understand it. I've missed something important in the interlude of the fourth and fifth day.

"Hello everyone!" He says to us. He too is very tan, he must have accompanied my mother to Florida. I wonder if they are together, it's the only thing I can conclude. And although I feel happy for my mother that she has found a companion in her later years, a part of it makes me sad that my father was never truly here, at least not for long enough for me to remember.

We slip into a sequence of cordiality and jokes as the table is set and we enjoy a delicious meal together. After eating, my mother goes over to light the candles of a cake and she walks back over with it, the tiny little flames dance as she brings it to me. They all sing, and the combination of their voices together is the sweetest thing to hear. I blow out my birthday candles and I wish for one thing: for none of the people in this room to ever leave me. And that can even include Mr. Sanders for all I care. When the festivities are finished, Ellie, Jeffrey and the kids offer to clean up the dishes and put everything away, so my mother and I step outside to the back patio and sit down in the plastic chairs to talk.

"Are you happy with Mr. Sanders?" I ask, as it is the question I wish to know about more than anything now that we are alone. It was far too inappropriate and out of place to ask in front of him.

The question may seem random to her, but she doesn't treat it so. She answers me, just as she would have answered any question I might have asked her back when I was young. "I am. I enjoy seeing him and we like spending time with one another. In a way Priam, I suppose I do love him. It's been years that the two of us have been like this. It's just a different kind of love. It's not what I had with your father, I know I will never have anything like I had with him, but that's okay. Regardless, Jeffrey's company helps to soothe the loneliness I felt previously. When you and Danny were here growing up, I never longed for a man's presence as much as I did when you both moved to New York and left me on my own. After your wedding, I realized that it would be okay to let go of your father, at least in some way. I know he would want me to be happy, and to feel love again, no matter the form it takes."

"I think you're right. I'm happy for you. And from the things you discussed over lunch it sounds like you both had a wonderful time in Florida. I guess I forgive you for missing my actual birthday after all," I say, teasing her.

"Oh, I really hope you'll forgive me for that. I can't believe I didn't realize it when I was booking our flights. I guess I am getting old. I hope today made up for it."

"It more than made up for it. It's a shame Danny couldn't come," I say, trying to find out where exactly my brother is now and how he is doing, without making it sound as if I actually am not aware. Nothing in particular has been brought up about him all day as of yet.

"Well you know how busy he and Rebecca are in the city. I'm sure they'll visit us soon," she tells me. "I know how much they love spending time with Charlie and Alma. It's such a shame they haven't been able to have any children of their own." When I hear this news it makes me sad, but in a way it makes sense all the while. Danny never had children during my life and if he had them here I don't know if it would have balanced out in the way I know everything has to. As I've concluded on my own terms, these second chances allow lives to lengthen and perhaps even shorten too, but they don't create new ones that never existed in the first place.

"They would have made great parents," I offer. "That's for sure."

"Indeed they would have. At least they are still able to be a fantastic Aunt and Uncle."

"Cheers to that," I say. "And who knows, maybe once Charlie and Alma are both done with high school, Ellie and I will move back to the city. We'd be able to spend more time with Danny and Rebecca then. I miss NYC quite a great deal at times."

"I'm not surprised. I've always felt the two of you belonged there more than anywhere else. Though I won't deny that I was ecstatic when you two chose to come back to raise your children here. It made me a happy Grammy."

"Well you know how I am, I live to please," I tell her with a smile as I reach out and grab her hand. "Especially you."

"Oh Priam, you're still just as charming as you've always been. Perhaps some things do get better with age. I sure have, don't you think?" She says with a laugh, and a wink.

I smile then, and take the moment for what it is, an experience of my life that has just begun it's forty ninth year, alongside the life of another who reigns in during the seventh decade of her life. The time that has passed us since the moment that we actually saw each other last in the life that I lived seems so different now. Chloe was right, as this journey goes on, the days that I am experiencing are changing much more from the framework of what they started as. I only wonder how much more they can change and if it is even possible for things to get any better than they are now.

I don't expect them to go any differently than they have been recently, I can't fathom that they'll go back downhill again, that they will actually get worse. For how can they, when I have all of the people I want to surround me? How can they, when I have made all of these changes and changes have made themselves? How can anything turn sour when it all feels so sweet? It's only because time trails on of its own desire and lifts the leverage above you that things are able to alter in unexpected ways. It's only in moving forward that time can push you back. It's only in never letting go, that you are forced to give up.

We drive home in the middle of the afternoon, after the celebration at my mother's ends and there is still enough sunlight left in the sky to take us back to where we belong. As I'm driving I revel in the company of the three people with me, as the good times continue to roll on. Ellie gets our children laughing about silly memories that I don't recall, but I know this body remembers them, at least in some way.

I realize as I drive that I am both the protagonist and antagonist of my story. The only real villain that existed during my life was myself. I was the one who messed things up, I was the one who did things wrong. Yet all the while I was the one who was trying to make things right. It's as if I've been split down the middle and the two sides have battled one another to try and find some common ground to settle everything, so that the subtle silence wouldn't end up all on its own. This journey has been similar to my original story. Even though these second chances have been so different from the life I remember, they still feel parallel too. Although the paths have diverged, I have to wonder if they will come back together, if they will ever recreate an experience that is perpendicular. If they do collide, I hope it is only in a beneficial way. I don't know if I can deal with any more heartbreak, even if my heart has already broken a hundred times before, it still hurts just the same.

"Lookie, lookie!" Alma cries suddenly as she points feverishly out her window to the side of the road, she has found something that has caught her attention. As we drive past what she has alluded to, I am only half surprised to look out my window to the left and see a golden retriever running alone along the road. I hadn't seen one yet today and I think I know by now that seeing one is a pattern on these second ways. The sighting is too short to recognize for sure if the dog is Chloe, the one I have known, the one I still do. I wonder what it means, but just as I ponder it, the dog is gone from my sight. However, the idea of her remains.

"Can we please get a dog?" Alma asks as sweetly as she can. "Pretty, pretty please?"

I know that they are all expecting only one kind of answer to come from me, and they assume they know what it will be. Except they don't, because I intend to tell them the opposite of what they think they'll hear. "Yes. I think we should. How about we go to the pet store tomorrow?" I ask them as they all gasp in an uncontrollable shock. Alma literally screams at the top of her lungs, she is unable to hold in the joy she feels. The small bag of fruit loops that she is holding in her hands falls to the floor.

"You're going to make us all deaf Alma!" Charlie says to her, half teasing, half serious as he shoves his finger into his ear and rings it around, as if he is clearing out the residue of the sound she has just made.

"Are you serious Daddy?"

"As serious as I could ever be," I tell her.

"I suppose even old men can change," Ellie says with a laugh as she looks my way.

I glance at my children through the rearview mirror and see that Alma is trying to reach for her bag of cereal that she dropped on the floor, but it is too far away. "I can't get it," she says, not to anyone in particular, but I know it will be Ellie who responds to her.

"I'll get it for you," my wife communicates to her as she reaches down to her belt buckle and pushes the red button that releases her from the grips of the moving vehicle. Even though she still remains within it now, amongst the three of us, she is no longer connected to the automobile as we are. She is free from what it holds on to. She turns towards me and then around to face the back where our children sit. "What should we name it? Maybe we can start thinking of some?" She asks them both. "I'm sure you two have thought of some by this point."

"What about Rose, or Gladys?" Alma suggests.

"Those are grandma names," Charlie says with a snort. "What are we going to do, adopt a hundred year old dog?"

"Now now, Charlie," Ellie says. "Be nice to your sister." She has reached the bag of cereal and hands it back to Alma and then turns around back into her seat. "What about Chloe?" She asks as she looks to me as I drive on, as if this suggestion is only for me. "I always thought Chloe would be a nice name for a dog." I take a deep breath that is both a mixture of something normal and something unusual as her suggestion is not what I anticipate to hear from her lips, but it is what comes.

Just as the truck collides with us then, it careens out of control and plows into us, tearing everything asunder. The last thing I recall before losing consciousness is the window on her side of the car shattering, the glass bursting through our space as if it is an unwanted intruder throwing daggers at our love and longing for what we have always wanted, but do not have.

My eyes feel heavy and I cannot open them. I hear Alma screaming, but it's not the same kind of loudness she has exuded earlier this day. She is shrieking out of pain and out of fear. I hear a grunt from somewhere behind me and I know that it's Charlie, as the tone of his voice registers in my mind.

A warm liquid is running over my eyelids and I finally decide that I have to see what I can, even though what I do is filtered by a crimson liquid that I know is blood. I lift my right hand up slowly to wipe some of it away. When I do, I realize that the sensation I feel is being caused by the fact that our car is lying on its side, as it must have rolled a few times from the impact of the truck that hit us. I remember it happening, but I don't all the while. I look in the rearview mirror and see that both Alma and Charlie are still strapped into their seats. They both have a few cuts on their faces, and they are bleeding a bit, but it's nothing that looks too serious. I thank God, if there is one.

"Are you kids okay back there?"

"I think so," Charlie moans. "I feel sore though. What happened?"

"A truck!" It's all Alma says, but I am happy to know she can still form words, as these two sounds let me know that she too will be okay.

"Where's Mom?" Charlie asks.

I wipe more of the blood off of my face and look to my right where my wife was only moments earlier. Her seat is empty. She isn't in the car. She's gone. I look forward for the first time, finally realizing that it wasn't only the passenger window that shattered. The windshield has been obliterated too, and from the amount of blood that is on her side of the vehicle, it appears she flew through it. She wasn't wearing her seatbelt when the impact hit. She was only a second away from clicking it back on, but there wasn't enough time. Time didn't give her the chance to do so, time didn't care....Ellie is no longer here.

I look down, as it's the only place I can look now as I feel I am beginning to lose everything. This can't be happening. There are shards of glass in my leg, and there is one large piece in particular that seems to have lodged itself pretty deep into my thigh that doesn't want me to move, but I ignore it. I need to get out of this car. I need to find her. I open my door, as my side is now the top of the car, the side closest to the sky. It isn't easy to get out this way, but I manage it, trying to forget about the pain even though it digs into me. I try not to think of the blood running down my face or the glass burying itself deeper within me as I move on. I tell myself that Ellie is going to be okay, even though I know she might not be.

I leave the kids in the car, which I know I probably shouldn't do, but at least I know they are okay, at least for the time being. I don't worry about the truck that hit us, I don't care about it to be quite honest. All I care about is her, and where she is, how she is and how I might have to save her. I have to save her. Then, I see her. Her body is sprawled out on the concrete about fifteen feet before me. As I get closer, dragging along the uncooperative body that houses me, I can see that she is surrounded by a large pool of blood. Her frame looks mangled, and before I am brave enough to look at her face, to check for signs of life that I know may not be there, I see her leg twitch, as only a dancer's leg does.

"Ellie? Honey, are you okay?" She turns over, ever so slowly and when she does, I realize she is nowhere near okay. Her face is just as bloody as mine, but somehow none of it has gotten into her eyes, they look into me and it's then that I know.

"Oh Priam..." she says with as much strength as she can, which isn't much. "I'm so sorry."

I reach out and lie down beside her, and as I feel the abrasive hardness of the concrete, I put one arm around her shoulder and take my other arm and place it next to hers so that our hands lace together. "You're going to be alright, just hold on."

"I don't know if I can."

"You can do anything."

"If only that were true."

"Make it true," I plead of her. "You can't go. Not like this. Not again."

Even through her pain she catches my words and the agony in her face shifts away for an instant "You're here Priam. You're here."

"I'm here. Stay with me. I can't lose you. I never want to lose you. My life is nothing without you."

"Your life is so much more than just Ellie Donahue, it always has been. You were just too in love with me to realize it."

"I could never be too in love with you."

"Maybe you were though, maybe I held you back."

"You did the opposite, you pushed me forward."

She gasps then, the suffering taking over her senses and invading them. "I don't want to leave you Priam, but I have to. I can feel it coming."

"Don't say that! Don't you give up on me Ellie. Don't!" I shout, my voice echoing around the stillness that surround us, but it disappears then, as I hear sirens approaching in the distance. The red flashing lights are on their way, but I know now they will arrive too late to do anything.

"I could never give up on you Priam. And I never will."

Her blue eyes look not at me then, but into me and

through. Those are the last words she speaks, as the pupils contained within the color of the sea where she once swam pulls the tide out and the blackness takes over. The hand I am holding doesn't go limp, but I can feel the life leave it. Ellie is gone. She's dead. I scream then, and the sound of my own screech scares me as it contains every emotion I've ever felt before and then some. This cannot be.

 This cannot be.

 I cannot...be.

 Tears don't come, as I am too angry for tears. This is all too much for anything. I don't want to turn away from her, but the pain within me is growing greater now, not only because of the chambers that wish to burst forth and apart from my heart, but because of the injuries I myself have suffered. I don't care for them and in a way I wish they would just take me too. I don't know if I can die again, but it's the only thing I can think of that would make this at all bearable. The opposite of living is all I yearn for, even though that itself is the opposite of what I have always feared.

 The glass shard within my leg is deeper than I thought, as I understand that the blood spilling from the spot where it entered my body is now merging together with the blood which emanated from Ellie. The living flow pouring from me mesmerizes itself by combining into the elixir that once forced her to live, to dance, to dream, to love. I don't let go of her hand. I won't let go of her hand.

 It's only when I look back to the car to see Charlie getting out and helping Alma to escape from the wreckage as well that I realize where we are. It's the same exact intersection where someone I knew once died before. These perpendicular lines are the ones that crossed and ruined my life when I was only thirteen, the place where the parallels stopped and decided to run into one another. The sight of this place, this spot where Ellie just left me, is one I have known and loathed before.

 The car crash has occurred at the exact spot where the Victoria was totaled all of those years ago. The place where my mother died in 1954 during my life is now the spot where Ellie has said goodbye in this year of 1990, which is contained within this continuation of my second chances. The trails had separated and diverged, but they always knew that they were going to come back together. I should have known that changing that first day and influencing things so that Moira Wood would live would come at a price. Everything is symmetrical in ways, as life, or the exact replica of something that is like it has to be defined, yet differentiated all the while in order to balance itself. There is chaos in the universe, but there has to be order as well. You can hold on to some, but be forced to let go of others. Time does not care who you are, or when you are living, all it knows is that it has to go on, and that the parallel lines will always become perpendicular. I saved my mother, only to kill my wife. What have I done?

I see Charlie and Alma approaching me as the sirens are almost here, as the red colored lights seem to bounce off of the blue sky and into my eyes. When I see my children, I go into a state of shock, realizing that I still have two days left and that neither of them were alive past this day and if they are now, I will have to lose them again too, in another way, on another day.

I can't. I can't. I can't.

I try to scream again, but it is impossible. The glass within my leg barrels into me deeper and it is then that I feel it pierce my heart, even though it is nowhere near that organ, the essence of my being. The loss of blood has been too much. I lose myself then, in more ways than one. I lose myself in every sense that a man can be lost, and I don't wish to be found.

Dealing with Charlie's death was like coming to the conclusion of a song that I never thought would end. When you have a child, you think about all of the things in their life that will happen before you. You imagine all of their firsts, but you never think that you will have to come to accept their lasts. It's impossible to move forward when you can't help looking back at the life that they had, the life that is gone. Losing a child while you are still alive is the most strenuous entity to understand. When Charlie died, when he decided to end his life, I wanted to give up. For the first time in my life, I didn't feel like trying anymore.

Leaving the room right after it happened was a challenge in itself. I didn't know how long I was unconscious after fainting, but when I came to it was well after midnight. I didn't want to let go of him. I didn't want to walk out of his room, because I knew that when I left him, I would have to tell Ellie.

I built up the courage and went into the bedroom where I knew she would likely already be asleep. When I saw her lying there, resting so peacefully, it felt like an atrocity to wake her, especially because I imagined she was dreaming. I didn't want to interrupt that harmony, so instead of stirring her immediately, I sat in the leather chair next to the bed and watched her for a while. I let her sleep a bit more, I wanted her dreams to extend further. Not a single part of me wanted to wake her and introduce her to this nightmare.

Even the sweetest of dreams come to an end though, and I knew that the longer I waited, the harder it would be for me to tell her what had happened. Eventually I went over to the bed and sat down on the edge of it, beside her body where she laid. I ran my hands over her skin delicately until she came back to me.

"Mmm....hello there," she said, utterly unaware and disconnected from the reality in the other room. I hated the fact that I was the one who had to introduce it to her. I hated that it existed at all.

"Hello dear. I'm sorry to wake you, but you need to get up. I'm afraid something terrible has happened." She sat up then and looked at me as if she knew. She didn't, but it's almost as if she had an idea. I fought back and forth with how I should tell her, or if I should even tell her at all.

I didn't. Instead, I showed her. For some reason my instinct was that she would rather see than hear. When I took her into Charlie's room and she was awakened by the reality that he was forever asleep, I knew I did the right thing by making her aware of it by showing her the vessel that once held his soul. The physicality of his body being empty and the lack of his soul remaining in our house was not something that I could put into words for her. How could I? I felt as if the entire situation was and always would be, my fault. So instead of telling her, I let her see. And still, as she came to know the fact that our son was no longer with us, it all became too much. Having to see her face become aware of it, that was what killed me the most. Knowing then that Ellie knew too, that was the hardest part of all.

The funeral was a few days later. It burned into me in a similar fashion as my mother's had, for his body laid in the same funeral home, in the same room, in the same position as hers once did. I stood in the same place, and felt the same kind of pain, even though it was a different kind of loss. When my mother died, it was like losing my past, as if everything I had ever known and understood was gone. When Charlie died, it was like losing my future, as if everything I had ever hoped to know and understand would never come to pass. All the while I had to remain in the present not knowing where anything would go from that point on.

It was a dark day and the rain came down as firmly as it could on that July afternoon. The weather fit my mood, but nothing could calm me down, not even the smell of wet asphalt, the scent that I used to love so much for reasons unknown. The black colored clothing of everyone who came wrapped me up within the gloomy day. I remember helping Ellie zip up the back of her black dress and covering her shoulders with the dark shawl she had chosen. Even under those circumstances I still couldn't help thinking that she looked radiant. No amount of darkness could ever extinguish her light. At least I would always have her.

She gave a speech that day, delivering words to all who came to let them know the kind of boy that Charlie was. We didn't keep the reason of his death a secret, and we didn't shy away from the reality of why he had given up. Charlie was gay, he always had been and he always would be. There was no reason to pretend otherwise. He felt misplaced, he felt alone and he felt misunderstood. Nevertheless, Charlie was great and his sexuality was not what defined him, even though it played a large part in what ended him. He had so much left to give the world, but unfortunately he never would. The tragedy of him taking his own life tore up my insides like a tantric tangled web of lies. I did not want to believe it could really be, but it was, it was.

A lot of people came to show their support and offer Ellie and I words of kindness about our son, and even though it made me feel a little bit better to see all of the people who cared about him, it could only do so much. Regardless of the memories they shared, the stories they told us of brilliant things Charlie had done, and what he had meant to them, it still wasn't enough. He was gone, and he was never coming back.

I remember seeing Danny walking in, emerging from the monsoon of rain and into the congregation room outside of where Ellie and I stood next to our son's hard cherry crafted casket. The tales that were being told to me then from a high school friend of Charlie's faded out suddenly, as all I could focus on was my brother in the near distance, getting closer to me.

Ellie noticed that I was regressing back into myself, as I couldn't focus on Charlie's friend in front of us. She listened to the rest of what the girl had to say though, and embraced her as she started to cry. "Charlie was the sweetest boy I ever knew. I still can't believe this," she had said. I started to cry too, more than I ever had before that day.

I pulled myself away from them and ran towards Danny, but not actually to him, passing the flowers that were still alive, as they had been cultivated and arranged to cover up the death that lingered there. My eyes were burning and Ellie was no longer beside me. It was the first time we had been apart all day. I knew then, as I took a seat in a private room and closed the curtain in the doorway shut, that when it opened again, it wouldn't be my wife who came to console me, but my long lost brother instead. I held my head in my hands, but I still felt his presence arrive when he pulled back the fabric and came in. I knew that he was there before he sat down next to me. He placed his arm around my shoulder and my body tensed from his touch. He was coming to make me feel better, but somehow, when I looked up at him, I felt worse.

"How are you holding up?" He asked.

I looked up at him with my tear soaked face and glared into his eyes. I couldn't help but feel angry, not only at Danny but because of what had happened to me, to us. "How does it look like I'm doing? My son killed himself for Christ's sake."

"I know. I'm so sorry Priam. I can't even imagine," he went on, as his hand on my shoulder started to apply pressure deeper into my skin. This was him trying to assert the situation as my big brother, to push into me to make me stronger, but I felt then that all he was doing was trying to comprehend something that I knew he never could. I pulled away from him.

"Of course you can't imagine Danny. You don't have a family."

He moved his body slightly away from me then too. My words plowed into him, like a cavalcade of tanks running over the garden that he had nurtured so thoroughly. Perhaps what I said was a little harsh, but I didn't give a damn. How could I?

"You're right, I don't have a wife, and I don't have a son or any children of my own for that matter," he told me. "But I think it's wrong to say that I don't have a family. I still have you. Don't I?"

I grabbed a tissue off of the coffee table in front of us and wiped the wetness from my face. My body was aching, not in a physical way, but from the emotions that were wrestling around inside me. I wished that I did not have to go through this day, all I wanted was for it to be over.

"You haven't had me for decades Danny. You gave up on me and forced me to give up on you. Don't think that Charlie committing suicide is somehow going to bring us back together. It's too late for that."

How I regretted those words later, when the years went on and more things crumbled, I wondered if I wouldn't have said it, if I could have had my brother back after all. But I said them and when I did, there was no taking them back, because in that moment when he sat beside me, as my son laid dead in the room adjacent to us, where my wife was on her own with all of the people who had once known Charlie, I didn't want to be there with him. On that day, I didn't want to be anywhere, I didn't want to exist at all.

"Okay, well maybe you're right," he said. Even though when I looked up at him I could tell that he didn't want to accept it, I could tell that the lines in his face and the ages that had passed us had caused him to regret things too. He had come here to help me and in doing so he had hoped that perhaps we could fix things between the two of us, as I once had. The roles were reversed though, just as he had once not cared about being my brother, I no longer gave a damn about him. At least not then, not on that day.

"Thanks for coming though. It does mean a lot," I said to him. Even in my grief, I wasn't blinded enough to see his kindness.

"Of course Priam, of course. There's no way I wouldn't have come."

"If it's alright though, I kind of want to be alone right now."

"Sure, sure, I understand," he said. "I just wanted to make sure you were okay. You're going to be okay. I know this is more than unbearable now, but you're strong enough to get through it. I believe in you." He stood up then and slowly walked away.

"I appreciate that Danny," I said to him. As he left the room he turned around so that his face looked towards me and he smiled so that the wrinkles on his face became more pronounced. I remembered riding our bikes together down Elm Street as if it were only yesterday, but we were getting old. He shut the curtain so that I was alone again. It was the last time I ever saw him.

A few months later, Ellie and I decided to move back to New York City. Without Charlie, Alden didn't feel right. The house we lived in reminded me too much of him and of my mother as well. We needed to get away, to return to the city that made us. We left Alden in the fall of 1990. We found a nice apartment in Brooklyn, not far from where I used to have my studio and we tried our best to reassemble our lives into some sort of normalcy.

Ellie returned to the American Ballet Company and started working as a choreographer. Her time of dancing on the stage was over, but her mind creating the movements still lingered on. With all of the contacts she still had there, it wasn't hard for her to reimmerse herself in that environment when we once again became citizens of the city.

I went back to Haversmith, as I had been working for them all the while in Alden anyways. When I walked into my old building again, it felt as if nothing had changed. I was promoted within two weeks after returning to the senior executive art director for advertising. The new position was a huge salary increase, but it was also a much bigger time commitment. I felt that time was all I had when I went back, because even though I was starting to come to terms with my own mortality, without my son life felt different. All I wanted was to be distracted away from the reality that I was living, so I stayed at the office for more hours than I ever had before and I was fine with that.

I stopped painting. I vowed to myself that I wouldn't paint after he died. I couldn't allow myself to, it just didn't feel right. Even though I knew that painting would be a release for me and probably make me feel better, I didn't think I deserved to experience any such kind of liberation. I decided I needed to punish myself for how I had led Charlie to the end. My art, the only thing that always made sense to me, was the one thing that no longer made any sense to me at all. For it couldn't, I would no longer let it. How life had turned around.

I had told Charlie that I thought being gay was wrong; even though I didn't even know what being gay really meant when I told him so. I thought it was something that wasn't right. After he was gone, I tried to understand it better, for I realized it was the thing that had caused him so much strife. I needed to try to come to terms with it, I needed to try and grasp what it all meant and I realized the only way I could really do that was to try and make amends in a way that I thought Charlie would have appreciated.

I should have known he was gay. I should have asked him about it. How could I have been so blind? I suppose I saw what I wanted to see and ignored everything else that I didn't. I knew Charlie so well, yet after he was gone, I felt like I barely knew him. I started to volunteer my time at a Gay Youth Shelter in the city. It just so happened that I passed one on my way home from work one day, walking in a way that I usually did not. It was as if the place called out to me, beckoning me in as if it knew that it could help me with all of the guilt that I felt. I originally decided to volunteer there because I felt remorseful about how I had talked to Charlie on the last night of his life. I thought that if I tried to help out other young people like him I would find some sort of reprieve, but what I ended up finding was so much more than that. I found a boy by the name of Robert, and even though I didn't know it then, or ever really, I saved his life...and in a way, he saved a part of mine.

I started going to the shelter once a week on Wednesdays, right after work. I didn't tell Ellie that I was going there. For some reason I decided to keep it to myself. She usually worked late on

Wednesdays anyways, so she never suspected anything. The nights I volunteered were always game nights. I didn't really do anything besides play monopoly. All I did was talk to these young kids and in doing so I tried to make them feel better about their lives. I tried to give them hope and in return, they gave me stories of what had brought them there and what their lives had been up until that point. In essence, they told me the kind of tales that Charlie never did. They helped me to come to terms with what it meant to be gay.

Then there was Robert. While all of the kids were mostly upbeat and lively, he was not. He arrived at the shelter about three months after I started volunteering in the summer of 1992. The first time I saw him he was sitting alone in a corner with his knees pulled up in front of him with his arms wrapped around them, as if he had to hold onto them so they wouldn't fall off. He looked scared. It was like he had nothing left to believe in. I waved to him. He didn't wave back. He looked right through me. I walked over to him. "Hello there," I said. "My name's Priam. What's yours?"

"Robert."

"Nice to meet you Robert."

"Why don't you fuck off?"

"Hey now, don't be like that," I said. "What's wrong?"

"More things than you could ever understand."

"Well, let me try."

He looked at me, and this time he didn't let his gaze push through my existence, instead he let his eyes register upon me. "Who are you?"

"I said the name is Priam. Priam Wood."

"That's a fucking weird ass name mister."

"Well your name is pretty fucking weird too," I told him, even though it wasn't.

He smiled then. Apparently all I had to do was match his attitude in order to speak his language. He understood me now. "Nicely said," he replied, warming up to me a little bit. "You're not like the other adults who volunteer here, are you? I doubt any of them would talk to me like that."

"I don't think I'm like anyone at all, period. I've never liked being compared to anyone else. What about you?"

"I feel the same."

"Well then, it looks like you and I have something in common Robert. Why don't we go play a game of Scrabble?"

"Okay. I guess," he said as he released his legs and got up from his chair in the corner to follow me over to a table where the board game was waiting for us.

Robert had run away from home at the age of fifteen. He hitchhiked all the way from Iowa to New York City, and now at the age of seventeen he was staying at the shelter after living on the streets and resorting to hustling for the past two years. His abusive father and alcoholic mother had disowned him the day he told them he was gay and that was when he decided he had to leave, that he could no longer stay with them. The life of good fortune and acceptance he had imagined for himself in the city had not come to pass. He was alone, and nothing seemed to be going his way.

He didn't trust very many people, but for some reason he trusted me. After the night that I met Robert, whenever I returned to the shelter every Wednesday, it was always him that I spent my time with. It seemed as if he needed it the most. This routine went on for many months, each time I went, I got closer to Robert, and he to me. Eventually, I told him about Charlie and although I was terrified as to how he would react to what I said to him when he told me he was gay, he actually ended up helping me come to terms with it more than I would have ever predicted.

"If only I would have accepted him, he might still be here," I had said.

He took a deep breath before speaking, and then spurted out his words as he always did, letting them come to meet the listener before he even listened to them himself. "No Priam. He wouldn't be here. Charlie had given up on himself a long time before you had ever given up on him."

"What do you mean?"

"I just mean, I don't think you should blame yourself for how it all happened. It's true that the way you reacted may not have helped the situation much, but Charlie knew that you loved him, just as he knew his mother did. The problem was too far rooted at that point, he was too unhappy with himself to move forward. So instead, he decided to stay where he was, never coming to know another point in time, never allowing himself to greet the future."

"But don't you think if I would have told him it was okay, that I didn't care if he was gay or not...don't you think he wouldn't have done it?"

"I can't say for sure. No one can, but what I can tell you is that I don't think what you said to him took him to the edge, I think his dissatisfaction with himself drove him there. From what you've told me about him, Charlie seemed like an amazing guy, but he was scared and I don't think there is really any reason for what happened. No matter how it happened though, I don't think he would want you to blame yourself."

"I do though. I blame myself everyday."

"But you're still alive Priam! You can't focus on it all of the time. You have to let him go, just as he let go of himself. He wouldn't want you to punish yourself for the rest of your life. He would want you to go on and see all of the things that he was never able to see. He would want you and Ellie to have a good life, he wouldn't want you to give up on your dreams just because his didn't work out."

"I can't."

"You can. If only you try."

The young man who sat in front of me then seemed older than I actually was, even though I was born decades before him. What he said to me made so much sense, yet none at all. Maybe there wasn't an explicit answer to why Charlie had done what he had done. It was possible that it had happened simply because it was always supposed to. Perhaps Charlie was just too good for this Earth.

"You know, I think you're going to be alright Robert. I've been coming here for months talking to you about everything from Sesame Street to Wall Street and even though it may seem as if not much has changed, I know it has. You are going to get out of here, you're going to get out of this predicament and you are going to save yourself in a way that Charlie was never able to. And for that, I do feel better. Not as much as I would feel if I could somehow save my son, but achieving some things are better than achieving nothing."

"Life will never make sense completely Mr. Wood. Not to you, nor to I, nor to any of us under the sun. But love will go on, with our without our comprehension. It will go on."

I said goodbye to him that night and when I hugged him he threw my scarf around my neck before I embarked out into the cold winter air. I wasn't aware that the next time I came to the shelter he wouldn't be there. When I arrived the following week, Robert had already departed. He had gone on, out there into the world, just as I knew he would. He was out there in the search to find his place, to make something of himself, to prove that he could. I had no idea where he had gone and he hadn't left word, but somehow, I knew to believe in him. I knew that Robert would make it. He hadn't given me any answers, but somehow his explanation of not needing to believe in reasons, but rather in the rationality of humankind and lack thereof made more sense to me than I had ever acknowledged being necessary.

When Ellie and I moved back to the city, I started to immerse myself into work more thoroughly than I ever had before. I never painted, but I still found other things to occupy my time at the office. I no longer created the ads all on my own, but there was still so much to oversee. Ellie did the same at the ballet, but in a different way. She still lost herself artistically, whereas I refused to allow myself to do so. I think she was happier than I was during those years after we came to get used to the actuality that he was gone, but of course she wasn't actually fulfilled. Somehow though, she was better at accepting the reality of it than I was.

As the years went on and we started to get farther away from when we had lived in Alden raising our son, I stayed at the office later and later. A few months after Robert disappeared from the shelter, I stopped going altogether, as it just made me sad that he was no longer there. Besides, by that point I had felt I had gotten all I could from it. I went on. At the same time, I didn't. I was stationary and I was slackened and loosened and stuck in New York in a way that I couldn't change. The rains were coming down, even though sunny days were all around me. Red souls were mitigating messages that were unable to be delivered. I was lost, and for the first time in my life, the sight of Ellie, the only being who always had the capability of calming me, was unable to do so. We started to grow apart. I don't know when it began and even if I tried I'm sure it would have been impossible to find an exact point in time where things started to change, but changing they were, and I didn't know what to do. I didn't try to do anything, thus the repetition only seemed worse as everything went on and I continued to lose myself in a realm where nothing existed. It all became harder to find.

The meals we shared at the dinner table were mostly silent. We would exchange pleasantries and kiss when we came home, but it was more of a formality than an act of love. I still loved her, of course I did, I loved her with everything I had, but for some reason I was no longer able to express it in the way that I once did. After Charlie died, we still slept in the same bed, but we never had sex again. The loss of my son put an end to so many things in my life, I gave up on a lot, while still trying not to give up on anything. Somehow, the paradox won. I still loved Ellie, but as we continued to get older, I felt as if I didn't know where anything was going. What were we aiming for? It was only us, just us. Even though she was enough for me and more than I actually deserved, I felt a longing for something more, and yet a subtraction of what we had.

I knew that my life could have been better than what it was, not only in regards to her as my love, my wife, but in other terms. I knew that if I had done things differently, perhaps I could have had my mother, my brother and my son too. I could have had it all, but instead, all I had was her. If only I would have realized that she alone should have been enough, perhaps it all would have turned out differently. Maybe then I wouldn't have died alone in the way that I did.

Our kisses felt different. Not in the way that the actuality of the kisses touched my lips in an unusual way, but rather the effort I pursed through my lips and pushed behind them were of an unknown occurrence. She still felt the same up against me, but it was almost as if I couldn't feel the spirit within her rise up anymore. I don't know if Ellie felt those differences then, or if it was only me, but things were changing, and even though I knew they were, I did nothing to stop the spiraling. I let it go. Eventually, she mentioned the distance that seemed to be separating us. She acknowledged that our boats were drifting apart and that the sea was claiming our love and drowning us in our sorrows. She acted as if we were only half righteous enough to recognize how things were stirring. It was after another silent dinner, when we had both gotten ready for bed and were lying next to one another in the darkness, our skin separated by the thick amounts of cotton and thread that lined up between us like walls built up for war, that the dam broke.

"What is happening to us Priam? I feel as if I lose a little part of you each day. I can't ignore this anymore. Do you still love me?" She said aloud into the night.

"Of course I do."

"That's not enough."

"Then what is?"

"I don't know, but I can't let this distance consume us. We have to do something to change it. Just because Charlie died doesn't mean you have to give up on everything."

Her words hurt me, but in a way, I knew she was right. I had to start trying again, but it just seemed like so much to do. She knew that I loved her. Wasn't that enough? "What can we do?" I asked.

"Something new. I think we need to do something together that we have never done before. Maybe something that we thought we would never do," she said as she wrapped her arms around my chest, holding me close to her and extinguishing the space of nothingness that had previously existed between us.

"Like what Ellie? We're fifty-six years old for heaven's sake. What haven't we done?"

"A great deal Priam. Do you remember when we were young and we always talked about traveling to far away places? Well last I remember the farthest place we've gone is Alden and that doesn't count at all. There are so many more places to see than this city and the place you were born. Let's go somewhere neither of us have ever been before. Maybe then, as we experience some place new together, we can reawaken whatever it is that we have lost."

"Like where?" I asked, not knowing whether or not to believe her idea of going away in order to find ourselves again.

"I don't know. How about London?" She asked as she kissed me on the neck. It's the first time she had kissed me in such a way in quite a while and it felt strange, but it felt good. "I've always wanted to go."

"London, eh? Bloody hell," I said in my best impression of an English accent, which wasn't very good. She giggled then and I turned to look at her, my eyes focusing through the darkness. I entangled my legs around hers and we laid there, two middle-aged lovers who were in the interior of everything and nothing all the while. Ellie was no longer the young girl that I had once met. Her hair was still that same warm colored chestnut brown, but it had streaks of gray. Her skin was no longer smooth, but contained lines from all of the love that she had held, and lost. She was so different, but she was still the one constant I had always known. Somehow, as I looked at her then, I knew that she would always believe in me, even if I couldn't myself.

"Okay," I said, speaking up again. "London. London.

London." I went forth, letting the name of the city roll around in my mouth, trying to get used to the idea to the point where it could become a reality.

"Red double decker buses, the River Thames, Princess Diana and the Queen. The Beatles, Big Ben and fish n' chips. I want it all, and I want to experience it with you. Say we can go?" She pleaded.

"We'll go. Let's go," I said, giving in and accepting that we needed to do something different in order to feel the same again.

"Oh Priam! Really? You'll go?" She squealed in delight.

"We'll go. We will." In so many words I made a promise to her that I could not keep. I thought then that things were looking up, but instead, they were just the beginning of the end. I delivered my life to myself as an idea that I thought I could create, but in reality I couldn't let go of what was and what could not be. I made up rhymes that didn't work and I forced the woman who loved me to stop believing in me, even though in actuality, she never would, she never could, but nevertheless, a part of her did. That night was the start of something new, but the end of what we had always known. We would leave our home, but lose the game.

When I wake up, I know that something is wrong immediately. I don't feel like myself at all, I don't even feel human. I feel insane, as if someone or something has overtaken my brain and captured control of my being. Either aliens have invaded or I've been possessed, or maybe something worse entirely. All I know is that I have never felt like this before, something is not right. I've risen thousands of days before this one, but this is the first morning I have ever felt like this, as in, I feel as if I can't feel at all.

I turn over in my bed, barely conscious of my body, but I am awake enough to know that Ellie isn't lying beside me. I rotate back around to my side where the small wooden bedside table rests. I look at the little clock perched upon it as if it is a mechanical white boxed bird. It reads that it is 11:30AM. I haven't slept in this late since I was a teenager. What the hell is going on? I feel like someone has drugged me. And that's when it all clicks. Even though I've never felt like this before, I realize I have somewhat, at least in a certain kind of way. My body has experienced this kind of sensation previously, but many decades ago, and at a much lower level than it is undergoing now. I'm high.

As I realize this, I wonder how it has happened, but then the midnight stupor of my own half awake, half sleepwalking charade comes back to me. I know now that those brownies I ate must not have just been normal chocolate fudge brownies. In fact, there is no way they were anything even close to the typical dessert.

In the middle of the night, I had awoken with a start to the sounds of my own stomach growling. I had worked late again and missed the dinner that Ellie had prepared, so instead of eating the leftovers she had placed for me in the fridge, I just came straight to bed, where I found her already fast asleep. Apparently my body was not happy with the decision I had made and thus, I got out of bed when it beckoned and went into the kitchen to find something to eat. I decided against the meatloaf that was waiting for me in the fridge and instead went for the container of brownies that Ellie had brought back home from the bake sale they had at the theater. They were so delicious that I ate three enormous ones and guzzled down a large glass of milk to chase them down my esophagus, before deciding I was satisfied. I returned back to bed, where my wife was still sound asleep, unaware that I had gotten up at all.

Somehow, the brownies that Ellie had brought home were not just your regular bake sale brownies. There was no way that they were, it was the only explanation that I could rationalize to understand how I was feeling now. Some young ballet dancing twit either was a complete jackass and actually sold weed brownies to my middle aged wife, or there had been a mistake and some mary jane loving hippie had accidentally brought their own magical mix of dessert to share without even realizing it. Regardless of how it happened, the madness had found its way to me and entered into my body. I lie here in my bed trying to rationalize how it happened, or why it happened. I realize I can't continue thinking like this, or my head is going to explode.

I look back to the clock and realize that it still reads 11:30AM. It feels as if though an hour has passed, but in reality not even a minute has gone by. I am losing myself within myself, unable to understand what is and what may be. I sit up and look around, everything seems to be morphing into one. I think I see someone in the corner of our bedroom, but it's just my bathrobe hanging from a hook. The dark blue material is heavily draping itself down from where it is connected to the wall as if it is about to release the hook entirely, sick and tired of being hung up.

Ellie is gone already. I know this to be true without even having to leave our room. She had errands to run, I recall her calling me yesterday at the office to let me know that she had to go pick up a few last minute things this morning before we headed off to the airport together.

The trip. London. Fish n' chips. Big Ben. The Beatles. The Queen. Princess Diana. The River Thames. Double Decker buses. All of the things she wanted us to see, to ride, to think about, to eat, to listen to, to yearn for, to experience and then some more. How can I be in this kind of predicament when today is the day? The day that we are supposed to take a huge leap forward and jump across the pond, or fly rather. This trip is meant to help us move forward, to crawl back out of the rut that we recently have been living in, and to rejuvenate our love to the way that it once was. How can that happen when I feel like this? If I start out the trip under these circumstances I don't think it will bode well for Ellie's plan. I have to fix this, but I don't know if I can. I should get up; I should get out of bed and try to focus on something, anything.

So I do. I stand up and then just as I have risen and become vertical, I quickly become horizontal again as I trip over my suitcase that is sitting on the floor at the edge of my bed. I'm back down once more. The entire world feels as if it is aiming to smother me. I can't pull it together, no matter how hard I try. This is going to be a major struggle, I recognize that now as the cold wooden floor pushes into my face which presses back against it. I look at the clock as I slowly stand up. It's still 11:30AM. How in the hell? The clock finally changes shape and morphs into another number: 11:31AM. Finally, I think. Only four hours and forty-nine minutes until our plane departs. It feels like a lifetime from now, so far away. I have all day, at least a while until I need to be prepared to leave. Certainly I will be better by then, I have to feel normal again, or Ellie might just kill me, if I don't kill myself first. I feel insane.

The numbers all of a sudden compute in my head and I recall that our flight leaves from JFK at 4:20PM. Four hours and forty-nine minutes from now. We'll be taking off at 4:20 in the afternoon. 420. The irony locks and loads and clicks itself into my head. I laugh, and when I do I feel as if my entire body is shaking uncontrollably, even though it is only bouncing up and down ever so slightly from the rumbling giddiness that is being released from me. I'm not exactly sure when Ellie said she was going to be back, and I can't remember what time we are supposed to be leaving to head to the airport, but I do know that I can't stay in this apartment until she returns. If I do, I'll be catatonic before the time comes for us to go, and well, that just won't work out for anyone.

I'm fifty-six years old and I have no control over my body. I smoked a decent bit in college and randomly at parties and get-togethers during my twenties, but Ellie never liked it so it was a very rare occurrence. How is it now, this late in my life that I am the highest I have ever been? At the same time, I feel so low, yet all the while, I don't really understand time at all right now. It is an essence of antiquity that has passed me by while reversing me back and bringing me forward too. Nothing makes sense. I go to my dresser and put on some clothes over top of my underwear. I pull on a pair of jeans and a white t-shirt. I look in the mirror and as I stare into the eyes of the old man before me, I wish that I was young again. I wish that this feeling I'm undergoing wasn't happening now, and if it had to happen at all I wish it would have happened back then, when I still had golden blonde hair and no rings or lines around my eyes. I long to be him again, the version of myself that still believed that everything would work itself out in the end. I remember him, the boy who never stopped trying. Now, as I near towards my sixth decade of life, I'm tired, oh so tired.

I push on my face as I look at it further in the mirror and I try to stretch out the lines that are there to make them disappear. They do for a moment, but then they come back just as quickly as I let go of myself. My green eyes still look the same though; the seeing beings themselves have never changed. Life goes on.

I hear a crash and I jump back into and out of my skin as I stretch my arms high above me and hit the top of the wall, literally leaping off of the ground and smacking the ceiling with my hands. When I come back down I feel tightened, so I twist and swivel my upper torso on my hips and my vertebrae crack at the tension that was created. I need to get out of this room. I look into the mirror once more, and then close my eyes, but when I do the darkness that I see and what I no longer do makes me feel ever weirder. I open my eyes again and say goodbye to the man who looks sad to see me go. I say goodbye to myself. I leave my apartment, and I wander out into the day. When I step outside, it is as if I am on another planet. This can't be right. The air hits me and it's like I'm taken over even further by whatever it is that has control of me. My senses are both prolonged and shortened. I don't know where I am going, but all I know is that I have to get away.

So I go.

Everything I have been feeling previously is amplified. The insanely uncontrollable urges and undergoings that were flowing over me when I was inside are exacerbated further now. I wonder where I am going, but I realize that I don't know, nor do I really care. If I am heading anywhere, I suppose it is to my office at Haversmith. Even though that is the last place I want to be, something is pulling me there. It's a Saturday and I know no one else will be in today, so thus the idea of entering into the space kind of thrills me. When I enter back inside again I wonder if I will feel similar to how I felt earlier when I first awoke. As I walk on, I realize that the outdoors are a whole 'nother world entirely.

I have plenty of time to myself before London and the plans that Ellie has made for us can consider me to be a renegade. I'll make it back to the apartment to fetch my suitcase and get in a taxi with her when we need to head to the airport. The day is mine in the meantime.

As I walk away from where I left, the sidewalk beneath me is moving, in the sense that I feel as if I am getting nowhere, and that the direction I am going is pushing back against me. I look down at the concrete that is organized into rectangles and even though I am passing the lines, which breaks the rock apart, it keeps on going. It's almost as if the sidewalk itself has turned into some kind of outdoor version of a treadmill. I turn around and see my apartment building behind me. I continue walking. I turn around again. The building doesn't seem to be getting any further away from me, yet I know I am moving all of the same. I exit my body and look upon myself as a bystander and I try to figure out if I am actually walking or simply just lifting my feet up and down and placing them back on the ground, staying in the same place. I am moving, but I am getting nowhere. People pass me and everyone I see I feel I know, but I don't.

A group of young Asian girls go by me in a fit of giggles. They have bright colored highlights in their hair; the pinks and purples contained up against the black pop off of them and catch my attention. I feel as if I am staring at them. I should stop. I want to call out to them and tell them to stop laughing. I almost do, but I lift my hand up to my mouth and press my fingers both on the top and bottom of my lips to close where the words could have escaped from, so that I don't say anything at all. My thoughts and my words are mixed. I can no longer tell if I am saying things out loud or if I am simply thinking them. Everything is blurring together. I resist the temptation to look at my watch, but I fail. When I do look at my wrist though I realize I don't even have one on. All for the better, the record of time and how it would revolutionize my mind doesn't matter much today anyways. Nothing makes sense.

"What the hell are you doing?"

I turn around when his voice booms from behind me. What I see is a bedraggled man who has wrapped himself in a thick woolen blanket. It is the middle of August, why he is covered in such a way is beyond me. His hair is matted down to his face; it looks as if it is covered in dirt and moldy glue. In fact, he is completely covered in filth and grime. When he opens his mouth again I see that his teeth are stained a pungent shade of yellow, as if I can smell the repulsive sight.

"I said, what in the hell are you doing?" He repeats, as I have not answered him.

"What does it matter to you asshole?" The sound of my voice frightens me.

"You look like you've lost your goddamn mind," he says, going on. "This is my spot. Get out of here."

I look down and realize that I am standing on top of a cardboard box that is laid out and flattened on the sidewalk at the corner of the street where we stand. I am standing on his home. "I look like I've lost my mind? Well maybe I have. But still, you've got to be shitting me."

"Well, I'm not."

"You have no reason to talk to me this way Rumpelstiltskin."

"That's not my name."

"It might as well be," I say to him. "You don't need to be so rude. You should get yourself cleaned up and make something of your life. Standing out here and bothering normal people like me isn't going to do you any good."

"You don't seem normal. You seem like a piece of shit."

I clench my fist and hold it at my side even though I can feel it wanting to raise itself up. "What is wrong with you? Maybe I'm a little weird...today, but you don't need to talk to me in such a way. I was minding my own business before you came up to me."

"No...you weren't. You're standing on my house."

I look down again and realize that I haven't moved from the cardboard that rests beneath my shoes, underneath my feet. "Maybe I don't want to move." He lunges towards me, his arms outstretched like a grotesque creature from the deep. The fist at my side rises up and impacts him in the face. I can feel his teeth crunching inside of his mouth and then falling out before they even do. "You dirty old bastard," I whisper to myself as he falls to the ground, shrieking deliriously. "Oh come on, I didn't even hit you that hard."

"You're crazy!" He shouts, his mouth filling with blood. "Get the hell out of here! Get off my damn house!"

The people who are passing us are staring at the situation now. Some of them have probably been watching it unfold. I flinch whenever a white car passes us, immediately thinking that it is going to be a cop and that I am about to be arrested for assaulting some deranged homeless man. Maybe I'm the disturbed one though, but still, wasn't it he who started it all? I don't want to be near this fairy tale monster any longer. I don't want to feel like this anymore, but I don't know how to make myself any better. I wonder what time it is, but I don't know.

So I go.

When I get to the office it is as empty as I thought it would be. Not a single person is on the floor where I work. It's a Saturday after all; I didn't expect anyone to be in. I sit down at my desk and rub the palm of my left hand over the knuckles of my right. They are bruised and cracked a bit, as the impact of the man's face which I hit singes through the edges of my senses now. I'm glad I left the spot where I came across him. Hopefully that was the worst part of my day.

Notes for a campaign are littered across my desk and I know I could work on them but I don't really feel like it. I needed to come here to get inside, to linger away from the outdoors where so many people could have interrupted me from going. I figured that the higher the chance of interacting with others, the bigger the risk of something going wrong. Haversmith Inc, where no one is except for me appears to be a better place to be.

If I could, I would light all of the candles that any amount of wax could weigh upon, but as I realize that the rationality of that doesn't compute, as it is the middle of the day and a quantitative amount of sunlight is already streaming through the windows now. I wish for some sort of darkness to appear so that I myself can control how much light dances from side to side, enlightening my mind. The seconds pass and then the minutes too, turning into hours that I don't know. I fade away. Before I'm gone completely though my office telephone rings. Who? The number that rings is one that I know. Ellie.

The droning sound of the recollection of the collection of the noise that I identify is one that I should respond to, but I feel it is too slow. It circles on, I let her go, unanswered. She calls again, a few minutes later. I reach out to respond to her request but my body doesn't want me to. I don't know why and I can't explain the lack of action from a physical sort of the entity that is my figure, but I let her go again, even though I know this time that I should not be doing so.

I wonder what time it is, so I look at the digital clock that resides on my desk. I see the numbers, but they no longer mean anything to me. I am past the point of recognition. The telephone rings again, and when I glance at the number I see that it is Ellie once more. She is not giving up. Somehow she knows I must be here. Then again, there is no other number she could call to try and reach me. I pick up.

"Howdy my lady."

"What are you doing Priam?"

"I'm sitting here."

"What? Why? I came home and you weren't here. We need to be leaving soon. Are you heading back?"

"Heading back where?"

"Home!" She says, her voice becoming more agitated up against the numbness of mine.

"Oh yes. Home. I left there earlier. It took me forever to get here."

"Well hopefully it won't take as long for you to return. London awaits," she says in a calmer manner. It's almost as if she thinks talking to me in a soothing way will make this all okay.

"I'm so lost Ellie. I don't know where I am or what I am doing."

"You're in your office. God knows why, but that is where you are. As far as what you are doing, currently you are wasting time, but soon you will be on your way back to me, so that we can head to the airport, to London, and be on our way."

"Are we just running away from everything?" I ask, as I lift my feet up, which feel as if they weigh thousands of pounds as they harshly slam back down upon my desk on which they begin to rest.

"Running away?"

"From our problems."

"Priam. We have been talking about this trip for months now. I've been planning it every step of the way and you have had a great deal of input too. If you ever had doubts about it, why in the world would you wait until now to voice them?"

"Because now is the first time I feel as if I am able to make my voice heard."

"In what way?" She asks, her speech cracking, the rapidity of her words are no longer strong, they are beginning to falter.

"I guess I am just having second thoughts about us going. How is being in London going to solve anything?"

"Getting away does not mean we are forgetting about our problems. It just means that we are going to be somewhere new, somewhere that I have always wanted to be, where I thought you wanted to be with me. I thought we agreed this would be good for us. Don't you want to feel alive again?"

"Do you mean because he's dead?"

"Don't you dare say that to me," she cries, and as that last word leaves her mouth it squeaks, entering into the air, into the mouthpiece, through the telephone line faster than I can even comprehend through the cords and into the earpiece, through the small amount of air and into my ear itself, into my head.

"Well, is that why? I've been thinking about him a lot today, all the while I haven't at all. When did we get so old? If he was still here, do you think he'd be older too? I wonder. I can't imagine him a day older than eighteen."

"He's been gone for seven years Priam. Seven years."

"He's not coming back. So what's to say our love will?"

Silence. Even in my current state I know that as soon as I have said it I am wrong, so wrong. Her breathing gets heavier, the fuzziness that is communicated to me by the lack thereof is my fault. I have no control of myself, but I know that is no excuse for how I currently am. I want to lift my feet up again and put them back down on the ground, but the idea of it all is too much and I can't talk to her and move my body at the same time. I wonder why she isn't speaking anymore, temporarily blacking out the memory of what just occurred, but then I remember. It's because of what I said. All of the words and the combinations and divisions of everything in between. Charlie is gone.

"Are you going to come with me to London or not?"

"Ellie..." I start, but I do not finish. Silence.

"We're going. We're going Priam. There is no way we are not going. What has gotten into you? I know things have been hard the past few years, but I didn't think we had come to this...not this."

She's crying, I know she is crying. I can't see her tears, but I know they are there. Even with all of the bodies and souls that are contained within the distance that fills in between us, I know how she is feeling now, and I know that I have caused it. I know why, but I don't at all. I've been invaded by a complex society that started a civilization that is crumbling all the while just beginning.

I should tell her that I am not in control, but that would

just be an excuse...a reason, but not a valid one. I am still at fault for what I have done. I want to say that "I'm really, really, really high and I don't understand anything right now but I will always understand that I love you." I don't though, instead I say "I just..." starting off.

"You just what? I'm going with or without you. I can't believe it has come to this, but apparently it has. You're not here, not a single part of you is here it seems. I've always put us first, but this time, I'm doing what I want to do, what I need to do. So either way, I'll wait for you, but I won't hold myself back. I'm heading to the airport in half an hour. I will see you there, or I won't. That part is up to you."

I want to give her a yes, or a no, or an answer at all of some kind. I want to apologize, I want to cry, to scream, to be somewhere in the middle. I want to let go, I want to hold on, I want to stay where I am. She hangs up. I am unable to do any of the things that I want to.

Time fades over me and pulls me under, I feel clocks counting backwards and overhear voices whispering to me and they slap me in the face with the tentacles of the trepidations that I know I should swallow. I'm separated by the essence that the flames contain, they are flying by my side. I lose myself, I don't let go, I just go letting on and I become lost.

My eyes falter and become heavy, my legs drop down, I isolate who I am from both what and where I am, and I halfheartedly decide to allow myself to go to sleep, even though I promise that it will only be for a little while, before I figure out what is going on and why I have lived the way that I have today. I wish to sleep, to fall away and to forget about what I have done wrong for the time being. I want to ignore the color and bleach myself into a state of white.

So I go.

In my sleep I dream of listless reveries that wish to hold onto me and never let me go. It's like a storybook that is written by someone who has no concept of what it means to have a beginning, a middle, or an end. The pages push together like that of a book that could not be written, not because there was not a decent story to be told, but because the content that needed to be created erased itself before it was composed.

The difference between when I am actually dreaming and when I awake from the dream are two separate things, but they feel connected and I suppose if it is by anything it is by the story that my mind wishes to tell me, even if it is only half reminded and truncated by the reality and the fallacy that delivers the images to me.

When I'm dreaming, it's as if my mind goes like this, it's as if the images that I see are relayed back to me in words such as these: anything of inside and around twirl diamonds and life inspired by art, art inspired by life and diamonds twirl around and inside of anything. The comma itself is the point where my mind breaks, and what comes before it flows one way towards it and what comes after it flows back in reverse. The comma is the center point of the symmetry that flows outwards. The pictures and the stories that are told unto myself are deliberated and delivered but they aren't decided upon. They are given to me and I get to do with them as I wish.

The typewriter pounds and the clicks, slams and dashing noises that it makes creates a song that the dancers drum to with their feet. The stage before me is lit with a purple light which quickly turns to orange as women appear naked as they walk out backwards and turn around to make me realize that their breasts are covered by black squares that are taped upon them, as if they are bras held up by invisible straps. Their nude colored skirts sway and make it appear as if their legs don't exist, except for when they move them in a way so that I realize they are there again.

A chain fence is pushed out from either side of the stage and it meshes together in the middle so that the dancers are trapped behind it. I examine each one of the links and realize that every single one of the diamond shapes of emptiness are connected to one another as the metal itself is all wrapped around intertwining and producing a dance of it's own. The women are screaming, in fact they are screeching as if they are black canaries with broken wings. Their calls hurt me and I become aware of myself again, yet I am unable to escape. They sprout out wings and they flit away, dancing on thin air as they rise up towards the ceiling and then dissipate completely.

The lights fade out, the purple and the orange are gone and from the crash emitted I conclude that the fence has disappeared too. The light comes back suddenly, flashing and then returning as a spotlight is shined right upon her. She is lying on the floor of the stage, as if she is dead.

The typewriter tune plays once again, and this time there is a harmony that lies underneath it that brings up the melody to one of a more rhythmic, if a more distressing tone.

She awakens, and as she does I realize that she is young again. The same age as the first day that I ever saw her, dancing in the park. I watch as Ellie dances to all of the dances that I ever missed, it goes on forever, as there were quite a few charades that I didn't show up for. I watch them all, as I am the only patron in the theater, where it is just the two of us. She looks out towards me every once in a while, but I don't know if she ever sees me. All I want is for her to know that I am here.

I get up from my seat and approach the stage as she dances on. The music and the sounds of the typewriter get louder as the melody underneath begins to fade away as I get closer. I am near to her so I try to reach out and touch her when a crashing sound interrupts me. The chain link fence falls back down from wherever it left to and it separates us. It protrudes into the ground and starts to spread, the metal links multiply and overtake us both. I look back to Ellie, and it is only then as the fence links get thicker and start to swallow us that I know that she has seen me. The metal melts and then begins to drown us. I reach out and desperately seek to grab her hand. Our fingertips are a centimeter away from touching before the final moment when we are both smothered by the weight and the heat of the hot magma metal kills us both. In the dream, we never get to touch, we never are reunited back together. She dies, as I die.

So I go.

I wake up, and for the first time today, I feel like myself again. Except as I become aware of the darkness around me, there is no light filtering into my open eyes. I realize it is no longer daytime. It is night.

My body trembles as the repercussions impact me and I slide out of my chair and down to the ground, as if I have liquefied and there is nothing I can do to move again. I am too late.

If it's dark outside, that means I must have fallen into some sort of sleeplike coma that kept me under, and prevented me from going anywhere at all, let alone to the airport, into a plane, up into the sky, or across the sea. I wonder if she stayed back, I wonder if she waited for me.

I get up off of the ground and sit back in my chair. The clock on my desk reads that it is 11:53PM. For the first time all day, time makes sense to me, but it is not the kind of sense that I wish to understand. Everything is wrong. I screwed up big time. I missed the flight to London, and even if Ellie did end up waiting for me, if she ended up not going, she's never going to forget this. Maybe she will forgive me, but this will always stay with her. I've let her down again.

The marijuana might have influenced me, but somehow I don't think I can use that as an excuse for my behavior, at least not entirely. Sure, it influenced me more than anything else did today, but I can't let a substance take the fall for my actions, not when the entity of my own being should be held responsible. I debate now whether or not I should tell her that the brownies she brought home had magical powers, life altering controls that manipulated how I acted today. A point clicks off of a board in my head and I decide immediately that I can't tell her, no matter what happens. I can't blame my mistakes on something else, especially when I have already made so many more mistakes before this one. No, I have to take the blame entirely. For even though outside powers were swaying me, it was still I who said those words to her on the telephone, it was still I who suggested that we were simply trying to run away from the hardships that are facing us. I was the man who made her cry.

The telephone rings and I know before I even hear her voice that it is she, even though I don't recognize the number at all. There are more digits listed on the caller id than what is normal. She's no longer in New York; she's no longer with me...she can't be.

"Hello?" I say, asking it as a question, beckoning for whomever is calling to give me some kind of news that will pull me out of this hole that I have fallen into.

"Priam, it's me. I...I..." her voice is echoing on top of itself. She can barely speak.

"Ellie, where are you? I'm sorry. I'm sorry."

"Don't apologize."

"I have to apologize, this is all my fault," I feel a burning sensation grow inside of me.

"No...don't. I'm in London. My plane just landed at Heathrow."

"You're...you mean, you're there?"

"I'm here."

"Ellie..."

"Priam..."

"I fell asleep, I'm sorry. I'll be on the next flight over, I promise."

"No. No...don't." She says to me from across the deep, in another instance where I am not with her. She calls from another place, another hour, another time. And even though I am able to comprehend the actuality of time itself again, I cannot understand how we are in different ones now. This is entirely my fault.

"What do you mean? I messed up. You don't deserve this, I know how much you wanted this trip Ellie and I should have been there at the airport with you. And I wasn't and I'm sorry, but I'll go to the airport right now and I'll get to London as soon as I can. We still have time."

"I think time has run out Priam."

"You- What?" I ask.

"I'm already here, without you. Priam...I never thought I would say this," she goes on, suddenly I can hear that she is gasping for breaths that won't come to her. She is barely holding on, teetering upon the edge, about to let go.

"Say what Ellie? Say what?" I ask, interrupting her.

She takes a deep breath, and some air goes in, but it doesn't seem like much. Regardless, it would be impossible to mistakenly hear the words she says next.

"Priam. I want a divorce."

Saturday, August 23rd 1997
*Day Six – **The Second Chance***

Even though it is what I remember as being the instance that affected me most recently, when I awake, the last word I heard, that word itself: divorce, quickly passes through my mind and then leaves me completely. This is the sixth day I have come across after all, I am nearing the end and I am used to how I feel when I wake up on these days in which I am in control. Although the relived day itself, the original way that this day went so wrong is burning through me now, I am not concerned about how Ellie asked for a divorce on this exact day in 1997. When I awake today, on this second way, the horror that has accompanied me and riddled me into some sort of requiem is the recollection I have from that fifth day, the one I had my way. Ellie is dead.

The car crash, the intersection of where everything upended itself and unheeded the wishes of how I wanted things to be. It faded to black as I passed out from the pain of it all, as the glass in my leg barreled deeper into my blood stream, my crimson color mixed with hers as her body continued to get cold. I knew then on that fifth day that she was gone. She had died in my arms. Somehow, as a result of the choices I had made on this journey of second chances, I killed the woman I loved, the woman I love. Is she really dead? I open and close my eyes again. I lie in an empty bed.

The room I am in is not the one I grew up in on Elm Street, and it is not the bedroom from the house that Ellie and I had raised both Charlie and Alma in on that fifth day either. It's not any of the apartments in New York that I had resided in during any lines of this experience that I both previously and currently am living. It's not a living place at all actually. As I sit up, I realize I am in a hotel room. Where, I'm not sure, but by the curtain to my right, which is open a bit, I am able to tell even from the small glimpse that is given to me, that I am in New York City. Why I am waking up in a hotel room in the city where I have lived for most of my life I do not know.

I am in a full sized bed, and as I examine the room further I see that there is an identical one beside the spot where I lie. No one is in it, but it appears as if someone was previously. The covers are rumpled up, the sheets are stretched out and the bed is unmade.

Someone was here, in this room with me, but I don't see anyone now. Who could it be? I wish to ask a million different questions, but there is no one to ask them of.

I get up quickly, and just as I go to put my right foot down onto the ground I am unheeded by gravity as I topple over and down to the floor. My left leg never gets a chance to touch down. Then again though, as I look at my lower body now, I realize my right leg hasn't touched the ground either, for I no longer have one.

My right leg is gone; instead where it used to be there is nothing but air. It appears as if my right leg has been amputated from the midsection of my thigh and down. I feel a phantom pain. I cry out. A part of me is gone. There is no getting it back. I cry out again. In standing up, I had acted as if nothing was out of the ordinary with my body or how things are connected. My mind was not aware of the fact that the part of it that I wished to put down to the floor is no longer able to do so, because it isn't there. As the recollections rebound, I recall that large shard of glass that entered into my thigh. I remember the blood pouring out of my right leg on that day she died. I lost more than Ellie, I lost a part of myself too, in more ways than one. I emit out songs of longing. I am sitting on the floor of a hotel room in which I know naught and no one is here to help me. I have no idea what is going on, or why things have happened in the way they have. I want to give up.

I call out again. I don't say words; I just let out sounds of unrest. No one heeds my calls. I stop calling. I start screaming. "Ellie!" It's the only word I can say, the only name my lips will know. I hear a door click open, not in a place I can see, but the sound comes nevertheless

"What on Earth?" Says the girl as she comes around the corner to find me where I am, all three-fourths of who I used to be.

The noise that I was producing is gone completely. As if the wind wasn't knocked out from me enough from the mistaken fall that I miscommunicated with my body previously, then all of the air has been ripped out of the room now. Standing before me is Ellie. She is wearing a white leotard; her chestnut colored hair is pulled up neatly into a ponytail. In her hands she carries a pair of pink ballet slippers. Her feet are bare. She's alive after all, and she looks exactly as she did the first time I ever saw her. She is only seventeen.

"Ellie? I- I- I don't understand. I thought you died. How-

How are you here?"

She looks at me; she tilts her head to the side and then lowers herself down to me so that she sits on the floor next to where I am. She releases her hair from the ponytail and it falls down to her shoulders. It is very wavy, as if it has been crinkled up. Although the color is the same as it always has been, it's not the kind of texture I remember it being. She wraps her arms around my waist and helps me back up onto the bed. As I push my hands off of the floor beneath me she guides me back to the place I awoke, I look at her face and realize that something is different. It is Ellie, then again, it's not.

"Dad, it's me. I'm starting to worry about you. I was only gone for a couple of minutes. When I left you were sound asleep, it looked as if you were dreaming."

"I was having a nightmare. I thought-"

She interrupts me. "So it seems. Maybe you should start to sleep with your prosthetic on, then you won't be tumbling out of bed anymore."

"Oh, don't be silly Alma."

I know now that the girl who sits on the bed beside me is not Ellie, but instead it is her daughter, my daughter...Alma Wood. She looks so much like her mother that I am not surprised that I was initially confused by the sight of her, especially because of what she is currently wearing and the age that she is now.

Dancing is completely correlated with Ellie in my mind and the remembrance of her as a seventeen year old girl is the first one that I had ever come across. In my shocked state in which I was reveling from the realization that I had lost my own leg, I momentarily abandoned myself and bounded back again by thinking that Ellie had lived. I know it is possible that in these second chances people can come back from the dead, but not like that. I had saved my mother, and in some way, my daughter and my son, but they were saved from ways where they were gone from those first days. I couldn't save Ellie and I don't think I can save her now, not when she has been lost during this journey of second chances. She really is gone, and I'm afraid it seems as if there is nothing I can do. The shade of blue that overcomes me now is the saddest of hues. Colors might as well not even exist anymore.

Alma gets up off of the bed and goes around the corner from which she had originally come. She returns with a large piece of plastic and metal in her hands. It is in the shape of a leg, and a foot...my leg, my foot. She helps me attach it to my body, the foreign appendage meshing into me where that part of my skin ends. I feel it connect into me, and as she helps me slowly stand up, I realize this piece of equipment will allow me to walk. Just as Ellie had to relearn how to walk after that third day when the ladder crashed down, it appears as if I have had to teach myself how to move from one place to another in a similar way.

"Easy does it," Alma says. Apparently I am walking around the room much faster than I usually do, but I can't help it. I am pacing before I even realize it. I will not let myself become a disabled individual. The only part of me that I will acknowledge as handicapped is that of my heart. For she is gone and there are no second chances of fixing it this time.

I want to ask Alma the questions that I have already thought up, but I know that I have to treat them delicately, just as I have done before with my mother, and with her mother. I have to talk to her in a similar way in the here and now. I can't come across as if I don't know the answers to what I wish to understand. For I should know all that has occurred in the interim, the only thing is...I don't. So I just start saying things, nothing that seems too strange, but I let out sentences that I know will get a certain kind of reply.

"Let's go home. I need to go home. I can't be here."

"Home? Dad...you know that we aren't going home for a few more days. Believe me, if Alden was only a few miles away I would take you there now, but it's not that easy."

So Alden is still home for Alma and I. I don't need to ask any more questions because as I ponder over it now I can conclude as to why we hadn't left the small town when Ellie died. Alma was only ten then, she wouldn't have wanted to leave the place where her mother was laid to rest. She would have wanted to stay near her, even if Ellie wasn't actually alive in that northwest corner of Pennsylvania anymore, the young Alma would have thought that she was. Charlie finished his final year of school and I imagine he moved to the city as I always pictured he would. Alma went on to conquer the art of ballet in a way that her mother would have been proud. We stayed in the house that Ellie and I had built together in Alden and we visited New York City often to see Charlie. Alma has attended various summer dance programs and has participated in a few shows as well. Alma has one year left at Alden High. I will move back to New York City then. I find this all out by the words my daughter tells me and from my own deductions too. Most of the facts she doesn't have to say, I am able to fill in the lines of what has occurred and what hasn't, even though I shouldn't be able to.

Hence the hotel room, we are in the city for the weekend. Alma had a ballet performance last night and the second showing is this evening. Charlie plans to join us for lunch in a few hours and then he will sit beside me as we watch her dance, just as I had once watched Ellie.

"Sometimes I still can't believe she's really gone," I say, professing it out as if it is a thing that I have undergone for ages. In reality it feels like only two days ago that she slipped away from me in a pool of crimson red on that molten concrete that pushed us up and tore us down, ripping us apart frantic and finally.

"I only knew her for ten years of my life, but I feel the same." Alma tells me. "I can't imagine what it must feel like for you Dad. If anything, in my loss, I try to remind myself of yours. She was my mother, but she was everything to you."

"Losing her in that way, in that finality, was the worst thing I ever underwent," I say, speaking both of this time now and the ways in my life that I lost her in multitudes.

"It's my fault, if I wouldn't have dropped that damn bag of cereal, if she wouldn't have taken off her seatbelt to help me, she would probably still be here with us."

"Don't talk like that. Her death wasn't your fault. If it was anyone's, it was mine."

"How could it have been yours?"

"I've done many things I'm not proud of Alma. Some of which are instances I am sure you have never heard of and never will. Maybe your mother's death was a way to chastise me for all that I have done wrong."

"But...don't you think her death was more of a punishment to her than to anyone else?"

"I'm not sure. I imagine Ellie is in a better place now," I tell my daughter, saying the name of the woman who helped me create her. "I don't think the pain of losing her I felt then, or that of what I feel now could be any worse on her end. She's gone and that longing that we yearn for her to return will always stay with us. We are unaware of where she is, but somehow, I believe she knows where we are."

"Do you really think that's how it works Dad?" She asks, as she sits back down on her untidy bed, setting her ballerina slippers down next to her as I continue to pace.

"One may never know." I approach the curtains and rip them open, letting the light of New York City infiltrate our layer and surround us entirely.

"At least we're all okay. I mean, it could have been worse. I don't mean to lessen Mom's death, but I guess I try to look more on the bright side of things as she taught me. Yes, you lost your leg, but you're okay, and so are Charlie and I. We're still breathing."

I feel the phantom pain return as if the glass that dug into me then is still digging into me now. I feel blood running out and dripping down from the limb that I no longer have. I feel an abnormality in the atmosphere. Charlie and Alma may be alive, but the thought crosses my mind: will they too die soon? I recall thinking about the idea that there was a certain balance in play that would decide how things would go and who would stay here with me and who would not. If Ellie is dead in this reality of second chances, when she lived many years beyond this day in my life, how can my two children, who both died long before the years they hold now be here with me for much longer?

Everything edges out onto the epiphany and upon the energy that I hold. There's no day that is guaranteed to greet me except for the one that I am currently navigating through. It's now, at this moment that I realize there is only one thing that Alma, Charlie and I can do. There is only one place on this Earth that we can go, today, for her.

"Alma, call your brother. I'm afraid we aren't going to be able to attend your show tonight."

"What do you mean?"

"We have somewhere we need to be, for your mother. She would have wanted it this way I think. There is a debt that I have to repay to her."

"In what way? What am I supposed to tell Charlie?" She looks as befuddled as she possibly can. Her confusion contorts in a different way than Ellie's would have, their faces contain similar instances, but they have variances that are all their own. I accept that Alma is her own person, no matter how much she looks like her mother.

"Tell him, that we are going to JFK and catching the next plane to London."

Her eyes light up, and even in the bewilderment of it all, and in the pieces of this plan that I know she can't understand, I see a part of Ellie then and I know that what I have decided is right. It has to be. Ellie may not be here, but I will still try my best to make up this day to her as I had originally planned on doing so. She may not be able to join me, but I will go to London today and I will take our children with me. I think it's what she would have wanted, every instance of her.

Alma calls Charlie and tells him to get to JFK as soon as he can. She doesn't give him any other specific orders, except for the fact that we are going to London so he needs to bring his passport. She tells him we will be meeting him there as soon as possible. There is urgency in her voice, and so, he is convinced.

I change into a pair of navy slacks and a gray buttoned up shirt. When I see my reflection in the mirror, I am reacquainted with my older appearance, as I am once again fifty-six years old. It feels different though, because I can see Alma changing out of her leotard behind me. Her youth counteracts the elderly sensation that I feel. When I was older like this in my life, I never had such a direct access to a youthful reminder. During our later years, Ellie and I had no children to harken back on us of how we once were, and how we were not then, as I am now.

There are many questions that I know Alma wishes to ask me, the foremost one being why I have decided to abandon the idea of this day in New York City and requested her and Charlie's company on a flight to London. She is aware that we are doing this for her mother and although I have only given her very few details, it appears that even in this way of living Ellie had always wanted to go over the pond to the capitol city of the United Kingdom. By the way that Alma looked at me when I told her we were going to London today in a similar way to that of how her mother had looked at me many times before, I could tell that she knew we were going to London to celebrate the life Ellie lived.

We didn't have much tact in planning or placing this adventure in time, but I could tell that Alma appreciated the spontaneity of the trip coming about all of a sudden, surprising us with its plans in a similar way that Ellie would have done. After our small weekend suitcases are packed, Alma calls her instructor and tells her that she won't be able to make it to the show tonight due to an unforeseen family emergency. She hangs up the phone and then we are on our way.

Walking out of the room and down the hall is a strange sensation as I continually place my unreal foot that is not actually mine onto the maroon colored carpet over and over again. It is still a part of me. We put ourselves into the elevator when it dings and the doors open before us. We take it down to the ground. A smarmy looking bellboy helps us get a cab. I can tell from the way that he looks at Alma that he is in love with the sight of her. He will never have her though. The taxi ride doesn't take long. Alma and I are mostly silent as we listen to the music on the radio that is mixed up with the story the driver tells us about his time in the Congo. We arrive at JFK a little before 10AM and I am warmed by the sight of Charlie who is waiting for us in the main terminal next to where British Airways is located. The strange sensation of seeing someone who is older than I ever remember them being is brought back to me, as the Charlie who hugs me now is a twenty four year old man. His shoulders are broader and the look in his eyes is a more confident one than I ever remember seeing. He has grown up into the person I always thought he would be. He looks like me too, I see a part of myself in him, but it is nowhere near the kind of reflection of Ellie that resides within Alma. My children look very similar to each other, yet they emit out energies all their own.

"Was this your crazy idea Alma?" Charlie asks. "What on earth are we going to London for?"

"Your mother always wanted to go and I never let her. I promised I would go with her and I never did. I've thought about going for centuries, and when I woke up this morning and tumbled out of bed, forgetting about the way I am, I realized there is no day but today. If I don't go to London now, I fear I never will." I tell them both matter of factly and how true my statements are. If I don't go now, the sites of red double decker buses and the River Thames will never greet me, except in some mixed up, made up memory. I desire London to be real for me, in the way it was for Ellie, in the way she was for me. I'm not sure if they really understand what I am saying, or what I mean. How could they? Regardless, they act as if they do and they accept the answer I have given them. They know that I believe wholeheartedly that we have to go to London today, for their mother, for Ellie. And thus, when I look into my children's eyes as we remain in this airport, where I am only able to stand on one real leg, I know that they trust me.

I approach the desk and tell the blonde woman at the counter that I need three tickets for the next flight to London. She looks at me in a peculiar manner, as I suppose she doesn't very often get requests for flights on the day of, especially to a place so far away. She doesn't ask me why I need to get there so quickly though. She doesn't know that today is the only day I can go, before I wake up on my seventh day, which will be four years from now. Today is the only day I can go to London, the only day.

"It appears as if we have a flight leaving at noon today sir, would you like me to book three tickets on that one? The next flight to London Heathrow isn't until seven o'clock this evening."

"Yes!" I shout. I can't believe my luck that there is actually a flight to London that leaves from JFK in the middle of this day, one that leaves in less than two hours no less. Soon enough we have our boarding passes and are making our way through the silver and gray colored security checkpoint, where officers with harshly strewn faces look us up and down and deem us suitable to pass on. When we get to the gate, we find seats to sit upon. Alma leaves to get a quick bite to eat, as we still have some time before we depart. So thus, I am alone with my son Charlie.

"How was Alma's show last night?" He asks. "Although I'm excited we are doing this, I have to be honest, I am a little bit bummed that I am not going to be able to see her dance in it."

"Oh it was extraordinary," I tell him, even though I have no recollection of seeing my daughter dance in the show he asks of whatsoever. I explain to him details that I half make up and half base on all of the numerous times that I saw Ellie dance. For in some ways, Alma and Ellie are one and the same. If I had to guess, I'm sure my daughter dances just as magnificently as her mother had. Alma received lessons from the best teacher of ballet after all: my wife.

"It sounds amazing, I wish I could have seen it."

"I am sure you will see your sister dance soon in another ballet. She will have many more days." I tell him, even though as I say it I am reminded of the fact that I am not sure how much longer either of them will live, not when they are already both so far past the days where their lives had originally expired. The balance of this is the most unstable equation that I will never be able to compute in any shape or situational form.

"I guess you're right."

"Anyways, how are you Charlie?" I ask, offering up a generic question in order to find out what I wish to know.

In talking to Charlie I find out that he is getting his Masters in English at NYU. He wants to be a college professor and teach poetry. He writes a great deal these days and has even had his work featured in a number of magazines and literary journals. A flashing image of him with another man smiling together bounces off of my occipitals there in the dark of my head and it is as if I recognize the young gentleman he is with, but I am not able to comprehend it long enough to know if I actually do.

"Things are wonderful Dad. Soon it's on to the PhD. And you know me, I'm always writing. There is an endless amount of things to be inspired by here in the city. I can't wait until you move back so that we can spend more time together."

"I look forward to that as well," I say to him, even though I don't know if it will actually ever come.

"Do you really think Alma is going to go to school in Pittsburgh instead of New York? I can't imagine her wanting to go to Point Park when she could easily go to a top-notch university here in the city. Why would she want to stay back there?"

This is all news to me, but I play it off as if I already know why, and really, I am able to infer the reasons of my daughter's ideas to choose her own liberty. "Maybe Alma just wants to stay closer to Alden. You know how she didn't want to leave after your mother died. I mean, that's why we still live there now. I do miss the city, but I wanted to do what was right for her, and I think she has done well at Alden High, just as you did."

"I guess. I suppose I'm being selfish by wanting you both here in New York with me. I want all three of us to be together as much as we can."

"Well we will be, today, and for the entire time we spend in London, and many more days after that I hope. Besides, wherever your sister decides to go, whether it be at Point Park or NYU or even Columbia, the most important thing is that she is happy. She will continue dancing on, either way."

I state that last sentence and then Alma returns from where she went as she sits down on the leather seats Charlie and I are at.

She begins to eat the ham and turkey sandwich that she purchased for lunch. "How soon until we board?" She asks, in between bites of her meal. "I can't wait 'til we get there."

"Only about ten minutes or so I would guess," Charlie says.

So we sit a while longer and as we do I watch all of the people rushing past, racing to get to their flights that they are late for. I can't help but to think of a similar situation on this exact day, when Ellie was in my position and I wasn't here. I think of this day when she stood at this very airport, perhaps even at this very gate and waited for me to show up so that we could fly to London together. I remember how I ignored her call when she tried to reach me, only to spit out words of uncontrolled bitterness when I answered her advances on her third try with my own insecurities.

I never made it to the airport on this day in my life. I was too high to function, messed up out of my mind and even though I hadn't purposely planned on missing the flight, I did so anyways. Ellie had gone to London without me and after the flight in which she flew across the ocean, she decided once she arrived in the land she had always longed to be in, that she could no longer be with me. It was in London that Ellie decided she didn't want to be married to me any longer. It was in London that Ellie finally gave up on me once and for all. So it is here and now that I sit beside our two children who are still alive even though a part of me feels as if it is all unbalanced and that they really shouldn't be, but I go on. They are here and she is not.

They died before her in my life, Alma first and then Charlie. Ellie should still be alive today. Why isn't she here? That fifth day went so awry; it went more wrong than I ever thought any of these days ever could. My second chances were meant to make things better, not worse in ways, but somehow, in parts, they had. Ellie is not here. It will be in London where I will somehow make things up to her, even though she no longer is with me, not at all.

Once we have taken off, when we are high above the sea somewhere over the middle of the Atlantic Ocean, a notion of the motion overcomes me.

Our flight took off a few minutes past noon in New York City. The duration of the flight is a little over seven hours, so we should get to London a little after seven o'clock in the evening. The only thing is, London doesn't follow Eastern Standard Time. The

Prime Meridian runs through it and the clock lies five hours ahead. It will be midnight in London before I get there, before we arrive, before this plane decides to touch down. The day will end while I am still in the air. This brilliant idea of mine, this idea I had conjured up for Ellie, will have been all for nothing. And even more so, I will have thrown away five hours I could have spent with my children back in the city. What have I done?

Alma and Charlie sleep for most of the flight. I can't bring myself to wake them even though I realize now that I won't see them again for another four years, if I ever see them again at all.

I look at my watch when we start to make the final descent down towards London after the captain announces that we will be landing in about twenty minutes. The only problem is that my watch already reads 11:55PM. I had changed it once I had realized earlier that we weren't going to make it in time. I'm used to how it feels to impact midnight at the end of these days at this point. There is no point in trying to hide from the one and the two followed by those doubled zeroes coming together. Midnight will arrive with or without my acknowledgement of it. It comes...and then it is gone.

Except this time I don't leave it. I look down at my watch in disbelief as I am actually able to recognize that it is 12:00AM without fading away into a realm of an in-between sort of nothingness. I don't understand how I am still here, or why, but yet, this is where I remain, up in the sky. Then it all clicks, as my watch ticks on.

It may be midnight in London, the place where I am going, the place where I am soon about to be with my children, but in New York City and in Alden, the places where I am from, it is only seven o'clock in the evening. The time may be different here, but as far as the rules of these second chances are concerned, this is still my day to relive the way I wish to. I still have time.

Alma and Charlie awake. I beam at both of them when they look at me. The plane lands on the ground. Brightness spreads within the cabin as the lights come on. We've just touched down in Londontown.

The first hour of what is considered to be Saturday night to me and early Sunday morning to the British is spent getting from Heathrow Airport to downtown London. We take a black colored taxi and go to The Sloane Square Hotel, which is the place I know that Ellie stayed at while she was here. We check in at the golden encrusted front desk in the main lobby and secure a room before taking our bags upstairs. None of us are tired, it only feels like eight in the evening for us after all, so we decide to explore the city in the dark, in the middle of the night.

Our hotel isn't far from Buckingham Palace, so we walk there, taking in the site of the magnificent home where the Queen resides. We walk further on towards Westminster, as the moon glows upon the greenery a drunken man plays a Beatles song out loud on his boombox at an outrageous level of noise. Charlie mentions that he is hungry so we stop at a small pub and each one of us orders fish n' chips. We gobble it down as if we haven't eaten in days. We ride a red double decker bus and crawl up the stairs so that we sit on the upper level of it. Alma and Charlie mention how high up they feel, as if they are soaring above the streets beneath us. The bus is heading towards the River Thames, so before we cross it we get off of the crimson colored machine and decide to walk some more again. I am entrenched by the sight of the water illuminated by the streetlights along the bridge, which rushes across it. The dark colors of its waters shimmer in my eyes.

"Turn around Dad!" Alma calls from behind me. "There's a better sight to see than the bloody river!" I turn around at her request and there he is: Big Ben. The clock itself is the biggest one I feel I have ever seen, hoisted upon the tower and connected to the bell that rings through it. As I stare at the hands I imagine them moving ever so slowly and as quickly as they can too. Time appears to be watching down on me. Time is all I feel I ever need. After walking around the houses of Parliament, which are all glowing in a orange kind of hue I ask a stranger to take a photograph of the three of us with Big Ben in the background. The picture is captured and the moment is solidified as a memory forever.

We decide to go on, to see even more of the city, even though I know we are living through the middle of the night and that twelve o'clock in New York City will soon approach. When it does, I will lose myself again, even though it won't actually be at the same time here as I normally would. In fact, it seems as if dawn approaches. The darkness is lessening as the three of us soldier on.

Before long we are outside of Kensington Palace, where Princess Diana lives. She isn't home though, instead she is on a yacht in the French Riviera. Soon she will be in Paris, France. I recall knowing this. Something will happen to her, but there is nothing I can do about that. No one can know, not here. As I remember the day the princess died, I recount all that we have done this night and all that I have seen, ridden, thought of, eaten, listened to, yearned for, and experienced: London. The Queen. The Beatles. Fish n' chips. Double Decker buses. The River Thames. Big Ben. Princess Diana.

Everything she had mentioned, every little thing that Ellie had wanted us to share in London together. Alma, Charlie and I have done it all, for her. If only she was here. The sunrise approaches and somehow I know that before it breaks the horizon, I will no longer be present. So thus, there is one last thing I want to do, before I'm gone. Something Ellie never mentioned, but something that I knew.

I take my children from the outskirts of Kensington Gardens and go into Hyde Park. We watch swans swimming in the pond and go on further still, until we reach the Prince Albert Memorial. It is located on the edge of the park, near the street. In the middle of the monument, sits Prince Albert himself, made up of gold, where he sits on his throne, the towered roof reaching off into the sky above him. The detailing that is on the structure is delicately ornate. At each corner of the memorial are white marble statues, that still somehow glisten in the dark. One represents Asia with an elephant and people of Asian decent. Another is a scene of Europe, with a horned cow and elegant women at it's side. The next is Africa, where a camel lies amongst African men. Finally, as we continue our circle around this magnificent monument, we come to America, where our fellow brethren are represented next to a buffalo.

We sit down on the steps. Just us three and I reflect on the day. My mind coagulates and as it does so I notice a golden orb appear in my periphery. I know that it has to be a canine creature, as I have not yet witnessed her appearance today. I'm not sure how Chloe can appear wherever she wants to, but I don't feel like giving her the satisfaction of noticing her completely. I recognize that she has appeared and then I let the notion pass.

"I wish Mom was here," Alma says.

"So do I," adds Charlie.

"She already was." I tell them, and then the day is done.

The phone conversation itself was brief. She told me she couldn't go on any longer with the way things were. She told me that she loved me, but she also told me that she didn't think she could be with me anymore, not like this, not with a life full of so many disappointments. She didn't want me to let her down any further, so she wanted to let go of me. She had called from a payphone in the airport as soon as she had landed. She hadn't been out into the city, she hadn't experienced all that it had to offer, all that she was longing for. I apologized wholeheartedly and begged her to reconsider. I was sorry, I was heartbroken, I was wrong.

Ellie didn't want to hear it though. She had heard the same kind of speech from me many times before. She needed something to change and since it seemed as if I wouldn't, she had decided that she would make the change herself, and break away from me.

"I have to go Priam, this phone call is expensive, but I wanted to call you and let you know that I've been thinking about this for a while. It's not like the fact that I am in London now on my own is the only part that made this decision for me. It didn't have to, all of the ways that we have fallen apart over the years has done that."

"Ellie I will make this up to you, I promise. Please, we can't- not like- not like this," I begged as I stared out my office window into the dark night that I could both see and could not.

"I'm sorry. I love you. I didn't want to do it like this, but I needed to get it off of my chest. I want to have a nice time in London, even if I will be experiencing it alone. I've wanted to come here for so long."

"I can be on the next plane in the morning!"

"No. No, Priam. I need to do this alone now. Don't try to reach me. I don't think I will be able to answer. I will talk to you when I return to New York. Goodbye."

"Ellie, wait-"

The click and the sound of the dial tone commenced within my ears. I was too late, as I had been so many times before. And this time, there was nothing I could do. She wasn't going to wait around anymore until I could find some way to fix it, to fix us. It seemed as if our love was broken beyond repair.

When she was gone, during the eight days that she spent in London, I often thought that she would change her mind. I believed that when Ellie returned and looked me in the eye, when she sat with me on our bed and we discussed everything, I accepted the idea that she would be convinced to let us go on.

Ellie arrived in London on a Sunday morning, the twenty fourth of August. She wouldn't return to New York City until the first of September. On her last day in London, Princess Diana died. I remember watching the news unfold on the television, and I wondered where Ellie was and what she was doing when she heard. I wondered if she was among the masses of people who lined up outside of Buckingham Palace to lay flowers down before the gates. I wondered if she accepted the death, or if she tried to deny that it had occurred.

The death of someone so ingrained within the world, in such a way that Princess Diana was, created some kind of parallel within me. If a woman of such high esteem and security like her could pass away so unexpectedly and die in the middle of her way, who was to say that the marriage that Ellie and I had deserved to live on any longer? It wasn't until the last day that Ellie was gone, that day when the Princess died, that I actually started wondering if I would be able to save anything after all.

The day that Diana died, I started to accept that maybe I had been wrong. With her death, and with the bouquet of flowers that Ellie laid down in front of the palace that I never knew about, nor did she ever tell me of, we both let the pieces of the puzzle go. Some things wouldn't fit or click together, no matter if they were made to do so.

Our love had gone wrong and with all of the reasons that had caused it to do so, it was on that last day of August in the year of 1997 when Princess Diana died, that we both realized separately, thousands of miles apart, that maybe we wouldn't be together anymore, maybe we couldn't, and maybe it was for no real reason at all. It just was...done.

I was at work when she got back to our apartment, when she moved out some of her things and wrote me a note that she left on the counter. I was at home, later as the day closed towards it's ending, when I found out. She hadn't taken all of her things, but she had taken enough of them that I noticed the presence of her being gone. The note on the counter was not long. It wasn't simple, but it wasn't complex.

Priam,

London was both an extraordinary experience and a very, very sad time for me. With all things considered, I am sure you can conclude why. I've taken some of my belongings; I'm going to be staying with Juliana for the time being until I get a place of my own. Please don't try to come over and see me.

I will call you tomorrow, so that we can discuss things and meet up and talk face to face. I'm not trying to be difficult, I just want things to be done in a civil manner. It is a shame that it had to come to this. I think we will both be happier though. And in the end, perhaps our separation may bring us back together in some way, whatever it is that may be.

Only time will tell, and as of now, time doesn't seem to want to share its secrets. Not with me, with you, or with us. Life will continue on, as it always does. And I will still hold you in the same place in my heart that you have always been, in the uppermost and protected chamber that it contains.

The beat goes on.

Ellie

I set down the piece of paper back onto the counter when I was done reading it and I did the most rational thing I could do at that time. Not surprisingly, I let the tears come. I was never a man who was able to hold anything in. They flowed down my face, falling down, as I fell apart, entirely. It was in that moment that I felt I had nothing left to live for. I did not yet know that I still had so much left to lose.

She called me the next day, and the day after that I saw her. We met in Central Park and sat on an oak colored bench that squeaked when we put our weight down upon it. The trees swayed as a colorless breeze passed their branches, holding up the sky. I remember every detail vividly, but after it happened, I let it slip away. I did not want to recall later on what it felt like to come to terms with the insufficiency of the selection she had chosen for us. It was like I had no say.

She explained her reasonings and they made sense, but I

didn't want to believe them. I wanted it to be the day when we were seventeen meeting for the first time. I wanted to watch her dance and I wanted to paint her doing so. As we sat there that day, I wished that I could do it all over again, if not for the bare necessity of it, then at least for the desire to do things the right way in the order that I wished I had originally, but I couldn't.

Her decision was adamant and she was not going to change her mind. That is what I learned that day when I saw her in the park, not one hundred feet away from the spot where I first laid eyes upon her.

When the conversation ended, and her presence left me, two specific things stuck within my mind, imprinting themselves onto my heart. The first was that she was wearing the maroon colored cardigan that I had given to her on her thirty-sixth birthday. The other being the last point she had to offer me before we said goodbye: "It's such a shame that Princess Diana died. When I first heard the news I cried and although I was sad about her passing, my tears were not occurring because of her loss, but rather, because of her death, I somehow knew that the solidification of our separation was actually going to occur." And so it did, even though I never wanted it to. The love we had once was still there, but it had changed too much, and I, I had not.

I refused to sign the divorce papers for over a year. I knew that it was over, but in not signing them, I thought that I could hold off the factual part of what was. After the day that we met in the park, I tried to see Ellie often, but she never agreed to see me. She needed space. I needed her embrace. Neither of us would win.

The struggle I strived for in trying to reunite with her was reminiscent of the first time I lost her, when she called off our engagement after I missed her performance. I went to Juliana's and sat on that same stoop waiting for her many a day. This time though, we were not young and we had no amount of youth to side with us. The bones within our bodies were stretching thin and as the days went on they felt like months. The wrinkles on my face pushed themselves in deeper, and I felt more alone than I ever had in my life. I was completely lost, all the while knowing exactly where I was. There was no way out. The future appeared bleak. Without Ellie, I didn't know how to live.

I went on living, even though it was hard to do so. I started to accept the fact that I wouldn't be seeing her anymore, but I never gave up on the idea of reuniting with her in some way. I woke up, I went to work, I ate, I dreamt of her.

A year or so after the talk we had in the park, the only time I had seen her since she returned from London, I saw her once again. It wasn't planned and perhaps it wasn't even meant to happen, but it did. I was on the subway going to work and as I sat there reading the printed black and white words written on the newspaper in my hands, I spotted a splotch of color come into my view. A woman with chestnut colored hair containing certain streaks of gray had just boarded the car that I was in, her golden hued jacket soothed my sight. I looked from the color and then to her as she turned around so that her face faced me.

Ellie.

We recognized each other immediately, and we both simultaneously gasped in a certain kind of way. She backed up from me and tried to walk down to the other side of the car, away from me. I stood up, "Ellie! Wait!"

We were both contained within the same container. There was nowhere that she could go and that played to my advantage. For it just so happened that the reason Ellie had only allowed for me to see her once, and only once, was because she knew she couldn't see me. She knew she loved me and that the only way she could go on living without me, was to not live with me as a part of her life, not at all, not even in the slightest. She didn't wish to cause me pain, but as our lives were heading towards where they would close, she had started to realize that she needed to not solely live for me. She needed to live for herself. She sat down in the corner of the car, and I stood before her. She looked down at the floor, not daring to make eye contact with me again, in fear of what would come of the connection. "Ellie," I said her name again. "It's me."

And then the character piece within her clicked, and she knew that she had to accept me, at least then. "Hello Priam," she had said.

"Can we talk?"

"Talk we can," she replied, reversing my words exactly.

I reached my hand out to her and she took it, my strength pulling her up from her seat as the train stopped and I got off the car, with her following behind me. We emerged from underground and I asked her where would be a good place for us to sit.

"I don't want to sit down Priam. Can't we just walk?"

"Sure. We can do that."

So we went on. I told her all of the reasons why I still hadn't signed the papers. I tried to make my case again, in the ways that I always had. I don't know if I thought there was still a chance of reconciliation in some way, but that is how I played it. She did not. As I heard birds tweeting on the lamppost above us we came to an intersection and stopped. She said what she needed to say to let me know how it was going to go.

"The pain of it all is too great. I love you, and you know I always will, but we can't be together any longer. You may want us to be, but I can't do it. I have to love you from afar. I know it hurts, but this way will hurt so much less than if we had tried to continue on in the way we were going. Our love is still there, but it doesn't work anymore Priam. I don't know, maybe I'm weak in wanting to let you go, but that is how it is."

"But doesn't this hurt you just as much?" I asked.

"It hurts in a different way. I miss you, but I don't long for you to satisfy me in the way that I used to. I don't have any expectations of you and so you are never able to disappoint me. That may be cruel of me to say, but it just so happens that without you in my life, I am able to remember all of the good times we had together and forget the bad."

"We could make so many more good memories together though Ellie, if only you would give me another chance."

"You had enough chances Priam and you didn't use them in the way you should have. The amount of chances given has to end somewhere. Everything ends Priam, even tales of love like this one."

"I don't know what to say."

"Perhaps it's best that you don't say anything. I have to go. I don't know if running into you and discussing things like this helped at all, but maybe it was meant to happen. I apologize for avoiding you for so long. Just try to remember that you are not the only one who is hurting in this. Even though it was me who requested things to be the way they are now, that doesn't necessarily mean it's any easier for me. I long for what we used to have, but that's just it, what we used to have is no longer here. And neither am I."

She leaned into me then and kissed me on the cheek. Even though her words may have sounded harsh, I knew that the soft interior of her being still remained. She didn't mean to break my heart, but she didn't know what else to do, as I had already broken hers so many times before. The fragments of the parts we needed so desperately didn't add up anymore. She left me then, once again. I stood at the corner and watched her go away, the yellow color of her coat was the only highlight I saw spring out from the mass of people who soon surrounded her.

Ellie became just another soul in the city that day. She walked away and became a portion of the metropolis that we together had helped make. I contemplated all that was and was not. I thought of the past that had already happened, the present in which I was, and where the future would go. As the yellow left me, so did Ellie. The light of my life left me that day, in finality. It would be the last time I ever saw her alive.

The next day, I signed the divorce papers and sent them on. The chapter of my life with Ellie as my wife had ended. The climax had teetered up to the top, and dropped off completely. I had lost. It had all come unspun. The strings that once crisscrossed and held one another together had separated and frayed. The meticulous measurements had melted into a feeling that had decided to fleet away. Nothing, not even New York City, could save me.

On the first day of 1999, I decided that I would write to Ellie. I committed myself to write one letter to her every single day. The turn of the century was only one year away. And before long, a new millennium would make us, and take us. I wrote her a letter every day, from January 1st 1999 and on.

She no longer lived with Juliana, but I had her new address, as it was on the divorce documents that I had so thoroughly scrutinized. I know she got the letters, even though I had no real confirmation of her receiving them. I believed that she got them all, and I told myself that she read them. Nevertheless, Ellie didn't respond to a single letter I wrote. She had let me go, completely, or so it seemed.

In November of 1999, I quit my job at Haversmith. I

decided it one day out of the blue, simply by the notion that I knew I would be far happier if I never had to go into the office again. The details didn't matter to me anymore. The everyday instances seemed lessened. The descriptions I used to paint for myself were only blank. I was getting on with age and I felt old. I still did not allow myself to paint, not a single thing. I did not deserve to be allowed to.

I quit by going to speak with David Haversmith, who was the son of Mr. Haversmith, the man who had hired me all of those years ago. I walked into his office without knocking and I approached where he sat at his desk.

"This job may have been looked upon as a good one for me, but all I can feel is the resentment towards it in the ways that it hindered me and the life I feel I could have had, the life I should have had. This job ruined my life. I realize now that I never should have abandoned my dreams. And so, I quit."

His mouth dropped open, and as he tried to higher it back up, I turned around and left before he could react, or say anything to me at all. I never went back.

Daniel passed away in the fall of 2000. He had moved back to Alden, and lived out his final years in our old house on Elm Street. He had written to me after Ellie and I had returned to the city and asked if it would be okay if he moved back into the house where we had grown up. I told him it was fine.

He had a heart attack. One moment he was alive, the next moment he was dead. I went back to Alden for the funeral. The casket remained closed. I didn't see him, I didn't cry, I couldn't cry. I loved my brother, but my feelings towards him were too complex to understand. I watched as his body was submerged down six feet into the ground. He was buried right next to my parents. Beside my parents, laid the bodies of Charlie and little Alma too.

As the rest of the people paying their respects faded away, I knelt there in the grass and thought about all of the people who were now lying beneath me: my father, my mother, my son, my daughter, and now my brother.

"You all deserved so much better," I said, and then I thought of her. She was the only one left alive. The last living soul that loved me, or at least the last one that once had. I didn't know if she did anymore. She hadn't even come to my brother's funeral.

Perhaps she had her reasons, then again...maybe she didn't.

Or rather, it could have just been that she didn't think I deserved them, just as I didn't deserve her. The amount of death that was ingrained within the soil below where I was then amounted up to more than I could handle. My life had turned into one tragedy after the other. All I wanted was some sort of release, my own kind of submersion into the depths below where I could join them. I wished to change how things had gone.

In the summer of 2001, after the first year of the new millennium had already left us and the rest of the world kept on living and dying as it had always done, I received a letter from Ellie one day. It was not a response to a letter I had written, nor did it address anything I had previously asked of her in the composed form. Instead it was an organization of characters and words all its own.

I read it, and so it said:

Dearest Priam,

I am dying.
I wish to see you again before I actually do.

Yours truly,
Ellie

Sunday, September 9th 2001
Day Seven – The Original Way

I don't know why I am the one who is still alive when everyone else I ever loved is already dead or currently dying. When I wake up, I exhale deeply and wonder if anything is ever going to change from this point on, or if I will always feel this saddened with every day that greets me. I am only sixty years old, but in some ways, I feel as if I have been alive for centuries. I am still in good shape for a man of my age, but as time goes on I feel the earth move beneath me differently. I often wonder when my life will end, but I try not to think about it too much. I wish I didn't feel so alone.

Then again, my lonesome life is a doing all my own. I've been the man who has messed up the magnificent colors by making them black, by using them too much and making the saturation slip and fade. I was greedy, I thought I could have everything. In doing things wrong I have brought myself to the point where now I have nothing except for myself and the memories of the life I once lived. The memories are gone, they are out of my reach.

I lean up and look to my bedside table, glancing at the small day by day calendar that rests upon it. I rip off the page from yesterday, and acknowledge today's date. As I do so, I think about the time that has passed me by, and one instance of the world going on in particular comes to mind. It has been two months since I received the letter from Ellie. When I got it and read it, I didn't know what to do. So, I did nothing. I stopped writing to her from that day on, putting an end to my daily letters that I had been writing her for years. I had wanted her to respond to me for so long, or at least to acknowledge that I still existed, but when she finally did, it was as if all things reversed. I wanted Ellie to love me again, in the way I knew she truly did. I wanted our lives to reconvene, but not in the way that they seemed destined to. I didn't want to see her on her deathbed, even though I knew she needed me.

I am afraid. I get up and walk into the bathroom. I sit down on the toilet seat because it is too hard to stand in front of it anymore. I don't have the balance or the energy to focus on my aim this early in the morning. I often wake up when it's still dark outside as it's hard for me to stay asleep for very long these days.

The nights come and go more quickly than they used to, all the while the days pass me too. I remember Grandpa Wood once telling me that the reason time goes by quicker when we're older is because one year to us when we are sixty is merely but one sixtieth of our life. While in comparison, one year to us when we are twenty years old is one twentieth. At my age time doesn't seem to matter very much, yet it is all I have.

I walk back into the bedroom and approach my dresser. I see my wedding ring lying on top of it, next to a photograph of Ellie and I. My hand goes for it and I slip it on my finger. Even though Ellie and I are divorced, I still wear it everyday, never at night though. I don't let it stay on my finger when I am not aware of what is occurring out in the world around me.

I still live in the apartment that we shared together those final years of our marriage. I thought about moving out and finding a new place, but I couldn't leave. This was our home after all and we did have some good memories here. I have only lived in three different places really, although the back and forth construction of where I resided may have been a strange one. There was the house on Elm Street in Alden when I was young, my studio apartment in Brooklyn before Ellie and I were married, then back to our house in Alden, and finally to this apartment where we returned to New York after Charlie died. The buildings in which my life has been contained mean something to me, even if they are only personified by the brick and mortar that makes them.

My feet take me out of the bedroom, and as I can feel the surfaces vary against the bareness of my soles, I enter into the kitchen and brew myself a fresh pot of coffee. I need it to waken me up and help me move on with the day. As the tiny little machine makes its weird noises, I think about her again. I've contemplated going to see her since the first instance that the letter was in my hands, of course I have. How could I not? As it remains though, I still have yet to see her. I do not know why she is dying, or what has caused her to be sick. What I do know though, is that she is still alive and that I must see her soon. I called her a few times, but I didn't say a word when she answered. I heard her voice and although it sounded the same as I always remembered it, the inflection that resided within the resonance had changed. It was Ellie, but it was as if it was a different version of her that was speaking through the telephone. She didn't know that it was I who had called those times though, as I had not spoken. I wished to hear her voice, but I did not know if I wanted her to hear mine.

I had already done so many things wrong in life. Perhaps she would just be better off if she never saw me again. Wasn't that what she had wanted after all? If not, wouldn't she still be here with me now? Wouldn't I be caring for her as the conclusion draws near? The questions commence, and I let them linger on. I want to see her more than anything. I cannot even bare the incredulity of my desire to be next to her once again. However, I have not moved myself forward to see her yet. Now that I know she actually wants to see me, it's as if something has forced itself between us. A concrete block the size of the Empire State itself has buried me deep down beneath it and I cannot escape the predicament that I am in, that of my monotonous and moonrise life, where I live alone and am alone in living. Something has been holding me back.

Then, that something within me changed. It happened eight days ago, on September 1st, four years to the day when she returned from London and left me the note on the kitchen counter. Four years ago to the day that she moved out of this place and I realized that things were never going to be the same. I called her. This time, when I heard her voice answer, I spoke.

"Hello?"

"Ellie," her name was all I had responded with.

"Priam?"

"Yes."

"Why have you taken so long?"

"You know me."

She stifled a giggle, but it sounded much deeper than I remembered her laughs being. "I guess that's right. Well I'm glad you finally reached out to me."

"Yes."

"You stopped writing. Why?"

"I don't know. Maybe because you finally wrote me."

"Is that all it took?"

"I suppose so," I had said.

"Priam."

"Ellie," I said her name back again.

"Are you going to come see me?"

"I would like to," I said.

"I would very much like to see you. It's all I seem to long for these days."

"I will come see you," I said to her, promising her a simple fact that I knew was far more complex than it sounded.

"When? Do you know how to get here?"

"I'm not sure when, soon. And yes, I think I know where your apartment is. If not, I'll find it."

"Okay. Priam?"

"Yes?"

"Please come soon. I don't know how much longer I have," she said, sounding faint and weak, her voice faltering and then silently fading.

"I will. Ellie, what...what is it?"

"Cancer of course. It's in my bones."

"I'm so sorry."

"It's okay. I've come to terms with it. I don't have long, I'm afraid. It's a shame. Don't feel sorry for me though. Just come and see me...okay?"

"I promise. Soon."

"Priam, you know...I still love you."

"I love you too Ellie. You've always been my ballerina, my love, my life, and you always will be." Then I hung up the phone. I didn't say goodbye, and neither did she, but we hadn't needed to. For once, or at least for the time being, the words were enough.

I decide that I will go to see her today. The warm coffee mug that resides in my hand feels too hot so I set it down and leave the kitchen. I go back to my bedroom and try and pick out a nice outfit, without having it be too over the top. I select something classy yet simple: a white buttoned down shirt, black slacks and a gray blazer that Ellie bought me for our twentieth wedding anniversary. I think she will be happy to see me wearing something that she picked out.

In going to see her, I know that she will be glad, but is going to see her on it's own good enough? No, I tell myself that I have to do something else to make her happy. I have to come up with an idea to surprise her in a way that she won't expect. I don't want to just simply delight her, I want to astound her and somehow make her live again. In all of the ways that living can occur, I need to deliver myself to Ellie along with an accompaniment of something more, something that she would never anticipate for me to bring her, yet all the while something she has always wanted. The bed falls beneath my bones as I sit down upon it and think. What can I do?

Then the idea arrives within my mind and I can't believe I haven't thought of it quicker. It's the perfect surprise and I can actually see it helping her feel better, somehow maybe even forcing her to live longer, as what I plan to give her is something that she always wanted, but I would never let her have: a dog.

Or rather, a puppy. I think of the soft and fluffy little creature that I have yet to find and I know that if I buy it for Ellie and bring it to her it will tickle her immensely. She had always loved animals but never had any pets as a child. And when we moved back to Alden, she requested for us to get one quite frequently. I never let her though. I didn't much care for animals and I didn't see the point in having one. I didn't think it was that big of a deal, but she continued to ask for one over the years and I continued to say no, stifling the possibility.

Buying a dog for Ellie would be the perfect thing to show her that I had been listening to her all of those years and that I still remembered how she wanted one so badly. A puppy might just be the right thing to cheer her up, and if not save her, at least it's company will delight her as her life comes to an end. I have to move fast if I am going to get one today, and be able to deliver it to her tonight. First and foremost, I suppose I should figure out what kind of dog she would want.

I know before I even have to think about it, a golden retriever. I don't know why I know, but somehow it is clear that this is the kind of dog she would want. The particular parts have all been shaken into place, I will see Ellie this evening and I will have with me a little lovable being that will make her smile. I will grace her with my presence, and give her something more, something she had always wanted. All I have to do now is find the right dog. Hopefully it won't be too arduous of a process. Out of the endless amount of animals that exist in the city, I am sure that I will be able to find the right one for her. I have to.

I leave my apartment and go down to the corner store to buy a copy of the New York Times. I ignore all of the people I pass, but I thank the man who sells me the newspaper with gusto, hoping beyond all hope that I will find what I am looking for to be contained within the pages I have just purchased. I take the newspaper back to my apartment and open to the classifieds in the back. I spread out the sheets so that everything is before my eyes all at once. I look for the words that I seek, and then they pop out at me: Pets for Sale.

Kittens – cute kittens of all different colors for sale - $35 No.

Kittens – healthy, inspected, and shots given, beautiful pets for your family, friendly and happy little cats - $40 No.

Iguana – two year old iguana for sale, I'm moving and can't keep him - $100 Hell no.

Dog – a one year old black Labrador for sale, she's very friendly and lovable. Has all of his paperwork. Would make a nice family dog. Closer.

Puppies – Five German Sheppard puppies for sale, $100. Even Closer.

Puppies – Seven golden retriever puppies for sale, only $250 each, beautiful and friendly dogs, have all their shots and are ready to find a good home and become your best friend. Bingo.

The address that is listed is located in Great Neck out on Long Island, but it's not too far outside of the city. I could take the train there and be back in enough time to see Ellie before it gets too late. I decide to call the number that is listed beneath the advertisement. The phone rings and rings, I am just about to give up and hang up when a surly sounding woman answers.

"Hello?"

"Yes. My name is Priam Wood and I'm calling about your ad in the Times about the Golden Retriever puppies you have for sale."

"Ah...yes. I'm afraid we've only got one left."

"That's okay! I'm not picky. Has anyone else called and shown interest recently? I'd like to come out to get it today, if that's possible?"

"Sure sir, that's more than fine. A few people have called, but no one was planning on coming today that I know of," her husky voice tells me what I wish to hear.

"Great. I live in Brooklyn, I can be there in an hour or so."

"Alrighty. Before you go though, there is something I should probably tell you about this pup before you come the whole way out here to see her."

"What's that?" I ask, my breath heightened, afraid that something might be wrong due to the even deeper tone of her voice. "She's been a little bit sick recently. I don't know what's wrong with her. She was the liveliest one out of them all until a few days ago. Maybe she's just depressed that all of the other ones have been bought and she hasn't. I don't know. Anyways, I figured you should just know that. Regardless, she is beautiful. You can come and see for yourself. She'll be waiting."

"Okay. I mean, yes, I would still like to come and see her. I'll be there soon. Thanks. Goodbye."

"See ya later Mr. Wood."

I put the phone back on the receiver and sit down upon my bed again, as I had been pacing the entire time I was talking to the woman with the raspy voice. I wonder if I should maybe search for another dog, or another place that has them. Will this dog be able to cheer Ellie up if it is sick itself? I contemplate on looking further, but then I decide not to. This is the first one I came upon and somehow, it almost seems as if it is meant to be.

This little puppy is sick, just as Ellie is. Perhaps, by some means they will both be able to heal one another. By chance, it may be that they are two towers of the same bridge, holding up the road that connects to them and crosses the water that flows underneath their stones. Maybe the only thing needed is a little bit of symmetry. In bringing this puppy to Ellie, I hope that the equilibrium of her living, as well as her faith in me, is restored and forged once again. I beg of the universe to let her believe, in me.

The train ride out to Great Neck is a gloomy one, as the city has decided to start pouring down upon us with heavy drops of precipitation to wetten the day. I stare out the window and watch as the towering buildings shrink away in the distance. As they get smaller, I wonder if my chances of succeeding in this venture, or any of my desires of this day will grow fainter too. I tunnel on, as a part of the electronic locomotive that is far more advanced than it was ever intended to be. I think of inventions that start as something groundbreaking, yet remain simple and are only later transformed into meticulous machines that are not able to be understood by the common man. Everything grows complicated in time.

It isn't a far walk from the Great Neck train station to the address that I have circled on a map of the town. The woman who has the puppy lives on a street called Piccadilly Road. I can't help but to think of London, and wonder where I would be now if I would have went on the trip there with Ellie like I was supposed to. Things would be different. Number 219 Piccadilly Road is a cute little yellow house, which looks as if it could belong on a farm. The white trim that goes along the borders of the edges that are created by the walls coming together give it a friendly feel. The front porch is covered in flowers, the most noticeable ones being the three big potted plants of mums, all of various autumn shades. Summer will soon be over.

I approach the dark green colored door and knock. And then I wait. The door opens and instead of seeing the hefty woman I was expecting, a little boy of around seven years old stands before me. His shaggy blonde hair is cut in the exact same way that mine used to be when I was young.

"Hello sir. How can I help you?"

"I'm here to see the puppy you have for sale. I-"

"My name is Max," he tells me, interrupting me before I can finish.

"Hi Max. My name is Priam. It's nice to meet you."

"You too sir. You're coming to see Little Star?"

"Little Star? Is that the puppy's name? Is your mother here?"

"Little Star. Little Star," he repeats again rather silently. And then he screams: "It's Priam! He's here!" nearly breaking my eardrums.

Max runs away then, his golden locks flopping as he goes. I remain where I am, waiting for his mother, or whoever the woman was that I talked to earlier to come and greet me. She emerges from the kitchen only a few moments later. She isn't the woman I expected to see, as she is thin and lovely. Her long blonde hair glows, even in the gloom of the day. Her figure is accentuated nicely by a pair of jeans and the white blouse she has paired them with. Somehow, she reminds me of my younger days. "Oh Priam, so glad you made it okay," she says to me as she motions with her hand for me to come in. "I'm Josephine," she tells me. She extends her hand when I enter, so I reach out to grasp it. Her voice is the same as I remember it, raspy, deep, and intricate. It doesn't fit with her appearance, but her overall beauty makes up for the strangeness of her voice. Nothing could sway the actuality of her being.

"It wasn't hard to get here at all. Thanks for letting me

come on such short notice," I say as I go to remove my shoes.

"Oh now, don't worry about taking those off. Sorry about Max, he gets a little excited sometimes. He can be rather rambunctious."

"Aren't all little boys though?" I ask.

"You have a point. Anyways, follow me, I can show you out to where the little girl is."

"Little Star?" I ask, wondering if the puppy indeed holds that name.

"Ah yes. That's what Max calls her. She has a white little spot on the top of her forehead. He likes to think that it's a star. Hence, the name."

I follow Josephine out into her garage where I am greeted by a large golden retriever who welcomes me by licking my hand.

"This is Matilda. She's the mother."

"She's a beautiful dog," I say.

"Isn't she?"

Josephine leads me over to a small area that is enclosed by a short metal gate. Within the gate the floor is covered in newspaper and tiny cotton pillows. Resting on top of one of the soft cushions is a little puppy that appears to be sleeping: Little Star.

I get closer and kneel down so I can peer at her through the gate. I see the small white patch on her forehead and the sight of it warms the inside of me. She is the cutest puppy I have ever seen. Not that I've seen many, but I would have to argue that this small creature is going to be a beautiful dog.

"I don't know what's been wrong with her," Josephine says then from behind me. "She's just been acting very strange and not eating very much of her food. And when she does, she throws it up most of the time. I'm sure she'll get better though. She has a strong spirit. She's Max's favorite. He'll be sad to see her go."

I turn away from Josephine and back to where Little Star rests. She remains still and unmoving, I look at her body closely and I notice that it doesn't look like she's breathing. The normal upheaval of her midsection that should be occurring from taking breaths isn't happening. Did I come to pick up a puppy that is already dead?

"It doesn't look like she's breathing," I say to Josephine as I stand up.

She comes over to the side of the metal fence where I am

and kneels down to look at her. "My eyesight isn't good, I can't tell from here. I'm sure she's breathing though; I don't think she was sick enough that she would have died. Go ahead and pick her up."

I step over the metal cage and sit down on the newspaper right next to where Little Star lies. I slowly reach down to where she rests and as I do so I think about the name of the puppy itself, and though it is a cute one, I know I am going to have to come up with something new before I give her to Ellie. If I am able to, that is.

My hand extends out to where she lies motionless and as it does I am still afraid that this little dog is dead. She isn't breathing, she isn't moving, she hasn't even acknowledged that I'm here. I touch her then and as soon as my skin touches her, from the moment we make contact, she comes alive again. Her eyes pop open and she bounds up from her lying position and lets out a squeak of a bark. She turns around and faces where I sit, heavily panting as she starts to run a few circles around me before she plops down right in the center of my lap, licking my hands over and over again. She moans a little bit, out of what appears to be happiness. She's found me, just as I found her. It's all we had to do.

"I'll be god damned. Lookie there," Josephine says. "The little girl seems fine after all. It appears that she's already in love with you."

"So it seems," I say, as I stroke the puppy behind her ears.

"What are you going to name her?" She asks.

"Chloe," I say, the name escaping from my mouth before I even think about it. It's as if the name itself was brought forward from a dream I once had, that I'm unable to remember. "I'm going to name her Chloe."

"How lovely." Josephine tells me. "I'm sure the two of you will have wonderful times together. Dogs are great you know. Chloe will probably end up being your best friend."

"I've never had a dog before. I'm actually...I'm planning on giving her to my wife, as a gift. She's always wanted one," I tell her then, admitting the reasons for wanting the dog in the first place. I do not acknowledge the fact that Ellie is sick, or that she is actually my ex-wife, those details don't seem to matter now.

"That's so nice of you. I'm sure she will be thrilled to meet Chloe."

"I hope so."

I pick Chloe up as I stand and hold her against my torso.

She squeals in delight and wriggles a little bit, but she lets me hold her without too much of a fuss. I step over the metal fence and follow Josephine back inside so that I can pay her. I hold Chloe the entire time I am inside the house. I don't want to let her go. I thank Josephine for everything and wish her well as I leave and go outside. I don't know if I can bring an animal on the train back to the city, but I don't really care either way because I am going to do it anyways.

As I walk away from the yellow house with the white trim, I turn back to look at it. When I do, I see a little boy with blonde hair standing behind the big bay window watching me go. For a second, I see myself, the seven year old version of who I once was looking out beyond the glass and watching me disappear. Then I remember that it is not I, as I am here walking away, holding Chloe. Instead, it is Max who longs for his favorite puppy whom I just took away from him. His face doesn't hold much emotion, but even at this distance I can tell by his longing expression that he is saddened. Before I turn back around to face the road in front of me, I see his mouth open, and he screams. I can't hear the sound, but I know that it has happened.

A few people on the train back to Brooklyn look at me funny for the fact that I have a puppy in my arms, but nobody says anything. Instead, they all look at Chloe lovingly and admire how cute she is. It's impossible for anyone to be angry at a puppy it seems. As I hold her in my arms on the ride home, I wonder why I hadn't wanted to get one before, not only for Ellie, but for myself.

My idea that having a dog as a pet would serve no purpose was entirely wrong. I have to add that to the list of all of the things that I was mistaken of. Even at sixty years of age, I am still learning about this life I am living, and how I could have lived it better. If only I could fix things.

When I get back to Brooklyn, I decide to go to a convenient store before making my way over to Ellie's apartment. Although Chloe is cute enough on her own, I want to purchase something to make my delivery even more special. I buy a giant red bow that I tie around Chloe's little neck. She looks adorable. I take her to Prospect Park and I let her run around for a while, with the giant red silk material still tied around her neck. I use the excuse of letting Chloe get some exercise as my reasoning for stopping in the park before we make our way to Ellie's, but really I know that I am stalling because I am afraid to see her.

Who will be with her? What will she think of my arrival? When did she become sick in the first place? Where has she been going for treatments? Why does she think she is going to die? How will she interpret me giving Chloe to her? The questions add up, as they multiply, before subtracting themselves from each other and dividing. I don't have any of the answers, all I have are the questions.

It's towards the end of the afternoon and I know that I have to go soon. I play in the park with Chloe for a while longer. The puppy appears to be perfectly healthy now; whatever was wrong with her has left her completely. She is fine. I however, am not, as I feel my insides eating each other.

The rain and gloom that hovered over New York earlier has left us, as the sun light has begun to shine through the overcast sky. The shadows of the trees fall upon the grass and make up monsters that fight with one another as the light shifts and sways them. People in the park admire Chloe and look at me, the sixty year old man who is by her side, watching her play.

I am waiting...for nothing...for everything...for all that is in between. I have to go. All of a sudden I pick up Chloe in my arms and then we are on our way, to Ellie.

The red colored stone that creates the structure of the place where Ellie resides is a bright burst of illusion compared with the drab shades of brown of the two houses on either side of it. I walk up the stairs with Chloe in my hands, and as I ring the bell I notice that the red color of the bricks are a very similar shade to the bow that is tied around her neck. They are the same.

I have to ring the bell a few times before someone comes to the door, and when they finally do and it opens before me, the person standing there is not Ellie, instead it is an older version of a person that I recognize: Juliana.

It is a shame the woman never liked me, and to be honest, she had never really helped out the relationship Ellie and I had. Regardless of whether or not how much her opinions swayed Ellie in the past, I wouldn't let her get in the way now. This wasn't about her.

"Hello Priam," she says as she beckons me to come in. "What's that you got there?" She asks, pointing to the puppy in my arms.

"Oh this is Chloe. I bought her for Ellie, you know how she always wanted a dog. I decided to finally get her one."

"How thoughtful of you."

"Where is she?"

"Upstairs. I'd like you to come sit down with me in the living room first however, I need to talk to you."

"Can't I just see her?" I ask, the last thing I want to do is delay any further. I don't want to talk to Juliana, not when Ellie is only right upstairs.

"No. You cannot," she says firmly. "Follow me please." She leads me into the living room, where she plops down onto a tan leather chair and I sit down upon the love seat next to her. I set Chloe down on the floor. She doesn't run away, she stays right beside me, nuzzling up against my leg. Juliana stares at me. The lines in her face are much deeper than I had realized they were before. Although she is well put together with her hair clipped neatly back and her outfit finely pressed, she appears to be very tired. It's as if she hasn't slept in weeks. I wait for her to say something for a minute or two, but she doesn't, she just looks at me. It's not a look of disgust, which were the only kinds of looks that I used to get from her, instead it is one of pity and oddly enough, sympathy.

"What is it?" I ask finally, not wanting the silence to overtake us and drag us under.

"I don't know how to say this without just saying it Priam. So that's what I'm going to do. I'm sorry you have to hear this from me, of all people."

"What?"

She takes a deep breath and even though she tries to suck in the oxygen that surrounds us, it's as if her lungs implode as she speaks the words that come next. "Ellie's gone Priam. She passed away a couple of hours ago."

The reverie that I had written and lived through collapses upon itself then. The words occur but they do not listen to the rules that have been laid down centuries before they were thought of. I feel a tearing inside of my chest and I know that it is my heart swelling and bursting as if each ventricle no longer wishes to exist. I don't want to believe the words, but I know they must be true.

Chloe whimpers on the ground beside me and lifts up her paw and places it on my thigh. I let out a noise that isn't anything I've ever exhaled before. Juliana remains motionless as I am taken over and everything I ever had is gone. The room is spinning around me as I am locked to the spot where I sit. I am temporary paralyzed as I am acquainted with the fact that has befallen me. I'm too late, she's gone.

I stand up suddenly and scream. It's a noise of primal fear, of pain and longing and misunderstanding. I wish to engorge all of the emotions that I am feeling and make them float away to a place that will never remain but I know they won't go. The house shakes as the sound that I've emitted bounces off of the walls and slams back into me.

Juliana goes to stand up, but I put my hand on her shoulder and make her stay where she is. Chloe starts to bark and the squeaks of her undeveloped voice ring within my ears as I start to run away. I have to see her. I bound out of the room and head for the stairs, where I jump up them, two, three at a time.

"Priam! Wait!" Juliana calls after me. I don't heed her request. When I get to the top of the stairs I hear a soft thumping coming from behind me, so I turn to see what it is. Chloe has followed after me, running up the stairs as quickly as she can. She doesn't wish to be left alone. She wants to accompany me.

I turn back around to the second floor that I have come upon and I see that there are many closed doors before me. I run to the leftmost one and open it. The room is dark and the bed is empty. The second door I open is the bathroom, the white tile shining as the sun pushes through the glass of the window that has been left ajar. The third door I push away from me is the one which contains her. It is where she lies. I see her lying in the bed and although I know it is her, I do not wish to believe it.

I approach the bed where she remains motionless and I fall to the floor, my knees hitting the wooden baseboards with a bang. I should feel pain in my kneecaps from the force I thudded, but the only ache I can feel is the one in my soul, which is ripping apart my heart. I wrap my hands around hers, and my skin tingles as it touches her flesh, which is cold. Her body has wasted away. The Ellie that I once knew and recognized is not the same person who lies here now. She is thin and frail; her chestnut colored hair no longer remains as it is now a silvery white. Her pale complexion is marked by dark spots. Her eyes are closed. Even though I am touching her and our cells are colliding and mingling up against one another, I know that the being of her body is just a physical remnant of what once was. From the moment we are created our bodies contain within them the contents of our destruction, yet it is up to time and fate to decide how we will leave this place. Ellie is gone and before she went, I failed her so many times.

I wish to bring her back to me, but I know that I cannot. I weep, but my tears are not enough, nor will they ever be. I feel as if I don't know how to exist any longer. I cannot imagine a world where Ellie does not reside.

I notice an enormous pile of letters on the other side of the bed which rest on her end table. I don't have to examine them closely to know that they are the ones I had written her. A clickity clacking noise emerges from behind me, and I know that it is Chloe who has found me without even having to turn around to see her. I feel her presence approach me and then her soft golden fur rubs up the exposed skin of my leg, which sticks out from the bottom of my pants. She lays her head on my lap where I sit on the floor, near the edge of the bed where Ellie is before me. She moans softly, as if she can sense the destruction that I feel.

"I'm so sorry Ellie," I say out loud over and over again. "You deserved so much better than me."

My body holds who I am inside of it all the while, even though I wish to escape from its reaches. It's as if I can see myself sit where I am from a third point of view, as if I can witness the longing and utter disbelief of the reality of Ellie being completely gone from me. I watch as I hold her hand, as she remains where she lies, as Chloe continues to cry for the both of us.

A life where Ellie doesn't exist is not a life worth living. I may have lost her years ago, and even though it was a certain sort of completion; there was still hope in being able to see her again. There was not this finality. Now it has come, and she is gone. The conduction of how this reduction has taken place offends me. If only I had gotten here sooner, if only I had had the chance to say goodbye, if only I had loved her better.

Time passes unbeknownst to me. I don't know how much has come and how much has gone, as it has reduced itself to something meaningless, even though it holds all of the power that exists here, there, or anywhere. Eventually, my body convulses one final time and I get up to go. Chloe whimpers as she removes herself from my lap and stands up where I was previously sitting. Letting my hand slide away from that of Ellie's, I stand overtop of her, lean down and kiss her on the forehead. It is the last time I will touch her. "Goodbye Ellie."

I walk out of the room with no knowledge of how to react further from this point. I am empty, as if all of my organs have disappeared. I feel hollow, as if I have been gutted of everything that was ever given to me. I have never felt more alone in my life. Through this life, all I have come to know is the death of those whom I loved. The only thing I have now I realize, is Chloe, as she follows after me. I reach down and scoop her up into my arms as I approach the top of the stairs. She cranes her neck upwards towards my face and licks my skin, giving me a kind of puppy kiss, returning the one that Ellie was unable to. Down we go.

I briefly talk to Juliana before leaving Ellie's house. I ask her what the funeral plans are through my stifled inflections of speech. Every sentence seems shorter. Nothing seems connected. There is going to be a viewing in the city in two days, on September 11th and then Ellie will be buried in Alden, next to Charlie, Alma, Danny, my mother and my father. And me, where I will one day lay. The entire destruction of the Woods will remain in the same plot. Together our bones will lie as the earth corrodes them. One by one, we are all eventually unspun. Before I go, Juliana tells me the last thing Ellie said before she slipped away. Her last words were just four: "It's Priam. He's here." So she tells me. They make no sense, because I wasn't. I wasn't here. I wasn't beside her when she left. I didn't make it in time. I didn't do enough. I didn't die there with her, but soon enough, I'll die anyways.

After I leave the house of red stone that I had never really known, I decide that there are two things that I need to buy immediately.

The faces of strangers on the street who pass me all intercept my delusion as if they know me, as if they are able to understand my pain. And just as I am about to speak out to each one of them, that is when they look away. Even though I live in a city that has millions of people, I feel completely alone. There is no one here but me.

I try to refocus on the two things I need. The first is for Chloe, who still resides in my arms. I forget that she is there from time to time momentarily, as she is calm, and does not wiggle around up against my flesh as I expect her to. The second is for me, who still resides within this body. Both of the places where Chloe and I exist will change, soon. It's time for two things, both of which are very different from one another. I buy a red leash for Chloe, and I buy a gun.

The bow around Chloe's neck is gone. I've thrown it away. I let her walk along the sidewalk now, as she is connected to me by the leash that remains in my hands. The gun, a small silver pistol stays in my pocket which is where I have put it. I don't know what to do with Chloe. I should probably take her to a shelter, or return her to Great Neck where I got her from, but I feel as if I don't have time for that.

It is getting dark outside and it won't be long before this day is done and I know that I don't want to live to see tomorrow. In killing myself, at least Ellie and I will cease to exist on the same day. Thus, in some way, we will be together. I hope beyond hope that all broken hearts end up in the same place once they are beyond repair and shattered completely.

I go to the park. I find the spot.

The spot we met, the spot I saw her dance, the spot where our souls collided and connected. I find the spot.

The spot where Charlie threw himself down, the spot where he started to give up on living, the spot where Ellie and I found him, but didn't find him enough. I find the spot.

The spot where I see that bench in the distance, the spot that I looked upon when she told me that it was over, the spot that remained in place then, even as she was letting me go. I find the spot.

I sit down upon it. This spot, up against the big maple tree, means so much to me. I cannot think of a better place to die.

I don't know the exact moment when I decided to commit suicide. It just sort of came to me, as the only plausible option, the only guaranteed end to all of the pain and undesirable longing that

I feel. No one will miss me, as no one is left on this Earth that loves me.

I've tied Chloe's leash around the tree and as I sit on this spot, waiting for it to get darker, waiting for all of the people who are around me now to go away so that there is no chance that they can stop me, she sits with me too, and she looks right at me with her amber colored eyes. It's as if she can see into me, knowing all of the knowings that I know. Somehow, she knows what I wish to do, and she, she will miss me when I'm gone.

If I'm gone. The longer I wait where I am the harder it seems to let go of everything, of anything, to give up, to stop trying for myself or for living. The thoughts are all just fragments, as my sixty year old body doesn't care about the descriptions or the details any longer. This is life, and what I wish for is death, the sweet release of nothingness to surround me. I long for a place where I can be with her again. Who is what and how is time will not collect in my head.

It's dark enough now. It has to be nearing towards midnight. I don't know how long I have been here. Chloe lays beside me, her front paws up against me. She doesn't move her gaze. She doesn't close her eyes. She doesn't want me to go.

I wait longer still.

And then the moment comes. I put the gun up against my head and I can feel the cool steel touch my skin. A flash occurs, but it's not because a bullet enters my brain, instead it is the recollection of the same kind of cool feeling as I touched her hand earlier today.

Ellie. She wouldn't want this. She wouldn't want my life to end this way. I start to hyperventilate. Chloe begins to whimper obsessively, unendingly. She wriggles her paws in a strange fashion up against me. If Ellie knew that I was going to kill myself, just as my son had done...but maybe she does. Maybe she does know. From somewhere, some place.

Charlie. He wouldn't want this. Even though he had given up himself, I know that he wouldn't want the same for me. He would want me to keep trying, even though he hadn't.

There have been so many things I have done wrong in this life: the last words I said to my mother before she died, the way I treated my brother, giving up on my dreams in order to gain some sense of false security, missing Ellie in more ways than one, leading Charlie astray and not reassuring him to believe in himself, not getting away and making it to the destination, being too late.

There are so many days in my life that I wish I could change. The gun still remains up against my head. Chloe barks. I shiver. I set it down. I cannot go. Not this way. I've made many mistakes, but I will not make my biggest one, no, not this way. Chloe calms down. I lean back and stretch out on the green grass that is darkened. She lies her golden head upon my chest. Instead of death, sleep comes, at the spot where the first and almost last knot of where everything once, or almost had begun to end.

The journey is coming to an end, I feel it before it even awakes me, in the still of the silence which lies on the edge of a dream, in the penultimate moment before I arise. I am in New York City. It is the atmosphere within my bones that know so, not the actuality of me realizing where I am. I open myself up to the space around me and although I do not recognize the room in which I lay right away, shortly the crimson colored memory comes back to me. I am in the house where Ellie died, on this same day, in that other way, the occurrence that I just experienced all over again. I am contained singularly within the room that she left, the place I came to say goodbye to her, even though I arrived too late.

Altered timelines and realities of being with my children who died decades ago in the faraway city of London come to me, as they are what I held closest to my heart when I was last in charge of these expressions of being. They are only able to stay at the forefront of it all for a while however, as the memory of Ellie dying here, in this very room, and me missing her come flooding back to me as a river that does not give a damn, nor will it ever be dammed.

It is a far-flung tragedy that has bounced itself off of the universe and come back to me; that of the punishment I have had to experience Ellie dying in two different ways, on two very dissimilar days. Neither was deserved, neither was right. I watched her go on that fifth day, during my second ways, in such an unexpected veracity, as she was thrown from the vehicle and faded away at the same spot where my mother had originally died when I was just thirteen. And then there was this room, this deathbed where she laid as I fumbled around the city trying to delve up a certain surprise to deliver to her: that of a little golden retriever puppy by the name of Chloe.

Ellie, my ballerina, my love, my life, she's gone, in more ways than one and in all of the realities that remain to exist. The fragments compartmentalize themselves and decide to go. This is the last day I have. It is my seventh day and this is the second way. Now, what I am experiencing and undergoing, is my final second chance. What comes next, what will occur after this day is done, I do not know. All I am aware of is that things coalesce in unexpected masses. What I always thought I would come to realize may never have even existed at all.

The telephone rings and with it's interruption, I lean up from my spot on the bed to accept it, even as the day withers me down to the pulp of a chord, I let the notes begin to play. Today, as I've come to realize, as I've been shown on every journey that has ever been led, is just another day.

"Hello?"

"Good morning Father, glad to hear you're awake," says the voice of a young man that is filtered through the wires and lines and into the receiver that rests up against my ear.

"Good morning Charlie."

I am elated to know that my son is still alive on this day, as I was afraid that the balance of how things worked out would take him away from me, and Alma too. Their mother was no longer here, so I figured that at this point there was a good chance that neither of my children would exist any longer, as they hadn't been present in this time period during the initial length of my life.

"I'm excited for the get-together today. It should be a wonderful time to visit I'm sure. I meant to ask you though, what did you want me to bring? I forget what you said the last time we spoke."

"What?" I ask, letting my confusion commence before I control it.

"For the picnic? What dish did you request of me?"

"Oh, right! The picnic," I say, covering my tracks that I didn't even know I had made. "You can bring whatever you want Charlie. Some sort of side dish would be nice. I have all of the major fixings." I tell him, even though I am not entirely sure of this.

"Okay Dad, sounds like a plan. I'll whip something up. We'll see you at noon then!"

"Goodbye son," I say and I hang up. I don't know how many people are going to come to this picnic and I don't know who exactly those people will be, but as I look to the clock and see that it is already 9:30AM I realize that I will find out soon enough.

This time, when I go to get up out of my bed I remember to look down first. Only one foot looks back at me. I find my prosthetic leg resting up against the end of my bed, I grab it and push it on and then I stand. I stare at myself for a moment in the mirror, my body is clad in a pair of tighty whities that could be better described as being a loosely fitting grayish brief. On this day, I am sixty years old and even though I look it, I don't necessarily feel it, at least not in the way that I should.

I open the bottom dresser drawer in front of me by pulling it open with my metal prosthetic foot. As I bend down to select a pair of jeans that are folded within it, my back cracks and I let out a sigh of discomfort. I forgot what it feels like to be getting old. Sure, I recall the oncoming pain that filled my joints and bones during my sixties and the instance of death that passed me over when I was a seventy year old man lying in that nursing home bed, but reliving these seven days and fast forwarding through decades of different versions of youth has muddled me up a bit. During this journey, time has played many tricks on me. What I have been, where I have gone, and who I will be, seems to still be unseen, at least partially.

I slip the jeans on over my real foot and my fake one. I wish to cover up the part of me that isn't really me, I wish to forget about the truth. They feel a bit snug around my waist, as the flat and toned belly that I once had is now protruding out a bit. The skin that used to be tight and smooth is now loose and bumpy. I am not the same dashing and handsome man that I once was. The golden hue still remains on my head and although I'm not bald, the color that rests overtop of my mind is more of a silvery yellow shade than what it used to be. As I look at myself further, I try not to think too much about how I appear, but instead I aim to concentrate on how I feel, although that doesn't bring me much solace either. I reach into another drawer and pull out a white t-shirt, plain and simple. Finally, I find the red cardigan that I had once bought for Ellie hung up in my closet. It was oversized on her, so it just fits on me. I place it over my shoulders, letting its warmth envelop me.

I walk out of the bedroom and into the hallway, coming to the stairs that I recall bounding up to find Ellie in the bed where I just recently awoke, the last place she ever fell asleep. I remember Chloe following up after me, not wanting to be alone. She had plopped down by my side and sat there with me as I tried to accept the fact that Ellie was gone forever. The walls along the steps that blurred past me then, come into focus now. I lower myself down one tiny platform at a time and as I do so, I look at the pictures that are framed on the wall beside me. There are seven of them, seven frames that were not there before.

At the top of the stairs where I stand, the picture that is closest to me is the most recent. In it, I sit in a sofa chair, holding an infant in my arms that is wrapped in a swaddling blanket. How I look in this image is pretty much the same as to how I appeared to myself just minutes earlier in the mirror. This photograph could have been taken yesterday for all I know. I wonder whose baby I am holding, but I do not know.

I go down another stair, and when I'm there, the next picture frame I see holds an image of Alma dancing in an exquisite apricot colored ballet costume. It is a scene that has been professionally captured, I can feel the reverberations of her movements just by looking at this lasting impression.

The next photo I come to is of Charlie, who stands in full graduation regalia. He has many sashes and colorful cords around his neck, showing that he graduated from NYU with honors. He looks elated as can be, with steel structures of the cityscape popping up behind him.

Then, as I am halfway down the stairs I come to a picture of us, a photograph of her and I. It is the centerpiece, resting in the middle of the incline that I am going down, with three photographs on either side. In this frame, there is contained an image of Ellie and me, on our wedding day, how it happened the second way. We stand before our white iced cake looking into each other's eyes, as all else around us fades away. All we ever needed was each other, or so we had thought.

I leave the reverie of our love and the beauty that we held within ourselves on that day and I come to the next frame further down, which is an image of myself in that old Brooklyn apartment I barely knew. I stand in the center of the room, as approximately ten various easels circle around where I am. All of the paintings are vigorously alive, full of color, vibrancy and life. I beam from the spot, completely content with the art that I had created.

The second to final picture that I see now as I head to the bottom of the stairs is an image of Danny and myself. I can't tell where it is, as we are sitting in the front two seats of a red convertible, but by the sunlight that bounces off of our laughing faces, I know that whenever this photograph was taken, we were having a wonderful time together.

The final picture, in the last frame, is the farthest back kind of memory that I can remember. For there stands my mother with her hands wrapped around a fourteen or fifteen year old version of myself. She is close enough to the age that she died, but far enough away from it for me to recognize that it is different. I am too big to be thirteen and her hair is longer than I remember it being when she was that final age. The giveaway that makes me sure, is the fact that I am wearing a costume that I never really wore before, that of Batman. Apparently I had given up on Superman after I had flown as a blonde version of him that Halloween, when she helped me take flight. I had grown up and she had watched me, and although things changed, apparently I still believed in superheroes. Regardless of those notions I had then about heroes, I realize that she was always my biggest hero. My mother Moira meant everything to me.

The firm flat ground rests beneath my one foot and my unreal appendage as I reach the bottom, I have made it the whole way down. As I think about all of the photos that I just walked past and admired, I realize that the seven days represented on this wall correlate to the way that these seven days went. As I think of this current day, and the number seven, my mind wanders back to six, to five, to four, to three, to two, to one. It's almost done.

I take a tour around the rest of the house and find that there are many paintings hanging on the walls that I have created over the years. When I walk into the living room, where Juliana told me the news of Ellie's passing, I notice that the painting I created on the day I met her in the park is resting on the mantle over the fireplace. The scene of Central Park and the figure of Ellie dancing in the corner of the painting appears just as I have always remembered it being. It is placed in a similar way as to where we put it on the day she came back to me, before we were married during my life. It seems some things come full circle: containing a beginning, middle, and an end. But what will this end be?

It's hard not to think about what will come next, as I wasn't able to get an answer from Chloe in that white abyss as to what happens when this seventh day is over. Will I return to her in that empty place and have to reevaluate all that has happened? I don't know what will come next.

Besides the veracity of my being and the paintings and pictures that hang on the walls, the house is empty. Sure, there is furniture and the space is tastefully decorated with an artistic vibe of bright colors and many things to catch the eye, but I still feel as if I have to continually fight off the feeling of restlessness. I look out the window to see the sunshine poking through the dark clouds, but it is still mostly hidden away. It looks like rain. The weather and the consequences of earth are unable to make up their minds. The picnic that is soon to occur within these walls will be good for me I am sure. Interacting with Charlie and whoever else joins him will help me to take my thoughts off of where I will go from here when this day is done.

I pass through the large dining room with its salmon colored walls. The large oak table that is located in the middle of the room is fully set with plates, cups and silverware. It is not extravagant by any means, but it is organized and concise. It makes me chuckle inside to think that I arranged everything in such a way, as during my life I was such a disorderly mess. Apparently things can change. There are eight places set and on the end of the table there sits a high chair. Seven guests will be joining me it seems, and a baby. I have no idea who will be in attendance besides Charlie, but it is nearing ten o'clock already, as I take note of the time from the grandfather clock that peers over me from the corner of the room. I will know soon.

I trace my steps away and walk into the kitchen. The clacking of my prosthetic echoes off of the floor, but I ignore it. I methodically put together a green bean casserole, as it is first thing I think of to make. From the looks of it, I have already prepared a lot of food to serve that is on the countertops and stored within the refrigerator. Perhaps I shouldn't even make anything else, but I don't want to wait around helplessly until everyone gets here. I open the can of green beans, empty out the water, put them in a pan, and mix in a cup of cream of mushroom soup, before putting the concoction into the oven. It's pretty easy, and when I am finished within seven minutes of starting, I realize that making the casserole hasn't taken much time away from what remains.

The light shines through a little bit from the kitchen windows, begging to catch my eye as it aims to push through the clouds that desire to hold it back. I leave the cooking center at the back of the house and walk towards the front again, to the living room where most of the paintings that I have created over the years reside. I see my old record player and I walk over to it, pulling out a vinyl record from the bookshelf beside it and placing the circular disc upon the turntable. The needle skids against it to make a melody for me to believe in.

I lay down on the couch that is shoved up unenthusiastically against the large bay window that leads to the outdoors. The sun that was just moments before trying to push through has disappeared and the raindrops are coming. I watch them fall slowly at first, before they pick up speed and assault the asphalt with their unusual trepidation. My eyes close as the rhythm of the blues soothes me. The tranquility of the moment seeps within and I drift asleep.

A wind rustles me, but in reality it is just the brushness of the touch of my brother that brings me back. When I open my eyes I see him before me, his eyes connecting with mine which are now restored to the light. The wrinkles on his face are not as deep as I imagined they would be, yet they are at an indention I never knew on him nevertheless. His thick dark hair that used to exist is no longer, as it is now thin and gray. I didn't know that he would still be alive.

"Howdy there partner," he says as I lean up from where I slept. When I do, I realize that it is not he alone who stands before me.

"Hello Danny," I say and then the rest of the room comes into focus, behind my brother stands Rebecca, still as beautiful as I remember her, none of what she held has faded with age, instead there is just a maturity that has been added to it. I haven't seen either of them during these second days since that fourth day, during my wedding to Ellie. Almost forty years have passed. They look so different from the reality that I knew them last to be in together, yet there are parts of them that remain the same. They are still in control of the breeze that has pushed their entities along.

"Took a little nap did you huh?" Another voice asks as she emerges from behind where Danny and Rebecca hover over me. I lean up more completely out of my reclining position to greet the surprise that is my mother, who resides in this room with us now, in all her elegance, grace and glory, at the brightly sprite age of eighty-six, an age I never thought she knew. After all of this time, she's still alive, and as I thank my heavenly stars or whatever it is that has brought me here, I conclude that they're all still alive and in that way they will remain through this seventh day...except for her, except for Ellie.

I lift myself up off of the sofa and release the dream I had been wandering through. I embrace my mother who comes toward me and as I feel her warmth I think of all of the things that have changed. I am ecstatic that everything is the way it is with the three of them, but I still can't ignore the pang in my heart that yearns for something more.

"I suppose we all need a little bit more sleep sometimes," I tell her, answering her question a few moments more after it has passed.

I try to take in the details of their features, how they look, how they appear, and how they are, but even though I notice them, I don't focus too much on the features they offer me, but rather I digest the reality that they are here, with me. I shake Danny's hand and embrace him as well and then I hug Rebecca too. I hold on a little bit longer than usual, as I never wish to let any of them go. It's been so long since we have all been together, yet at the same time it's only been a few days for me. Time doesn't understand my rhyme and I have to admit it has no reason. It just is. What I know is hidden by a tree, but then it's brought back to me.

I wish to speak to them all further, to learn more of what has happened in the in between, but before I do so, there is a knock on the door and they turn their attention to where the noise has come from. Before I get to the entryway, another familiar voice lets itself be known in the cacophony of the house as it joins us.

"Hello?"

I turn out of the living room and into the hallway where I see my son Charlie entering, in his arms he is carrying a baby girl who is adorned in a pink and green colored jumpsuit. She is a little strawberry that he holds dearly up against him. I go to speak out, but before I do she looks at me and I feel my senses cool.

"Hey there buddy," I say to my son as I give him a one handed hug as to not crush the little girl in between our shoulders, which collide slowly. I reach my hand out and place it on her head, pulling it down to caress her soft skin. I kiss her on the forehead, "And how is this little girl doing?" I ask as I wrinkle up my nose and tickle her chin gently.

She offers a small giggle and not much else. She can't be any older than a year. Her skin is a dark olive and as Charlie pulls off her hat, I see that her hair is dark brown, almost black. It's obvious that this is Charlie's little girl, the baby from the picture, but it appears he was not the one who created her.

"Oh Estelle is doing just fine. She slept the whole way over here, but woke right up with a smile when we arrived outside."

"Isn't that cute," says Danny who has joined Charlie and I with Rebecca and my mother. "Both Priam and Estelle got a little shuteye before today's picnic."

"The girl knows how to live properly. What can I say? I've taught my granddaughter well."

They all laugh, and as the heartiness fades, another person enters into my home. The screen door slams behind him and he comes up beside Charlie. Although he is not a stranger, I am beyond confused as to why he is here, why he has entered my home, and how.

The man who puts his arm around Charlie now was once a seventeen year old boy that I met in the following months after my son killed himself. The boy I knew then was someone who helped me to cope with the loss and confusion that had commenced after Charlie was gone. In the gay youth shelter where I volunteered I met this boy, this man who is now my son's partner. He had helped me and tried to reconstruct my mind and somehow make up for the emptiness that I felt inside, and in a way, he had succeeded. The man beside my son is none other than Robert. The young gay teenager I had met after Charlie was gone in my life has ended up being the person he has fallen in love with.

I can't help but to accept the simplicity of it. It makes sense, and I think of the full circle again, wondering if things like this were always meant to be, but were simply interrupted by tragedies that we were unable to stop, unable to change, until now, until here, until this untilment.

"What took you so long?" Charlie asks Robert, wondering what had delayed him outside from coming in immediately with him and Estelle.

"Oh, I was just admiring the street and this beautiful red stone house. I got lost in the moment, you know how I do. It's been a while since I've been here last."

Charlie looks away from his partner with a smile that spreads itself ear to ear. It's as if he blushes from all of the adoration that he contains for the man, and when he looks back to me, I know that my son has found the love that he thought he would never have, and for that, I am content. Out of the mistakes I have made, the changes that have been changed, and the losses that have been deducted, at least there are forms of love that still exist such as this.

I count the guests in my head then, those who surround me, as if I am the focal point. Five have arrived and little Estelle too, but as I recall the number of places set at the table, I know that we are still expecting two more.

"When's Alma getting here?" My mother asks as she moves forward and puts her hand on my back ever so lightly.

"She's going to be a little late, right?" Charlie asks of me, somewhat rhetorically. He doesn't wait for me to reply as he continues on answering his grandmother's question. "They drove all the way from Pittsburgh to Philadelphia last night for a show, and then they were going to drive from Philadelphia into the city this morning. That was so nice of her Professor to give her a ride, wasn't it Dad?"

"Splendid indeed," I say to him as I try to access some sort of information as to who this Professor is, but I am unable to form up a complexion of her, I can't see her face or recall her name.

Charlie goes on, "She's more than just her Professor though, she's the head of the dancing department at Point Park, and according to Alma they have become very close. She used to dance at Lincoln Center, in the same ballet troupe that Mother once had."

I interject then, adding things I pretend to know: "And now she's acting as a wonderful role model for Alma. Who knows, perhaps soon enough we will all be watching our little girl dance on the same stage that Ellie once did."

"Wouldn't that just be lovely?" My mother says as her hand leaves my back.

"Come now everyone," I say as I turn to walk out of the hallway, letting my mother's suggestion hang in the balance. "Let's get out of this cramped space and spread out, we do have the whole house after all. Make yourselves at home, we can take all of the dishes you've prepared into the kitchen. Alma will be here shortly I'm sure."

As we walk on, I feel a warmth that has emanated from my family around me. When my daughter arrives I know the point of it will expand even more, but even then it still will not be complete. How can my love of this second life I have constructed for myself ever be complete when the most important aspect of it is not present? How can I love this life when it does not hold the depths of my ballerina, who once danced here? I should feel as if I have everything, I know this. Yet without Ellie, I have nothing.

We all get comfortable and I talk to my guests both together and individually. In doing so, I find out more of what has happened since I have seen them last.

Charlie and Robert adopted Estelle about six months ago from the Dominican Republic. They had been in the process of trying to adopt for about a year before that and when the agency told them that they had finally been approved and would become parents to the little girl they were thrilled. From the moment they were united with Estelle when they went to go pick her up in Santo Domingo, they felt like a family, they felt whole. Apparently the two of them have been together since their undergraduate years at college and when I hear this passing remark, I am surprised to not have found out they were together during that sixth day that I spent with Charlie and Alma in London.

My mother is still seeing Mr. Sanders and she seems content with him being a part of her life, as he now lives with her. She mentions him in a caring way, but she still brings my father up more in conversation. Even though Patrick Wood has been dead for sixty years, you would never know by the way my mother talks about him, because to her, it's like a part of him is with her everyday. She still volunteers her time at the local theater and helps with the plays at Alden High, offering her expertise and advice to the shows that are put on within our little community in northwest Pennsylvania. Even after all of these years, she's still got it.

Danny and Rebecca appear to be happy, from the way their eyes connect when they look at one another, I know that they are fulfilled. When the topic of adoption is discussed however, it seems to make them slightly uncomfortable, for the two of them were never able to have children of their own. I'm not sure if my brother and his wife ever tried to adopt and I don't ask, leaving this remain something that I will probably never know. They're both retired now, and have been traveling the world, to faraway places such as Thailand, Brazil and South Africa, just to name a few. They have each other and for them, it seems to be enough.

They all mention Ellie, at least in some capacity and although I enjoy hearing about their different perspectives of her in stories that I would never have known otherwise, I would be lying if

I said that it didn't dig deep within me. Even through their love, the subtraction of her from this current equation still rings true. I wish it was a lie that I could undo.

The minutes pass and I long for Ellie to join us as we all banter on about the stories we have already created and the ones that have yet to come. And then she finally does, at least in part, as I hear the front door push open and Alma walks into the middle of the floor, putting herself at the center of where we all are seated, twirling around, shouting exclamations of excitement and embracing us all one by one. It's uncanny how much she looks as her mother once did, I wouldn't be able to recognize the difference between the two of them if it weren't for the subtle inflections of myself that she holds in her face.

Even though she embraces me last, it's as if she did so on purpose because she wanted to hold onto me the longest. She is a beautiful girl, and although I feel somewhat ashamed in the fact of not knowing her well, as I've only had two previous days with her, I can tell that we are close and she admires me dearly, and for that, I am glad. When we separate I feel a violet colored shadow enter into the room from the corner of my eye as the rain outside thunders on. I pull away from Alma more completely and when I focus onto the person that has entered, it clicks back in my head that the woman who stands here and has joined us is none other than Alma's Professor. It just so happens that she is someone I've never met before here, as she introduces herself to me when I walk over to her and extend my hand. Nevertheless, as I look upon her face, I know her name before she says it.

"Hello Mr. Wood. My name is Marjorie. It's so nice to meet you, Alma has told me so much about you and the rest of your family."

"It's a pleasure to meet you as well Marjorie, but please, call me Priam."

Although it doesn't seem like she knows it, once in my life I helped Marjorie, as she practiced her ballet and tried to balance on a black metal railing before falling to the ground. On that fourth day, I came to her assistance when she was a young girl. I made her feel better, as we waited for her mother to come and pick her up. This isn't the first time our skin has touched. She told me of her dreams then, of how she wished to dance and how she wanted to succeed. Decades have passed, but I can still recognize the achievement in her eyes, I can still see the face of the seven year old girl that she once was, even though she is older now. I think back to the day when I met Marjorie before this one and how meeting her pushed my life astray.

I wonder how everything here is connected to the life that I led, in such random yet beautiful repetitions that I myself could never put together. I wonder how Robert and Charlie have fallen in love. I wonder how Marjorie and Alma dance alongside one another. I wonder how the tide will turn from here. Perhaps all of these things were always meant to be, but time and the seven sins that I had created had gotten in the way of what should have been present, what should have been right. Will there be any more connections that surprise and delight me? I wonder. And as I do, the only one I wish could come true is the most impossible one of all, that of wishing that Ellie was still here with me. She's not though, and I tell myself now as Alma introduces Marjorie to the rest of the family that I have to give up on fanciful ideas like these. I have to be happy with the love of all of those around me, all of the people in my life who are in this room now. It should be enough. They should be enough. It's not though, they aren't.

The love seeps into me and then it pours out, in faster and thicker amounts from which it came in and the light that I saw earlier this morning feels farther away than ever before. I feel myself sinking into a dark and murky pool of muck, which drags me down like quicksand. I wish to get out of it, to free myself from sinking, but I can't. Everything is perfect, but Ellie is still missing. The kiss of her lips that I felt those days I fear I will never feel again. My eyes roll back into my head. I fall to the floor.

When I open my eyes for the third time today after an extended period of darkness, more people surround me than I've ever experienced waking up to before. I can tell from where I lie that I'm propped up by some pillows on the floor.

"I guess I fainted," I say, passing it off if it is no big deal.

"Are you okay?" Alma asks, she looks worried. "Did that damn leg trip you up again?"

"Oh I'm fine dear. It's not that. I guess I just got a little overwhelmed."

"He's getting old you know, just like me," Danny quips from above.

"Neither of you two are very old if you ask me," my mother says, and this causes everyone to laugh a little bit, easing the tension that was previously in place. Charlie extends his arm out to me and pulls me up slowly.

"I'm fine, honestly. Now that everyone's here, let's prepare the meal. I think I could use some food in this belly of mine," I tell them all. "Let's eat!"

We take the platters from the kitchen and place them on the large dining room table that is already set. Before long, we take our seats and my mother suggests that we all grasp hands and say a prayer. I sit between her and my brother, directly across from me are my children, Charlie and Alma. Robert, Rebecca, Marjorie and little Estelle fill the gaps in between. The meal is a delicious one and I take pleasure in it wholeheartedly, as I shovel down the food quickly, I hope that it's sustenance will help me to remain more grounded than I've felt previously. I try to let my worries slip away, and focus on this occurrence now. We enjoy the meal.

I realize that love is all around me, coming in all different forms from every person that is here. My mother has love for us all, in her unending way, as she is the person that in one way or another has brought us here. If it weren't for her, some of us wouldn't even exist and the others wouldn't be connected to us. Danny and Rebecca love each other as husband and wife and in doing so they know that their love for one another alone is enough. It has gotten them through. When I look to Charlie and Robert, I realize now that they fact that they are gay doesn't bother me as I once proclaimed it would. When Charlie came out to me on that fifth day, the last day of his life, I rebelled against his proclamation that he was homosexual. I didn't understand it, and I didn't want to, but now I see him in a loving relationship that is displayed before me with Robert and the young girl named Estelle that they are raising together, my granddaughter. I am able to accept that love is love and it shouldn't matter what pairings of gender that it comes in. Alma and Marjorie have a different kind of love, through friendship and mentoring one another in various ways, they join together in a special kind of union that helps them learn from each other and to grow as women. Finally I recognize there is also the love that has been lost, the kind of love that I feel more than any, the kind that has continued to tug on my heartstrings all day. There is the love that I have for Ellie, the love that will never leave me.

I think of this day, my seventh way, and my mind drifts back to all of the days on this journey that have come before. I can't hold it in anymore, as it has reached the tipping point and it has become far too much for me to endure all on my own. So, I do something that I have not yet done during these second chances. I do something that I never thought I would do during this ride. I bring it up: what I'm thinking, what I've been going through and how I have gotten here. At least in certain ways, I deliver a topic to them that encases the undertaking on which I have been traveling. I look up and I ask a question aloud to all of them: "If you could relive seven days of your life and change the things you regretted the most, would you?"

I'm afraid I have done something terribly wrong when no one answers me. The silence settles for a few moments, as I feel beads of sweat forming on my forehead. I feel as if I am about to be yanked out of the seat where I sit at the table for ignoring the balance and trying to rectify it into something of my own accord. Then, they begin to answer me, one by one, the souls around the table let their voices be heard.

"There are days I wish I could change, of course there are," my mother begins from the spot next to me, "but I don't know if I would be brave enough or concise enough to pick just seven, that would be a challenge. And in coming to change the things that I had done wrong, what if I were to somehow mess up the things that I had done right?" She asks.

"I agree," Danny goes on. "There are moments in my life that I regret, but what is a life without regret after all? Can a trail of perfection even be called a life if it contains no strife whatsoever?"

"If I hadn't done what I had done in the moments up until I met your brother, I don't know if I would have ever met him," Rebecca says, addressing me directly. "Even though I was a mess during my teenage years, I don't think I could take back those mistakes rightfully. I would lose myself in doing so, I would lose who I was."

"Mistakes are the moments that make us," Charlie offers, and he leaves it at that.

"I've fucked up a lot in my life, pardon my French," Robert continues from where Charlie left off, but no one seems to mind his use of language. "But I have to admit I feel the same as the others. I don't know if I would have the courage to select a certain amount of days to change, that would be hard. Sure, there are individual regrets, but there are also those that add up in multitudes."

"I guess I'm a lot younger than the rest of you are to have a clear idea about what I would do if given the chance to relive seven days of my life, but I would be lying if I said I've never thought about it," Alma tells us as she looks deeply into my eyes, trying to connect, she searches for the reason why I asked this question in the first place. I imagine it is written on my face, but the look she gives me stays the same. She is confused by me and the way that I am currently behaving. "There are things I wish I could change, but as we all sit here Daddy, I think about all of the good that we still have, nevertheless what the bad holds, and I just, I don't know."

"And from an outsiders point of view, I think I would have to agree with the consensus. Life is a conglomerate of memories, listlessness, mishaps, misery and lumps of undecipherable loveliness. If there is no confusion contained within our days, weeks, months, and years, then there would be no reason," Marjorie admits, as if what she has said is a simplicity.

I digest what the seven of them have told me, and I think hard about the opinions offered to me that apply upon the question I have asked. Although they vary, they all have a similar kind of message for me: Yes, life is disorderly and we all have things we wish to change, but if it really comes down to it, if we're happy for the most part in what we have, would we really try to change anything at all if given the chance? It's not enough. "And what do you think she would have done?" I ask them, hoping that they will somehow know. "What would Ellie have done if given the chance to change things? Would she?"

"Daddy..." Alma trails off, swooning amongst the sadness that has befallen the air around us.

"Would she have been able to save herself from the fall that broke her back? Would she have been able to dance on into further days in the way she was meant to? Could she have saved herself? Could she have saved me?" And then I tremble, as a ghostly cold hand grasps my spinal chord and snaps it like a whip, getting me to stop what I am saying. I freeze...and then I'm reawoken.

For out of nowhere in the midst of this conversation I remember one of the most important things that happened to me on this day. I think back to how it originally happened, and how I actually am reliving seven days of my life in a way that I just discussed with everyone else, who are all experiencing my version of it now unbeknownst to them. The inception overloads and I moan a sigh of grief, realizing that I might be too late on this day yet again. "Chloe!" I shout out her name as I get up from my chair and aim to go. Everyone looks at me as if I have lost my mind completely, and perhaps I have. I can't believe it, but somehow I have forgotten that today was the day that I found the golden retriever who kept me sane in the final years of my life. Today was the day that I went out to Great Neck, regardless of whether or not I was too late to deliver her to Ellie, she found me and I found her. It was all we had to do. I realize now that I have to leave my family who sit at this table, I have to go and find the golden creature who was the last soul to love me.

A ringing begins then, interrupting my escape and instead of bolting for the door furthermore as I was on my way in doing, I let the noise go on. The buzzing is coming from a device in Marjorie's pocket. She apologizes for the disruption and moves to pull out her cell phone and answers it anyways. I stand where I am and I look to her, watching her mouth as it moves, listening to the words of the conversation from the only side I can hear.

"Hello? Yes. I'm still in Brooklyn. You're what? You're coming here? Sure I can give you the address. The family cancelled on you? You mean they don't want her? Is Max with you? Just come here and I can drive you back to Great Neck. I'll take the puppy if you need me to. We'll find her a home. I'll make sure she gets better. Tell Max it's going to be okay. How long has he been crying for? What? I'm sure she's still breathing. The address is 54 Berkeley Place. How far away are you? I'll be here. See you soon Josephine."

Marjorie's voice and the words she delivers are all I need to hear, without even being signaled a single sound of the raspy voice of the woman on the other line that I know is there. Without a doubt the woman she just talked to, her sister, is the woman that I met in Great Neck that day, today. Somehow, the connections continue and bring themselves to me. I realize as I turn back to rejoin everyone at the table that there are no such things as coincidences. Everything happens for a reason. I am about to ask questions as everyone stares at me so I can be sure of what I believe I already know, but I don't have to, as Marjorie starts to inform us all of the conversation that has just occurred before I ask anything.

"I'm sorry about that everyone, that was my sister. Her dog had puppies recently and she's in the city today because someone in Brooklyn was supposed to buy the last one she had left. I guess they just backed out of it last minute though. Her little boy is throwing a fit, and she knew that I was here visiting with you all, so I'm afraid I have to meet up with her and be on my way," she says as she gets up from her chair. Alma rises from beside her and places a hand on her shoulder.

"Wait...did you say you need a home for the puppy, because I think I have an idea." My daughter looks at me then, and she reads me for what I am. She knows.

"Yes, we do. She was hoping to sell it today. My nephew Max doesn't want to get rid of it, as he has grown rather attached to her, she was his favorite. So my sister has decided the sooner the better so that he can start adjusting to being without her."

"Well, my idea might benefit us all," Alma tells Marjorie, and then turns away from her slightly, letting her hand slide off of her shoulder as she faces me again. "Daddy, are you okay? I'm worried about you, you don't quite look like yourself. Who is Chloe? And why did you shout her name in such a way? Why did you get up like that as if you were going to leave and then return when Marjorie's telephone rang?"

"Oh Alma, don't worry about me. I've just...had a lot going on recently." Nothing could be closer to the truth, yet farther too.

"You sure you're alright honey?" My mother asks me, seemingly agreeing with the sentiment that Alms ponders on at this very moment.

"I'll be alright."

"Well, I think this might make you feel better," Alma continues. "Remember how Mom always wanted a golden retriever? Didn't she always want to name her Chloe? Just as you called out that name, Marjorie's telephone started ringing. What if this little puppy is meant to be yours? Maybe it would be good for you to have a companion with you in this house so that you weren't always on your own. Mom wouldn't want you to be alone."

The knock at the door comes sooner than expected and I have to turn away from Alma before answering her, as I hear the deep soprano voice of Josephine call out "Marjorie?" I know that this is it. They let themselves into my home and I hear Max's footsteps run over the hardwood floors and approach where I am.

His mother chases after him, but he is too quick for her. As they walk down the hallway and turn the corner they come into my view as I shift in my chair. I see that Josephine is a few feet behind him, and it's unlikely that she will catch up before he gets to me. Within his hands is a small golden retriever puppy, one that is motionless, seemingly not alive, yet still shining so bright nevertheless.

Estelle cries out in delight somewhere from behind me, and the voices of the ones I love surround me in a muffled way. Their words are unintelligible and I realize now at this moment that I won't be able to comprehend anything else that is said. It's Chloe. I know that it is, without a single doubt in my mind. Without even seeing her face directly, I can feel her presence, I sense the connection. My guide has arrived to take me home. Max comes straight towards me, as if it is his mission, as if it is the only thing he has ever been taught to do. The people around me disappear one by one, my mother first, then Danny and Rebecca, followed by Charlie, Robert, Alma and Estelle, so that none of my family members remain. Marjorie drifts away, and Josephine does too. Only Max is left, with Chloe in his arms, and then he is before me.

I reach out to touch her and as my arm extends I am reminded of that fourth day when Chloe came to visit me on my wedding day, but ran away before I was able to impress my digits against hers. I knew then, after she ran away from me that our cells couldn't collide too soon. My skin gets closer to hers now, and I know that when our senses come together, it will be done. Max disappears right before me and Chloe falls from where he was holding her and lands right into my arms which form a perfect cradle to collect her within. As soon as her soft golden fur brushes up against my arms and I grasp her tight, I feel my heart seize up, and corrupt.

I have a heart attack. Though it feels to me as if my family has disappeared, in reality they are still there and they surround me then as I fall to the floor. Chloe licks my lifeless lips when I land. I die again, at the exact same moment as Ellie passed away on this original day. The journey concludes and I am encased completely within the black. The paint won't wash away, for it covers me whole. I am dead, and the second chances that I've been given have come to an end.

On September 11th, 2001, two days after Ellie died, two thousand nine hundred and seventy seven other people were killed as a result of terrorist attacks on my city, and on America itself. The loss of life put everything in perspective and pummeled me down even deeper into depression as I watched the smoke billow up into the air that day, as it spread over New York City, clogging up the sky, refusing to leave us completely.

I remember when I first heard the news. It was a little after nine in the morning, I was standing in front of the mirror, putting my tie on, as I was getting ready to go to Ellie's house to attend the viewing that was scheduled to be held at eleven o'clock. The television was on CNN in the background, as I always had it tuned to that station every morning in my later years. When I woke up, my routine consisted of reading the New York Times while drinking a cup of coffee, with Chloe resting at my feet, as I had the television on in the background so that I could fully inform myself as to what was going on in the world from all viable angles. I hadn't paid much attention to it that morning when I first switched it on as I wanted to make sure that I looked my best for the viewing. Eventually I situated the cloth that hung from my neck just right, deeming it adequate. Thus, I left the looking glass to sit at the chair in front of the TV. What I saw on the screen astounded me.

Footage of the Twin Towers was being shown, both of them were funneling a massive amount of smoke upwards into the sky as it appeared that the buildings had either been bombed or hit by something massive that exploded upon impact. But what? And more importantly, why?

I turned the volume louder as Chloe perked up from where she laid in the corner on a little dog bed that I had bought for her the day before. She ran over to me and jumped into my lap. I petted her golden coat intently as I listened to what was being said. I tore my eyes away from the image of the tallest buildings in New York City that were in flames, and I looked down at the breaking news headline to find the what, but not the why: Two Planes Crash Into Towers of World Trade Center. It made no sense. Chloe began to whimper, as if she knew.

I, as a man of many emotions, ones that I was never very

good at holding back, began to cry. Not only for the lives that I was sure had already been lost, but for the families that would lose them. I knew what it was like to lose the person you loved the most. I began to mourn with the city...my city.

Millions of questions ran through my mind, but I couldn't answer them. I sat there glued to the television, listening to the news anchors give updates as they came in, but not really giving me any answers. After a while, I decided that I couldn't stay put any longer. I had to get out. I grabbed the red leash and I attached it to the collar around Chloe's neck. We left the apartment together and ventured out into the wild and destructive wilderness that was New York that day.

I never experienced anything like it. Everything was slowed. The city that usually moved faster than I could comprehend was stagnant and paralyzed. I could hear sirens coming from every direction, even in Brooklyn, the noises were churning at hazardous levels. I made my way towards the Brooklyn Bridge so that I could see the sight for myself. When the skyline of lower Manhattan came into view, I couldn't believe my eyes. I blinked a few times, but what I saw didn't change.

Although I had seen the exact same thing on the television only minutes earlier, actually seeing it in front of me made it all the more real, while all the more unbelievable and unbearable. Chloe struggled to pull me forward, so I followed where she led and immersed myself into the middle of a crowd of fellow New Yorkers who had gathered at Brooklyn Bridge Park. We all stood there in awe, saying nothing, only gasping, and aiming to catch our breath occasionally, as it repeatedly was knocked out of us, over and over again. This couldn't be happening, we kept telling ourselves silently...but it was.

I picked Chloe back up into my arms to stop her from struggling. And when my eyes left the ground and refocused back up into the sky as I held her, that's when it happened. That's when the South tower fell to the ground. As it began to collapse the red headed woman next to me screamed. Not some kind of stifled exclamation of remorse, no, I mean she really screamed, in horror, in exasperation, in disbelief. The shrill sound rung through my ears and reverberated within them continuously.

The rest of the people around me covered their mouths and moaned, they groaned, and they wished to turn back time. We all did. We all tried to think about what we could do, but there was nothing. All we could do was stay where we were, watch, and wait. The smoke started piling up into the sky and growing larger as if it was some kind of black fire monster that would envelop the entire city, gorging itself on the hearts and desires of every New Yorker until it's appetite was satisfied. I knew that it would spread to where we stood shortly enough, but it hadn't reached us yet.

Another half an hour or so passed and then the North tower fell too, just as the South Tower had. The smoke was creating a stain on the clear blue day and enveloping the city within a case of more dust and debris. My city was beginning to decay. The Twin Towers were gone. New York City and the millions of people who lived in it, would never be the same. I would never be the same.

The second tower had plummeted to the ground and I still stood there surrounded by strangers, all of us rooted to the spot. I held Chloe in my arms and all I could think about was one thing: thank God Ellie didn't live to see this happen. It was the only renaissance that had been achieved with her death, the only reason that I could accept that it had happened when it did, but that was the only one.

After the towers were gone from the sky and the gray cloud of destruction expanded further thus, I came to the conclusion that I had to leave where I was. I didn't know if Ellie's viewing would be cancelled, but I was close enough to her house that I decided to go in person to find out the answer. It was the only answer I would be granted on Tuesday, September 11th 2001.

New York City was on fire and I burned there that day, right along with it.

When I walked into Ellie's red stone house I noticed that it was full of people. It appeared that the viewing was still going to happen, regardless of what was occurring in the city. Apparently everyone had collectedly decided that just because there was more death in the air, that didn't mean that we were going to let it triumph over remembering the life of someone who was so dear to us. In mourning Ellie, in missing her, and in paying tribute to the life that she had lived, we all together did the same for the other citizens in New York who died that day. It was a celebration of life, and a hope for the future where things would be better.

I knew mostly everyone in attendance, and so many people

gave me their sympathies. It was like a replay of my mother's funeral all over again, except this time I was actually able to comprehend what was going on, even though I couldn't say the same for what was going on in the rest of the city as we said goodbye to Ellie once and for all.

Tears didn't serve me any longer that day, as their point seemed meaningless. The loss I felt was too great to take any form. It was something that the world would never be able to understand. New York City and I were the same on September 11th 2001, as we both came to terms with losing what was most important to us. Our wills were broken, and our love was damaged, but we would never give up.

Other people cried and not only did their eyes form tears, but they wept openly and hysterically. I kept Chloe in my arms the entire time the viewing went on, as I figured that Ellie would have wanted me to, and in doing so I was able to elicit a few smiles into faces which were previously heartbroken. I didn't want to let her go.

After the viewing, I went back to my apartment and watched the news for the rest of the day. As the hours droned on, things still didn't make sense, and when the darkness came, overwhelming our city entirely, I wondered what the morning would bring. I fell asleep that night with Chloe snuggled up in the crook of my arm, and I thought to myself, maybe some things can never be explained.

The next day, the ash in the sky still remained and although it frightened me, I didn't let it intimidate me. I went for a walk with Chloe, through every neighborhood in the city. From Brooklyn, to Manhattan, to the Bronx, to Queens and finally to Staten Island. I wanted to get a perspective of how the entire city was feeling as a whole and that was the only way I could think how to do it.

There were signs everywhere, on every street, on every corner, on every telephone pole and storefront. Everyone was looking for someone, hoping and praying that their loved ones would be okay. They were stuck in limbo, unsure of who was alive...and who wasn't. Random collections of flowers accumulated in different places to honor those who had been lost in the terrible tragedy. And even though Ellie had died two days before the rest of these people had, I still bought a bouquet of flowers in Brooklyn and set it on the pile with the rest of the bright colored bundles before I called it a day.

She may not have died beside them, but she had still died with them. To me, Ellie was New York City. Just as the Twin Towers had represented what the city meant to so many people, Ellie represented the metropolis for me. Without them, it would have a completely different identity. I had lived day to day without Ellie for many years, but knowing that she no longer existed in the world whatsoever made me feel incomplete. A part of my skyline had been torn down, my heart had been impacted by a plane causing it to flame and crumble. The focal point of my city, the central piece of my life had been destroyed without reason.

By the end of the day, Chloe was exhausted from walking everywhere with me, so I took off her red leash and put it in my pocket, carrying her the rest of the way home. When I finally got back to my neighborhood I was drained too, and rightfully so. As I reached the steps in front of my apartment building, I realized that today was the first time I had ever been to all five neighborhoods in one day. It had been almost fourteen hours since I had left my building that morning, but I had achieved what I had wanted to nevertheless. I had been to all five boroughs, I had seen things I had never seen before, and I met people that I never thought I would.

When I sat down on those cement stairs with Chloe at my feet, it was then that it hit me. Ellie was no longer alive, but I, I still was, and even with a broken heart that was beyond repair, there were still many things I had left to live for. If not for someone, than for myself. On that day, the one that came directly following the aftermath of 9/11, I thanked intervention for preventing me from killing myself, for it was on those steps of stone that I realized I could go on without her if I had to, and I did.

Even without the Twin Towers, the five boroughs still made up New York City and that's the way it would always be. Some things could never be taken away. Ellie was gone, but I still held onto her memory, for the rest of my days and more.

I took Chloe everywhere with me, literally everywhere, and during the first few months that I had her it wasn't much of an issue in doing so. After all, everyone loves puppies. Strangers often came up to pet her and speak to her in baby voices. It was a way for me to interact with others too, a chance to talk to my kind again, even though the conversations never lasted very long.

After Ellie was buried in Alden, next to the rest of my family who had passed before her, I was alone, utterly and completely, except for the little golden gal that accompanied me everywhere that I went. Eventually though, it started to become a problem.

I didn't just take Chloe with me on walks outside, and in the subways and taxis I rode, I took her into the restaurants, stores and city buildings that I entered too. There was no place I went that she didn't go with me. Although I got strange looks from people often when she sat with me underneath my table when I went out to eat, no one ever asked for me to take her outside...until one day.

It was early in March of 2002 and Chloe was no longer a puppy. She wasn't yet full grown, but she was big enough that she had lost a sense of her youth and her undying cuteness as she had begun to transform into the frame of her adult self. I walked into a diner not far from my house where I always got breakfast on Sundays. I sat at my usual table and had her lay down underneath me. I had become a man of habit. George, the owner of the diner who had become a joyful acquaintance of mine came over to take my order as he always did.

"The usual today Priam?"

"You got it. Scrambled eggs, three sausage links, French toast and a cup of coffee, black."

"Coming right up."

I pulled the New York Times out of my bag and began to peruse its pages. Chloe took a deep breath beneath me, huffing and slightly puffing out the air. Ten minutes or so passed and then George came back, delivering my food to the table. I thanked him and he asked me if there was anything else I needed. I told him no, but he did not leave.

"George?" I had asked, inquisitively.

"Priam. I hate to say this, but I think we have a problem."

I looked up from my heaping plate into his gray eyes and tried to figure out what the issue was, but I couldn't see it. "Did something go wrong with the order? I don't mind if it did, it looks fine to me."

"No, no, it's not that. It's just- I'm afraid you can't keep bringing your dog in here. I've gotten some complaints from my other customers. She's just gotten so much bigger. You know, she's not a puppy anymore. I know she's your best friend and all, but you can't bring her in here anymore. I'm sorry, I could get in trouble with the Health Department."

I suppose I was naïve in thinking that this conversation would never happen. The only thing was, it hadn't yet up until that point, so I had just pretended like it was never going to. "Okay George, I won't bring her in here again. I guess I'll just have to figure out something else. I don't want to have to leave her alone. Maybe I just won't go out anymore."

"Don't say that. I'm sure you can make it work somehow."

"Thanks George," I said and I turned away from his face, returning my focus to my breakfast. I looked down at Chloe as he walked away. Her amber colored eyes pierced right through me. She whimpered. She knew. I picked up a piece of sausage and lowered it down to her mouth. She gobbled it up.

I never trained Chloe, but she was very smart and somehow knew when I wanted her to sit, to lay down, and to come over to me. She even went the bathroom where and when I wanted her to, without me ever having to command or teach her how. It didn't make much sense, but I just assumed that she was intelligent and I never really questioned it. Due to how clever of a dog she was, I came up with the solution to my problem of taking her along with me everywhere I went. It was a simple fix really, although perhaps a morally ambiguous one. Chloe became my guide.

One beautiful spring day while walking with her along the city streets on our way to Central Park, I came across a kiosk that was selling sunglasses. I had lost the last pair I had and was in desperate need of a new one. The sun was showing itself more frequently then and I needed to shield my sensitive eyes.

I bought a pair of thick black ones, the kind that are rectangular in shape, covering the eyes completely in the front and on all sides, not letting a single speck of light get in. When I put them on and looked into the little mirror hanging there, what I saw staring back at me made me chuckle. For the reflection of myself made it seem as if I was a blind man, covering his eyes so that no one would look at his vessels which could not see, attached to his golden retriever guide dog who helped him get where he was going. That was it. Bingo.

Chloe became my guide dog that day, and for everyday that followed for the rest of her life. From the spring of 2002 and on, whenever I went out in public, I pretended to be blind.

I knew from the beginning that it was wrong and that I was probably breaking some law and could be fined heavily for it, but the truth was I didn't give a shit about the risks or the consequences. I was alone in my life. She was all I had. I got away with it. Once I had those sunglasses on my face, and I purchased the proper kind of harness for Chloe to connect to me and make the completion of it all the more convincing, no one ever questioned it. I didn't want to be alone, and with Chloe joining me everywhere I went, I never was. In my scheme, I freed up a part of my life. For up until I devised the plan of making Chloe my guide, there was one kind of place that I had never even bothered trying to take her to: art museums.

Through my many experiences with the art community, I knew better than to try and take an animal into the spaces and places where valuable works of art were on display. There was no way they would have had it, no matter how cute she was, there was no way they would have let me. However, when I put those sunglasses on and attached Chloe as an extension of my being, I eventually decided to give it a try...and it worked.

I still wouldn't let myself paint. I hadn't created an original piece since that day Charlie had killed himself. As I continued to tell myself, I was not worthy of the liberation the art of creation would grant me. So instead, I went to enjoy the works of others during the final years of my life. Together, Chloe and I went to a different art gallery in the city every week. It wasn't always on the same day of the seven days that stretched before me, but the experience did always happen at least once during the seven layers that built themselves up. I never failed to attend, or to see something new. I am sure I looked ridiculous and the people who saw me go into those galleries in the way that I did were most likely befuddled to say the least. For what in the hell was the point of a blind man going into a gallery when he couldn't even see?

It's kind of funny how people feel towards strangers. Never wanting to question those that are less fortunate than them. Trying not to stare at their deformities or wrongness, even though in not trying to look they just end up looking more. In my case, the people who were looking at me were under the assumption that I couldn't see them, but in fact I could. I saw them, I saw them all.

As the years went on technology started to advance and

most galleries began to have audio guides which you could listen to while looking at the paintings. So to help ease the confusion of the other art patrons, I began to listen to the voices telling me about the works when I looked at them, because to everyone else who saw me, at least this made a little more sense. They felt bad that I couldn't see the artwork, but they didn't question my request of knowledge of what I could listen to. They pitied me for not having the eyesight that they had, and they often looked at Chloe longingly, wondering if she was my only friend. They were right, about Chloe anyways, because she was it. Yet, they were wrong in the other, because even though it appeared to them as if I was a blind man, in reality I could see. And I saw. I saw what was before me and what had passed me, but I didn't know what was yet to come. The days outnumbered my ways, but I still went on.

The years faded past me all the same. There was no colorful dignation in my days, nor was there any true sense of release. Chloe continued to get older as I did too. She became my trusted accomplice, my final friend. Eventually I pretty much stopped talking to people altogether. I lost myself within myself and never was found again. There wasn't anything remarkable that happened to me between the years of 2003 and 2010, at least nothing that I cared enough to imprint deeply within my mind. I had Chloe and she had me. I experienced art, and I wandered around my city. I witnessed the world happening on and on as I pondered what it meant. All of the people I loved were gone. It was during these final years that I would constantly think of my regrets as they dug into me, breaking my skin and pouring my blood out as a sacrifice. I wished to change what I had done wrong, but it was already over and done with. There was no going back.

In the summer of 2011, right after I turned seventy years old, I started to become very ill. It was strange however, because I reacted in an unusual way to the sickness that was so obviously spreading through me. I welcomed it. I didn't want to be alive. It's not that I necessarily wanted to die, a fact that had become obvious when I didn't have the audacity or brashness to kill myself, but I had realized that I wouldn't mind meeting the stillness that I figured death would grant me. I hadn't given up completely, but I didn't care too much for going on.

When I started to get sick, Chloe became noticeably weaker

too. It was as if our bodies were in synch, so attuned to one another that our souls decided we would perish at the same time. She was getting old as well, ten years for a dog is nowhere near ancient, but it was up there nevertheless. I planned on taking her to the vet to get her checked out, but every time I tried to take her to go, she would vehemently react in an unusual way, refusing to leave the apartment or walk anywhere at all. So I, in my weak state, gave up on trying to make her go. I therefore decided I wouldn't go to the doctor either. Except, that plan didn't really work out for me.

September 9th 2011 came around, and when it did, it meant a lot to me. It was the tenth anniversary of Ellie's death and the tenth year that I had Chloe with me. I felt both a warmth and an unrelenting chill. It was also the day I found out that I had cancer.

Chloe and I left the apartment, with my sunglasses on my face and her harness attached to my hand. I don't know if it was a mistake or I had somehow just actually becoming partially blind in pretending to be so for so long, but without even realizing it, I let Chloe lead me right into the last place that I wanted to be: the hospital.

It was as if I had momentarily lost all of my senses, becoming blacked out by the shades that covered my eyes and because of this, I had let my golden retriever trick me. She was my guide after all, but I never wanted her to lead me there. Yet when I got there, I decided I should maybe just get myself checked out after all. There was no use in denying it any longer. They did some tests, they got results and they told me the tale that the machinery had spun for me.

"I'm sorry to tell you this Mr. Wood, but you have pancreatic cancer. It's stage four. There isn't much we can do at this point, but we can try. I wish you would have come to me sooner. Why did you wait so long?" The young man of around thirty asked me. He was my doctor, at least that day anyways.

"I don't have anything left to wait around here for. I guess that's why."

Chloe got up from the ground beside me where she was sitting and pulled herself away from my grip. She was angry. This is not what she wanted. The doctor patted her on the head and after he did so she calmed down and returned to me. I had long ago gotten used to the way that Chloe could read the reactions of what was going on from the people around her. I never once thought it was strange, it was just how she was.

"I see," he said. "Well, we can start treatment immediately and see what we can do for you."

"No thanks. I don't want treatment. What's done is done."

I got up from my seat, shook his hand, thanked him again and went on my way. The young doctor stood there flabbergasted, surprised to think that I didn't want to try at all to save myself. He had yet to make the kind of mistakes that I had. He had yet to yearn for the people that he would one day lose. He wasn't anything like me, at least not yet.

That night I allowed myself to paint again. It was the only thing I could do. In finding out that I would be dying soon, I released myself from the chains that I had once created. It was time.

Directly after leaving the hospital I went to the art supply store and bought a large white canvas, twenty-five different colors of paint and seven brushes. I took it all back to my apartment and began to search for my easel, which I eventually found packed away in the back of a closet. It hadn't been touched in ages. I set it up in the living room, placing the white canvas on top of the wooden frame and legs that lifted it up. I prepared things in an organized way, unlike how I usually did. The mess of my meticulousness had melted away. Chloe laid down beside me and watched me paint.

The scene that unfolded before me was a landscape with two central figures. I painted the Brooklyn Bridge, gray and vast, its stone unfolding across the river, connecting my heart and my mind together. I focused my brush on detailing the structure of it and highlighting the walkway which I had crossed so many times before. In the background, I painted an orange sky, one that was mixed with blues of a setting sun, letting the day become undone. I focused on the light and thought about all of the different times that it had set on me, darkening my days and bringing me into the night. And on that walkway I painted those two figures, taking the most amount of time to create them. On the left, in a white dress, with chestnut brown hair down, long, and flowing, with a smatter of rogue redding her lips, I painted Ellie, dancing free, just like on the day that I had met her, and on all of the days that followed. In my painting she danced. To the right, a little farther back on the walkway I painted Chloe, golden and glowing, running straight towards where I sat, as if she would be able to leap right off of the canvas once she reached the edge. I created a certain sort of synchronic symphony, and when I was done with it, once I put the paintbrush down, I backed up from it and admired what I had created. I took it all in. It was my masterpiece.

2012 came, and when we greeted it, Chloe and I both knew that it would be the last new year that we would ever meet. We were both so weak, so frail, so unnervingly unaffected, but in reality, we were both dying a little more each and every day.

The last museum we ever went to was the Met, and the last painting I ever really looked at was a print created by a famous artist that I had once met: Andy Warhol's Marilyn Monroe. I stood in front of it for over an hour, with Chloe by my side and all the while, all I could think when I looked at the face of one of the most famous women who ever lived was this: What had happened to her?

I tried to compare the tragedy of her life to my own, but then I realized it was useless. We all have our own loneliness, it's all different. I left the museum that day, covered in shade, with Chloe tugging me along, with me tugging her, filled with more questions than when I had arrived, and none of the answers in sight.

I was extremely sick and Chloe was worse. Come January 15th, I couldn't even get Chloe to get up, not at all. She stopped walking, and she stopped eating. I knew that she wouldn't be with me much longer.

She died on January 17th 2012 and I cried harder than I ever had before, the last soul to ever love me was gone. That night, I used all of the final strength I had to take her body to where I wished her to always lay. In the dark, I took Chloe and I buried her right at the spot in Central Park where I first laid eyes on Ellie Donahue. I knew I could get in trouble for doing it, but no one saw me and I was successful at making a hole to contain her within, covering her with the earth that had helped to create her. I said goodbye to her, to that spot, and to everything.

Right before midnight, before the eighteenth day of January could come to meet me, I checked myself into a home for the elderly and I started to prepare myself for my death, which was surely going to come. I remained there for seven nights. I lived there for seven days and then I died.

I died, on January 24th, 2012.

There is blackness, but then it decides to let me go, entrenching me with what soon is pure white and I feel it's desire cover me whole. The white abyss has returned again, but this time, it is different. The vastness it had previously contained has changed. For although I cannot see anything but emptiness, it is as if there are invisible corners on all four sides, holding me in this specific place yet begging me to wish for something more all the while. The blank canvas on which my body lies is quite the contradiction. As I look down at my digits and my appendages, I realize that I am seventy years old again, encased within the body from which I originally passed away. I am back to where I started; yet I don't feel the same. This time, I have the past two weeks with me, or what felt like as much anyways. I recall the back and forth pattern of my seven days alternating between how they originally happened and how I organized them into second chances of what I wished them to be.

I get up from where I sit, putting my two feet in front of me and pushing my palms off of the surface on which I rest, motioning my body forward so that I can stand. I feel crooked and the pain that was with me in my last moments on both accounts reverberates within me now. I begin to walk forward, into the nothingness. It isn't long however until something appears: the seven painted frames.

They come into focus before me, all seven of them in a straight horizontal line just as they were the first time I ever saw them. The colors yellow, green, blue, indigo, violet, red, and orange are brighter than I ever thought they could be. I continue to walk on, and when I come up to where they rest, upon the nothingness of white that they contrast sharply against, I see that within their painted wooden frames images of each of my seven days flash past. This time though, there aren't just pictures of how they originally happened. No, now the seven frames contain images and visuals of both versions of my seven days, the original ways and my second chances. They go back and forth between their differences, forming their own kind of charade on how the events really went. As I look at them, the various versions jumble up within my mind and I try to recognize how it was and what really happened. I touch the yellow frame, of my first day, and when my finger collides with the images of what transpired there, the slate bares itself blank, washing away the day and all that happened on it. I walk away, touching the others in similar ways, each one becoming barren and white, letting the moving pictures that were held slip away suddenly. I reach the end of the line, and look back to my left at the seven painted frames, all which now rest upon the emptiness, vacant.

I move my feet backwards, shuffling away from where the colored rectangular outlines hang. They start to bleed, not crimson pools of rich liquid, but instead they all separately melt, their individual colors spreading down and then ramping up the speed in which they strain themselves further. All seven colors coalesce and coagulate, creating a colorful and hectic chaos that is ever so quickly covering every inch of the white abyss and making a palette of pungent and painted precipitation encompass the reality where I reside. The white is outnumbered as the colors overcome the emptiness that was all that existed just moments before. The liveliness and personification of my days have released themselves upon the desolation that was here, as the temperament of the seven frames overcome the overbearing similarity of the nothingness. The blank canvas where I have returned to has decided to paint itself, with the help of my touch, with the imprint of my life, which I both followed and led.

There is a ruffled noise that comes from behind me and as I turn, a voice emanates from the being that is there. "Hello Priam."

It's Chloe. She sits on top of the colors that have taken over and when I hear her voice it rings inside of me in a different way. I haven't seen her speak, and even if I were to, I know her mouth won't move, but it's the actuality of remembering how her voice came to me from before when I first died that tingles deep down within me now.

"Hello Chloe. I feel, as if I saw you so recently, yet so long ago."

"That's understandable, the journey you went on was by no means an easy one, but it was what you wanted. Wasn't it?"

"I suppose you could say so," I tell her. "Even though it didn't end up the way I had hoped. Even when things went right, they still went wrong. I fixed some of the things that I had longed for, but I lost just as much. My mother lived longer than I did, and I had the relationship I always wanted with Danny. I didn't give up on my art dreams, I married Ellie and we had a beautiful wedding day. Charlie never committed suicide and knew that I loved him. Alma lived a full life and I took her and her brother to London with me. Yet even with all of that, it doesn't feel as if it was enough, because of what I did, and what I changed during my second chances, I somehow made it so that Ellie died far sooner than she was supposed to. I couldn't save her. In fact, it's because of me that she died in that car accident. I killed her. And I have to admit, as I stand here now in this jumbled mess of colors that were previously white, I feel as empty as I ever have. I feel as lost and confused as when this journey started when I first met you here. It all ended without Ellie regardless of what I did. Every change I made through all of the second chances I was given still didn't matter, because although the ways I died in each way differed, I might as well have been alone on that seventh day, because she wasn't there. She wasn't there."

I take a deep breath as the words have escaped me one after the other without much oxygen pushing through. Chloe cocks her head to the side and stares into me. Thinking about all that has gone on from the day that I died alone and to how I got to where I am now is a lot to handle, let alone discussing it out loud for the first time. The repetition of it might as well be random, but I know that it isn't. The way things went has to be for a reason.

"What have you learned from it all?" She asks me then.

I don't know what to say. What can I say? Was there anything to learn? The two different sets of my seven days couldn't have been more different, and while I compare them in my mind I know there are hundreds of lessons that I could repeat back to Chloe, but I don't think that is what she really wants me to do. She knows, she has to. Rather, I think what she desires me to do is to look inside myself, and to search for the purpose of it all; life, love, longing, and how one goes on from here.

I do recall something in particular though, something that I wished I could have had answered while it was still going on and it applies directly to her. As my guide, I feel I have a right to ask Chloe as many questions as I can think of, even if she doesn't necessarily have the answers.

"You were there. You were there Chloe, on every day. Weren't you? I saw a golden retriever in some way on every day that I was able to relive and in some instances I know it was you, while in others, I only caught passing glimpses. It was you though...wasn't it?"

Her amber colored eyes blink heavily, her gaze slowing down as she looks up at me. "Yes, it was me Priam. I did indeed make an appearance on each of your days and I did so with reason."

"What reason could that be?" I ask, raising my voice. "Half of the times you showed up you ruined things! You ran across the street when Danny and I were driving to New York and put us hours behind! You chased the black lab so that it ran right into the ladder that Ellie was perched upon, knocking her down and breaking her back. And you were there moments before she died on that fifth day, but you did nothing to stop that truck from colliding with us! You ruined so many things for me Chloe. Why did you do it? I thought you loved me. We were friends, those last years of my life. You were there for me when I had no one else."

"I wasn't trying to destroy your plans Priam. I showed up on each of your days for a reason, and as a matter of fact, it was to help you and to teach you a lesson," she tells me. Her voice isn't stern, but it is of a more serious tone than it has been previously. I look at her mouth as the words come, but again it doesn't move. The voice only emanates out of her, in a mystical way that I cannot completely comprehend.

"What in the hell kind of lesson was breaking my wife's back going to teach me? What kind of lesson is that? You let her die! You might as well have killed her directly the second time around!" I am yelling now, raising my voice and shaking my hand in her face, my right pointer finger scolding her. I am angry and I don't understand why Chloe has done what she has. It makes no sense to me.

"Priam, it may be hard for you to understand, but everything I did on each of your days was to help you. It was the chaos of reasoning that guided me. The reason why things occurred in the ways that they did may not easily compute for you, but I can explain them to you one by one, if I need to do so."

"Please." The one word is all I offer.

"Of course. You see, everything happens for a reason, even during your second chances. Even though some of it may seem wrong at first, I can help you to understand that all of it happened because it was necessary.

"If I hadn't chased that rabbit outside of your classroom window when you were thirteen to make you notice me, you would have eventually sent a spit wad back in Jimmy's direction only to get caught by your teacher, granting you detention for the following week. You would have been so upset that you never would have went to the old Miller place at all. Your mother would have stayed home all night with you, never going to the grocery store. She would leave the house though, one week later in the interim, to pick you up from detention. She would have gotten into a car accident on the way and died, never to see you again.

"If I hadn't run in front of the Victoria while you and Danny were driving to New York, the car would never have had it's issues and you wouldn't have stopped and visited at the diner for hours like you did. You never would have mentioned moving to New York together and he never would have left Alden. Your relationship wouldn't have blossomed further and you never would have become the kind of brothers that you always wanted to be.

"If I hadn't chased that Labrador and caused it to knock the ladder over, it is true that no one's back would have been broken, but you never would have moved back to Alden either. Your wife wouldn't have agreed to move back to raise your children like you had done so originally because her dance career would still be ongoing. She would have convinced you that since you too were still working on your art, that it made no sense to leave the city and you never would have gotten away, returning to the small town that created you.

"If I hadn't showed up on your wedding day, you wouldn't have remembered to remain calm in the way that you did, and you wouldn't have been able to get her to dance with such elegance and grace.

"If I hadn't ran alongside the road right before the car crash that killed her, it is true that she wouldn't have died, but then, your second chances would never have become what they were always meant to be."

I want to interrupt her then more than any point previously, and when I motion to do so, right as the words are on the ends of my vocal chords and ready to strike out the sound, she lifts up her paw and touches the air with it, letting me know that she is not done.

"If I hadn't passed you and your children by at the Prince Albert Memorial in London, where you sat at the spot and basically ignored me, you never would have believed fully without a doubt that I was showing up every single one of your days deliberately. You wouldn't believe me now as I speak to you that I was and always have been, watching out for you.

"And finally, if I wouldn't have come back to you as the little puppy that you met me as on your last day, it never would have come full circle and the parts of your life that you always questioned wouldn't have made as much sense to you as they do now. If I hadn't come back to you, even when you had forgotten about me, you never would have believed what is about to happen now."

I let the silence stay in the stillness for just one second, and then I burst forth out into it. "But how Chloe? How were you there in all of those ways? How could you simply appear and intercede on my second chances and make that much of a difference? How can I believe it? Why do you so freely admit that your meddling is what resulted in Ellie's death? How can you sit there and look at me when you know your actions have caused me so much heartache?"

"Because Priam, I am not what you think and I am not what you see. Instead, I am a being that you have always known, just not what you recognized me as. I am not a normal dog, I am not a golden retriever, and I never was. Not in your life, not during your second chances, not at all...not ever."

"What the hell do you mean you're not a dog? You most certainly are!" I shout at her, my voice quivering. " You are exactly what you appear to be, you are just as you exist before me. Chloe, this is what you have always been."

"Oh Priam, some things are not what they may seem."

Chloe lifts up her right paw into the air and follows it with her left one. She haunches her weight back so that her golden coat shifts and shimmers up against the light that is reflected off of the colors that bounce about the room. Her back legs extend and begin to push her body up, and then something happens. She starts to change, slowly at first, but then faster and faster. Her hair begins to recede and her body begins to lengthen, growing up towards the sky. Her face shifts and slackens, relaxing into what can only be classified as human. Her paws transform into feet and hands, her fur lessens and then disappears completely to become silken soft skin. Her snout leaves her face and transforms into a button nose; her mouth and teeth shift so that they become encased in a pair of red ruby lips. Her eyes slide from amber colored orbs into the deepest of sapphire blues. Her shoulders straighten and then she is there before me, utterly altered into another being, yet as I look at her before me, it all makes sense. She is the same.

"Ellie!" I scream, as I reach out and embrace her naked body, pulling her into me. The second clicks and then she wraps her arms around me too, taking me in. I begin to weep and I bury my head into her shoulder as the tears flow. I am not aware of anything except for the realization that Ellie has been with me all along, in one way or another, watching over me and protecting me from myself.

After a few more moments pass, I release her from my grasp and take in the sight of her. She appears to be twenty-seven years old, at the height of her beauty. Her fingers snap and crack against the colors that spray across the space where we stand. A white silken dress falls down out of thin air and lands onto her outstretched arm. She places her feet into it and pulls it up and on. She then turns around so that I can zip it up for her. When I have taken the zipper to the middle of her back I rub my fingers up against the small of it. The white fabric of the garment snugly cinches her as she spins around to face me once again.

"There is so much to explain," she tells me, speaking for the first time since the transformation occurred, and when she does, I realize that Chloe's voice was hers all along. Even from the initial instant in the white abyss, Chloe and Ellie were always one and the same. I was too blind to notice, to ingrained within reality to think of things as how they could be and not how they should. Some things are not what they may seem.

Ellie walks away and beckons for me to join her. We walk a hundred feet or so into the colors that surround us, and eventually she finds a spot that she deems suitable for us. She snaps her fingers again and this time, two wooden chairs appear out of thin air, one next to the other. She takes a seat and motions for me to do the same.

"What is this place Ellie? Where are we?"

"All in due time Priam. First, I have to tell you how I happened to meet you here. I have to tell you how I became Chloe."

"I don't understand how that is possible. I mean, I suppose you making your appearances on each of my days to intercede and cause things to go my way, or whatever you decided needed to occur can make some sort of sense, seeing as this journey was never anything ordinary. But, do you mean to tell me that you were always Chloe? Even during my life, from the time that I purchased the puppy until the day she died?"

She reaches out and takes my hand, pulling it into her lap and tracing circles around the top of it with her fingertips, soothing me with her touch and calming me.

"Yes Priam. I was always Chloe. My soul was contained within the body of the golden retriever from September 9th 2001, until I left you, seven days before you died. That's not to say I was reborn as a dog. No, it wasn't reincarnation or anything like that. Instead it was something more similar to your story, yet all the while more complicated.

"Please Ellie, make me understand. It's all I desire."

"I will try my best Priam," she says, holding my hand within hers as she begins to tell her tale, the story of her existence in this afterlife and how it so intricately connects with mine. "Just as you were granted the wish that your heart desired the most when you died, so was I. You longed to make changes to your life, to prove that you loved me and the rest of your family wholeheartedly. You wished for days that you could relive so that things would go right, or rather, you wished to have second chances so that you could feel as if you had lived your life as a good man. My wish, or rather the first part of it, was for you to no longer be alone. I never wanted to get a divorce Priam, I never wanted to live without you, but during my life and from all of the confusion that commenced from it, I felt that I could no longer be with you. It was my mistake to leave you, and while I longed for you endlessly those final years of my life, I never made it known to you, and then it was too late.

"I died before I was ever able to tell you that I had been wrong. I left my life wishing things had been different, in not too unlike a manner that you did. However, while you felt your entire life had been messed up, what I was concerned about most was my relationship with you. I wished to make it right, and the only way I could think to do so, was to hope that somehow I could be with you during the final days of your life, to protect you, and to guide you through. When I died, I came to the white abyss just as you had, and I was greeted by our son, Charlie. Just as I explained to you as Chloe, he explained to me what this place was and what would happen from here. I tried to ask him questions, but he was unable to answer most of them. He told me that I would learn more eventually, and ultimately I did, but it took time.

"I wished to be with you back on Earth. I wished to be together with you once again. I told Charlie, as the last soul to pass who had loved me, that all I wanted was to be your guide throughout the final days of your life. Of course, there was no way I could be brought back to life and live with you as myself. It wouldn't be possible, for even in the afterlife there are rules as to how things can happen, as you know. Charlie had come up with a way though, as the actions you were carrying through on the day that I died had left us an opening.

"Do you remember how Little Star was sick, the puppy that you purchased out on Great Neck that day? From the first moment you heard about her, you were informed that she was not doing well, and had been acting strange recently. The truth is, Little Star was dying, and she was never going to be alive when you touched her. Even without our meddling, her soul would never have met yours. When you saw her for the first time, her spirit was weakening and drifting away. She died the second before your flesh touched hers and in that second my soul was sent into her body, taking over the vessel of the golden retriever's being and becoming an entity all anew: Chloe.

"All the while, I died on Earth at the exact same time that Little Star did. Our souls left the planet simultaneously. You see, time here is not of the same accord as time is on Earth. Even though Little Star and I died at the same time, and my soul was sent back to the dog's body in a flash right before your eyes, I still had time here to meet Charlie once again, to tell him my greatest wish and be informed of what would occur before anything down there could happen.

"I was Chloe. I was with you from 2001 until 2012. Yet, I feel I should also tell you that I was Chloe on one other day too during the course of our lives, and that day was during the summer of 1990. Before I left the white abyss and said goodbye to Charlie prior to when my journey with you would begin again, I added one final request: to be present somehow in the moments before he committed suicide. I wanted to appear to him in some form as a beacon of hope. I knew that I couldn't change what had happened and how he had chosen to give up, but I wanted to appear as a symbol of everlasting life to him. So, in this ever expanding second that so much occurred in, before I came back to you as that puppy, I first roamed the green acres outside of our house on Elm Street in the year 1990. I ran outside of the window that our son sat in front of, writing his suicide note. I was the golden retriever he saw, the spirit he spoke of that appeared so free. I gave him something to yearn for and in doing so, in some way, things became complete.

"Now I must admit, I was surprised you never noticed how intelligent of an animal you had at your side. I mean sure, I could tell that you knew I was a different kind of dog, but you never fathomed anything was amiss and how could you? During life we don't think of the impossible, it is only after our life is over that we yearn for what we previously deemed absurd. My senses were heightened at your side and although I could not speak to you or let you know that I was beside you, it was enough to be with you for me. I was both impressed and amused how you never let me leave your side, even devising a way to get around the regular rules of society to make sure that I accompanied you everywhere you went. I was your guide, and I couldn't have been more fulfilled.

"Sure, of course I wished I was still alive in human form with you, and I longed to go back and change things so that I never left you, but I had to settle for the immensity that I had already been given. I couldn't stay until the moment you left your life though, as I knew I had to return and be informed of it all just as you are being informed in a similar way now. So, my lease was up and I left you in life seven days before you died. The same amount of days which you would be given to relive. It was planned that way. When I died again as Chloe, I returned here and met with Charlie once again. We talked for a great long while, mostly though, I listened to him and it all started to make sense. I realized that things have to go wrong sometimes, in order for them to become right.

"He told me that when you died, I would be your guide and at first I was ecstatic to be reunited with you in the way that I always wanted, but it wasn't so simple. For although I originally imagined greeting you in this body, as the woman that you had always known, he informed me of the rules. I had to be present as the last soul that loved you, and to you, that was Chloe, for you were unaware when you first got here, when you first died, that Chloe and myself were one and the same. You didn't know that I was with you that last decade of your life. So, I greeted you as a golden retriever, and I was unable to tell you who I really was. I knew that I had to wait until your second chances were done to reveal myself. However, even then as I explained the process to you, I knew that I would be appearing on each of your second days, interrupting and inflicting myself upon what you were changing so that things would occur in the ways they needed to.

"Although so much of this can be explained, there are still so many parts that can't. I know I've talked an awful lot now, but it was necessary in order for you to have the complete story of how things happened and why they did. I don't know if it makes more sense to you now, but I imagine that these details have enlightened you further. Do you feel you understand better Priam?"

I look at her more deeply then through my seventy year old eyes and I reflect upon the beauty that is looking back at me. She has said a lot and explained a great deal. Although I do understand it in some ways, there are a large amount of complexities contained within what she has just described to me. Chloe and Ellie were one and the same all along, I get that much, and I suppose it makes sense to me. For just as I was granted the wish I desired most, she too had a desire to fulfill, and that was to be with me throughout the end of my life. I'm sure when she requested this wish she never imagined it would be in the way that it actually occurred, but then again when I first asked to be granted a second chance at life, I never thought I would be given seven days that would bounce back and forth against the real days of my life that I would have to relive. I say nothing. I do not know what to say. I rub the underside of her youthful hand that still rests up against my liver spotted one, her soft palm impacts my coarse digits and smoothes them over. I wonder why I still exist here as an old man, appearing the way that I died, while she is at the peak of her loveliness.

"What is the lesson of it all Priam? What have you learned from your second chances and from what I have told you?" She asks me, begging me to deliver something. "Should we change things?"

"I don't know Ellie," I sigh. "There are moments from this journey that I am grateful for. I had so many lovely memories that were added into my mind that I never would have experienced otherwise. I was able to see my mother in all different stages of her life and bond with her in ways I never dreamed possible. I was able to have the kind of relationship I always wanted with my brother, and I saw him fall in love, in the same kind of way that you and I did. I was given the chance to see what my life would have been like if I never would have given up on my art dreams, and I was able to give you the kind of wedding that you deserved. Charlie and Alma lived longer than either of them had during our lives and they gained happiness I was only ever able to think of previously. So in those respects, I am happy that I relived my seven days and made these changes. There were many wonderful moments and memories I gained from them. All the while however, it was lessened drastically when you left me once again. You died Ellie, you left my side earlier than you ever had before when everything else was so perfect. You died on that fifth day, and as I lost a part of my heart, I also lost a part of myself, my leg left my body and I became less of a whole. I have to wonder now why you did that to me, as if what I gathered is correct, you were Chloe during my life, but you also showed up as her during my second one too. If that is the case, then you yourself caused your own demise on that fifth day...didn't you?"

"I suppose you could say so in certain words," she tells me and when those words reach me, I release her hand. This is something that I cannot understand.

"Why would you do such a thing? It's as if you in some way killed yourself, and took yourself away from me in such a disastrous and painful way. I never thought I would feel such emptiness and remorse again as I had when you died during my life, but that fifth day, when that truck crashed into us, and I had to lose you all over again, in a pile of blood and heaping madness, that dug into me deeper then, deeper even than the glass that barreled into me. Why would you do that Ellie? Why?"

"I had to do it Priam. I didn't want to and it pained me to see you hurt, but if I wouldn't have left you and things during your second chances would have been perfect, you never would have been able to understand what I am about to tell you now."

"And what is that?" I ask, standing up from the chair and backing ever so slightly away from her.

"That things will never be perfect. Even with a love like ours, things will always go wrong and there is nothing you can do about it. Even with the mistakes of your past and the lessons you have learned from them, the life you so longed for and all of the things you wished to accomplish can never be. If you achieved everything that your heart desired, your life would not be a life, it would be a dream."

"So you left me on that day to prove that it was impossible for me to have everything I wanted? Couldn't you have done that in a less dramatic way? I don't want to accept this Ellie. I can't."

She gets up from her chair and comes towards me. I want to back away, but I don't. I stand rooted to the spot, the colors around us swirl and make me dizzy. "Let's put it this way Priam. If you had to choose between the original seven days and the second chance days that you were given, which set would you chose? If I were to ask you right now to select one course of events over the other and to implement one of them as being the real days of your life, being able to select either one, which would you chose?"

"I-I-I," I stutter as I think about the two sets of seven days and how they compare to one another. All I can think about is the original days and how so many things went wrong with them, yet nevertheless I know that they were seven days of my life, seven days that I lived without having anything to compare them to. Sure, my second chance days were better overall, but could I really accept them as the actuality, when in some way, they had the benefit of the doubt, as they had all of the mistakes I had already made attached to them? And furthermore, Ellie still died during my second chances, and in a much more terrible way. We may have been together until the end that second way, but does that even matter if she died anyways?

"It's difficult isn't it?" She asks me.

"It's impossible," I say. "I don't think I can do it."

"And luckily, you don't have to. It was just a question to make you realize further. Do you think your second chances were real Priam?"

Again I stutter, wondering what she means by this. Of course they were real, they felt just as detailed and ingrained within my being as any of my original days did. I know that I had to relive my original days for a reason, for the comparison, and to learn from my mistakes. I felt similar senses and impressions during my second chances as I did on those first days when I compare them within my mind. So how could my second chances not be real?

"Does it matter?" She asks me, not waiting for my answer.

"I don't know Ellie. They felt real for me, and maybe they weren't real in the sense of them being normal days of my life, but they still mattered to me, and I still lived them as if though they were days of a life I never lived. At least that is how I thought of them while I was experiencing them. Everyday was about you Ellie, even the one before I knew you."

"And us too," a voice says from somewhere behind where I stand. I look into Ellie's eyes before me and through the reflection of her seeing beings I can tell that the person who has spoken is someone I will recognize. I turn slowly and am greeted by the face of my mother, she stands before me appearing exactly how she did the day she died, in her blue and white polka dotted dress. She is at the height of her beauty. On either side of her stand both Danny and Charlie. They too look better than I ever remember them being. Danny wears a finely pressed chocolate covered suit, existing in a body that can't be a day older than twenty nine, and Charlie appears at the age of eighteen, exactly how old he was when he left us, yet glowing more predominately, his features more perfected than they ever were.

I embrace the three of them, one by one. Their youthful flesh touches my old wrinkled skin, as I wonder again why everyone I see is so beautiful while I still remain in this old sickly looking vessel. I am an old man, a man who has died twice and still somehow is alive in a certain sort of the way. My family is around me and the questions I have to ask of them all still outnumber the amount of thoughts that I can actually comprehend, but for the first time since the colors melted before me, I have to wonder if every question has an answer. For maybe, just maybe, some things can never be explained completely, and maybe it doesn't matter.

It's an overwhelming feeling to be amongst the four souls I was closest with in my life, and even more so to think that they exist now in their truest form, while I still reside within the body of a decrepit version of myself. I wish to be as good as they are, and as pure, but I don't know if I will ever be.

"I'm so sorry, for everything that I have done," I say to them then, and I say it to Ellie too, although I am aware that she already knows how regretful I am of the mistakes I have made, as she had helped me to arrange my seven days. "I messed up so much with each of you. If I would have been a better man, maybe things would have been different. During my second chances, I tried to make things up to each of you, but I guess...well, were you there?" I ask, realizing now that I have no idea if they experienced my second chance days in the way that I did. Was it really them there with me, or was it just some manufactured entity of how they would have reacted if things had occurred in the way that I reworked them? As

Chloe, Ellie had led me to believe that I couldn't reveal the true nature of my journey to any of them while it was happening. Then again, had she ever really said that to me? Or had I just made up that notion myself?

"We were all there Priam, on every day that you saw us. It wasn't just some autopilot version of our existence. We were there, in the same kind of way that you were," my mother tells me. "You see, we all passed before you did. Your second chances were as real as they could be."

"In a way though, I may have misled you," Ellie says then as she steps up and stands beside the other three, so that the four of them are in a straight line before me, organized and simplified as the chaotic colors still bounce around in the background. "When I greeted you here, as Chloe, I wasn't able to explain all of the details, some things had to be left unsaid and some elements couldn't be revealed until you were brought back here."

"But why?"

"So you could learn. So you could change," she continues on. "During your journey you believed that the versions of us that you interacted with had no idea that the days that were going on were manufactured ones. You held your tongue and tried your best to understand the days as the entities they were, all the while trying to fill in the missing days from the interim."

"The truth is Priam," Danny says as he takes one small step towards me, speaking for the first time. "There was no interim. You were only given seven days and seven days it was. The versions of us that were there all knew what was going on, for we were there on each of your seven days, reliving them along with you. Just as you had all of the knowledge of your life and the understanding that these were seven days of second chances that were given to you, we too went through them with the same information. We were never in the dark."

I am dumbfounded. To think that all the while the loves of my life were simply making the motions as if these days were completely self contained and compartmentalized within an entire second life, of which I only got to live through seven days, astounds me, and not necessarily in a good way. I am confused and rightfully so, but I also feel betrayed. Why would they do this?

"We knew this was the trial you were undertaking Dad," Charlie tells me then, as Danny takes one step back and my son steps forward. "And, at Mom's guide we played along. Not in a halfhearted or cruel way, but we took the steps that were necessary to make you see, to try and make you understand what your life meant. We lived through your second chances as if we were unaware of anything except for the new life you thought you were living. Our desire all along was to help you, to teach you a lesson, and to guide you to the answers you sought. It was us, we were there with you, on each of your seven days, all along."

He steps back and they all stand in the line again, in some way ordered, and I begin to wonder. If they were there, and the entities that existed along with me on my journey of second days were actually them, just as I was me, could these really be counted as second chances after all? For how could they, if they were only playing along? Throughout all of the pain and heartache that I underwent because of how I thought my actions were making them feel, they knew what I knew. These second chances were not real days as the seven original ways were, they were something different. While I was living through them, I felt as if I could barely comprehend them, but now they feel even more enigmatic to me. There is a chance that I will never be able to understand what they meant fully, but maybe, I don't have to categorize them singularly.

"Do you want to know the main reason why I wanted to relive the days of my life that I regretted the most?" I ask all of them then, pushing the question out into the air and letting it hang in the balance. It spreads and it goes to them, as it continues out further and clings to the colors on the nonexisting walls. "I wanted to prove to each one of you that I wasn't a bad man, and that even though I messed up, I still loved you all so dearly. There were many things that I did wrong, that I could have done better. All I wanted was to give you each the life you deserved, and the happiness that I sought for you. It was all my fault, I was the antagonist who broke your spirits and ruined everything. I'm so sorry."

I burst into an uncontrollable rhythm and my body shakes. I tremble and I start to feel as if I will faint. My seventy year old body is not capable of handling this, and I wish I would die again, once and for all. I don't though, instead the four of them surround me, placing me in the middle of their circle and they support me, bringing me up.

"Don't you see Priam. We've always loved you. Even through your mistakes, and the things you did wrong, we still recognized you for the good man that you are," Ellie tells me then as she lays her head upon my shoulder. "You have to stop being so hard on yourself. No one is perfect. No one in life has ever been able to achieve all of the things that they wished to."

"But I could have done better," I say through my constricted vocal chords.

"You did well enough," my mother tells me. "My death was not your fault."

"I ruined our relationship more than that flame you set ever did. The destruction of our brotherly demise was caused more by my jealousy and anger than anything," Danny says.

"I killed myself Dad. You didn't push me to the edge, I guided myself there. Sure, I was confused the night that I ended my life and I felt alone, but I ignored all of the times that you had been there for me, and only focused on that one. I am not proud of what I did, but I never wanted you to blame yourself in losing me. I lost myself," Charlie admits.

"And as you know Priam, even at times when I was not with you, all I ever longed for was to be by your side, no matter what shape or form that would be. I may have guided you, but even at times when our path was strangled and strewn apart, you guided me. You are my love, my life, my everything," Ellie confesses and kisses my cheek.

The four of them separate from around me and let me stand on my own again. "You are not to blame for all that went wrong during your life. And as you so realize from the seven days that you were given to live through again, nothing can ever go according to plan and not every mistake can be rectified. Life will never be perfect, no matter how desperately you long for it to be," my mother says.

"Your second chances were as real as you wish them to be," Danny offers.

"What you take from them, is up to you. We were there then, and we are here now," Charlie tells me.

"The second chances of Priam Wood were not for us, my love," Ellie whispers into my ear. "They were for you."

The colors coalesce and in a way it starts to make sense to me, why the days went the way that they did, and why the people I loved were there in the way that they were. I can accept the elements of my second chances and recognize them for the entity that they most directly stand for, that of showing me that my life went the way that it did with reason, even if I didn't want to accept the choices it made for me. I realize now that I was never going to be able to live a life where everything went according to plan, not the first time around and not during my second days either. The interruptions were necessary in order to make me a man.

"And Marjorie and Robert showing up on that last day in the way that they did, how did that happen? Or I suppose I should ask, why did it?"

"To show you that things come full circle," my mother says.

"The lesser players in your life still made a difference and impacted you significantly, even if they were only present for a small amount of time. As humans, we can affect each other over decades, or within seconds. The lasting impression we imprint upon each other is what truly matters," Danny tells me.

"You made a difference in each of their lives, and they asked to be there your final day, as a way of thanking you for leading them to a happy life. Even though you never witnessed it, both of them found similar contentment while you lived," Charlie says.

"Do you mean to tell me that they both died before me too? If they were present there, they would had to have...right?" I ask.

"No my dear," Ellie goes on, trying to explain what is hard to rationalize. "They died years after you did, they both lived on for quite a while after 2012, but you see, time doesn't exist here as it does on Earth. And so, Marjorie and Robert were there, just as we were present with you too. The afterlife does not follow after life directly; the planes are continuous, intersecting, and overlapping. Time is not of the essence, as here it exists in an unexisting way.

I rectify this in my mind, and although it is confusing, it somehow falls in line in a similar way as to how Ellie explained how she met Charlie in the white abyss right after dying, while coming back to me as Chloe simultaneously, as the original soul of Little Star died. Time overlapped then, as in my life it was one singular second that passed, while here, I'm sure it felt to Ellie as if she was speaking with Charlie for over an hour before she came back to me. I realize now, that time does not matter.

One thing still stands in the way of me letting go however. I can accept the reality of Chloe and Ellie being the same entity, and I can understand why as that golden being, Ellie intercepted me on each of my days and made a change to influence me, but there is one crooked puzzle piece that will not fit. The jigsaw rips.

Why did Ellie leave me in the way that she did on that fifth day? Why did she let herself die in my arms, with blood pulling and spooling all around us? Why did the love of my life tear my heart asunder when the biggest regret she had during our existence was that she left had me in the first place? Why?

"Ellie, I still cannot comprehend why you left me." She sighs then, not in an exasperated way, but in the kind of fashion to show that she had her reasons. Her lips become a brighter shade of red when she speaks, and I listen with intent as she tells me while the three others look on, their youthful bodies still very close to my ancient one.

"To show you that nothing can be perfect, not even our love, which you so often considered as being so, regardless of it's faults. I had to show you that no matter how hard you tried, even through your struggling and yearning you could not achieve the glory you hoped for. I once told you how much I loved you for your spirit and the fact that you never give up. I knew from the beginning that you would do the same on this journey of seven days, and that you would strive until the end, trying your best to accomplish what you set out to do. The only way I could show you that the mistakes you made in your life were not as wrong as you thought they were, was to leave you all over again, even when it was all going so well. In order for our love to endure, we had to be without one another in ways, during life and during this second journey. In the end it strengthened everything. I swear that it did."

"Couldn't you have left me in a different way though?" I ask of her. "Why did you do so in such a fashion? It was terrifying, it was horrid, the thought of it now alone is a nightmare I never want to think of again." My breathing becomes heavier and I begin to wheeze. My lungs feel as if they are turning into stone and closing completely. Ellie takes my hand in hers and as I feel the warm touch of her soft skin against my calloused casing I calm down a bit, but parts of me still feel lost.

"I had to leave you in order for you to realize the mistakes you made and the regrets you had were simply parts of your being that made you a man. A good man, I might add, regardless of how you felt about that fact yourself. In life, I died without you and I was never able to say goodbye, even though I died as an elderly woman in my comfortable bed. The second time around, I passed in what you describe as a horrible fashion, but I died in your arms nevertheless. Who is to say what version is better? Even with all of the blood, I would choose the second version over the first any day. To die in your arms, no matter how it occurred, could never be a nightmare to me. Only the idea of dying alone terrifies me."

"You mean like how I died?" I ask of her then, with tears in my eyes. As they go, each drop that falls feels like such an enormity.

"Like you died Priam. You were alone then, but you are not so now. And you never will be again. The mistakes you made that chased us away, yes they were your mistakes, but each of us had our own too," she tells me as my mother, Danny and Charlie come closer to us again. "You did not make them on purpose. Life got in the way. We were all wrong in ways. Even if you did not see it, I am sure that you can recognize it now."

At her words, I feel myself letting go, not of my existence, but of all of the trials and tribulations I have faced that have held me back. In that moment, the colors that surround me register deeply within me and I accept the different hues and shades as being part of the way. The four souls that I love the most are near, and they are telling me that I was a good man, and for the first time, I believe them. I have to. I acknowledge the pureness, serenity and beauty that they all contain now, as I would be a fool not to do so. When I look at each of their faces, I see reflections of myself in their eyes. They are a part of me, and I am a part of them. I paint a picture in the sky.

"It's the moments where things go wrong that make us who we are," Ellie continues. "Without your seven days, without your second chances, you never would have been able to understand this principle of life and how it affects our existence. Without the journey of your second chances and experiencing them the way that they happened, you never would have been free."

A spark within me ignites then, as I accept the undertaking for what it is, and what it was. I feel my body lessen and then strengthen. I melt a bit, only to solidify further. I push my feet forward off of the nothingness and everything beneath where I stand. I kiss Ellie's luscious red lips before me, and when my mouth touches hers, I know that our love will last forever. As I pull away from her, I look to the faces of the other three members of my family and I see their eyes sparkle as they smile. Something is changing within me.

I look down at my hands and see that the liver spots are disappearing, the veins that were pronounced and gray are sliding away. My posture becomes straightened as I grow a few inches taller. I lift my hand up to the top of my head and feel my hair becoming thicker, and coarser. My chest becomes broader and my shoulders rise up. I feel my body tighten and become muscular again. I look into Ellie's eyes, and when I do, I see the reflection of my youthful face and my golden hair shining back to me. I laugh, and as I do so I wrap my arms around the woman I love and I twirl her around. She giggles with delight.

I exist within the body of my twenty seven year old self once again. Just as she, and everyone else looks to be their most beautiful self, I too have been restored to the height of my physicality. I have reached peace, and understanding, and in doing so, I have left the seventy years of pain behind.

The rest of them come then, from behind the colors to where the five of us stand. One by one souls who existed during life join us where we are. First, my father, Patrick Wood emerges and he shakes my hand, before embracing me. He gives me no words, but his look is enough to tell me that he is proud. He joins my mother's side encased within the vessel that he left the earth within, in the third decade of his life. He grasps her hand and I see the love they share.

After him, comes Alma and she looks just as I remember her on that sixth day when we traveled to London. She appears to be seventeen years old, innocent and beautiful. She hugs me and says, "I'm so happy you're here Daddy. I'm so happy you made it! I knew that you would be okay in the end." I place my hand on her head and gently smooth out her soft chestnut colored hair.

Grandpa Wood comes next, followed by the rest of my grandparents. They are younger than I have ever imagined them being, but they still appear to be a few years older than my parents, at least to me. I thank each one of them for all that they have done.

And finally, the last person to join us is Rebecca. I had never met her in my life, but regardless I feel as if I know her well now. She hugs me and then stands next to my brother, reuniting with him, as she was the love that he had lost. They are reunited together and I am elated to witness it. I lace my hands with Ellie's and I look at the faces that surround me. I feel complete, but where do we go from here? How do we spend this time without end? I am just about to ask the question when I hear a squeak and a golden blur emerges from the fray.

Little Star comes forward and nips at my heels. I pick up the puppy as everyone laughs with glee. I pat her on the head and pet her for a few seconds as Ellie leans down and scrunches up her face in front of her in a playful way. Little Star gives her a kiss, licking her face. She doesn't speak, but it is clear that she is conscious of everything as we are. I set her down and she prances around happily.

"And now what? What happens from here?" I ask my love, my life, my everything.

"We go on, together. Do any of the other details really matter?"

"No, I suppose they don't," I admit.

The colors collide and then shift. They start to accumulate together in certain ways to build something new. Each element forms a structure and the buildings start to rise up. I watch as all of the shades spin around, as I stand with my family in the middle of it all. It is a magnificent sight to witness, for it feels as if I am in the middle of a canvas as a painting is being created automatically around me. I remain where I am and watch as the colored conclusion comes forth. They form a new place, a combination of everything I had ever hoped for and more. The white space and the colors are gone, as what has replaced them now is our house on Elm Street. It isn't exactly as I remember it though, as the street on which we stand extends out and flushes perfectly with the outside world, which just so happens to be the city that I have always loved. In this place my house on Elm Street, the home I always had, is located on a street corner in Brooklyn, not more than four blocks away from where I can see the Brooklyn Bridge in the distance. It is a synchronous harmony that I only could ever have dreamed of previously. I realize that anything can exist here. I take one more look at the house, as everyone admires the scenery that has created itself around us, and then we head towards the bridge.

I walk towards the light, hand in hand with Ellie and as we walk on, I think about how life lists the places we will go and the people we will know, but it was never able to offer me anything that could compare to the glory of now and how it feels to exist in this moment, how it feels to be free.

Acknowledgements

This book wouldn't have been possible if it weren't for the people in my life who helped and supported me from its inception. I want to thank everyone who listened to my ideas and encouraged me to keep writing during the year that it took me to complete this novel.

I have to thank the three women who were the first ones to finish reading my manuscript. To my mother, Christine Rigby, my sister, Nicole Severyn, and my grandmother, Teddie Cowan, I can't thank you enough for all of your critiques and the opinions you gave me to make this book the best it could be. It warms my heart to know that three strong women such as you were the first people to become acquainted with this story. This novel is many things, but what I think it represents the most is the love that exists between family. I am blessed that you are a part of mine, and I am in awe of the strength that each of you represent amongst the three generations that you are a part of.

I also have to thank Michael Ploetz and Kara Knickerbocker. The two of you have always been familiar with my writing, and it was extremely helpful to me to get feedback from you both. I like to think that our friendships are strengthened by our mutual love for literature and writing. I look forward to the day when I am reading the novels that I know both of you will write in the future.

And to Charles Bonge, thank you for inspiring me and for believing in my talent as a writer. I'll never forget sitting next to you at the symphony when the ending of this story suddenly formed in my mind, almost bringing me to tears as the orchestra played on. Your assessment of my manuscript and the ideas you gave me were so detailed that they benefited my editing process significantly. The words you delivered meant so much to me.

I appreciate the support all of you gave me and I want to thank you from the upper most chamber of my heart for helping this project come to fruition. Here is to hoping that this is only the first of many novels that I will write, only the first of a score of acknowledgement pages that you will be listed on.

About the Author

Alexander Rigby has been writing since the age of nine. These written works have ranged from stories about witches and warlocks, to magical trees, sagas set in outer space, adventures of freshmen in high school, and a tale of two gay best friends struggling with life in the city. When he was young, his parents used to punish him by taking away his books, as they were the things he loved the most. Little did he know at that time, he would end up writing some. As a recent graduate of the University of Pittsburgh, Alexander has finished writing his first novel *The Second Chances of Priam Wood*, a story that he is extremely proud of and believes in wholeheartedly. Although he has written various pieces before, even completing some, this is the first time he wishes to share this story with anyone who desires to read it. He lives his life by a few simple rules: to treat each day as it could be his last, to try to experience as many new places and meet as many different people as is possible, and to do more than just exist.

29919214R00311

Made in the USA
Middletown, DE
08 March 2016